THREE COMPLETE NOVELS

LORI COPELAND

THREE COMPLETE NOVELS

LORI COPELAND

AVENGING ANGEL
PASSION'S CAPTIVE
SWEET TALKIN' STRANGER

WINGS BOOKS
NEW YORK · AVENEL, NEW JERSEY

This omnibus was originally published in separate volumes under the titles:

Avenging Angel, copyright © 1987 by Lori Copeland
Passion's Captive, copyright © 1988 by Lori Copeland
Sweet Talkin' Stranger, copyright © 1989 by Lori Copeland

This edition contains the complete and unabridged texts of the
original edition. They have been completely reset for this volume.

This 1994 edition is published by Wings Books,
distributed by Random House Value Publishing, Inc.,
40 Engelhard Avenue, Avenel, New Jersey 07001,
by arrangement with Dell Publishing, a division of Bantam Doubleday
Dell Publishing Group, Inc.

Random House
New York • Toronto • London • Sydney • Auckland

Printed and bound in the United States of America

BOOK DESIGN BY CAROL MALCOLM-RUSSO/SIGNET M. DESIGN, INC.

Library of Congress Cataloging-in-Publication Data
Copeland, Lori.
[Novels.   Selections]
Three complete novels / Lori Copeland.
p.   cm.
Contents: Avenging angel — Passion's captive — Sweet talkin' stranger.
ISBN 0-517-12194-8
1. Historical fiction, American.   2. Love stories, American.   I. Title.
PS3553.06336A6   1994
813'.54—dc20
94-30316
CIP

8 7 6 5 4 3 2 1

CONTENTS

AVENGING ANGEL
1

PASSION'S CAPTIVE
159

SWEET TALKIN' STRANGER
321

AVENGING ANGEL

To the many dear friends who lent me their encouragement and unfailing support in this new endeavor. I wish I had room to call you by name, but I want you to know you have a very special place in my heart.

To Lydia E. Paglio, for her continuing faith in me and who virtually made this book possible. I hope I never fail you, babe.

To Denise Marcil, who found a home for my new baby. It's been a pleasure working with you.

To Olivia Ferrell, for taking my hand and leading me through the unknown. I'll never forget your friendship.

To Norma Brader, who has been with me from the beginning, strengthening, sustaining, and always there with a kind word or a pat on the back when none was due. Thank you is so inadequate, but I want to say it anyway.

And to my wonderful family for putting up with me. Lance, Randy, Maureen, Rick, Kathe, Russ, Opal, James, and Joseph. You're my whole world and I love you . . . I love you . . . I love you.

CHAPTER 1

July 1865

*W*YNNE ELLIOT COUGHED AND DABBED HER HAND-kerchief daintily at her nose as another cloud of choking dust swept in through the stagecoach window. She smiled for what seemed like the hundredth time at the gentlemen across from her and fervently wished the tiresome trip were over.

Gazing out the window, she compared this almost harsh Missouri countryside to her own beloved Georgia. It was July, a time when flowers were blooming back home, when the breezes were moist and balmy, and when moss was draped through the trees to create a kind of fairyland picture.

Here the ground was hard, the grass depressingly dry from lack of rain. And while there seemed to be little evidence of the kind of death and destruction which her dear South had suffered, there were still scars.

The farther they traveled, it seemed, the more rugged the contour of the land became. The Ozark mountain country, she'd been told, was a land where people either survived or didn't, and given the landscape, she could well imagine why.

She could see low mountains with virtually untouched forests in the distance. And the road they were traveling over twisted and snaked through gaps and valleys, revealing endless walls of shale and limestone.

On at least two occasions the coach had stopped so the driver and guard could remove fallen rocks from the way. Why, it seemed that at any turn a group of outlaws could have been hidden behind those massive boulders to waylay the coach. At the last station she had heard mention of the name of Alf Bolin and his men, an unsavory group that seemed to relish jumping out at unwary travelers, and the men's casual conversation had made Wynne's pulse flutter nervously.

Of course, since her journey began in Savannah, she'd heard many such shocking tales. The men at the way stations seemed to delight in relating such stories to stun and distress the lady passengers.

But anything she had been told had failed to prepare her for Missouri's rugged beauty. And it was beautiful, Wynne admitted reluctantly. Great oaks and maple trees, which by their size had to be a hundred years old, lifted strong arms out over the trail and sank roots into soil which was alternately black and rich clay red, but so stony that no plant could hope to survive. Still, inhabitants of the area seemed to eke out an adequate living from the earth. And apparently in Springfield, a regular metropolis she'd heard, there were thriving businesses. She had been told just yesterday that the railroad as well as more stores, and hotels would be there soon. But if this were true, then Missouri would come out of the great conflict in much better shape than her own beloved Georgia.

She sighed as the stagecoach continued to toss its passengers about. How much farther could River Run possibly be? Her bones felt as if they were coming through her skin. Traveling by coach had not been easy, what with the jostling about, the dust, and the heat. How she longed for a bath, a long, hot bath, with scented soap, and a shampoo. . . . She sighed longingly. Revenge could indeed be tedious at times.

Absently she rubbed the smooth, strange-colored stone she'd grown accustomed to carrying in her pocket. Cass had given it to her. Odd that she hadn't rid herself yet of this one last painful reminder of him. But the trinket had become a kind of worry stone, worn smooth by the continual wash of river water. Her thumb fitted perfectly in the little hollow which looked as if it could have been carved for just that purpose. Her fingers had moved over it for the past few months in a kind of silent litany: *I'll get him . . . I'll get him if it's the last thing I do . . . I'll get him. . . .*

But it had been a long, tiresome journey to fulfill that promise, and it wasn't over yet. She tried to bolster her sagging spirits with the promise that it wouldn't be much longer. As soon as she caught that devil . . .

Wynne wiped ineffectually at the small trickle of perspiration that escaped from beneath her hairline, then adjusted her hat.

Her attention settled on the flamboyant young woman in red sitting next to her. Now there was an interesting example of womanhood.

Miss Penelope Pettibone was on her way to a new job at Hattie's Place.

According to Penelope, Hattie's Place was where a man could go for a drink, a hand of cards, and "other gentlemanly pursuits." At the mention of "other gentlemanly pursuits," Wynne's eyes had widened knowingly, and her face had flushed a pretty pink. Never in her nineteen years had Wynne ever met one of . . . "those" women, and she had found she had a certain unwilling fascination with Miss Pettibone, one that made her wonder how it would be if she were the one headed for the job instead of Penelope. Wynne fanned herself more quickly at the titillating thought and then turned her attention to the reason for her trip to Missouri.

Only that scoundrel, the dishonorable Cass Claxton, occupied her thoughts now. The mere thought of that man left her breathless with anger. Not only had he left her standing at the altar in complete disgrace, but he'd also managed to walk away with every penny she had except the small pittance she kept in a tin box under her mattress for extreme emergencies.

True, she'd been foolish to fall in love with a man she knew so little about and even more foolish to offer financial assistance on a business venture he was about to embark upon, but Wynne had always been one to put her whole heart into everything—especially in matters of love.

If it hadn't been for the war and her suspicion that Cass had enlisted the day they were supposed to marry, she would have tracked him down long ago and put a bullet straight through his thieving heart for doing her the way he had.

Her temper still boiled when she thought how gullible she'd been. Well, she was no longer gullible, and the war was over now. Quite by chance she'd been told by a close acquaintance of Cass's that he had indeed enlisted, and survived, and had been seen in Kansas City a few weeks ago. The friend had said Cass was en route to his home in River Run and should be there any day now.

Wynne clenched her fan in her hand; her eyes narrowed pensively. It had been a long time coming, but Mr. Cass Claxton would soon pay for his sins, she vowed. A satisfied smile crossed her pretty, heat-flushed features. Yes, very soon Cass would rue the day he'd ever heard of Wynne Elliot.

If there was one lesson she'd learned from this, it was that *no* man could be trusted, and though she wasn't necessarily soured permanently on men, she would certainly never allow herself to be fooled by one again.

The coach lurched along as Wynne studied the two male passengers dozing in the seat across from her. Undoubtedly they were no different, she speculated.

She did have to admit, though, she liked to watch the way stuffy Mr. Rutcliff's fat little jowls jiggled every time the stage hit a rut in the road. But when it came to women, she'd bet he was just as unpredictable as all men, even if he was nearly seventy years old.

She'd had to cover her mouth with her handkerchief to keep from laughing out loud a couple of times when a bump had nearly thrown him out of his seat. He'd snorted himself awake and angrily glanced around him to see who had been the culprit that had dared interrupt his napping.

Henry McPherson, the other gentleman traveler, was younger than Mr. Rutcliff and boringly polite. He constantly tipped his hat and said, "Yes, ma'am," and, "No, ma'am," in response to any comment either she or Penelope made.

Actually Wynne had the impression the two men had been scared to death of Penelope since they'd overheard her discussing her destination with Wynne.

The coach began to pick up speed, and Wynne glanced out the window at the scenery that was now swiftly rushing by. "Does it seem to you we're going faster?" she asked of no one in particular as a frown creased her forehead.

"We can't go fast enough for me," Penelope said with an exasperated sigh. "I can't wait for this trip to be over." She made another useless effort to knock the layer of dust off her dress and grimaced in distaste when it only settled back on the light material.

Puzzled by the increasing speed of the coach, Wynne leaned her head out the window and immediately jerked it back in. "Hell's bells! I think we're about to be robbed!" she blurted out in disbelief, almost instantly wincing at her own statement, one of many of her father's salty expressions.

At her exclamation both men's eyes instantly flew open, and Mr. Rutcliff craned his neck out the window to verify her statement. "Oh, my! I do believe you're right!"

Penelope sent up an instant wail. "I knew it! I knew it! We'll all be killed!"

Wynne shot Penelope an irritated glance. Over the past few days she'd noticed that optimism did not seem to be the girl's strong point. "Penelope, really! I'm sure we are well protected." There was the guard, the driver, and the two male passengers. There was certainly no cause for alarm; besides, the coach could probably outrun the outlaws without the slightest problem.

But a few minutes later her optimism sagged. Her heart was beating wildly as the sound of gunshots filled the air and the riders drew steadily closer.

Glancing worriedly at the gentlemen seated across from her, she noticed they didn't look overly optimistic either. "Shouldn't we do something?" she asked fretfully. She clutched the worry stone in her hand as the two men peered out the coach window apprehensively.

"There's nothin' to do but pray," Mr. Rutcliff replied in a barely audible voice.

Pray? Wynne blinked back a sudden urge to cry as she realized that all of them just *might* be killed.

Pray! Suddenly she found herself doing just that as the masked riders slowly but surely gained ground on the wildly swaying coach.

Like a flat iron on a hot stove, the noonday sun bore down on the two dusty riders as they sat atop their horses on a small rise looking out across the land.

Only a faint, teasing wisp of a breeze grazed their horses' manes. The heat was so stifling it was hard to draw a deep breath.

"Just look at it, Beau. We're finally home." The baritone voice, husky with emotion, spoke first.

The two men sat on tired horses overlooking the rolling hills of their southwest Missouri home, savoring the smell and feel of being back.

"It looks good, doesn't it?" The older one almost breathed the words reverently. Letting his reins go slack, he slumped wearily in the saddle as he relaxed for a moment, his eyes hungrily drinking in the familiar sight spread before him.

The gently sloping terrain was no longer the lush, fertile green that would have met their eyes if it had been spring. The blazing summer sun had taken its toll on the land and burned it to a dry cinder. But it was still a delectable sight to one who had seen nothing but death and destruction for the last few years.

Four years. Four years of hell. Four years of never knowing if they would ever see home again. Four years of watching men die by the thousands and wondering if they would be next, living with the unspeakable horrors of war day after day after day . . .

Home. The word held a new and even more precious meaning to the two men as they breathed silent thanks to their Maker for bringing them intact through the carnage and destruction.

"You know, Cole, there were times when I thought I'd never see this again," Beau confessed.

"I know," his older brother answered quietly. "I had those times too."

"We were lucky, you know. There are so many who won't come home—"

"Hope Ma and Willa have some of those chicken 'n' dumplin's waitin' for us," Cole interrupted. He'd had enough dying and sorrow to last him a lifetime. All he wanted to do was forget the last few years, not relive them.

Anxious to forget the past himself, Beau released a long sigh of longing as he thought about his ma and the Indian housekeeper's delicious cooking. Willa had been with the family since he was a baby and as much of a mother to the three boys as their own ma had been. When the family had moved from Georgia to Missouri back in the late forties, they'd established a home and hoped to build a new life. Unfortunately their father, Samuel, had died early, leaving his wife with three young sons to raise. No one could argue that Willa had been nothing short of a godsend to Lilly.

"I want six pans of corn bread and three dozen fried apple pies before I even hit the front door." Beau's mouth fairly watered at the thought.

"Yes, if I were you, I'd eat the pie and corn bread even before I went over to see Betsy." Cole teased him with a knowing wink.

"You're right," Beau said solemnly. "That would be the only sensible thing to do." Then they broke out in laughter. Both knew the first place Beau would head for was old man Collins's place. Beau and Betsy had been about to be married when the war intervened, and now the wedding would take place as soon as possible.

"Who wants ol' Betsy when they can have Willa's cookin'?" Beau grinned mischievously, his eyes twinkling. He'd always been the "scamp" of the family, as Willa put it. "You know, now that the war's over, you ought to think about settlin' down, too, Cole."

His brother chuckled softly as his gaze returned to caress the valley below them. "Betsy's the prettiest girl in the county, and you're claimin' her. Who would I marry?"

"Aw, come on." Beau chided him. "You know you wouldn't marry Betsy if you could." Cole and Betsy had always gotten along well together, but Beau knew that no woman had ever captured Cole's heart. "I'm beginnin' to worry about you, Cole!"

Cole chuckled again. "Well, don't. Now that the war's over, when the right woman comes along, I might give marryin' some serious thought."

"It'll never happen," Beau said, knowing that finding the right woman for his overcritical brother wasn't going to be an easy task. "You're never going to find a woman who'll suit you because you're too picky."

"I'll run across her someday. I just happen to like a woman with a little spirit," Cole said distractedly as his eyes continued to drink in the familiar surroundings. The war had been an ugly, evil blight on the land, but mercifully here the scenic hills of Missouri had remained virtually untouched. "And I haven't met her yet." This was a familiar argument, one his whole family had memorized. Cole's mother and Willa were fond of questioning when he, the eldest, was going to marry and produce offspring.

"Spirit, huh? Well, what about Betsy's sister, Priscilla? Now there's a fine figure of a woman if I ever saw one." Beau grinned at his brother. "She's strong as a bull moose, healthy as a horse, and sturdy as a oak fence post. Why, I've seen her and her father cut a rick of wood in a couple of hours and never raise a sweat. She'd make some man a fine wife," Beau said encouragingly. "Got a *lot* of spirit too," he added for insurance. "Saw her hand-wrestle an Indian brave once, and she didn't do bad!"

Cole's mouth curved in an indulgent smile. "She didn't win, did she?"

"No, she didn't win, but she didn't do all that bad," Beau insisted.

Cole smiled wider at the younger man's sincerity. "Beau, somehow the thought of a woman hand-wrestlin' a brave, cuttin' a rick of wood in a couple of hours, and never raising a sweat just doesn't appeal to me."

"Well, *what* does? I've seen you go through more women than I can count, and not one of 'em suits you. You're just too damn picky!" Beau repeated sullenly.

Cole shifted in his saddle. His bones ached, and he was dead tired. "Don't start naggin' me, Beau," he said good-naturedly. His little brother could nag as hard as any granny when he set his mind to it, and Cole was in no mood for a lecture on women. "When I find a woman who can wrestle the Indian brave and *win*, then turn around and be soft as cotton, smell as pretty as a lilac bush in May, and forget all about being a lady in bed, that's the day you can stop worryin' about me."

Beau shook his head in exasperation. "I've never known a woman to smell like a lilac bush in May after she wrestled an Indian brave!" he complained.

Cole chuckled, took off his hat, and wiped away the sweat on his brow. The clear blue of his eyes carefully scanned the valley below, then narrowed and lingered on the cloud of dust being kicked up in the far distance.

"Looks like the stage comin'," he noted.

"The driver's sure got the horses whipped up." Beau leaned forward slightly in his saddle, his eyes narrowed in his handsome face. "Will ya look at that!"

Leather creaked as the horses moved restlessly beneath the men's weight. Their gazes followed the path of the coach barreling along the dusty road. The driver was whipping the team to higher speed, and the coach careered crazily as it tried to outrun the small band of riders galloping toward it.

Beau released a low whistle under his breath. "Looks like they're in trouble."

Putting his hat back on his head, Cole took up his reins and glanced back over the hillside at the frantic race. "We'd better see what we can do to help."

Both men spurred their horses into action, and the powerful steeds sprang forward. The horses covered the ground with lightning speed, steadily gaining on the swaying coach.

By now six masked riders had brought the stage to a halt and the passengers were filing out with their hands held high above their heads.

The leader of the motley pack had dismounted hurriedly. While he held a gun on the driver and guard, the others began pulling luggage off the top of the coach.

"Don't nobody make a move and you won't get hurt," the second rider informed them in a gravelly voice. "Driver! You and shotgun throw down your guns and the gold box."

The driver and guard looked at each other, then foolishly made a move to pull their guns. Two shots rang out. The women screamed and covered their eyes as the bodies of the two men fell from their perch. Even to the inexperienced eye, it was apparent they were dead by the time they hit the ground.

Three of the bandits immediately returned to dragging valises off the top of the coach and ripping through the contents in search of valuables.

The passengers watched in dismay as their personal items were strewn about in the frenzied search. Wynne stood in shock. Her undergarments were being handled by rough, dirty hands, the lace pieces thrown into the dust with no regard, ripped and torn.

In a vain effort to stop the robbery, Penelope stepped forward and batted her eyes coyly at the leader. "Really, sir, we have nothing of any value. Won't you please let us pass—"

The man angrily pushed her aside. "Out of my way, woman." As he shoved her, his hand caught the large emerald broach pinned to the front of her dress and ripped it off harshly.

Wynne gasped at his audacity. For a moment she forgot her own paralyzing fear and rushed over to stand protectively in front of the sobbing girl. "You brute! Why don't you pick on someone your own size?"

Wynne's heart thumped loudly in her chest as the robber's eyes narrowed angrily. It nearly stopped beating altogether when the bandit jerked her up close to him and made a thorough search of her body with his beady eyes. He quickly relieved her of the pearl ring on her left finger, scraping her knuckle painfully in the process. Rummaging in her purse, he removed all the coins, then focused his attention on her. "This all you got, lady?"

The snapping green of her eyes met his coolly. "I am not a fool! Of course, you have it all . . . and please get out of my face." Her nose tilted upward in an effort to avoid his offensive odor. Thank goodness he had a mask over his face to dull the stench of his odious breath!

"Aww, am I offendin' Her Majesty?" He chuckled wickedly and jerked her closer, lifting his mask above his mouth. The sight of his yellow, tobacco-stained teeth made her stomach lurch.

Slowly his greedy gaze lowered to the gentle swell of the décolletage of her emerald-colored dress and stopped. "What's the matter, honey? Ain't I pleasin' 'nough for you?" He laughed mirthlessly as she continued to keep her face averted from his rancid smell. "Hot damn. You're a pretty little thing." He breathed against her ear. "How's about givin' ol' Jake a little kiss?"

"See here! Rob us if you will, but I must insist on your treating the ladies with respect!" Henry McPherson stepped forward in Wynne's defense. He was promptly knocked unconscious by the butt of a gun wielded by one of the masked men.

His body slumped quietly to the ground as the assailant waved his pistol menacingly. "Don't no one else try nothing foolish if you don't want to get hurt."

"Come on, Jake! Cut the crap and get on with it," one of the riders ordered, casting an apprehensive glance at two riders fast approaching from the west. "We got company comin'."

Jake laughed once more and shoved Wynne away from him. "Sorry, honey. We'll have to make it another time."

"In a pig's eye we will," Wynne said scoffingly but retained enough sense about her to do it under her breath.

The bandit paused in his work, and his evil eyes narrowed menacingly. "What'd you say?"

She grinned weakly. "I said, yes . . . some other time . . . maybe."

"Damn, Jake! Would you quit socializing and come on!"

Jake forced his mind back to the business at hand. After another sweep of her body with his cold dark eyes Jake brutally ripped the fragile gold chain from around Wynne's neck. She winced, then straightened her small frame into an angry stance. "You give that back!" she screeched, and snatched at the necklace. But he stuffed it into the bag he was carrying and laughed at her again.

"Sorry, Red, but I just got a sudden hankerin' for little gold chains." He chuckled again and strode in a rolling gait over to his horse and mounted quickly.

"That necklace isn't worth anything," she protested angrily, "except for sentimental value to me! My father gave that to me just before he died—"

Her words fell on deaf ears as the man tipped his hat to her in a mocking salute. Then the six riders spurred their horses back into action.

"Well, okay then! Take the necklace, but I won't forget this!" she shouted into the cloud of dust their horses kicked up.

Stamping her foot in exasperation and grabbing at her tilting hat, she stared at the robbers' retreating backs. *Damn-damn-damn*, Wynne muttered under her breath. Seconds later two other riders appeared over a rise and quickly took up hot pursuit of the culprits.

The dazed passengers stood about stupidly as Wynne rushed over to kneel beside the injured Henry. He was just beginning to come to and moaned before opening his eyes to look around in bewilderment. "What happened?"

"Just lie still, Mr. McPherson," Wynne said, reaching for one of the pieces of scattered clothing to place under his head. "You were knocked out by one of the ruffians, but they're gone now." Glancing around, she saw the others hadn't moved at all. "Someone had better check the guard and driver," she said briskly.

Mr. Rutcliff snapped out of his stupor at the sound of her voice and knelt between the two shot men. Shaking his head sadly, he glanced back to meet Wynne's questioning gaze. "Dead as a doornail. Shot 'em both clean through the heart."

Penelope collapsed in tears, and Wynne absently reached over and patted her shoulder. "It's all right, Penelope. They're gone now. Why don't you go sit under that tree until you get yourself under control?"

"But we all could have been killed," Penelope wailed. "I tried to stop them, but you saw what happened—"

"Yes, but we weren't killed," Wynne said in a soothing tone. "Mr. Rutcliff, are you all right?"

The elderly man looked pale and mopped at the perspiration trickling down inside his collar. "Why, yes, I believe so. Quite a disturbing turn of events, wouldn't you say?"

"Yes, I would say that," Wynne replied blowing in exasperation at the wisp of hair that had escaped from beneath her hat and hung loosely in her face.

As Wynne and the other travelers tried to gather their wits, Cole and Beau were pushing their horses to the limit, but the gang of riders had already disappeared into the distance. The long legs of the brothers' animals swiftly ate up the dusty miles, but the other riders had too much of a head start on them.

"What do you think?" Beau shouted a few minutes later as he reined up beside Cole.

"We're not going to be able to catch them. We'll only wind the horses," Cole responded as he pulled his mount to a halt.

Beau's gaze continued to follow the cloud of dust in the far distance until it topped a rise and disappeared altogether. "No, I suppose not. Well, let's go see what we can do to help the passengers."

They pulled their mounts around abruptly and started back toward the stage.

When the two riders came back into view, Wynne paused in picking up her scattered clothing. She watched warily as they approached. Spying one of the guns still lying on the ground, she picked it up and carefully leveled it on the approaching pair. One robbery a day was all she was going to put up with, thank you. If these two ruffians had come for the same purpose, she was going to be the one to take care of them this time.

Penelope was beside herself with fright and would be no help at all. She sat under a nearby tree, crying and fanning herself. Mr. Rutcliff was trying to comfort the injured Henry McPherson. That left only Wynne to defend what was left of their meager possessions.

Beau glanced over at Cole worriedly, then back down both barrels of the twelve-gauge shotgun she was pointing at them as they rode up and cautiously reined to a halt.

"Throw your guns down, gentlemen," she commanded in a firm voice.

"Now, ma'am," Beau said patiently, "we don't make a habit of partin' with our guns—"

"Now!" She hefted the shotgun up an inch higher on her shoulder.

Beau looked at Cole and sighed. Both men slowly unbuckled their gun belts and let them slide to the ground.

"Now your rifles."

"Ma'am . . ." Beau protested again. He wasn't about to let the Springfield .58 caliber be taken by this slip of a girl. He almost laughed. There she stood, her collar torn, dust smudges on her face, and that silly hat! A wide-brimmed thing with a bird in a nest. And it kept tipping forward so she kept nudging it back, causing the gun to wave dangerously. And no matter what she said, that charming southern drawl took out a great deal of the sting. He'd heard enough of that speech pattern to know she was Georgia born and bred.

"I said throw down your rifles." The gun waved menacingly again.

With a tolerant glance at Cole, Beau slid his beloved Springfield carefully to the ground. Only then did she lower her weapon a fraction. "Now, state your business; then be movin' on."

"Afternoon, ma'am." Swiping off his hat, Beau flashed what he hoped was a winning smile. "Me and my brother was wonderin' if everyone was all right here."

In Wynne's opinion, this newest set of strangers didn't look a whole lot better than the last ones. They were rumpled and dirty, both in need of shaves and haircuts. The only difference she could discern between these two and the other band of unsavory hoodlums who had just fled was that they didn't smell as bad—at least not quite.

Both men were large in stature and impressively muscular, if one liked that sort of man. But they were the exact opposites in coloring. They were still wearing the ragged blue uniforms of the North. Wynne prayed that on top of everything else this rotten day had brought her, she hadn't had the misfortune to meet up with two carpetbaggers.

She studied them carefully. The one who had been doing all the talking had hair streaked whitish blond by the sun and dancing blue eyes. He sat in his saddle with a rakish air. The second man was older, his skin toasted to a deep nut brown, and his hair was jet black with just a trace of unruly curls softening his rugged features. Wynne swallowed hard and tried to steady her hand as she kept the gun directly turned on the miscreants. Lordy, the thing was unbelievably heavy!

"Don't come any closer," she warned as the men's horses edged nearer.

"Ma'am, why don't you put the gun down?" Beau said in his most persuasive tone. "Someone might get hurt."

She narrowed her eyes and took a menacing step forward to show them she was not in the least intimidated by their presence. She meant business.

"It's quite possible someone might—namely, you. Now, I'm warning you, mister, you'd better not rile me. You'd best state your business and move on, or I'll have to use this."

"I really don't think that'll be necessary." Beau turned slightly in his saddle so he could see Cole's face. It was expressionless, but Beau noted that Cole was keeping an uneasy eye on the woman's trigger finger. "I think I'd better state our business, Cole."

Beau started to dismount and stopped short as the girl's voice rang out again. "Just stop right there!" she demanded.

Deciding she'd better let them know in no uncertain terms who had the upper hand, Wynne marched forward with a steely glint in her eye. Unfortunately a discarded valise was in her path. After hitting her shin painfully, Wynne pitched forward. Still clutching the gun, she twisted to one side and fell to one knee.

Cole and Beau ducked frantically as the gun went off, sending a spray of buckshot zooming over their heads. For a moment confusion reigned as Wynne fought to gain control of the gun and her destroyed composure as well as her feet. Beau and Cole rolled out of their saddles onto their knees while still hanging on to the reins of their horses, which were wide-eyed and dancing by now.

Seconds later Wynne was primly straightening her gown, grumbling a pretty unladylike "hell and damnation" under her breath, but the gun was firmly back on her targets.

"Gentlemen, don't be misled." She cautioned them in her most superior, even if it was shaky, voice. "I assure you I *do* know how to use this gun and shall not hesitate to do so if the need arises. So I suggest you move on. My fellow passengers and I have nothing left but our clothes in the road, so you're wasting your time if you've come to rob us."

Wynne glanced uneasily at the dark rider who was slowly coming to his feet. His face was grim, and his eyes narrowed. She didn't like the set of his mouth.

She hoped she wasn't making a complete ass of herself. But after all, she had the gun and he didn't.

The electrifying blue of the man's eyes was directly on her as he studied the scene before him and remounted his horse.

"Ma'am," Beau protested with a weak grin, "I think you've got the wrong idea. We're here to help, not rob, you."

"Oh, really?" Wynne's eyebrows lifted skeptically. He did have a point, though. These two men had chased the robbers off, but it could very well have been for their own evil purposes.

"Honest," Beau declared solemnly. "We're only sorry we weren't in time to prevent this unfortunate mishap." A little of his southern heritage came through as he swept his hat off and bowed gallantly. She was once more the recipient of his radiant smile.

"That may be so, but you're still a Yankee!" She spit the words out as if they left a vile taste in her mouth. "And I wouldn't believe a thing a Yankee said!"

"Ma'am," he said coaxingly, "the war's over. Can't we let bygones be bygones?"

"That's easy for you to say," she pointed out. "*You* won."

Beau shrugged his shoulders. "True, but I had some help," he said modestly.

Wynne shot him a dirty look. He wasn't taking this whole situation seriously. Beau slowly eased his way over to her. "Now, why don't you just calm down and let me and my brother take you and the other passengers on into town?"

Wynne surveyed the lifeless bodies of the driver and guard and realized she was at this man's mercy even though she was holding the gun. It was obvious that neither she nor Penelope could drive the stage, and the two other men were in no condition to attempt such a feat.

"Well . . . maybe that would be a good idea, but bear in mind I'll have this gun pointed at you all the way in case you try something underhanded." She shot the other man a warning look. "And that goes for you too."

Cole shook his head in disbelief at the way his brother was handling the situation. He calmly took a cheroot out of his shirt pocket and lit it. If it had been up to *him*, he'd have taken the gun away from her ten minutes ago and turned her across his knee.

"What's the matter with him? Can't that pompous ass talk?" Wynne whispered crossly, motioning with her head to Cole. All the man had done since he arrived was stare at her as if she were a raving maniac!

Beau glanced over his shoulder toward his brother. "Who, Cole? Sure, he talks, when he wants to." Then his gaze returned to focus on her, studying the hat, which was tilting dangerously again. "You don't have to be afraid of us," he told her reassuringly, noting the cautious look in her eye. "Do we look like the type of men who would take advantage of a lady?"

Wynne's eyes studied him for a moment, then drifted involuntarily over to the other man. His eyes and stance remained aloof as she met his direct gaze.

No, this one didn't seem the type to take advantage of a woman, but the other one certainly looked questionable.

"Nevertheless, you've been warned," she stated simply, then turned toward the stage. Once again fate intervened. Her feet became entangled in one of Penelope's stray petticoats lying on the ground. Her own skirt wrapped itself around her legs, pitching her forward. When she threw out her hands to keep from falling, the gun spun in the dirt and landed at Beau's feet. Dust puffed up into her nose, and she sneezed, barely halting the automatic move to rub her nose. As she looked up from her prone position, the first person she saw, naturally, was that dark man watching her as if she were something in a sideshow.

Fortunately it was Beau's boots that were right in front of her face. With a courtly bow he reached down and handed the gun back to her with a polite smile. "Allow me, ma'am."

"Thank you . . . sir." She felt her face flood with color. After scrambling to her feet, she snatched the gun back and reached up to straighten her hat, which had gone askew in the turmoil. She had no idea why she was so clumsy today! "I'll just get the other passengers in the stage," she announced.

"That would be fine, ma'am," Beau drawled with a grin.

He made his way back over to where Cole sat on his horse watching the fiasco.

"What do you think you're doing?" Cole asked calmly.

"Gettin' ready to escort the stage back to town," Beau answered innocently.

"Why did you give that gun back to her?"

"Oh, that," he scoffed. "She's not gonna shoot anyone. She's just scared."

"I *know* she's not going to shoot anyone intentionally," Cole growled, "but I think we're in serious danger of getting our heads blown off by her stupidity!"

"Come on, Cole. Look at 'em. They're—they're helpless." Beau's gaze returned to the shaken passengers, beginning to climb back into the coach. "Let her feel like she's runnin' the show. It's not gonna hurt a thing."

Cole took a drag on his cigar and studied the situation for a moment. In his opinion, everything was under control and one of the men passengers could take the stage on into town.

"Boy, you're a born sucker when it comes to a pretty face," he said accusingly. The woman undoubtedly was a looker. She stood barely five feet tall with the prettiest red hair and snapping green eyes Cole could ever recall seeing, but she still seemed like a menace to him.

"No, I'm not," Beau said. "I just think it's our duty to get 'em into town safely. Look at 'em, Cole. Neither one of those gentlemen looks like he could handle a team of horses, and I know the women can't."

Cole wasn't heartless, nor was he inclined to spend one more moment with a gun waving in his face. He had made it all the way through the war without an injury, and he wasn't about to have some snip of a woman ruin his perfect record less than ten miles from home. "There's no reason for us to get mixed up in this," Cole contended. "We can send someone out here to help them when we ride through town."

"No, I don't want to do that," Beau argued. "We can't just ride off and leave the ladies out here to fend for themselves. It won't take long to escort them back to town, and then we'll be on our way."

"I still say we stay out of it."

"Okay. If you don't want to help, then I'll do it myself."

Beau could be stubborn as a Missouri mule, and no one was more acutely aware of that fact than Cole. "All right, all right. But I don't like it," he said.

"Thanks." Beau grinned with relief. "I just wouldn't feel right about leavin' them alone." He watched as the last passenger clambered aboard the coach. "Now, you drive the stage and I'll load the driver and guard on our horses and be right behind you."

Cole dismounted with a grumble and strode over to the coach as Beau took care of the dead men.

Gripping the cheroot between his teeth, Cole had planted his foot on the wheel of the stage and started to climb aboard when the cold barrel of a gun tapped him on the shoulder. He tensed and turned around to meet Wynne's calculating eyes.

"Don't forget. I'll be watching you." She reminded him as curtly as her southern accent would allow.

He bit down on the end of the cigar impatiently. "Ma'am, I'm quivering in my boots," he drawled in a mixture of Georgia softness and Missouri twang.

Well, Wynne thought irritably, he could talk! Then her eyes suddenly narrowed. There was something vaguely familiar about him, although she was certain she had never met this man before. In spite of herself, she found herself noticing how very even and white his teeth were, and though he had obviously been riding for some time, he was not nearly as dirty and offensive as the bandits had been. The heat had curled his dark hair attractively around his tanned face, and his eyes—well, she had never seen such a strikingly clear blue color before. . . . For a brief moment she tried to imagine what he would look like with a shave, a haircut, and clean clothes, and the new image was of an extremely handsome swain.

She shook the disturbing image away. But she couldn't shake the feeling that he reminded her of someone else.

"Good. See that you remain that way." Wynne primly tucked herself and the gun into the coach and slammed the door. But a moment later an ominous steel cylinder was slid out of the window and carefully positioned in the direction of the driver's seat.

Cole shot a dirty look at Beau, who had just ridden up on his horse. "I don't know why I let you talk me into these things!" he snapped.

Beau was still grinning as Cole climbed aboard the stage. With an impatient whistle and a slap of the reins he set the stage in motion and, the barrel of a shotgun pointed straight at his head, headed for town as fast as he could.

CHAPTER 2

THE STAGE PULLED INTO TOWN WITH A LOUD JANGLE of harness and a cloud of boiling dust. The townspeople, surprised to see Cole seated in the driver's seat, ran to meet the new arrivals.

"Cole, boy!" Tal Franklin, the town sheriff, climbed aboard the coach and slapped him soundly on the back. "Good to see you, son!" Cole could have sworn Tal's eyes grew misty for a moment before he dragged out a large handkerchief and wiped hurriedly at his nose. The last few weeks the townsfolk had seen the sons of River Run return home—at least the ones who had survived the war—and it had been a heartwarming sight.

"Good to see you, Tal." Cole grinned widely, clasped the man's hand, and pumped it affectionately. Words seemed very inadequate for the feelings that swelled within him as he looked at the familiar face he'd known for most of his thirty years. God, it was good to be home!

"Looks like you come through without a scratch." Tal beamed; then his smile faded a little. "Have you seen either of your brothers?" Tal hated even to ask the question, dreading the answer he'd heard too often in the past few months. So many of the boys who had made it home were nearly destroyed by their experiences of death. They were bone-weary and disillusioned.

"One of 'em's right behind me." Cole smiled and set the brake before leaping off the driver's seat. "I ran into Beau about a couple hundred miles back, and we rode home together."

"Aw, your ma's going to be beside herself. Two of her boys comin' home the same day!" Tal slapped him on the back again. "But what in the world are you doing driving the stage?"

At that moment Beau rounded the corner by the saloon, leading Cole's horse with the bodies of the stage driver and shotgun guard draped across the saddle.

A buzz of excited voices reached the sheriff as he turned to peer over his shoulder. "What's going on here?"

"The stage was robbed about five miles back," Cole reported as he walked back to open the door of the coach and help the first passenger down. He waved at the sound of several friendly voices that called out to him, and his heart swelled with happiness at being back among familiar faces.

There was old Nathan at the blacksmith shop, grinning at him with his gold tooth shining in the afternoon sunlight. Nute Walker was sweeping the front porch of his general store and watching all the commotion that was taking place. A holiday mood was evident in the crowd.

Mary Beth Parker, the town spinster, sat in the window of the post office and waved her handkerchief at him. He remembered her smile from when he was a small boy and his ma would send him in town to pick up the mail each month. Mary Beth had been the postmistress of River Run for more than fifty years, and it wouldn't seem right to see anyone else sitting in her place.

Familiar sounds, familiar faces—how good it was to hear and see them all again.

Jerking open the stagecoach door, Penelope stepped lightly into Cole's waiting arms. He swung her small frame down easily, then quickly doffed his hat in the first show of manners Wynne had seen from him. "Ma'am, I hope the ride wasn't too uncomfortable for you."

Penelope's sultry gaze took in the width of his shoulders and the broad expanse of his chest as she removed her arms from around his neck ever so slowly. She batted her eyes at him demurely. "Why, thank you, sir. I surely do appreciate your bein' such a gentleman. I'm feelin' much better now, thank you." Her soft southern accent floated lightly on the air, along with the enticing scent of her jasmine perfume.

Cole felt his smile widening to a silly grin, and he mentally berated himself for getting so flustered in the presence of a pretty girl. But it had been awhile since he'd been so close to a female, and he could feel his body reacting accordingly.

His grin was still spread all over his face as he reluctantly set Penelope aside and turned to the next passenger. Instead of warm flesh, his hand came in contact with the cold metal of a gun. And his grin died a sudden death.

Wynne forced the burdensome gun ahead of her as she tried to work her billowing skirts and the hatbox she was carrying out the narrow doorway. Naturally the brim of her hat scraped the doorframe, and it tilted alarmingly. She had watched the sickeningly courteous treatment the dark, silent man had bestowed on Penelope, and when he just stood back and watched her struggle out of the coach on her own, Wynne's irritation became evident.

Intent on maneuvering herself, her purse, the hatbox, and the gun out the narrow door, she missed her footing on the bottom step. The hatbox crushed against the doorframe, and the gun barrel reared upward as she came flying out nearly headfirst.

All effort at trying to remain graceful disappeared while she concentrated on not killing herself by falling out of the high-set stage.

An unwilling witness to this minifiasco, Cole ducked quickly to one side and automatically flinched against the blast he expected to hear as Wynne's gun waved about wildly. He straightened just in time to see her plop into the dust, flat on her fanny, the gun and the hatbox beside her, her purse dangling from her wrist. Her face flamed a bright red when she glanced up to see the definite smirk on his face. This had to be the most humiliating day of her life! What must this man think of her when she kept falling all over the place like a complete idiot?

Cole drew a deep, resigned sigh, then picked up his hat and dusted it off on his thigh. Jamming it back on his head, he walked over to Wynne and leaned down until his face was level with hers. With as serious an expression as he could muster, he spoke in a perfectly controlled voice. "Excuse me, ma'am. Could I assist you with your hatbox?"

Swallowing the peppery retort which sprang immediately to mind, Wynne allowed something like a growl to escape her tightly compressed lips. Struggling to her feet, she steadfastly refused to look at the gathering crowd. There were definitely a few smothered chuckles, and she felt like a total fool. This was absolutely the last straw! She had no idea why she was being besieged by such bad luck today, but she was beginning to resent it highly! "Thank you . . . sir, but I believe I can manage by myself." She certainly had done so up to now with no help from him at all!

He'd helped Penelope out of the stage like a porcelain doll, then let *her* fall out on her face. She was completely mortified, but she wasn't about to let on that she'd noticed the difference or that it bothered her.

She shook the dust from her skirt and was reaching for the hatbox when Cole's hand snaked out. Before she knew what was happening, he'd snatched the gun away. "Please, I insist on bein' of service, ma'am. At least let me carry your gun."

His blue eyes danced determinedly, and again her face flushed brick red as she thought about how bumbling she had been during this whole ordeal. With some effort she gathered the shredded remnants of her composure, squared her shoulders, and lifted her small chin. "Yes . . . well, thank you. That would be most helpful." She acceded gracefully, her nose tilting up a fraction. Lifting the hem of her skirt and holding her purse, she swished past him in her most haughty manner. Assuming she and the other passengers were perfectly safe now with the sheriff present, she could afford to let down her guard a little.

Tal Franklin stood with Beau, discussing the details of the robbery, as Wynne approached. "I'm certainly glad to see you, Sheriff," she confessed, dropping her hatbox onto the ground beside him. "Do you think there's any possible way you can catch those thieves and return my money today?" She peered up at him hopefully while adjusting the precarious tilt of her hat and tucking up stray strands of hair which trailed over her dusty, damp face.

Tal had witnessed the whole performance of this young woman's getting off the stage and wondered about the obvious animosity between her and Cole. And that hat she was wearing! Eastern fashions were slow to get to the Midwest, and generally the ladies were interested in seeing the new styles; but he'd bet his last dollar not one of them would wear that bird's nest. "Well, I'll try my best, ma'am, but they've got a pretty good head start on me. One of my men's roundin' up a posse right now. We'll be on our way soon as they get here."

Wynne's shoulders slumped. "I'd hoped you'd know who they were."

Tal's heart immediately went out to her. "From the description Rutcliff gave me, sounds like it's the Beason gang. They been giving us a peck of trouble lately. If it is them, they'll head straight for the hills, and it'll be a mite hard to get to them," he said in a resigned voice.

"But you'll have to get to them," she replied. "They took every cent I have plus my jewelry. I haven't anything left except my clothes!"

"Sure sorry, ma'am. We'll do everything we can." His attention was diverted momentarily, and he stepped over to help one of the men lift the lifeless body of the guard off Cole's horse.

Wynne sank down dejectedly on her hatbox to think for a moment. The sun beat down unmercifully, and the dust hung in the air. Her dress stuck to her moist skin, and she fanned her heat-flushed face with her handkerchief as she tried to think. Without any money she didn't have the slightest idea what to do next. She'd been carrying every last cent she had left, but at best it would have been enough to see her only through a few months. By then she'd planned to have her revenge on Cass Claxton and be on her way home to try to sell the only asset she had left in this world: the land her family home had been built on.

Now she was stranded in a strange town, penniless, and without the vaguest idea of what to do next. Since her father's death the only family she could claim was a distant aunt in Arizona, and she didn't think her aunt would even remember her name, let alone wire money to her. She could get a job, but she wasn't trained for anything other than being a lady.

After spending the last few years at Marelda Fielding's Finishing School for Young Ladies in Philadelphia, she knew all the genteel manners and actions befitting a proper lady, but Miss Marelda had hardly prepared her to be sitting in the middle of the street on her hatbox, alone and flat broke.

Wynne fanned herself harder and forced down an almost hysterical giggle. Miss Prim and Proper Marelda Fielding would positively swoon if she could see the fine mess Wynne'd gotten herself into this time.

Cole and Beau were talking in undertones when she glanced in their direction. Somehow she had the feeling they were discussing her situation, and it unnerved her.

"What are we going to do about her?" Beau asked worriedly.

"Penelope told me she's here to work at Hattie's," Cole said. "She didn't say, but I assume that's where the crazy one's headed too. So you can stop playing mother hen."

Beau's gaze studied Wynne's small, wilted form, and he felt disappointment as Cole's words registered. "Oh? I wouldn't have thought she'd be one of . . . those kind of women."

"Well, apparently she is, so let's just play it smart and move on." Cole resettled his hat and turned toward his horse. "If you want to spend time socializin' with her in the future, you can always ride back to town."

"The devil I can," Beau said, but he sounded awfully wistful to Cole. "Betsy would wring my neck."

The sheriff motioned to Cole as Beau strolled back over to where Wynne sat and knelt beside her. "I think we're just about through here. The sheriff will notify the families." He paused and surveyed her worried face. "Are you gonna be all right?"

Wynne sighed and plucked absently at the drawstrings of her purse. She was indeed in a pickle and needed someone to advise her on what she should do now. After debating the question, she had decided that this man seemed harmless, even though he had fought on the wrong side during the war.

"To be honest, Mr. . . ." She paused, searching for a name. There'd been no time for the pleasantries of exchanging names.

Remembering his manners, Beau swept off his hat gallantly. "You can just call me Beau, ma'am."

"Thank you, Beau. And my name's Wynne Elliot, but you may call me Wynne."

"Wynne. That's a right pretty name, ma'am."

"Thank you . . . Beau . . . but as I was saying, I'm afraid this robbery has left me in quite a quandary." Taking a deep breath, she shot him a timid smile.

"Oh?" Beau was instantly sympathetic. "Well, I know you must have been real scared, but you're safe now," he assured her.

"Oh, I'm not concerned for my safety," Wynne answered quickly. "It's just . . . well, they took all my money, and now I'm not quite sure what I'm going to do." With tears precariously close to the surface, her drawl became more pronounced.

Wynne couldn't help noticing the abrupt way his gaze dropped from hers, almost as if he were suddenly embarrassed. "Oh, uh, why, I don't imagine you'll have to worry none about your keep." He consoled her rather weakly. "Hear tell Hattie takes right good care of her . . . girls."

Wynne stared at him vacantly. "Hattie?"

"Yeah . . . you know, Hattie Mason . . . she runs the local saloon and . . . well, you know, the lady who owns Hattie's Place—"

Suddenly what Beau was implying dawned on Wynne. "Hattie's Place!" She sprang to her feet indignantly as Beau's head snapped back.

He rose more slowly. "Well, yeah . . . Cole said he thought you and Miss Pettibone were headed for the same . . ." His voice trailed off meekly when two red flags of anger bloomed high on her cheeks.

"Oh, he did, did he?" She shot a scathing glance in the direction of the gossipy culprit. "Well, you can just tell *him* he'd better get his facts straight before he starts maligning my good character!" she snapped.

"Now, ma'am," Beau said, trying to pacify her hurriedly, "my brother didn't mean no harm. He just sort of assumed since you and Miss Pettibone were traveling together . . . you know, you two being such pretty women and all—"

She stamped her foot angrily. "Well, he assumed wrong!"

"Yes, ma'am. I'll tell him." Beau agreed quickly, suddenly realizing what a nice, even-tempered girl his Betsy was.

Shooting visual daggers at Cole, who was still talking to the sheriff and Penelope, Wynne snorted. "Hattie's Place! How dare he!" She stamped her foot in disgust, again raising a cloud of dust.

Cole glanced in Wynne's direction at the sound of her upraised voice, and she glared at him bitterly.

"Now, don't you be frettin' yourself none, ma'am." Beau hastened to change the subject. "Cole and me will be happy to take you to your folks, and in a few days the sheriff will find the men and return your money and then ever'thing will be all right again."

She was barely listening to his optimistic predictions as her angry gaze bore into the tall dark-haired man, who had returned to making idle conversation with Penelope in front of the saloon. She seriously doubted if Cole would be too thrilled about Beau's generosity.

Her temper continued to simmer when she noted the polite way he was treating Penelope. She couldn't help comparing his courteous manner toward the petite blonde with his arrogant manner toward her a few moments earlier. His gentility had taken wing when he had let her fall out of the coach on her fanny and make a complete fool of herself for the second time today!

"But you don't understand." She interrupted hastily as Beau tried to soothe her ruffled feathers. "I don't have any family out here."

Surprise flickered briefly in his eyes. "You don't?"

"No," Wynne said in confirmation. "In fact, I really don't have any family . . . anywhere."

"You're not from around here?" He knew he hadn't recognized her, but a lot of things had changed, he was sure, since he'd been away.

"No, Savannah is my home . . . or was until Papa died a few months ago."

"You're from Georgia?" Beau asked, surprised. "Well, what on earth is a young lady like you doing traveling out here all alone?"

"I'm . . . looking for someone," she said vaguely.

Beau looked relieved. "Good, at least there's someone. A lady friend?"

"Wellll . . ." Wynne shrugged her shoulders lamely. "Not really. I'm looking for a man. I heard his home was in River Run. Even though I know he's been off fighting the war, I understand he's coming back here now that it's over."

"Oh." A devilish light twinkled in Beau's eyes. "A beau, huh? Well, take heart, Miss Elliot. Me and Cole have lived in these parts all our lives, so we know just 'bout everyone around here. If he lives around here, no doubt we can help you find him."

Wynne's face lit up expectantly, her cares suddenly seeming much lighter. "Do you think so?"

"Why, sure!" Beau affirmed. "And as for you havin' no money, don't worry about that! We'll just take you home with us," he said. "Ma always has room for one more, and she'd be ashamed of us if she found out you was in trouble and we hadn't done our Christian duty."

"Oh, no. Really, I couldn't impose on you like that," Wynne protested.

"Impose!" Beau warmed to his idea. "We'd be right proud to have you come along with us. Soon as me and Cole get settled in, we'll start lookin' for your man." His face creased in one of his irresistible grins as he offered Wynne his arm. "Now I don't want to hear no more arguments. You're coming home with us."

He picked up Wynne's hatbox and escorted her to his horse, assuring her all the while that everything would work out. "You can ride with me," he said. "I'll get Cole to carry your bags."

Wynne wasn't at all sure she was doing the right thing, but she suddenly found herself being lifted up and placed firmly on the back of his horse.

Her relief wavering, she leaned over to catch Beau's arm. "Uh, Beau, don't you think you should check with your brother before you offer to let me go with you?" She could well imagine what *his* reaction was going to be to this latest piece of news.

Beau swung his large frame up behind her and grinned in encouragement. "Oh, don't fret none. He won't care. After being gone four years, all he wants to do is get home. He don't care who goes with him."

"I still don't think he'll be too happy about all this," she protested.

"He won't care," Beau insisted.

Beau nudged the horse's flanks gently and set them into motion. Seconds later they ambled up beside Cole and Penelope. Cole glanced up, and surprise flickered across his face when he saw Wynne mounted in front of Beau.

"You about ready to go?" Beau inquired pleasantly. "Wynne's coming home with us."

Wynne could have sworn Cole's mouth dropped open for a minute before he quickly recovered from his brother's casual announcement.

"I thought she was headed for Hattie's," Cole blurted.

"Well, it just so happens you thought wrong!" Wynne answered curtly. Then she proceeded to bestow on him one of her loveliest and snootiest smiles, one Miss Fielding would have been proud of. "Your brother has kindly offered the hospitality of your home until I can regain my money." She batted her eyes in obvious flirtation, just to see that look of irritation sweep across Cole's features. "Beau said you wouldn't mind carrying my valises." She crossed her hands over her breasts in mock admiration. "My, you're such a wonderful gentleman."

Cole glanced at Beau sharply, then back at Wynne with a grim set to his mouth. "If you ladies would excuse us for a minute, I'd like to have a word with Beau."

Beau obediently slid down off the horse and handed the reins to Wynne with a knowing wink. "Be right back."

The two brothers walked around the corner of the building while Wynne said her good-byes to Penelope.

The minute the two men were out of sight, Cole grabbed Beau's arm and demanded, "What in the hell are you doing this time?"

"Hey, just calm down," Beau said cajolingly, glancing back over his shoulder worriedly to see if they could be heard. "I knew you wouldn't be too happy about this arrangement, but the poor girl's up a creek, Cole."

"I fail to see where that's our responsibility," Cole replied stubbornly. "Let Hattie take care of her!"

"She told you. She wasn't coming to work for Hattie," Beau said patiently. "Penelope is the only one going to work there."

"Then what is she doing out here all alone in the first place? Damned crazy woman—" He broke off in a grumbling voice.

"She's looking for some man."

Cole snorted. "God help him! Let's hope, for his sake, she doesn't find him."

"What have you got against her?" Beau asked. "She hasn't said ten words to you, and you act like she's done something wrong."

"She's careless and a little addlebrained, don't you think?"

"No, I don't. So she doesn't know how to handle a gun very well. Lots of women don't. Betsy and Priscilla don't—"

"I don't want to hear any more about Priscilla! Okay?"

"Okay, okay. But you can't hold not being able to handle a gun well against Wynne," he pointed out. "For the life of me, I can't understand why you're so dead set against helping her. You're usually a little more gentlemanly when it comes to women," Beau added. "Ma would be ashamed of you."

"I think you're asking for trouble," Cole argued. "I think we'd better turn her over to Tal and be on our way."

"I can't do that."

"You can't do that," Cole repeated in exasperation. "Why can't you do that? It means nothing to us one way or the other. We stumbled on a robbery! We didn't take her to raise!"

"I know, but somehow I sort of feel responsible for her, Cole. Don't ask me to explain. I'm gonna take her home to Ma for now, and then I'm gonna help her find the man she's looking for," he stated flatly. "All I'm asking you to do is carry her valises on your horse. Now, is that askin' too much?"

"Yes, it is, and you're a fool," Cole grumbled, pulling his hat off and wiping his forearm across his forehead.

"Maybe so, but that's the way I'm gonna do it. Now, are you gonna carry her bags, or am I gonna have to make another trip back into town to get them?"

Cole raked his fingers through his dark hair in annoyance. "I don't know why I let you talk me into these things," he muttered. "She's only gonna be trouble for us. You mark my words."

"I'm marking as long as you're carrying her bags." Beau grinned and slapped him on the back good-naturedly as they walked back around the corner.

"I'll tell Tal she'll be out at our place if he needs her," Beau announced. "I won't be but a minute."

Cole grunted an answer and went over to pick up the two bags sitting on the ground in front of the stage. After hefting them up onto his shoulders, he went back to his horse and started tying them on.

Wynne sat on Beau's horse and watched him work, noting he did so with very little enthusiasm. She fanned herself energetically, trying to lessen the growing heat and distract the flies that were buzzing around her head. She almost envied Penelope, who had disappeared into the cool interior of Hattie's Place. Almost envied her, but not quite.

Even though this Cole had not made the slightest effort to be pleasant from the moment they met, Wynne decided as she got off the horse that she should at least introduce herself if she was going to be spending the next few days in his company.

"Excuse me," she said.

Cole glanced up, and once more she unwillingly noted how very strikingly blue his eyes were. Against the deep tan of his skin they looked as blue as a cloudless sky on a bright summer day. And he was handsome, Wynne had to admit. Devilishly handsome—although he had the temperament of an old goat.

Strange, but she suddenly had the nagging feeling again that she had met him before. There was something about him that jarred her memory, yet she couldn't quite put her finger on what it was. Before she could pursue the puzzling thought, Cole returned his attention to his work, totally dismissing her.

Wynne cleared her throat and tried again, thinking perhaps he'd not heard her the first time and had glanced up only accidentally. "Uh, sir?"

This time he stared at her, and Wynne smiled back timidly.

"Are you talkin' to me?" he asked curtly.

Her smile faded. "Well, of course, I'm talking to you," she stated. "Who did you think I was talking to? The horse?"

"It wouldn't surprise me none." He went about his work, making no effort whatsoever to continue the strained conversation.

Swallowing her exasperation, Wynne tried again. "I, uh, I thought since we would be in each other's company for the next few days, we should introduce ourselves."

He grunted something unintelligible again.

"Uh, I'm Wynne Elliot." She extended her hand.

"And I'm Pompous Ass," he replied evenly, cinching the rope around her bags tighter and ignoring her hand.

A flush of embarrassment rose from her collar, and her gaze slid away in embarrassment. "Oh, my, I didn't know you heard that."

"I heard," he said tersely.

"Well, I must apologize—is it Cole?"

He shot her another irritable look and continued his task.

"I suppose this whole ordeal has unnerved me, and I have completely forgotten my manners." Once again she extended her hand toward him in a friendly gesture, forgetting that it was covered in dirt from her fall out of the stage earlier. "My name is Wynne Elliot, but you may call me *Miss* Elliot." She was going to give only so much until he showed a greater interest in being civil.

Cole stared at her slightly grubby hand and, after a moment of hesitation, gingerly accepted it. "*Miss* Elliot." He bowed mockingly. "I wish I could say it was an honor to make your acquaintance," he said dryly.

She ignored his continuing despicable manners. "I'm . . . sorry about calling you a pompous ass."

"And I'm sorry I called you . . . what I did," he said generously.

Her forehead wrinkled in a frown. "What did you call me?"

" 'Addlebrain' and 'careless' are the two that come to mind right off," he confessed with a grin playing about his lips.

Her frown deepened. "Addlebrained! You called me addlebrained!" She jerked her hand out of his. "I suppose you think I'm addlebrained just because I dropped the gun and tripped over it!"

"No, I think it was because you fell out of the stage," he said blandly, controlling the grin with some effort. "Then I added 'careless.' "

He watched with amusement as she shook her head angrily, causing her hat to slip down over her nose. She shoved it back on her head impatiently, and the bird rocked precariously in its nest.

"Well, I can assure you I am *not* careless or addlebrained," Wynne sputtered. "You just happened to catch me at a bad moment!"

"If you say so . . . Miss Elliot." Cole picked up the reins of his horse and swung into the saddle as Beau came out of the sheriff's office.

"I'll follow you," Cole called as Beau, holding his horse's reins, walked up behind Wynne. "Let's try to make it home for supper."

"Sounds like heaven to me!" Beau whistled as he helped Wynne up onto the horse and lifted himself up behind her. He gave a loud rebel yell as he kicked his horse into action.

Wynne shot one more cross look in Cole's direction, then held on for life as the trio rode out of town in a cloud of dust.

Addlebrained indeed!

CHAPTER 3

*F*UNNY HOW LIFE HELD SUCH STRANGE TWISTS AND turns. Not so very long ago the only thing Wynne Elliot had to worry about was the color of her next ball gown.

As she bounced along on Beau's horse, she thought about how wonderful life had been back home in Georgia before both Mama and Papa had passed away. She had been an only child, raised in an affluent home by doting parents. Moss Oak had been one of the biggest cotton plantations in the South before the war broke out. The plantation had been in the family for generations, and her father, Wesley Elliot, had run it as he had run his family, with a firm but loving hand.

Then the war had come, and Papa had sent her away to school. For a while she could ignore the rumors of the terrible atrocities going on and concentrate solely on learning the fine art of being a lady, which Papa thought she sorely needed. She was a little too independent for his liking. Since she'd followed him about the plantation from when she was a child, she'd picked up a few habits he disapproved of—like his penchant for swearing.

But all too soon her idealistic bubble burst, and she was faced with the harsher realities of life. Mama had taken ill with a strange sickness, and Papa had brought Wynne back home to comfort her.

With a feeling of complete helplessness, Wynne and her father had stood by and watched as each week Rose Elliot struggled to overcome the devils that were ravaging her body. There was nothing anyone could seem to do to still the nausea and the swift weight loss that beset her. Then came the terrible pain. Wynne was still tormented by the sound of her mother's soft sobbing in the night and her father's agonized voice trying to ease her torment and contain his own. Weeks seemed like years then.

At times Wynne would spend hours praying that the good Lord would relieve the suffering and take away the agony they all were experiencing. How she longed to hear laughter and the sound of gaiety rumbling through the old mansion once more instead of the hushed whispers of the servants and the almost tangible smell of death. At other times she would cast away her own selfish feelings and cry out for someone, anyone, to give her mother peace.

When the end came, Rose Elliot simply went to sleep and never woke up.

If Wynne had thought her mother's sickness was heartbreaking, it was nothing compared with her father's grieving his life away after her mother's death. He roamed the halls at night in search of something that Wynne never quite understood. Her heart broke even more when she passed his study late in the evening and heard the tortured weeping of a man who had suffered an unbearable loss, one he could not seem to cope with. The day Rose died, she took the biggest part of Wesley with her. Left behind was the lonely shell of a man merely serving out his time on earth until they could be together once more.

It was then that Cass came into Wynne's life. He was a gentle, loving man who helped her through that terrible time with his sunny disposition, quick wit, and unusual charm.

She'd met him through a mutual friend at a Christmas ball. When she questioned why he hadn't enlisted in the southern cause, Cass had explained that since he had family obligations, he had paid someone to take his place. While it bothered her that he had paid the $400 for another man to fight on his behalf, she conceded that it was customary practice for men of means to do so.

And undoubtedly Cass came from an affluent and prosperous family. At the time he was in Savannah, visiting relatives, prominent, wealthy pillars of the community, and Wynne had been so totally captivated by his impeccable manners and his courtly ways that all else faded from her mind.

It was such a rare treat for the belles of Georgia to have such a fascinating, eligible young man in their midst that Wynne simply forgot about the war and let her heart be won by the dashing young man whose pretty words dripped off his tongue like rich, warm honey—lying, deceitful words that she still didn't believe she had actually been gullible enough to believe!

A scant six weeks after Rose's death Wesley chose to join her. Wynne had heard the shot ring out as she lay in her bed that fateful night. For months she had heard the reverberation over and over again. . . .

She was left totally alone and more frightened than she had ever been in her life.

The Yankees came through and burned Moss Oak and all the surrounding buildings. Mercifully they had left the main house standing, but they had ransacked and stolen all the furnishings as Wynne and the servants had stood by and surveyed the devastation in stunned silence.

The loyal family servants had stayed on, erecting makeshift housing to live in so they could work the land for her, but it was hopeless. The fields were charred and desolate, and it would be a long time before cotton would blossom there again.

"Are you comfortable?" Beau's voice broke into her painful thoughts and brought her quickly back to the present.

Immersed in her sad memories, Wynne had almost forgotten her uncomfortable perch in a saddle too large for her and the closeness of the man riding behind her. She plucked at the material of her dress, attempting to allow some air to circulate against her skin. The sun was a ball of fire in the sky, making her nearly limp with heat, and she was anything but comfortable; but considering how kind Beau had been, she decided it would be ungrateful on her part to complain.

"I'm fine, thank you." She shifted slightly, increasingly aware of the pressure of Beau's arms around her as he held the reins. Surely it couldn't be much farther. "Are we almost there?"

"Just another three miles or so," he answered. "We can stop and let you rest a spell if you'd like."

"No, that's all right. I'll be fine."

She was most appreciative of what this man was doing for her. Not all men would have taken her under their wing the way he had.

She turned her head slightly, her eyes fastening on the rider trailing a safe distance behind them. He certainly would have left her for the buzzards.

Her mind unwillingly brought Cass, another tall, handsome devil, to the surface once more, and the picture set her to seething all over again.

The only good thing Cass Claxton had done for her was to be there for her to lean on during the most tragic time of her life. And in all honesty he had never failed her once back then. He helped her face reality, always there for her when she swore she couldn't, wiping at her tears and telling her that she could. For a young man of twenty-two, he readily admitted he didn't know all the answers, but together they would find them.

Then one day Cass was offered an opportunity to go into business with one of his cousins. They wanted to buy a business that manufactured gunpowder, and Wynne was ecstatic. It meant Cass would be staying in Savannah.

She immediately began dropping hints of marriage, seeing that as a way of salvaging her broken life. In further enticement she offered the money from her inheritance as bait for such a venture, and it wasn't long before she was able to persuade Cass to accept her generosity. The night before they were to be married, Wynne gave him all her money—with the exception of a meager amount she kept in a small tin box under her bed—assuming his business venture would be concluded early the following morning.

Looking back, she wondered if Cass ever really loved her or if he had asked for her hand in marriage simply to appease a girl for whom nothing in life had gone well lately. Certainly his family could have lent him the money to go into business, but instead, he had asked Wynne to marry him.

A shiver of embarrassment rippled through her as she recalled her wedding day. It had dawned cold and gray with the promise of rain in the air. Tilly, her mammy since childhood, had lovingly dressed Wynne for the ceremony, fretting over her like a mother hen.

Wynne had smiled and glanced at herself in the large looking glass she was standing before. The soft, delicate folds of her mother's ivory wedding gown billowed out around her and swept to the floor. Her eyes grew misty as she stared back at the reflection that could have been Rose's nineteen years ago.

"Do you think Mama and Papa would have approved of what I'm doin', Tilly?" she had asked softly.

Tilly had heaved a big sigh and patted her shoulder reassuringly. "You got to do what you think best, baby." Seeing that Wynne's face still held worry, she added tenderly, "I'm sure your man will be real good to you, darlin'."

And she was right. Cass probably would have been good to her—if he had made it to the wedding.

The pain and humiliation still stung sharply as she thought about how she and the guests had waited at the church for him to arrive that day. They had waited and waited and waited. . . .

The very next morning Wynne had returned to Marelda Fielding's Finishing School, a feeble effort on her part to put her life back to what it once was.

But never again had she found the carefree life she had known. The death of her parents, the war, and Cass's rejection—all had taken their toll. And it seemed to her she just had to take some sort of revenge.

Slowly a plan—a very simple plan to avenge her pride and uphold the Elliot name—began to take root. She would find Cass Claxton and kill him for what he had done to her. Not only had he stolen her blind, but he had made her the laughingstock of Savannah in the process! Surely such parody could not go unpunished.

Wynne jerked her thoughts back to the present, assuring herself that Cass Claxton had not seen the last of her. She would find him if it was the last thing she did, and before she killed him, she would demand an explanation for his despicable behavior.

Squinting against the glaring sun, she turned her attention back to the man riding behind them, trying to make out his dusty features beneath the dark beard. It was either her vivid imagination, or else *he* even *looked* like Cass. No, that couldn't be. They only looked alike because she had been thinking about her former fiancé, she thought as she fanned herself rapidly.

But her imagination wasn't playing tricks on her. Now she realized why she had thought she'd met him before. Both men had similar characteristics. Cass had the same blue eyes and curly black hair as Cole. Unwillingly she found herself leaning back in the saddle, peering more closely at the trailing brother. Even the set of Cass's chin suggested the same stubborn streak she now saw in Cole's. Her eyes skimmed down his face and paused at the opening of his uniform. Thick wisps of the same dark hair on his head peeped out of the opening of his shirt, and her pulse quickened.

Powerful and ruggedly virile, Cole sat his saddle with the same aura of authority that Cass had, and for a moment Wynne found her heart thumping at the remembrance of being pressed against the broad expanse of a chest much like the one she was now practically ogling.

Her eyes narrowed speculatively. *I wonder what* he *would look like with his shirt off.* . . . She caught herself shamefully. Whatever made her think a thing like that?

She wasn't quite sure what made her gaze lift suddenly; but it did, and she found herself staring into a set of mocking blue eyes that held ill-concealed amusement at her disgraceful surveillance of him. Her face flooded with color, and she hurriedly snapped her head around to face the other direction.

That moron! She could practically feel his arrogant eyes boring a hole in the back of her head, but she refused to give him the satisfaction of looking at him again.

She was sure her face was bright red as she thought of what Cole must be thinking!

"Did you say something?" Beau called.

"No, nothing!"

For the remainder of the ride she carefully kept her eyes straight ahead and her thoughts a complete blank. When the two riders finally turned into a winding lane and let their horses have their head, Wynne breathed a great sigh of relief.

The horses thundered down the lane as Cole and Beau grinned at each other mischievously and reverted to their childhood days, when they would try to outrace each other home. Wynne held on as tightly as she could, fearing they both had taken leave of their senses.

With a burst of speed, Cole's horse shot by them and raced the remaining half mile to the farmyard. With a whoop of sheer joy, he sprang out of his saddle before the horse had even stopped and enfolded in his arms the woman who had just run out the door to see what all the excitement was about. Lifting her high above his head, he swung her around and around, his face breaking out in a wreath of smiles. "Hi, Ma! I'm home!"

"Cole!" Tears of relief filled the woman's eyes as her laughter joined his, his words of greeting resounding through the air. How long she had yearned to hear those words again.

Her eyes searched her son's face, looking for signs of the young man who had left home four years ago. She found none. The familiar features greeted her, but she could see he had grown much older in the time he had been gone and she couldn't help noticing the age lines gathering around the corners of his eyes. He looked so much like Sam it was all she could do to remember this was her firstborn, not her deceased husband, who stood before her.

"Beau? Have you heard from Beau?" she questioned.

"Beau's with me, Ma." Almost before the words had left his mouth, Beau and Wynne came riding into the yard.

There was a second round of shouting and laughter as Beau tumbled off the horse and wrapped his mother in his arms. With two burly men as sons, Lilly didn't have a chance to stand on her own two feet. Beau tossed her up into the air and nearly broke her bones as he caught her back in his arms and hugged her tightly. He then gently set her on her feet.

"Beau and Cole! Back home in the same day. Praise the Lord!" The tears in her eyes spilled over as she reached over to clasp her arms around Cole's neck and hug him tightly.

"It's so good to be home, Ma," he confessed in a husky, emotion-filled whisper.

"And your brother . . . have you seen or heard from him?" Her eyes pleaded for the answer she longed to hear.

Cole met her question with surprise. "No, isn't he here with you?"

"No—no, I got a letter a few months ago. Said he had joined up—"

"Damn!" Cole said irritably. "I thought he was gonna stay here and help you!"

Wiping at the corners of her eyes with her faded apron, she tried to defend her youngest son. "I know, but you know he always had a wanderin' streak in him . . . just like your pa."

"Well, don't worry, Ma. Now that the war's over, he'll be ridin' in any day." Cole tried to console his mother, but Wynne noticed his face was unusually solemn.

Lilly's arms went back around her boys' shoulders, and she hugged them simultaneously again. "Well, I thank the Lord you're here. I can't believe you're both home at the same time. When we heard the war was over, we started looking for you to come home, but since we hadn't heard anything from either one of you in so long, we didn't know what to expect."

Beau and Cole hung their heads sheepishly. "I would have wrote, Ma," Beau said apologetically, "but I figured I'd probably get here before the letter did."

"And what's your excuse?" Lilly put her hands on her hips and turned on Cole those accusing eyes that only a mother can conjure.

"Ah, Ma . . . you know me. I never was good at writing letters." Cole grinned with a lame shrug.

For the first time since all the excitement had broken out, Lilly glanced up at Wynne and smiled. "Land sakes! All this excitement, and we plumb forgot our manners. Who have you brought home with you?"

"Ma, this is Wynne Elliot." Beau walked over and lifted Wynne off his horse and set her down on the ground. "She was on the stage to River Run when it was robbed. They took all her money, and since she don't have no kin around here, we brought her home to stay with us for a few days."

"Robbed! Why, that must have been real frightenin'." Lilly reached out and pumped Wynne's hand warmly. "I'm glad Beau brought you home. You're welcome to stay as long as you like."

"Thank you," Wynne murmured gratefully. "I should be able to move on in a few days." She purposely avoided meeting Cole's eyes. "The sheriff is out looking for the bandits right now."

"Well, don't you fret yourself none. Tal will find them if anyone can. He's a good man. Now, come along, and let's all go in the house," Lilly suggested, wrapping her arms around her sons' waists and giving them another motherly squeeze. "It just so happens Willa and me have a big pot of them chicken and dumplin's you're so fond of simmerin' on the stove. Course, you're not either one goin' to sit at my table till you shave and wash some of that road grime off you." She tugged affectionately at Cole's beard.

Beau's face lit up happily. "No kiddin', Ma? You really got some chicken and dumplin's! I was just tellin' Cole this morning how I hoped you'd have some."

"Luck!" Lilly scoffed, hugging him tighter. "Why, we've had a pot of them chicken and dumplin's on the stove since we heard the war was over. We've just been a-prayin' and waitin' for you two to come home and eat 'em!"

As suddenly as it appeared, the laughter drained out of her voice, and her eyes grew misty. "I guess I'm just gonna have to stay down on my knees an extra long time tonight and thank the good Lord he seen fit to send you back to me." A tear suddenly slipped through her veil of happiness as she grinned and pinched Cole's cheek once more. "It's good to have you back, boys."

Cole looked down at his mother and said in the most heartfelt voice Wynne had ever heard, "Thanks, Ma. It's sure good to be here."

CHAPTER 4

LORD A'MIGHTY, IT WAS HOT! HE THOUGHT AS HE mopped his forehead again with a lank handkerchief. The blazing late-afternoon sun beat down on the lone rider without mercy as he entered the hot, parched streets of Springfield.

Bertram G. Mallory reached up and took another swipe at his dusty brow as he cast his eyes upward for some sign of rain, but there was none in sight. Only the endless blue of a summer sky met his gaze as his weary horse plodded along. It had been more than three months since it had rained in these parts, he'd heard. Too long. The countryside was brown and scorched, and the man's patience was wearing thin—not only with the weather but with Wynne Elliot.

Every time he got near the damn woman, she somehow managed to slip through his fingers. But she wouldn't do it again. He ran a long, lean hand over his dirty face. No, sir, he'd make sure of that this time.

He reined in the horse, with a low, painful groan slid out of the saddle, and hitched the animal to the rail. His hand automatically went to shield his still-tender left side. The result of the untimely accident he'd experienced a few weeks ago was still sensitive to the touch, not to mention the thought.

Bertram's eyes narrowed as he recalled the harrowing incident that had left him with three busted ribs and a splitting headache for days.

At the time it had seemed like a good idea to hop that train. After all, when he'd heard that Miss Elliot was reportedly attending a finishing school for ladies back east, he had been riding for days and been bone-tired. He would have tried anything to make the trip shorter.

But when he'd finally arrived at Marelda Fielding's Finishing School

for Young Ladies in Philadelphia, he'd been told by Miss Fielding that
Wynne wasn't there. Apparently the Elliot woman had decided to pay a
visit to Missouri. River Run, Miss Fielding had said. Well, he knew right
then that meant a peck of trouble unless he could get to her before she
got there.

River Run was a good several weeks' travel from Philadelphia by stage,
but not by train. Since it was imperative that he catch up with her as soon
as possible, and with the least amount of discomfort on his part, he
decided to hop the first train going south and hoped it would carry him to
within a reasonable distance of Missouri.

With a sense of elation he'd quickly sold his horse and pocketed the
money. He figured when he arrived in Missouri by train, several days
ahead of her, relaxed and completely rested, he would buy another horse
while he waited for Wynne Elliot's arrival. At the time he'd grinned
smugly.

It was a good plan, he decided. And there was no need to waste his
money on a ticket. He'd simply wait until the train passed under a big
bluff and then jump on the top of the car and ride there until the conduc-
tor collected the fares. Then he would casually blend himself in with the
other passengers and enjoy the ride.

He flinched as he again felt the sharp, excruciating pain ripping
through his side. It would have worked, too, if his timing hadn't been a
fraction off and if the train had run as far as Missouri.

He'd jumped just as he'd planned. He'd hit the top of the rail car
with the speed of a bullet, but the train had been traveling faster
than he'd calculated. Not much—but just enough to throw off his rapid
descent.

The jolt splattered him painfully into a spread-eagle position flat
against the top of the fast-moving train. Then his eyes had widened as he
frantically clutched for some sort of a hold and the train shot around a
bend in the track. Even now Bertram could almost feel all over again the
terror he had felt as his fingers began to slip and he'd realized he and the
train would soon be parting company. Even his toes had dug in for
support. At the deepest bend of the curve he lost his grip. He was ruthlessly flung off the side of the car, and his life had flashed before his eyes
as he'd been hurled through the air. His poor body was flung like a rag
doll to the ground, where he rolled for what must have been fifteen
minutes down a deep, briar-blanketed ravine.

When he regained consciousness, there had been an old prospector
bending over him. It was dark by then, and he was certain every bone had
been broken in his throbbing body. Bertram winced again as he recalled
the agonizing ride to town, slung over the back of the old man's donkey.
The prospector left him with the doctor and, after waving off Bertram's
gratitude, disappeared out the front door.

But to Bertram's amazement not quite every bone had been broken. He'd come out of the harrowing brush with death with only three cracked ribs and a cracked head, but they had been enough to lay him up at the local hotel for several weeks.

To add to his embarrassment, he'd found out that all the pain and inconvenience had been for naught.

The train had gone only twenty miles down the road before service ended. How was he to know that? Because of the difficulty merchants were experiencing throughout the country trying to get their goods overland by wagon, not to mention the financial loss of trying to cope with losing their animals to injury as the result of the terrible road conditions in most states, almost every town had railroad fever. Tracks were springing up all over the country, and the city fathers were crying for rail service. He'd been certain he could get to Missouri with no problem. . . .

The unexpected hotel expenses, having food brought in, and doctor's fees had taken the meager amount of money he'd brought with him, so he was faced with yet another costly delay while he found a job. He worked long enough to buy another horse, and then once more he set off in pursuit of the elusive Miss Elliot.

To begin his search anew, he'd been forced to go back to Miss Fielding's Finishing School for Young Ladies, hoping that by now she might have returned. He'd listened with a sinking knot in the pit of his stomach as Miss Fielding told him she had not seen Wynne since he had last been there and she assumed Wynne was still visiting in Missouri.

Bertram had sagged against the long white column on the porch as the door closed and fought the overwhelming feeling of yet another failure. He could smell the roses that were twining up the columns in a red blaze of color, and drifting tantalizingly through the air was the mouth-watering smell of someone baking corn bread.

He wondered again why he didn't just give up and go back home to Savannah. It would certainly be the sensible thing to do. But he knew he wouldn't give up. Bertram released a long sigh and pushed himself away from the column. He'd give anything for a bath, a shave, and a soft bed to sleep in tonight. And a woman to keep him company. That would be nice. A soft woman to hold in his arms and ease his aches and pains.

But he had given his word, and Bertram G. Mallory was a man to whom a promise meant something. He would go to any lengths to fulfill an obligation. But by the good Lord, this one was almost more than he could cope with. Yet a promise was a promise. And his promise was to find Wynne Elliot, no matter how long it took.

Wearily Bertram pulled himself back into the saddle, and once more he pushed himself and his horse hard. By his calculations he knew, now that he was in Springfield, his mission was finally nearing an end. And none too soon. He winced painfully as his hand went to shield his side again. River Run was just down the road apiece. By late tomorrow afternoon, he hoped he and Miss Elliot would meet face-to-face.

But tonight he'd rest a spell. He sure wished he had the money to find a good, clean hotel and have the bath, the shave, the hot meal, and maybe even the woman he had been longing for. But he knew that was foolish wishing. He certainly didn't have the funds for that sort of luxury. No, he'd settle for a cold beer or two, then camp somewhere on the outskirts of town for the night.

Bertram glanced around him, surprised to see so much activity on the streets at this hour. Pulling a watch from a side pocket, he noted it was getting close to 6:00 P.M. Most folks would be home taking supper about now. He rewound the stem, then carefully placed the watch back in his pocket.

He was right proud of that watch. His grandfather had given it to him many years ago, and even through the thick of battle he'd managed to hold on to it.

These big towns must have a faster way of life, he decided as his gaze lingered momentarily on a group of ragged-looking women who were standing next to the livery.

Although it wasn't unusual to see hundreds of Confederate female refugees swarming about the towns, looking for food and shelter, it still worried him. They were a destitute, heart-wrenching sight, and he didn't like to think about their being so alone. Women should be taken care of, pampered and held gently. It always saddened him to see those women. After what he'd experienced during the war, he'd have thought he would have become accustomed to the poverty and degradation that had been brought upon the people, but he hadn't. He guessed he never would. He had fought for only a few weeks, then been wounded and sent back to Savannah. But it was all he'd wanted of the killing.

Picking up the reins of his horse, he threaded his way along the fringes of the crowd that milled about, talking in low tones. They all seemed to be waiting for something. He wondered if one of those medicine shows might be coming to town.

Suddenly the hushed murmurs stilled. Everyone stood quietly waiting. His puzzled gaze studied the small crowds gathering in the doorways and alleys surrounding the square, and his brow furrowed with interest.

As far as he could tell, there was nothing unusual happening, yet the crowd seemed apprehensive and watchful.

He threw the reins over the nearest hitching post and stepped up onto the porch of the general store, where he spoke to one of the old-timers leaning back in a chair, whittling on a piece of wood. "Howdy."

The old-timer's knife paused as he glanced up at the newcomer and gave him a friendly grin. He had a battered old hat on his head and a snow-white beard that was stained with tobacco juice, and from what

Bertram could tell, he didn't have a single tooth left in his head. "Howdy," he answered, then leaned over the rail and spit a long stream of brown liquid into the dust.

Bertram stepped back out of the line of fire, then pushed his hat back on his head before he hunched down beside the man's chair. "Hot, ain't it?"

"Sure is."

"Could use some rain."

"Yep." The old-timer leaned over and spit again. "It'll rain soon, though. Saw a black snake in a tree this mornin'." He spit once more and wiped at his mouth with the sleeve of his shirt. "Hit's a sure sign rain's on the way."

"Yeah. Sure is." A black snake in a tree was about as accurate a prediction of rain as Bertram could think of, with the exception of birds flying low or walking on the ground. They always meant rain, and he was grateful for any small sign the drought would soon be over.

"You're a stranger to these parts, ain't you, boy?"

"Just passin' through."

"Humph." The old man grunted, then leaned over and spit again.

Bertram surveyed the scene in the square. "What's going on out there?" He nodded his head toward the people still gathering on the street, his curiosity aroused once more.

"Gonna be a shootin'," the old man stated calmly, his gnarled hands gently rubbing the piece of carving he was working on.

Bertram wasn't sure he'd heard right. "A shootin'?"

"Yep."

Once more his worried gaze sought the milling crowd. "Who's gonna be doing it?"

The old-timer looked up and gave him his toothless grin again. "You ever heared of Wild Bill Hickock, boy?"

Bertram blinked in surprise. "Hasn't everyone?" It was a well-known fact that Wild Bill's reputation and skill with a gun had made him the constable of Monticello Township, Illinois, when he was still a teenager. Rumor had it that he had been working as a Union sharpshooter and scout during the past few years, and Bertram had even heard speculation that Wild Bill had been a spy for the Union, posing as a Confederate throughout southern Missouri and Arkansas.

"Well, Wild Bill's gonna git his watch back today," the old-timer announced gleefully.

Bertram frowned. "Someone took his watch?" He let out a low whistle under his breath. That sounded mighty daring to him. Most men gave Wild Bill a wide berth when they met him. He couldn't imagine anyone being foolish enough to steal the man's watch.

"I guess you could say that. Him and Tutt ain't exactly the best of friends. They've had hard feelin's over Savannah Moore, a woman they both had a hankerin' for, but that's not what they're fightin' about."

"Oh?"

"Nope, they ain't fightin' over her this time. They were aplayin' cards the other day, and after Hickok had won most of Dave's money, Dave reminded him of the thirty-five dollars Wild Bill still owed him from another time when they had been aplayin'. Well, Wild Bill said he owed him only twenty-five dollars, and he laid it on the table in front of Tutt."

The old man warmed to his subject, his fingers fondling the piece of carving as he ran the sharp knife blade over the soft wood. "Now Tutt took his money all right, but he also took Wild Bill's gold watch that was alayin' there, saying that he figured that would about make up for the other ten Wild Bill owed him."

Bertram was completely engrossed in the story the old-timer was telling. Having heard of Wild Bill's reputation, he'd have sworn that Tutt would have been a dead man before he could have gotten the watch in his pocket. "And Wild Bill let him have the watch?"

"Oh, I wouldn't say that exactly. Bill jumped up and told Tutt to put the watch back down on the table. But Dave jest ignored him and left with the watch anyway. Th' air's been real thick betwix the two ever since."

"And that's what's the shootin's gonna be about?"

"Yep. Wild Bill warned Tutt not to wear the watch in public, but he paid Bill no heed. He went ahead and wore it anyway. We knowed somethin' was bound to happen, and sure enough, it has."

A stream of tobacco flew across the porch and raised dust beside the walk. "Some of Tutt's men sent word to Wild Bill that Dave would be acrossin' the square around six o'clock tonight if he wanted to try and get his watch back. Hickok sent word back that Dave couldn't be carryin' his watch across the square unless dead men had started walkin'."

Bertram fumbled in his pocket and hastily withdrew his own watch, noting with dismay that the appointed hour was upon them. "It's six o'clock right now. Why, Dave Tutt's a fool for tauntin' Hickok like that. He'll kill him for sure."

The old man leaned over and spit once more. "Maybe, maybe not. Dave Tutt ain't 'zactly shabby with a gun hisself. But there's one thing for certain. All hell's agonna break loose in a minute."

If there was one thing Bertram had no desire for, it was to become remotely entangled in a shoot-out on a public street with two known gunslingers. Even watching the spectacle held no interest for him. "Well, I think I'll just mosey on—" His words were interrupted as a breathless hush fell over the crowd.

Up the street to one side a bearded man stepped into view of the crowd. About the same time another man with shoulder-length dark hair and a long brush of mustache appeared on the opposite side. The flat-crowned hat, black coat, and tucked shirt identified the second man as Wild Bill Hickok.

"You'd better stay on that side of the square if you want to live, Tutt," Hickok warned.

Bertram could do nothing but watch now as Tutt made no effort whatsoever to reply. Bertram held his breath, watching the men as if he were watching a play. Except it wasn't one. One of these men would be dead in a few minutes.

But Dave Tutt didn't dally. He merely stepped out into the street, drawing his gun as he went. As he drew, so did Hickok, and both men fired at the same time.

The bullet from Hickok's gun went straight through Dave Tutt's heart, and he fell dead in a crumpled heap in the dusty street.

Hickok quickly whirled around and pointed his gun in the direction of Tutt's friends, who by then had drawn their own guns. "Put your arms up, men, or there'll be more than one man dead here today."

Bertram had seen enough. As if Hickok's words had freed his paralyzed body, he spun and started for cover. But as luck would have it, his foot caught on a loose board. As if a hand had come out of the sidewalk and grabbed his ankle, he was jerked to a sudden halt. The momentum was such that Bertram reeled off the porch into the street. He landed with a thud beneath the watering trough, his ankle throbbing with excruciating pain. He swallowed a painful moan, and his eyes squinted shut with agony.

The old-timer jumped up from his chair on the porch and peered over the trough. On the square Tutt's men slowly holstered their weapons and melted into the crowd.

With one final glance around him Wild Bill calmly walked over to Tutt's body and recovered his gold Waltham watch and chain, then turned and walked to the courthouse to surrender his pistols to the sheriff.

"Here, boy. Let me help ya. Are you bad hurt?" The old man rolled Bertram over onto his back.

Bertram groaned and held on tightly to his rapidly swelling ankle. If he didn't get that boot off soon, he knew he'd have to cut it off, and he couldn't afford another pair of boots.

"I think I busted my damn ankle." Bertram gritted the words out. The pain was a searing heat, and he was having trouble breathing, let alone talking.

The old man squatted beside him and gingerly rotated Bertram's foot.

"Aaagh!" Bertram screamed.

"I believe you're right," the old-timer said. He motioned for some of his cronies still sitting on the porch, whittling, to lend a helping hand. "We'll have to git you over to Doc Pierson's and let him have a look-see."

"Damn! Damn! Double damn!" Bertram railed. A broken ankle! That was all he needed now to lay him up again for another who knew how many weeks!

He was still cursing a blue streak as four elderly men gathered around him. They seemed hardly strong enough to support their own weight, let alone budge him, but each one dutifully scooped up an arm or a leg. He bit down as they unceremoniously hauled him across the street to the doctor's office like a wilted sack of flour and folded him onto the doc's operating table.

"Take care o' my horse," Bertram shouted as the old men melted back out the doorway.

"Sure will. He'll be at th' livery," his one new friend assured him.

Bertram groaned again. Now a livery bill! What else?

The doctor leaned over him. "Now, son, let's see what's happened here."

A firm hand clasped his boot as Bertram closed his eyes in renewed agony and prayed to pass out.

CHAPTER 5

"**Y**ES, THE WAR'S OVER, BUT THERE'S STILL MEN OUT there in the bushes who don't know that yet." Cole glanced up and smiled at his mother, who had just cut him another thick slice of gooseberry pie. "Lord, Ma, you're going to have me so big I can't get back on my horse," he complained good-naturedly, but Wynne noticed he had no trouble polishing off the second serving of dessert.

"You're as thin as a shitepoke," Lilly said, then quickly turned to slip another piece of pie onto Wynne's plate before she could stop her.

Wynne eyed the man sitting at the table across from her, and the thought that she wouldn't describe him as thin skipped through her mind. He was powerfully built, with broad shoulders and an expansive chest beneath the blue chambray shirt he was wearing this evening. Now that he was freshly bathed and cleanly shaved, Wynne had to admit he was quite a handsome man. It was only his deplorable disposition that spoiled everything.

"Thank you, Lilly, but I really couldn't eat another bite," Wynne protested. For two days she had sat at the dinner table and nearly burst. Willa's meals had been large and plentiful. She was surprised at such an abundance of food on the table each day, especially when it seemed every other homestead she had passed while riding the stage seemed to be in a depressing state of shortage of even the barest essentials.

She had been surprised by the house too. True, whitewash and repairs were needed, but it reflected an affluent life-style she'd not expected to find. The house was quite large with the parlor and family rooms on the main floor and the upstairs five bedrooms, each furnished with a double bed, clothespress, nightstand, and full-length mirror, again much like her own at Moss Oak.

There was also a gentility present, almost a southern flavor to their life-style. Meals were at set times, and manners were observed religiously. Like tonight, china, glass, and silver had been used on the night of Cole's and Beau's return.

Suddenly Lilly's voice wafted through her thoughts. "Nonsense. It wouldn't hurt for you to have a little more meat on your bones," she told Wynne as she busied herself refilling their cups with the dark chickory coffee that Wynne had come to despise. It was tangy and bitter, and she would just as soon do without than to have to drink it. "Praise the good Lord the garden's doin' well," Lilly murmured, almost as if she had read Wynne's mind. "And Elmo Ferguson's been seein' that we have fresh meat on the table at least twice a week."

"I'll have to stop by and thank Elmo for lookin' out for you," Cole said with a mischievous twinkle in his eye. "But I bet he's been invited in for a piece of sweet potato pie every now and again."

"Oh, occasionally I've had one cooling on the windowsill," she said absently. "So, you're a captain now." Lilly's eyes shone once again with pride as she hurried to change the subject. She didn't like to be teased about Elmo, and Cole knew it. "I'm real proud of you, son."

"Thanks, Ma, but I'm lookin' forward to bein' just a plain farmer again."

He glanced over at Wynne as she quietly pushed the second piece of pie aside. She didn't want to offend Lilly, who had immediately taken her in and treated her as part of the family, but she was stuffed as tight as a tick. "If you don't mind, I think I'll save this for a little later on," she murmured as she saw the way he was looking at her.

A cool, distant set of blue eyes locked obstinately with hers for a moment before they dropped back down to his plate. "A lot of people would be glad to get that pie, Miss Elliot," he said curtly.

For two long days Cole had purposely gone out of his way to ignore her, speaking only when forced to and, in general, treating her as if she were something he had picked up on his boot in the barnyard instead of a houseguest.

Because he was beginning to fascinate her, she had taken the opportunity to observe him and his relationship with his mother. With her, he was kind and thoughtful, even nice.

And the relationships between Lilly and her son still amazed Wynne. Cole and Beau treated their mother with the utmost respect, while there was a genuine, honest warmth among them, evidenced daily by the continual bantering that volleyed back and forth in the household.

If one were around Lilly very long, it wasn't hard to see where Beau had gotten his soft heart and sense of humor. Wynne only wished some of that goodwill had washed off on Cole.

The tension between them had seemed to grow with each passing day, even though Wynne had gone out of her way to be pleasant to him. Well, if not out of her way, then she had at least made a conscious effort to be polite to him, far more than he had done for her.

"I'm aware there are people going to bed hungry tonight," she said challengingly, daring him to look her in the eye again, but when he complied, his eyes stern, her hand reached feebly back for her fork. "Well . . . maybe just a few more bites."

"That's all right, dear. I'll put the pie in the warming oven, and it will be there when you get hungry again." Lilly took her place at the end of the table and reached for her cup. "I wish Beau and Betsy would hurry up and get back."

Lilly smiled when she thought about her middle son and his intended bride. She heartily approved of the woman Beau had chosen to be his wife.

When Beau had found out that his fiancée had taken a teaching job in a small community about fifty miles from River Run and was over there cleaning her schoolroom for the fall session, he had immediately set out to bring her back home for a few days.

Lilly reflected sadly on how the war had affected all of them. There had been a state of martial law in many areas during the past several years. Schools had closed, and churches had disbanded. But the small community of Red Springs, where Betsy taught, had not been directly affected by the fighting during the war. Although the community could barely afford to provide a roof over the new teacher's head and three meals a day, it wanted its children's education to go on uninterrupted, and Betsy had answered the call.

She was a woman to be proud of, and Beau was a lucky man, Lilly thought with delight. She only wished Cole could find a woman who would be as suited to him.

"Stop frettin' now. They should be back anytime," Cole said when he finished off the pie and pushed away from the table.

Outside, the sound of hoofbeats shattered the peaceful silence of early twilight as several riders rode up to the house and reined to a halt.

"Now who could that be?" Lilly frowned. "It's nigh on to dark, and I can't think of a neighbor who would come callin' at this hour."

Cole automatically reached for his gun belt hanging on a peg next to the back door as Lilly hurried over to pull the curtain aside to peek out.

"Why, it's the sheriff," she announced, her face breaking out in a friendly smile. She pulled the door open and hurried outside onto the porch, leaving Cole and Wynne to follow.

As Lilly stepped off the porch, Tal Franklin smiled at her, and she felt her pulse give an excited little extra beat.

No one could argue that at fifty-two the sheriff of Laxton County wasn't still a fine figure of a man. His six-foot-three frame sat in the saddle with an air of undisputed authority. There was just a suggestion of gray in his sideburns now, but his dark, hazel eyes were as clear and sharp as they had been thirty years before. His body was honed as hard as steel, and the elements had tanned his skin to a deep bronze. It was no wonder he could make the ladies of River Run blush with delight when he turned his smile in their direction, and Lilly was no different from the rest.

"Evenin', Lilly." Tal tipped his hat politely, his warm gaze taking in the soft curve of her breast against the worn calico dress. She always looked fresh, and she always smelled good. Even now he knew that if he were just a bit closer to her, he would be able to smell that faint lemon smell she always had about her.

Wynne had followed Cole out the back door, and she watched with growing amusement as Lilly's face blushed vividly pink when her eyes met the handsome sheriff's. It wasn't hard for her to see there was an attraction between the sheriff and Cole's mother, and somehow that didn't surprise her.

The two looked about the same age, and they both were unusually attractive people. Cole's mother still had a youthful, trim figure, beautiful, laughing blue eyes, and pretty dark blond hair with only a few threads of gray running through it to give away her age. Wynne thought she was beautiful.

It was plain to see the sheriff was of the same opinion. She wasn't sure, but if she were to hazard a guess, she would say that Elmo Ferguson wasn't the only one vying for Lilly's attention.

Lilly was busy discreetly fussing with her hair as Tal slid out of his saddle and handed the reins to one of his deputies.

"Are the sheriff and your mother . . . attracted to each other?" Wynne asked in a whisper when Cole came to stand behind her. She certainly wasn't on good enough terms with him to discuss such personal matters, but it was plain for all to see that Lilly and Tal were looking at each other in that special romantic way.

Cole glanced at her coolly. "I wouldn't know."

"Oh, they are," she said. "Can't you see the way they're lookin' at each other?"

The revelation took Cole by complete surprise. He had never thought about his mother's looking at another man that way—at least no one other than Elmo. And he wasn't at all sure he liked the idea.

"No, they're not," he said curtly.

Lilly's and Tal's heads snapped up at the sound of his annoyed voice. "Did you say something, dear?" Lilly called.

"No." Cole gave her a weak grin and lowered his voice to a deep growl next to Wynne's ear. "You have an overactive imagination, Miss Elliot. And remember, that's my mother you're talking about."

Wynne glanced at him over her shoulder. "I know it's your mother. I wasn't casting any aspersions on her." The man obviously didn't have a romantic bone in his entire body! "I was only making a simple observation."

"Well, stop. It's gettin' on my nerves."

Doesn't everything? she thought resentfully, but decided to hold her tongue.

Cole reached in his pocket and withdrew a cheroot as he watched her flounce away. He stuck it between his teeth and angrily lit a match with the end of his thumbnail. His pa had died in a hunting accident just after his youngest brother had been born, and as far as Cole knew, Lilly had never looked at another man except old Elmo, and that was purely in a friendly manner—nothing more. Leave it to Miss Elliot to make more of it than it was. The bird on her hat must have pecked a hole in her brain.

"Won't you and your men come in and have some supper with us?" Lilly asked as Tal reached for a small leather pouch tied to his saddlehorn.

"No, thanks, Lilly. The men are wantin' to get on home before dark. I just stopped by to bring Miss Elliot something." He was holding the bag in his hand now, but his attention was still centered solely on Lilly as Wynne approached them.

"You have something for me, Sheriff?"

Diverting his attention from Lilly slowly, Tal colored slightly before he was able to get his mind back on the business at hand. "Uh, yes, Miss Elliot, ma'am." He quickly extended the small pouch to her. "We brought your ring back."

Wynne's face lit with relief as she hurriedly undid the bag and dumped the pearl ring out into the palm of her hand. "Oh, this is marvelous! Where did you find it?"

"Down the road apiece from where the stage was held up," he explained. "Must have dropped out of the bag when they was tryin' to make their getaway." He nodded at Cole, who had stepped off the porch to come stand beside Wynne. "Evenin', Cole."

"Evenin', Tal." Cole glanced down at the ring in Wynne's hand. "Was this all you were able to find?"

"I'm afraid so. They seemed to have gotten clean away this time. But just as soon as me and my men get a little rest, we're going to go out again."

Wynne's newfound hopes were suddenly dashed as she realized with a sinking sensation that she would probably never recover the rest of her belongings. It had already been two days since the robbery had taken place, and the men were probably long gone by now. "Well, thank you anyway, Sheriff." She sighed. "I'm grateful that you were able to recover my ring."

"As I said, ma'am, as soon as me and my men rest up, we'll try to pick up their trail again," he told her.

"You sure you won't come in and at least have a cup of coffee with us." Lilly invited him again, but he swung up into his saddle.

Wynne looked over at Cole and grinned smugly. He shot her a disapproving look.

"I'd love to, Lilly, but we have to be getting along. Some other time, I promise."

"Thanks for your trouble, Tal." Cole shook the older man's hand.

"No trouble. Just wished I could have gotten the rest of the little lady's things back for her," Tal said. He tipped his hat politely at Wynne and Lilly. "Evenin', ladies."

Wynne watched with a heavy heart as the small group of riders left the yard in a cloud of dust.

Cole and Lilly had already started back to the house when Wynne's gaze dropped to her tightly clasped hand. She opened it slowly, feeling a mist rise unexpectedly to her eyes. One little pearl ring: That was all she had left of her personal possessions. All her money was gone. Her other jewelry, which would have been worth much more than the ring, was lost. Of course, there was still Moss Oak, but that was of no value at all right now. It was merely a piece of land with charred fields and no owner to care lovingly for it. Even sadder was the fact that she didn't have one soul to care, much less to help her with her plight.

She sighed wistfully. What in the world was she going to do now?

CHAPTER 6

I<small>T</small> WAS LATE SATURDAY AFTERNOON BEFORE BEAU returned from Red Springs with Betsy. He lifted his fiancée down from the buckboard as carefully as if she were a rare jewel and stole a brief but thorough kiss before he set her lightly on her feet.

Her face blushed a pretty pink, but her eyes shone with the same radiating love as his while she primly straightened her hat and tried to pretend disapproval of his rowdy ways. But she loved him for it. Beau's spontaneity and zest for life had been one of the first things that had attracted her, and she wouldn't have him any other way.

Lilly made a big fuss over Betsy, telling her how much she had missed seeing her in church on Sunday mornings and taking her around to the side of the house to show her how well her flower bed was doing this year.

"I have to water it every evenin'," Lilly confessed. "If it don't rain soon, I'll have to stop. I can't have the well goin' dry, and the vegetable garden's goin' to need waterin' more than these ol' flowers do." Lilly sighed and leaned down to touch a delicate lavender petal lovingly. "They sure are pretty, though." The world had seen too little beauty since the war began. Too little beauty, too little happiness, too many tears, but thank God it was over now, Lilly thought.

"They're truly lovely," Betsy said as Beau joined them. He'd taken care of the horse and buckboard quickly, and his stomach was reminding him he hadn't eaten since early this morning.

"Hope we haven't missed supper, Ma."

Lilly laughed. "No, Willa's frying chicken, and I was just gettin' ready to put the biscuits in the oven."

Beau sniffed appreciatively as the aroma of meat sizzling in hot fat filled the air. "I hope she's fixed enough." He'd never forget that when he was fighting, long days had gone by with bare rations and little or no meat.

They started for the house, catching up on the news as they walked. "Cole rode into town this morning to see what kind of supplies he could buy. He should be back anytime now," Lilly told them.

"Oh, it will be so good to see him again." Betsy smiled. "Beau says he's fine."

"He is. And he looks real good." Lilly beamed. "Thin, like this one here, but I'll have 'em both filled out in no time at all."

"Is Wynne still here?" Beau asked. He'd told Betsy about the girl he and Cole had befriended on their way home, and she was anxious to meet her.

"Yes. She's in the house helping Willa." Lilly shook her head thoughtfully. "Don't know what's gonna happen to the poor little thing. Tal hasn't been able to recover any of her money. But he did find the pearl ring she was wearing and brought it back to her."

"Well, that's more than I thought he would find," Beau said.

"What about her family?" Betsy questioned.

"Don't seem to have any. Her mama and papa're dead. She says there's an old mammy she can go to back in Savannah, but she don't seem inclined to want to do that right now."

"No, she's lookin' for someone," Beau said.

"Oh? Who?" Lilly asked.

"I'm not real sure. Some man, but she never did get around to tellin' me who."

"Well, that's a relief," Lilly said. "At least when she finds whoever it is, she'll have someone to take care of her."

The three went inside and found Wynne busy setting the large oak table in the dining room. Introductions were made, and Betsy decided she liked Wynne immediately. She asked Wynne to accompany her upstairs so she could freshen up before dinner, and Wynne complied willingly.

Sitting on the side of the bed, she listened attentively as Betsy chattered on about how she had known all of Beau's family since she was born and how she had been in love with Beau for as long as she could remember.

Cole rode in from town just as they were starting back down the stairway.

"Now that's another man that's going to make some lucky woman a fine husband one of these days," Betsy confided in hushed secrecy. "Isn't he about the most handsome devil you've ever seen? I mean next to my Beau, of course."

The part about his being a "devil" Wynne was more than inclined to agree with, but she hesitated to dash Betsy's high opinion of Cole by telling her she wasn't impressed with Beau's older brother in the least.

"I suppose he would appeal to some women," she replied evasively.

"Some women? Are you serious?" Betsy laughed, a delightful clear, tinkling sound. "My older sister, Priscilla June? Why, she would absolutely faint away if he would give her the time of day."

"Really?" Wynne forced her tone to remain pleasant. "What's the matter? Can't Cole tell time?"

Betsy looked blank for a moment, then broke out in a fit of giggles. "Oh, Wynne, you're so funny!" Her blue eyes widened expectantly. "Listen, are you spoken for yet?" Maybe the man she was looking for was her fiancé.

"No." Wynne smiled. "Not yet." Maybe when she got to know Betsy a little better, she would feel inclined to tell her about Cass. Somehow she sensed Betsy would understand and sympathize.

"You're not?" Betsy's grin widened.

"And I don't care to be," Wynne added quickly. "I've decided to be an old maid." She had even given serious thought about going into a convent as soon as she found Cass and took her revenge. By then she would have a whole list of grievances to be forgiven for.

Betsy's face wilted with disappointment. "Oh, my, what a shame. . . ."

Willa was setting huge platters of fried chicken on the table when the two women entered the dining room and took their places.

Beau smiled at Betsy as she picked up her napkin and placed it in her lap daintily. Cole picked up a bowl of potatoes and completely ignored Wynne as she took the chair opposite him.

"We'll have prayer first," Lilly admonished sternly, and Cole set the potatoes back down promptly, and they all bowed their heads.

"Lord, we thank you for this bounty we are about to receive and for giving us another beautiful day of life," Lilly said softly. "We thank you that you've seen fit to put a stop to this terrible war, and I want to tell you again how much I appreciate you looking over Cole and Beau and sending them back home to me, safe and sound. I'm mighty beholdin' to you, Lord. If it wouldn't be no bother, I'd ask that you send my baby home real soon, 'cause I'm worryin' about him something real powerful, too, Lord. But I know you must have a lot of things on your mind now, and I want you to know I'm not demandin' anything. I just wanted to remind you 'bout my baby in case you might have forgotten. If you have time, Lord, we could sure use some rain. Garden's gettin' awful dry, and the well's threatenin' to do the same.

"Well, guess I'll close now. Supper's gettin' cold. Just wanted you to know we love you and hope you'll forgive us for anything we might have done today that you wouldn't be right proud of. We didn't mean you no harm, Lord. You've been mighty good to us, and we won't be forgettin' that. Amen."

"Amen." Cole and Beau solemnly added their deep voices to hers.

"Now"—Lilly looked up and smiled—"you may pass the potatoes, Cole."

"You know, Wynne, I've been doing some thinking about that

robbery," Beau announced while he spooned pole beans onto his plate. "You think you could recognize those men if you ever saw them again?"

Surprised, Wynne glanced up. "I guess so. Why?"

"Well, I was just wonderin' . . . Cole, you don't think Frank and Jesse had anythin' to do with it, do you?"

"Frank and Jesse?" Lilly answered before Cole could. "Why, those boys wouldn't do anything like that!"

Cole spared his mother an indulgent look. "Ma, Frank and Jesse's been ridin' with Quantrill's Raiders and they certainly ain't been holdin' Sunday school picnics."

"Cole, since when have I gone addlebrained? Their pa was a preacher, if you remember. And those boys were good boys, at least they was until th' Jayhawkers took it in their heads to persecute 'em."

Wynne's mind was not solely on the conversation but rather on how she was going to get through another meal without popping the buttons on her dress. "Who are Frank and Jesse?" she asked, passing the bowl of potatoes on.

"Frank and Jesse James." Beau repeated the names as if they should mean something to her.

She smiled. "Sorry, I've never heard of them."

"Well, of course, she hasn't," Betsy said. "The James boys live up around Jefferson City. In fact, they live only a couple of miles from my aunt Marabelle. When I was a small girl, I used to visit my aunt during the summer, and me and Jesse would play together—that is, until their mother, Zerelda, married that horrible Ben Simms."

"Terrible man," Lilly murmured sympathetically.

"Yes, he was. Ben Simms was some sixteen years older than Zerelda, and he treated Jesse and Frank terrible. In fact, he was downright cruel at times," Betsy said. "I remember Aunt Marabelle telling how he whipped Frank so bad one time that he had to miss school for several days."

"How awful," Wynne commented. Cruelty was foreign to her. Wesley Elliot had rarely raised his voice, and Rose Elliot had always preferred talking rather than a leather strap. "Is that when they started to get into trouble?"

"No. Ben Simms died, and then Zerelda married a doctor named Samuels—Reuben Samuels, I believe his name was. He was from Kentucky and a kind man, but"—Betsy laughed—"Zerelda was a woman who ran her own house, and I don't know if he was a happy man or not."

"Zerelda had a hot temper, is what she's tryin' to say." Beau grinned. "And she passed that temper on to Jesse. Frank, now, is more like his real pa—calm, slow to anger . . . more brainy. But Jesse is actually the clever one."

"The boys were fairly ordinary farm boys," Betsy remarked as she buttered a biscuit. "Jesse was real religious, like his pa. But when the war was first brewin', there was a lot of bitterness about the border warfare bein' waged between Kansas and Missouri. It was over whether Kansas should come into the Union free or slave."

Lilly shook her head thoughtfully. "Family against family, brother against brother, just like the Good Book says."

"The people of Missouri were mostly southern sympathizers," Beau told Wynne. "They would up and march right over the border and kill all the Kansans they could find. Of course, the Kansans didn't take right friendly to that sort of doin's, so they up and marched right back and knocked a few Missourians' heads together. Missouri men were called bushwhackers and the Kansans were called Jayhawkers or sometimes Redlegs—"

Cole glanced up from his plate and commented dryly, "Or sometimes sons of bitches."

"Cole!" Lilly exclaimed. "Watch your language! There are ladies present at this table!"

Cole and Beau grinned at each other as Beau continued. "The Redlegs were not attached to regular uniformed forces. They operated on their own, rode and robbed and slaughtered as they pleased. Quantrill is a Missouri leader of one of those forces."

"And Frank and Jesse James ride with him?" Wynne asked.

"Frank rides with Quantrill occasionally, but Jesse rides with one of Quantrill's rebel bands," Cole said.

"Well, anyway, durin' the war they were attackin' farmers. Just out of the blue they'd swoop down and demand to know if there was anyone there from the other side. If there happened to be, they'd up and kill him."

"How horrible!" Wynne gasped, her whole attention focused on the story now.

"It is awful," Betsy said. "But probably no more so than all the other things that happened durin' that miserable war." It was still hard to believe it was over.

"Actually just two Missouri counties were real actively involved in the war," Beau continued. "And one of them was Clay County, where Frank and Jesse and Betsy's aunt Marabelle lives."

"You see, Frank and Jesse's mother was originally from Kentucky," Betsy added. "And she was a confirmed southerner. With that temper of hers and her set ideas, she wasn't shy about sayin' what she thought either. To her, Union sympathizers were scoundrels, and southerners were God's people.

"Unfortunately she had northern neighbors, and Zerelda told 'em where they could go—on more than one occasion. When Fort Sumter was fired upon, Frank decided to join up. He was eighteen at the time. I remember hearing he was at Wilson's Creek for a while. He came back home all full of victory and pride 'cause his regiment had won that battle.

But Aunt Marabelle said it wasn't long after that before he was seized by the Unionists and took to Liberty to jail."

Betsy laughed. "But his ma came to his rescue real quick. She went to the commander of the Union forces in the county and asked him to release Frank. He said he would if Frank would sign an oath of allegiance and if the Stars and Stripes were flown in the yard of their house. Frank finally signed the oath, but the commander was transferred shortly after that, so the flag never flew over Zerelda's house."

"You forgot to tell her that the new commander tried to recapture Frank and that he had to go back into the bush," Beau pointed out. "From what I've heard, that's when he decided he couldn't go back with General Price again, so he joined Quantrill's guerrillas."

"Jesse was at home, farming while this was goin' on," Betsy said. "And, one day a squad of Union soldiers rode up to the Samuelses' cabin. Dr. Samuels was busy out back, but he must have heard the horses comin'. He came around front and asked what they wanted. They said they wanted him and his wife—that they'd been talkin' too much. Zerelda was out back makin' soap and didn't know what was goin' on. So the Unionists got a rope, seized the doctor, and bound his hands behind his back. The rope then went around his neck, and they marched him to a coffee-bean tree and threw the end over a limb. They jerked him off his feet and left him hangin' there."

Wynne suddenly felt faint. "How . . . horrible."

"That's not all," Betsy said soberly. "As soon as they left, Zerelda ran around the house and cut him down. Amazingly he survived, but he was in bad shape for a long time. The men thought Jesse was hid in the barn. They finally found him in the field plowin'. Now, mind you, he was only fifteen at the time. Two of 'em seized Jesse, and a third tried to beat him to death with a rope. Finally, they went back to the house, and when they discovered Samuels wasn't hangin' in the yard, mercifully they rode away."

"What happened to Jesse?" Wynne whispered.

"Jesse finally managed to get to the house. He was hurt bad, and so was the poor doctor. Zerelda took care of the both of 'em, wouldn't hardly leave their side until she was sure they were gonna make it. Aunt Marabelle says that's when Jesse changed. He went off to join one of Quantrill's bands right after that. All through the war the Unionists kept comin' to the Samuels house, lookin' for Frank and Jesse, keepin' the family on edge all the time."

"So Jesse finally decided to ride with Quantrill," Wynne murmured. "Can't hardly say I'd blame him any."

"No, he didn't." Cole patiently tried to keep the facts straight. "He had to be seventeen before he could ride with Quantrill. So he joined one of the side commands under the direction of Quantrill, Bloody Bill Anderson."

"You sound as if you know them personally," Wynne said.

Cole shrugged. "Our paths have crossed a few times."

"Frank and Jesse floated in and out of Missouri all durin' the war," Beau told her. "There's not a better place to hide than in some of these hills and hollers. We got some of the roughest country you'll ever see. A man could get lost a hundred feet from his cabin in a few of those valleys, and down around the White River country is about the best place to start. There's where you'll see Frank and Jesse, if you're lookin' for 'em."

"Well, I'm not," Wynne affirmed. "And I hope I never have the occasion to meet up with them."

Lilly shook her head again thoughtfully. "Next thing you know, they'll be robbin' banks."

Beau gave Betsy another moonstruck smile and picked up the bowl of poke greens and extended it to her. She shook her head and smiled back at him winsomely.

"Well, have you and Betsy thought about a date for your wedding?" Lilly inquired pleasantly, hoping she could change the depressing conversation.

"We was thinking about maybe the last Sunday in October." Beau grinned. "It'd be kinda coolin' off by then."

Betsy's face flamed bright scarlet as she hurriedly groped for her water glass to avoid choking on the bite of food she had just put in her mouth.

"I mean . . . well, what I meant is . . . I just thought . . ." Beau stammered, his face turning as red as his fiancée's.

"I think we know what you meant, Beau," Cole said dryly.

"Well . . . no . . . you see what I meant was—"

"What he meant was he and Betsy want to wait until early fall to get married so that Cass will be back home by then." Lilly intervened mercifully. "There'll be no marriage in the Claxton family unless the whole family's present to wish Beau and Betsy well."

The sound of Wynne's fork clattering off the side of her plate caused four pairs of eyes to rivet on her all at one time.

Cass Claxton! Had she heard wrong? She fervently prayed she had.

"Is there something the matter, dear?" Lilly's fork paused in midair as she peered over it anxiously. Wynne's face had suddenly turned as white as a ghost.

"No . . . I . . ." Her mind was churning with confusion. Had she actually heard Lilly say Cass Claxton was her son? No. She couldn't have, yet Lilly had clearly said *Cass* would be home and the *Claxton* family would be together. Hell's bells, fickle fate had dropped her right into the viper's own nest this time.

"Wynne?" Betsy's concerned voice slowly seeped through Wynne's stupor. "Are you ill?"

Even Cole had stopped eating now, and she could feel his probing eyes on her as she removed her napkin from her lap and carefully rose on shaky limbs. "Uh, if you'll excuse me, I think I need a bit of fresh air."

She turned and bolted out of the room without another word, leaving them staring at one another in bewilderment.

"My word, what do you suppose happened?" Lilly asked worriedly.

"Why, I just can't imagine!" Betsy exclaimed.

"Maybe all that talk of war and Frank and Jesse upset her," Beau said anxiously.

"Well, I'd better go see about her—"

"Let her be, Betsy!" Cole's voice sliced authoritatively through the air. Betsy whirled and faced him. "But, Cole, she might be ill. . . ."

"Go ahead and finish your supper," he commanded tautly. "If she had been sick, she would have said so."

Betsy glanced at Lilly expectantly.

"He's right, dear. Maybe the past few days have finally caught up with her and she just needs some time alone," Lilly said. "Why don't we give her a few minutes to herself and then one of us will go check on her?"

Betsy wasn't at all sure that was the right thing to do, but one look at Cole's stern face and she began to sink back down in her chair obediently. "Well . . . maybe just a few minutes, but then I'm going to see about her."

The remainder of the meal was finished quickly and in strained silence. When Willa brought dessert, Cole stood up and excused himself curtly, then left the room. A few moments later they all were relieved to hear the back door open and snap shut.

CHAPTER 7

*T*HE AIR WAS STILL WARM AND HUMID, SO HEAVY IT WAS almost difficult to breathe. A slight stirring of the wind touched Wynne's flushed cheeks as she stepped out the back door of the Claxton farmhouse.

She stood on the porch, her hands clenched together. She paced without knowing it, looking around helplessly, seeing nothing. *Where do I go from here?* she asked herself. *Oh, why?* Why did it have to be Cass's brothers who had befriended her?

Swiping angrily at the tears that suddenly threatened her composure, Wynne stepped off the porch. She looked up at the sun, which was just sinking in a big, fiery orange ball behind the grove of cherry trees on the west side of the house and headed in that direction.

When she was a little girl, she'd healed small disappointments and cried out her frustrations in the arms of a gnarled tree at Moss Oak. Somehow she'd drawn strength and security from that old tree. The cherry grove here seemed to beckon invitingly as if it would offer a refuge for her inward turmoil, a haven for the chaos that had again come upon her unexpectedly.

Once she'd reached the shelter of the grove, Wynne sank down in a thick carpet of grass beneath a tree. Above her, fruit was sparsely scattered about the branches. The aroma of dry grass, sweet cherries, and the sultry end of a summer day taunted her senses. Overcome with sadness and defeat, Wynne dropped her face into her hands.

After a few minutes she managed to regain control of herself. Sniffing and rubbing the backs of her hands across her cheeks, she stared around. Lilly was right, she thought dismally. If it didn't rain soon, everything was going to dry up and blow away. She hiccuped. Maybe, if she were lucky, the wind would take her right along with it.

Throwing her head back, Wynne stared up at the clear blue sky through the tree branches. *Fool! Fool! Fool! You've done it again! Made a complete fool of yourself by stumbling right into the arms of Cass's family*, she berated herself. She raised her face and chuckled mirthlessly, then irritably snapped a loose thread off the waist of her dress. *Literally thousands of people between here and Savannah, but who does Lord Providence send to rescue her?*

She laughed out loud. *Cass Claxton's brothers! That's who.* If it hadn't been so ironically funny, she would have bawled.

She leaned back against the tree and rested her head against its trunk. A hopeless sigh escaped as she pondered the disturbing similarities in Cass and his family. No, not his whole family. Lilly was nice, and so was Beau. But that rotten Cole was just like his brother—cold, calculating, and totally heartless. He'd never done anything spontaneous in his life, she'd bet. And he thought her the most foolish thing in the world—and he just might be right.

She was always reacting without thinking things out. But she'd thought out well what she'd do to Cass Claxton. And nothing would stop her, Wynne decided again.

It didn't matter that his family had taken her in when she had no one else to turn to. Cass Claxton couldn't toy with her feelings and steal her money without paying for it! And she could no longer delay putting her plan into effect.

For days she had been hoping that Sheriff Franklin would be able to recover her money. But now that she knew she was staying with Cass's family, she would have to move on. Oh, granted, she should just sit right here and wait for the rat to return to his nest. That would be the easiest way to handle the situation. Cass would undoubtedly return home one day soon, and she could shoot him and then be on her way. Her hand absently toyed with her worry stone. But she had to face facts. If she stayed around until Cass returned, it was possible she would let slip what she was about to do, and then Cole would try to intervene in her plan. She shot a dirty look toward the house. That would be just like him!

No, the pearl ring the sheriff had returned would have to be her ticket to freedom. She would go into town first thing tomorrow morning and see if the bank would accept it as collateral on a small loan.

Wynne felt better now that she had a plan. The bank would lend her a small sum. She'd need only enough to live on for a few weeks while she continued her search for Cass. It wouldn't take a great deal. Only enough for food and lodging, and she would assure the banker that she ate very little and required a minimum amount of sleep. She was aware it was a rather slim hope that she might encounter Cass while he was on the trail, but at this point she really had little other choice.

And who knew? Maybe she would be lucky and locate him right away. Wynne sat up straight. Maybe she would get even luckier and he would still have a portion of her money on him. After all, she was overdue for a stroke of luck. Long overdue.

Her stomach turned slightly queasy at the prospect of removing personal belongings off a dead man, for that's exactly what Mr. Claxton would be when she found him: dead as a doornail.

Once her mission had been accomplished, she could return to Savannah and try to rebuild her life or maybe even enter that convent. A life of servitude would be her penance for killing a man even if he did deserve to die for what he'd done.

Oooh! Why had she not realized immediately that Cole was Cass's brother? Why had she thought it was just her imagination? They looked so much alike it was almost scary, but she had been so preoccupied with all her other problems she never dreamed fate would throw another Claxton in her path!

Her ears picked up the sound of a match being struck. Before she could turn to see who it was, the fragrant aroma of cigar smoke filtered softly through the evening air.

"You didn't finish your supper," a man's deep voice stated dryly.

Wynne started at the unexpected intrusion, then stiffened with resentment. The last thing she needed was to put up with *his* company. "I suddenly lost my appetite," she answered curtly.

"So I noticed." He took a long drag off the cheroot and leaned against the tree opposite her. Smoke curled in a tiny blue furl around his head as his gaze narrowed on hers suspiciously. "I hope it wasn't anything we said that caused your sudden . . . indisposition."

She eyed Cole squarely. "Certainly not. What would make you think that?" She might be in the serpent's nest, but they weren't aware of it and wouldn't be if she had anything to say about it.

"Oh, no reason," Cole replied easily. He stood with his hat tipped back on his head, his arms crossed over his chest, quietly studying her.

Feeling uneasy beneath his penetrating gaze, Wynne looked down at her hands, which were now folded primly in her lap. Distressingly long moments passed before she finally lifted her head back up to meet his unnerving scrutiny.

"Do I have something on my face?" she snapped.

"No."

"Then why are you staring at me like that?"

Cole shrugged. "I was just wondering how you could keep such a straight face and lie the way you do."

Her gaze dropped back to her hands guiltily. "I have no idea what you're talking about."

His tongue made a clucking sound as he shook his head disapprovingly. "Now, now, Miss Elliot. Didn't that fancy school you went to back East teach you that a real lady never tells stories? At least not the big whopping ones you've been tellin' lately."

Her eyes blazed with fury and frustration when she looked at him again. "Mr. Claxton, did you want anything in particular, or did you just come out here to annoy me?"

"Annoy you?" He took another thoughtful drag on his cheroot. "I don't think I'd waste my time doing that. A prissy little old thing like you 'annoys' too easy."

"I'm not prissy." She pouted, locating another loose string around her waist. She jerked at it angrily again, and it unraveled a bit further. Hellfire and damnation! Now her clothes were even trying to come apart on her! She turned her eyes upward guiltily. *Papa, I am sorry for all this cursin', but you can surely see I'm bein' sorely tested,* she thought in apology. She felt better then. Actually Papa would have been saying things much worse, she rationalized, if he'd been in this revolting predicament.

Cole studied her, sitting under that tree, picking at a string on her dress. Soft hands, pale skin, had never done a day's work in her life. All fluff and ruffles and a bird on her hat. His mouth quirked in near disgust. He pitied the man who hitched up with her, and it was on the tip of his tongue to say so; but he wasn't inclined to start another argument. He had more important issues to discuss with Miss Elliot.

He pushed away from the tree and edged over to where she sat wrapping a loose thread around her finger absently. "Mind if I set a spell?" he asked casually.

She shrugged.

"Gonna be a nice night," he observed pleasantly as he sat down on the ground next to her.

She shrugged again.

"Willa can sure fry chicken, can't she?"

Wynne hazarded a sideways glance at him. Why was he being so pleasant all of a sudden? She jerked another string off her dress. "I suppose."

He removed his hat and laid it on the grass beside him. Wynne couldn't help noticing what nice hair he had. It was coal black and had a nice, healthy sheen. The high humidity caused the curls to roll up in tight little kinks around his neckline and damp little loops in the front where his hat had creased them almost flat. Tonight he was bathed, clean-shaved, and dressed in freshly washed denims and a steel blue chambray shirt that turned his eyes almost the exact same shade, a far cry from the first time she'd seen him.

He leaned back against the tree trunk, gazing off into the western sky, which was ablaze with purples and oranges and golds, and he sighed contentedly. "It's good to be home."

The words were said wistfully, thankfully, and it put Wynne a little more at ease with him. "Were you away long?"

"Yeah, four years, but it seemed like forever."

"And Beau was gone that long too?"

"Yes, we left about the same time."

"Oh."

Cole studied her from beneath lowered lashes. "But my youngest brother, Cass, hasn't returned yet."

Wynne's back stiffened perceptibly at the despised name. "How sad. Where has he been?"

"Fighting, just like we have."

Wynne's mouth dropped open in surprise. "He's been in the army?"

"So Ma says." Cole hunched down more comfortably. "I was surprised when I heard about it. When I left, Cass was supposed to stay around and help her with the farm. We even paid to have a man fight in his place, but it seems he took off awhile back to visit family in Savannah and then all of a sudden decided to join up." He glanced at her. "You sounded a little surprised yourself, Miss Elliot. Any particular reason?"

So she had been right! Cass must have hightailed it to the first regiment he could find and joined up after he'd left her standing at the altar.

"No, I—I'm just a little surprised. I thought he was just away somewhere."

"No, he's been in the war," Cole repeated. "He didn't join until late in the conflict. Ma's pretty worried about him. You heard her at the supper table. She's hoping he'll come ridin' in any day now."

Wynne pulled at another string on her dress. "She hasn't heard anything from him lately?"

"No, but he'll not keep her worryin' for long," he said.

Ha! He had not been nearly as gracious with her! "How gallant of him!"

Cole's eyes snapped up to meet hers again. "Gallant?"

Realizing how sharp she must have sounded, Wynne immediately set out to rectify her hasty observation. "I mean, that will be very considerate of him," she said. "I hope he's fared as well as you and Beau have." She had to strain to get that particular lie past her lips.

Cole momentarily turned his attention back to the glorious sunset. "Yeah, that's what we're all hoping. How old are you, Wynne? Seventeen, eighteen?"

"Nineteen," she said curtly.

"Nineteen? Hmm, I didn't think you were that old. That's about Cass's age. He's twenty-two."

"I suppose he followed your leadership and became one of those damn Yankees." She turned her gaze on him accusingly, bitterly remembering the blue uniform Cole had been wearing the first day she met him.

Cole continued to study her as he drew on his cheroot. "Damn Yankee?" He shook his head tolerantly. "No, as a matter of fact, Cass chose to fight for the South. If you'll recall, Missouri was a little divided in its opinion of the war, and so were the Claxton men."

"Cass was the only one of you who knew right from wrong!" she said defensively, but that was only where the war was concerned. Otherwise he'd been a real jackass. "He worried about the war all the time, even though he'd paid someone to fight in his place and how it was goin' and about gettin' back to take care of your mother. . . ." Her voice trailed off lamely as she realized what she'd said.

"Oh?" Cole's brow lifted thoughtfully. "Do you know my brother?"

"Oh, heavens, no," she said quickly.

"Then how do you know what he thought?"

"I was . . . just guessing." She laughed nervously.

"Amazing." His lips pursed thoughtfully as he studied Wynne. "For a moment there it sounded exactly like you might have met him. You did say you were from Savannah, didn't you?"

"Yes . . ."

"And Cass was in Savannah for a while," he said thoughtfully.

"Really, Cole." She gave another cheery laugh. "Savannah is a large city. I couldn't possibly know everyone who goes there." Her fingers flew over her worry stone nervously.

In the blink of an eye the cheroot was gone, and she was in the grass, held down by strong arms across her shoulders. His blue eyes locked angrily with her startled ones as he demanded in the deadliest voice she had ever heard, "Then what in the hell are you doing with his worry stone?"

"His . . ." Her mind churned feverishly as the stone dropped out of her hand like hot lava.

Good grief! How stupid could she get! She had been sitting there with the blessed thing in her hand, talking to him!

Wynne peered up at Cole while her mind worked furiously. Should she continue to lie her way out of this newest crisis, or should she just tell this overbearing, conceited, boorish clod the truth about his precious brother?

Cole's voice was menacingly low when he spoke again. His face was so close she could feel the warmth of his breath on her face, see the tiny lines fanning out from the corners of his eyes. His body on hers was hard and masculine, yet she took no pleasure in its tantalizing presence.

"Come on, Miss Elliot. I'm dying to know how you happen to have my brother's worry stone, yet you say you've never met him." Cole's steely gaze bore into hers relentlessly as his fingers pressed into her shoulders.

"You're hurting me," Wynne said between clenched teeth. She struggled, attempting to break his hold, but the effort was useless. He had her pinned solidly to the ground, and she could barely breathe, much less dislodge his weight.

He shook her to emphasize his words, and her head bobbed crazily. "I'm waiting, Miss Elliot."

"You're hurting me!"

Once more they glared at each other defiantly, each gaze a silent stalemate. His breath was soft and sweet against her face, and he smelled fresh, like soap and water and shaving cream.

He threatened her again in a stern voice. "I can stay here as long as you can, lady."

Wynne twisted beneath him then and succeeded in getting her hands free from between them. With a lurch her curved fingers clawed at his face. They struggled again, and Cole easily caught her wrists and, while holding her body still beneath him, thrust her arms up over her head and pinned them to the ground.

"Ohhh, let me go!" Wynne demanded. She would dearly have loved to spit in his face, but he'd have probably spit right back at her! She decided on another approach. Feminine wiles had never worked in the past with him, but maybe they would now. At least she had to chance it.

Forcing her body to go limp, Wynne feigned sudden, subdued submission. "Oh, all right." She batted her big green eyes at him prettily. "Is all this brute force necessary, Cole?" She made sure her voice was soft and her drawl as sugarcoated as possible. It made her sick to do it. "I do declare, you're crushin' the little ol' life right out of me." She blinked her wide eyes again coyly. "Surely a big, strong man like you doesn't have to pin a poor innocent girl to the ground to ask her a simple question."

He blinked back at her mockingly. He was absolutely the most maddening man. "Innocent? Like hell you are! You tell me where you got Cass's worry stone and I'll let the 'poor little innocent girl' go about her business—but not until she learns to tell the truth," he snapped. "If she doesn't tell the truth, she just might get her pretty little ol' fanny whipped right here and now."

"Why, you big jackass! Get off me!" Feminine wiles flew right out the window right along with her temper. Because he was momentarily surprised by her lurch, Cole's grip was knocked loose. Overcome by her own fury, Wynne rolled over on top of him and pounded her fists on his chest.

Deciding retreat was the better maneuver at this point, Cole covered his head with both arms. When her blows continued to rain on his chest, he lost all patience and with one swipe of his arm knocked her aside. But before he could pin her down, Wynne had twisted away and was on her knees.

Once again her long skirts were her undoing. Before she could get to her feet, Cole had caught her around the waist and pitched to one side, pulling her with him. Determined to escape, Wynne twisted again. This time she lost her balance and rolled over the edge of a slight incline. But before her momentum could give her any advantage, Cole's arm snaked out and flipped Wynne over onto her back again. His forearm resting against her chest and his powerful leg thrown across hers successfully halted any further escape attempts.

"I am sorely getting out of patience with you!" he grunted as he planted himself squarely in the middle of her squirming body.

"Get off me, you big—" He was crushing her for sure this time.

"I will," he said pleasantly, "just as soon as you answer one simple question." He reached into his shirt pocket, withdrew another cheroot, and lit it while she seethed angrily beneath him. "Where did you get Cass's worry stone?"

"What makes you think that silly stone belongs to your brother?" she grunted.

"Because I gave it to him and Beau and I each have one to match. I found all three of them in a riverbed not too far from here when I was just a kid. Cass would never willingly part with it, so save yourself another lie."

"He gave it to me!" she shouted in a most unladylike display of temper.

Cole's face exhibited brief surprise at her outburst. "He *gave* it to you?"

"That's right. He gave it to me." She pushed at his heavy weight once more and grunted painfully. "Now get off me!"

He studied her hot, flushed face thoughtfully. "Not yet. When did he give it to you?"

"In Savannah. Two days before we were to be married."

This time there was no doubt of his surprise. His mouth went slack, and his hold on her loosened. Wynne quickly seized the opportunity. Pushing with all her might, she pulled away from him, and Cole let her go. Drawing in a deep breath of fresh air, Wynne brushed damp tendrils of hair off her face as Cole stared at her in disbelief.

"Cass was going to marry you!" he said.

"That's right." She sat up and irritably tried to straighten her hair, which by now was tumbled about her head wildly. He made it sound as if he thought his brother had completely lost his mind. "But don't worry, Cole. He didn't marry me. Your precious little brother left me standin' at the altar," she said bitterly. "But not before he made off with almost every cent I had in the world."

By now Cole had managed to regain his composure and was looking at her as if he didn't believe a word she said. "Now I know you're lying. Cass wouldn't steal anyone's money, let alone a woman's," he said sharply.

"Well, that just goes to show how much you know. He *did* take my money," she contended. "And when I find him, I'm going to shoot him first, ask questions later."

Cole's eyes narrowed in sudden realization. "Then Cass is the man you're looking for?"

"That's right." Her defiant gaze met his steadily.

"And you're going to shoot him when you find him?"

"That's right!"

"So . . . that's what you're doing out here," Cole said musingly, "looking for my little brother."

"So I can blow his thievin' head off," she said.

"I doubt that."

"Don't. I'll do it. I promise."

"Not if I can help it, you won't."

"You won't be able to do a thing to stop it," Wynne stated smugly. "First thing tomorrow morning I'm going to take my ring to the bank and secure a small loan. Then I'll buy another stage ticket and be on my way. Unless you want to trail me all over the countryside, there's not one blessed thing you can do to stop me."

She knew as well as he did that he wouldn't follow her.

"Just where do you think you're going to find Cass?" Cole asked. "None of us know where he is."

Wynne pushed herself to her feet. At the tone of Cole's voice her bravado wavered. "I—I know that, but I've been inquiring about his whereabouts everywhere the stage stopped, and I know he was seen in Kansas City a few weeks ago and he was supposed to be on his way home. That's why I came to River Run. But obviously he hasn't made it yet, so now I'll just head toward Kansas City and hope to find him somewhere along the way."

Cole's face sagged with relief. "Then he's alive?"

She glanced at him guiltily. "Yes. He's alive—for now."

Cole shook his head warily and thrust long fingers through the riot of thick, damp curls which framed his face. "Ma will be relieved to hear that."

"Are you—" Wynne straightened her spine defensively. "Are you going to tell Lilly about me?" she demanded. She'd hate to hurt the woman. Lilly had been awfully good to her, and so had Beau. She wouldn't want to cause them any more worry, yet Cass had caused her more than her share of heartache.

Cole studied her for a moment, then chose his words carefully. "I don't know what happened between you and Cass, but I do know my brother is an honorable man. Whatever he's done, he had good cause to do it. That's why I'm not gonna say anything to Ma about any of this, but not because of you. Number one, I don't want her to worry any more than she already is. Number two, I think my brother can take care of himself"—his eyes ran over her coldly—"especially when it comes to little eastern finishin' school girls."

She stamped her foot at him irritably. "You'd better fear for his life!"

"Cass can take care of himself," Cole stated flatly, rolling to his feet. "And number three, you haven't a prayer of findin' him in the first place. In case you haven't noticed, lady, there's a lot of territory between here and Kansas City, and a woman travelin' alone is just askin' for trouble."

"I'm nineteen years old, and I am perfectly capable of taking care of myself. I made it out here alone, didn't I?" Wynne pushed again at her hair, which seemed determined to fall in her face. Somewhere strewn about the grass were the rest of her hairpins.

"You did—just barely. But I'd have to argue with you about bein' able to take care of yourself."

"Why?" Her mouth firmed, and her chin raised automatically as she challenged his statement.

"For one thing, you're standing there in nothing but those frilly little breeches you women wear—"

"Frilly breeches! What are you talking about?" Wynne's gaze dropped to her waist, and her mouth dropped open with astonishment.

The skirt of her dress had slipped to the ground and lay in a puddled heap around her feet. Apparently the loose strings she had been jerking away at had been there for a purpose, and in all the scuffling the material around the skirtband had completely given way, leaving her standing in nothing but her linens!

"Oooooooh! How dare you!" Her face flamed as crimson as her hair as she swooped down to pick up her skirt and step back into it, shooting him a glare that would have felled an ordinary man. "I hope you were enjoyin' yourself!"

A smile played about his lips as Cole observed her growing frustration with maddening composure. "No, as a matter of fact, I wasn't. And if you call gettin' robbed and bein' stranded in a strange town without a penny to your name takin' care of yourself, then I guess you have," he said, going right back to the conversation as if nothing unusual at all had happened. "But next time you might not be so lucky. Next time you might run into highwaymen who are lookin' for a little more than money or you might meet up with bushwhackers who haven't seen a woman in a few months or there're still splinter groups of Quantrill's raiders ridin' in these parts. One of them might take a fancy to a pretty face and want to bring her back to camp for all his friends to enjoy."

The more he talked, the more uneasy Wynne became. "You're— you're just trying to scare me!" Still, she couldn't help recalling the earlier conversation at the dinner table about such men.

"You think so?" Cole's face was as solemn as a preacher's now. "There're a lot of men ridin' these roads nowadays, Wynne. Most of 'em have been away from home for a long time, and they wouldn't be too particular who they took their ease with."

A rosy blush flooded Wynne's face at his bold insinuations. "You can talk all you want, but I'm leaving tomorrow morning," she said firmly.

"All right." He shrugged indifferently and reached down to pick up his discarded hat. If she wanted to be bullheaded about it, then it was her skin she was risking, not his. "Have it your way." He turned and started to walk away, then had second thoughts. "Oh, by the way. Tell Cass, if you happen to see him, Willa's keepin' his supper warm."

She wasn't about to give that dirty scoundrel any message, Wynne thought resentfully as she watched Cole turn once more and head back to the house. But she'd cheerfully tell Mr. Cole Claxton a thing or two! One being that the next time *he* saw his baby brother he'd be in a pine box!

And with that Wynne gathered the waist of her skirt in one hand, the hem in the other, and marched to the house behind Missouri's *second* biggest scoundrel.

CHAPTER 8

DAWN WAS JUST BREAKING OVER THE HORIZON THE following day as Wynne tripped lightly along the rutted path, carrying her two brown valises with her. Her heart was lighter than it had been in several days.

It was going to be another scorcher, but she comforted herself with the thought that it couldn't be a very long walk into town and she would enjoy the peace and solitude.

She almost laughed out loud when she thought about the way Cole had accused her of not being able to take care of herself. She could take care of herself as well as the next person. Maybe even better.

If he could see her now, he'd certainly have to change his mind. She was properly dressed in a pale blue sprigged dress with tatted lace trim, the waist nipped in to emphasize its narrowness and the fullness of her bosom, her hair was brushed up with small curls nested at the crown of her head, and she was on her way into town to take care of her own affairs. She was a woman well versed in the business affairs of running a plantation. Papa had made sure of that, so dabbling in the business world was not new to her.

Granted, the overseer at Moss Oak had been experienced and especially conscientious, considering that many overseers had up and deserted the plantations during the war, leaving their employers helpless in the care of the servants staying behind and the crops in the field. Many owners had simply sat and watched their heritages disintegrate before their eyes.

But Moss Oak had survived, not without a great many problems plaguing it, but the land was still there and in the Elliot name. The fields were parched, no crops in the ground other than the small truck garden which fed the servants who remained on the place, but someday it would be brought back to the fertile land it once had been. She'd see to that. And she sincerely hoped that whoever bought the land would love it as much as Wesley Elliot had.

She sniffed disdainfully. The nerve of Cole Claxton trying to tell her she couldn't take care of herself.

Mercy, it was hot! Wynne glanced skyward at the sun, beating down pitilessly. Already the lace around the collar of her dress was clinging to her skin. Her black, high-top, buttoned shoes were certainly fashionable, but they were not meant for walking any distance. When she had progressed a few miles down the road, that fact was achingly plain.

Even the perky bird sitting serenely on top of her hat looked slightly more wilted than when her journey first began, and her hair was beginning to straggle down her neck.

Wynne had lain awake half the night, thinking about her predicament. But having firmly made up her mind, she'd risen early and tiptoed around her room. She'd hurriedly washed and dressed in her Sunday best and pushed her clothing into the two valises. She wanted to be out of the Claxton household before anyone noticed her absence.

While she didn't want to create a scene by leaving as the family gathered for breakfast, she couldn't just disappear without any explanation, and she didn't want to hurt Lilly. Cass's mother had been so giving, so accepting. Penning a neat note to Lilly, Wynne said that she had decided to resume her search for the man she had been looking for and had left the house early because she didn't want to disturb Lilly's rest. Explaining that she was going to sell her ring, then take the first stage out that morning, she cautioned Cass's mother not to be concerned for her welfare because she was sure it would be only a small matter of time before she found the man she was seeking.

She thanked her for the kindness that the Claxton household had shown her and forced her pen to include Cole's name as one of her generous benefactors. Actually she did feel a certain sense of loss in having to leave. It would have been lovely to be able to extend her stay so that she would have been there to see Beau and Betsy married. While she was sealing the envelope, it occurred to her she was going to miss Lilly too. Funny, but she felt no animosity toward her. After all, she couldn't help it if she had two loathsome sons.

Nevertheless, Wynne was thankful Cole had remained silent about her past association with Cass. She assumed, and hoped, he would continue to do so now that she'd left.

Just remembering how she'd made a fool of herself in the orchard the night before made her cheeks burn with embarrassment. When she'd returned to the house, Wynne had entered through the front door and slipped upstairs to make the necessary repairs to her dress before joining the others.

Cole had been sitting at the table eating a piece of pie when she came downstairs thirty minutes later. Although there were a lot of fretful glances coming from Betsy, nothing had been mentioned about Wynne's earlier, somewhat abrupt departure from the dinner table, so she felt certain that Cole would remain discreet to spare his family worry.

The sun was a blazing ball of fire now. Wynne dabbed at the perspiration gathering on her brow with a dainty lace handkerchief.

Although she had only a meager amount of clothing in her valise, it seemed to weigh ten pounds more than it had when she started.

Five more miles down the road a large blister was forming on her right toe, she was hot and thirsty, and her arms ached from carrying the burdensome bags.

Another two miles found her angrily sorting through the two bags and stuffing only the essentials into one, then discarding the other in the middle of the road.

By the time the town of River Run came into view, her disposition could best be described as something less than sunny.

Behind her the sound of approaching hoofbeats reached her. The animal wasn't coming very fast, just a smooth, ground-covering pace. Curious, Wynne turned to see who might be on the road this early.

Oh, no! she groaned. Him again! She'd recognize Cole Claxton's arrogant posture anywhere. What was he doing out here? Coming to drag her back no doubt. Well, he had another think coming, she thought, seething.

The horse drew nearer as her chin rose a notch higher and she mentally prepared a scathing refusal for when he demanded she return to the Claxton homestead.

When his mount was abreast of her, her mouth shot open to refuse his offer, but damn the man, he rode right past her! Didn't even look her way.

Before she realized it, she had been standing in the road for a full five minutes watching that—that arrogant fool's retreating back. She stamped her foot indignantly. Damnation! That man got under her skin even when he ignored her. To make matters worse, the moron hadn't even asked her if she wanted a ride! Might have known it, she grumbled to herself. The man had the manners of a dolt! And with another muttered oath learned at her father's knee, Wynne picked up her one valise and continued her trek toward town.

Banker Elias Holbrook glanced up from his desk as the tinkle of the bell over the bank door announced his first customers of the morning. Business had been mighty slow since the war began. Some banks had even had to close their doors, but Elias had somehow managed to keep his business afloat.

With pride he watched Nute Walker stride to the teller window to make a deposit. The new owner of the general store was doing well, and here was old Mrs. Groves again this morning. Only butter-and-egg money, but she faithfully put her few pennies in her account every week.

Suddenly Elias blinked. The striking young woman who had made such a town spectacle of herself a few days earlier, getting off the stagecoach, staggered through the door, dragging a dusty brown valise. Her face was flushed as red as one of the stripes on Old Glory, which flew over the courthouse, and she wore a hat with a strange-looking bird on it. The little hat was cocked crazily on the side of her head, and strands of her red hair hung limply from beneath. Her dress was soaked in perspiration, and dust lay heavily on the hem of her shirt. Her lovely green eyes were ringed with dirt, reminding him of a worn-out raccoon.

Wynne dabbed at her cheeks and neck as she sagged weakly against the polished pine railing and let the cooler air of the bank's interior wash over her.

Regaining his composure, Elias spoke to the young woman pleasantly. "It's gonna be a warm one."

She smiled lamely. "Yes, quite warm." It wasn't even nine o'clock in the morning, and the heat was already suffocating.

Moved to compassion by the pitiful sight of her road-stained face and dress, Elias poured a glass of water from a pitcher sitting on his desk and handed it to her. Wynne accepted his offer gratefully. Even the tepid water felt cool to her parched tongue. She emptied the glass in one long swallow, then, drawing a deep breath, returned the glass to the corner of Elias's desk.

Her foot hurt abominably. There was a chair right next to a big oak desk, and without thinking, she sat down and peeled off the offending shoe. The petite foot she withdrew had a blister the size of a silver dollar throbbing painfully on its big toe. Emitting a huge sigh of relief, she tucked the skirt of her dress under her bottom and then brought the injured foot up to her lap to poke gingerly at the puffy spot.

Amazed by her actions, Elias leaned over Wynne's shoulder and peered at the proceedings with growing interest. This was the first time a lady had ever come into his bank and removed her shoes, especially such a lovely young lady.

"My, my. That looks terrible." He clucked sympathetically.

"It hurts like the blue blazes," she said with a groan. Almost immediately she realized what she'd done. Hell and damnation! What must he think of her?

Her foot slid very slowly off her lap, and as circumspectly as possible under the circumstances, Wynne tucked her bare foot and her shoed one beneath the dusty hem of her skirt.

A true lady would never enter a bank and take her shoe off in front of a man! She could just hear what Miss Fielding would have to say about that!

Clearing her throat nervously, Wynne set the shoe in her lap on the floor and crossed her hands in her lap. She pasted an utterly charming smile on her face. "Would you perhaps be the man I would talk to about obtaining a small loan?"

Elias straightened automatically and tugged at his vest. "A loan?" His

face brightened. It had been years since anyone had been in his bank
wanting a loan! The war had stopped nearly all transactions of that sort.
No one had any money, so no money could be lent.

"Why, yes, my dear! I certainly am." He extended a cordial hand.
"Elias Holbrook, here."

"Mr. Holbrook." Wynne accepted his hand with a graceful nod of her
head. "How nice to make your acquaintance, sir. My name is Wynne
Elliot." Just as she shook his hand, her hat tilted dangerously to one side.
Her hand flew up to steady the hat.

Elias smiled at her obvious discomfort. She was a charming, beguiling
young woman, and he wanted to put her at ease. "Wynne. That's a lovely
name, my dear."

"Thank you."

"You're staying out at the Claxton place, aren't you?"

"Yes . . . I don't know if you heard about my minor inconvenience. . . ."

"Yes, yes, I did. I'm terribly sorry." There wasn't anyone in town who
hadn't heard about the stage being held up or who had missed the
spectacle this young lady had created by falling out of the stage with her
rifle.

"Yes . . . well, about the loan. Your establishment has been quite
highly recommended to me," she said hoping he wouldn't suspect how
desperate she really was.

Actually the part about someone's recommending his bank was not
entirely true. Not one person had suggested she try the bank, but she
thought it might sound more businesslike if she took this approach.

"Oh, my. Why, that's wonderful," Elias proclaimed. He scurried
around his desk and sat down, reaching for a pen and paper. "Now, what
amount did you have in mind, Miss Elliot?" Of course, it would be out of
the question for a woman to secure a loan with the bank, he thought
fondly, but the Claxton family was a real solid investment, and he could
issue the loan in Cole or Beau's name.

"Well . . ." Wynne wrapped her handkerchief around her forefinger
tightly. "I think perhaps twenty dollars would be sufficient."

"Hmm . . . twenty dollars . . . yes . . ." Elias was scribbling as they
talked. "And what sort of collateral would you be able to offer the bank?"

"Oh, I have this pretty little ring my father gave me for my sixteenth
birthday." She hurriedly slipped the ring off her finger and handed it to
him. "Isn't it nice?"

Elias stared at the tiny ring lying in the palm of his hand, then glanced
back up at her. "This is all the collateral you have?"

She mustered up the most winning smile she had. "Yes, that's all I have
with me right now, but it is truly a lovely ring, don't you agree?"

She could see the seed of doubt begin to sprout in Elias Holbrook's
eyes, and her heart sank. "Well, yes, my dear. It is lovely, but I would

need more than the ring to make such a loan," he said. "Have you nothing else of value?"

"Oh, yes! I have a whole plantation back in Savannah," Wynne answered.

"A plantation!" Elias's face brightened once more. "Well, well. Now that's more like it. May I see the deed, please?"

"Deed?"

"Yes, the deed. You do own the land free and clear?"

"Yes, but I don't have the deed with me," Wynne said.

"Oh?" Once more doubt clouded Elias's face. "Oh, dear me."

"But I *do* own the land and I could send for the proper papers—"

"Yes, but that might take months," he pointed out gently.

"But I still have the ring as collateral. . . ." Her voice trailed off weakly as he began to shake his head negatively, and she realized with a sinking heart he wasn't going to give her the loan.

For the next ten minutes she tried everything she could think of to make him change his mind, but he remained firm. The bank could not issue the loan in her name.

"Miss Elliot, may I make a suggestion?" he said kindly. "Why don't you talk this over with Cole Claxton and then you and he come back in? Perhaps something could be worked out—"

Wynne was on her feet in an instant. "Cole Claxton! Never!"

"Now, my dear"—Elias could see he had said the wrong thing—"it pains me greatly to have to refuse you a loan, but you must realize the bank is not in the habit of making loans to women—"

"It pains me too," Wynne replied angrily. She stuck her foot in her shoe and sucked in her breath painfully as the leather slid across the blister. "Thank you for your time, sir!"

"Miss Elliot . . ." Elias watched feebly as she limped across the bank lobby and snatched up her valise, then slammed out the front door.

"Yes . . . good day, Miss Elliot," he added under his breath sheepishly as he glanced around at the other early-morning customers and smiled.

The temperature felt as if it had shot up even higher than before when Wynne stepped out of the bank.

Oh, yes, Banker Holbrook had thought the ring was lovely but completely inadequate collateral for a twenty-dollar loan just because she was a woman! But it wasn't until he suggested that Cole come talk to him, that perhaps he would be willing to issue the loan in Cole's name, she'd known her goose was cooked for sure.

No matter how she'd argued—presented her case, she amended, for Miss Fielding's sake—Banker Holbrook had not been persuaded. Well, she wasn't beaten yet.

Shifting the valise in her hand, she stepped off the sidewalk and limped toward the general store.

Mr. Holbrook had suggested that she find a private investor. He'd said Nute Walker sometimes made small loans in exchange for personal property. But Mr. Walker didn't need a pearl ring.

Nor did Tom Clayborne or Jed McThais or even Avery Miller, for that matter. It seemed as if not one person in River Run had use for a lovely pearl ring or any money to lend either.

Wynne slumped down on a bench in front of Hattie's Place and glumly surveyed the ring on her right hand. Tears sprang to her eyes. She'd always thought it was the prettiest ring she'd ever seen.

The interior of the saloon was extremely quiet. She supposed Penelope would still be sleeping. For a moment Wynne toyed with the idea of marching right in there and rousing Hattie out of bed and asking for a job. After all, she was completely alone, broke, in a strange town, and didn't even know where her next meal was coming from. It was a time for desperate measures.

She stood up and went over to the saloon door. Standing on tiptoe, she peeked inside. She couldn't ever recall seeing such an establishment before. Papa would have never permitted it, and it was quite possible he was changing positions in his grave right now because of her brazenness.

Barely visible in the dim interior was a lone man sweeping the floor. Chairs were stacked neatly on top of tables, and a low ceiling fan was trying its best to move the stagnant air in the room. The strong odor of stale cigarette smoke and brackish beer filled her nostrils. Her nose wrinkled as she thought about what it would be like to work in a place like this.

If you're going to kill a man, Wynne, then you certainly should be able to give yourself to one in order to survive, she reasoned.

For a moment she felt a mild stirring of apprehension at the thought of actually killing Cass. What would it be like to walk up and point a gun at his big, broad chest, then deliberately, coldly, cruelly pull the trigger? A ripple of revulsion snaked through her. This was the first time she'd ever really stopped to think about the act.

When it happened, would he look at her with amusement, or with scorn, or maybe even with a tiny bit of remorse? Or would that devil throw his dark head back and laugh at her, his even white teeth glistening in the sunlight, having his own revenge, even as he stood at death's door?

With a long sigh she stepped away from the door and sat down on the bench again. Well, she'd never know how Cass would react until she found him, and she couldn't find him until she had some mode of transportation, and she couldn't get that transportation unless she sold her ring.

Across the street a small crowd had gathered at the general store. They were signing up for a wagon train that was due to leave the following morning, heading west. Mr. Walker had suggested she try to sign on, but when she'd inquired about that prospect, she'd been told she would have to have a husband or a guardian of some kind, preferably a family member.

She sighed again, long and wearily. Well, she obviously didn't have a spare "uncle" around, and her chances of finding a husband by daybreak the next morning were about as slim as selling the pearl ring.

Her gaze fell on the livery stable, and it occurred to her that she hadn't tried there yet. Now there was a possibility she hadn't thought of before. Of course, how stupid of her! She probably wouldn't be able to sell the ring there, but perhaps the owner would have a nice horse he would trade for it.

Riding a horse wouldn't be the most comfortable way to travel to Kansas City, but she supposed she could do it if she had to. She'd ridden nearly every day on the plantation before she'd gone away to school. And other women braved their way across the rugged frontier, didn't they? She'd gotten this far on her own, hadn't she?

Feeling slightly better about the whole situation, Wynne picked up her valise and hobbled across the street toward the stable.

The blacksmith was busy shoeing a horse as she walked up and smiled brightly at him. He was a huge, burly sort of man with a big gold front tooth. Sweat shone on his wide face, and he towered over her small frame from an eminent height.

Combined with the heat of the day, the forge made the inside of the stable oppressive. Not a thread of the smith's clothing was dry. Rivulets of sweat poured freely off him and ran in streams down his body, and his muscles bunched and relaxed in rhythm as his hammer beat a steady tattoo to shape a red-hot horseshoe. Glancing at her only briefly, the smithy kept his attention trained on his work.

Clearing her throat, Wynne smiled again and said, "Good morning, sir."

His answer was barely more than a passing grunt.

"It's extremely warm," she said pleasantly, then realized how ridiculous a comment that had been.

Again he grunted and moved away to pick up more shoeing nails and put them in his large, soiled apron.

"Could you perhaps tell me how far it is to Kansas City from here?"

"Over two hundred miles."

Wynne's face fell. "That many miles?"

He nodded and kept on working.

She cleared her throat nervously and looked about the stable. There was a lovely horse standing in one of the stalls. It was large, *and* sturdy-looking, and the most beautiful rust shade. It looked as if it would be easy to ride and as if it were gentle, and she desperately hoped the horse was both if she was going to travel 200 miles!

Wynne cleared her throat again. "Sir, I was wondering. Would that horse over there happen to be for sale?"

The blacksmith's gaze followed to where she was pointing. "It is." Then he returned to the job of shaping another horseshoe.

Wynne set down her valise and walked over to the stall. The horse stuck its nose over the gate and whuffed at her. Wynne smiled and rubbed its nose. "Pretty boy," she murmured. *Oh, yes, this one would do nicely*, she thought.

Stiffening her resolve, she quickly turned back to the smithy. "Well." She spoke again, more loudly.

"Well, I'm sure you've heard about the stage being robbed. I was on that stage and the thieves took all my money and now I have no way to travel on to Kansas City," she explained all in one breath. "But I do have this lovely pearl ring I'm sure you'd like. I would trade it in even exchange for this horse—"

The blacksmith's eyes promptly narrowed, and his mouth firmed with obvious resentment that she would think he would be interested in a pearl ring!

Wynne's eyes widened, and her mouth went suddenly dry. "Uh, oh, no! I didn't mean that *you* might be interested in the ring," she said hurriedly. "I thought perhaps you might know someone you would like to give it to. . . ." She trailed off hopefully as she saw the man's attention unwillingly focus on the ring that was on her hand. Quickly she thrust it out toward him, willing her trembling to stop.

His dark eyes took in the fragile object with little sign of any real interest. Leaning forward a fraction more, he surveyed the piece of jewelry more closely, and Wynne held her breath.

Her heart beat so strongly she was sure he must see it beneath the thin fabric of her dress. If he wouldn't trade the horse for the ring, she'd have no choice but to go to Hattie's and ask for a job.

Straightening, the smithy scowled at her sourly. "What'll I do with a little play pretty like that?"

"Oh, you could give it to your wife—"

"Don't have no wife." He interrupted curtly.

"Oh. Well, you could give it to—to a lady friend," she suggested cheerfully.

She waited for him to deny he had a lady friend, realizing instantly that had been a bad suggestion. It would be a miracle if he had such a female acquaintance.

But apparently he didn't find the suggestion that preposterous because his gaze had gone back to the ring and was lingering there as he seemed to be seriously considering the offer. Finally he spit out a stream of tobacco juice that whizzed by her ear as if it had been fired out of a cannon. The spittle had come so close to her cheek she was sure she could feel a remnant of the repulsive moisture still lingering wetly on the side of her face. It was all she could do to refrain from wiping her cheek with her hand.

"Well . . . I don't know . . ." he said thoughtfully.

Trying to keep from gagging, because Miss Fielding had repeatedly warned that a lady does not gag in public, Wynne fumbled hastily in her pocket for her handkerchief and smiled at him brightly.

Hell's bells and fiery damnation! She had to have that horse!

"Any lady would looove the ring," she said encouragingly, turning her hand from one side to another to make the ring glow in the dim light of the stable.

Fifteen minutes later she came riding out of the stable on the back of a glorious white mule, grinning ear to ear. She'd made a good deal and she'd done it all on her own.

The blacksmith wouldn't trade the horse for the ring, but he would trade the old mule for it. It seemed the animal had wandered into town on its own a couple of weeks ago. It was speculated that a prospector had previously owned it. Perhaps he'd died somewhere out on the trail and the mule had wandered wild for a while. The animal was of no value to the smithy, just one more mouth to feed, and the ring had miraculously caught his eye.

The trade had come complete with the prospector's pack equipment. There were two dirty old blankets, various mismatched eating utensils, a pick and a shovel, three pie-shaped pans, for gold panning—should she happen to run across any gold—and even an old rusty gun. The unexpected weapon would be a godsend if she were to complete her mission successfully, for she had wondered where she would get a gun. After all, she was sure she couldn't run Cass down and club him to death, although if it had come to that alternative, she'd have done it.

There was also various other paraphernalia that Wynne couldn't readily identify, but she was sure it all would come in handy once she was out on the trail. All in all, she thought with a satisfied smile, she'd driven a very shrewd bargain.

The only problem at the moment was that she'd always ridden sidesaddle. Because she suspected he had felt sorry for her, the blacksmith had thrown in a very worn saddle with the deal, and she had to ride astride. Getting accustomed to that was going to be a little tricky, and the animal had a strange gait, more of a lurching from side to side than the smooth stride of the horses she was accustomed to at Moss Oak.

The blacksmith had helped her mount. At first she thought about insisting upon riding properly like a lady, hooking her knee around the saddlehorn to make it a kind of sidesaddle, but the smith had warned her that would be a poor choice. "You'd better set like a man," he'd said, "or th' gall dern thing will pitch you right in the middle of the road."

Of course, she didn't want the "gall dern thing" to do that, so she'd primly tucked her skirt up around her legs and shinnied up on the back of the mule as gracefully as the situation would allow.

"Uh, just exactly what direction is Kansas City?" she asked just before she started out on her long journey.

The blacksmith scratched his head absently, then sent another brown stream of juice flying by the mule's head. "You sure you ought to be doin' this, lady?" If she didn't even know what direction Kansas City was in, he didn't think she should be setting out for it all alone.

"Thank you for your concern, but if you would just kindly point the way."

He shook his head again worriedly. "Just keep bearin' north, little lady. Just keep bearin' north."

Oh, what a glorious feeling it was to ride down the center of town, knowing she was once again a woman in charge of her own destiny.

The colorful procession of two made a good deal of noise as it progressed down the main street. The pack was tied firmly behind the saddle, but the utensils were tied on loosely and clanged together noisily as the mule and its rider ambled slowly out of town.

The only thing that spoiled her newfound paradise was the fact that *he* was there to witness it. Cole was standing outside the general store, taking note of her departure with irritatingly cool detachment. Leaning insolently against the porch railing, he calmly placed a cheroot between his teeth and watched indifferently as she rattled her way past him.

Wynne ignored how blue his eyes were against the dark tan of his face. It didn't matter that the white muslin shirt was open at the neck to reveal the shadow of dark hair across his chest. Or that his sleeves were rolled back to reveal corded forearms. His hat was tilted rakishly to the back of his head, and a fringe of hair that was a bit too long framed his strong face, and he was so handsome it nearly took her breath away.

None of that made any difference, she told herself. Cole Claxton was ill-tempered, arrogant, and a completely egotistical old goat. But there was something about him that commanded her respect too. There was no way she could get around that. There were strong family feelings among the Claxtons. That alone was enviable. They'd come from a background of wealth and gentility. Their home had reflected that as much as had the ingrained southern mannerisms Lilly had exhibited.

From listening to conversations around the dinner table, she'd learned the Claxtons had indeed come from Georgia. They were even from near her home, not far from Savannah. When Cole and Beau were very young, Samuel Claxton and his wife had liquidated all their assets and moved to the West. They'd found the fertile Ozarks mountain area and had been taken by its beauty. They had settled there, determined to raise a family without the blight of slavery, and they'd succeeded.

Another painful stab of resentment attacked her as Wynne thought about the different natures of the handsome Claxton men.

Cole, at thirty, was the eldest. The strong, silent one, he made Wynne incredibly angry by being so practical, but she knew Lilly depended on him to be the strength and steady hand of the family. Beau, at twenty-five, was beguiling and charming, always out to help and please. But at twenty-two, Cass Claxton was rotten through and through. Oh, he'd been as genteel and well mannered as his two brothers—actually more so. A perfect "southern" gentleman at all times. Apparently he'd been the only one of the family to cling to its Georgia roots and fight for the South—when he'd finally decided to fight. *The miserable wretch*, Wynne thought. He'd been a handsome devil and, oh, so cleverly charming.

It was a constant thorn in her side that Cole and Cass bore such a striking resemblance to each other.

But she wasn't going to let him dampen her enthusiasm. She was back on course, and nothing would stop her now from completing her mission. Before long there would be only two Claxton men for the women of the world to defend themselves against.

With a decided lifting of her nose she nudged the old mule to a faster gait and loped past the general store with not so much as a glance in his direction.

And the last Cole Claxton saw of Wynne Elliot was her fanny bouncing along in the saddle like a proud little prairie hen flouncing over the horizon, heading west.

CHAPTER 9

"*W*EELLL, GUESS WE COULD ALWAYS GO CROSS THE street and wet our whistles," the old-timer suggested as he shot a wad of tobacco juice cleanly off the porch, then wiped the remainder of the brown stain still lining his mouth on the shoulder of his shirt.

It never ceased to amaze Bertram how a man could be so neat yet so untidy at the same time.

"No, we was over there earlier." He winced and shifted his broken leg around to a more comfortable position. The splint was cumbersome, and his leg was beginning to itch like crazy. And the insufferable heat wasn't making it any easier on him.

"Weelll, we could go wet a line, if you was a mind to." For some reason, ever since Bertram had fallen off that blamed porch a couple of weeks ago, Jake seemed to think it was his responsibility to take care of him. From the day he had broken his leg, the old man had befriended him even to the point of insisting that he stay at his home until the leg mended. Since Bertram was once more at the mercy of fate and low finances, he had little choice but to accept the generous offer.

Jake lived by himself in nothing more than a shack on the outskirts of town. His wife had died back in '51, and his only son had been killed in a gunfight the year after. In short, Jake was lonely, and he welcomed the young stranger's company. And it hadn't been too bad for Bertram either, except Jake talked a lot and got on his nerves every once in a while. Still, the old man was good to him, so he couldn't complain.

"I could put you on back of ol' Millhouse and walk you down to the river," Jake was saying.

Every morning Bertram was put unceremoniously on the old horse's back, and Jake led it into town. The rest of the day they sat on the plank porch in front of one of the local establishments and whittled with the other idle citizens of Springfield. It was not a comfortable journey, but it was better than lying in bed all day with nothing to do and no one to talk to.

"No, thanks, Jake." Bertram refused listlessly. "I'll just sit here and finish this cow I started." He held up for inspection a piece of wood that was poorly fashioned in the form of a four-legged animal. It wasn't that he didn't appreciate Jake's efforts to keep him busy; it was just that he was getting awfully bored. He wanted to get on with his mission of finding that fool Elliot woman. Once he got his business with her finished, then maybe he would be able to resume a normal life.

"Why, that's right nice, boy." Jake paternally praised the misshapen image Bertram was holding.

Well, it wasn't, and Bertram knew it. The miniature carving didn't look anything like a cow. More like just an old notched-out piece of pine. But Jake had tried so hard to teach him to whittle that Bertram didn't have the heart not to try at least to master the art.

This afternoon the porch was full of Jake's counterparts, all whittling and spitting periodically. Bertram hadn't taken up tobacco chewing yet, but he suspected that would be next if he didn't get out of there pretty quickly.

All eyes centered on the white mule that came lumbering through town just before noon. A young, pretty red-headed girl wearing a silly little hat with a bird on it was riding the animal or at least making a stab at it. She seemed to be having a hard time getting the beast to do what she wanted.

Rising slowly to his feet, Bertram winced as he heard the woman shout an unladylike command to the mule as it suddenly stopped dead still in the middle of the road. The girl almost pitched forward on her head but finally managed to keep astride.

You filthy, stubborn piece of dog meat! I ought to—Wynne fumed, then glanced around her in embarrassment. Lord, there was a whole porchful of men staring at her! And one in particular whom she noticed leaning against a post, with a splint on his leg. Quickly regaining her composure, she pushed her hat back out of her heat-flushed face and smiled cordially at the men staring at her from the porch. "Afternoon, gentlemen," she called sweetly.

They all hurriedly tipped their hats and gave her friendly, toothless grins.

For the next few moments she sat on the mule, jabbing it in the sides with her toes and bouncing up and down just as if she were actually going somewhere.

Leaning against the post, Bertram grinned at her obvious dilemma. "Need any help, ma'am?"

The girl shot him a lame smile, but about that time the mule decided to move on, and it did in such a rapid fashion that the last Bertram saw of the girl was a white streak bounding out of town amid a loud clamor of pots and pans.

Shaking his head in amusement, Bertram hobbled back to his chair and picked up the wooden cow once more.

"Here comes that Fancy Biggers woman," Jake said out of the corner of his mouth a few minutes later.

All heads snapped up to watch the young woman coming across the street. She worked at the saloon, and Bertram had noticed in the two weeks he had been there how the other women of the town picked up the hems of their skirts and made sure they didn't touch any part of Fancy's gown as they passed her.

Bertram didn't like that. Fancy Biggers might not be living exactly by the Good Book, but he didn't think it gave the other women cause to treat her so badly.

She couldn't have been much older than eighteen, maybe nineteen, Bertram guessed. Couldn't hardly tell with all that war paint on her face. But she was pretty. He was sure of that. She had really nice red hair, too, that shone like a shiny new copper penny in the afternoon sunlight. Her eyes were a sort of brownish yellow, kind of strange-looking but pretty.

She was thinner than she should be. Looked to him as if she could stand a few more square meals under her belt. And the dress she was wearing was indecent. He couldn't argue that. It was bright red satin and made her waist look like about the tiniest thing he had ever seen. Why, his hands could span her waistline and still have room left over. And the neckline—well, it dipped deep in front to reveal small, firm breasts.

There was a small brown mole on her left one. Course, he didn't mind the dress all that much, but he could see where the other womenfolk might get a little upset with her prancing around in front of their men the way she did sometimes. She was carrying a matching red umbrella and twirling it absently around her head as she walked, sort of in a flirty manner.

All in all, Bertram liked Fancy Biggers. In the two weeks he had been in Springfield, she had been nice to him.

Fancy stepped up onto the porch, and the men's chairs came back down on all four legs with loud thuds. "Afternoon, gentlemen," she said pleasantly.

There was another outbreak of toothless grins and nervous twittering as the men made their appropriate responses.

She turned her attention to Bertram and smiled. "Afternoon, Bertram."

"Afternoon, Miss Biggers." Bertram had managed to rise respectfully to his feet again as she had stepped up onto the porch. He felt his stomach flutter nervously, and he didn't know why.

"Lovely day," she remarked conversationally.

"A little hot."

"Yes. We could certainly use a good rain."

"We sure could, Miss Biggers. Looks kinda cloudy back in the west. Maybe we'll get a shower before the day's over." He grinned at her warmly and forced his eyes off the small mole he had located almost immediately.

"I wouldn't mind at all, but it's still a lovely day for a drive, wouldn't you think?" Fancy smiled at him again, and Bertram felt his face flush deep red as he heard the other men's knowing chuckles behind him.

"Uh, yes, I guess it is. Real nice." Was she asking him to take her for a ride?

"I know you're not exactly up to driving a team at the moment; but the saloon has a buckboard I could borrow, and I was wondering if you might like to go for a ride with me," she asked boldly.

Fancy Biggers had always had to ask for everything she got, so it didn't bother her in the least to extend such an invitation to Bertram. They had talked many times since he'd come to town, sitting out in front of the saloon while she was taking a break from the fast-drinking, fist-fighting patrons who frequented the establishment.

He was the only man she had ever met who didn't seem to want anything from her, although he was at liberty to buy her favors just like any other man. But he never once suggested such a thing. Bertram was always polite and extremely nice to her. He told her about his family and what he'd been doing since he left his home in Savannah. He was older than she was, nearly twenty-eight, but that didn't bother her either. She loved to hear him talk. He had such a nice, deep, rich voice, and she could listen for hours when he told her about how his mother used to bake apple pies for him three times a week because she knew that was his very favorite.

Fancy couldn't imagine having someone bake a pie specially for her. She'd been an orphan since birth, being raised by first one stranger, then another. Most of the women had been mean to her, and the men had taken her youth and innocence away before she was fourteen years old. Bertram Mallory was like a breath of spring air to her with his genteel manners and soft-spoken conversation.

"Well, yes . . . a ride might be real nice," Bertram said quickly, wishing the other men would stop their dad-blasted giggling! They were worse than a bunch of old women.

"Fine." Her wide grin couldn't hide her pleasure. "I'll get the buckboard and be back for you in a few minutes."

Bertram had to take a lot of ribbing before Fancy finally appeared again, but he decided it was worth it. The old-timers got him loaded in the buckboard, and soon he and Fancy were leaving the town behind them for a pleasant afternoon in the countryside.

Those old geezers could laugh all they wanted to, Bertram thought as he stole a secret glance in Fancy's direction. A day in the countryside with Fancy Biggers was a whole lot better than trying to carve out another one of those blasted cows.

A little more than two miles away another young woman was spending the day in the countryside, but it wasn't quite as pleasant.

The mule had been nothing but trouble from the moment Wynne left River Run. It didn't want to walk, and it didn't want to sit down. It just seemed to want to exist—nothing else.

Two miles out of Springfield she'd had to slide off the mule and practically drag it another few feet before she realized they were going to have to get a few things straight, one being that she was the boss and the mule was going to have to bow to that fact.

By now the heat was unbearable. Wynne angrily jerked off her hat and fanned her face for a moment. The blister was paining her again, so she hobbled over to a grassy patch and took off both shoes. Relieved, she wriggled her toes for a moment, then hobbled back and stuffed her shoes into her valise, which she had tied on the mule's back.

Now she felt a little better, and after a sip of tepid water out of the canteen, she turned her attention back to the problem at hand: the mule.

Perhaps if she tried to explain her predicament to the animal, it just might listen to reason. At least it was worth a try. The horses at home had liked to have her talk to them.

"Now, mule, you and I have got to have an understandin'." Wynne began in her most cajoling voice. "I've got a job to do, and you're here to help me do it."

It didn't seem overly interested.

"Now I know you had a nice stall in that stable, but I've brought you out here in the hot sunshine, and we're goin' on an adventure." That was it. Lie to it. Perhaps . . . Oh, fie! It didn't really matter what she said. The danged animal didn't understand a word she was saying!

Besides, whom was she trying to fool, herself? Adventure, ha! She was out to kill a man, and she was beginning to wonder if she was really equipped to handle the job.

Wynne sat down again, one hand holding one rein while the mule sat facing her with a simple placid look on its face.

Cold reality was beginning to appear, and some of her earlier enthusiasm for the task she'd set herself was beginning to seep away. "If the truth be known, mule, I think I may have bitten off more than I can chew," she confided.

"Miss Fielding was very strict about things like servin' tea properly and carryin' on a charmin' conversation, but how do you kill a man? Even one you hate with all your bein'?" She was quite sure *Godey's Lady's Book* had absolutely nothing to say about the way to handle that task. In fact, it said quite the opposite. A proper young woman did not attempt revenge. She was above that.

"Such triflin' with a lady's heart should be avenged by the men in her family," Wynne assured the mule. A deep sigh escaped her. There were no men in the Elliot family now. They all were gone, and a tear dampened her eye.

A long, low roll of thunder rumbled across the western horizon. "Oh, flitter, mule. If it rains, I don't know what I'll do." She stood up and tugged on the reins. "Come on. Please, please cooperate," Wynne begged but the mule didn't budge.

She shielded her eyes against the bright sunlight and looked around her. Other than the ominous-looking dark clouds on the horizon there was nothing but trees and scrub brush and hundreds of grasshoppers surrounding her. The lack of rain had made the pesky creatures abundant this year. They clung to her skirt and hopped around her feet with the most unnerving exuberance as she scanned the grove of hickory trees off to the right. Her eyes narrowed when they focused on what seemed to be some sort of shelter nestled between the trees. The dense foliage almost hid the old building, but on closer inspection Wynne decided that it must be an old log cabin.

Perhaps if she were lucky, the owners wouldn't mind her taking refuge when the storm broke. But the first thing she had to do was get the darned mule to move.

Turning her attention back to the animal, she tugged on the rope halter and tried once again to force the beast to move its feet. The beast, of course, was not inclined to do so. "Ohhh!" Wynne jerked on the halter and was rewarded with a long, loud bawl which split the air with a sound resembling Gabriel's last trumpet's blast. "Oh, my Lord!" And she dropped the reins to cover her ears, completely unaware of the lone rider who appeared in the distance.

Cole slowed his horse to a walk as he surveyed the scene below him. The blue of his eyes turned to a deep indigo as he rested his forearm across his saddlehorn and watched with growing amazement.

Wynne was standing in front of the mule, which had set itself squarely in the middle of the trail. They hadn't made it much past two miles out of Springfield, but somehow that didn't surprise him.

What did surprise him was that she was standing there shaking her finger in the animal's face and from the look of it preaching it a sermon. *Damn fool woman*, he thought irritably. Reaching into his shirt pocket for a smoke, Cole asked himself once more why he was wasting precious time following her, time that could well be spent on a hundred other things. Since he'd been gone, the farm had gone steadily downhill. Ma had done her best, and he'd hoped Cass would stay there to help out, but he'd gone off to Savannah and then the war. There were fences to be mended, ground to be tilled, crops to be planted, and what was he doing?

Chasing a crazy woman, that's what. He'd cursed himself all afternoon for even giving her a second thought. When he'd seen her in town, he'd laughed at the spectacle she'd been, bouncing around on the back of that mule, pans clattering. He'd told himself then that whatever happened to her was her just due. But as the day wore on, her pitiful plight kept coming back to him. It didn't matter that she was a woman unused to the roughness of the Ozarks, but it had suddenly occurred to him that she might be more dangerous than he was giving her credit for.

Oh, he didn't actually think she had the skill it would take to kill his brother, even on the remote possibility that she could find him. But there was always the chance she could accidentally kill him if she came upon him unexpectedly. Not with any expertise, but through sheer clumsiness!

The thought had nagged at him all day, and by late afternoon he'd decided that since he was the only one who knew what she was up to, he would have to make sure that didn't happen. So, instead of working to get the farm back into shape, here he was trailing Wynne at a discreet distance, and it was getting ready to rain.

Damned woman. She'd been nothing but trouble from the day he and Beau had come across her, and now he was going to be following her across the state for the next few weeks. His purpose was not to protect her —whatever happened to her was her own blamed fault—but there was Cass to consider. He found it hard to believe Cass was the man who'd left Wynne at the altar, but if he were, he would be made to answer to Cole when he found him. Cass was the youngest, and Cole had always been protective of him since he'd never known their pa; but he'd brook no such actions from either of his brothers. If a Claxton man gave his word, then it was to be honored.

But it seemed there was no end to the trouble that Elliot woman caused. Not only had Wynne delayed their arrival at home, but she'd made him lie to Ma. It was ridiculous, but having to lie to Lilly made him feel like a kid again. He'd had to make up some farfetched story about needing to ride to Kansas City to conduct unexpected business.

Beau had looked at him as if he had suddenly taken leave of his senses. Cole had refused to offer any other explanation and had promptly gathered his supplies, saddled his horse, and ridden off without another word, leaving a puzzled mother and brother gaping after him.

He drew on the cigar in annoyance and shook his head disbelievingly at the scene continuing below him. The little twit sat in the grass, her feet firmly planted as she pulled on the mule's halter. The animal suddenly lurched forward, knocking Wynne flat on her stylish fanny, then stood over her, braying.

A tiny grin threatened Cole's stern features as he heard Wynne's screech of angry indignation. She was living up to the reputation of redheads' having a bad temper. At first he wanted to applaud the mule, but on second thought he nudged his horse forward and walked it down the slope.

Wynne might have guessed the rider approaching was none other than that miserable Cole Claxton. Squinting up at him, she was never more aware of her rumpled dress, the dirt on her hands, which had probably been transferred to her face, and the strands of hair which were falling about her face. Her shoulders slumped in dejection.

Eyeing her bare feet coolly, Cole reined the horse to a stop and peered down at her in ill-concealed amusement. Taking another drag on his cigar, he inquired in a pleasant voice, "Having a little trouble, Miss Elliot?"

"What are you doing here?" she snapped.

Once again the smile teased the corners of his mouth. "Why, Miss Elliot, you act as if you're not happy to see me," he said dryly.

"How astute of you. I'm not." Wynne jumped to her feet and tried to brush the dust and grasshoppers off her skirt while trying to conceal her toes beneath the hem.

Cole watched while she fussed with her appearance and muttered what sounded suspiciously like some very unladylike obscenities under her breath. Her hair had come totally loose from its pins, and limp curls hung down her back.

"I thought you were going to take the stage to Kansas City," he said provokingly.

"I decided it would be better to travel by . . . mule," she replied curtly. She would die before she would let him know she hadn't had a choice in the matter. "If I'd gone by stage, I might have missed Cass on his way back," she added defensively.

"Oh? Well, here I was thinkin' maybe you couldn't get a loan at the bank, so you went all over town tryin' to sell your pearl ring and that didn't work either, so you finally had to go over to the stable and swap the fool thing off for this old mule and backpack."

"Well, obviously you thought wrong," she said huffily. Now how did he know all that? There undoubtedly was a bunch of busybodies in River Run!

Shifting in his saddle, Cole had to grin at her growing frustration. "Where's your little bird hat?"

She had had about enough of his sarcasm! Jerking the hat out of her valise, she flung it at him hotly. "Right here!"

Cole ducked when the hat came sailing past his head, but he was still grinning as he straightened up and clicked his tongue. "Did anyone ever tell you you have a nasty temper, Miss Elliot?"

"Mr. Claxton, I'm sure you have not ridden all the way out here to discuss my personality traits," she replied icily. He was just trying to get under her skin, and she was dismayed to find out he was well on his way to accomplishing his purpose. "What do you want?"

Those devastatingly blue eyes skimmed over her lightly as he placed the cigar back in his mouth. "Oh, I don't know. Maybe I missed you and I decided to ride out and see how you were doin'," he answered.

"Very amusing." She wasn't buying that in the least.

"Maybe I wanted to make sure you had a rain slicker." He was delighted by the way her green eyes sparkled brighter with anger by the moment. He motioned with his eyes toward the west. "Looks to me like it's gonna rain, and maybe I got to worryin' about that little bird on your hat," he lied. "I sure wouldn't want that little bird to get all wet, so maybe I come ridin' out here to—"

Once more he was forced to duck quickly as a woman's black shoe came flying past his head.

"Oh, my!" He clucked. "There you go gettin' all riled again. And I'm just tryin' to be nice to you," he said patiently as he sat up straight again.

"Ha! That's a laugh!" He'd never been nice to her willingly, and she was quite sure he wasn't starting now. "Now will you kindly move on, Mr. Claxton, and leave me be?" she demanded. She turned her attention back to the stubborn mule.

"No." His weight shifting in the saddle made it creak. All humor left his face as she stared up at him. "I can't do that, Miss Elliot."

"And why can't you do that, Mr. Claxton?"

"Because now that I know you're out to kill my brother, I have to do somethin' about it."

"Such as?"

"Protect him from your . . . oh, shall we say, ineptitude as a gunslinger?"

Her mouth dropped open in outrage. "How dare you imply that I'm inept with a gun?" She was, of course. In fact, she didn't recall ever having actually shot a gun. But he didn't know that. She glanced around, searching for an example of her shooting abilities. "I'll have you know I can shoot a—a grasshopper's eye out at a hundred feet!" she boasted, and prayed he wouldn't insist that she prove it.

He gave a whistle of mock admiration. "A grasshopper's eye at a hundred feet, huh? Well, I have to admit, that's pretty fancy shootin'," he said with growing amusement.

"That's right. It certainly is," she replied smugly as their gazes locked stubbornly.

"But you'll have to do better than that, Miss Elliot, because I can shoot out a grasshopper's eye at a hundred and fifty feet."

No one would argue that Cole Claxton was not deadly accurate with a gun, but he seriously doubted anyone could *see* a grasshopper from that far away.

Of course, neither one pointed out the fact that there would be nothing left of the grasshopper as evidence to support this boasting should they actually engage in such a childish duel.

Wynne stared at Cole belligerently, his amused face like a needle in her flesh. "I do not want your despicable company on this trip."

"I don't want yours either," he stated calmly. "And don't make the mistake of thinkin' I'm here for you. I'm here for Cass. So don't come runnin' to me when you get yourself in a peck of trouble you can't get out of. I'll be right behind you all the way, Miss Elliot. I want you to be aware of that. And if you do happen to run into my brother, I'll be there lookin' over your shoulder," he said, all trace of teasing now gone from his voice. "I'm givin' you fair warning, Miss Elliot, I will not stand by and watch my brother killed, even if it means one of us gets hurt in the process."

Wynne paused in rearranging the pack on her mule as a shiver of apprehension moved slowly up her spine. By the tone of his voice she knew Cole was not making idle threats. He would prevent her from shooting Cass any way he had to. She studied him again at length. Cole's gaze met hers steadily.

If she was guessing, Cole Claxton was a superb poker player. There was not one flicker in his eye to which she could pin a hope he wouldn't do exactly what he said. He held all the cards, and obviously he had just upped the ante.

A small warning voice from deep within wondered if it wouldn't be smarter to fold while she was ahead.

CHAPTER 10

*I*F SHE DIDN'T BEAT ALL HE'D EVER SEEN. SHE WAS crazy! A silly, inexperienced woman who was going to get herself killed—if she didn't starve to death first.

For two days he'd been following Wynne Elliot, and in that short span of time she'd been caught in a brief but drenching rain, had fallen in the river twice, and, when shouting at her mule, used words that matched anything he'd heard in the war. All that had been just a prelude to the screaming fit she'd pitched when she discovered she couldn't start a campfire because she had insisted on swimming her mule through the deepest part of the streams during river crossings and invariably got everything wet, including her matches, and her clothes, and bedding.

She must have slept in wet blankets every night since leaving River Run, Cole guessed. True, he admitted to himself with a small smile, the fool mule wouldn't walk half the time. Its stubbornness, he decided, could be bested only by its mistress's.

Cole rested easily on his horse and watched Wynne ahead of him on the trail. As far as he knew, the woman hadn't eaten a bite since her trip began. If she had, it would have had to have come from that dirty-looking pack strapped in a lumpy bundle behind her saddle.

She was a mess by now, clothes limp and seemingly permanently wet, her hair hastily thrown up on top of her head. But he was bound and determined he wasn't going to help her.

He had followed her from a safe distance during the day. Every night they had made camp not 200 yards from each other. But while his fire was easily built, with coffee bubbling over the coals and bacon and beans sizzling, the simple but filling fare's aroma wafting toward her, Wynne had steadfastly ignored his presence. And he had ignored hers.

Tonight was a little different, though. Tipping his hat forward, Cole noted with disgust where Wynne had chosen to camp and kicked his horse into a walk.

Naturally she'd pick an open space, too far from water and without a shelter should something dangerous approach. If she did happen to get a fire started, anyone could see it from miles away.

Why couldn't she just give up this whole thing? Why was she so stubborn about killing Cass? And why was she so blamed certain he was the man who'd jilted her? Such action was unlike his younger brother, at least the brother he knew.

When Cole chose his own campsite, Wynne had already pulled her pack off the mule and spread her blankets. From the way they sagged heavily when she tried to spread them, they were still sopping wet. Cole concealed another unwilling grin. Her hair was falling down again, her dress was dirty a good two inches up from the hem, and the rip in the skirt had increased and was raveling.

It reminded him of that night in the cherry orchard when she'd accidentally unstitched her skirt from her bodice and stood there in her frilly underwear. In spite of himself, Cole hesitated in building his fire and allowed his mind to dwell on the memory. There she'd stood, that unruly cloud of reddish hair making her face appear even younger than the nineteen years she admitted to, in her bodice and white cotton bloomers. He'd never seen a woman look more vulnerable or more attractive.

Later Cole clasped his hands behind his head as he leaned back against his saddle and closed his eyes. The gentle hissing of the campfire was a soothing balm to his weary body as he felt his muscles slowly begin to relax.

Overhead the stars glistened like tiny diamonds, while back to the west there were occasional flashes of heat lightning. The tantalizing smell of rabbit roasting over the fire, and coffee boiling in the pot, drifted delectably through the air.

For some reason he felt guilty that she was sitting in the dark beside an unlit pile of sticks, hungry and probably scared. But if she was, it wasn't his fault.

He shifted against the hard ground uncomfortably, unwilling to admit his conscience was bothering him just a little. He'd warned her about making this useless trip, but she'd refused to listen. The chances that she would find Cass were close to nil, and every day he expected her to give up her crazy vendetta and go back to Savannah.

Maybe after she'd spent one more night of being hungry and listening to the coyote's howl while she sat alone in the dark, she would reconsider what she was bent on doing.

Cole let his thoughts drift aimlessly. He couldn't imagine what had gotten into his younger brother. If anything, Cass was like Beau, generous to a fault. He wouldn't think of stealing a woman's money. The Claxton men had been raised to be gentlemen, with Cass being the gentlest of the three.

Beau had his tender side. He was always the one to take in injured animals and defend the smallest child in school. Then again, like Cole, he could be angered when provoked. Cole had to admit, though, that Cass was the ladies' man of the three. Ma had spent more time with him as the youngest, had taught him more of the "southern" way of living than he and Beau had absorbed. That was one reason Cass had gone to Savannah to visit relatives he and Beau had never met and the reason Cass had joined the southern sympathizers when he'd enlisted.

Cole sat up and tested the rabbit on the spit; it was almost ready to be eaten, and his stomach rumbled with hunger. As he settled back against his saddle again, his thoughts returned to his family. He guessed that of the three, he was just about the orneriest. Being the oldest, he'd appointed himself the defender of his younger brothers, becoming the man of the family too early to enjoy a childhood.

But none of that could explain why Wynne believed Cass Claxton had been the man she'd been about to marry. There had to be some reasonable explanation. Maybe someone using Cass's name had deceived her. Yes, Cole decided, that had to be it.

Feeling better now, he tested the rabbit on the spit and decided it was done. He gingerly tipped the cross stick loose and off the forked stands, blowing on his scorched fingers. Someone had been posing as Cass. That was the only logical answer, but if that was the case, where was his brother now? Cole shook his head in dismissal. Cass could take care of himself.

Whoever had taken advantage of Wynne had not been a Claxton. He would bet money on that.

The meat popped and sizzled as the fat dropped in the fire, which flared brightly for a moment as Cole pulled a leg free and tasted the succulent meat. His conscience tugged at him so he could barely enjoy the tasty fare. She had to be hungry. And while the days were blistering, the night air could seep uncomfortably into the bones without a fire. Maybe he should give her a few of his matches.

That couldn't hurt anything. It wouldn't be contributing to the approaching murder of his brother. She could build a fire and—no! Cole snapped his thoughts stubbornly back to his previous ones. The quicker she gave up this ridiculous escapade, the sooner he could get back home to rebuilding the farm and the sooner Wynne Elliot would be heading back to Georgia where she belonged.

Wynne was miserably hungry—wretchedly, pathetically starved!

The tempting aroma of roasting rabbit drifted toward her on a gentle breeze as she sat huddled next to a large rock and watched the glow of Cole's campfire flickering in the night. It looked so warm, so comforting.

Her stomach growled painfully as she drew the thin blankets she had found in the pack up around her tighter. Their dampness kept the warmth from being any comfort, and her skin felt clammy and dirty. Her head itched, and her face felt gritty, and her dress was destroyed. All because of that damned mule!

She glared at it as it stood not ten feet away, placid and docile. "Why can't you look like that in the morning when I'm ready to ride instead of being so blamed stubborn? Stupid mule," Wynne muttered, and pulled the blanket tighter around her shoulders.

Her stomach rumbled again. That meat smelled so good, and the coffee's rich, full aroma filled the air with fragrance, making her mouth water. It was probably some old stuff he had made with chicory, she told herself. But she wouldn't have minded having a cup. For the last two days she'd lived on nothing but the tough jerky she had found in the miner's supplies.

At first she had been too squeamish to think about eating it, but as the hours wore on and her stomach began to hurt from being empty, she'd decided that trying to chew the leathery stuff was better than starving to death.

Wynne rested her head against the rock and fought back the urge to cry. She wasn't one of those crying ninnies, she reminded herself. It took a lot to make Wynne Elliot cry, and it sure wouldn't be over the smell of Cole Claxton's old coffee.

Rebel tears trickled down the sides of her cheeks as she sniffed and pulled the blanket up tighter. Why was he following her anyway? Did he think he could keep her from killing that worthless brother of his? If so, then he'd never dealt with an Elliot before.

Tomorrow she would practice shooting her gun. The blacksmith had been kind enough to include plenty of bullets in the trade, so she didn't need to worry about running out. And she couldn't argue that she needed the practice. She had to make sure that when she found Cass, she could outshoot him and his contrary brother.

Her gaze was drawn back resentfully to his firelight as she absently licked the salty wetness creasing the corners of her mouth.

By tomorrow night she would be a good enough shot to kill her own supper and then she'd just see whose mouth was watering!

If it killed her, she would get a fire started, even if she had to resort to rubbing two sticks together. Of course, she'd already tried that numerous times in the past two days, and it had not yet worked for her.

But if she did kill a rabbit, she would get a fire started one way or another, she vowed.

He was not about to get the best of her. She jerked at the blanket again and winced as she felt the water ooze down her neck. In exasperation she flung the wet material away from her and huddled down closer to the rock.

The next morning Cole was awakened by the sound of a gunshot and a bullet loudly ricocheting off his coffeepot.

With movements finely honed by years of sleeping lightly with an ear tuned to the sounds of battle, he scrambled behind the large log he'd drawn up beside his fire and pressed as close to the ground as a man his size could. After a moment, when no further sound was heard, he peered cautiously over the log toward the fire. "Damn!" He muttered. Black liquid was trickling out of the gaping hole in the coffeepot into the faintly glowing ashes of his fire.

When his gaze swiveled upward again, Wynne stood before him. Her red hair was tumbled wildly about her head, her green eyes sparkled angrily, and her mouth was set with determination. "Give me what's left of that rabbit!" she demanded.

"Wha—" Cole was wide-awake now, but he stared back at her blankly. Every muscle in his body was taut and ready for a fight, but instead of a bushwhacker or some other burly miscreant standing before him, there was merely a five-foot piece of fluff. And she was pointing a gun straight at his head.

"Don't argue with me!" She took a menacing step forward, the metal of her gun barrel glinting wickedly in the early-morning sun. "I said, hand me that rabbit!"

Still trying to figure out what was going on, Cole cautiously stood.

"Don't come any closer," she said warningly, her eyes glittering wildly.

Immediately Cole's steps faltered. Deciding he'd better do as she said, while the gun was waved about dangerously, he picked up what was left of his dinner and what would have been his breakfast. "All right, here's the rabbit. Now put that gun down before you hurt someone."

"Now pour me a cup of that coffee before it all seeps out," she ordered, hefting the barrel of the gun higher.

"Well, hell!" Cole said heatedly. "How do you expect me to pour you a cup of coffee when you've just shot a hole the size of Texas right in the middle of the pot?" He jammed his hands on his hips irritably. "Just what am I supposed to do for coffee now, Miss Elliot!"

"You'll do just what I've been doing," she said without the slightest trace of pity, "without. Now, pour that coffee before it all runs out on the ground."

If it hadn't been for the fact that she had the gun, he would have put a stop to this nonsense once and for all. But he valued his life more than he did the coffee, so he obliged her request grudgingly.

When he handed her the tin cup, Wynne nodded and started slowly backing away from his camp.

Cole stood with his hands still on his hips, watching her irritably. Robbed by a woman. It was too much.

"Oh . . ." She paused in flight. "I want some matches too."

"What!"

"You heard me!" She stamped her foot authoritatively. "I want some matches!"

Cole forgot all about the fact he'd been ready to give her matches the night before. "I'll be damned if I will give you any matches!"

Leveling the gun barrel directly at his chest, Wynne repeated her order in a low, ominous growl. "I said I want some matches please." She waved the gun at him, her finger on the trigger.

Cole wasn't certain how tight that trigger was set. If it was loose, he could be dead where he stood before the fool woman realized what she'd done.

With a grunt of disgust Cole bent and flipped open his own pack. He tossed a small packet of carefully wrapped matches toward her. But when they landed in the dust, Wynne waved the gun at him again.

"Pick them up and hand them to me. Carefully."

Moments later she had her matches and was backing her way out of camp. When she was in safe running distance of her own camp, she turned around and fled the enemy territory.

Cole stood watching her, disbelief still dominating his handsome features. "Damn!" he muttered. She'd done it again. The woman was a menace to society!

As she hurriedly sat down on the rock and began to eat the cold meat, Wynne had to admit that what she'd done was not very nice. But at the moment she really didn't care.

It was only after she had eaten her fill of the delicious fare and drunk the barely warm, bitter coffee that remorse began to set in.

It seemed her life of crime was increasing every day. She sighed hopelessly as she licked the remnants of the tasty rabbit off her fingers.

It had started with her simple, and completely understandable, determination to avenge herself and get her money back. Then she had decided to kill the man in the process, and now she had resorted to robbery.

Lordy, lordy, Miss Marelda Fielding would have a fit.

Having a woman best him just wasn't sitting well with Cole Claxton. The very thought that a pint-size woman weighing a hundred pounds less than he did could waltz into his camp and demand he hand over his food at gunpoint was nothing short of humiliating.

Had she been a man, she would have lived just long enough to see the muzzle of his gun pointed at her chest. Cole squirmed uncomfortably in his saddle as he reached in his shirt pocket for a smoke.

Damn. He was hungry. He had purposely eaten only half that rabbit last night so he could have the remainder for breakfast. But Miss Elliot had taken care of that.

Well, she wouldn't take him by surprise again. And the next time the fact that she was a woman, a pretty woman, would make no difference.

By evening both riders were exhausted. The heat had sapped their spirits along with their energy, and when Cole noticed Wynne making camp earlier than usual, he was relieved.

At least this time she'd chosen a decent camping space. She had halted in a grove of trees with a clear stream of water running through it. The peaceful setting looked cool and inviting. Much more so than the bare expanse of dusty ground he would have to bed down on if he were to keep her in his sights. Of course, there was nothing to stop him from taking advantage of the better location. Contemplating the thought, Cole sat on his horse. Why should he be uncomfortable just because she was in the lead?

Having made a decision, he rode to within fifty feet of where Wynne was bent over trying to start a fire. Noting the new arrival with only a passing interest, she quickly turned her attention back to her quarrelsome task.

She was no longer concerned Cole would take action against her for stealing his breakfast. If he had intended to do that, he surely would have done so earlier. There'd been plenty of opportunity. He'd followed her more closely today than before.

If the egotistical boor wanted to camp next to her, Wynne supposed there was little she could do to stop him.

With an efficiency that galled her, Cole made camp and had a good fire going long before she had fanned her tiny flame to life.

Moments later he remounted his horse and rode out of camp. Two clear shots rang out over the quiet countryside, and in a few minutes he returned with two plump rabbits dangling from his saddlehorn.

She supposed he was going to sit over there and stuff his face with two rabbits tonight just to annoy her. But he was only fooling himself if he thought she would even notice. So he'd got lucky and killed the rabbits on the first two shots! So what? Wynne carefully kept her face emotionless as she calmly went about spreading her bedroll beside the frail wisp of smoke just beginning to rise from her fire.

No doubt he had heard her trying to kill her own supper all day. All the rounds of ammunition she had shot would have been pretty hard to miss, especially as closely as he had been trailing her. And he could clearly see that she'd failed to come up with any fresh meat. He had probably snickered and laughed at her revolting lack of expertise with a gun, but that didn't bother her. She would get better. That's what he had better be concerned about. Then they would see who was laughing at whom!

Placing her hand at the small of her aching back, Wynne straightened up and watched as Cole took the rabbits down to the edge of the stream and began to clean them. She didn't watch the process, knowing it would only upset her stomach and ruin any success she might have in killing her own dinner.

But the stream was inviting. She was tired and dirty. Her hair was whipped and matted by the dry wind, and her skin felt about to crack from the heat. She felt as if she had never been clean.

Deciding that since she would obviously be going to bed hungry again tonight, she could at least be clean, she gathered up a tiny bar of soap she had packed in the valise and the last of her clean clothing and walked downstream in search of privacy.

While he worked, Cole watched from the corner of his eye as Wynne picked her way along the bank of the river. It was clear she wasn't going to be eating again tonight, but that was her own fault, he told himself. Anyone who wasted twenty rounds of ammunition to try to kill one rabbit deserved to go hungry.

Several minutes later, when she still hadn't returned, Cole found himself unwillingly glancing downstream, wondering what she was up to. Finally he wandered in the same direction. No telling what sort of trouble she had gotten into this time.

Around a small bend in the stream there was an inviting clear stream. Cole stood hidden in a patch of bushes not far from the edge and watched as she waded out into the water.

The setting sun was bathing the tranquil waters in a fiery orange glow as his gaze followed her graceful motions. Her clothes were in a small pile lying on the bank, and she wore only a thin chemise. The water had dampened the delicate material, which now clung suggestively to her rounded breasts as she began to lather with the piece of soap. The lowering sun bathed her dampened skin in gold, and with her body half turned from him the swell of her breast drew him strongly. His gaze was riveted to her. He watched her feminine movements as her hands cupped water and let it flow over her shoulders and arms. He swallowed hard as rivulets flowed between her breasts, making the material of her only scrap of clothing almost transparent. It was as if someone had unexpectedly rammed a fist into his middle. He sucked in his breath, and he swallowed the groan which began low in his throat.

It had been a long time since he'd seen a woman like that and even longer since he'd held a woman close. His mouth went dry as Wynne bent and wet her hair, working the soap into a lather. Eyes as blue as sapphires traveled from the tip of her head to the curve of her waist to the gentle flare of her hips, and he swallowed again. He could only imagine what her skin would feel like lying softly beneath him. He forced himself to turn away, but he couldn't will his legs to ease his discomfort and remove him from the scene before him.

A few moments later he found himself watching her again beneath lowered lashes. She was still lathering her hair, working the rich creaminess through the crimson mass. She was turned fully toward him now. Her eyes were closed in pleasure, and she had a sensual look on her face as she luxuriated in her bath.

The sun had turned her fair skin to a warm honey. It occurred to him that when he had seen her this morning up close, over the muzzle of her gun, her nose had been sunburned and her cheeks were sprinkled with freckles.

Get your mind on something else, Claxton, Cole warned himself as his body made him uncomfortably aware of its reaction to her nearly nude body. She would be the last woman he would make love to even if he wanted to.

But damn, he suddenly found himself actually wanting to. *Now who's actin' like a fool, Claxton? This is the woman who is on her way to kill your brother.* There were other ways of relieving his frustration, he reminded himself as he slowly began backing away from Wynne's bath.

In a few moments he was back at his fire and spitting the rabbits, wishing he were anywhere but where he was.

When Wynne still failed to return, he made certain the meat was roasting properly, then gathered his own clean clothing and went to bathe farther downstream.

Later that night Wynne lay in her bedroll and forced herself to ignore the smell of Cole's supper lingering in the air. His campfire had been banked, and she presumed he was fast asleep by now.

They had not exchanged one word since they'd made camp, but that wasn't unusual. They rarely spoke to each other unless it was to argue.

In a way Wynne wished that weren't so. She was lonely and maybe just a little bit afraid if she would let herself admit it.

This trip was the first time she'd ever been so alone, and she wasn't sure she liked it. She glanced at the other campsite and wondered if Cole had ever felt so lonely. He was probably used to being out in the dark night, beside a campfire with only the sounds of crackling bushes and wild animals.

Did he ever wonder what those strange sounds were or if they were dangerous? No, probably not. He was a man of experience. She could tell that. A man who'd experienced war, death, killing, and probably love. Love of a woman, of many women. Wynne stared up at the stars. How many times had he lain out on the battlefield wondering if he would see another day? It was difficult to imagine Cole Claxton as a man who had natural fears, but surely he did. The only reason he was following her now was concern for his brother.

She could understand why Cole would feel resentful toward her, why he must hate her. She would have felt the same way if someone were trying to kill one of her kin, yet it would seem that since they were traveling in the same direction, maybe it wouldn't hurt for them to talk a little once in a while. They could discuss the weather, or he could tell her where he had fought in the war, or maybe they could just talk about nothing in particular.

Once more the ache in her stomach reminded her of how hungry she was. And the thought that Cole still had one whole rabbit left over there for his breakfast the next morning didn't help any.

She knew she didn't dare try to take it from him again. He had let her get away with it once, but she probably wouldn't be as lucky the next time, especially since he had witnessed her deplorable accuracy with a gun today. He'd probably laughed all day at her bumbling antics. How embarrassing. Her cheeks burned in the darkness. How utterly stupid he must think her.

Propping herself up on her elbow, she squinted toward his campfire. She tried to locate the leftover rabbit. It was lying next to the fire—all brown and juicy-looking.

No, get your mind off that rabbit! She scolded herself as she let her head drop back down on the lumpy bedroll. *He would break your arm if you tried to steal it from him again. Surely tomorrow you'll be able to kill your own*, she told herself.

But her gaze drifted involuntarily back over to Cole's camp a few minutes later, and she sighed wistfully. She was so hungry! He had at least enough rabbit left for two people, and if he were any kind of gentleman at all, he would have offered to share it with her.

She bit her lower lip pensively. Maybe she could just sort of sneak over there and take a small piece of the meat while he was sleeping. He would never miss it. She would take a piece so tiny he would never even know it was gone.

After slipping out of her blanket, Wynne tiptoed on bare feet across the short space between her camp and Cole's. Holding her breath, she crept closer to where he lay sleeping peacefully. The sound of soft snores helped still her growing apprehension of what she was about to do.

Once again her steps faltered uneasily. She'd better make sure he was actually asleep. He could be trying to trick her. She certainly wouldn't put it past him. She leaned over and studied his sleeping features intently. No, he wasn't trying to trick her. He was asleep.

The plump rabbit drew her magnetically as Wynne tiptoed closer to the fire. Just one teensy little piece. He would never know the difference, but it would mean that she wouldn't have to lie awake all night with an empty stomach.

Holding her breath nervously, Wynne reached out to capture a plump, succulent morsel.

Her fingertips were actually touching the rabbit when, from out of nowhere, a bolt of lightning slammed into her and knocked her flat on her back. "Oh, no, you don't, Miss Elliot!"

For a moment Wynne was so stunned by the impact that she couldn't see straight. Her ears were still ringing when her vision finally cleared. She swallowed hard and looked up into Cole's angry face, his weight pinning her squarely to the ground.

"Get off me, you fool!" she demanded hotly when she finally managed to regain her voice.

"You were trying to steal my rabbit again, weren't you?" he asked curtly. He grabbed her flailing arms and held them over her head.

Their bodies strained against each other, and Cole knew immediately he'd made a mistake by controlling her in this manner. She lay beneath him, her small body tense with surprise, then with anger. But now he was more aware of the softness of her breasts, the warmth of her feminine body than of the straining pull of her arms against his confining grip. It was as if they both held their breaths for a moment, but then Wynne broke the tense moment.

"I most certainly was not!" she said indignantly. Their eyes bore into each other's defiantly.

"Oh, yes, you were," he said accusingly. "And this time you're going to get your fanny whipped for it."

She glared at him defiantly. "You wouldn't dare!"

Turning a deaf ear to her angry shrieks, he calmly flipped her over his knee and began to paddle her squirming behind. Amid all the screams and threats of dire consequences that she supposedly was going to inflict on him in the future, he taught her her first valuable lesson on the inadvisability of stealing another man's meat.

When it was over, she sat before him sobbing, tears rolling down her cheeks, shooting him looks that would singe the hair on his chest.

"Now"—he reached in his back pocket to take out his handkerchief— "from now on, if you want anything that's mine, you come and ask me— nicely." He was gently wiping the crocodile tears from her cheeks as he talked.

"You're . . . a . . . big . . . bully," she said, sniffling.

"No, I'm not. I know that's what you think, but I'm only trying to help you. You can't just go through life snatching things that're not yours from other people. You're goin' to get yourself killed."

"But I was hungry and you wouldn't let—"

"I know. And I'm sorry I wouldn't help you shoot your meat." He replaced the handkerchief back in his pocket and reached out to place his hands on her shoulders. His eyes met hers almost tenderly. "From now on I'll see that you have enough to eat, okay?"

She sniffed and nodded. "And a fire?"

This time he couldn't hold back the grin. "And a fire." His gaze focused on her mouth. Damn! It looked so kissable.

She stared back at him longingly. Her bottom still smarted from his big, rough hand, but that didn't make him any less handsome at the moment.

Back off, right now, Cole warned himself, but it was too late. Slowly his head leaned forward, and his mouth touched hers.

She sighed, a soft, kittenish sound as her arms automatically wound around his neck and he pulled her nearer. Then his mouth closed over hers in a deep, hungry kiss that left them both pale and shaken a few moments later. His touch had been electrifying and exciting, so much so that it left her breathless.

"Uh." Cole cleared his throat nervously as he forced himself to release her. "Sorry about that, Miss Elliot." He had no idea why he had done that!

Wynne quickly jumped to her feet and began to fuss with her hair. "It's—it's quite all right, Mr. Claxton." Whooee! Cass had never kissed her that way!

"Listen." He stood up and moved over to the fire to retrieve the extra rabbit. "You take this and go on back to bed."

"No, I couldn't," she said nicely. "It's your breakfast."

He glanced at her in disbelief. Women! Ten minutes ago she was ready to steal it from him. "No, I insist." He generously extended the meat to her.

Her hand immediately flew out to accept it before he could have second thoughts. "Well, if you're sure . . ."

"Yeah," he said dryly. There was that grin again. "I insist."

He watched as she hurriedly carried the rabbit back to her camp with an air of triumph and a sneaky smile on her face.

Ha! She thought smugly. *I guess I finally brought him to heel!*

Ha! Cole was echoing, with his own smug grin. *Little did she know that I killed the rabbit for her in the first place.*

CHAPTER 11

THE FOLLOWING MORNING WYNNE WAS AWAKE LONG before the sky slowly began to shed its heavy mantle of darkness. She lay in her bedroll, watching the eastern horizon with a strange sense of detachment from the beauty unfolding before her.

Her mind was still on the kiss Cole had given her last night. "Taken" would be a more appropriate description. For she would never willingly have allowed that man such liberties with her!

It never occurred that she'd done very little to stop the unexpected embrace or, in fact, that she might have actually encouraged him in the matter. Instead, she chose to think of herself as the victim who had once more been made to suffer at the hands of a Claxton.

The longer she lay and thought about what had happened, the easier it was to convince herself that she'd had nothing to do with the kiss and that Cole had had everything to do with contributing to her damaged pride.

Oh, she would grudgingly admit the kiss had been nice. But certainly not pleasant by any means, a bit stimulating, perhaps, but only mildly so.

Most gentlemen would not kiss a woman in the way Cole Claxton had kissed her! All fiery and hungry . . .

The man should be ashamed of acting like such an—an animal!

Still . . . Her hand came up gingerly to touch her mouth, which was still bruised from his virile assault. She had to admit she had never, in all her nineteen years, been kissed that way.

But the only reason the kiss had stimulated her in the least was that Cole resembled Cass so strongly. That was the only reason why her mouth still tingled and she grew slightly breathless when she thought about the night before, the only reason her body grew warm and liquid with the memory. Fool. Cole Claxton had probably had a hundred women.

Wynne rolled over onto her side and glared in the direction of his camp. She couldn't see him, couldn't see that devilishly handsome face. But she could see in her mind those penetrating blue eyes, that thick hair which curled at the slightest provocation.

Oh, yes, Cole Claxton was breathtakingly handsome—Wynne groaned aloud with frustration—but he was also cruel, unrefined, uncivilized, and a big bully with little regard for a woman's gentle nature.

But considering her own eagerness to fall under the spell of his younger brother, it was little wonder that she was probably only one of a number of women intrigued by Cole.

Still, she wasn't about to make the same mistake twice. She wanted Cole Claxton out of her life. She was good and tired of his following her day after day, taunting her, laughing at her lack of experience in the wild. And she intended to do something about it, starting today.

She rolled out of her bedroll, talking to herself as she folded the blankets and tried to smooth some of the wrinkles out of her dress. She was going to lose that scoundrel if it was the last thing she did. She was more than capable of taking care of herself, no matter what he thought.

Once she had made up her mind, it took very little time to wash her face and hands, change into a fresh dress, and break camp. In a few minutes Wynne was urging the mule out of the grove of trees just as the sun started to rise over the hilltops.

"Giddeyup, you ornery mule!" she commanded in a hushed tone, giving the animal a smart kick in the ribs. For once the animal complied with her wishes and set off in the bone-jarring trot which rattled her teeth and jerked her neck about painfully.

Leaning against a spreading oak, whose base was shielded by a thick undergrowth of wild grapevines, Cole watched the mule lope away with its ungainly rider. He shook his head tolerantly as he reached in his shirt pocket for a smoke.

Now what in the hell was she up to? he wondered wearily.

He'd had a hunch she would try to make a run for it this morning. From where he'd concealed himself he'd been fully aware of the moment she'd awakened and had watched in amusement as she'd studied his camp and mumbled to herself.

He'd almost laughed aloud as she'd carefully smoothed her hair and perched that silly hat back on top of her head. Why on earth she insisted upon wearing that hat and the corset he knew was beneath that Sunday dress he'd never understand.

Pushing himself away from the tree trunk, Cole moved toward his camp in his easy stride. What he ought to do was turn around and go home, he told himself. He was tired of sleeping on the ground and having to hunt for every meal. He'd lived like that for the past four years, and he was tired of it.

Going home was such a tempting thought that it almost brought him pain, but then another equally disturbing one worked its way back into his mind. For a brief moment Cole let himself think about how good Wynne had felt lying beneath him last night. All soft and fragrant, all woman. Even having been on the trail for days, she still smelled feminine and nice, like the lilac bushes that grew wild across the countryside. And her hair. The crimson strands had felt like that piece of material he'd bought Lilly for Christmas one year. The tinker had had a bolt of it in the back of his wagon. Silk he'd called it, and it was really pretty. Yes, her hair had lain across his bare arm like rich, elegant silk, and it made a man long to run his fingers through it.

Cole irritably slapped his bedroll onto the back of his horse and stared in the direction she had taken. His body followed the direction of his mind, and for the first time he found himself wishing Wynne had been one of the new girls Hattie had hired. That way he could have followed through on his instincts without thought of the consequences.

Pulling his thoughts back to the problems at hand, Cole sighed and flipped his half-smoked cigar out into the stream. He was tired, tired of responsibility, tired of duty.

Just once he wished there were a simple answer to a problem. But he'd looked after Beau and Cass since the day Pa died, and he guessed he wouldn't be stopping now.

Not—and a smile curved his mouth—when Wynne Elliot was running around the countryside, threatening to blow one of his brothers' brains out.

It was truly a glorious morning. The birds were chattering in the trees, and the sound of an occasional woodpecker held Wynne's attention as the mule trotted along.

Taking a deep breath, she turned her face up and smiled happily. It felt marvelous to be free of the specter of Cole Claxton following her within hailing distance.

Urging the mule in a more northerly direction, Wynne concentrated on making her trail harder to follow. By the time he woke up, she wanted to be only a memory.

She prayed she could keep her sense of direction and not become hopelessly lost. The blacksmith had said to steer north, and that's what she had been doing.

She had to laugh when she thought about how incensed Cole would be when he realized how easily she had rid herself of him.

It only served him right, she thought smugly. It was high time he was made aware he wasn't dealing with a complete imbecile. No sir, Mr. Cole Claxton was dealing with Wynne Elliot, a courageous woman who had survived the deaths of her parents, who had held a plantation together, if only for a little while, and who could take care of herself on the trail and could do just fine without a man's help.

Her delighted laughter rang out clearly and sweetly over the hillsides. He might not believe she was capable of anything other than making a fool of herself, but Mr. Claxton would know differently soon enough. Oh, would he ever!

By midafternoon the sun was a blistering red ball again, the heat so oppressive that Wynne could hardly breathe. The mule had slowed to barely a walk now as it picked its way along a narrow path that was overgrown with prickly briars and thickets. Vines trailed across the path, brushed at her face, and caught her hair. She had abandoned the main road hours ago to ensure her getaway but was still careful to travel northward.

Periodically she reached up to swipe halfheartedly at the moisture continuously beading on her flushed features. She would have given anything she still owned for a drink of cool water, but in her haste to break camp she had forgotten to fill the canteen.

Ordinarily water shouldn't have been that hard to come by, but with the recent lack of rain, most streams and gullies she had crossed had been bone-dry.

And she thought she really should stop and throw this blasted corset away before she fainted clean away from the heat. She wasn't sure what was causing her the most agony: the pantaloons, the corset, the layers of petticoats, or the lack of water. But she wasn't about to part with any of the three items of apparel. A woman must maintain some bit of propriety even in this wilderness, she told herself as she dabbed daintily at her cheeks and throat.

If and when she ran into Cass, she wanted to look her best, although she had to admit her dress was becoming wilted and dirty.

Of course, she had two other dresses packed away in the valise, but they were not nearly as nice as the one she was wearing. It was foolish to dress so nicely every day just on the remote chance she might actually encounter Cass, but her pride prevented her from traveling in comfort.

Her hand absently reached up to readjust her hat, and a thin layer of dust trickled off the brim and brought forth a sneeze that resounded loudly around the still countryside. When he saw how beautiful she looked, Cass would be absolutely sick that he had walked out on her just before he became absolutely dead, that is.

There were still several hours of daylight left when Wynne finally admitted she couldn't go another mile. She halted the mule on a hill which overlooked a deep valley. A growing sense of despair threatened to sap what little fortitude remained. She was tired, hot, sticky, and convinced by now that she had no idea where she was or if she was even going in the right direction.

Dominating the air now were gnats, which flew around her face and stuck to her bare skin. The sun had burned her face and cheeks in spite of the hat, and the tops of her hands were beet red too. The tip of her nose itched and was peeling, and she didn't even want to guess what it looked like. It was impossible to go on, yet she didn't know what else to do.

The combination of heat and the lack of food and water made her head swim. It was all she could do to hold herself upright in the saddle, and she still had to make camp and try to find something to eat before darkness fell.

For a moment she almost wished the "pompous ass" were still following her. She turned in the saddle and peered almost longingly back in the direction from which she'd just come. He wasn't behind her, of course. She had been too thorough in her escape. By now he was probably on his way back to River Run, where in a few days he would have a wonderfully clean bed to sleep in and huge plateful of Willa's chicken and dumplings to gorge himself on. The thought of all those rich dumplings swimming around in a golden gravy with plump pieces of tender chicken made Wynne's stomach rumble with protest.

Well, this was no time to start feeling sorry for herself, she thought. Straightening her shoulders with some effort, she forced herself to think. She had a goal, and she was going to reach it come hell or high water.

There were two remaining matches and plenty of bullets left. Surely to goodness she would be able to kill one small rabbit for her supper. She was getting better at hitting the targets she chose.

Nudging the mule with her heels, she urged it down a steep incline and held on tightly. Rocks tumbled over the mountainside and hit the walls of the lower canyon, but she refused to look down. She was dizzy enough as it was. It was all she could do to hold on because the fool mule kept trying to brush her off on the trees which crowded close to the narrow path. Vines and limbs reached out and snatched at her clothes and hair. At one point the mule nearly succeeded in knocking her off against an old oak just covered with strange-looking vines.

Wynne decided to plan her next steps as a means of keeping her wits about her. She would camp at the bottom of the valley tonight. With luck there would be water available. She closed her eyes and prayed that would be the case. Then she would try to find something to eat, a rabbit or a squirrel, but most likely just berries again. Her mouth watered at the thought of fresh meat roasting over a fire.

It seemed it took forever for the mule to make its descent, but the path finally widened and became more level.

The air was a bit cooler down there. The tall limestone bluffs gave partial shelter from the sun's burning rays. She pushed at the thick mass of hair on her neck and vowed to find something to tie it away from her face before she started out again in the morning, even if it meant ripping a piece of cloth from her petticoat. She brushed at the leaves which had settled and caught in the material of her dress.

By now she had removed the hat, her one concession to ease her agony, and tied it on the saddlehorn. She could always put it back on should she run into Cass unexpectedly, and it was sheer heaven to let the small breeze that was faintly stirring blow freely through her heavy mass of hair.

Suddenly there was a new aroma permeating the air. Her nose lifted slightly as the unmistakable smell of fatback sizzling over an open fire filled her senses.

Cole! He had followed her! But jubilation quickly turned to smoldering resentment. How dare the man continue to follow her when she had made it perfectly clear she didn't want his company?

Still, the aroma of his dinner tempered her anger somewhat as she urged her mule into a faster gait. Perhaps he would be kind enough to share his meal with her tonight, although that might be pushing optimism to the very limit.

In her eagerness for food she let the mule break through the clearing with the grace of a runaway stage. But she quickly yanked the animal to a halt as six revolvers were whipped out of their holsters with astonishing speed and pointed directly at the center of her chest.

Wynne's eyes widened as she stared almost openmouthed at the tattered, dirty men standing before her. The realization slowly dawned on her that it was not Cole's fatback she had smelled cooking, but rather these frightening-looking men's.

"Oh, lordy!" she muttered, and yanked the mule's head around and kicked his flanks. While she knew it was futile, she at least had to try to correct this newest blunder.

The mule hadn't taken three strides before she was hauled off and flung roughly to the ground. With another part of her mind, Wynne was aware that the sleeve of her dress was ripped from the bodice and the buttons down the front torn loose with the violence of her fighting. Kicking and screaming, she tried to scratch out the eyes of the ruffian holding her down, but to no avail. Recognizing defeat, Wynne lay still, staring up at the bearded face of her captor.

"Well, well, boys, look what we got here," the assailant crowed as the other men slowly slid their guns back in their holsters. His dark eyes stared at her face. Then his gaze slid over her shoulders and to the shadow between her breasts. Her heart beat so heavily that her skin moved with it, and she struggled to control her breathing so he would look somewhere else. His thin mouth smiled knowingly as he noted her efforts and the reason for them. A strange gleam came into his eyes, and his face tightened. A thread of real fear raced down Wynne's spine.

She twisted and kicked as the bully hauled her over his shoulder and carried her to where the others stood around the campfire, drinking coffee. The odor of his unwashed body was so strong it made her empty stomach roll, and she had to swallow hard several times to fight the growing nausea that threatened to overcome her.

"Why, looks like you got yourself a little hellcat, Sonny." The other men laughed as Sonny flung Wynne down on the ground like a bag of grain and eyed his new possession greedily.

For the first time in her life Wynne lost her voice as cold, paralyzing fear rendered her speechless. The men surrounding her were a terrifying sight to a lone woman. Besides the one standing over her, four stood around the fire, with another sitting on a large rock. He caught her attention momentarily. It looked as if he were reading a book!

A fifth man, stood away from the group. He was almost hidden in the shadows at the edge of the small clearing. Apparently he was on watch while the others ate their supper.

Wynne swallowed hard and sat up a little straighter, determined to look death right in the eye. Even while she willed her pounding heart to quiet down, her mind took in impressions automatically. None of the men looked more than twenty-five at the oldest. But they were dirty and unkempt, their clothes worn and dusty. Their hair was long, and their beards were untrimmed. They stared at her with a callous observation that made her feel like a "thing" rather than a woman. She was afraid even to guess what they might be thinking.

One of the men called out, "Right pretty-lookin' red-headed she-devil, Sonny. You gonna share her with us?" The man stepped over to examine Wynne more closely. Her breath caught as he reached a dirty hand out toward her. He took a lock of her hair and slid the shiny mass through his fingers absently, all the while staring into her terrified eyes. "Real pretty," he murmured again, and there was something in his eyes which compelled her to study him a little closer. He looked young, terribly young.

"Please," she finally managed to say, "let me go—"

"Ah, Jesse, you'd think anybody was purty after that woman in

Kentucky. Why, she was ugly 'nough to vomit a buzzard," one of the other men said, chortling.

They all broke out in a new round of laughter, but the young man holding a lock of Wynne's hair was unruffled by their friendly jesting.

"That may be rightly so, but this one's real purty." He seemed to be speaking more to her than to the men, and his voice was soft and soothing.

"Now, look, Jesse, I got her first," Sonny whined when he noticed the way Jesse was looking at her.

"Yeah, maybe so, but I'm not sure I'm gonna let you have her first," Jesse said over his shoulder. He kept his attention centered on the frightened girl standing before him. "Where ya goin' in such a hurry, honey?"

"Nowhere—to Kansas City." She corrected herself hurriedly when his eyes narrowed warningly.

"Kansas City? That's a mighty long way for a woman to travel alone," he said chidingly.

"Well, I'm not exactly alone," Wynne lied. "I—I have this man with me. He'll—he'll be along any moment now, so I really must be running along."

The men laughed again at her attempt at bravado.

"I'm supposed to be making camp while he hunts our supper." She continued her bluff. "And he probably would be quite upset if he finds out you have detained me, gentlemen. He's a big, short-tempered jackass —uh, man"—she hurriedly corrected herself again—"and he doesn't put up with a lot of nonsense." She began to edge slowly back toward the mule.

"Ohhh, me, oh, my! He probably will be real upset if we detained her, gentlemen." One of the men mocked her in a feminine voice. They all roared again and once more goose bumps rose on Wynne's skin.

The man reading the book glanced up at all the boisterous laughter and frowned. Laying the book down carefully on the rock, he stood up and stretched.

Wynne's eyes widened in disbelief as she noticed the title of the book was *Venus and Adonis* by William Shakespeare.

Jesse turned and grinned at his brother good-naturedly. "Where ya going, Frank?"

Frank and Jesse. The names rang a bell in Wynne's muddled mind, yet she couldn't think where she had heard them before. But she knew she had.

"Thought I'd check the horses," Frank announced.

"Ah. Did we bother you?"

"No," he said. "Just thought I'd stretch my legs for a bit."

"Do you mind if I go with you?" Wynne piped up in a shaky voice. She had no idea if this man was as bad as or possibly worse than the rest of them, but anyone who read Shakespeare didn't seem as frightening to her.

"No! You can't go with him," Sonny exclaimed indignantly as he jerked her back to him. "You're staying right here, sugar face."

Having regained some of her spirit, Wynne sent him a sour look. She'd sugar his face. First chance she got.

But Sonny was only amused by her dour expression as he dragged her over next to the fire and shoved her down onto an old blanket. "How about some supper, honey pie? We was jest about to 'dine' when you dropped in."

"No, thanks."

"Aw, have we spoiled your appetite?" Sonny grinned at her. "Better eat a bite so's you'll have some strength." He glanced at his buddies, and they all laughed again. "I have a feelin' you might need it later on."

Jesse smiled with the other men but decided to let the issue of who had first claim on her lie for the moment. He went back to his watch, but she still sensed his gaze lingering on her.

Fear had eliminated her hunger, and she shook her head mutely at Sonny's urgings to eat something. Staring into the fire, Wynne tried to bite back the urge to cry.

"Better eat, woman. You're gonna need it." He taunted again wickedly, for her ears only.

Wynne shivered. At her stony silence Sonny shrugged and turned his attention to his meal.

Turning her back to the men, she sought to fasten her bodice again with the few buttons left and plucked ineffectually at the torn threads of her sleeve. Hell and damnation, what was going to happen to her now? Tears were again very near the surface, and she blinked them back. These horrible men, every last grimy one of them, were most likely going to rape her, and then leave her for dead. And there would be no way she could prevent it.

The gun was in the saddlebags on the mule, and the one they had called Frank had led it away a few minutes earlier. There was no way she could get to it without drawing their attention.

It hurt her pride even more when Cole's numerous warnings about the likelihood of such an occurrence began bouncing loudly in her head.

A small sob almost escaped. Oh, why hadn't she listened to him? Why had she undertaken such a ridiculous venture in the first place? And this time she couldn't hold back the tears.

It was growing dark when the men finally had eaten their fill. Some had stretched out on the ground to let their meal settle while the others continued to drink coffee. They had eaten like swine, belching and smacking, eating with their fingers since there apparently were no utensils.

She had found herself comparing the motley group before her with the way Cole and Beau had looked the first time she had met them. Actually there was no comparison. The Claxton brothers had been dirty but not bone-deep nasty, the way these men were.

Cole's image kept recurring in her mind, and she suddenly, desperately wished she hadn't been so foolish that morning. Even if he did annoy her and she got on his nerves something powerful, and she had to take food away from him by gunpoint, and he had taken her over his knee and whipped her soundly, she knew he would have protected her from a fate like this, no matter how much he disliked her.

A low rumble of thunder broke into her miserable thoughts. She glanced up at the sky and saw that dark storm clouds were beginning to roll overhead. The thought of rain held no elation for her now. It would never be able to wash away the pain and degradation she was about to experience.

And the reminder of what was about to happen caused her to bury her face in her hands and weep in silent despair as a sharp bolt of lightning streaked across the ever-darkening sky, and the storm moved in.

CHAPTER 12

WITH THE THUNDER AND LIGHTNING CAME THE wind. Cool, blessedly welcome gusts of air snaked through the treetops and sent showers of red sparks from the campfire skipping across the parched earth.

"Looks like we're in for a big one," one of the men shouted above the roar of the approaching storm.

Jesse scanned the ever-darkening sky with troubled eyes. The clouds looked ominous. They boiled and churned and puffed out periodic gusts of wind that bent the tops of the trees nearly to the ground.

Wynne's hair whipped wildly around her face as she tried to knock the sparks from the fire off her dress. The men were running about, trying to quiet the animals, which were becoming increasingly spooked by the thunder and lightning.

Chaos reigned as the wind began to reach almost gale force. Realizing that the men's attention had been momentarily diverted, Wynne whirled and started to run toward the canyon. But before she'd taken two steps, a burly arm reached out and wrapped itself around her waist.

"Let me go!" she screamed, fear and desperation giving her the strength of a wildcat. She struggled wildly, scratching and kicking, as Sonny dragged her back to the camp. His maniacal laugh blended with the howling wind as his hands bit cruelly into the tender flesh of her arms.

"No need to run, honey. Ol' Sonny'll take care of you!" Again he laughed, raising his voice to the sky and whooping loudly as his hand reached out to squeeze her breast.

Wynne screamed in protest and sank her teeth into the meat of his forearm. But he only laughed harder and jerked her up against his hard body, his eyes glittering with aroused passion. "That's it, honey pie. Fight me. I love it when my women fight me."

She spit in his face, then gasped as his broad hand connected sharply with her cheek. For a moment the sound of the wind was forgotten as she actually saw stars.

"I think that'll be about enough." A new voice had entered the fracas now as a tall man stepped into the clearing, a Springfield rifle leveled squarely at Sonny's head.

"Let her go, Morgan," he commanded calmly.

Cole's ice blue gaze swept the group, making certain the six he'd seen from where he had been hiding were well within the range of his rifle. Wynne couldn't have picked a worse group to fall into. He counted Frank and Jesse James and several others who'd ridden with a splinter group of Quantrill's Raiders during the war as some of the orneriest men around. And of course, she had found them.

Wynne moaned and sagged with relief when she saw Cole standing not ten feet away. He looked unusually tall and commanding, and she couldn't remember ever being so glad to see anyone. The pompous ass looked incredibly beautiful to her.

Sonny Morgan was startled by the new arrival and slow to comprehend what was taking place. "Claxton, what the hell you doin' here?" he demanded irritably. Now there was gonna be another one he'd have to share her with!

The other men had begun to move in closer when Cole stepped back and motioned for them to throw down their guns. Belts were reluctantly unbuckled and quickly dropped to the ground.

Cole chanced a hurried glance at Wynne, his snapping blue eyes sending a clear message that she had foolishly gotten them into this sticky situation and she was going to hear about it if they made it out alive. "Are you all right?" he asked curtly.

She nodded sheepishly.

"Okay, Morgan. Just let her go, and there won't be any trouble."

"Ah, hell, Claxton, what's it to you?" Sonny argued, pulling Wynne possessively to his chest. "I found the little woman first, and I figure that makes her mine."

Cole's gaze never wavered, and his gun was steady as he raised it a fraction more to encompass all of Sonny's broad chest. "Well, you figured wrong this time."

Comprehension was still slow to dawn on Sonny. "How come?"

"Perhaps what Cole is tryin' to say is that the little lady is his." Jesse spoke up as he tipped his head in a mock salute to the man holding the gun on him.

Jesse James had met Captain Cole Claxton during the war. He knew him to be a fair man when it came to a fight, but a deadly force when he was threatened, so he knew it was best to hand the girl over to him without a fight. Especially in view of the fact Cole had a rifle and he didn't.

Sonny looked at Cole resentfully. "She your woman?"

That was a tricky question, one that Cole didn't know how to answer. The first drops of rain began to fall as he shrugged noncommittally. "Let's just say I'm lookin' after her interests at the moment." His hand never wavered. "Just hand her over real gentlelike, Morgan, and we'll be on our way."

Sonny glanced expectantly at Jesse, who nodded his silent agreement. After weighing the situation for a few moments longer, Sonny finally shoved Wynne roughly away from him. "Well, hell! take her then. She weren't nothin' but a peck of trouble anyways."

"You noticed that too?" Cole noted dryly.

Wynne shot him a look that should have struck him dead in his tracks. But moments later she found herself edging next to his towering bulk. When it came to choices, she'd rather be with Cole than against him in this situation.

Slipping his arm around Wynne's waist, Cole started backing out of the camp slowly. "Nice to see you again, Jesse," Cole said pleasantly.

"Nice to see you, Claxton." The blue-eyed young man wore a slight grin, but there was that air of danger about him which spoke louder than the smile.

"Frank doin' all right?"

"I'm fine, Cole." The man standing to the side answered quietly. "Good to see ya again."

Cole nodded briefly at Frank James and kept on retreating in measured steps. He could feel Wynne trembling in his arms, and he squeezed her waist in quiet assurance.

"Looks like we're goin' to get a good rain," he continued conversationally, and Wynne thought she was going to scream. The tension in the air was so thick you could have cut it with a knife and *he* was talking as if they were at a Saturday night social!

"Sure could use it," Jesse agreed mildly.

The rain was beginning to pepper down on them now as Cole reached his horse. Never taking his eyes off the other men for a moment, he helped Wynne into the saddle and then swung up behind her, still keeping the gun leveled at the group that stood looking on.

Tipping his hat politely, he said. "Take care now."

"You do the same . . ." came Jesse's reply.

Reining his horse around, Cole spurred the animal into action, and they left the camp just as the sky opened up in a thunderous deluge.

"My mule!" Wynne shouted above the pounding rain.

"What about it?" Cole yelled back as he raced the horse at breakneck speed through the canyon. He doubted any of the men would try to follow, but he wanted to make sure there was plenty of distance covered in the shortest possible time should they saddle their horses and decide to try to take back their "property."

"It's back there!"

"You want to go back and get it?" Cole asked.

"No! But now I won't have anything to ride or wear. And my gun! What about my gun?" she yelled, trying to keep the pouring rain out of her mouth. "Hell and damnation! I'm about to drown," she exclaimed irritably. "Can't you slow down a little?"

"Just pipe down, lady!" he yelled back. "I'm a little out of sorts with you as it is."

"Me!"

"Yes! You! That was a crazy trick you pulled this morning, and you're damn lucky I was around to save your little tail!"

"Why, of all the nerve!" she said, bristling. "I didn't need your help in the least!"

"Oh, no? Well, it sure looked to me like you did!"

"Well, I didn't! I was just getting ready to make a run for it when you showed up," she said.

"Yes, I saw how well you made the break," he snapped.

She sucked in her breath indignantly. Her pride wouldn't let her concede the argument. "Just how long had you been standing there, Cole Claxton?"

He'd been there almost from the first moment she had been captured, but he'd decided to teach her a valuable lesson, provided she wasn't in any real danger. Perhaps from now on she'd listen to what he said. "Long enough to see you were in over your head." His arm tightened around her waist.

It suddenly dawned on her they were riding back in the same direction they had just come from. "Stop!" she screeched.

For one brief moment Cole automatically pulled back on the reins, and the horse slowed. "What in the hell is the matter this time?"

"You're going back the same way we came," she said.

"Oh, for—just dry up, will you!" Cole spurred his horse forward, but she continued to complain.

"We've already covered this ground," she said, grousing. "Now we'll have to travel it all over again."

That's right, Cole thought smugly. If he could delay her silly mission by even an hour, he'd jump at the chance.

The horse raced through the dark night, carrying its two riders as if the hounds of hell were chasing them. Deafening claps of thunder shook the earth, and lightning zigzagged angrily across the sky as they rode on. Wynne's clothes were plastered wetly against her skin, and her hair flapped wildly about her head as Cole pushed the horse harder. She could feel the imprint of his maleness pressed tightly against her spine as she struggled to scoot up closer in the saddle.

"Sit still," he commanded gruffly, fully aware of what she was trying to escape.

He would just as soon not be in such close proximity with her either, but at the moment he had no choice. He could only hope he wouldn't make a fool out of himself by letting her see how she was affecting him.

Although her experience with men had been limited, she knew that the ride was taking its toll on Cole as a man. She could feel the strength of him at her back, the warmth of his breath against her cheek as his strong arm held her against him. Unbidden, the memory of his kiss the night before, of his mouth touching hers, pushed its way to the forefront of her mind.

A tiny shiver sent goose bumps popping out all over her when she thought about his making love to a woman. No doubt he would be masterful and exciting, she was forced to admit. He would hold her, and his low voice would murmur words she could only imagine, and when his body . . .

She blushed when she realized where her thoughts had led her. It was only because he reminded her so much of Cass that she let herself think about such things, she told herself again. Yet she found herself smiling with smug satisfaction a few minutes later as the evidence of his discomfort continued to mount to almost alarming proportions, and now it was Cole moving restlessly against her. By his every action he had denied that he was aware that she was a woman. Instead, he had treated her like some pesky fly that he couldn't shake.

Her smile widened mischievously as she purposely squirmed in the saddle and caused him to be the one to back away this time.

"I told you to sit still," he growled.

"Sorry. I was uncomfortable," she replied innocently.

Yes, Cole reminded her of Cass quite often, but the two brothers were as different in nature as corn and sweet rolls, she found herself thinking a few moments later. And she had also come to the conclusion that their looks weren't all that much alike either. Now that she had been around

Cole more, she saw that he was the handsomer of the two brothers. He had a certain maturity about him that Cass had yet to achieve, and his hair was thicker, curlier, and coarser than Cass's.

And their eyes—well, they both were blue, but Cole's had a deeper, more vibrant hue than Cass's. And Cole was taller and heavier while Cass had the body of a young man yet to develop fully.

It suddenly occurred to her had she met Cole first, she might never have given Cass a second glance.

Except she could never put up with his ill-tempered, old-goat personality, Wynne reminded herself. Cass had him beaten in that respect.

The mere thought of how he had treated her prompted Wynne to decide to torment him a little more. It wouldn't be the thing most ladies would do, but then he deserved a lesson in humility. After all, he'd just stood cruelly outside that clearing and watched those men mistreat her. And she bet he'd enjoyed every minute of seeing her frightened and shaking in her boots!

She wiggled again. Miss Fielding would surely understand, given the circumstances.

Snuggling back against the warmth of his chest, she faked a graceful yawn and settled her head in the curve of his shoulder. "I do declare I'm plumb tuckered out from all this rowdiness."

Behind her, Cole stiffened with surprise as he reined the horse to a slower pace. The storm was beginning to abate now. There were still distant, low rumbles of thunder, but the rain had slowed to where it was falling only in a fine mist.

He wasn't sure what to make of her unexpected friendliness. She was lying in his arms, totally relaxed, humming softly under her breath. It was as if they were two lovers out on a moonlit ride instead of making a run for their lives. The feel of her against him was unnerving. The ache in his loins was so intense he was in complete misery now. At one point he had about decided to stop the horse and switch her to his back so he could get some relief. But now she was lying against him like a soft, purring kitten, and he couldn't for the life of him make himself move a muscle. It had been too long since a woman had been in his arms this way. Way too long.

And it didn't help matters any that her dress was soaked to the skin and the outline of her small breasts were much more clearly defined than they should be. He carefully moved his hand an inch lower on her waist so there would be no chance of encountering anything he shouldn't. But he couldn't make himself let go of her.

Wynne wiggled again and smiled to herself at his quick, soft intake of breath. She turned and peered up at him beguilingly. "Am I disturbin' you by leanin' back on you this way?"

Cole shook his head mutely, not trusting his voice. *Damn! Claxton,* he told himself, *don't let her get to you this way! Whatever little game she's playing, ignore it!*

The moon peeked out from behind a dark cloud, bathing the two riders in its soft glow as she smiled up at him demurely. "You just tell me when you get uncomfortable."

Like the complete dolt he had always accused her of being, he found himself nodding he would while grinning back at her stupidly. He didn't like how she was affecting him, but he seemed powerless to prevent it! What he should do was set her little fanny right in the middle of the road and let her walk to Kansas City! That's what he should do, he thought angrily. After all, she'd been nothing but a thorn in his side from the moment he'd met her. She wouldn't listen to a word he said. She was constantly goading him. Not to mention the woman's unmitigated gall!

Taking his rabbit by gunpoint was not something he was going to forget very easily. She could count on that. Nor would he forget the reason for this asinine trip across Missouri. She was trying to kill his brother, and he wasn't about to forget that either. Even if she did smell like lilacs.

For the next few moments they rode along in silence. By now exhaustion had erased her teasing mood. Her eyes drooped, and she snuggled closer to Cole's broad chest. It felt terribly good to lie there against him and forget some of the overwhelming problems that this adventure had brought. She had no idea where they were going, but at this point she really didn't care. The horse just kept plodding down the road, and Cole wasn't saying anything.

Only his body continued to relay the silent message that he was aware she was still there. The memory of the kiss they had shared the night before made her pulse suddenly beat faster, and she forced her thoughts back to her newest dilemma.

Now her mule was gone. So were her clothes and even her gun. She supposed she should be frantic, but strangely she wasn't.

If Cole had been decent enough to save her from a fate worse than death from those horrible men, then he would surely see that she was taken care, at least for tonight. Tomorrow she could start worrying again.

Having a nice man around might not be all that bad, she thought as she grew drowsier. That is, if a woman was lucky enough to find the right man. Where Cass was concerned, she was beginning to realize that she might have just made a bad error in judgment, that's all. Surely all the men in the world weren't like Cass Claxton.

Wynne sighed softly. Perhaps she would reconsider going into a convent when this was all over. Perhaps she would find a man someday who would love her and respect her the way Beau did Betsy.

For the first time Wynne noticed that her resentment of Cass was actually beginning to be more trouble than it was worth. Try as she would, she couldn't seem to summon that terrible, gut-wrenching agony she had experienced toward him only a few days before. There wasn't even the anger she'd clung to so desperately the past few days.

"You haven't eaten again today, have you?" Cole's stern voice broke into her daydreaming.

"No, how did you know?"

"I've followed you all day."

This revelation should have upset her, but somehow it didn't. "You did? I didn't know that."

"I didn't mean for you to."

"If you followed me all day, how come it took you so long to come to my rescue?" she asked crisply. The knowledge that her clever plan had failed stung sharply.

"I wanted you to learn a lesson," he stated calmly.

"You would." She sighed hopelessly again. "And I'll admit I probably have learned a lesson. From now on I'll listen more closely to what you're saying."

"I'll have to see that to believe it. You want a drink of water?" He knew she'd been without that precious commodity all day too.

"Please." She'd decided to be cooperative. What choice did she have?

Cole leaned sideways to unsnap his canteen and handed it to her. "Don't drink too fast," he said.

The water was cool and delightful going down her parched throat. She drank long and greedily until he pulled the container away from her. "That's enough for now. You'll make yourself sick."

Recognizing his authority, Wynne lay back against his chest once more and gazed up into the sky. Low clouds were racing across the horizon, and in the distance she could still see traces of lightning periodically flashing.

"Who were those horrible men?" she asked as Cole replaced the lid on the canteen.

"Frank and Jesse James, plus a few men they ride with."

Wynne shuddered. "Are those the men Lilly and Beau and Betsy were talking about at dinner the other night?"

"They're the ones."

She shuddered again. "They were disgusting. All except the one called Frank. He seemed a lot quieter than the rest of them."

"They were just a bunch of horn—" Cole caught himself before he said "horny" in front of her. "They were just a bunch of men looking for a good time," he said brusquely.

Wynne lifted her eyes back to meet his. "You mean, all men do that sort of a thing when they're out on the trail?"

"No, not all men," Cole said. "But a woman's just askin' for that kind of treatment if she's runnin' around the countryside without the protection of a man."

She could have argued with him, but the past few hours had made her realize that he was probably right. She nestled back more comfortably in his arms.

He smelled nice, like rain and warm flesh and faint cigar smoke. She nearly gagged when she thought of how those other men had looked and smelled.

"Where are we going to camp tonight?"

Cole swallowed, his mouth suddenly dry as renewed recognition of her femininity assaulted his senses. "We passed what looked like a deserted cabin earlier this afternoon. I thought we might hole up there for the night." His eyes scanned the sky briefly. "My guess is it'll rain again before morning."

"Is the cabin very far away?" She didn't recall seeing any such lodging.

"Couple of miles more."

For the rest of the trip Wynne dozed peacefully. The air was cool now and smelled of damp earth and moist vegetation, and she was so tired she couldn't think straight any longer.

When they arrived at the cabin, Cole suggested she stay on the horse while he checked to see if the dwelling was occupied. In a few moments he was back with the good news that it was empty.

As he lifted her off the horse, it occurred to Wynne that a temporary truce had apparently taken place between them. By the way he was acting, Cole planned to share the cabin with her tonight instead of camping somewhere nearby, as he usually did. And she wasn't about to complain. Her emotions were still rattled from her earlier capture, and she personally didn't plan on letting him out of her sight any sooner than she had to.

It was entirely possible that the gang of men had followed them and might attempt to take her back. She shuddered to think what would happen then. This time Jesse and Frank James might not be quite so polite, and Cole would be a captive, too, and not able to stop whatever they had in mind. She followed Cole closely as he carried the saddle into the cabin.

The cabin was barely adequate shelter. There were a few stray pieces of furniture strewn about the dirty room. Dust and cobwebs dominated the corners and rafters, and the sound of rats scurrying for cover as they entered was a bit disconcerting.

Yet it looked like a castle to Wynne. At least it would be a roof over her head tonight, and that was more than she had been used to the past several days.

Her teeth began to chatter as Cole knelt in front of the hearth and began to build a fire. Her dress clung to her uncomfortably and felt wet and clammy. Her shoes felt as if they were coming apart and pinched her toes as the leather began to dry. A fire would feel wonderful. Some other weary traveler must have used the cabin before them because the wood-box was filled with dry wood.

"You'd better get out of those wet clothes."

Wynne agreed. The rainstorm had cooled the air down until it was almost chilly. She glanced about and located an old blanket lying on a bed in the corner of the room. It wasn't clean, but it was better than wearing those wet clothes and catching her death of cold. Her nose was tickling already with a sneeze.

Her fingers paused uncertainly as she started to unbutton the front of her dress. She swallowed nervously. "Turn your head."

Cole glanced up from the fireplace. "What?"

"I said, turn your head."

"Oh."

Wynne could have sworn she saw him smile as he obediently did as he was told.

A few minutes later she had peeled off her wet dress and underthings and draped the blanket about her shoulders modestly.

By now the fire was going and the room had lost some of its dampness. She busied herself hanging her clothing around the room so it would dry. "What about you? You're soaked to the skin too."

Cole spread out his bedroll and retrieved a blanket. Wynne flushed, knowing that while his blanket had been protected by a piece of canvas, hers must have been just as wet as the clothes on her back since she'd not taken the precaution of having either oilcloth or canvas in which to wrap her things.

Wynne turned her head, pretending to be busy with the fire, while Cole slipped out of his clothes. A few minutes later they were toasting themselves by the fire.

"Have you looked around to see if anyone might have left anything we could eat?"

Gathering the blanket around her more securely, she stood and nearly tripped over the ends. Glaring at Cole, knowing he hid a grin, she went to rummage through the old cabinets. After searching each one thoroughly, she only managed to come up with a bottle of what appeared to be discarded corn liquor.

Holding it up to the firelight, she examined the contents with a frown. "It's half empty."

"Bring it over here," Cole said. "I prefer to think of it as half full."

In a moment she was seated back at the fire and he had uncorked the bottle with his teeth. Extending the bottle to her first, he noticed a slight hesitation on her part. "You first."

She eyed the bottle worriedly.

"Go ahead. Take a sip," he said encouragingly. She was huddled deep in her blanket, and he thought she needed the extra warmth. All he needed was for her to get sick.

Wynne wasn't at all sure she should drink the liquor. On rare occasions her papa had allowed her a small glass of peach brandy, but she'd never partaken of hard spirits.

"I don't know . . ."

He grinned widely, and his eyes twinkled with merriment. Wynne noticed the rare occurrence made him even more breathtakingly attractive. "It won't hurt you."

"Well . . ." She took the bottle and brought it to her mouth. She tipped it up cautiously to let a small amount of the liquid trickle down her throat, then gasped and gagged. The stuff burned like fire. Tears immediately welled up in her eyes, and she fought for breath.

Cole burst into laughter as he scooted over next to her and patted her firmly on the back. "Good, huh?"

"It's—it's . . . hor-r-ible!" Wynne croaked.

Cole shrugged and took a long swallow of the fiery whiskey. Holding the container away from him, he looked it over carefully. "Not bad. I prefer mine a little stronger."

She looked at him sourly. He chuckled again and held the bottle out to her once more. "It'll taste better the second time."

She doubted that was true, but a pleasant warmth was beginning to settle in her stomach as she took another small taste. It still felt as if she were pouring scalding water down her throat, but the liquor actually wasn't as bad as the first time.

The rain began falling again. They could hear it on the roof as they settled back to relax. The day had been long and arduous, and other than being hungry, they both began to feel pretty good. The bottle changed hands regularly, its contents slowly diminishing.

Everything was suddenly becoming quite fuzzy, and Wynne wasn't seeing well at all now. But her eyes seemed intent on lingering on the man who sat across from her. The blanket he had thrown carelessly around him covered only his hips and legs now. The top had slipped down to reveal his brown, bare torso.

Very few times had she ever seen a man with his shirt off, just her papa and a few of the slaves who worked in the cotton fields. But Papa's chest had not looked anything like Cole's. While Papa's had been broad, it had not been nearly as broad as Cole's. Wesley's chest had been rather pale and flaccid, but Cole's was firm and tanned. Papa's had only a few wisps of hair, but Cole's chest was covered by dark, thick hair that curled sleekly against his skin.

Wynne ran the tip of her tongue around the corner of her mouth and wondered what it would feel like to be pressed against him, against his potent maleness. Her mouth went dry with the images floating through her mind, and she closed her eyes momentarily to let them flow freely.

Cole was not unaware of Wynne's preoccupation with him. He was achingly aware, in fact, of the trail her gaze took over his body, uncomfortably aware. And this time he allowed his own imagination to spin.

The liquor was beginning to work its magic, and he found himself slowly unwinding as he lay back and studied her from beneath lowered eyelids.

The firelight played across her hair, picking up the red glints as it dried. It tumbled across her shoulders and spilled down her back in glorious profusion. The creamy skin on her shoulders compelled him to follow the curve and shadow which pointed to the swell of her breast. When she moved, it was with a delicateness and quickness which reminded him of a colt just getting its legs—an uncertain, beautiful grace. The flickering shadows from the firelight played across her face, emphasizing the hollow of her cheek, the curve of her eyelashes when she lowered them over eyes that were becoming too bright from the liquor.

Cole suddenly found himself wanting to touch her. She was clutching the blanket protectively around her, yet he could discern the curve of her small waist and the following swell of her hip. For her size her legs were long, and the ankle revealed in the fold of the too-short blanket was delicately curved. Even in a dirty, tattered blanket it was painfully obvious Wynne Elliot was a lush, very desirable woman.

There were a million reasons why it was foolish to entertain such ideas of touching her, and Cole knew every one of them by heart. But the drinks had mellowed his feelings to the point where he was actually thinking of kissing her again, and he allowed the thought to linger.

He had never met a woman who could annoy him so quickly yet make him forget all about that anger when she leveled those strange-colored green eyes on him. She was feisty, unreasonable, bullheaded, and had the endurance of six women. Yet she was one of the most beautiful creations he had ever met. At least it seemed that way to him tonight.

Their gazes met and held in the soft glow of the room. Why was he looking at her so strangely? she wondered in her sensual fog. The blue of his eyes turned to dark turquoise as his gaze began slowly but thoroughly to travel over her. Wynne didn't know what to make of it. The liquor had hit her empty stomach with the impact of an oncoming train, and she found herself unable to think clearly.

His eyes were making her feel hot and flushed, and she had a funny ache deep inside. It was as if her bones had turned to water. All she did was think of how good his mouth had tasted on hers last night and that funny ache got stronger and stronger. . . .

She mustn't let her thoughts dwell on him, she cautioned herself. She broke their eye contact and quickly turned her face toward the fire. Somewhere deep inside she remembered there was some reason why she shouldn't think such things about Cole Claxton. Yet for the life of her she couldn't remember what it was. It had to be important because the feeling was too strong.

A loud clap of thunder shook the cabin as Cole finished the last of the liquor. He set the empty bottle very carefully to one side as if it were very important not to move too quickly. Once more his gaze found hers, and he asked softly, "Are you warm enough?"

Yes, she was. In fact, she was becoming overheated, and she let the blanket slide down her arm a fraction more. "Yes . . . thank you."

He grinned at her lazily. "You might be more comfortable over here." His baritone voice was velvety and slid over her senses like silk over her skin.

She stared at him. "I'm fine . . . thank you."

"You look sleepy." He nearly whispered the words, compelling her to come nearer. She had never seen him this at ease, and the new experience was pleasant.

"I am . . . a bit."

"Why don't you come over here closer to the fire?" he suggested again lightly.

Her pulse raced faster. If she moved any closer, she would be touching him, and she wasn't certain that would be a good idea.

"I'm all right—" But her words were interrupted as Cole reached for her hand and began to pull her closer.

Unnerved, Wynne reacted more quickly than she should have and jumped to her feet. To her dismay the blanket unfolded and slipped to the floor with a brief whisper. Cole's sudden sharp intake of breath rasped in the quiet of the cabin. Instinctively she bent to retrieve the covering, but his hand snaked out to catch her arm.

Once more their eyes locked, and she felt herself growing weak when she saw the way he was looking at her.

"Wynne." He spoke her name in a husky voice as his gaze devoured the beauty before him. "You're . . . so lovely."

He could think of only one thing as he looked at her slender frame. If it had been Cass who had run out on her, then he must have lost his mind.

She was like the picture of a goddess he'd seen in a book one time. She was slender, and her womanhood was obvious against the paleness of her skin. Shadows from the firelight danced on her body, taunting and tempting. Almost unconsciously she straightened beneath his gaze, a woman answering a man's unconscious command. Her hands hung to her side, drawing attention to the soft curve of her breasts, which were small but temptingly firm. They were just the right size to fit in his hand.

"Cole . . ." She whispered his name, knowing she should pick the blanket up and move away from him. A lady would never permit a man to see her unclothed. But she didn't want to move away.

Still watching her, Cole stood up slowly. His blanket dropped away, but he ignored it as he drew her to him. Their bodies met, and he held her against him tightly as he buried his face in her hair. She smelled of freshness, rain and woods. "Wynne . . ." He breathed her name again, and his breath was warm against her skin.

Automatically her face turned toward him, her eyes drifting closed as she drank in the wonders of the feel of his body pressed up against her. His rugged strength made her even more aware of her femininity, and she began to tremble.

"Don't be afraid," he murmured. "I won't hurt you." With those simple words his mouth gently sought hers. He didn't overpower her with his passion but kissed her tenderly at first, his tongue teasing her mouth open to receive his again and again.

The ache deep within her had begun to build again, and she stretched up, draping her arms around his shoulders. Her body moved against him automatically, her breasts aching with desire as his large hands found and molded them. She touched him, moving her palms against his firm flesh. She wound her fingers through the dark hair on his chest and held on to him tightly as his kisses started to deepen. She lost all sense of propriety, forgot everything that had seemed important just a few minutes before.

Cole widened his stance and drew her even closer, pressing her hips flush against his. A groan grew deep in his chest, and he smothered it with her mouth, reveling in the freshness and immediacy of her response.

She had been kissed many times before but never been so totally consumed as she was now. And then they were lying on the floor, one of the blankets spread under them. Cole was whispering things to her she had never heard before, exciting, titillating intimacies, and his hands and mouth were building within her body a tide of passion that threatened to sweep her into oblivion.

Sighs of pleasure mixed with the occasional rolls of thunder as he took her higher and higher. She had never seen a man's bare body, and he allowed her to discover his with a sense of freedom she had never known. He was the first man to make love to her, and he took his time to make sure she found the experience one of total joy.

She pleased him beyond his wildest dreams. He discovered an earthiness about her he'd never suspected lurking beneath that prim exterior. She experimented with an almost childish curiosity, and when she discovered something which pleased him, she explored further and further until he was nearly over the edge of reason.

In return, Cole made love to Wynne as if she were the greatest treasure on earth, and she responded with an abandon that made him laugh with enjoyment and gasp with surprise and pleasure. He'd never made love with a woman who laughed, and he found it an experience he'd never forget. And when she was finally his in the completeness of their lovemaking, she was everything he had ever imagined a woman should be.

When the tides of passion finally abated, he rolled over with her in his arms, and their mouths still sipped at each other languidly. "Mmm . . .

sorry about that, Miss Elliot," he murmured guiltily. He felt strangely compelled to say that. After all, a gentleman did not take a woman's virginity unless he planned to make her his wife, and Cole had no such plans at the moment.

"Oh, that's quite all right, Mr. Claxton," Wynne answered in a drowsy voice as her small hand patted his bare chest comfortingly. She wondered why he always felt that he had to apologize when he kissed her or now, after having made love to her? But she didn't let herself dwell overly long on the troubling question.

Soon they fell into an exhausted sleep as the rain pattered gently down on the rooftop and the fire flickered brightly on the hearth.

CHAPTER 13

SHE AWOKE THE FOLLOWING MORNING TO FIND HER-self cuddled tightly up against his bare chest. He was still sleeping soundly, one arm draped limply around her waist. The sun had been up for hours, but a delightfully cool breeze was blowing through the open window. She blinked her eyes a couple of times to clear her head.

When the haze slowly began to recede, her gaze focused on his hand resting on her bare stomach. It was wide and strong with blunt-cut fingernails that were clean and well cared for. His dark, work-calloused skin made a startling contrast with her alabaster coloring.

The events of the night before suddenly rushed in on her. Hell's bells, how much lower was she going to sink in her pursuit of Cass? Not only would she have to answer to the good Lord for thinking about murder and actually having committed a theft, but now she had given herself to a man without the sanctity of marriage. And they hadn't even made it to the bed!

Wynne sighed hopelessly. There wasn't a convent in the whole world that would have her after she had finished confessing all these iniquities.

Still, with a smile curving her lips, she couldn't make herself regret this newest act of sinfulness.

Tipping her head up, she looked at Cole's slumbering features, and her pulse did that funny little cadence again. Giving in to her curiosity, she let her finger lightly caress the smooth dark skin on his left cheek. Last night had been a new experience for her, one she would forever hold dear in her heart.

In those incredible hours she had forgotten all about Cole's being Cass's brother. Instead, he had been an exciting yet incredibly gentle lover who had brought her into full womanhood in a wild and wondrous way. She sensed that no matter how many men would come and go in her life, she would never forget the joy Cole had brought to her in those few magical hours.

He stirred, his arm tightening around her possessively. He looked different in sleep. The tired lines around his eyes and mouth had softened, making him look much younger. It was hard to believe this was the same man who had angered her so in the past.

It was even more painful when she thought about the fact that he was a Claxton. Perhaps, if things had been different, if Cass had not broken her heart and trampled on her pride, then she might seriously consider the idea that she might, in time, fall in love again.

That new and disturbing thought brought her foolish meanderings to an abrupt halt. Her hand reached down to scratch her arm absently. No, that was ridiculous. She couldn't be falling in love with Cass's brother! Up until last night she hadn't even liked the man, for heaven's sake. You would think that after the misery she'd been through the past few months, she would have learned her lesson concerning men. Yet, strangely, it seemed she hadn't.

That Cole and she had shared such intimacies the night before was due entirely to the liquor, she thought.

She scratched her arm harder, and it felt heavenly. She had never drunk such hard liquor, and combined with an empty stomach—well, she had been—well, taken advantage of again! That's all. The more she thought about it, the more firmly convinced she became that that was what had happened. Cole Claxton, the uncivilized, egotistical ruffian that he was, had taken advantage of her inebriated state and imposed himself upon her—again! Otherwise, she never would have succumbed to his dubious charms.

She glared at his sleeping form resentfully. The nerve of him, taking such liberties with her! Sitting up, she jerked the blanket off, then hurriedly covered her nakedness once more. She couldn't get up and go prancing around the room like this. Cole might wake up any minute, and she would die if he were to see her this way.

He stirred again, and she watched fearfully as, in his sleep, he began to scratch a small patch of redness on his chest. A moment later she found herself scratching her arm again.

Glancing down, she frowned as she surveyed the large, irritated area spreading up her arms with long pinkish fingers. Holding the arm up for a closer look, she studied the tiny, watery blisters with growing concern. What in the blue blazes was that?

Whatever it was, it was becoming quite annoying and painful. Once more she thoroughly scratched the area but found little relief in the action.

By now Cole was scratching again, mumbling unintelligibly under his breath. Bending over to examine his misery, Wynne saw the same watery blisters erupting in patches all over his chest.

When she raised her head, it was to encounter a pair of arresting blue eyes now open and staring at her. "What are you doing?"

"Uh, looking at your chest."

A slow, incredibly sexy grin spread across his drowsy features. "Oh? Well, come over here and take a closer look." He reached out without thinking and cupped the back of her head, bringing her forward to meet his mouth in a long good morning kiss.

It never occurred to her to pull away. Instead, she found herself returning the kiss and enjoying every moment of it.

Only when he began to pull her back down beside his naked length did she remember the strange rash on her arm.

"Cole, look." She hurriedly held her arm up for him to inspect. Last night had been wonderful, but she couldn't permit it to happen again.

Cole's sleepy eyes tried to focus on the arm suddenly shoved in his face. "What is it?"

"I don't know, but whatever it is, it's on your chest too," she said lamely.

"My chest?" Cole glanced down to see what she was talking about. His eyes widened in disbelief. Then he quickly grasped her arm to peer at it more closely. "Oh, hell."

"What? What is it?" she asked expectantly.

"Oh, hell!" he stated emphatically again as he sat straight up in the bed. "It looks like poison ivy!"

"Oh." She let out a sigh of relief. The way he had been acting she had halfway been expecting him to tell her it was some sort of horrible plague. A simple case of poison ivy wasn't fatal. "Oh, is that all?"

By now Cole was busily inspecting his chest for further signs of the growing affliction. It didn't take long for him to spot the trouble areas, and he swore under his breath irritably. "Oh, damn! I'm sensitive to this stuff," he complained.

"Then you should have stayed clear of it," she said, thinking at the same time it was rather endearing that there was something to which he was particularly susceptible.

"I do stay clear of it! I always have since I nearly died with it as a kid. You must have given it to me," he said accusingly.

"Me!" Once again she was put on the defensive. "Why does it always have to be me who causes all the trouble?" Jumping to her feet, Wynne jerked the blanket off him and wrapped it tightly around her. She glared down at him angrily. "Just what makes you so sure I gave you poison ivy? You could have given it to me, you know."

"No, I couldn't have given it to you because I'll ride five miles out of my way to avoid getting the juice of the damn stuff on me," Cole replied. "Can you say you've been as careful, Miss Elliot!"

Wynne felt herself blushing to the roots of her hair as she tried to avoid his indicting gaze. It was hard to keep her mind on the argument with him lying there naked and so—so . . . stunningly male. "I—I don't even know what poison ivy looks like," she said.

"Obviously not," he grunted. "To get a case this bad, you must have rolled in it somewhere!" He surveyed her arms, which were becoming puffier by the moment, with bleak resignation.

Wynne's temper was flaring, but she had to admit he could be right. The past few days had been a nightmare, and she had waded through endless thickets and briars. She'd even fallen off the mule a few times, and there had been those strange-looking vines on that old oak tree the mule had brushed her against.

Suddenly it was all too much. Nothing had gone right since Mama and Papa died, and she burst into a fit of inconsolable tears.

Cole hastily rolled to his feet. Watching Wynne closely, he picked up his discarded pants and slid into them. "Hey, now look. Don't start cryin'. It's not the end of the world."

"But I'm—I'm for-e-ev-er doin-g su-c-h stu-pi-d th-in-gs," she sobbed. From the moment she'd met him she'd acted like a blithering idiot. No wonder he disliked her so! Now she had given him poison ivy, and he would never forgive her.

"Come on, stop getting yourself all upset." He fumbled in his back pocket for his handkerchief and handed it to her. There were very few things in Cole Claxton's life that could bring him to heel, but a woman's tears was one of them.

Wynne could tell she was making him uncomfortable by all her blubbering and sniveling, but she couldn't make herself stop. Snatching the cloth out of his hand, she buried her face in it and bawled even harder.

For a few moments he let her cry it out, casting uneasy glances in her direction every once in a while. All that squawking and bellowing were going to make her sick, but he didn't know how to put a stop to it without bringing on more of the same.

When the storm finally began to abate and Wynne lifted red-rimmed eyes to meet his, his face sagged with visible relief. "Feel better?"

"N-o," she said, and hiccuped.

"Well, you'd better hurry and get it all out of your system," he said, but in an unusually nice tone—for him. "We have work to do."

She looked at him skeptically as she blew her nose loudly. "Wh-a-t wor-k?"

"We have to find a whole lot of pokeberry leaves."

"Pokeberry leaves! What for?" She wouldn't know a pokeberry leaf if it came up and spit in her face!

"We can make poultices out of them and hope they'll keep the poison ivy from spreading." He paused and, to her growing amazement, smiled nicely at her. "Mind you, I said hope that it won't spread any farther."

"But you think it will?" She would have thought that he would be angrier than ever with her, but he seemed to be taking this newest crisis in resigned stride.

He shrugged his broad shoulders as he absentmindedly scratched his chest again. "With my luck lately? Yes. It'll spread like wildfire. By night we'll both be as miserable as hell." The woman was a hex. There was no longer any doubt about it. He'd come through the entire war without a sign of an injury, nearly four years of unbelievable luck when he led his men into battle, day after day, watching them fall around him in droves, yet always managed to escape unharmed. But now, after having spent one, *one* measly night with her, he was faced with a threat he feared even more than death. Poison ivy. The words struck total fear in his heart.

When he was a kid, he had been flat on his back in bed with the dreaded ailment for more than three weeks. After that Lilly made sure he was dosed heavily each spring with sulfur, molasses, and a pinch of saltpeter.

He'd come to recognize the little three-leaved vine from a mile away and to avoid it. Naturally Wynne wouldn't have recognized the vines, and probably the juice had been all over her clothing. If he knew her, she'd hung her clothes on the vines, thinking they made perfect clotheslines.

Well, it was too late to worry about it now, Cole conceded silently. He could only hope there was a mess of pokeberry leaves growing somewhere nearby.

His eyes drifted back to Wynne. She was hastily trying to pin her mass of tousled hair up on top of her head with the remaining pins she had managed to hold on to.

The tempting curve of her breasts were silhouetted against the sunlight shining through the window, and he felt a swift tightening in his loins as he recalled the memory of her lying in his arms—sweet and unbelievably giving. A stab of guilt sliced through him. He should be ashamed of himself for losing control like that. She was obviously not used to drinking, and he was. He supposed he had taken unfair advantage of her, but she hadn't put up a fight. If she had, he would have stopped. He was sure of that.

But in a way she had led him on, looking at him with those wide green eyes, all soft and inviting, seductively running the tip of her tongue around her lips after each drink out of the bottle, making them wet and shiny . . . Hell. *She*, not he, was the one responsible for last night, he convinced himself. He'd been minding his own business when she started looking at him that way. Besides, how was he to know she'd never been with a man before? She had sure been acting as if she'd known what was going on.

He deliberately cast the memory aside. Whoever was at fault, last night had not been worth a case of poison ivy. Or had it been?

He was astounded to find his hand trembling as he reached in his shirt pocket for a smoke. If she had been any other woman, he would have had his answer without a second thought. Women were a dime a dozen to Cole, and the last thing he wanted was a prissy little thing who couldn't even shoot her own dinner.

But because he couldn't convince himself that last night had not left him untouched, it unnerved him even more than her crying had.

"Is the pain any better, Bertie?" The soft, familiar voice alone was soothing balm to Bertram's misery.

"I think it's gettin' bearable." He rolled to his side and tried to ease himself into a more comfortable position as Fancy gently tried to assist. "Agghhh . . ." A low groan escaped him as a sharp stab of pain ran up his spine.

"Doc said if you needed any more laudanum, he would send you over some."

"Have I taken the whole bottle already?" He peered at the brown glass container sitting on the table among all the wooden animals he had carved these past few weeks and frowned.

"Almost." Fancy plumped his pillows and fussed over him for a few moments. "Brought you dinner. Hope you're gettin' your appetite back."

"I am." He sniffed the air appreciatively and eyed the tray covered with a red-checkered cloth she had set on the table earlier. "What'd you bring me?"

"Just some stew and corn bread."

Bertram grinned. Stew was his favorite, and she knew it. "Wouldn't happen to be a piece of blueberry pie on there, too, would there?"

Fancy grinned back at him, her features blushing a pretty pink. "There just might be."

"You're gonna spoil me, Fancy."

"I want to, Bertie."

Bertram Mallory was about the best thing that had ever happened to her. In the few weeks he had been delayed in Springfield, she'd fallen deeply in love with him. He was about the kindest, gentlest man she had ever met, and it made her want to cry when she thought about how empty her life would be when he left town.

Fancy wished she knew what was so important about his getting to

River Run. That was all he talked about, getting there and finding some woman he'd been trailing for the past few months.

The fact that he was looking for a woman worried her a little. He sounded desperate at times and frustrated at others when he talked about his leg's healing so he could go on with his trip. She couldn't imagine his being on a spiteful mission. He was too kind to be an evil man. Yet every time she tried to question him on why he was looking for this woman named Wynne Elliot, his eyes narrowed and he gritted his teeth and stubbornly refused to tell her. Just said it was personal and he had to find her. If fate didn't get him first.

He talked funny like that sometimes, and she didn't really know what he meant, but she was sure it was important for Bertie to find that woman.

And he would have been on his way again right now if he hadn't stopped to help Elmo Wilson fix a wheel that had come off his buggy Sunday morning.

Bertram had been leaving for River Run really early when he come across Elmo and his wife, Sadie. They were sitting in the middle of the road all hot and sweating in their Sunday best. Bertie said he could tell Sadie was about to expire, so he got off his horse and offered to help. Elmo was grateful and he had told Bertie that if he would just lift the side of the buggy up carefullike, then Elmo would slip the wheel back in place and they all could be on their way.

Well, Bertie had agreed that was simple enough for a strong man like himself. He had proceeded to heft the left side of the carriage when all of a sudden his back went out and he screamed like a castrated bull. Said he got mad and just cussed a blue streak right then and there in the middle of the road because he knew that throwing his back out was going to delay him another few weeks.

Fancy knew his cursing must have been pretty bad that morning. He could come out with some pretty colorful phrases at times, but she never minded. In fact, she was used to that kind of talk. You could tell if a person was really mad or not by the way he sort of phrased things.

Bertie said poor Sadie like to have jumped right out of her skin he scared her so badly, but he swore the pain grabbed him around the middle something fierce. Even worse than the times he fell off the train and broke his leg combined. And he just couldn't help letting out that holler and cussing.

And what with his leg's being out of the splint just that morning, the jolt had set it aching like all get-out.

Elmo and Sadie had brought him back to Springfield and taken him to the hospital. Then they'd rushed over to get the doctor and sent someone to tell Fancy about the accident.

Although Fancy hadn't relished the idea of Bertram's being hurt again

—poor man seemed to be having an ungodly run of bad luck lately—she was elated that she would have him around for a while longer.

Bertram caught her hand in the middle of all her fussing and brought it to his lips lovingly. "You're mighty good to me, Fancy."

"Ah, I'm not, Bertie. You deserve so much more than somebody like me caring for you." Her head dropped down shyly as the grasp of their hands tightened. She'd known a lot of men in her time, but somehow this quiet, almost naïve man could make her feel like a schoolgirl again.

"I don't ever want to hear you say such a thing again," he said. "Why, you're the finest woman I've ever known, Fancy."

And she was. Oh, she might let men do things to her body that Bertram didn't approve of, but he knew what made her let them do those things, and he understood. Other people might judge her harshly, but Bertram didn't. He saw beyond the saloon girl paint and glitter. He saw into her good, kind heart. Bertram loved her.

"Thank you, Bertie. It's not true about me being nice, but I surely do appreciate you thinkin' so." Her fingers soothed his hair back from his face tenderly.

"You *are* nice," he whispered adamantly, "and as soon as I finish what I started out to do, I'm goin' to come back and get you, Fancy. Then I'm goin' to marry you and take you back home with me."

Fancy smiled. Bertram had begun to talk like that lately, making all those silly promises that made her heart start to pound with excitement. But she didn't take any of them seriously. She knew that when he left, she would probably never see him again. No one had ever cared enough about Fancy Biggers to come back for her. But she didn't mind. Bertie had been nice to her, nicer than any other man had ever been. When he made love to her, he treated her as if she were something special. He'd say such pretty words to her—just as if she were a real lady, not just that bad girl who worked down at the saloon.

And he didn't make her do things just to please him when they were making love, vile and ugly things, the way other men did. Instead, he always cared about seeing that she was pleased, and that was nice. Really nice.

He never made demands. He always seemed happy to be with her, whether he was making love to her or just holding her in his arms while they lay on an old blanket and looked up at the stars. He'd make up silly stories about people who would travel out there among the stars someday, and she would laugh and declare that he was becoming addlebrained.

No, she never let herself believe that she would someday marry Bertram G. Mallory, but lordy, how she wished that could be.

Seeing the doubt clouding her pretty features, Bertram kissed the palm of her hand and winked at her. "You just wait and see. One of these days you're goin' to be Mrs. Bertram Mallory or I'll eat my hat."

She knew it was an impossible dream, yet it seemed to her no harm would come if she let herself hold it for a bit. "And we'll live in a big house sittin' on top of the hill—"

"With a big white fence around it—"

"And lots of flowers and a big vegetable garden—"

"And kids—"

Her eyes shone brightly as she grasped his hand tighter. "At least six kids, Bertie . . . maybe more."

Bertram grinned. "However many you want, Fancy."

"And we'll have three meals a day, three big meals with potatoes and meat and carrots—I love carrots, Bertie. Do you?" Never in her life had Fancy had enough carrots to eat.

"You'll have all the carrots you can ever eat," he said solemnly.

"Oh, Bertie." Her eyes were glistening with tears now. "It all sounds so wonderful."

"It will be. As soon as I get my business taken care of, then we'll start our new life." He had decided he was even going to change professions when this was all over. The one he had was too harrowing. "I'll take care of you, Fancy. From now on you don't ever have to worry about a thing."

Resting her head on the pillow next to his head, she sighed and let the tears slip silently from her eyes. It all sounded so wonderful. "Bertie—about you going to River Run . . ."

"Yes?"

"Well, I know you're lookin' for someone, but maybe they won't even be there anymore," she said carefully. "After all, you've been here nigh on to six weeks now, and you said this Wynne Elliot was just supposed to be visitin' there."

Bertram's brow creased worriedly. "I've thought about that."

"Well, what if this woman's gone somewhere else by now."

It was Bertram who let out the long, weary sigh this time as his hand absently stroked the top of his head. "Then I suppose I gotta keep on goin' until I catch up with her."

"Oh, Bertie, I wish you'd tell me why it's so all-fired important for you to find her!"

"Because Bertram G. Mallory is a man of his word!" he stated firmly, and she knew without asking he wasn't going to say anything more.

CHAPTER 14

*I*T WAS HARD TO BELIEVE. THEY WEREN'T MORE THAN twenty miles out of River Run, and they had been gone for almost a month! For the past two and a half weeks they had been holed up here, and Cole was about to go nuts.

He lay on the old bed in the cabin and stared at a wasp circling the ceiling. His face was a mass of red puffy welts, he ached all over, and he felt as if the entire Confederate army, including General Robert E. Lee himself, had tramped over him.

He could hear Wynne humming happily as she worked around the cabin. Well, she *could* hum, he thought resentfully, and gritted his teeth to keep from scratching. Her case of poison ivy had turned out to be mild, while his had raged out of control for days now.

His gaze went back to her puzzledly. He figured she surely would have left him there to suffer a quiet death while she stole his horse and went on in search of Cass, but surprisingly she had stuck around to care for him. Each day she had fed him, bathed him, against his indignant protests, and made new pokeberry poultices to apply to his swollen body.

Not one square inch of him had been spared. Even the shaft of his manhood had oozing little blisters on it, and he thought he would die of the searing pain every time he had to stagger outside the cabin to relieve himself.

In the long, tortured hours of the night, while Wynne had slept peacefully on the floor beside him, Cole had plotted to get even with his little brother for putting him through this nightmare if it was the last thing he did!

"Hello." Wynne had noticed Cole was awake and came over to check on him. "How are you feeling?"

"Like hell," he said grouchily.

"Oh, you always say that," she replied brightly. She was getting used to his complaints, and they no longer annoyed her. "Surely you're feeling a little better today." She tried to examine the progress of his rash, but he brushed her hand away grumpily. "All right. But I'm only trying to help."

She straightened and went back to arranging a large cluster of wild daisies in the empty whiskey bottle.

While Cole slept during the heat of the day, she'd taken to searching the area, looking for wild roots and berries for their supper. Up until now she'd been successful, but all she had come across today had been the lovely flowers. She'd taken them back to the cabin in hopes of cheering up the grump, but it looked as if her efforts had been wasted.

Wynne knew the enforced illness had been extremely hard on Cole, so she didn't begrudge his being a little touchy. At any other time she would have felt the same way. But the unexpected turn of events hadn't bothered her in the least.

Actually she welcomed the short reprieve. It was wonderful to sleep with a roof over her head each night and be able to walk down to the pond and bathe each morning.

At times she even found herself forgetting why she was here in the first place. Even more amazing, there were times when she was beginning to realize she no longer really cared whether or not she ever found Cass.

The bitterness and anger were slowly ebbing away, and suddenly she found herself—well, almost happy once again. Even thinking about Cass failed to dampen her spirits now as it once had.

"What would you like for dinner tonight?" she asked chattily.

"Since when is there a choice?" For days they had eaten nothing but berries or poke greens or some sort of stew Wynne had concocted from wild roots.

"There isn't actually. I tried to catch a fish out of the pond this morning, but I'm not fast enough with my hands," she said.

He grunted and closed his eyes again. He hated being incapacitated in this way, and escape through sleep seemed the easiest way to cope with his pain and frustration at the moment.

"When I was a small girl, Papa used to take me fishing. We had this large pond that was close to the house, and it was stocked with all sorts of interesting-looking fish." Her hands carefully arranged the flowers as she talked. "You know, fish are really interesting. Have you ever noticed that?"

Cole grunted again but didn't open his eyes.

"Some of them are truly magnificent, with nice, plump bodies and charming characteristics. And then there are those poor things that are just plain ugly and have nasty dispositions—big, bloaty-looking eyes and horrendously fat lips."

Cole's stomach rolled over in disgust.

"It's just a shame people don't eat the mean ones and leave the cute ones alone." She glanced down at him. "Don't you agree?"

One blue eye opened with pained tolerance. "With what?"

"That the ugly fish should be eaten first."

"I've never thought about it."

It suddenly occurred to her he might be trying to rest. "Am I bothering you?"

"No." She was. He was trying to get to sleep so the rash wouldn't bother him so badly, but he didn't have the strength to start another argument.

"Well, as I was saying—"

"What about supper?" He interrupted hurriedly before she could continue her conversation about ugly fish.

"Oh." Her thoughts promptly returned to their earlier discussion. "Well, I could always make stew again."

He sighed. "Anything but those damned berries."

"Cole! You really should do something about that vile cursin'." She rebuked him firmly. The man had a terrible mouth on him at times.

"I'd talk if I were you."

She frowned at him guiltily. She didn't do so badly herself at times. "Well, I couldn't find any berries today, so you're in luck."

Cole didn't consider that lucky. He was sick of the berries, but she couldn't hit the broad side of a barn with a gun, so that meant they would have to eat that unappetizing root stew until he could get back on his feet and kill some fresh meat. But it didn't really matter. He'd had very little appetite lately.

"If you would lend me your gun I could go and try to kill a rabbit for our dinner," she said. It irritated her that he had hidden his gun from her and she couldn't find it.

Cole rolled over to his side, and the pain took his breath. A new round of itching assaulted him. "I'm not letting you have my gun."

"That's not fair. You're sick, and I'm the only one able to provide our food," she said argumentatively.

"And if I give you the gun, either you'll run away and leave me stuck here without a horse or way to protect myself, or you'll shoot yourself and I'll have to get up and bury you. I don't feel up to that yet."

Her hands rested on her hips in irritation. "I'm hungry, Cole. Now give me that gun. I won't run away. If I had wanted to do that, I would have left days ago!"

"I said no."

"Then I'll just have to think of another way to kill our supper because I'm not going to bed hungry again tonight!"

"Good luck."

The door trying to be slammed off its hinge signaled him the slaughter was about to begin.

For the next couple of hours he dozed off and on. The cabin became an oven, and he woke up once drenched in sweat, and the itching began all over again.

It was late afternoon when he heard a terrible ruckus erupt in the front yard. The sound of some feathered wings flailing the air and Wynne's horrified screams mixed with terrified squawks shattered the peaceful stillness.

Cole fought to clear his groggy mind as the fracas grew louder and more intense. After pulling himself weakly up onto his knees, he dragged himself over to retrieve the gun he had hidden under a loose board in the floor, then slowly back to the doorway while the fight outside raged on unchecked.

He had no idea what the woman had gotten herself into this time, but it sounded as if the Battle of Vicksburg were being fought all over again outside the doorstep.

Just as he reached the doorway, Wynne burst through, a triumphant grin on her flushed face. Her dress was even more torn and soiled than before, and her hair was matted with twigs and chicken feathers, but in her hand dangling limply was the proof of her earlier words that she would not go hungry again tonight. "Just look what I have, Mr. Claxton!"

Cole stared blankly at what looked like a chicken, minus its head, dripping blood all over the floor of the cabin. "How in the hell did you get that?"

"I ran it down," she exclaimed gleefully. "And then I swung it around and around until its head popped off!" She had seen the Moss Oak servants do that many times. Getting the head off hadn't been as easy as it looked, but she had managed. "It was wandering around in the woods and I ran until I finally caught it and then I brought it back here. Isn't that marvelous?"

"Well, I'll be—"

"I don't need your gun anymore, sir," she informed him loftily, then grinned impishly as she swirled the chicken in a wide circle as if it were one of those drawstring purses women carried. "Why, hell's bells, I think I've finally got the hang of it!"

Cole groaned as he sank weakly back down on the floor. "God help us all."

It was another week before Cole's rash showed real signs of improvement. During their extended stay Wynne had settled in the cabin as if it were to be their permanent home.

She had ripped off the lower half of her petticoat and made several cloths to clean with. The cabin was spotless now. The old floor was scrubbed clean, and fresh flowers adorned the table each day. She'd managed to stretch the chicken over an entire week and then miraculously went out and found another one.

She had even discovered an old root cellar in the back of the house that held a leftover bushel of apples and two jars of honey. Somehow she managed to turn the fruit and sweetening into a tasty dessert.

Cole lay in bed watching her move about the cabin, and he began noticing that all of Miss Fielding's teachings had not gone astray. There was a certain beauty and elegance about her that he had failed to notice in the past. Somehow, no matter what the circumstance, she went about her work with the grace and refinement befitting the most dignified southern lady, even when she was down on her hands and knees, scrubbing the rough wooden floor with a scrap of petticoat.

Instead of the clumsy, addlebrained girl he'd first encountered, she was proving every day that she was indeed the southern, genteel lady her papa had raised her to be.

They had never spoken of the night they had spent together. But it was on Cole's mind day after day as their forced confinement began to take its toll on him.

At night they lay in the dark and talked as the sounds of night filled the old cabin. Wynne told him stories of her growing up on a large cotton plantation, while he regaled her with stories about the war. They had grown so comfortable with each other that one night Wynne even found herself telling him about Cass and how they had met and fallen in love.

When she started weeping as she talked, Cole had rolled over and pulled her up beside him. He had held her tightly as she poured out all her bitterness and grief, and when the tempest had past, they had talked long into the night. Cole found he now believed that his brother was the one partly responsible for her unhappiness, but he still couldn't account for why.

He told her all about Cass and how he had been as a boy. With each word Wynne could feel more of her rancor slowly ebbing out of her. Reading between the lines, she learned that Cole was the strong one, Beau the optimist, and Cass the dreamer of the Claxton family, and she found herself feeling almost a part of his family, a family that had produced three similar yet diverse men.

Then, one morning, Cole forced himself out of bed and took Wynne outside the cabin and gave her a lesson in shooting.

"Why are you doing this now?" Wynne asked, puzzled.

"If anything happens to me, you'll be able to take care of yourself." He resisted the impulse to scratch.

"But nothing's going to happen to you," she protested, the mere thought of something bad happening to him making her grow weak.

"I don't plan on it," he assured her. "But you need to know how to take care of yourself anyway."

They were sitting in the yard, she pressed tightly up against him as he steadied her arm and aimed at the target he had constructed earlier. For a moment their gazes met and held, and each one remembered how the other tasted and smelled. Cole's face still had signs of poison ivy, but he was so handsome it fairly took her breath away.

Reflected in both eyes were admiration and yet another light, a new radiance that had encompassed both of them in the past few days. "Aren't you afraid that I'll use this new knowledge to harm Cass?"

His gaze did not waver. "I know you'll do what you have to, Wynne."

It was the closest he had ever come to saying he understood why she was doing what she was, but it was enough.

"Thank you, Cole. I appreciate your faith in me."

He nodded briefly and returned his concentration to the lesson.

But that night Wynne once again warmed water and brought it to him. Every day of his illness she had given him a sponge bath to help alleviate the pain. But the past few days he had been well enough to tend to his own needs. That was why he was taken by surprise when she set the water down before him and began to roll up the sleeves of her dress.

"What's this?"

"Your bath?"

"Oh." He waited, his breath caught in his chest, as she crossed the room to get a piece of her torn petticoat. His eyes carefully followed her movements as she returned.

"All ready?" Wynne smiled. Her voice had a whispery, excited lilt, and he wasn't quite sure what he was supposed to do.

His eyes narrowed thoughtfully as he brought his cheroot up to his mouth and studied her for a moment. "I thought I was on my own now." He was propped back in the kitchen chair, his dusty boots perched atop the table, watching her.

She moved closer, her fingers reaching out to begin unbuttoning his shirt casually.

The chair came slowly down to all four legs. "What are you doing—"

"I told you. I'm going to give you a bath." Wynne eased down onto his lap and continued her task. Her warmth seeped through, taunting him, tempting him. She smelled of green grass and creek water, and a soft wisp of hair brushed his cheek as she leaned closer. Her nimble fingers, now roughened with the scrubbing chores and from picking berries from prickly bushes, were agonizingly slow in slipping free the buttons of his shirt.

"I don't think that would be a good idea."

But she only smiled at him and concentrated on her task.

Moments later it was clear she was actually going to go through with her threat. He finally threw his cheroot into the fireplace testily. "You're a shameful woman, Wynne Elliot." His low voice caressed her senses, and she smiled again.

Dropping her eyes away from his shyly, she knew full well he spoke the truth. What she felt for Cole might be shameful, and she had no idea where all this wantonness had come from, but right now she didn't really care. She just knew she wanted him to make love to her again. Her body clamored for his touch, to feel his lips on hers again, and to know the completeness of his loving. "I know. Do you find that undesirable?" For a moment she was afraid he might not want her.

Cole shook his head, searching for the right words to tell her this had to stop before it went any farther. Making love to her once could be blamed on drinking too much liquor. But now he was stone-cold sober, and he would have to make a rational decision.

As the fabric of his shirt fell away, the dark hair across his chest unfolded before her. And it was a magnificent chest—all broad and wide and masculine. Spreading the lapels wide, Wynne placed her arms around his waist and rested her head against his comforting warmth. He felt so good. How many times had she lain awake on the floor beside him, listening to his restless movements and the soft moans of discomfort while the poison ivy was at its worst. She'd longed to reach up and touch him, longed to lie beside him, but she'd resisted for two reasons. Cole was miserably sick, and then there had been the guilt. But even while she knew it was wrong, she obeyed the impulse to risk his possible rejection. This time she wanted to make love to him.

Her hands roamed his torso absently. He was hard and strong. He was like Moss Oak, something to give shelter, to believe in, something lasting. At least that's what she wanted him to be. Whether he would or could be all those things for her was yet to be seen. But just for tonight tomorrow didn't exist. All that existed was Cole.

His arms automatically came up to enfold her as lips gently traced the edge of her hair. "Damn . . . damn . . ." he whispered. "This is all wrong . . ." but he couldn't stop himself. She was too close, too warm, too willing, and the memory of her body beneath his was too fresh and too potent.

Cole hadn't wanted this to happen. For days he'd watched her moving about the cabin and lectured himself on how foolish it would be to let his feelings get out of hand again. The first time he had made love to her could be excused, but tonight he would be well aware of what he was doing. And God help him, he couldn't stop himself and didn't want to.

Even as he held her, Cole knew he was making a mistake which would probably follow him the rest of his life. He didn't want her in his heart—but she was already there, a small voice argued. Somewhere between here and River Run he'd fallen in love with this winsome woman/child, and he no longer had the will to ignore it. Yet he had no idea how he would deal with it. How could he have let himself fall in love with a woman who had vowed to kill his own brother?

When his arms tightened around her, Wynne smiled softly and drew back from him. She dipped the cloth into the water. Her battle was won. She knew it.

He knew it. But he still didn't like it.

Moments later he felt the first trickles of warm water dribbling down his bare chest as an involuntary shudder rippled through him.

"Wynne . . ." His voice was nearly pleading now, but she spared him no mercy.

"I wish I had soap." She apologized as her fingers gently administered to the small patches of redness still evident among his chest hair. She wanted to do so much for him, please him, make him so painfully aware that she was all woman that he would never forget the lesson. But she was terribly inexperienced, and she didn't know where to begin.

"It doesn't matter," he said in a voice that had suddenly grown husky. He was so touched by her actions he found it hard to speak. Her small hands ran across his bare skin, sending hot surges rushing through him as he reached out hesitantly to trace the delicate curve of her jaw. It was the first time he had really touched her in the light, and her skin looked as smooth and rich as honey.

Blue eyes looked deeply into green ones. Then, as if in surrender, his mouth slowly lowered to cover hers. They kissed—a warm and lingering exploration that made both their breaths come a little bit faster. In their hunger for each other, one kiss wasn't enough. It was as if he wanted to devour her, and she him. Pausing only briefly in the gentle assault, Wynne smiled and touched Cole's face reverently with roughened fingertips. "Forgive me, Cole Claxton, but I'm truly about to become a shameful woman," she whispered, the words trembling upon lips that were becoming swollen by his passionate kisses.

Cole chuckled, a deep rumble from low within his chest, and he pulled her to him for another long kiss. Her mouth opened willingly beneath his, and he made a soft sound in his throat as he suddenly rose from his chair, swinging her up in his arms.

"Your bath," she murmured as she wrapped her arms around his neck snugly and held on.

"We'll both take one later."

Then he was carefully laying her on the old bed, and their clothes suddenly began to come off as throaty sounds of ardor were muffled by two mouths that hungrily sought each other.

Her hands explored all there was to know of Cole Claxton. He murmured her name almost incoherently and pressed moist lips to her closed eyelids, nearly drowning in the growing haze of sensuality.

Words came rushing back to him in a thunderous roar, words he had said to Beau not so very long ago: "When I find a woman who can wrestle the Indian brave and *win*, then turn around and be soft as cotton, smell as pretty as a lilac bush in May, and forget all about being a lady in bed . . ."

With a low groan Cole rolled her over onto her back and his hand found the womanly softness of her as her breath trembled between her parted lips.

"Cole," she whispered, "I . . ." There were so many new and conflicting emotions raging inside her. His hands and his mouth were setting her on fire, and her body was crying out for fulfillment. She moved beneath him to a silent rhythm which he alone directed. His touch was exquisite torture. He found her innermost places and revealed their secrets, and she wanted more . . . more . . . more.

She had never come close to being with Cass like this. He'd been handsome and had brought her first recognition of desire. But she'd felt nothing like this. "Love me . . . Cole . . . love me . . . I can't—"

"Shh." Her cries merged with his as he built their passion to frightening proportions. She arched against him when his warm mouth suckled her breasts, then gasped as his lips teased a taunting trail across her bare stomach only to pause and tantalize her navel. His boldness fanned the fires of passion to even greater heights until she cried out and boldly drew herself up to meet his searching hunger.

He took her swiftly and without hesitation, and the world tipped crazily as they became one. She held nothing back from him but gave of herself as if she had been waiting all her life for this moment, this hour, this man.

"Cole . . ."

The whispered word was a demand, a prayer, and he responded. "I'm here," he whispered back. "Touch me . . . stay with me. . . ."

And she did, matching him movement for movement, cry for cry.

They were in a world where nothing existed except them, and the bed beneath them was silken—and there was no tomorrow, no Cass, no problems.

When they reached that moment of total completeness, it was as if they were suspended in space for one incredible second, and they clung to it stubbornly.

"Wynne . . ." He placed delirious kisses on her mouth, and when fulfillment finally subsided, they collapsed against each, and she held and stroked him, tenderly wishing the moment never to end. Very slowly they drifted back to earth, still clasped tightly to each other.

Wynne pressed soft kisses into the curve of his neck and whispered her happiness as she felt him slowly begin to relax.

"Uh, Miss Elliot, I'm sorry about—"

She reached over and clamped her hand over his mouth. "If you tell me you're sorry one more time for making love to me, I'll—I swear I'll scream!"

Couldn't he just for once admit that what they had shared was wonderful and exciting and certainly needed no apology?

He grinned at her, a lazy, sensual grin. "All right. I'm gettin' tired of lyin' to you about that anyway. I'm not sorry. I never have been."

She sighed and smiled back at him. "That's better, Mr. Claxton. Neither have I."

His arms squeezed her lovingly. Then, moments later, he was sound asleep.

The sounds of tree frogs and katydids closed in around them as she reached over and quietly snuffed out the flickering candle, then cuddled down in his arms to sleep.

The following morning Cole was sitting at the table smoking when she finally awoke.

"Hello." She smiled.

"Hello."

"Why didn't you wake me?"

He shrugged noncommittally. "There was no need."

Wynne sat up and stretched lazily, not at all concerned that it was broad daylight and she was stark naked. She had come to feel as comfortable in his presence as if they were man and wife. "Did you sleep well?"

"Yes."

She noticed he seemed pensive this morning, but that wasn't unusual for Cole. He was a thinker. Wynne smiled at him lovingly. "I did too. Your rash looks almost all gone this morning."

Shoving back from the table, he rose and began to pull on his boots.

"Where are you going?" She was wishing he would come back to bed for a while.

"Home."

"Home?" Wynne asked blankly. It was as if a cool breeze had brushed her skin, and she shivered.

"That's right." The boots were on, and he straightened up to face her.

"But what about me?" Her mind was whirling. If Cole left and took the horse, she would be left alone, without any transportation—without him. The thought caused a shudder to ripple through her.

Cole leveled his gaze on her, and she noticed how clear blue his eyes were in the morning sunlight. "I think you would be wise to come with me."

"But why?" Suddenly she realized that their time together was about to end, and the knowledge was incredibly painful.

His face lost some of its earlier harshness as he knelt beside her. "Give it up, Wynne. Come back to River Run with me. There's no tellin' where Cass is. By now he may be back home, and it would be crazy for you to keep on lookin' for him. You don't have a horse or a gun."

"You could stay with me," she pleaded. Cass no longer mattered to her. It was the thought that Cole would not be with her any longer that was causing her heart to pound. "And when I find Cass, you can be there to warn him about me." She was desperate, grabbing for any feeble excuse to keep him with her.

"No. I can't do that." He turned away in exasperation, running long fingers through his unruly hair.

"Why?" Her hands grabbed the sleeve of his shirt and turned him back around to face her.

"Because, dammit, I just can't." He had already gotten in deeper than he'd planned to. "Now, I'm tellin' you, Wynne, I'm leavin' in thirty minutes. If you want to go with me, then I promise to see that you get back to Savannah safely. If you don't want to come"—he forced his gaze away from her—"then I guess you're on your own."

His words were so cut-and-dried, so unemotional, so final.

Tears began to gather in her eyes as she absently toyed with the end of the blanket. The past few weeks had meant nothing to him. She had been the fool, falling in love—and with another Claxton yet.

"Well?" Cole towered over her ominously as she blinked back the tears.

"All right," she said lifelessly. She kept her face carefully averted so he couldn't see her pain.

His face sagged with relief. "You'll come back with me?"

"Yes." She didn't see where she had much choice. Cass no longer mattered, and Cole had never cared.

Cole walked to the door. "I'll saddle the horse."

CHAPTER 15

*T*HE RIDE HOME WAS DEPRESSING. THE WEATHER WAS gray and overcast, befitting both their moods.

Although Cole rode with Wynne sheltered in his arms, they spoke very little. At night they lay beside each other, aching to touch yet not allowing themselves the pleasure. They were lost in their own private worlds, and as morning dawned after another sleepless night, they carefully avoided each other's eyes, speaking only about the mundane, going about their business as if the past few weeks had never happened.

Wynne reminded herself a thousand times a day that Cole meant no more to her than Cass did. He had used her just as cold-heartedly as his brother had, and she had only thought she had been falling in love with him. There was no longer any doubt about what she had thought she felt for Cass. She had not been in love with him. Not really. He had just been there for her to lean on in a time when there had been no one else to turn to.

Cole rode behind Wynne, repeatedly challenging his sanity as he thought about how he had let himself fall in love with this woman. Even if she were to give up the foolish idea of killing his brother, she would always bear a deep seed of resentment toward Cass. The family would be divided, something he found intolerable.

The Claxton family had stood together through thick and thin. It was inconceivable that an outsider in a crazy little bird hat could waltz into his life and come between him and his younger brother. Yet, if he were to be honest, the thought of putting Wynne on the stagecoach to return to Savannah tore him apart as much as the thought of a divided family did. After sharing the past few weeks with her, he couldn't imagine what his life would be without her.

Toward evening of the second day they stopped to water the horse. Wynne knelt beside the stream and splashed a handful of the cool water against her grimy face. The trail dust was thick and ground into her dress. She longed for a hot bath and a clean bed.

Cole watched as she closed her eyes and trickled the water over her neck. She had been no trouble at all lately. She'd done her share of the work and never uttered a word of complaint. Instead, she'd been submissive and unusually quiet. She was not at all like the fireball he had found standing in the middle of the road one day, waving a gun at him, and the change served only to deepen his agony.

Shading her eyes against the setting sun, Wynne peered across the small stream and watched another rider approach. He carefully dismounted and led his horse to the water as her forehead crinkled with a frown.

The young man was familiar to her, and she remembered him as the man she'd seen standing on the porch leaning against the post and who had greeted her when she had passed through Springfield a few weeks earlier. Only that young man's leg had been in a splint.

The rider maneuvered himself down on his knees with stiff, careful movements to ease his thirst, and Wynne decided he must be wearing some sort of brace on his back now. He didn't turn at the waist, and bending seemed quite an effort.

"Is that someone you know?" Cole asked when her attention seemed not to leave the stranger. A well-defined stab of jealousy sliced through him when he noted Wynne's continuing interest.

"No, but I think I've seen him before," she said thoughtfully.

Cole's brow lifted sourly. "Oh?"

"Yes . . ." She watched for a few moments longer, causing Cole's growing jealousy to simmer.

A few minutes later she shrugged and dismissed the rider, deciding that she must be mistaken. It would be too much of a coincidence.

"Let's move on." Cole waded the horse out of the stream and waited while Wynne took another long drink, then rose and walked over to him slowly.

Their eyes met, and she waited for him to help her mount the horse.

On her nose was a stray droplet of water and Cole's attention was drawn to it. His eyes softened and grew tender as his finger reached out to brush it away, but he suddenly changed his mind and let his hand drop back to his side.

She gazed up at him expectantly. "What's the matter?"

"You have water on your nose," he said brusquely. What he had wanted to say was she looked too damn kissable! He knew the texture of her mouth beneath his, how it tasted, how it blended with his until he thought he would take leave of what little senses he had managed to hold on to when she was in his arms.

"Oh." Disappointedly she reached up and removed the droplet, then smiled at him. "There. Is that better?"

Keeping his gaze averted, Cole nodded yes and quickly lifted her back into the saddle.

She was incredibly close, close enough for him to see the black specs in the green of her eyes. And Cole's resolve faltered. Wynne couldn't have looked elsewhere if her life depended on it. She wanted so badly for Cole to hold her again, to whisper those wonderful things he did when he made love to her.

"I wish you wouldn't look at me that way," he said uncomfortably, careful not to reveal any of the tension growing steadily inside his trousers.

"And I wish you didn't look the way you do!" she replied defensively, but both their tones were tempered with something close to affection.

Gathering up the reins, Cole turned away quickly.

"Aren't you going to ride?" she asked with surprise as he began to walk the horse at a fast pace down the rutted lane.

"No, ma'am. I'm walkin'." The last thing he needed right now was to ride in that close saddle with her molded to him as tightly as his pants were!

By the time the Claxton farm came into view the next morning, Wynne and Cole released audible sighs of relief. Their close proximity of the past few days had their nerves humming as tautly as telegraph lines.

The household seemed to be all aflutter as Cole lifted Wynne off the horse. "What's going on?" he wondered aloud, his attention focused on the tables and chairs that had been set up in the cherry grove.

"Looks like your mother's havin' a party."

Cole led the horse toward the barn while Wynne took a deep breath and tried to gather her courage. Willa was hanging wash, her large body dipping up and down rhythmically as she retrieved the wet pieces one by one and pinned them onto the line. She momentarily glanced up at the new arrivals and grinned a friendly welcome, then went back to her chore.

Wynne shuffled slowly toward the house. The thought of facing Lilly and Beau again crept over her like a dreadful blight.

But it shouldn't have as Betsy, her face alight with pleasure at seeing her new friend again, burst out through the back door.

"Wynne! I do declare, you're a sight for sore eyes!" The young woman threw her arms around her exuberantly as they hugged hello. "Where in the world did you disappear to?" Betsy demanded.

Hearing all the commotion, Lilly poked her head out the back door to see what was going on. Seeing Wynne happily ensconced in Betsy's arms, she flew out the back door, her feet barely touching the steps. "Wynne, darlin', how good to see you back!"

After a tight hug Lilly held her away from her bosom and surveyed her disreputable condition with growing distress. "Oh, dear, I suppose this means your trip has been unsuccessful. You didn't find your friend?"

Wynne's eyes fell away guiltily. "No, I wasn't able to find a sign of him."

"Oh, I'm so sorry."

"It's all right. I've changed my mind about trying to locate him." She lifted her eyes back to Lilly's. "I've decided to go back to Savannah instead."

"Well." Lilly heaved a sigh of relief. "I must say I think that would be for the best."

Amid a new round of female chatter Cole came out of the barn and was quickly caught up in the homecoming festivities.

"Land sakes alive! You're home too?" Lilly peered over his shoulder hopefully. "I don't guess you ran into your brother anywhere along the way?"

"No, Ma, but I heard Cass made it through the war." Cole smiled wearily, glad to be able to give her that small ray of hope.

"You did!" Lilly clapped her hands together gleefully. "Well, praise the Lord! I just knew he would. Surely he'll be ridin' in any day now."

Cole grinned lamely and shrugged. "I reckon anything's possible."

"Why, course, it's possible," she said. "He'll be home anytime now. You just wait and see." She turned her attention back to Wynne. "How did you get here, dear?" Lilly had heard only one rider enter the farmyard.

"I ran into Wynne a ways back on the road. Her, uh, horse had bolted and run away, so I gave her a ride," Cole said before Wynne could answer.

"Your horse ran away?" Lilly's face was instantly filled with concern as her eyes ran over the bedraggled young woman standing forlornly beside Betsy. "Why, I thought you left on the stage."

"No—no, I decided to buy a horse instead," Wynne said meekly, leaving out the fact that a quarrelsome mule had been her traveling companion.

"Great day! I'm glad I didn't know that." Lilly sighed. "I'da worried myself to death. I hope you weren't hurt when the horse threw you, dear."

Wynne smiled. "No. I'm fine." Her fingers dug into her dirty dress embarrassedly. "But the blasted thing took all my clothes with it!" she snapped heatedly. "Now I don't have a thing to wear."

Draping a protective arm around her, Betsy rushed to allay her worries. "Now don't you worry a bit." She consoled her as she led Wynne to the house. "We'll get you into a hot tub of water, and after you're bathed, you can borrow some of my things. I'm a little larger than you, but I think I have a blue calico that will look just wonderful on you!"

Wynne smiled gratefully. "Thank you, Betsy. I surely would appreciate it." She glanced at Cole, then dropped her gaze away shyly. Betsy was still chattering like an old blue jay as the two women disappeared in the house.

Wrapping an arm around her son's waist, Lilly followed at a slower pace. "You think she's really all right, dear?"

Cole's eyes had followed Wynne until he could no longer see her. "She's okay, Ma."

"Well, she's sure a lucky little ol' thing to have you coming along to save her just at the right time," Lilly said, hoping her older son might take a closer look now that Wynne was back.

"Uh-huh, I suppose," he said distractedly. "Where's Beau?"

"Mending fences. He'll be along after a while to eat his dinner. How'd your business go in Kansas City?"

"Fine." His eyes took in the cherry orchard once more. "What's goin' on?"

"Oh, Beau and Betsy was gettin' all astir to announce their engagement, so we thought we'd sort of have an informal party so's they could hint around to all their friends that the weddin' was still on."

"You were goin' to have an engagement party without me and Cass!" Cole said with mock astonishment, knowing full well Lilly would never consider such an event without having her entire family present.

"Oh, no, dear. It isn't an official engagement party! Just sort of a Saturday night shindig. The actual announcement of Beau and Betsy's weddin' won't be made until the fall sometime," she told him quickly.

Cole squeezed his mother's shoulder affectionately. "I was just teasin' you, Ma. I know you wouldn't do that."

She reached up and tugged the three-day wiry growth that lay dark and thick across her eldest son's handsome face. Sam. He was Sam Claxton all over again, and it made her want to shout for joy that the good Lord had left a small part of her deceased husband on this earth to give her such comfort. "You think I don't know you and your tomfoolery by now?" She smacked him on his backside playfully. "Now you get on into the house and tell Willa to fetch you some bath water. There's gonna be a party tonight." Her eyes sparkled brightly with anticipation of things to come. "There's gonna be singin' and dancin' the likes of which you haven't seen or heard for five long years!"

CHAPTER 16

LATE IN THE AFTERNOON A CROWD BEGAN CONVERGing on the Claxton ranch. Everyone was ready for a celebration and came with a lightness of heart that left not one somber look on anyone's face. Music filled the air, and the sound of laughter bubbled over the hillsides as the party got into full swing.

Wynne could hear the sounds of women's laughter, mixed with the deeper sounds of men's baritone voices, while she finished dressing in her room. She smiled at her reflection in the mirror as she heard a woman's high squeal and a man's booming laughter.

Tonight was supposed to be a happy time, and she didn't begrudge the silly shenanigans going on down there. But her smile slowly faded as the pain of reality closed in on her once more. She wished only that she and Cole could be a part of that lightheartedness.

What a wondrous delight it would be if they could forget what lay between them, and he would swing her up in his arms and haul her off to the barn to steal a kiss from her or whatever else he might be inclined to steal. But Cole would never do that. He never teased, he never showed what he was feeling except for the brief moments when passion overrode his pride, and he would most assuredly never haul her off to the barn in front of everyone. Yet it would be nice if he were that sort of man.

Wynne's musings were interrupted by the soft tap on the door and Betsy calling her name.

They had talked long into the afternoon as Betsy had helped her bathe and dress. Betsy encouraged Wynne to stay on in River Run while she arranged her newly washed and dried hair in a mass of shiny curls on top of her head, but Wynne would not be swayed. She would leave on the morning stage, and her decision was final. There was absolutely no reason for her to remain where she was not welcome, and Cole's quiet estrangement on the ride home had assured her that he would make no effort to try to change her mind.

When she'd told him of her decision earlier this evening, he'd met her announcement with the same calm indifference he had exhibited when they first met. All he'd said was that she should be ready by first light and he would take her into town and purchase a ticket for her if that was what she had a mind to do.

So tomorrow morning she would be on her way back to Savannah with a broken heart, but at least it would be a fresh one.

Betsy and Wynne walked down the stairway together and were greeted by whistles of male admiration. But there was only one man's reaction Wynne longed for, and he was nowhere to be found. In fact, it was late in the evening before Cole finally made an appearance at the party.

Wynne's heart threatened to stop beating when she saw him walk down the stairway and pause to speak to Betsy's sister, Priscilla June. He looked unbearably handsome, and Wynne was sure her love for him was written so clearly on her face that the whole room would soon know her secret.

She wasn't the only woman in the room who had spotted his entrance. A small crowd of women had gathered by the stairway, vying for his attention, but Priscilla had already staked her claim as she cooed and fussed over Cole until Wynne wanted to march right over and snatch her hair out by the roots.

He glanced up from saying something to Priscilla and their eyes met and suddenly every other person in the room disappeared.

She fought to hide her feelings but knew she was failing miserably. She could only stare back at him with her heart in her eyes and pray he wouldn't turn away from her.

The blue of his eyes darkened as they ran lazily over the dress she was wearing. The blue dress with tiny pink flowers hugged her breasts and accentuated her tiny waist. Cole felt the ever-familiar painful tightening in his loins that inevitably occurred when he was around her.

For a moment they stood transcended in time. It was as if the world held no one else but them. And then he smiled at her, a slow, incredibly intimate smile that told her that no matter what their differences, he had not forgotten what they had shared, nor would he ever.

She smiled back, a trembling, not at all certain smile, just enough to let him know that she understood and fondly shared his remembrances.

Then the magic was broken when Priscilla took his arm. Shattered, Wynne moved on through the crowd, trying to bite back the welling tears.

The night became a blur as she danced and laughed and tried to forget that after tomorrow she would never see Cole Claxton again.

Finally around midnight she gave up all pretense and slipped quietly around the corner of the house to go to her room. Cole's voice stopped her as she reached Lilly's flower garden. "Turnin' in so early?"

The familiar aroma of his cigar permeated the air. Wynne's footsteps faltered, and she shut her eyes in emotional pain. She didn't think she could stand another encounter with him tonight. "Yes. I'm . . . a little tired."

"Uh-huh," he intoned. "I can imagine. It was a long trip, and tomorrow you have another one facin' you."

She couldn't see him, only the tip of his cheroot glowing in the shadows. "Yes." She gathered her light shawl closer to her bosom and started to walk on.

"What's your hurry, Miss Elliot?" he asked in an easy voice.

Once more her steps slowed, and she paused. "I told you. I'm very tired."

He finally stepped out of the shadows and joined her. Her breath caught and held as she gazed up at him. The rays of the silvery moonlight played across his face, and she longed to have him take her in his arms and tell her that he loved her, that it didn't matter what she had been about to do to his brother at one time, that the only thing that really mattered was that she was in love with him now and it would be so foolish to throw away that rare, wondrous miracle simply because of her past stupidities.

He could do worse in a bride, Wynne assured herself. She could make him proud. She would use all the skills Miss Fielding had taught her until one day he would look at her as a lady, not some bumbling nincompoop! If he would only give her a chance. But how did she tell him that without making another absolute fool of herself?

It was plain to see he didn't return her feelings. No, he would only laugh and tell her she obviously didn't know what man she loved. First Cass, now him.

She could never bear that.

She turned and started away again, but his hand reached out to stop her. "Dammit, Wynne, don't go in yet." His voice had suddenly lost its earlier arrogance. Instead, it held a soft, almost urgent plea. Her breath caught as he swung her roughly around and took her in his arms, his mouth hungrily seeking and finding hers.

She melted in his arms like soft butter. This was what she'd wanted, what she'd longed for all evening as she had gaily danced with first one man and then another. She returned the kiss with such fervor it made Cole groan with newly aroused need. He pulled her closer, crushing her breasts against the solid wall of his chest in an embrace that threatened to overpower her.

Where the kiss would have ended, she could only guess because it was sadly interrupted a few moments later by Beau's calling her name.

"Don't answer," Cole murmured raggedly. "We have to talk." His mouth took hers again with fierce possession.

But Beau's voice persisted as it came closer to where they stood sheltered in the shadows. "Wynne?"

"I have to answer," she whispered. "In a few more minutes he'll see us, Cole."

Cole swore under his breath as he realized the wisdom of her words and reluctantly released her. A moment later she stepped quietly out of the shadows. "Yes, Beau?"

"Oh, there you are." He came forward with a large grin on his face. "There's someone here lookin' for you."

"Me?" Wynne asked with surprise.

Beau shrugged. "Yeah. Some guy came ridin' in awhile ago. Said he would have been here earlier, but his horse threw a shoe—oh, hello, Cole. Didn't see you standin' back there." Beau's grin widened knowingly.

"Who's lookin' for her?"

"Don't know. Some fellow says it's real important that he talk to Wynne."

"She's not talkin' to any man tonight," Cole stated flatly, a new round of jealousy overtaking him. "Tell him to come back tomorrow morning and call on her proper."

"Good heavens, Cole. He's not calling on me," Wynne protested lightly. She was thrilled to hear jealousy seeping into his tone, yet she couldn't imagine who her unknown visitor was. She didn't know anyone in River Run. "Where is the man, Beau?"

"Out front. Ma made him sit down and drink something cool. He looked a mite peaked when he got here."

Wynne glanced at Cole expectantly. "It wouldn't hurt for me to see what he wants, would it?" She couldn't bear the curiosity until morning.

When she looked at him like that, Cole would have given her anything she wanted. "I don't like it, but go ahead. See what he wants."

She smiled and slipped away as Cole reached in his shirt pocket for another cigar.

"Aren't you going to go with her?" Beau asked lightly.

"I got no claim on who she sees," Cole replied curtly, but his insides were tight with the thought of another man demanding her time.

The young man awaiting her managed to paste a pleasant smile on his face in spite of his discomfort as Wynne entered the parlor. The back brace the doctor had rigged up was hot and bothering him something fierce, and it was the end of a long and particularly tedious day. When Wynne approached him, his face immediately went slack with astonishment.

For a moment Wynne surveyed him quizzically. Then she smiled in recognition and moved across the room to take his hand. "Well, hello again." He was the same young man she had seen twice before, once sitting on a porch, whittling, as she had ridden through Springfield, and only yesterday, when they'd stopped to water their horses.

"*You're* Wynne Elliot!" His voice cracked and sounded as if he had just entered puberty again.

She smiled expectantly. "Yes."

She noticed his large Adam's apple bobbing up and down nervously as he tried to regain his composure. Leaping lizards! For months he'd been chasing this woman across country, and she had passed him twice already!

"Miss Elliot . . . I had no idea that was you . . ." His voice trailed off weakly.

Wynne continued to smile at the pale young man, wondering what in heaven's name he wanted with her.

Remembering his manners, Bertram wiped his hand nervously on the side of his trousers, then politely extended it to her. "Bertram G. Mallory, ma'am."

"Mr. Mallory." Wynne tipped her head and accepted his hand graciously. Perhaps this was another one of the lawyers from her father's estate, though he certainly didn't look like a lawyer.

"Oh, ma'am, you don't know how nice it is finally to meet you!"

"Why, thank you." She smiled again. "I believe you wanted to speak with me?"

"Oh, yes, ma'am." He could still hardly believe Wynne Elliot was finally standing there in front of him. "I'm with the Pinkerton Detective Agency—you've heard of us, haven't you?"

Wynne nodded. She had read about Alan Pinkerton in a paper one time. He was a man from Glasgow, Scotland, who now lived in Chicago and had made a name for himself by recovering a large sum of money for the Adams Express Company. The paper had said he was also credited for uncovering a plot to murder the late President Abraham Lincoln.

"Well, ma'am, I was hired by Mr. Claxton to return this to you." He began to search through his pockets, extracting his billfold, a comb, a pocketknife, and his gun, all which he promptly handed to her. "Excuse me, ma'am, could you hold these for a minute?"

"Yes, certainly." Wynne took the items, and he continued his search. "You said Mr. Claxton sent you?"

"Yeah . . . yeah . . . now wait . . . I know it's here somewhere." His face suddenly brightened. "Yes! Here it is!" He quickly slapped a leather pouch into her hand and immediately felt as if a ton of weight had just been lifted off his shoulders.

"Cass . . . Claxton?" she asked again as her smile began to fade.

"Yes, ma'am. It's the money you lent him."

Wynne's hand clasped the pouch and the wallet and the comb and the gun tighter as her eyes narrowed in anger. If this was someone's idea of a joke, it wasn't very funny. "The money I lent him. What are you talking about?"

"It's all there, ma'am. Every cent of it. Cass gave it to me, to give back to you, the day you two was supposed to be married." Bertram peered back at her from eyes that were bloodshot and ringed with road grime, but they were good, honest eyes. "I've tried real hard to find you, ma'am. Honest I have. I had been in bed with a bad case of the miseries the day Mr. Claxton came to my door, so I couldn't bring the money back right then. I got up early the next morning and went to your house, but you were already gone back to Miss Fielding's school, so I went lookin' for you there, but I missed you again." He sighed hopelessly. "From then on every time I got close to you, either you disappeared again or I had another one of them damn—oh, pardon my language, ma'am—accidents."

The mere thought of those flukes made his ribs, his leg, and his back begin to pain all over again. "Then I heard you was on your way to River Run, so I figured I'd try to catch you before you got to Mr. Claxton's folks, 'cause he told me River Run was where he originally came from and he had just been visitin' kinfolks in Savannah. I was afraid you'd get here ahead of me and tell them what you thought he had done to you, and it would all be a big mistake 'cause Mr. Claxton didn't really take your money like you must be thinkin' he did." Bertram hung his head sheepishly. "Sure sorry I didn't make it in time. I know you must be thinkin' all sorts of bad things about him—and ma'am? About his marryin' you? Well, I was supposed to tell you he loved you an' all, but he just sort of got cold feet and decided maybe he wasn't quite ready to get hitched yet, only he didn't have the heart to tell you. He told me he knew he was probably makin' a big mistake 'cause you was one of the prettiest and nicest women he'd ever met, but he thought maybe he had a lot of growin' up to do before he settled down to raisin' a family."

While Bertram rattled on, Wynne's face was a mask of conflicting emotions: disbelief, jubilation, incredulity, exultation. If what this man was saying was true, then these horrendous past few months had been for nothing! She had been running around vowing revenge on a man who was guilty of nothing more serious than being afraid of the responsibility of taking a wife and of hurting her even more by going through with an ill-advised marriage.

Wynne frowned, her eyes going to the gun she was holding. Good Lord, *what* if she had been able to find Cass and actually carry out her threat? No, she realized now that she would have never actually been able to kill him. Wring his neck as she had that chicken maybe, but kill him? No, never! Then her face lit with renewed elation. In a way Cass's deserting her at the altar had been a blessing because she realized now that what she had felt for him was not love, not in comparison with what she felt for Cole. Her smile faded again. And what was *he* going to say, other than "I told you so," when he learned that his brother had made provisions for her money to be returned all along but she had been too busy seeking revenge to stop long enough for Mr. Mallory to find her?

Wynne breathed a long, deep sigh. It all was very confusing.

"Ma'am?" Bertram was keeping a careful eye on the rapid play of emotions across her face, and he wasn't quite sure how she was taking the news.

She glanced up. "Yes?"

"Are you . . . all right?"

"Oh, yes, yes. I'm just fine." Or at least she would be as soon as her mind was able to digest the past few moments. "I can't thank you enough, Mr. Mallory, for finally locating me. You've made me a happy woman."

"Oh, that's all right, ma'am." Bertram began to gather up his wallet and comb from her safekeeping. "Mr. Claxton paid me handsomely, and I'm just doin' my job." Of course, he had spent every penny Cass had given him, plus his own substantial fee while trying to locate her; but that wasn't her fault, and Bertram was too much of a gentleman to tell her about all his problems.

Outside, someone let out a loud war hoop as the sound of approaching hoofbeats thundered into the farmyard. A crescendo of voices rang out as Wynne heard "Cass! Cass is comin'!" being shouted in excited voices.

Bertram stepped over to the window and lifted the curtain. "Oh, my, looks like Mr. Claxton could have delivered the money a whole lot easier himself," Bertram said uneasily. He'd best try to slip out the back way before he had to face Cass and have him find out he had just now returned the lady's money.

Wynne suddenly came back to life, the shock of the past few moments finally wearing off. "Good heavens! Cass is home!"

Funny, an hour ago those words would have meant very little, but now all she could feel was extreme joy. Cole and Beau would have their brother back, and Lilly's youngest son would have returned home safely.

Letting out a squeal that would have shocked Miss Fielding right down to her prissy old corset, Wynne, still carrying Bertram's gun, bolted out of the room in order to be one of the first to greet him. Cass was home, and he wasn't the scoundrel she had thought him to be at all! She had to tell him she forgave him and make peace. Then maybe she and Cole . . .

Wynne skidded to a stop halfway across the parlor and whirled around to rush back over and give Bertram a large, energetic hug. "Oooooh, thank you, Mr. Mallory, thank you ever so much," then spun around again and raced out the two wide parlor doors at full speed.

"Ma'am, my gun." But Wynne had already disappeared out the doorway. With a resigned sigh he rushed out after her.

Cole was just on his way to check on Wynne when she buzzed by him like an angry hornet, flailing the gun in the air, nearly knocking him over in her hurried exit.

"Hey, what's the hurry?"

He reached out to slow her passage, but she only shrugged his hand away and yelled over her shoulder as she flew out the front door, "Can't stop now! Cass is comin'!"

"Ma'am, the gun!" Bertram said again as he hurried along to keep up with her, but to his dismay she still wasn't listening.

The smile that had been on Cole's face drained away to a weak facsimile as the meaning of her words sank in. And she had been waving a gun. Oh, hell. His feet suddenly went into action as he tore behind her and the man following close behind.

"Wynne, wait!" he shouted.

But she ignored him, too, and kept on running.

Oh, Lord, she'll kill him! he thought as he ran faster.

Her total being bent on reaching Cass first, Wynne, a radiant smile on her face, had burst through the crowd on the porch and down the steps, running toward the rider who had just entered the yard. All she could think of was the fact that she wanted to thank Cass for being so honest! Not only had he restored her faith in men, but maybe, just maybe he had just provided a future for Cole and her!

Bertram was making his way out of the house as Cole rushed by like a streak of lightning, nearly knocking him off his feet in his hasty exit.

"Oh, sorry, fella." Cole hurriedly steadied his swaying form. Then the front screen slammed loudly as Bertram straightened up and readjusted his hat. Oh, lordy. If he could just get out of here and be on his way back to Fancy without further injury, then he would swear he would change profession first thing tomorrow morning. He decided to forget the gun and just pray he wouldn't need it until he got back to Springfield. He pushed open the screen door and headed directly for his horse, hoping to make a quick exit from this madhouse.

Cole was gaining on Wynne as he jumped the porch railing. "Wynne!" he shouted again, drawing everyone's attention to the chase. "Stop!"

By now Wynne had nearly reached Cass, and Cole exerted every ounce of strength he had to overtake her.

Bertram had managed to get outside and to his horse. Watching the two crazy people chasing each other across the yard from the corner of his eye, Bertram got one foot in the stirrup just as his horse began to shy.

The crowd was standing still, watching the spectacle of a red-headed woman running across the yard toward the new arrival and a man following close behind, shouting for her to stop! Bertram swore irritably under his breath and fought to control his horse, trying to swing his stiff body into the saddle.

"Wynne!" Cole yelled again. "I won't let you do it."

In one huge flying leap he shouted, "No, don't, Wynne!" then tackled her just as Cass reined his horse to a skidding halt.

Surprised by the number of people at the house this late at night, Cass watched openmouthed, trying to control his prancing horse, as a man who looked suspiciously like his older brother tackled a young red-headed woman who was waving a gun in the air. No, it couldn't be! Was that Wynne Elliot?

Bertram had managed to get one foot in the stirrup, but his horse was prancing so frantically from the unaccustomed clamor taking place around him that he couldn't finish mounting, nor could he get his foot loose.

"Oh, please, Lord! Not again." Bertram begged, still trying to convince the horse to stop jumping around. "If you're ever gonna help me, do it right now!" he beseeched, pulling the reins to get his animal at least going in a direction he could control.

With his back held immobile, Bertram couldn't bend enough to mount unless the horse stood still. With a quick glance over his shoulder, he saw the fiasco continuing and strove even harder to control his horse so he could get his foot loose. His ankle was still a little weak, and now his back was killing him again, and these fool people were intent on murdering one another in front of their own house! Once again he fervently wished he'd never met up with the Claxtons.

"Hold it, horse. Whoa, boy, whoa!" Bertram pleaded.

The impact of Cole's landing on her had not only surprised but hurt Wynne. And it made her mad! Darn mad!

"Get off me!" she screeched, kicking and elbowing him. "What in the world is the matter with you?"

"Don't do it!" Cole was trying to still her flailing limbs, fighting to gain control of the gun. His heavy body pinned her to the ground as he grasped her wrists tightly. "Don't . . . Wynne."

"Don't what?" What on earth was he babbling about? It never occurred to her that she still had possession of Mr. Mallory's gun, or that Cole had no idea what had taken place in the parlor a few moments earlier, or that she had neglected to tell him on the ride home that she no longer wanted to kill Cass, that she now loved Cole Claxton, not his brother.

"Don't shoot him—please." A "please!" From Cole Claxton! Wynne felt she'd just witnessed a miracle.

"Shoot him? Whatever are you talking about?"

Cole's eyes were locked with hers pleadingly as his words began to seep in and she finally noticed the gun was still in her hand. "Oh, darling! I wasn't going to shoot him!" she exclaimed as she flung the weapon away from her. "I was only going to thank him for being so honest and nice. . . ." Her words trailed away meekly as she saw the pleading look in Cole's eyes begin to change.

"Thank him!" Cole exploded. Here he had nearly killed himself these past few weeks trying to prevent his brother from being ambushed, by her, and now she was going to "thank" him for being so nice!

"Well, yes . . ." Wynne knew she had a bit of explaining to do as Cole slowly stood back up and pulled her to her feet. "You see that man who wanted to see me in the parlor . . ."

While she was explaining Bertram's mission, he still had one foot caught in the stirrup and was bouncing about helplessly, swearing under his breath and trying to protect his one good leg as the horse shied away from him.

As Cole listened with amazement, the sound of running horses caught their attention. With a boil of dust and a loud "Ho! Ho, there!" a buckboard driven by a rather flamboyant woman swung crazily into the yard. With a flash of red satin she bounded down and immediately rushed to Bertram's rescue.

"Fancy!" Bertram blurted, seeing his fiancée rushing toward him.

"Oh, Bertie, darlin', let me help you." Grabbing the reins of the horse, she managed to still the animal while he jerked his aching foot free from the binding stirrup.

"What are you doin' here?" he said gratefully, a big grin covering his face now that he was safely out of harm's way with no new injuries.

She reached out and touched his cheek reverently. Fully aware of Bertram's uncanny ability to harm himself, she'd followed at a close distance, curiosity as well as love prompting her. "I just sort of thought you might need me, Bertie."

Although he had faithfully promised he would return for her, she wasn't taking any chances. Bertram G. Mallory was a rare man, and he was *hers*.

"Aw, Fancy, I do need you"—Bertram grinned humbly—"for the rest of my life."

By now Cass had dismounted and was enveloped in Lilly's tearful embrace. He had no idea what was going on; but he was finally home, and that was all that mattered.

Lilly had no idea why Cole had been wallowing in the dirt with Wynne, nor did Cass, but they supposed that in good time it all would come out. Those two were going to make a fine couple, Lilly thought jubilantly as she and Cass stepped lightly around the warring couple and merged into the happy crowd.

"—and so you see, I don't hate Cass anymore," Wynne was saying lovingly. "He didn't steal my money or my heart. I just thought he did."

"Oh, honey." Cole heaved a relieved sigh. "Then you've finally got all this avenging nonsense out of your head?"

Wynne nodded repentantly.

"And you'd be willing to listen if another man said he loved you?"

She grinned. "Only if *you* say it."

"Okay, here goes, but I don't know how good I'll be at sayin' it. . . ." Cole had never told any woman he loved her, but he was going to make a stab at it.

"Just say it," she begged, her hands framing his handsome face.

"I—I love you," he admitted gruffly. "I know that you thought you had reason to doubt those words coming from a Claxton, but I mean them, Wynne." His voice lowered intimately as he pulled her up closer to him, his mouth only inches away from hers. "You know I mean them."

She wasn't sure how many surprises she could stand in one day, but this one was even more thrilling than the last. "You really do?"

Cole's face suddenly grew playful. "Are you strong as a bull moose and healthy as a horse? Can you wrestle an Indian brave, cut a rick of wood without raisin' a sweat, and forget all about being a lady in my bed?" He already knew the answer to that one.

She smiled at him sweetly. "If you want me to, I certainly can."

"Then I really do love you, lady," he said, "and I want you for my wife."

"Well, there is Moss Oak . . . I don't know . . ." She wanted ten seconds to think it over, as a matter of principle, but she knew Cole would help her settle the problem of the plantation.

"You'd better," he said with a knowing wink. " 'Cause you're gonna have my baby."

She blinked indignantly. "I am not!"

He ran the tip of his tongue around her lower lip suggestively, hoping he spoke the truth. He had made sure there was a strong chance she carried his child before they had left the cabin. "Well, we'll see come next May."

She touched her tongue to his and brought forth the low groan she was seeking. "You think that bothers me?" She would gladly settle for being his wife and having Claxton children by the dozens, rather than run around the countryside trying to avenge her honor. It *had* to be a whole lot easier.

"It doesn't? Then I suppose we'll just have to make darn sure I got the job done," he whispered suggestively against the sweetness of her mouth.

Scooping her up in his arms, he grinned and winked at his brothers as he proceeded to carry her down toward the barn, kissing her breathless with every step he took, right in front of all those people!

Well, wonders of wonders, Wynne thought, grinning at his handsome face. Cole Claxton was romantic after all!

PASSION'S
CAPTIVE

To
Janet and Tom Colliatie:
CHERISHED   FRIENDS

CHAPTER 1

Missouri, September 1867

THE DAY HAD STARTED LIKE ANY ORDINARY ONE.

The pungent aroma of earth mixed pleasantly with the tangy smell of sweat rolling in rivulets down the back of the tall, powerfully built man who gently urged the team of oxen to pull their heavy load. Overhead, the bright sun hammered down on man and animals as they steadfastly went about furrowing the ground for fall planting.

Nature's elements rarely bothered Beau Claxton. Truth be, nothing much bothered him because he was an inordinately happy man. The good Lord had provided a roof over his head, food on his table, close family ties, and the prettiest, sweetest woman in all of Missouri for his wife.

As far as Beau was concerned, he had everything a man could ever want.

Oh, he had to admit that times were still hard. The country was trying to put itself back together since the War Between the States, and many people still went to bed hungry each night, but Beau knew he and his family had fared better than most.

Beau's mother, Lilly, still lived on the old homestead a couple of miles down the road. His father, Samuel Claxton, had moved his wife and their two sons from Georgia to Missouri when Beau and his older brother had been small.

Cass, Beau's youngest brother, had been born shortly before Samuel had died. Beau's eldest brother, Cole, and his wife, Wynne, lived two miles on the other side of Beau's land. Fifteen months ago they'd produced a baby boy named Jeremy who was growing like a weed and cute as a bug's ear.

Beau had to grin when he thought about how downright silly Cole was about his wife. They both acted like lovestruck youngsters whenever they were together. Beau would've bet his spring crop that no woman could have worked Cole Claxton into such a lather, but two years ago the feisty little woman from Savannah had waltzed in and stolen Cole's heart, and the man hadn't been the same since.

But Beau understood how Cole felt. As he gave a sharp whistle for Sally to yaw right, Beau's grin broadened. Hadn't Betsy Collins done the same thing to him? He recalled how they'd no sooner decided to marry than war had broken out. Beau had left to join the fight, and when he returned, Betsy was still waiting for him. Though they'd married two years ago, Betsy could still make his insides go soft when she smiled up at him with those big blue eyes.

Just the thought of holding her in his arms and making love to her caused a familiar ache to tighten his loins. Any day now, they'd be having their own child—a son, he hoped, though a little girl wouldn't upset him any. It had seemed to take forever for Betsy to get in the family way, but the Doc had said she was healthy as a horse and should be able to have all the babies they wanted. And Beau wanted a large family.

"Easy, girls, easy." Beau turned the oxen and leaned over to wipe his dusty face on the sleeve of his sweat-dampened shirt. The days were still hot, even though they were nearing the end of September. Beau would welcome the cooler days and crisp nights of October. There was still a lot of work to be done before winter. He had to butcher the old sow, lay in a good supply of firewood, and stock the root cellar. . . .

The sound of Betsy's voice made him glance up and slow the team's pace. He grinned at her and waved. Must be close to noon, he thought, and she's bringin' my dinner. His mouth watered at the thought of the fatback and cornbread she'd have in his dinner pail. She'd been making fried apple pies when he'd left the house. No doubt she'd packed a couple of those too.

He heard her call to him again, and Beau whistled for Kate and Sally to halt. Strange, he thought, Betsy wasn't walkin' toward him like she usually did. He enjoyed watching her move. The enticing swing of her hips always managed to get his juices flowing, even when they shouldn't be. After their meal, they'd often lie under the old cottonwood tree and kiss. Like as not, they'd end up making love, and it'd be well past his allotted rest hour when he'd finally go back to work.

Betsy called his name a third time, and Beau's smile began to fade. He dropped the reins and shaded his eyes against the hot sun to see her more clearly.

Her slender frame, swollen with child, was silhouetted against a broad expanse of blue sky. For a moment he hesitated, expecting Betsy to start toward him again. But she lifted her hand feebly in the air, and then dropped to her knees.

A cold wave of fear shot through him, and his feet began to move. Something was wrong. The baby. Yes, that's it, he reasoned, as he began to pick up speed. The baby was coming, and Betsy was scared. How many times had he told her not to be afraid; he'd be there with her when their child was born. He'd be there to share her pain, to hold her hand, to tell her how proud he was that she was the mother of his child. Together they'd share an incredible joy when their son or daughter came into the world.

Beau was running fast now, taking long deep breaths as he watched Betsy slump down on the ground. His feet covered the hard-packed dirt with lightning speed. "I'm comin', Bets!" he called to her.

She raised her head once as if she were trying to answer him, but with growing horror Beau saw her fall back limply to the ground.

God . . . oh, God . . . Beau's lungs felt as though they'd explode as he raced to her. Something deep inside told him that this was more than their baby coming, but Beau refused to listen. On he went, over rough tufts of ground, his boots gouging the dry, crusty earth, his eyes never once leaving the silent form crumpled close to the woodpile.

It couldn't be anything serious . . . she was teasing him . . . no, Betsy never tried to scare him . . . it had to be the baby . . . maybe she was going to have a harder time than most . . . the pains were sharp, and she'd dropped to the ground to wait for him . . . that must be it. . . .

Gut-wrenching fear clutched his windpipe as Beau pushed himself faster. Betsy wasn't moving. She lay on the ground in deathlike stillness.

When Beau finally reached Betsy, he fell to the ground and gathered her in his strong arms. His heart was pounding, and his breath was coming in painful gasps as he cradled her head and called her name.

At the sound of his voice, her eyes opened slowly, and she smiled at him. With trembling fingers she reached up to touch his cheek and felt his tears drip gently on her hand.

"What is it, sweetheart? The baby . . . is it the baby?" he prompted in a voice husky with emotion.

"My baby . . ." she whispered softly, so softly that he could scarcely make out her words. "Dear God, Beau . . . our baby. . . ."

"Bets, what's wrong? Tell me, sweetheart. Should I get Ma or Wynne?"

She lifted her hand to cover his lips. "Snake . . . over by the woodpile . . . rattler . . . don't worry . . . it's dead now. . . ."

Rattler! The word hit him with the force of a bullet, and suddenly he felt his heart drop to his stomach.

He whirled around, his distraught gaze searching the woodpile by the house until he saw the sickening evidence. A large timber rattlesnake, almost seven feet in length, was stretched out on the ground. Its head, severed by a hoe, lay in the dust some five feet away. The small pile of wood Betsy had been gathering was scattered about the ground, mute testimony of what had happened. Betsy had encountered the snake unexpectedly while gathering wood to prepare dinner.

Immediately, Beau began searching for the bite. If she'd been bitten by a rattler, there wasn't much time.

"Where's the bite, Betsy?" Beau's voice trembled, but he fought to remain calm. He didn't want to scare her more. She moaned softly, and he remembered that she should be still. The more she moved, the faster the poison would spread through her body. "Don't move, sweetheart, I'll find it . . . I'll find it!" His eyes and hands searched her body. It didn't take long to locate the two small puncture marks on her right arm. He bit back a shout of despair as he saw the angry swelling. My God, it had hit the vein squarely.

Beau swallowed the knot in his throat. He knew without being told that the poison would go straight to her heart; there was nothing, *nothing* he could do to save her.

But he'd try. Swiftly, he pulled his knife from his pocket and cut two small slits across the vein. He brought her arm to his mouth and sucked the venom, then spat it on the ground, while he stemmed the tears brimming in his eyes.

When he'd done all he knew to do, he talked to her in soft, reassuring tones, telling her how much he loved her, reminding her of the good life they'd share with their baby. He whispered to Betsy not to be afraid. He'd protect her and never let anything hurt her again. He apologized for being neglectful, and promised her that from now on he'd make certain there was sufficient wood in the box before he left the house every day. He should have done that anyway, he agonized, though Betsy had insisted on carrying the wood herself.

"Don't leave me, Bets," he pleaded as he heard her moans growing weaker. "God, I have to go for help," he murmured a few moments later when he saw her face turn a ghastly shade of white. "I have to get the Doc out here—"

"No . . . no . . . don't leave me, Beau." Her hands clasped him anxiously, and he rested his head on the swollen mound of her stomach as both began to sob softly. They knew what was happening, and Betsy needed him with her now.

Beau began to pray. Lifting his face to the sky, he begged and pleaded and promised until he became outraged. Then he threatened. Tears streamed down his cheeks as he railed against the unfairness. He'd been taught that there was a God who cared, a God who watched over him, a kind, benevolent God. Surely such a God wouldn't take his wife and child from him in such a cruel and senseless way.

Paralyzed with terror, Beau clutched Betsy and crooned to her, rocking her back and forth, gently back and forth, back and forth, until the sun began to dip low on the western horizon. The golden rays spread across the parched earth, enveloping the young couple in an ethereal glow. Still Beau wouldn't let go.

He didn't know the exact moment she left him. His arms had grown numb from holding her, yet he could not release her. If he put Betsy down, she'd be gone from him forever, and he couldn't accept that.

It was his brother, Cole, who found them.

Cole had known something was wrong when he rode through the newly furrowed field and saw the oxen, Kate and Sally, still hitched to the plow. His tall frame swung out of the saddle slowly as he dismounted and walked to where Beau sat cradling Betsy in his arms.

"Beau?" Stunned and puzzled by the pitiful sight before him, Cole hesitantly knelt beside his brother.

Beau was crying openly, deep, heart-rending sobs that shook his entire frame as he clasped his young wife tightly to him, murmuring her name over and over.

Cole glanced around him, then he saw it. The object responsible for such overwhelming grief lay lifeless on the ground beside the woodpile.

It took a moment for it to register, but when Cole understood what had happened he swore softly under his breath and dropped his head helplessly. "Oh, Beau, hell."

Cole struggled to regain his composure, but when he had he reached to remove Betsy gently from his brother's arms.

"No . . . no . . . don't take her, Cole." Beau spoke for the first time, his voice steady—almost serene.

"Beau, I have to take her."

Beau's grip tightened possessively around his wife's body, and he shook his head.

"Beau, give her to me," Cole commanded softly. Since the day Sam Claxton had died of a heart attack, Cole had been both father and brother to Beau and Cass. He'd been there for them through the good and bad times, and they still looked upon him as head of the household. It was no wonder that after years of strict obedience, Beau reluctantly began to relinquish his hold.

"Don't hurt her," he whispered hoarsely.

"I'll take good care of her."

Carefully lifting her in his arms, Cole stood and carried Betsy into the house that Beau had built for her two years before.

The Claxtons were a prominent family in River Run, so everyone turned out for Betsy's funeral. Such a lovely young thing, the townspeople whispered among themselves. Why had tragedy struck such a fine couple when they'd only begun to live? What would poor Beau do now? She was so young . . . and the innocent baby she was carrying . . . why, it would have been born soon . . . it's horrible . . . just terrible . . . simply unthinkable. . . .

Beau hadn't shed a tear since the afternoon Cole had found him holding Betsy. Standing straight and tall between his two brothers, Beau kept his face an empty mask as the preacher droned on.

At the graveside, Lilly Claxton wrapped her arms around Betsy's mother and suffered with her. To Lilly, Betsy had been more than a daughter-in-law; she had been like one of her own.

Beau showed no emotion until the first spade of dirt fell atop the simple pine coffin. As the sound reached his ears, he flinched as if he'd been burned, but his eyes stayed dry and his face stoic. After the burial he turned and walked away without a backward glance.

Wynne Claxton, flanked on either side by Cole and Cass, approached Beau. Such strong men, the Claxton brothers, she thought fleetingly. It hurt her to see one of them brought to his knees by tragedy.

She loved all three men, each in a different way.

Her husband, Cole, was the love of her life, with his solid ways and curly dark hair and incredibly blue eyes. He'd made her the happiest woman on earth for the past two years.

And Beau. He was exceptionally handsome with his golden hair and eyes the color of a bright summer sky. He was the sunshine in the Claxton family. Before Betsy's death, Beau had always looked at the good side of life. Happiness had bubbled over in his eyes, eyes that always caught her attention, laughing eyes, eyes that twinkled devilishly and flirted outrageously. Dear, sweet Beau. He'd been so kind to her at a time when she'd needed kindness the most.

And then there was young, lovable Cass. Every bit as handsome as his older brothers, Cass seemed destined to give some girl a run for her money before she got him to the altar. He was the lover in the family, and at one time he'd nearly broken Wynne's heart, but that had been long ago, and since then she'd forgiven him.

The Claxton brothers were strong but gentle men, incredibly tender in the way they loved their women. Wynne had seen the love Beau had shared with Betsy, and she knew how deeply he was grieving.

Handing baby Jeremy to his father, Wynne enfolded Beau in her arms and hugged him tightly. "I want you to know we share your pain and that we love you very much," she whispered.

"I don't know how I can go on. . . ." Beau's brave façade shattered, and his voice filled with raw emotion.

"But you will. You will, Beau." He was young and strong, and with time his wounds would heal. Wynne had to believe it, even if Beau couldn't yet.

For a fraction of an instant Beau's arm tightened around Wynne to show his appreciation, then it dropped back to his side and he walked on.

Cole matched stride with his brothers as Beau marched to his horse. "Why don't you come over and spend a few days with Wynne and me?" Cole invited. It was unthinkable to him that his brother would return to an empty house.

"Thanks, but I think I'll be leavin' for a while." Beau paused and turned to face his brothers.

"Leavin'? Where you goin'?" Cass demanded.

Beau's gaze rested upon the small mound of newly turned dirt as he spoke. "I don't know. Just away somewhere."

"Aw, Beau, I can understand you feelin' that way, but don't you think this is a bad time to be runnin' off?" Cass protested gently, looking to Cole for support when he spotted a bedroll and pack behind Beau's saddle. "Tell him, Cole. He shouldn't be wanderin' around by himself . . . at least not right now."

Cole's clear blue gaze met Beau's with silent understanding. "I think he should do what he feels he has to, Cass."

Beau nodded gratefully. "Thanks, Cole. Bets . . . well, she'd have appreciated all you've done. . . ."

Cole reached out and clasped Beau's shoulder reassuringly. "Let us know when you're ready to come home."

"I will. I want you to take Kate and Sally and the rest of my stock."

"I'll see to them for you."

Beau reached out and touched Jeremy's nose, drawing a happy gurgle from the baby. "Take good care of this little fella." Bright tears stood in Beau's eyes as he thought about his own baby and what might have been.

"I will," said Cole. "You take care of yourself."

Beau nodded. "Tell Ma not to worry." Slowly, Beau mounted his horse and pulled his hat low on his forehead.

"She'll worry anyway—you know Ma," said Cass, still not sold on the idea of Beau's leaving. The way Cass figured it, a man should stay with his family at a time like this. "Listen, let us know where you are, you hear?" Cass commanded anxiously.

Beau's eyes returned to Betsy's grave and lingered as he said a final good-bye in his heart. "I hear."

CHAPTER 2

"SHOO! SHOOEEEE! GET OUT OF HERE YOU—YOU Shoo! Shooeeee! Get out of here you—you miserable . . . ungrateful . . . ham hock!" Charity Burkhouser was determined to show no pity as she swatted the old sow across its fat rump and herded it right back out the front door. It was a sad day when a woman couldn't step out to hang the wash without being invaded by pigs!

She slammed the heavy wooden door and leaned against it to catch her breath. She *had* to do something about getting the fence back up.

A woman alone in the world just doesn't have a chance, she muttered to herself. Her husband had died in the war three years ago, and since Ferrand's death Charity had been on her own. Not that she wanted to be—far from it. She wasn't equipped to homestead a piece of land in this godforsaken place they called Kansas, nor had she *ever* had the least desire to do so.

Shortly after they'd married, Ferrand had decided to take advantage of the federal government's Homestead Act, signed into law in May of 1862.

Charity could still remember how excited Ferrand had been the day he'd come home, swung her into his arms, and announced they were moving to Kansas. "A hundred and sixty acres, Charity. Just think of it! They'll *give* us a hundred and sixty acres of whatever land we stake out."

"But, Ferrand, *Kansas*?" For a girl who'd spent all of her life in Virginia, Kansas sounded like the end of the earth. Charity fanned herself as she paced the parlor of her ancestral home. "I don't know why you want to run off to some foreign land when we have a perfectly good home right here with my parents."

"Charity," he reminded her patiently, "Kansas is not a foreign land."

"Well, it would surely seem so to me, Ferrand." Charity was accustomed to nannies and servants who attended to her every whim without a moment's hesitation. Somehow, she had a strong feeling Kansas wouldn't have those essentials.

"But that's my point. It would be *our* land, darling, not your parents'," Ferrand pointed out tactfully. He'd gotten along well enough with Sherman and Lareina Pendergrass, but he wanted a home and land of his own now that he was married. "Under the Homestead Act, all a person has to do is begin improvements on the land within six months of the time he files for application, remain a permanent resident there for five years, and the land becomes his, free and clear." Ferrand pulled Charity against his chest to kiss her soundly. When their lips parted a long moment later, he winked at her and gave her bottom a reassuring pat. "Come on, Charity, where's your spirit of adventure? We'll raise a family of pioneers. You'll love it."

"But, darling," Charity protested, "why do we have to go to Kansas to have our own land?" Ferrand Burkhouser came from an old, aristocratic line in Virginia. His father could well afford to buy any amount of land his son desired. Why, even her own papa had offered to purchase a plantation for Ferrand on their wedding day three months ago. Her husband didn't need to travel hundreds of miles to acquire just a hundred and sixty acres.

Charity didn't understand her man sometimes.

"Well . . . this is all so sudden, Ferrand." Charity bit her lower lip pensively. She felt obligated to at least consider her husband's dream. She did love Ferrand, and her papa always said a man was the undisputed head of his own household, but still . . . "Would I be able to hire my own help? I wouldn't want to take up . . . housekeeping and . . . and farming myself."

Charity couldn't imagine worse punishment. Why, she didn't know the first thing about farming!

Ferrand threw back his head and laughed at his young bride. She was a pure delight. Her beauty was unsurpassed, with those clear, snapping green eyes and black, shining curls that cascaded down her back. And her disposition, though at times a bit trying, gave him his greatest joy. He'd give her the moon if he could. "Of course you will, my darling! Your life won't change that much. I'm sure there'll be plenty of people looking for work in Kansas."

"But I'll miss Mama and Papa and Faith and Hope. And what about the war, Ferrand?" So far, he'd miraculously escaped the fighting, but Charity feared he might have to leave any day.

"After we're settled, your parents and sisters can come and visit us," Ferrand promised. "And as for the war, we'll worry about that when the time comes."

As it turned out, there'd been virtually no one looking for work in Kansas. Lordy, everyone had had enough to do just trying to survive on the rugged frontier, Charity recalled. She and Ferrand hadn't lived on their new settlement for more than a few months when Ferrand decided it was his duty to join the fight for the Confederacy. Then she'd been left to face the bewildered looks of her neighbors when they found out Ferrand had decided his loyalties still belonged to the South.

And since Kansas was so far away, her family had never once been able to make the long trip to visit their eldest child.

After they'd learned of Ferrand's death, Charity's parents had written, urging her to come home. When Charity informed them she was staying on to claim the land, her family had begged her to reconsider such a rash decision.

But Charity was a stubborn woman. She was determined to remain in Kansas, though at times she hated every waking hour in this wild, uncivilized land, where the winds were fierce and the winters long and unbearably cold. The heat could be suffocating and the droughts endless. There were tornadoes and grasshoppers and Indians. And wolves. She hated the wolves. They prowled around her little soddy at night, snapping at her dogs, Gabriel and Job, while Charity huddled in a corner, grasping Ferrand's old rifle tightly, praying they wouldn't come through the door.

Still, Charity couldn't bring herself to relinquish her right to the homestead because, in a strange, inexplicable way, she felt a certain pride to think she owned the land, or would, if she could hold on just one more year.

Then maybe she'd go home and visit her parents. The thought was mighty tempting. There hadn't been any servants or nannies out here to take care of her. In truth, she'd barely been able to manage.

She felt herself smiling, something she rarely did anymore, as she thought of how poor Ferrand had struggled to mold her into a pioneer woman.

Lordy, he'd been good to her. He'd seen her through her crying spells and days of loneliness. Sometimes weeks would pass before they'd see another human being, and at times Charity thought she couldn't bear the solitude.

But she'd survived. And when the news of Ferrand's death had reached her, Charity had had a good long cry, but by then she'd begun to adjust to the harsh realities of the world.

Oh, she'd been furious at Ferrand for getting himself killed in that foolish war and leaving her all alone to care for a miserable chunk of worthless land. But that feeling had passed, and she'd started remembering what a really good man Ferrand was, and then Kansas didn't seem all that bad.

It was home now, her home, so she guessed she'd best make do and quit feeling sorry for herself.

What she and Ferrand had shared had been special. Despite all her domestic failings, Charity knew she had to do this one last thing for him. Ferrand had worked too hard in the brief time they'd been granted together for her to be fainthearted now. She'd see this thing through. Though she had to admit, she couldn't see how she was going to do it.

She needed a man. Not for the same reason a woman usually wanted a man, but Charity needed a man from a purely practical standpoint. She had to make improvements on the land just to keep her claim, but she simply didn't have the knowledge, the strength, or the skill necessary.

Thanks to Grandmother Pendergrass's personal tutelage, Charity knew how to piece a pretty quilt and bake a tasty blackberry pie, but she didn't know how to build a barn or plow a field. Oh, she'd tried. Her hands, once lily-white and soft as rose petals, were now calloused and beet-red.

When it had come to setting posts and planting wheat, she'd done an atrocious job. Ashamed for anyone to see the way her fence posts leaned westward when they were supposed to stand straight, Charity had ripped them out and cried herself to sleep one night.

No, a man was her only answer.

But a man was a rare commodity around these parts. It was unlikely that anyone would walk up and knock on her door and say, "Well, hello! I hear you're looking for a husband, Mrs. Burkhouser. Take me."

Though the town of Cherry Grove wasn't far from her land, Charity rarely socialized. Once a month she made the trek into town to purchase staples and yard goods from Miller's Mercantile, but suitable marriage prospects weren't plentiful. Oh, there were the usual cattle drovers who came through town, bringing their longhorns up from Texas to ship them out by railheads. Of course, the travel-worn herders were always looking for female companionship. But Charity despised their slovenly ways and drunken antics. They carried on like the devil himself. Their cattle brought them a good price back East, but Charity wanted nothing to do with such men. They were rovers and drifters, and she needed a man who'd stay around for a while.

But she was going to have to find someone soon or lose her claim by this time next year.

She sighed in despair and turned her face upward, as she did increasingly these days. "Well, it's up to you, Lord. I'm at the end of my row."

The lone rider slowed his horse beside the stream and paused to let the animal drink his fill. The man was unkempt and dirty. A dark blond stubble marred his formerly clean, handsome features. He seemed older than his twenty-eight years. Fatigue lined his face, and nature hadn't been kind. The sun had cooked his skin to a dark, golden bronze, and blue eyes that had once danced with merriment now stared in blank acceptance of a life that no longer held purpose.

Beau knew he looked bad.

He didn't eat the way he should. He was at least forty pounds lighter than he had been a year ago. During that time, he'd rambled down one winding road after another, going wherever the next road took him. He'd just tried to get through one day and then the next and then the next. Sometimes he'd notice when he crossed a state line, but if anyone had asked him where he was, Beau wouldn't have known or cared. Life was just one long dreary day after the other.

Betsy had been gone a year now, or close to it. Beau didn't know what month it was, but it seemed to him the heat was letting up some, so it was probably September again.

He smiled at the memory of his wife. Their baby would've been almost a year old by now. Wonder if it would've been a boy or girl? Suddenly, he realized he'd never let himself ask that question. Well, it didn't matter now. Nothing mattered anymore.

He slid from his horse. Reaching into the stream, he cupped his hands for a cool drink of water. When he finished, he splashed a handful of wetness down his neck to ease the heat.

Straightening, he prepared to mount again when his horse began to shy nervously. "Whoa, girl, easy." Beau gripped the reins and pulled himself into the saddle as the mare whinnied and sidestepped again. "Easy . . . easy. . . ." He glanced toward a wooded area, and a strange wariness came over him.

"What's the matter, girl?" Once more, his eyes scanned the area. Suddenly, Beau felt a tightness in his stomach. Standing not twenty feet away, partially hidden in the undergrowth, was one of the biggest timber wolves he'd ever seen.

The horse trumpeted in alarm and started to bolt. The wolf's lips curled back above his fangs, and he gave a low, ominous growl. His eyes had a bright, feverish sparkle to them, and his back paw dangled limply.

Beau could see fresh blood dripping from the wounded paw onto the dusty ground.

The wolf had been caught in a trap, Beau surmised. Slowly, he backed his horse out of the stream, taking pains not to make any sudden moves. The wolf would be in no mood for socializing, and neither was Beau. He could shoot it, but his draw would have to be lightning quick, and he didn't want to chance it.

Before Beau could choose his next move, the decision was out of his hands.

With one tremendous lunge the wolf sprang from his hiding place as the horse reared wildly in fright.

Beau tried to control his horse and reach for his gun at the same time, but the wolf charged, and suddenly the air was alive with the screams of man and crazed animals pitched into a life-or-death struggle. Angry snarls and shrill squeals of rage and terror surrounded Beau as the wolf viciously tore into the meaty flank of the horse. Swearing violently under his breath, Beau managed to pull his gun from his holster, but the

wolf sprang again. This time he took the rider out of the saddle, and
Beau went down into the water, trying to shield himself from the wolf's
ferocious jaws.

Man and animal thrashed about in a frenzied battle as the wolf repeatedly ripped and slashed Beau's body. The water swirled and churned
and turned red with blood.

Some three hundred yards away a young woman stopped kneading
bread and cocked her ear toward the open window. The dogs were setting up a howl on the front step, and in the distance she could hear what
sounded like animals in some sort of terrible fight.

Charity wiped the flour from her hands and moved to the mantel.
Darn pesky coyotes, she thought irritably, reaching for the rifle. They'd
probably attacked a stray dog or calf.

The noise increased in intensity as she stepped out of the soddy and
started toward the stream.

She'd be forever grateful to Ferrand for choosing this particular piece
of land. In this part of Kansas, a shortage of rain, coupled with high
winds and low humidity, sometimes left a pioneer at a serious disadvantage. But the Burkhouser soddy was built near an underground spring
that provided a stream of cool, clear water year round.

Charity's footsteps quickened as she heard a horse's shrill squeal rend
the air. Good heavens! Something had attacked a horse!

Her feet faltered as she entered the clearing, her eyes grimly taking in
the appalling sight. Before her, a large timber wolf was ripping a man
apart as his horse danced about him wildly.

Regaining her composure, Charity hefted the rifle to her shoulder
and took careful aim. Seconds later, a loud crack sliced the air, and the
wolf toppled off the man into the water. The gunfire spooked the horse,
and it bolted into the thicket as Charity hurriedly waded into the stream.

She flinched as she edged past the fallen wolf, but the gaping bullet
hole in the center of its chest assured her that her aim had been true.
The first thing Ferrand had taught her when they'd moved here was
how to be a deadly, accurate shot. She'd learned her lesson well.

Kneeling beside the injured man, she cautiously rolled him on his side
in the shallow water and cringed as she heard him moan in agony. He
was so bloody she could barely make out the severity of his wounds, but
she knew he was near death.

"Shhhh . . . lie still. I'm going to help you," she soothed, though he
could neither see nor hear her. As his eyes began to swell shut from the
nasty lacerations on his face, he passed out.

She glanced around, trying to determine whether to hitch Myrtle and
Nell to drag him out of the water. He was a tall man, but pitifully thin.
Though she was small and slight, she was a lot stronger than when she'd
first arrived in Kansas. She decided she wouldn't need the oxen to move
him from the water.

It took several tries, for he wasn't as light as he looked. She tugged and heaved inch by inch, pausing periodically to murmur soothing words of encouragement when he groaned in pain. Though she handled him as carefully as she could, his injuries were so great that he suffered excruciating pain.

Once she had pulled him onto the bank, she hurriedly tore off a small portion of her petticoat and began to clean his wounds. He tossed restlessly, fighting her when her hands touched his torn flesh.

"Please, you must let me help you!" she urged.

Charity was accustomed to patching wounds on her stock, but she grew faint looking at his injuries. In her whole life she'd never seen such mutilation of a human body, but she shook off her queasiness and administered to his needs.

As her hands worked, she studied him carefully and recoiled not only at his injuries but at his general condition; he was so unkempt, so dirty, so . . . slovenly. She wasn't used to that. Ferrand had always kept himself clean and neat. No doubt this man was a drifter, or perhaps one of those drovers. He certainly hadn't had a bath in months—maybe even years—and he was in need of a shave and a haircut.

She peeled away his torn shirt and washed the blood from the thick mat of dark blond hair that lay across his chest. Though his chest was broad, she could count his ribs. Obviously, he hadn't had a square meal in a long time. With more meat on his bones he'd be a very large man . . . powerful . . . strong. . . . Strong enough to build a barn and set fence and work behind a team of oxen all day. . . . Her hands stilled momentarily.

Good Lord. A man. Here was a man—barely alive perhaps, but a man all the same. He could be the answer to her problems.

Her hands flew about their work more feverishly. She had to save him! Not that she wouldn't have tried her best anyway, but now no matter what it would take, by all that was holy, she'd see to it that this man survived.

As far as men went, he wasn't much . . . disgusting, actually, but she reminded herself she wasn't in a position to be picky.

She'd nurse him back to health, and once she got him on his feet, she'd trick him into marrying her. No, she amended, she wouldn't trick him . . . she'd ask him first, and if that didn't work, *then* she'd trick him.

But what if he has a wife? an inner voice demanded.

Don't bother me with technicalities, she thought irritably. I'll cross that bridge when I get to it.

Her hands worked faster, a new sense of confidence filling her now. He *would* live. She just knew he would. The good Lord wouldn't give her such a gift and then turn around and snatch it back, now would he?

He moaned again, and Charity lifted his head and placed it in her lap possessively.

He was a gift from God.

She was certain of that now. Who else would so unselfishly drop this complete stranger at her door?

Once more she looked down at her unexpected gift, and her face lit with a radiant smile. Closing her eyes, she lifted her face heavenward, and sighed with relief. Maybe now she would be able to claim her land after all.

Then in her most reverent tone, she humbly asked for the Lord's help in making this man strong and healthy again, at least strong enough to drive a good, sturdy fence-post.

She closed her petition with heartfelt sincerity. "He's a little . . . well, rough looking, Lord, but I'm sure not complaining." She bit her lower lip thoughtfully as she studied the ragged, dirty, bloody man lying in her lap. With a little soap and water, maybe he'd be tolerable. She shrugged, and a big grin spread across her face. "I suppose if this is the best you have to offer, Lord, then I sure do appreciate your thoughtfulness."

CHAPTER 3

CHARITY DRAGGED THE STRANGER UP THE RAVINE, and then the quarter of a mile or so to the soddy. By the time she managed to pull him onto her bed, she was gasping for air.

Sighing, she surveyed his pitiful state. The nearest doctor was over an hour's ride away. The stranger would die before she could make it to Cherry Grove and back.

No, if his life were to be spared, she'd have to use whatever skills she possessed, and she had to admit they were deplorably few.

It would take a lot of nursing, and the mercy of a higher power, to see him through this, she realized.

Though he remained in a fortunate state of unconsciousness, the man's face was swollen and contorted with pain.

The angry six-inch gash across his chest was oozing blood in a red stream, and Charity knew the stranger would bleed to death if she didn't tend his wounds soon.

Rolling up her sleeves, she moved to the hearth. Without hesitation she tore an old petticoat into soft bandages and filled a wash pan with scalding water from the kettle.

She'd stitched up livestock, she reminded herself, as her hands automatically went about her task. When Sally had gotten tangled in Ansel Latimer's fence last year, Charity had been the one who'd cleaned the torn flesh and stitched it back together. From her sewing basket, she took her scissors and a needle. Of course, Sally's wound had been nothing like this poor man's, but the ox had healed beautifully.

And she'd assisted with a few births. Right now, she decided, helping a woman have a baby seemed easier than sewing a man together after he'd been mauled by a wolf. She selected a spool of black thread and absently closed the lid on the basket. Doctoring wasn't her favorite thing, but then she had no choice if she wanted the man to survive.

It took a half hour to cut away his clothes. As she began bathing his wounds in cool water, her stomach lurched ominously, and she rushed to the window. Drawing deep breaths of fresh air helped to quell the urge to empty her stomach. His wounds were ghastly; tender flesh was torn open in large, gaping holes. The front of her dress was splattered with his blood, and she nearly gagged as she rubbed her palms across her apron and saw huge red stains.

Charity wasn't sure she could go on. Most likely the man would die in spite of her efforts. No one could survive such injuries, she told herself. Then she thought of her own miserable plight and resolved again to save his life.

Inhaling deeply, Charity strode to the washbasin. The water turned a bright red as she washed her hands. Determinedly, she refilled the basin and resumed her gruesome task.

A laceration across the middle of his back was the deepest, she decided. Grimacing, she carefully rolled him onto his stomach and cringed as she poured a small amount of carbolic acid into the wound as an antiseptic. The man stiffened and screamed in anguish as he tried to knock her hands away. But Charity held firm, throwing her slight weight against his large frame, pinning him down until he drifted back into unconsciousness.

She found herself biting her lower lip till she could taste her own blood as her hands worked feverishly to stitch the wound. When she finished repairing his back, she rolled him over and continued to stitch the other wounds. At any moment he could wake up and overpower her, and then what would she do?

The darning needle, which she'd held in the fire, slid in and out, in and out, in and out . . . until she thought she'd surely faint. The room was stifling, and flies buzzed about her head, lighting on his wounds. She shooed them away and dipped a cloth into the bucket of clean water and pressed it to her flushed features. After the lightheadedness had passed, she continued.

Her damp clothes clung to her as her hands mechanically went about pulling flesh together and carefully sewing it into place. Her stitches were neat and small, and she was surprised to feel a rush of pride as she gazed at her work. He might not live, but if he did, he'd have few scars.

The afternoon shadows began to lengthen. Charity's back felt as if it would break, but she worked on. She heard Bossy standing near the front door, bawling to be milked.

"Not now, Bossy," she called out softly, hoping the old cow would wander away.

It was nearing dark when she finally finished. Tears stood in her eyes as she listened to the sounds of his suffering. She dropped weakly into the rocker and stared unseeingly at the dying embers, numb with fatigue. She'd felt every agonizing prick the needle had made in his bruised flesh as surely as if she'd been the one injured.

Her body, as well as his, was sticky with sweat and blood, and she knew she must bathe the both of them before she could rest.

The man began to mumble and thrash about on the bed, and Charity feared he'd reopen his wounds. If he did, she wasn't sure she'd have the strength to sew them again.

There was nothing to ease the stranger's agony except the bottle of brandy Ferrand had kept for special occasions.

If this wasn't a special occasion, Charity thought desperately, she didn't know one. Hurriedly, she pulled the bottle from the cupboard. She scooped his head from the pillow and cradled it in the crook of her arm. Tipping the bottle to his lips, she let the strong brown liquid trickle down his throat.

When he started to choke, Charity set the bottle aside and patted him soothingly. He screamed in torment as the wound across his chest threatened to escape the bounds of the slender thread she'd so meticulously sewn.

When he regained his breath, she tipped the bottle again, and the nerve-racking choking began again. It took several minutes to get enough of the liquor down him to dull his senses.

He'd fought her with a strength that was surprising for a man so gravely injured. Twice he'd nearly knocked the bottle out of her hand, but Charity was as determined as he. As the liquor took full effect, he lay so still that Charity leaned forward to be sure he was still breathing.

Assured that he was, she released a long sigh and absently tipped the bottle to her mouth. *He's going to make it,* she thought. *He has to.* If she could clean and stitch his wounds without fainting, then by all that was holy, he could live! She took another long sip from the bottle and eyed the unconscious male lying in the middle of her bed.

He sure was a pitiful sight. His chin was covered with dark stubble, and his ribs poked through his sides like those of some half-starved animal.

But it didn't matter, she reminded herself, trying to bolster her sagging morale. He *was* a man, and she was going to see to it that he lived. He obviously needed someone to take care of him, and she needed a man. Surely a satisfactory arrangement could be worked out, once he regained his health.

She tipped the bottle again. The harsh liquid stung her nose and burned her throat, bringing a rush of tears to her eyes. She coughed and thumped her chest solidly, then paused to observe his condition. He was still breathing, she confirmed, taking comfort in the thought. By morning he'd be awake, and she'd find out who he was, and where he'd come from.

Mustering up enough strength to walk to the woodbox, she tossed a couple of logs on the fire, then stumbled back to the rocker and dropped into an exhausted sleep.

CHAPTER 4

THE WIND WHISTLING DOWN THE CHIMNEY PENEtrated Charity's dulled senses. Her eyes opened to slits, then closed shut again.

For three nights, she'd hovered over the stranger, alternately bathing him in cool water and changing the bandages.

His wounds didn't look good. The long, angry lesions were beginning to fester, and Charity's heart pounded with fear every time she looked at them.

The man was hot and feverish—delirious at times, calling out for "Betsy." If Charity had known a Betsy, she'd have gladly fetched her. She'd try anything to ease his torment, but nothing seemed to help.

Only once had he shown any sign of consciousness. Last night, when she'd been sponging his burning forehead, his eyes had opened to stare at her with a blank plea in the deep, tormented pools of indigo.

Charity had smiled and spoken to him in soft, reassuring tones, running the damp cloth gently across his reddened skin. "There, now, you're going to be fine."

Her heart had skipped a beat when his eyes had grown incredibly tender as he'd returned her smile.

It had been so long since a man had looked at her that way. Then she realized that it wasn't Charity Burkhouser he'd been seeing but his "Betsy," as his feverish mind had continued to play tricks on him.

The stranger had grasped Charity's hand and brought it to cradle lovingly against his stubbled jaw. His eyes had slid shut, and she'd heard him whisper faintly, "Bets, I knew you'd come back, darlin'." Charity watched with an aching heart as tears rolled from the corners of his eyes to the pillow.

Slowly his eyes had opened again, and she'd caught her breath as he pulled her head down to meet his.

Charity had been transfixed as their lips touched and lingered. Because he was so ill, the kiss had lacked passion, but nothing could have disguised the love he'd been transferring to her. His kiss had caused her pulse to flutter erratically, and she'd felt herself growing weak all over.

When their lips parted, Charity had seen a look in the stranger's eyes that she'd seen before in Ferrand's.

It had been a look of love . . . and desire . . . desire so strong that Charity felt warmed by the heat shimmering in the tormented depths. Then he smiled at her again and said softly, "Bets, I love you."

Charity had never seen such striking eyes, clear, vibrant blue . . . the color of morning glories on the trellis beside the porch when the first rays of daylight nudged them gently awake.

Instinctively she knew those eyes bright with fever could sparkle with merriment during better times.

Despite his pitiful condition the stranger was the handsomest man she had seen in a long while.

And he loved a woman named Betsy, Charity realized with a sinking heart.

The wind was rising, and Charity noticed a slight chill in the air as she rose to throw another log on the fire. Stoking the glowing embers, she thought of the stranger again, and a frown played across her features. Maybe he wouldn't be able to help her after all. Then what would she do? She'd lose the homestead after everything she'd done to keep it.

Her thoughts wandered back to Ferrand and how hard they'd worked together to build the soddy. It hadn't been easy traveling to the Great American Desert, as Kansas was sometimes called.

Charity remembered the steamboat they'd taken part of the way. My, what a glorious time that had been, churning up the wide Missouri on a big old paddle-wheeler. By then, Ferrand had convinced her that an exciting new life awaited them; all they had to do was reach out and take it.

Charity walked back to the rocker and sat. It was still early; the sun wasn't up yet, so she could dawdle for a spell before she milked Bossy. Rocking back and forth, she let her thoughts remain on the past.

Lordy, how she'd loved Ferrand Burkhouser.

When they'd arrived in Kansas, they'd immediately found a piece of land, staked their plot on good level ground, and stripped the spot of grass. They'd worked from daylight to dusk, smoothing the site with a spade, then packing the dirt down to form an earthen floor.

From sunup to sundown, they'd cut the heavy sod into blocks to build the one-room soddy. She smiled, recalling the way she'd followed Ferrand behind the plow, carrying a sharp spade to cut the strips of earth into individual blocks, one foot wide, two feet long, and four inches thick. After the blocks had been cut, she'd loaded the heavy bundles into the spring wagon. Ferrand had driven Myrtle and Nell as they pulled the grasshopper plow that sliced the strips of sod from the earth.

At times, Ferrand had stopped to wipe the sweat from his brow, and feeling playful, he'd picked up a handful of sod and tossed it at Charity. With her impish grin she'd returned the barrage, and soon they'd lost a good hour. When they'd paused to catch their breath, Ferrand's expression had changed, and he'd carried Charity to the large old walnut tree where they'd made love.

Tears sprang to her eyes as Charity remembered how happy they'd been. Dabbing her eyes with a corner of her apron, she tried to push her memories aside.

What good did memories do her anyway, she scolded. Ferrand was gone, and crying wouldn't bring him back. She wouldn't cry again. She was just feeling tired, that was all. Sitting up with the stranger for three nights straight had taken its toll.

She walked to the bed and touched the man's forehead. Still hot. She didn't know how much longer the fever could rage before it either disappeared or killed him. It had to do one or the other soon.

As she settled back in the chair, memories returned. She sighed wistfully. Ferrand seemed to hug the fringes of her mind this morning. Perhaps, she conceded, it was because he'd always loved this time of day. Charity let herself think about his quiet strength, and somehow that eased her pain.

Leaning her head against the smooth wood, she thought about how he'd made the rocker and given it to her on their first Christmas together. She tried to remember Ferrand's eyes . . . blue, like the stranger's . . . no, they were hazel, weren't they?

The slow creak of the rocker paused momentarily. Blue . . . no, hazel. She frowned again. Blue or hazel? Which one was it?

Strange, she couldn't seem to recall. Setting the chair in motion again, she thought about how tall and handsome Ferrand Burkhouser had been. She could remember clearly what an attractive man he was. Oh, he might not have had a broad-shouldered frame like the stranger, but Ferrand had had a gentleness about him that she'd cherished.

And he'd held his own when it had come to working the land. He might've been raised in a home where servants had done all the back-breaking chores, but Ferrand hadn't been afraid of hard work.

The sod blocks had been heavy and burdensome, and Charity had thought her back would surely break in two, but Ferrand had helped her lift them, and daily the pile of earth bricks had grown.

Earthen bricks had been stacked with the grass side down, one layer after another to form walls two feet thick. Since they'd had no mortar or nails, they'd packed loose dirt and mud into the cracks and crevices. They'd covered the walls with a simple frame of cottonwood poles and willow brush, topped with the rest of the strips of sod. When they'd finished, Charity had felt sure there wasn't a finer house in all of Kansas.

Charity's eyes wandered lovingly around the room. The soddy was all she had left of Ferrand, and if she lost it, she feared she'd lose what remained of his memory.

Oh, she knew this house they'd built with their hands wasn't fancy like her ancestral home in Virginia. The soddy was dark and it lacked proper ventilation. When it rained, mud dripped down on the few pieces of furniture she had.

Charity's gaze surveyed the meager furnishings. Not much, that was for sure: an old, worn cowhide carpet on the floor, a wooden bed with a straw-filled mattress, some goods boxes fashioned into tables, and a few barrels Ferrand had shaped into chairs.

But she'd managed to save enough egg money to make some pretty gingham curtains, and the two richly patterned patchwork quilts that had once belonged to her grandmother brightened the room.

All things considered, Charity loved this house. That's why she had to keep the stranger alive. He might be pitiful, but if she could enlist his strength after she built him back up, he could help save her homestead. She didn't know how she'd make him stay after he recovered, provided he did recover.

This "Betsy" would be an obstacle, but perhaps the stranger could be persuaded to help out while he was mending. It would take a long while for him to regain his full strength, Charity thought.

Suddenly she slapped the arm of the chair as her frustration erupted. Oh, it cut her to the core to depend on someone else to bail her out! Everything should have been so different. Damn the war! Damn the miserable, senseless act of war that had snatched Ferrand away from her!

The wind whistling down the chimney added to her fury. While she was cursing everything, she thought angrily, she might as well include the Kansas grasshoppers, tornadoes, and blizzards, along with the incessant wind that had withered what little crops she'd planted.

Wearily she rose from the chair and blew out the tallow candle on the kitchen table. The sun was up now—a new day. Maybe this one would shine more favorably on her and the stranger.

Pouring water into the washbasin, she washed her face and hands, then pulled the pins from her hair. The soft black cloud fell like a silk shawl around her shoulders as she picked up a brush and began to pull it through the tangled locks. She paused and stared at her reflection in the mirror. Frontier life had been hard, and she feared her beauty—what there was left of it—was fading quickly.

Her hand absently fingered the faint crow's feet around her eyes. Come next month, she'd be twenty-three years old. Twenty-three years old! It was hard to believe.

Most women her age were busy raising families and tending husbands, but Charity had neither. Instead she had a dead husband, a small piece of land, a few chickens, a few old sows, a dog, a cow, two oxen, and a sick stranger about to go to his final reward. Sometimes life was so unfair.

The sound of a buckboard rumbling into the yard caught her attention. Charity hurriedly repinned her hair, wondering who could be calling at this hour. She surveyed herself one final time in the mirror, then quickly smoothed the wrinkles on her dress and answered the knock.

She was surprised to find her neighbor, Ansel Latimer, standing on her doorstep, his face pale, his mouth set in a grim line.

"Good morning, Ansel," said Charity, peering on tiptoe around his large frame. "Is Letty with—"

"Letty sent me to fetch you," Ansel interrupted curtly. "She's—she's feeling right poorly this morning, and I don't know what to do for her."

"Oh, my. Is it the baby?"

"I don't know. It ain't time for the youngun to be born, but Letty— she's been hurtin' all night."

Ansel and Letty Latimer had been Charity's nearest neighbors until a few months ago when the Swenson family had staked their new claim.

The Latimers lived a good five miles away, but Letty and Charity visited back and forth once a month, happily planning for Letty's new baby due in late November.

Being about the same age, the two women had developed a close friendship while the Latimers and Burkhousers homesteaded their properties. Ansel and Letty were the closest thing to family Charity had, now that Ferrand was gone.

Charity was reaching for her shawl when she remembered. "Of course I'll come, Ansel, but will you step in for a moment?"

Ansel removed his hat and walked into the cool interior of the soddy, trying to adjust his eyes to the dim light as he spoke. "We'd best hurry, Charity. I hate to leave Letty alone any longer than need be."

"Of course. I'll only take a moment." Charity motioned for him to follow her to the bed. "I want you to see something."

Ansel Latimer strode across the room. He was a tall man, still handsome at forty-three, with brown eyes and dark hair streaked with gray. He was twenty years older than Charity, and she valued his intelligence and common sense. Many times she'd gone to him with her problems since Ferrand's death. If anyone would know what to do about the stranger, Ansel would.

Slowly his puzzled gaze surveyed the man lying deathly still, and a frown crossed his rugged features. "Who is he?"

"I don't know. Three days ago I found him in the stream where a wolf was attacking him. I shot the wolf and managed to drag him to the house."

Ansel leaned forward and lifted one of the bandages, and Charity watched his frown deepen. "Infection's set in."

"I know," Charity confessed in a low whisper. "I've tried to keep the wounds clean, but they look worse each day."

Ansel lifted the other bandages and shook his head as he viewed the angry, pus-filled lesions. "He needs a doctor, but even then, I don't believe he can make it."

"I know. Oh, Ansel, what should I do?" Charity pleaded, her voice trembling. "I'm afraid he's going to die!"

Ansel patted her shoulder reassuringly. "Looks to me like you've done about all you can, girl." Ansel had never seen a better job of stitching. "But the man's wounds are too serious. It'd be better to let him go to his reward in peace."

Charity's eyes filled with tears as she stared down at the stranger's flushed features. His face was pathetically swollen and hot with fever. She felt such a closeness to the man, yet she couldn't explain why; he was a complete stranger. But she'd fought so hard to save his life that it seemed impossible to let him go.

Still, she knew Ansel had spoken the truth. Wouldn't it be kinder to let him pass away? In three days she'd managed to get only a few drops of water and a couple spoonfuls of broth down his throat, and he hadn't kept it down.

Though she sat next to the bed, the man was so weak Charity could barely hear him whispering for Betsy. She wondered how much longer she could bear to watch his suffering.

Ansel gently touched her arm. "Let him go, Charity. You've done all you can. He's in the Lord's hands now."

Charity nodded, tears of resignation beginning to trickle down her cheeks. Ansel was right. She had to let the stranger go. There was no mercy in letting him suffer this way.

"Come with me, Charity. We'll tend to Letty, then I'll bring you back this evenin' and help you bury him," Ansel said, certain the stranger would be dead by sunset.

Charity nodded, reaching to tuck the sheet tenderly over the man's chest. "I know it's best, but it . . . it seems awful just letting him pass away, alone." Her voice caught as her tears began to run in swift rivulets.

"Nothing more you can do," Ansel comforted, putting his arm around her shoulders and leading her away from the bed.

She knew he was right. Ansel was always right, but it seemed wrong, leaving a man like this. Charity wanted to be with him when it happened. . . .

"Letty needs you," Ansel reminded her gently, as if he could read her thoughts.

"Oh . . . yes, Letty . . . of course." Charity had almost forgotten her friend. Letty should be her first concern, but Charity's eyes raced back to the still figure lying on her bed as Ansel helped her with her shawl.

"Best bundle up real good. Chilly out this morning."

"Please put plenty of wood on the fire. I—I don't want him to be cold."

Ansel did as she asked, then opened the door and commanded quietly, "Charity, Letty needs our help, girl."

"Yes . . . yes, of course, Ansel." Charity glanced one final time at the bed before she turned and walked through the door.

"May the mercy of the Lord be with you," she whispered, wishing desperately that Betsy could be there to see him home.

CHAPTER 5

THE OLD BUCKBOARD RUMBLED ALONG THE RUTTED road, bouncing Charity back and forth on the wooden seat uncomfortably, but she barely noticed. Her thoughts were still with the stranger as she wondered how long it would be before he went to meet his maker.

He could be dead at this instant, she realized, and the thought made her shiver in her shawl. At another time a ride in the crisp fall morning would have been a source of pleasure, but not today.

The roadbed ran along Fire Creek, and Charity found herself recalling the times she, Ferrand, Letty and Ansel had enjoyed picnics here on Sunday afternoons after church.

The riverbank was lined with willow trees, grapevines, and hazel bush.

Charity and Letty used to spend hours gathering the wildflowers that grew in colorful profusion along the roadbed, while the men discussed their crops.

A killdeer sang his tuneless note, and a meadowlark called as the old buckboard lumbered across the shallow stream and rattled up the steep incline toward the Latimer homestead.

Charity noticed Ansel had said little during the ride, commenting only occasionally on the weather. His face remained pensive, and the worry lines were grooved deeper at the corners of his eyes.

Charity knew how much Ansel loved Letty, and she sympathized with his concern for his young wife. She knew he and Letty had looked forward to their first child like youngsters waiting for Christmas. Charity sighed deeply, wishing she and Ferrand had had a child.

Her thoughts drifted back to her friend. Charity couldn't imagine what was ailing Letty this morning. She'd seemed fine at church on Sunday. After the service Letty and Charity had lingered outside, discussing the new dress they'd make for Letty after her baby was born. They'd use the fine blue and yellow sprigged calico they'd dawdled over the last time Charity had ridden to Cherry Grove with the Latimers for supplies.

Charity suspected Letty's weakness for green apple pie was the source of her discomfort, but she didn't think Ansel was in any mood to hear her opinion.

The buckboard clattered along the prairie, and soon Charity could see the sod chimney of the Latimer dugout poking out of the ground. Whenever Charity visited Letty, she always came away thankful that Ferrand had built a soddy instead of a dugout.

Letty was forever complaining about her home being dark and damp year round, and she said it was practically impossible to keep her home clean with dirt from the roof and walls sifting down on everything. Whenever it rained, water came pouring in through the roof and under the door, and Letty had to wade through the mud until the floor could dry out.

Bull snakes got into the roof made of willows and grass, and Letty said sometimes a snake would lose its hold at night and fall down on the bed. On those occasions Ansel would jump up, take a hoe, and drag the snake back outside.

Charity shuddered at the thought. There were no snakes in her soddy. In summer it was cool as a cavern; in winter, a snug, warm refuge from the howling Kansas blizzards.

"Looks like Letty's let the fire burn down," Ansel remarked uneasily as he drove the buckboard alongside the dugout and drew the horses to a halt. Only a faint wisp of smoke curled from the chimney.

Ansel set the brake, jumped down, and lifted Charity from the wooden seat. "I'll bet Letty will have dinner waiting," she predicted, trying to ease the worried look on his face.

But when Ansel and Charity stepped inside the dugout, Charity's optimism began to fade. It took a moment for her eyes to adjust to the small room. A ray of sunshine filtered through the one window in the room, and Charity squinted to locate Letty, who lay on the bed, her hands crossed over her swollen stomach, her lips moving silently.

Charity moved swiftly across the room and knelt beside the straw-filled mattress, reaching out to smooth back the damp tendrils of carrot-red hair. "Letty, it's me, Charity."

For a moment she thought Letty hadn't heard her. Then Letty's lips moved, and Charity leaned close to understand her words. "Ansel . . . make him go outside. . . ."

"What?" Charity's heart started to hammer. Something was terribly wrong. This was far more serious than a case of eating too many green apples. Charity touched her friend's delicate hand reassuringly and discovered it was unusually cold. "Ansel's here, Letty, and so am I. Can you tell us what's the matter?"

"Ansel . . ." Letty's voice was stronger this time. "Make Ansel . . . go outside," she repeated weakly.

"But, Letty . . . why?"

Letty's tears fell across cheeks sprinkled generously with girlish freckles. "Just make him go, Charity . . . make him leave. . . ."

Charity turned in bewilderment to face Ansel, who was standing quietly in the shadows of the room. "She wants you to leave."

"I heard." Without questioning his wife's unusual request he turned and walked out.

Charity turned to Letty and began smoothing the rumpled sheets. "Now, let's get you comfortable." She paused and frowned when she felt a warm, sticky substance on the sheets. A jolt of shock moved through her as she stared at the blood on her hand.

Gently, Charity moved Letty's body. The girl was pitifully thin except where she was swollen with child. Charity pressed her hands to the bottom sheet and discovered it was saturated with Letty's blood. Her gaze flew back to Letty's pale face as the young woman on the bed whispered softly, "It's the baby, Charity. It's comin' . . . and there's somethin' wrong."

Letty cried out, then bit her lower lip and muffled an agonized scream as she reached to grasp Charity's hand. Letty held on tightly until the spasm passed.

Charity grabbed a cloth from the basin on the floor beside the bed and gently sponged Letty's flushed face while she spoke in low, soothing tones. "There now, everything will be fine," she promised. "The baby might be a few weeks early, but I'm sure it'll be strong and healthy. Perhaps Ansel should go for the doctor?"

Letty reached up and halted the movement of the wet cloth, her dark eyes fraught with anxiety. "There isn't time, Charity. Something's wrong."

Charity smiled assuringly. "Nonsense, Letty. I'm sure everything's fine. You're just nervous about having your first baby."

Charity hushed as another violent seizure racked Letty's slender frame. Sweat broke out across the girl's brow, and she buried her face in Charity's shoulder to muffle her scream. "Don't . . . want . . . Ansel . . . to . . . hear," Letty panted as the spasm slowed.

"Don't worry about Ansel," Charity soothed. When the pain abated, she ran the wet cloth across Letty's pale features again. "How long have you been in labor?"

Letty shook her head as she stiffened with the onset of another contraction. This time the seizure was so violent, so savage, that Letty screamed and clung to Charity's hand so tightly that Charity bit her lip to keep from crying out. The baby was very near, she thought frantically. She needed to tell Ansel to stoke the fire to bring the kettle to boil. . . .

But Letty's amber eyes grew wide with fear, and her body began to shake convulsively as she called Charity's name. Still trembling, Letty began the Lord's Prayer with whispered fervor, "Our Father, who art in heaven . . . hallowed be Thy name . . ."

Charity's hand flew to her mouth as she watched blood pour from Letty onto the sheet and gather in crimson pools.

". . . Thy kingdom come . . . Thy will be . . . done . . ." continued Letty until she screamed again and clutched the sides of the bed.

Charity couldn't think straight. She knew it shouldn't be happening this way. She'd assisted at other births, and they hadn't gone like this.

". . . Give us the day . . . our daily . . ." Letty whispered till another contraction seized her. "Ansel!" she pleaded in a high-pitched wail.

The door to the dugout flew open and Ansel rushed into the room, his eyes wild with fear. "Letty . . . my God!"

"Leave!" Charity tried to shield him from the pitiful sight. Letty was thrashing wildly on the bed, screaming Ansel's name over and over as her life's blood gushed from her and ran down the side of the bed onto the dirt floor.

"My God—do somethin' for her!" Ansel watched his wife in stunned horror. Letty's body was consumed with spasms as his child was pushed from the confines of its mother's womb.

". . . And lead us . . . not . . . into . . . temptation. . . ." Letty murmured, stopping to pant, her eyes squeezed tight in torment. "Oh-hhh . . . Ansel, help me!"

Throwing her full weight against his frame, Charity tried to shove Ansel toward the doorway, hoping to spare him from what was happening. "Go outside," she pleaded, raising her voice above the sound of Letty's terrified pleas. "I'll tend to her. She'll be fine . . . she'll be fine. . . ."

Ansel let Charity push him through the doorway, and he stood outside as she slammed the heavy wooden door in his face. "My God, she's dyin'," Ansel mumbled hoarsely to himself. "Letty's dyin'."

He sagged against the door frame, then slid down in a crumbled heap on the dirt stoop. He threw his hands over his ears to block out his wife's screams, tears of helpless frustration rolling down his cheeks.

Inside, Letty was splitting apart with the pain. Charity's hands reached to support the baby coming out bottom first.

Letty's screams ran together as she clawed the sheets, her eyes bright with terror. "I'm goin' to die, Charity. Take care of . . . my . . . baby . . . take care of my baby. . . ."

"No!" Charity protested, her own voice rising in hysteria. She couldn't permit Letty to die! "You have to hold on, Letty—you have to fight!" The baby was nearly out now as Charity grasped the small mound of flesh and pulled, blinking back her tears.

"Tell Ansel . . . I . . . love . . . him . . . take care . . . of . . . baby!"

Before Letty could finish another plea, she convulsed violently one final time as the baby slid free of her body into Charity's waiting hands.

"It's a girl, Letty! You have a daughter! Look! She's beautiful!" Charity held the squalling, red-faced bundle up for Letty to see, her words slowly dying in her throat.

She blinked back sudden tears as she realized Letty would never know she had a fine, beautiful daughter.

She lay peacefully in the folds of the bloody linen, her screams finally stilled.

Ansel wasn't sure how long he'd sat before the door finally opened again. He glanced up and saw Charity holding a bundle in her arms. He could see she'd been crying.

"Ansel?" she spoke softly, her eyes welling into emerald pools.

"Yes?"

"You have a lovely baby daughter." She carefully pulled back the folds of the blanket and held the baby so that her father could inspect her.

Ansel stared awkwardly at the tiny wrinkled face. "A little girl?"

"Yes. She looks real healthy."

Ansel's eyes slowly lifted to meet Charity's expectant gaze. How young and vulnerable he looked, she thought. "Letty?"

Charity shook her head as tears trickled down her cheeks. For a moment the anguish in Ansel's eyes was more than she could bear.

Two tears rolled out of the corners of his eyes and he looked at Charity, heartbroken. "She's . . . gone?"

Charity could only nod, her own tears blinding her.

His sad gaze dropped to the baby. "A little girl. Me and Letty was hopin' for a boy," he said thoughtfully, all trace of emotion suddenly gone from his voice.

"Would you like to hold your new daughter?"

"Oh . . . no . . . not now. . . ." He turned and nearly stumbled off the porch in his grief. His shoulders slumped as he moved away. "Think I'll take a walk right now," he murmured.

"Ansel, are you all right?" Charity's heart was breaking. She wanted to go to him and lend him comfort, but she hesitated. He needed time to grieve.

"Oh . . . yes. I'll be all right. You'll—you'll see to my wife's needs, won't you?"

"Of course." Charity would bathe Letty and dress her in her Sunday best for viewing.

"Good, good." Ansel stopped and took a deep breath, looking up into the sky. "My, it's a fine day, isn't it? Couldn't ask for any finer. Letty would have found it real enjoyable."

"Ansel." Charity watched numbly as he ambled off alone. She looked down at the tiny bundle in her arms and saw Letty's pug nose and thatch of bright red hair. Letty would live on in this child, she thought with sad jubilation. Letty would live on, but what would happen to poor Ansel?

She lifted her tearstained face to the glorious blue sky—and as if Letty could hear her, Charity finished Letty's last thought in a heartfelt whisper. "For Thine is the kingdom, and the power, and the glory . . . forever . . . amen."

CHAPTER 6

*T*HE DOOR TO THE SODDY SWUNG OPEN SLOWLY, A head popped around the corner, and a pair of coal-black eyes traveled intently around the room.

The gaze, dark as midnight, surveyed the chairs, the table, the mirror over the washstand, then moved reluctantly to the cold ashes in the fireplace. Then the eyes moved slowly back to the bed where a large mound lay still in the middle.

"White Sister sleep."

The door creaked open and an Indian squaw moved into the room, followed by a second squaw. Both were unusually large in stature and impressive in girth. Many buffalo had been consumed by these women in their respective thirty-one and twenty-nine summers.

The first squaw, Laughing Waters, crept silently toward the bed to see if White Sister was sleeping soundly. It was unusual for White Sister to be asleep while the sun was still up.

Laughing Waters and Little Fawn knew they could quietly browse as they pleased, examining every nook and cranny, satisfying their natural curiosity, and White Sister wouldn't scold them.

She'd let Laughing Waters and Little Fawn come into the soddy many times without invitation. The two Indians would pop in every week or so for an unscheduled visit.

They'd peek at the cooking utensils, pry open the storage bins, and if White Sister wasn't busy, she'd let them watch her work the big wheel by the fireplace that spun round and round throwing pretty yarn into a basket.

Sometimes White Sister would snip a piece of yarn or colorful ribbon and give it to them, and the two squaws would leave delighted with their new treasures.

The women drew the red blankets they wore around their massive bosoms and crept closer to the bed. The cabin was chilly, and Laughing Waters was puzzled. Was White Sister sick?

Moving closer, the two women peered intently at the form lying on the bed. Then Little Fawn looked at Laughing Waters and frowned. "This no White Sister," she whispered.

Laughing Waters was just as surprised as Little Fawn to find a strange man lying in White Sister's bed. She leaned closer and suspiciously eyed the man, whose face looked as if it had been pecked by a buzzard.

Little Fawn looked at Laughing Waters expectantly, then laid her head on the white man's chest and listened. When she was certain she'd heard a faint heartbeat, she looked up at Laughing Waters and grinned, displaying a wide, toothless gap beneath her upper lip. "Gold Hair lives, but sick."

"Ohhhhh, big sick," clucked Laughing Waters maternally as her hands gently peeled back one of the bandages on the man's chest. She shook her head sadly as she viewed the infected wounds. "Heap big sick," she agreed.

Little Fawn thought the man, despite his illness, was the handsomest white man she'd ever seen. Her sharp gaze ran admiringly over the powerful, broad shoulders. His hair reminded her of the golden stones she'd found in the stream one day. The sun had shimmered and danced on the rocks, mesmerizing Little Fawn with their unusual beauty. She couldn't imagine where White Sister was and why she'd left behind such a treasure.

Her hands touched the long, golden locks, stroking them carefully. "This good man," she told Laughing Waters. *"Good."*

"Man White Sister's," Laughing Waters reminded her sternly.

Little Fawn shook her head stubbornly, her two long braids fanning out in the air. "White Sister gone. She leave Gold Hair to meet Wah-kun-dah alone. I take care. Make Gold Hair strong again." Little Fawn looked lovingly at the man on the bed. Gold Hair mine, she thought fondly. He fine, strong buck. When he well, Little Fawn call him Swift Buck with Tall Antlers. He be good father, make many papooses.

Laughing Waters recognized the determination in her little sister's voice and knew it would do no good to argue with her. Little Fawn wouldn't let Gold Hair pass on to the Great Hunting Ground in the Sky without doing her best to prevent the journey.

Besides, Laughing Waters thought Gold Hair fine man too. She make white man well. Then he be hers, and she call him Brave Horse With Many Wounds. He and Laughing Waters make many strong papooses.

Little Fawn turned to Laughing Waters and spoke rapidly in Kaw, the native language of their tribe. Laughing Waters listened, nodding her head as Little Fawn outlined her plan to save this splendid specimen.

Both women hurried into action. Laughing Waters slipped out of the cabin to gather the roots and herbs they would need for the healing poultices, while Little Fawn rushed to get the fire going again.

Beau stirred uncomfortably on the bed. Damn! It was hot.

He wanted to force his eyes open, but the effort was too painful. Every inch of his body ached, and his mouth was so dry he could spit cotton.

Where was he? He willed his legs to move but found them so heavy they refused to budge. A trickle of sweat began to run down the side of his head, and when he tried to wipe it away, he realized his hands wouldn't move.

Paralyzed. He was paralyzed! The image of the wolf with its slobbering jaws came rushing back, and Beau realized with a sinking sensation what had happened. He was dead. The wolf had killed him.

The thought was strangely painful to him. Beau had to admit that he hadn't wanted to live since Betsy's death, yet he hadn't necessarily wanted to die either. But that must be what had happened.

Beau drew a shaky breath and found the air stifling and arid. A new, even more disturbing thought came to him. If he was dead . . . and it was this hot . . .

He groaned and willed his eyes to open. If he was where he thought he was, he might as well face it.

Slowly, his lids fluttered open, and he looked around in the dark. He was lying in some sort of bed . . . in a room. His heart began hammering, and he felt the sweat roll in rivulets down his forehead and drip into his eyes.

The rosy glow of red hot flames danced wickedly across the wall in front of him, and he groaned again and clamped his eyes shut tightly. Oh, God, thought Beau, feeling limp with fear. So that's where he was—in hell.

Well, it wasn't fair, he thought dismally, resenting the fact that he hadn't even had a chance to explain the bad things he'd done in life—not that there'd been all that many.

There had been a few times when he and Cole had been with some pretty questionable women.

And he had fully intended to pay that hundred-dollar gamblin' debt, once he got back to Missouri. . . .

It was his understanding that he'd at least have a chance to tell his side of the story, even if He did have all transgressions written down in some big book.

No, it just wasn't fair, he railed silently. Ma had taught him to obey the Ten Commandments, and with a few minor exceptions, he hadn't been all that bad. Cole had been worse.

Beau wondered if he could talk to someone to get this mess straightened out. He hadn't seen anyone when he'd opened his eyes. Maybe he'd been left down here to roast all alone.

He carefully opened one eye and moved it slowly around the room, surprised to discover hell looked much like the inside of a dirt soddy. Of course, he'd never stopped to think what hell would look like, since he'd never had any intention of going there.

But damn, it was *hot* down here. Preacher Slystone had been right about that.

Again he tried to wipe the sweat off his forehead with the back of his hand, only to discover he was wrapped tight as a tick in some sort of blanket. He moved around, trying to jerk his hands free of the cocoon. Suddenly he glanced up, and his heart jumped into his throat.

Standing over him was the biggest Indian he'd ever seen. On closer examination he saw it was a squaw, and she was smiling a wide, toothless grin at him.

"Gold Hair wake. Good."

Beau grinned back lamely, wondering if he was supposed to say something, though preferring not to. He might be in hell, but he didn't have to socialize with the other residents this soon.

A second Indian woman suddenly loomed above him, her massive bulk blocking the flickering flames on the walls as she began unwrapping the tight blanket.

Beau groaned and jerked away. "No! Don't!" he pleaded weakly. They were going to finish him off before he could state his case to the proper authorities. "Listen, there's been a mistake."

"No talk, Gold Hair," the second woman grunted. "Save strength."

Beau's eyes widened as the first woman reached out and touched a lock of his hair, smiling as she fingered the silken softness. "Pretty, like rocks in water."

"Listen, who's in charge here?" Beau demanded. He wasn't sure what was happening. A terrible stench filled his nostrils as the second woman hurriedly stripped off the blanket, blatantly baring his naked body in the light of the dancing flames.

Beau self-consciously jerked the blanket back over himself.

"No hurt, Gold Hair. We make well," Little Fawn soothed.

Amid Beau's indignant protests the women tossed the blanket aside again, then dipped their large hands into a pail beside the bed and slapped moist, vile-smelling mud all over his body.

Beau gagged and winced as a series of sharp, excruciating pains ricocheted through him like stray bullets. He realized frantically that this must be part of his eternal punishment, though he'd never have imagined it would be administered by a pair of Indian squaws.

Preacher Slystone had never mentioned any such thing. That neglectful omission was Beau's last rational thought before he mercifully slipped back into sweet oblivion.

CHAPTER 7

*F*RIDAY DAWNED DARK AND DREARY. A COLD GRAY MIST fell from the leaden sky and surrounded the travelers riding silently in the buckboard.

The young woman held a small bundle in her arms. Occasionally she crooned to the tiny infant as the man beside her drove the team of horses with methodical movements.

Had it been only two days since she'd traveled this same road? To Charity it seemed an eternity had passed since Wednesday, the day Ansel had come to fetch her for Letty.

Dear, sweet Letty. It was still hard to comprehend that the fresh mound of dirt behind the Latimer dugout was all that remained of her friend.

LETICIA MARGARET LATIMER, BELOVED WIFE, MAY SHE BRING AS MUCH JOY IN

HEAVEN AS SHE BROUGHT HERE ON EARTH. With a sad heart Charity had watched Ansel lovingly carve the inscription onto a wooden cross and place it on Letty's grave that morning.

Charity had dressed Letty in her wedding gown, made of the finest ivory silk. Unpacking the dress, she'd found a tiny pair of kid shoes tucked beneath the folds. Slipping the shoes on Letty's feet, Charity had thought of Letty's well-to-do family back East, who'd married their daughter to Ansel Latimer in grand style.

When Letty's hair had been brushed until it was the color of a fiery sunset, Charity tied a cameo brooch at the base of her neck, remembering that Ansel had given the cameo to Letty on their first Christmas. It had been Letty's most cherished possession.

As she gazed down at her friend, Charity's eyes filled with tears. Letty looked so small, so young . . . so helpless.

Charity had draped the kitchen table with Letty's grandmother's lace tablecloth. She'd called Ansel in from the lean-to, where he'd been building the small pine box.

As Ansel stepped hesitantly into the room, Charity had slipped past him to go outside, giving him time alone with his wife.

Later, the two had hoisted the simple pine box onto the middle of the table. Gently they'd placed Letty in it. Charity lit a single candle that burned until Letty's burial the following day.

Charity stood for a few moments looking down at her friend, fondly recalling how they'd sat around that same table, laughing and giggling like two schoolgirls. For hours on end they'd made plans for the new baby, stitching tiny gowns, lace bonnets, and knitting booties. So many dreams had come to an end with Letty's death; so many hopes would be buried with her.

The funeral was small. Only a handful of neighbors stood in a circle around the open grave, singing "Amazing grace, how sweet thy sound, that saved a wretch like me. . . ." The haunting strains still echoed in Charity's head as the baby began to fret. Charity looked up at Ansel. "She's hungry again." Without the benefit of her mother's milk the infant seemed insatiable.

It bothered Charity that the baby hadn't been named yet. When she'd mentioned the subject at breakfast, Ansel looked at her blankly. Instead of answering her he'd responded vaguely about his crop for next spring.

Letty had wanted to name the baby Mary Kathleen, if she should have a girl, but Charity wanted Ansel's blessing on the name.

Ansel glanced down at the baby, and Charity wondered if he was aware it was his child. At times, she didn't think he knew. Leaving the sole care of the baby to Charity, he'd barely acknowledged that the infant had been born.

She was sure Ansel was acting strangely because his grief was so profound. He didn't cry or express his sorrow overtly. Charity was almost certain that if he'd just hold his new daughter, somehow a small part of Letty would return to him.

The babe looked so much like her mother, Charity could swear those were Letty's laughing, amber-colored eyes staring back at her.

"We'll be at your place soon," Ansel said quietly, his tone unchanged by the noises of the baby sucking loudly on her tiny fist. "The child can eat then."

Charity shifted the baby to her shoulder and bounced her gently. The soothing motion stilled the baby's fretfulness for the moment. Charity worried how Ansel would care for the child alone, once he returned home. Perhaps, she sighed, it would be good for father and daughter to be on their own. She'd promised to help Ansel find a woman to live in and care for the baby, but she knew that could take time.

In some ways, though, she felt that might be for the best. Ansel could become acquainted with his daughter, and Mary Kathleen could help fill the void in his life.

The baby began to whimper as the buckboard topped a rise and the Burkhouser soddy came into view. Charity's thoughts turned to another, even more perplexing problem: the stranger in her house. He would have to be buried immediately. She'd been gone much longer than she'd expected to be, and his remains would have to be disposed of quickly.

She glanced at Ansel and prayed he'd spare her the unpleasant task. Her heart still ached from having left the man to die alone.

When the buckboard rumbled into the yard and Ansel brought the horses to a halt, Charity noticed a heavy plume of smoke coming from the sod chimney.

Ansel jumped off the wagon and lifted Charity and the baby to the ground. "Someone has built a fire," she remarked, glancing in puzzlement at the rising smoke.

Could the stranger still be alive? she wondered. A thrill of expectation shot through her though she quickly suppressed that improbable hope. There had to be a more reasonable explanation for the fire.

She glanced around the yard, looking for a clue. The stack of firewood next to the house was the exact height it had been when she'd left two days ago. The oxen and old Bossy, her bag heavy with two days' milk, grazed in the small pen beside the lean-to. A few sitting hens roamed outside the soddy, scratching in the dirt and clucking contentedly.

Gabriel and Job lay in front of the door, wagging their tails lazily, waiting for Charity to come scratch behind their ears.

Everything seemed exactly as she'd left it, except for the strong smell of woodsmoke in the air.

She turned to ask Ansel how he'd explain the strange occurrence and was surprised to see him climbing back onto the seat of the buckboard.

"Oh, Ansel, why don't you rest for a spell before you unhitch the horses," she urged, knowing he'd need the wagon to carry the stranger's remains to the gravesite.

"No, thank you, Charity. I'd best be gettin' along." Ansel picked up the reins and released the brake.

Charity stared at him open mouthed. "But, Ansel," she protested lamely, trying to make sense of his behavior. "You can't be leaving!"

"You take care now, you hear?" Ansel whistled and slapped the reins across the horses' broad rumps. The buckboard began to roll noisily out of the yard amid the jangle of harness and creaking leather.

Charity watched in stunned silence as the wagon moved off in the direction it had just come. She glanced from the bundle in her arms to the cloud of boiling dust. Great balls of fire! He *was* leaving, she thought frantically.

"Ansel, wait!" she shouted, running after the wagon. "You forgot your baby!" But in a few moments she was out of breath, and her footsteps began to falter. The buckboard disappeared over the rise and was completely out of sight.

Charity let out an exasperated sigh and stared down at the infant in her arms. If this wasn't a fine kettle of fish! How dare Ansel ride off and leave the child in her care!

The baby began to cry, thrashing her fists angrily in the air, demanding her dinner as Charity started trudging toward the soddy, wondering what in blue blazes had gotten into Ansel! Surely he'd have the good sense to remember he'd forgotten his baby and come back; meanwhile, she was left to care for the infant and face the unpleasant task of burying the stranger by herself.

As if her thoughts weren't disconcerting enough, the baby was screaming at the top of her lungs when Charity finally reached the soddy. She pushed the door open and sucked in her breath as a blast of hot air nearly knocked her off her feet.

"What in . . ." Charity pushed the door wider and stepped into the room, trying to adjust her eyes to the dim light. Once she could see, Charity surveyed the scene before her with amazement.

Two Indian squaws sat beside the fireplace, chanting and passing a large pipe back and forth between them. They had built a roaring fire, and the flames were licking wildly up the chimney.

Charity wrinkled her nose, her attention momentarily diverted as she noticed the several large pans of herbs and roots bubbling on the stove, filling the room with a vile odor.

The stranger lay on the bed. Swathed tightly from head to toe in a bedsheet, he resembled a picture of an Egyptian mummy Charity had once seen in a book.

The room was so stifling hot she could barely breathe, and the odor coming from the stove made her stomach lurch. She stood at the door, clutching the baby against her bosom.

When Little Fawn caught sight of Charity, she gave her a wide grin. "White sister return?"

Then Little Fawn wondered what Charity's return would mean to her claim on Gold Hair. Her smile faded as she scrambled to her feet, dragging Laughing Waters behind her.

"Little Fawn? Laughing Waters?" Charity surveyed the two disheveled squaws with growing bewilderment. The heat in the soddy had flushed the women's face to a bright red. Their buckskin dresses clung to their massive frames. Sweat rolled from beneath their dark hairlines, and the tailfeather in Laughing Waters's hair was cocked at an odd angle.

"What on earth is going on here?" Charity glanced to the bed where the stranger lay, writhing in agony. Her heart leapt when she heard him moan weakly as he tried to break free of the bindings. Realizing he was alive, she went weak with relief.

Little Fawn, seeing the unmistakable joy on Charity's face, crossed her arms over her ample bosom, and a combative glint came into her eyes. "We make Gold Hair better."

Charity could hardly believe he was still alive. It was nothing short of a miracle, but the man *had* survived. "He's better . . . he really is? Oh, thank God!"

Laughing Waters grunted. "*Little Fawn and Laughing Waters* make Gold Hair better," she clarified curtly, lest Charity misunderstand who'd actually saved the man's life.

Charity hurried to the bed, trying to control her rapid pulse. Yes, he was alive, though only his eyes, open now and staring at her wildly, were visible through an opening in the sheet.

"Why is he wrapped so tightly?" she asked in a whisper, unaware that the man was fully conscious.

"Make medicine work," Little Fawn explained. She scurried to the bed and edged Charity out of the way with her large hip. Her fingers picked up a stray lock of his hair, and the man's eyes widened fearfully as she smiled and stroked the golden strand. "Pretty, like rocks in water. Me keep."

The man groaned and clamped his eyes shut. "I think he's trying to say something." Charity reached to unwrap the bandage wound so tightly under his chin that it prevented him from speaking, but Little Fawn's hand shot out and stopped her. The squaw sent Charity a stern look. "*We* help Gold Hair!"

Charity glanced up, surprised to detect the possessive note in her voice. Laughing Waters and Little Fawn visited her often. They were the last of a friendly band of Kaw Indians who camped about five miles on the other side of Fire Creek. For months the two squaws had made a habit of visiting the soddy, making themselves at home whenever they came.

Apparently they'd happened to visit two days ago and discovered the wounded man. But Charity certainly hoped they didn't think he'd become their property!

"Thank you very much for tending . . . Gold Hair . . . while I was away," she said carefully, hoping she could convince them that the man was hers, not theirs.

"Gold Hair heap good man," Little Fawn proclaimed with another grin.

"Oh, yes . . . yes, I can see that. He's very . . . nice, and he's . . . mine."

Little Fawn's face fell.

Laughing Waters's eyes narrowed. "Why you leave Gold Hair? Heap big sick."

"Yes, I know he is." Charity wasn't sure how much they understood but sensed they were waiting for her explanation. Remembering the baby, she smiled and unwrapped the blanket and proudly displayed a grumpy Mary Kathleen. "See? I've been away helping my friend have her baby. That's why I had to leave Gold Hair."

The women lowered their heads in unison and looked at the child. "Oh, papoose," Little Fawn crooned, tickling under the baby's chin.

Charity noticed Laughing Waters wasn't impressed. "Gold Hair heap big sick. We fix; we keep," she calmly announced.

Since the Indians had never seemed threatening to her, Charity didn't feel alarmed. Apparently the two squaws had been able to do for the stranger what she hadn't, and she was grateful.

But not grateful enough to let them have him. "No, you see, my friend was very ill. She was about to have her baby, and she needed my help," Charity explained patiently. "Since Gold Hair was asleep, I thought it would be all right to leave to help my friend." That wasn't exactly true, but Charity knew the women would have no way of knowing otherwise.

Laughing Waters was clearly skeptical. "Where mother of papoose?"

"She . . . died," Charity admitted painfully.

Laughing Waters still wasn't convinced that Charity should have first claim to the man. "Where papoose's father?"

"He's . . . not here right now . . . but he'll be back soon. Because my friend died, I was gone longer than I intended to be. I'm thankful to see you and Little Fawn have taken such good care of Gold Hair."

Little Fawn and Laughing Waters exchanged a noncommittal look. "If you'll show me what to do, I'll take over now," Charity bargained, praying they'd buy her story. "You see, he was attacked by a wolf, and I haven't been quite sure how to care for him. I see you have him on the mend."

Laughing Waters grunted disgustedly, and it seemed unlikely the two would relinquish their rights to the white man. They went off into a corner of the soddy and gestured animatedly as they whispered to each other.

While Charity held her breath, she glanced over at the bed and found the man eyeing all three of them warily. His eyes were as blue as she remembered them, and she tried to reassure him with a nod.

Laughing Waters returned and grudgingly handed Charity a large cup of vile-smelling tea. "Make Gold Hair drink."

Charity nodded and released a sigh of relief. "Thank you, I will."

"We be back Big Father's Day," Little Fawn stated firmly.

The baby began to fuss, and Charity nervously rocked it back and forth in her arms. She thought she'd faint from the heat. "Sunday? Yes, Sunday will be fine," she said agreeably, realizing the squaws were not going to give him up so easily.

"Keep fire going. Heap big sweat. Make Gold Hair better."

"Yes . . . yes, of course," Charity promised, wondering why she hadn't thought to try and sweat the poison out of him herself.

"Put medicine on hurts."

Charity stared at the bucket of herbs and roots next to the bed. "I will."

Little Fawn walked back to the bed and touched a strand of golden hair once more. As Beau looked up helplessly, she gave him a flirtatious wink and proudly displayed the wide gap of missing front teeth.

"We go now," Laughing Waters announced.

"I'll take good care of . . . Gold Hair," Charity promised.

Laughing Waters started past her, then paused to look at the baby again. "Gold Hair make stronger papoose," she grunted.

Charity watched as Little Fawn and Laughing Waters opened the door.

"We be back Big Father's Day," Laughing Waters warned again.

"Yes, fine. We'll be here."

The door slammed, and Charity sank weakly onto a chair as the baby began to scream. What a disagreeable day, she thought numbly. Most disagreeable.

CHAPTER 8

THOUGH SHE KNEW THE STRANGER NEEDED ATTEN-
tion, Charity warmed a bottle and fed Mary Kathleen. At the moment,
the baby was more demanding than the man, and he seemed momentarily
comfortable.

Casting worried glances toward the bed, she rushed around the soddy,
trying to soothe the baby's wails, which were growing more frantic by the
minute. No doubt about it, Mary Kathleen had turned hostile.

Even the warm bottle of milk Charity tried to feed her did nothing to
appease the baby. She screamed at the top of her lungs, her tiny face
turning red as a raspberry as Charity paced the floor, jiggling her up and
down in her arms.

The more Charity jiggled, the louder Mary Kathleen cried.

Beau, still trussed up like a Christmas goose, lay on the bed calmly
watching the growing ruckus.

When the infant suddenly flew into a full-blown tantrum, holding her
breath until her tiny features turned a strange, bluish white, the woman
panicked and broke into tears of frustration. Both woman and baby were
sobbing noisily as Beau cleared his throat, hoping to get the woman's
attention.

He'd felt relief after discovering he wasn't in hell—at least he wasn't in
the huge fiery pit described in the Good Book. But just exactly *where* was
he? he wondered.

Wherever it was, it was strange. Two Indian squaws fussing over him,
slapping foul-smelling mixtures on his wounds had been bad enough;
now he was faced with a baby howling like a banshee and a woman who
obviously didn't know the first thing about raising a child.

Again Beau cleared his throat loudly and squirmed about, but the
woman and baby were too busy sobbing to notice. Glancing around, Beau
focused his gaze on a tin cup filled with tea sitting on the stand beside the
bed. Slowly, he inched his way across the mattress and nudged the cup
with his shoulder, knocking it off the table.

The contents splattered on the bed, leaving a dark stain on the white linens, but the cup had the desired effect of hitting the floor with a resounding clatter.

Both Charity and the baby ceased their wailing at the same instant. Charity glanced at the bed through a veil of tears, and saw the man motioning with his eyes for her to remove the tight bandage confining his chin.

Deciding the loud interruption didn't concern her, Mary Kathleen resumed screaming while Charity hurried to the side of the bed.

"Were you speaking to me?"

"Ohmmhgtynm."

"You want me to untie the bandage?"

"Ohmmmhgtynm!"

"Oh . . . yes, of course."

With one hand Charity began loosening the knot in the bandage, while trying to converse over the baby's screams. "I'm sorry, I know we're disturbing you, and I'm *trying* to get her to hush, but she just won't!"

The knot came undone, and Beau felt as if he'd been released from a bear trap. He worked his jaws back and forth, wincing at the painful stiffness yet grateful for the blessed freedom.

"I just don't know what's gotten into her," Charity apologized. "Nothing seems to help."

"Get the scissors and cut me out of this damn sheet," Beau whispered hoarsely.

"Oh, I don't think I should. Little Fawn and Laughing Waters said—"

"I know what they said!" Startled by the snap in his voice, the infant screamed louder. "Just get me out of this!"

"You're scaring the baby." Charity patted Mary Kathleen on the back, to no avail; the baby only cried harder. "If I remove the sheet, it'll disturb your wounds." Pleased the stranger was improving, she didn't want to do anything to hinder his recovery.

Trying not to frighten the baby again, Beau made a conscious effort to lower his voice and speak calmly. "Just get me out of this, and I'll help you with the baby."

Those were the magic words. At this point Charity would have done anything to stop the baby's crying. Quickly she took scissors in hand and snipped away at the sheet as Mary Kathleen lay on the bed beside Beau, kicking and bellowing at the top of her lungs.

When the last of the cloth fell away, Charity blushed and averted her eyes. He was completely naked, and the sudden sight of his superb male body flustered her more than the baby's cries.

"Your . . . bandages need changing." Her hands were as shaky as her breathing. Beau sucked in his breath as Charity lifted the fabric Little Fawn and Laughing Waters had carefully placed over the tender wounds.

"Damn! That hurts. Take it easy!"

"Cursing won't make it any better." Gingerly she peeled away another bandage.

"You let a damn wolf gnaw on you for supper and see if you don't feel like swearin'. Ouch! Dammit, woman, that hurts!" There was a time when he would have apologized for swearing in a woman's presence, but much had happened to change Beau Claxton in the past year. So he swore again and gritted his teeth in renewed agony as his raw wounds were exposed to the air.

"There, now . . . just one more. . . ." Charity removed the last bandage and chanced another glance at his bare body before averting her eyes.

Beau sat up slowly and jerked the blanket over the lower half of his body. Charity knew he was watching her. Moreover, she knew he'd seen her looking at him. She had to break the awkwardness and tension surrounding them. "You remember the wolf?" she asked, staring at a far corner of the room.

"I try not to." He winced as the baby's howls continued. "Hand her to me."

Charity glanced at him in surprise. "You feel like holding her?"

"I can hold her better than I can stand to listen to her."

She hurriedly gathered the baby in her arms and carefully handed her to him. Beau caught his breath when Mary Kathleen's flailing fist hit one of his wounds.

"Oh, I'm so sorry!" Charity started to remove the baby, but Beau shrugged her away and eased the tiny bundle into the crook of his arm. He laid his head back on the pillow limply. The exertion of the past few moments had broken a fine sheen of sweat across his forehead. Mary Kathleen promptly ceased crying and snuggled deep against his side.

The room became quite peaceful as Beau gazed down at the infant in his arms. "You know, little one, you're pickin' up some bad habits," he said softly. "Some man's gonna turn you over his knee someday if you don't control that nasty temper."

Mary Kathleen hiccuped, then stuck her fist in her mouth and began sucking it loudly.

"She's hungry," Beau pronounced.

"I know she is, but she refuses to take her bottle."

"Give me the bottle."

Charity fetched the bottle and handed it to him. In moments the baby was contentedly sucking the contents dry.

"How did you do that?" She was awed by the way he handled the infant.

Mary Kathleen nestled snugly next to his large frame, her big amber eyes beginning to droop with exhaustion.

"I've always been good with kids. I have a nephew I used to visit every day. We got along real well." Beau refused to think about the child he'd lost.

Charity watched with amazement as Mary Kathleen slowly dropped into a peaceful slumber. "Would you like me to move her?"

"No." Beau tucked the baby's blanket around her snugly. "She'll be fine right here."

"I need to put clean bandages on your wounds."

"In a while."

Charity tried not to stare at his chest, but her eyes kept wandering back to the bare expanse of masculine flesh. It was impressively broad, covered in a cloud of light-brown hair. She felt an unexpected rush of desire when she remembered how protected, how wonderful, she'd felt when he'd held her, even if he had thought she was his "Betsy."

She suddenly realized that she missed having her own man, missed being held and kissed, and made love to.

After Ferrand's death she'd sworn she'd never love another man, never again risk the hurt he'd caused her by going off and getting himself killed in that senseless war.

It occurred to Charity that she'd been angry at Ferrand for a long time. Now she could feel that anger subsiding.

For the first time since his death she found herself thinking that maybe it would be possible to love again.

She wanted to be made love to again, to be a cherished wife and bear a man's child. Her gaze drifted wistfully back to the stranger, and she wondered again why she found him so attractive. His hair was shaggy, he hadn't shaved in weeks, and his large frame was whipcord thin. The two large wounds across his middle were covered with a thick, sticky poultice, and his ribs were poking through his skin. Still, she found him extremely desirable.

Charity found the admission disturbing. Would her growing feelings for him only serve to bring her new heartbreak?

"I guess we should introduce ourselves." She willed herself to take one step at a time. She drew her palm across her dress to dry the moisture from it, and extended her hand. "I'm Charity Burkhouser. I shot the wolf and brought you here."

The man glanced at her extended hand, but made no effort to take it. "You shouldn't have bothered."

"Oh . . . no bother." Charity was puzzled. She thought he'd be immensely grateful she'd saved his life. She paused, waiting for a thank-you, but when it appeared she'd have to wait all night, she let her hand drop to her side.

"What did you say your name was?" He hadn't said, but she thought it only decent he supply some sort of information about himself.

"Claxton."

Charity smiled. "Just . . . Claxton?"

"Beau. Beau Claxton."

"Beau. That's nice. I'll bet your mother chose that name." Charity noticed he was losing interest in the conversation.

"Well, Beau, I must admit, there were times when I thought I'd never know your name." She watched his eyes begin to droop with fatigue. "Are you from around here?"

"No." His voice sounded weaker than before.

"Oh. I'm sorry I had to leave you, but Letty—the baby's mother—she needed my help. I'm so thankful Laughing Waters and Little Fawn happened along when they did."

Beau wasn't sure he was thankful, but he was too weary to think about the horror of the past few days.

"How long have I been like this?" he murmured.

"Almost a week, but you're getting better." It was a relief to see his wounds weren't looking so angry.

He was silent for a moment. "You said the child's mother died?"

"Yes, I'm afraid she did."

"That's too bad. A baby should have its mother."

The image of Betsy, heavy with child, drifted painfully back into Beau's thoughts. God, he didn't want to think about Betsy again . . . he didn't want to remember it could have been his child tucked safely against his side. . . . He could feel a weight of sadness that had been his for over a year creep back into his heart.

"Would you like some broth? I see that Laughing Waters and Little Fawn left some on the stove for you."

"I'm not hungry." Just tired. Bone tired.

"Well, just rest a spell. We can talk later." Charity leaned to tuck the sheet around him and the sleeping baby. His eyes drifted closed as she stood and gazed fondly from the baby to him. After a moment they were sound asleep, his large arm wrapped protectively around Mary Kathleen's tiny shoulders.

I sure hope there's no Betsy waiting for you to come home, Charity found herself thinking. Startled by her errant thoughts, she realized how selfish she sounded.

Of course, if he was married, Charity would write and inform his wife of her husband's injuries. It would only be right. And yet . . . As she reached to brush his hair from his forehead, she sighed.

Perhaps Betsy was his sister? But no, he wouldn't kiss a sister the way he'd kissed her the other day, she realized. Maybe Betsy was just an acquaintance? Even that possibility sent a pang of jealousy through her.

Well, no matter who Betsy was, Beau Claxton was a fine man, Charity decided. If there was no legal Mrs. Claxton, there'd be one soon—if she had anything to say about it.

CHAPTER 9

BEAU AWOKE TO THE TANTALIZING SMELL OF CORN-bread baking in the oven. The tempting aroma drifted through the soddy, making his empty stomach knot with hunger. How long had it been since he'd last eaten?

He glanced down at the small bundle cuddled protectively against his side, and a smile formed at the corners of his mouth. The baby was still sleeping peacefully.

Without disturbing the infant, Beau shifted around to ease his stiffened joints. The maneuver hurt him, but not as much as before.

Settled more comfortably, he let his gaze drift toward the window, where he noticed the last rays of sunshine glistening on the windowpane. It must be late afternoon, he thought, realizing this was the first time he'd been able to distinguish the hour of day since his injury.

His gaze moved on, roaming aimlessly about the room. The bright gingham curtain hanging at the window looked freshly washed and ironed. The buffalo rug covering the floor was swept clean, and everything was tidy.

The room had all the signs of a woman's touch, he reflected. The colorful red-and-blue patchwork quilt draped across the foot of the bed reflected long hours dedicated to the intricate rows of tiny stitches.

Beau knew little about such womanly pursuits, but he'd watched his mother sit beside the old lamp in her parlor, working late into the night on a coverlet much like the one he was saw now.

The sound of a woman's voice humming "Dixie" momentarily distracted him. His head turned slowly on the pillow, seeking the source of the clear, sweet notes filtering through the room.

He saw a young woman standing at the stove, stirring a large pot with a wooden spoon. Instead of the foul-smelling brew the pot had contained before, there was a delicious aroma of meat and vegetables.

Who was this girl? Beau searched his memory for her name. Charita? Cherry? He couldn't remember.

"Well, hello. You've finally woken up." Charity's voice interrupted his thoughts as she set the spoon aside and wiped her hands on her apron. "Dinner will be ready soon. I hope you feel up to eating a bite."

"Yes, I think I can." His gaze drifted back to the pot on the stove. The smell of the simmering stew made his mouth water.

"Well, good!" Charity brought her hands together enthusiastically. His returning appetite was the most encouraging sign of recovery so far. She immediately began ladling the thick stew onto a plate. She added a piping hot wedge of cornbread and a slab of freshly churned butter, then arranged everything on a tray along with a large glass of milk.

The baby was beginning to stir as she approached, so she sat the tray on the small table beside the bed and gently scooped Mary Kathleen into her arms. "Best you eat slow," she cautioned, fearing the rich food might upset Beau's stomach.

"Aren't you going to eat?" His eyes were on the cornbread. It was thick and crusty—just the way his mother used to make it.

"I'll feed the baby, then I'll eat." She returned to the stove and removed the bottle of milk she'd warmed earlier. "You and Mary Kathleen had a nice long nap," she remarked.

Beau picked up the piece of cornbread and took a cautious bite. The exquisite flavor made him close his eyes with pure pleasure. It'd been a long time since he'd tasted anything so good.

"Looks like rain to the west." Charity sat in the rocker and held the baby, who was eagerly sucking from the bottle. "Sure could use a good soaking. It's been real dry."

Beau took another bite of the cornbread and chewed it slowly. "What time of the year is this?"

"October." Charity cocked her head to one side. "Why?"

"No reason." Beau picked up the spoon and brought a bite of stew to his mouth. God, he'd been wandering for over a year! The realization astounded him, and he felt a pang of guilt. His family must be sick with worry. "Exactly where am I?"

"In my soddy."

"No, I mean, am I still in Missouri?"

Charity laughed warmly. "No, you're in Kansas. Not far from a town called Cherry Grove."

"Kansas?"

"Yes. Are you from Missouri?"

"Yes."

Charity thought his questions odd and wondered if his memory had been affected by the accident. In a way, it would be to her advantage if he didn't remember his past. If he couldn't remember who he was, then he might be more easily persuaded to stay and help her. She decided to face her biggest obstacle first.

"Who's Betsy?"

The stew in his mouth suddenly tasted sour. He lifted his head slowly, and a defensive light came into his eyes as he met her inquiring gaze. "Who?"

"Betsy. You kept calling for her while you were unconscious." Charity held her breath, praying Betsy would be anyone but his wife.

A tight knot formed in the pit of his stomach, and Beau pushed his plate away though he'd barely touched it.

"You're finished already?" Her tone rang with disappointment.

"I've had enough."

"But you barely touched your food."

"I lost my appetite."

Charity hated to hear that. If he didn't eat properly, she knew he'd be slow to regain his strength. "Perhaps if I put your plate in the warming oven, you'll feel like eating more later."

Beau seemed to ignore the suggestion as he settled back on the pillow and closed his eyes again.

When Mary Kathleen finished the bottle, Charity lifted her to her shoulder and patted her back gently, savoring the sweet fragrance of the baby's skin. Once more her thoughts turned to Ansel, and where he could be.

All afternoon she had been expecting him to return for his daughter, but it was getting dark, and she feared he wasn't coming. If he didn't show up tomorrow, she wasn't sure what she'd do. Send someone to fetch him? She didn't know who it could be. And it would be impossible to leave Beau and the baby alone.

Grief had made Ansel temporarily forgetful, she tried to reason. It was the only explanation she could come up with for his puzzling behavior.

Surely tomorrow he would return for his daughter.

Turning back to the present, Charity remembered that Beau hadn't answered her question about Betsy. Was it an oversight or had he deliberately avoided her question? There was only one way to find out: she could be what Ferrand had always called downright nosy. She decided to chance it.

"You never told me about Betsy."

This time, Charity was sure he was deliberately avoiding her question. He lay on the bed, eyes closed, hands folded peacefully across his chest—totally ignoring her.

The baby burped loudly, filling the silence that had suddenly crowded the room, but Beau said nothing.

"Well?" Charity prompted.

Finally he took a deep breath and opened his eyes. With pained resignation he met her gaze across the room. "Betsy is my wife."

Disappointment ricocheted like heat lightening across Charity's face. She'd known it was a possibility he was married, hadn't she? Hadn't she warned herself not to get her hopes up? But nothing could dull the dismal feeling of frustration closing in on her.

"Oh . . . I—I thought maybe that's who she might be." Her voice sounded high and hollow even to her own ears.

Well, Charity, *you've no one to blame but yourself for getting the foolish idea in your head that he was sent to you as a personal gift*, she scolded silently. It was plain he wouldn't be any use to her now. He had a wife named Betsy waiting for him when he recovered.

She sighed and squared her shoulders. "First thing tomorrow morning, I'll write your wife about what's happened and where you are."

Beau stared at the ceiling for a moment with expressionless blue eyes, and then Charity thought she detected a veiled sadness began to creep into them. "Yeah, you can do that, but I don't see how you're going to have it delivered," he said softly.

"Shouldn't be too hard. It's about time to go into town for the mail. I'll send the letter then."

Beau said the words slowly, as if trying to make himself believe them. "No, you can't do that. Bets is dead." It was true. Betsy was dead and a year was a long time to wallow in self-pity. His wife had been taken from him, and, like it or not, he was going to have to accept it.

Charity's gaze lifted expectantly to his. "She is?"

"Yes."

Dead. Betsy was dead! Relief surged through her, and she was instantly ashamed of herself for being so heartless and selfish. It was plain to see from the look on his face that his wife's death had been unbearable for him. "Oh . . . I'm very sorry," she apologized, the sincerity of her tone indicating she truly was.

"Yeah." He took a deep, ragged breath. "So am I."

"How long ago?"

"Over a year."

Strange, this was the first time Beau had been able to talk about Betsy's death without weeping like a child. To say her name didn't even hurt as much as it once had. "She was carrying our baby, and a rattlesnake . . . bit her," he continued cautiously.

Charity knew this couldn't be easy for him. Memories of Ferrand's untimely death flooded back as she listened to Beau talk about his wife's accident in quiet, almost reverent tones.

"It—it didn't take long for her to die. . . ." His voice broke momentarily, then he cleared his throat. Charity was stunned to see him reach for his plate again. He calmly picked up the spoon and ladled a bite of vegetables into his mouth. He chewed for a moment, absently savoring the flavor of the stew. When he glanced back at Charity it was almost as if he'd forgotten she was there. "I loved my wife very much."

"Yes, I'm sure you did," Charity said softly, feeling his pain as deeply as she'd felt her husband's loss. "It's hard to get over something like that. I lost my husband three years ago."

"Oh?" Beau was surprised that with each bite, his appetite increased, and his spirits lifted. "The war?"

She nodded. "Ferrand was riding with Sterling Price's Confederate raiders in the fall of sixty-four. When the Confederacy made its last offensive west of the Mississippi, Curtis Stewart, with the help of Alfred Pleasonton's calvary, whipped the Confederates and drove them back into Arkansas. Ferrand was killed near Westport, Missouri."

"The Confederacy?" Beau glanced up. "Your husband fought for the South?"

"Yes. Ferrand's decision was very hard—especially on me. But I understood his reasons. Naturally, there was a lot of talk. You must remember, in the Civil War Kansas sent a larger number of Union soldiers to the field, in proportion to its population, than any other state. But my husband and I came from Virginia, and your upbringin' is hard to forget. Our families still live there. Ferrand was torn at first, but when it came right down to it, he felt he had to fight for what he believed in. Of course, all he did was go and get himself killed."

"It must have been hard on you," he murmured sympathetically.

"It was," she said with a sigh. "We had barely started homesteading this piece of land when Ferrand decided to join up. For a long time after his death I didn't know what I should do. My family wanted me to move back to Richmond, and that would probably have been wise. But Ferrand always said I was as stubborn as a Missouri mule when it came to holding on to what's important to me. After all the hard work we'd put into this soddy, it sure seemed frivolous to walk away and leave it for someone else."

"You been tryin' to work the land by yourself?" It wasn't unusual to find a woman homesteading land—the war had left many widows as heads of their families. But Beau couldn't imagine this tiny woman driving a team of oxen.

"I've been doin' a miserable job of it," Charity wasn't too proud to confess. "The fences are mostly down, I haven't had a decent crop in two years, and I haven't begun to make the improvements required by the state to grant me a title." She looked down at the baby thoughtfully. "I must admit, I was near my wits' end when you happened along."

Beau finished the stew and cornbread and drained the glass of milk. The meal was sitting easily in his stomach, and he felt his strength slowly begin to return.

From what he could tell, she was still young. Seemed to Beau that she was pretty enough to land another man. She was small and slender, with hair the color of a raven's wing, nice green eyes, and a wide, generous mouth—certainly nothing about her appearance to turn a man away. He suddenly realized he hadn't noticed whether a woman was good looking or not for a very long time. "Why haven't you remarried?"

Charity shrugged. "We have a real shortage of men out here, Mr. Claxton. Besides, other than Ferrand, I've never met one I'd want to share my bed—" Charity caught herself, then cast her eyes down to the baby shyly. "Never met one I'd want to have underfoot all the time," she corrected.

"Yeah." Beau knew the feeling. "Since Bets died, I haven't been with a woman—" He caught himself quickly when he realized what he was saying. "Well, I guess it doesn't matter. I'm never going to marry again."

Charity arched her brow slightly. "Oh?"

"Yeah, I loved Bets. No one could come close to taking her place."

"Oh, yes. I feel the same way." Somehow his pessimism gave her a feeling of foreboding. "Do you have family in Missouri that should be notified about your accident?" She wondered where his roots lay.

"I have family, but you don't need to bother gettin' in touch with them. I've been wandering around ever since Bets died." He paused for a moment before continuing. "I'll write and let them know where I am, soon as I'm up and around."

"You've just been driftin' all this time?"

"Yeah, just driftin'."

Glancing at Mary Kathleen asleep on Charity's shoulder, he seized the opportunity to change the subject. "Where's the baby's father?"

"I'm not sure. Ansel brought me home yesterday, then just up and disappeared."

"Disappeared?"

"Yes, and I don't know what to make of his strange behavior. You see, Ansel's wife, Letty, died giving birth to the baby a few days ago. Now Ansel seems so lost—not like himself at all. When he brought me home yesterday, I thought naturally he'd take the baby with him, but he didn't. He just climbed back in the buckboard and drove off." Charity shook her head, still puzzled by Ansel's peculiar actions. "But I figure once he comes to terms with his grief, he'll be back for the baby."

Charity rose and walked over to lay the baby at the foot of Beau's bed, her mind returning to what Beau had said about no other woman ever replacing his wife. She didn't know why his statement bothered her. It was natural for him to feel that way, she reasoned. She wouldn't be asking for his love. All she wanted was his strength and stamina for the next few months to clear her land and set fences.

After all, it was just as likely that no other man would ever replace Ferrand in her heart. She supposed if he'd agree to marry her, they'd be starting out even. And she supposed she shouldn't be beatin' around the bush about her intentions either. Now was as good a time as any to involve him in her plan.

"Mr. Claxton," she began formally.

"Just call me Beau." He'd closed his eyes again, wanting to doze. He felt relaxed and comfortable, ready for sleep.

"I understand how you feel about the loss of your wife, and I can sure sympathize with your feelings about not wantin' to marry again. I loved Ferrand with all my heart. But I've discovered that sometimes you have to put personal feelings aside and go on with life. . . ." Her voice trailed off anxiously.

"Yeah, that's what they say." Beau knew it wouldn't be easy, but he was going to have to try to make a life for himself again. Life went on, whether a man wanted it to or not, and the time had come for him to stop grieving. As soon as he got back on his feet, he'd head back to Missouri. Maybe he'd bring his mother and their housekeeper, Willa, home to live with him. They could help tend the house while he worked the fields. It wouldn't be the rich, full life he'd had before, but it would be livable.

Charity was trying to gather enough courage to proceed with the conversation. Asking this man to marry her was going to be one of the most brazen things she'd ever undertaken, but she'd never before faced losing everything either.

Necessity could override her fear in this instance, and she knew she had him at a certain disadvantage. He was still too weak to get up and walk out on her if he didn't take to the idea right away. If he did balk—and she was fully braced for that possibility—she would at least have a few days to try and make him change his mind.

"What are you wondering about?" Beau finally asked.

The heavy meal had made him feel complacent and drowsy. He was thinking how good it was to carry on a simple conversation again. He'd been on the trail for over a year, and although a few months earlier he would have argued otherwise, he felt beholden to this woman for saving his life.

Charity took a deep breath and shut her eyes. There was no easy way to approach it. She'd simply have to be blunt and forthright before her courage failed her again. "Well, I was wondering . . . would you marry me?" Her voice suddenly sounded downright meek.

For a moment her words failed to register. Beau's eyes remained closed, his head nestled deep within the pillow.

"Ordinarily I'd never be so brazen," she rushed on, determined that he wouldn't think her a sinful, immoral woman. "But I'm afraid I'm in a terrible quandary." Her voice picked up tempo, as she interpreted his continued silence as a hopeful sign. "You see, if I don't make the required improvements on my land within a year, I can't claim title to my homestead. To be blunt, Mr. Claxton, I need a man. That's why I think it was fate—you know, the way I found you in my stream. I dragged you back to the soddy, and worked day and night to save your life—although I suppose most of the credit should go to Little Fawn and Laughing Waters. Nevertheless, I worked just as hard, and if it hadn't been for Letty needing my help so desperately, why, I would never have dreamed of leaving you here alone . . . to die. . . ." She paused and sighed. "But, of

course, you didn't die, and I'm tremendously grateful you didn't. Now"
—she paused again for air, preparing to make her next recitation in one
long breath— "you'll find I work hard, cook decently, bathe regularly,
and make a good companion." She hurried to the side of the bed and sat
down, sounding more enthusiastic as she explained her plan. "You see, I
figure if you'd be so kind as to marry me, then at the end of the year, I can
claim my land and you can be on your way."

Beau's eyes remained closed, and she prayed he hadn't fallen asleep.
"Of course, I realize I'm asking you to spend the whole winter here, but I
think it will take a while for you to fully regain your strength. In the
meantime we can make the needed improvements on my land. Naturally,
I'm prepared to pay you well for your time and effort," she promised.
"While I'm not a rich woman, I do have a small nest egg, and I can assure
you I'll see that your generosity is handsomely rewarded." She paused,
leaning closer to see if he was listening at all. She couldn't tell. "It
wouldn't take very long, and I'd be most grateful for your assistance."

Beau's left eye opened very slowly.

Charity held her breath. If he refused, she wasn't sure what she'd do
next.

Both eyes opened wide, staring at her in disbelief. "Marry you!"

"Yes." Her smile began to wilt as she realized she might have been a
bit hasty in revealing her plan. Maybe she should have waited a few days,
let him get to know her better. . . . "I realize this may have come as a
bit of a shock, but you see, Beau—"

"Mr. Claxton," he interrupted curtly.

Her chin tilted stubbornly as she ignored his frosty attitude. After all,
she understood this might be disconcerting for him. She *was* a complete
stranger. "Mr. Claxton, I'm afraid my unfortunate circumstances have
forced me to come directly to the point, though to be honest, I don't
know any other way to be. Now, I've been truthful by revealing to you
why I'd make such an unusual suggestion, and, while I can't fault you for
being taken by surprise, I don't think you have the right to act like I've
escaped from an asylum for the insane. It's just that I'm . . . desperate."
Her tone had gone from meek to pleading.

Beau found the sudden turn of conversation incredible. "Let me understand . . . you're *seriously* asking me—a complete stranger, a man
you know nothing about—to marry you?"

How ludicrous, he thought. Why, for all this woman knew, he could
be a worthless drifter, a debaucher, a hired killer, and there she sat
innocently offering to be his wife—and pay him for the privilege?

"I am, indeed," Charity stated firmly. "I need a man."

He shook his head with a frown. "Can't you find someone to—"

"I don't *need* a man, not in that way," she shot back, her face flushing
scarlet with his bold insinuation. "I need a man's strength, not his . . .
you know. . . ."

"No, I *don't* know. Why in the world would you ask a complete stranger to marry you? Are you addlebrained?" Now that Beau had regained his composure, he was angry. A woman should never ask a man to marry her, no matter *what* the circumstances.

"I'm not addlebrained, and I told you why," she returned calmly. "I don't want to lose my land, and I'm going to unless I come up with a man soon."

"So you propose marriage to the first man you meet?"

"You're not the first man I've met. You're just the first *available* man I've met," she corrected.

The baby began to fret, and Charity rose to pick her up. "Besides, you're not a stranger—not really. In fact, I feel rather close to you." There wasn't an inch of his body she wasn't already familiar with, and the thought of his masculine, naked physique made her stomach turn fluttery. "I know your name is Beau Claxton, and I also know that once you've recovered from your accident, you'll be a strong, healthy man—healthy enough to clear land and set fence posts and drive a team of oxen. I know you come from Missouri, you're widowed, and, because of your injuries, you're going to be laid up here for a while." Charity turned and smiled at him. "That's all I need to know, Mr. Claxton."

"This is the most ridiculous thing I've ever heard." The woman *had* to be addlebrained, Beau thought irritably. "You don't know a thing about me, and I just told you, I don't plan on ever marrying again, let alone to a woman I've just met."

"Are you refusing my offer?" She had the sinking feeling he was.

He looked at her again in disbelief. "Of course I am."

"Oh. You won't at least think about it?"

Beau shut his eyes again, trying to dismiss the entire unpleasant conversation. He felt obligated to her for saving his life, but not enough to marry her. "Certainly not."

The room grew silent for a moment as Charity tried to digest his words. He wasn't going to marry her, that was plain as the nose on her face. Well, she hadn't wanted to take advantage of the situation, but he was leaving her little choice.

Beau glanced over at the rocker and found his temper simmering again. She had no right to ask him to marry her, but that damn whipped-dog look on her face annoyed him even more. "Look, if you're so desperate for a husband, what about Mary Kathleen's father? Seems to me he could sure use a wife right about now." The silence had grown ominously thick.

"Ansel?" Charity looked up in surprise. She had never considered Ansel. He'd be the logical choice, but it would be months before he could think of taking another wife. No, she quickly discarded the idea. Ansel was out of the question. She needed a man *right now*.

"No, Ansel isn't my answer." Charity hated to resort to underhanded tactics, but it seemed clear she'd have to force Beau's hand. At this point she wasn't above double-dealing.

"Then I'm afraid you're up a creek without a paddle," Beau predicted.

"I guess so, but I figure you're in about the same shape."

Beau looked at her sternly. "I don't see how you figure that."

"Well, if you won't at least consider my proposal, I'll have no other choice than to turn you over to Little Fawn and Laughing Waters."

Beau's eyes widened. "Those two women who—"

"The Indian squaws who took care of you in my absence," she confirmed, feeling almost shameful for being so mean. Almost. "They're very enamored of you, you know. I had a terrible time convincing them you're my . . . man. They feel they have a certain claim to you since they had a part in saving your life."

"I'll be damned if they do!" Beau's chin jutted stubbornly. This mess was growing more ridiculous by the moment.

"I know it's disconcerting." Her tone was soothing, but she planned to be just as heartless as he if he wouldn't cooperate. "But I'm afraid if you don't marry me, then I'll have no alternative but to give you back to them. They're returning Sunday, you know, and I'll just tell them you're not my man after all. They'll take you back to their camp, nurse you back to full health, and then—" Charity's eyes narrowed, and her voice dropped ominously low— "you'll be on your own, Mr. Claxton, because they *both* want you for a husband." All traces of pleasantness had suddenly evaporated. She straightened her back with a satisfied smile. "Of course, if you'd prefer being a husband to Laughing Waters and Little Fawn to staying here and helping me save my land, then I suppose there's no point in talking."

Feeling he had to get out fast, Beau struggled to the side of the bed. As he sat up, his head suddenly started spinning, and he felt so weak he couldn't keep his balance. He groaned and toppled back on the pillow. If those two squaws got hold of him again, he didn't know what he'd do. He didn't have the strength to outrun them . . . and yet, by the same token, he refused to be cornered like a damn rat by this woman!

"I could still die," he threatened.

"Oh, I don't think so. You've already missed your chance. Besides, I can't understand why you find marrying me so offensive. You obviously don't have anything else to do; you said so yourself."

"This is blackmail, you know." His voice was muffled in the pillow. "And I'll be damned if I'm going to let you get away with it!"

"Suit yourself." Charity walked to the rocker and sat down. She gently rocked the baby back and forth as she hummed "Dixie."

She knew she had him. He was sensible enough, she thought, just a mite stubborn, that was all. When he thought it over, he'd prefer marrying her to facing his fate with Laughing Waters and Little Fawn.

"I mean it!" Beau eyed her sternly. He was sitting up again, his head bobbing weakly back and forth. It didn't take much for him to see that she hadn't given up yet. She was a mean, pigheaded woman. "I'm not marryin' anyone, let alone two crazy squaws or an addlebrained girl."

"We'll see. You do know what day this is, Mr. Claxton?"

Actually, he didn't have any idea. "No."

"Saturday." Charity sent him a smug look. She should be ashamed of herself; he was still very ill and could do little about the circumstances facing him. But she was desperate, and he was the only available man she knew.

"So?"

"Big Father's Day is tomorrow." She began humming softly.

Beau slumped back on the pillow, her words sinking in. He vaguely recalled the two Indian women saying they'd return on "Big Father's Day."

Tomorrow was Sunday.

His hand absently touched his hair as he remembered how the Indian squaws had constantly fussed over him. Damn. His gaze shot back to Charity, and he saw that she was ignoring him.

Well, fine. Let her, he thought. She could threaten all she wanted, but she couldn't make him marry her. She was bluffing, that was all.

Just bluffing, and he wasn't about to fall for it.

CHAPTER 10

THE NEXT MORNING THE SUN ROSE EARLIER THAN Beau would have liked. He'd lain awake most of the night, trying to figure a way out of this entrapment. Sleep would have been impossible anyway: the baby had screamed the entire night.

Beau had to admit he felt sorry for Charity. She'd paced the floor, trying everything she could think of to quiet the baby. Nothing had worked. The infant had only stiffened in anger and cried all the harder.

The birds outside the soddy began to chirp noisily when Mary Kathleen finally dropped into an exhausted slumber. Charity placed the infant in the small crib she'd fashioned from a drawer and tiptoed to the rocker, dropped numbly into it, and fell into a sound sleep.

Beau lay quietly staring at Charity, feeling renewed resentment at the predicament she'd gotten him into. Still, he couldn't say he didn't feel sympathy for her own unpleasant predicament.

Stranded on the Kansas frontier with a seriously injured man and a baby who wasn't hers didn't seem rightly fair. With her tending his needs and the baby's, she'd barely had time for her other chores.

And not only did he sympathize with her, he was beginning to feel guilty because he'd permitted her to sleep in the rocker the past two nights, allowing him the luxury of the soft, straw-filled mattress.

Of course, neither of them had gotten any rest, he recalled, what with the baby crying all the time.

As he watched Charity awaken and begin to move around in the soddy, it occurred to him again how unjust it was that so much misery could fall on one woman. However, he wasn't about to let compassion overrule common sense. Her marriage proposal was out of the question.

While he could pity her plight, he wouldn't permit himself to become part of it.

And as far as her threatening him with those Indian squaws was concerned, she was downright crazy if she believed she could *scare* him into marrying her.

She wouldn't actually turn him over to them, and he knew it. He figured no one would be that callous. He was a sick man, unable to defend himself. No matter what, she wouldn't do that to him.

As soon as he was able, he was going to hightail it out of here and head for Missouri. At least the women back there were sane.

Charity served Beau his breakfast, and they both carefully avoided the subject of marriage. Still, Beau kept one ear tuned to the door, listening for signs of Laughing Waters and Little Fawn.

He agreed to keep an eye on the baby while Charity went to the stream for fresh water.

After she returned with the buckets full, she set out to gather chunks of dried dung left by grazing cattle and buffalo. The chips would be fuel for the cooking stove, along with dry twigs, tufts of grass, hay twists, woody sunflower stalks, and anything else she could find to burn.

Later, while Beau and Mary Kathleen napped, Charity built a fire outside the soddy and set a large black kettle over it. With a bar of lye soap and a washboard, she scrubbed the baby's diapers, then hung them to dry.

Normally she'd never dream of washing on Sunday, but this Sunday was different. She had very few diapers for Mary Kathleen, and the baby's needs came first.

By the time Charity had finished the wash, the baby was awake and demanding to be fed again.

"I'll do that," Beau offered, as Charity warmed the bottle and bounced the baby on her hip to still her hungry cries.

Charity glanced at him gratefully, her hair hanging limply in her face. "Are you sure you feel up to it?"

"I'll manage."

Beau thought it was the least he could do. He didn't suppose Charity felt much better than he did after the morning she'd put in.

When Charity placed the baby in Beau's arms, Mary Kathleen quieted down immediately. "She seems to like you." She handed him the warm bottle of milk and tucked Mary Kathleen's blankets around her snugly.

"You're gonna squeeze the life out of her," Beau complained. "Give her room to breathe." He began loosening the blanket, and Charity could have sworn Mary Kathleen heaved a sigh of relief.

"I don't want her to take a chill," Charity fretted.

"She won't. Babies don't need so much mollycoddlin'." When Beau put the bottle in the baby's mouth, she began nursing hungrily.

"She's real cute, don't you think?" she asked.

The woman always smelled fresh and lemony . . . and feminine, Beau thought as Charity leaned over his shoulder and peered at the baby with maternal pride. He studied Mary Kathleen's wrinkled, reddish face and decided it reminded him of a scarlet prune. "Not really . . . but she might be, given a few more weeks."

"Oh, what would you know about babies?" Charity teased as she moved to the stove and began preparing their dinner.

"I told you: my brother Cole, and his wife, Wynne, have a baby." Charity noticed a tenderness lit his eyes when he talked about his family. "Jeremy must be gettin' nigh on to three years old now."

"Do they live in Missouri?"

"They have a piece of land not far from my place."

"Is your brother taking care of your farm while you're gone?"

"He said he would." He gazed down at Mary Kathleen thoughtfully. "Don't you think someone should see about getting the baby's father to assume his responsibility?" Beau didn't think it was fair for Mary Kathleen's father to have waltzed off and left the baby with Charity, even if he was grieving over his wife. If his and Betsy's baby had lived, Beau was certain he'd have seen to its care.

"I thought Ansel would be here by now." She sank down wearily in a chair by the kitchen table and began peeling potatoes. "I'll ride over to his place this afternoon while the baby's napping—"

There was a sudden knock on the door and both Charity and Beau looked up.

"Maybe that's Ansel now." Charity hurried to the door, and Beau held his breath, praying it wouldn't be Laughing Waters and Little Fawn.

When Charity found Ansel on her doorstep, hat in hand, a pleasant smile on his face, she gave a sigh of relief. "Ansel, where in the world have you been?" Her voice sounded more critical than she'd intended, but she was bone tired.

"Morning, Miss Charity. I hope I'm not disturbin' you?"

"Of course you're not disturbing me," Charity said curtly. "I've been worried about you, Ansel. Where have you been?"

"Worried about me?" Ansel looked at her blankly. "Why?"

"Why? Because you rode off yesterday and left Mary Kathleen with me."

"Who?"

"Mary Kath—oh, never mind. Come in, Ansel." Charity ushered him into the soddy and closed the door. She could explain the selection of the baby's name later.

Ansel saw Beau lying in the bed and glanced back at Charity with a puzzled look. "Didn't know you had company."

"Company?" Charity eyes darted around the room expectantly. "I don't have company."

Ansel's gaze returned to Beau accusingly. "Who's he?"

Charity glanced at Beau, then back to Ansel. "He's the man I found in the stream." Charity was more confused than ever by Ansel's odd behavior. It was as if he'd forgotten all about the stranger. "You know—the one the wolf attacked?" *And the one you left* ME *to bury*, she wanted to add but didn't.

Ansel walked to the table and sat down, seeming to dismiss Beau for the moment. "It's cold out this morning."

"Ansel, are you all right?" Charity moved to the table and knelt beside his chair. "I've been so worried. Where have you been?"

"Been? Why, I've been at home, why?"

"Home . . . well, I've wondered . . . Are you sure you're all right?"

Ansel looked at her and smiled. "Yes, Letty, I'm just fine. How are you today?"

"I'm fine." She frowned. She'd noticed he had called her Letty. "And the baby's fine, Ansel. Would you like to hold your daughter?"

Ansel's face brightened. "Why, yes, I think that would be nice."

Charity felt encouraged. This was the first time Ansel had shown any sign of wanting to hold his daughter. She hurried to the bed to retrieve Mary Kathleen from Beau's arms.

Charity hurriedly introduced Ansel to Beau, who'd been watching the exchange with interest.

"I know you'll be glad to hear Mr. Claxton is doing fine now. When I got back, I discovered he was being nursed by Little Fawn and Laughing Waters—I think I've mentioned them to you before. The two women happened to find Mr. Claxton and knew exactly what to do." Charity settled Mary Kathleen in Ansel's arms. "There now, isn't she beautiful?"

Ansel looked down at the tiny bundle in his arm, his face growing tender with emotion. "Oh, she's real pretty."

"She truly is." Mary Kathleen opened her eyes and stared at her father angelically. He returned her smile and hesitantly reached to touch his forefinger to her rosy cheeks. "She looks like you, Letty. Just like you," he whispered softly.

Charity wasn't sure if he was speaking to her or his deceased wife. "Yes, she does look exactly like Letty. She has the same eyes, the same color of hair. . . . Letty would be proud," Charity acknowledged tenderly.

"Yes, yes, she would." Then, as quickly as he'd accepted the baby, Ansel handed Mary Kathleen back to Charity and stood up. "Well, I mustn't overstay my welcome. My chores need tendin'."

"You're always welcome, Ansel, but I understand your wanting to get back home." She began gathering the baby's belongings. "She's a bit fussy at night, but I think you'll get along fine. She's been eating about every two—"

The sound of the front door slamming shut caused Charity to whirl around in disbelief.

The room was empty, except for Beau and herself—and Mary Kathleen. Charity faced Beau. "Where'd he go?"

He shrugged.

Charity raced to the door and jerked it open just in time to see Ansel's buckboard rattling out of the yard. "Hell and damnation! What in tarnation is wrong with that man?" Charity slammed the door shut, making the baby jump with fright. Mary Kathleen puckered up like a thundercloud and began squalling.

Beau tried to quiet the baby while Charity stormed around the soddy, mumbling under her breath about the injustices of life. She slammed the iron skillet on the stove and angrily dug a large spoon of lard from a can and flung it into the pan.

"I *can't* imagine *who* he thinks he is to leave me with his baby! I *can't* take care of a baby and fix fences and drive oxen and—Letty was my friend, but there's a point—*hell* and damnation!" Charity irritably questioned Ansel's sanity—and her own—as she chopped potatoes and onions and dropped them into the sizzling fat.

Beau managed to calm Mary Kathleen but left Charity alone. He figured only a fool would try to talk to her now.

He had no idea what was going on, but it was plain to him that Ansel wasn't in full control of his faculties.

The realization did little to soothe Beau's jangled nerves.

If Ansel Latimer had gone off the deep end because of his wife's death, Beau was going to be left as the only candidate to help Charity save her land, and that grim prospect made him even more uneasy.

As if she understood his turmoil, Mary Kathleen burst into tears again.

Beau heaved a weary sigh as Charity sent a bowl clattering on the table and began mixing a batch of cornbread, still mumbling heatedly under her breath.

"I know just how you feel," he confided to the baby dryly. "It's a hell of a mess, isn't it?"

And, as if he didn't have enough trouble, Laughing Waters and Little Fawn appeared right after dinner.

CHAPTER 11

*L*AUGHING WATERS AND LITTLE FAWN ARRIVED IN their usual unpretentious manner.

Beau had just drained the last of his coffee when the front door to the soddy opened wide. Heart plummeting, he stared mutely at the dark outline of two large squaws silhouetted starkly against the noonday sun.

Both women had their arms piled high with firewood.

The memory of Charity's earlier threat closed in on him: *If you won't marry me, I'll have no other choice but to hand you over to Laughing Waters and Little Fawn. . . . They are enamored of you. . . . They both want you for their husband. . . .*

"Laughing Waters, Little Fawn, how nice to see you!" Charity turned from washing dishes to cast a pointed look at Beau. Wiping her sudsy hands on her apron, she stepped forward to greet the two women.

"We come. See Gold Hair." Little Fawn stated their purpose, and Laughing Waters's stern, austere expression reinforced it.

"Well, how nice. Please come in." Charity smiled pleasantly at Beau as she reached for her shawl hanging on the hook beside the door.

Beau shot her a warning look, but she ignored him. "While you visit with Mr. Claxton, I'll feed the chickens and gather the wash."

"Charity!" The sound of her name snapped authoritatively across the room.

"Yes?" Charity faced Beau with a look of wide-eyed innocence.

"You have company. It's not proper for you to go gather the wash." Though his voice remained firm, there was a distinct plea in it as well. "Besides, the baby will be wakin' up anytime now."

"Little Fawn and Laughing Waters aren't here to see me." She paused to tie the strings on her sunbonnet. "They've come to visit you, Gold

Hair," she pronounced carefully, "and don't worry, I'll listen for the baby. You just go right ahead and enjoy your visit." She smiled graciously at the two squaws. "Make yourselves at home, ladies."

Laying their bundles of wood by the doorstep, the squaws solemnly entered the soddy and stood by silently as Charity reached for her egg basket. Knowing the women had brought wood as a gift to please Beau, Charity smiled at them. "The wood is nice. I'll see that Gold Hair is warmed by it."

Beau couldn't believe Charity was callous enough to desert him! "Charity . . . now, wait a minute!"

"Papoose asleep?" Laughing Waters asked suddenly.

"Yes, she's sleeping soundly. Would you like to see her?" Charity invited.

The squaws edged toward the table where Charity had placed the baby's makeshift crib. Intently their dark eyes surveyed the infant until their curiosity was satisfied, then they slipped back to stand quietly at the doorway.

"Well, I'd best get to my chores," Charity announced.

As soon as Charity slipped out the door, Little Fawn, with a wide grin, began creeping toward the bed.

Beau winced, realizing he'd just been unsympathetically thrown back to the wolves.

Gold Hair heap better, Little Fawn was thinking, rejoicing that Beau was no longer so pale. He looked healthier now, and he was still handsomer and stronger than any other warrior. Her dark eyes moved to Beau's hair, and her fingers wiggled involuntarily, itching to touch the soft yellow mass.

While the men of other tribes let their hair grow long, it was the custom of Kaw men to shave their heads, leaving only a well-curved tuft on the crown where they could wear their warrior's eagle feathers.

Only when grieving a death would a tall, raw-boned Kaw suffer his hair to grow as proof of his inconsolable sorrow. But Little Fawn had never once seen such striking golden hair on any man. Her heart beat faster with anticipation. Soon, Swift Buck with Tall Antlers would be hers, and she would give thanks to Wah-kun-dah, the "All Powerful," for sending her such a fine, strong brave.

Beau saw the possessive light in Little Fawn's eyes, and began to draw back into his pillow defensively.

The squaw's toothless grin always made him uneasy. He knew something about his hair fascinated the two, but he wasn't sure what.

"Now, don't you go messin' with my hair," he warned in a voice that brooked no nonsense.

"Gold Hair speak! See! See! Gold Hair speak!" Laughing Waters quickly joined Little Fawn at Beau's bedside, and the two smiled down at him.

"Ohhhh, Gold Hair heap better," Laughing Waters proclaimed, thinking it wouldn't be long now before she and Little Fawn could take Brave Horse With Many Wounds back to their camp. Laughing Waters eyed Beau proudly. She knew that White Sister claimed Gold Hair, but the two squaws, after much discussion, had decided that would change.

They reasoned that they'd helped save Gold Hair's life; therefore, he belonged to them as much as he belonged to White Sister.

Laughing Waters and Little Fawn had been without a man's protection for too long. Speckled Eye, Little Fawn's husband, had died of smallpox during the past winter. Handsome Bird, Laughing Waters's husband, had ridden off on a buffalo hunt three years before and never returned.

The squaws had made a pact. They weren't going to relinquish their claim to this male just because White Sister wanted him too.

No, Gold Hair was theirs by all rights, and they planned to have him. So they'd concocted a clever plan.

Everything was set. They'd make Gold Hair drunk, then carry him off to their camp before he knew what was happening.

The plan was a simple one, and it had nearly worked on at least one other occasion.

But this time, it couldn't fail.

If White Sister tried to prevent them from taking Gold Hair, they would run like the wind, and Laughing Waters and Little Fawn knew Charity wouldn't be swift enough to overtake them.

Then Gold Hair would be theirs.

"We bring you gift," Little Fawn announced.

"Now listen, ladies." Beau knew he had to put a stop to their ambitious interest and quickly, or he could find himself running around half naked, hunting buffalo for the rest of his life. "I don't want to hurt your feelings, but—"

Laughing Waters slyly withdrew a bottle from beneath her red blanket and handed it to him. "We bring *pi-ge-ne*. Make you heap better!"

Beau cautiously took the bottle of amber liquid and examined it closely. "What's this?"

Little Fawn proudly displayed another toothless grin. "*Pi-ge-ne*—firewater!"

"Whiskey?"

Laughing Waters and Little Fawn bobbed their heads enthusiastically.

"Where'd you get this?"

"Trade pony and two buffalo robes," replied Little Fawn.

Beau couldn't deny that a shot of whiskey would ease his pain and anxiety, but he knew he couldn't accept their gift. He had a feeling there'd be strings attached. He quickly handed the bottle back to Little Fawn. "Listen, I appreciate the thought, but I can't drink this."

In unison their faces fell. "You no like *pi-ge-ne*?" Little Fawn asked.

"Sure, I like," Beau hedged, "but I can't accept your gift."

"White Sister no like *pi-ge-ne?*" Laughing Waters prodded.

"Yeah, that's it. White Sister no like *pi-ge-ne.*"

Why not pin the blame on Charity, he decided. After all, if it hadn't been for her, he wouldn't be in this mess. She wasn't listening, so what could it hurt? He figured if he let the squaws think he belonged to "White Sister," they'd be on their way and out of his hair. Literally.

Little Fawn turned to Laughing Waters, her eyes frankly puzzled. "Gold Hair no want *pi-ge-ne.*"

The gift had cost them one pony and two buffalo robes, no small sacrifice for two lone women.

Beau could see the squaws were distressed by his lack of gratitude, and he began to feel guilty. Despite their absurd infatuation with him, he had to admit that if it hadn't been for their dedicated care, he'd probably be dead by now. They'd been good enough to stay with him in Charity's absence, applying the healing poultices to his wounds, stoking the damn fire until it'd nearly melted the walls, and here he was, treating them unsociably.

The least he could do was take a drink of their "*pi-ge-ne*" to show his appreciation. But he'd make it clear from the start: the idea that he belonged to them because they'd saved his life was totally out of the question.

"Okay ladies, now listen. I'll drink your *pi-ge-ne*, but I'm not going to marry either one of you." Surely, he thought, if he were brutally frank, there'd be no misunderstanding.

The squaws looked at each other, startled that he knew of their intent. "White Sister tell," Little Fawn whispered sharply to Laughing Waters.

"She no fair," Laughing Waters complained. Dark eyes suddenly riveted on Beau as Laughing Waters immediately turned sullen. "Gold Hair no be husband to Little Fawn and Laughing Waters?"

"No," said Beau firmly. "I'm beholden to both of you for savin' my life, but as soon as I'm able, I'll be movin' on. I'm not going to marry anyone."

"No be husband to White Sister?" Little Fawn asked, reluctant to abandon hope of snaring this fine brave.

"No, no be husband to White Sister," Beau confirmed, noticing the squaws' faces swiftly light with renewed expectation. "*No be husband to anyone*," he stated. "But if it will make you feel any better, we'll drink some of the *pi-ge-ne*, then you can be on your way," he offered in a more conciliatory tone.

It was as charitable as he could be, under the circumstances.

"Drink *pi-ge-ne*." Little Fawn nodded enthusiastically at Laughing Waters, and her sister's head bobbed cheerfully.

Now they were getting somewhere.

The squaws weren't ignorant of the effect strong liquor could have on

Gold Hair. They knew firewater would not only make him docile and willing to accompany them to their camp, but Laughing Waters and Little Fawn knew the *pi-ge-ne* could make a man amorous, a condition they would not be at all averse to in Gold Hair's case.

"Heap good, Gold Hair. You like." Laughing Waters snapped the cork off the bottle with her gums and grinned as she handed the bottle to Beau.

He accepted the bottle cautiously. "One drink, then you go . . . and not come back," he added.

Little Fawn and Laughing Waters nodded agreeably.

Keeping his eyes trained on the squaws, Beau wiped the rim of the bottle with the corner of the sheet, then carefully tipped it to his lips and took a swig. The strong whiskey brought a rush of tears to his eyes as he took a couple of swallows. Slowly, he lowered the bottle.

"Heap good?"

"He-a-p g-o-od," Beau agreed, his voice breaking off in a suffocating strangle. He rolled to his side to catch his breath.

The squaws grinned knowingly at each other. Little Fawn handed the bottle to Laughing Waters, who promptly took a long, noisy swill.

When it was Little Fawn's turn, she drank deeply, and Beau was astounded at their amazing tolerance. Neither of them had even blinked an eye.

"Good!" Little Fawn wiped her mouth with the back of her hand and extended the bottle to Beau again, who by now had recovered his composure.

He took the bottle and carefully wiped the rim again. He hoped the second swig would go down easier than the first.

The warmth of the liquor snaked its way down his throat pleasantly, and he could feel his veins begin to hum.

He glanced out the window and saw Charity throwing corn to the chickens.

Smugly, he thought how shocked she was going to be when she discovered how easily he'd outfoxed her and the two squaws. She really thought she'd backed him to the wall with her threats of "marry me or else." He smirked. Well, once more, he'd proved you couldn't tangle with Beau Claxton and come out on top. At least, not a puny little woman like Charity Burkhouser.

The bottle made the rounds again, and by the time Beau had drunk his fill a third time, he was relaxed and enjoying himself.

"*Pi-ge-ne* good, Gold Hair?" Little Fawn couldn't resist reaching out and touching Beau's hair.

He drew back defensively, but the liquor was beginning to make him feel mellow, so he tried to be diplomatic. "Don't touch my hair, ladies." He flashed them both a winning grin. "Just drink your firewater and leave my hair alone."

Laughing Waters grinned. "Goooood *pi-ge-ne*, Gold Hair?"

Beau's grin was a bit uneven. "Yeah, not bad." He blinked, noticing his words seemed slurred. But when Little Fawn handed him the bottle again, he decided he'd imagined it. Actually, he felt better than he had in months. He gave the squaws a lopsided grin. "Thank youuu, laaadies. You are most kind." He winked at them, his blue eyes shining, then tipped the bottle and took another long swallow.

A few minutes later, Little Fawn's hands crept up to touch his hair again. This time he smiled tolerantly, deciding he didn't mind her affections all that much. So she wanted to touch his hair, what could it hurt?

"Pretty," Little Fawn cooed.

"Thanks." His eyes locked on the sway of her massive bosom, and he felt a hint of uneasiness. Damn, was he getting drunk? The squaw was beginning to look good to him—at least, from the neck down.

In another ten minutes the bottle was empty.

Where'd those ugly squaws disappear to? Beau wondered. In their place were two beautiful Indian maidens, with hair as black as night and dark mysterious eyes that made his blood sing.

They sat by his bed, smiling and twining locks of his golden hair between their nimble fingers. Beau felt a quick, long-suppressed tightening in his loins.

"Wheeers Liitle Fwam and Laughin' Waters?" he asked, grinning stupidly at the lovely apparitions that had magically appeared from nowhere.

They were the most exquisite creatures he'd ever seen!

Little Fawn and Laughing Waters looked at each other, covered their mouths, and giggled girlishly.

As they'd planned, the firewater had paid back its cost.

At this moment the *pi-ge-ne* was worth more than *four* ponies and *six* buffalo robes to them.

CHAPTER 12

CHARITY WAS BEGINNING TO FEEL GUILTY ABOUT leaving Beau with the squaws. Although she was desperate for a man's help, her conscience told her it hadn't been right to leave him to the mercy of Little Fawn and Laughing Waters.

Her hand dipped into the corn bucket. As she scattered the kernels on the sunbaked ground, she admitted she'd been heartless to threaten him with the squaws if he didn't marry her.

Ferrand would have been ashamed of such underhanded tactics. He'd always said a person was only as good as he was honest. Charity had to face it; she'd seriously jeopardized her integrity lately.

She'd apologize to Beau for behaving so brazenly. Furthermore, she'd assure him that she wouldn't hinder his return to Missouri, once he'd recovered.

Perhaps she would even consider asking Ansel Latimer to marry her. She knew he was strong and kind. After he weathered the initial shock of losing Letty, he'd need someone to help him raise Mary Kathleen, and Charity would love the child as dearly as if it were her own.

But in truth, Charity knew a marriage to Ansel would be disappointing. He'd never make her stomach turn upside down the way Ferrand had. No, she thought, no one would ever give her that delicious, giddy feeling again, and she might as well accept that.

Ferrand could just smile a certain way, and her pulse would race with heady anticipation. . . .

But Ansel would be good to her, and she knew Letty would be pleased to know Charity was raising her daughter—her thoughts broke off and she glanced up as she heard a door open.

She stared open mouthed, watching Laughing Waters and Little Fawn haul Beau out of the cabin spread eagle. His backside nearly dragged along the ground, and he had a silly, stupefied grin on his face.

The corn pail rattled to the ground as Charity sprinted toward the soddy.

The squaws wasted no time in their wily escape, their short, squatty legs pumping, their flat feet thundering across the crusty ground.

"Hold it!" Charity skidded to a stop and brought her hands to her hips, sternly.

At the sound of Charity's voice both squaws glanced her way but made no effort to slow their rapid departure up the hillside.

Beau grinned at Charity and waved happily. " 'Lo, Mrs. Burkhouser!"

"Ladies! I said, wait a minute!" Charity's feet went back into motion when she realized the squaws had no intention of stopping. She couldn't imagine what was going on.

She'd been fully aware that Little Fawn and Laughing Waters were smitten with Beau, but she'd had no idea they'd carry their whimsy to this appalling extent!

And Beau! Beau not only appeared unconcerned about his abduction, but it looked to Charity as if he was a willing participant in the escapade.

"We go, White Sister," Little Fawn puffed over her shoulder. "One sleep, come back," she lied.

Finally overtaking the two, Charity reached out and jerked Laughing Waters to a sudden halt. "Now see here! You can't just come in here and tote this man away like a sack of flour!"

"Gold Hair no mind." Laughing Waters stubbornly planted herself in front of Charity, keeping a firm hold on Beau's bare feet. Charity was relieved to see that the women had at least had the forethought to put trousers on him.

"Well, we'll just ask Gold Hair if he minds or not!" She leaned over Beau's limp body. The strong smell of liquor assaulted her nostrils as he leered up at her drunkenly.

"Hallo there, Mzzz. Bursshouser. Didja feed all them chickens?"

"You're drunk!"

"Me?" Beau looked properly insulted. "I certaaainly am not! I've jusst been havinng a litttle *pi-ja-nnee* with thesse twoo bootuful maidens." He flashed Charity an apologetic grin when he saw she wasn't buying his explanation. "Wall, maybe I have had . . . jest a little too much . . . but they made me—"

"I can't believe this!" Charity confronted the two squaws again, her sudden anger making red flags bloom high on her cheeks. "You carry him back into the house—immediately!"

Laughing Waters and Little Fawn had no intention of obliging her wish, and their stoic expressions proved it.

"Gold Hair come with us," Laughing Waters proclaimed, lifting Beau's foot as a signal to Little Fawn to move on.

"Hold on." Charity spread her feet and blocked their path. "He can't go with you. I thought I made it clear: Gold Hair is *mine*."

Little Fawn looked to Laughing Waters for direction.

"Gold Hair say he no marry White Sister," Laughing Waters announced.

"But he no marry Laughing Waters or Little Fawn either," Charity reasoned.

"Ladieees, ladieees, don't fight. I no marry any of you," pronounced Beau in a lofty slur.

Charity could see the squaws had their hearts set on having Beau, and she knew he'd give her no assistance in saving himself in his disgusting condition.

It was clear: if Beau were to be delivered from this fiasco, it would be solely up to her. She frantically searched her memory for a bartering tool. She had so little left.

The brooch. Ferrand's grandmother's emerald brooch. It had been his gift to Charity on their wedding day, and Little Fawn and Laughing Waters had admired it extensively since the first day they had discovered it in the tin box she kept under her bed. It was her greatest treasure, but she couldn't idly stand by and let the poor man be abducted this way, especially since he wasn't even aware he was being abducted!

"Ladies, let's hold on a minute. Surely we can come to some satisfactory solution."

The squaws held their ground and watched Charity suspiciously.

"What White Sister mean?"

"I agree you helped save Gold Hair's life, and I suppose you could argue that he is partly yours."

Laughing Waters eyed Beau possessively. "We save Gold Hair. We like. We take."

"But I saved Gold Hair too."

"You leave Gold Hair to meet Wa-kun-dah, alone."

"But I had good reason. I was called away to help the papoose's mother, remember? She was very ill too."

They remembered, but didn't care to.

"Gold Hair heap good man. We want," Laughing Waters repeated sullenly.

"True, that's why I'm prepared to make you a trade."

Little Fawn hurriedly shook her head. "Gold Hair make good papooses. We keep."

Charity glanced at Beau and frowned. "Yes, I'm sure he would . . . but I'm prepared to offer you my brooch. The one in the tin box. Remember how much you liked those pretty green stones? You said they looked like sky sparkling at night?" Charity glanced down at Beau, who was dozing, and scowled. The nerve of the man. His very future hung in the balance, and he was asleep!

Laughing Waters exchanged a dubious look with Little Fawn but then curtly nodded.

Charity smiled sadly. "I will trade you my emerald brooch for Gold Hair."

"Green rocks for Gold Hair?" Little Fawn's eyes immediately lit up.

She was a complete fool when it came to bright, shiny things, and White Sister's green rocks sparkled like morning dew on the grass.

Drawing a deep breath, Charity closed her eyes and repeated again, before she lost her nerve, "The brooch for Gold Hair."

Little Fawn and Laughing Waters knew they'd have at least to consider her tempting offer.

"We talk. White Sister stay."

The squaws dropped Beau's limp body in the dust, and he landed with a resounding thud, bringing him wide awake.

"Damn!" Irritably he sat up and rubbed his smarting backside. "What is going on?"

"Serves you right," Charity snapped. "Because of your foolishness, I'm going to have to give up Ferrand's grandmother's brooch."

"Whose what?" Beau was befuddled, and his head was splitting.

"Ferrand's grandmother's . . . oh, never mind." Charity knew he couldn't possibly understand anything in his sorry state. "You'd just better hope they accept the trade or you're in serious trouble, Mr. Claxton!"

Beau looked around him in a daze. "What?" He wished somebody would make some sense. What was he doing sitting in the middle of the road? It was hot, and suddenly he didn't feel well at all.

Charity glanced over worriedly to Laughing Waters and Little Fawn still conferring in hushed tones beneath a large thorn tree.

Occasionally, one would raise her voice, and the other would shake her head and wag her finger angrily.

The tense conversation went on for a full ten minutes, and Charity was beginning to despair. If they refused the brooch, she didn't know how she'd prevent them from taking Beau away.

Beau had curled up in the road and was sound asleep again, blissfully ignorant of what was taking place. Gazing at him sourly, Charity wondered if he was really going to be worth giving up her brooch for.

Finally, Little Fawn raised her arms, shook her hands in the air in exasperation, and stalked away. With a satisfied smile Laughing Waters scurried back to Charity. "We trade Gold Hair for roach."

"Brooch."

Laughing Waters grinned. "Yes. Roach."

Charity heaved a sigh of relief. "Good. And Little Fawn? Does she agree?"

"She no care."

Charity seriously doubted that. "Now, when we make our trade," she warned, "it's final. You must leave Gold Hair alone, for he will be all mine."

"Laughing Waters no see Gold Hair again?"

"That's right, and Little Fawn must agree to relinquish her claim as well."

Laughing Waters thought for a moment, then smiled agreeably. "Me tell Little Fawn: Gold Hair White Sister's. We no take."

"Very well."

They reached down in unison and picked up Beau's feet and hands.

"We make good trade," Laughing Waters proclaimed proudly as they started carrying Beau's limp body back to the soddy; but Charity found it hard to be as optimistic.

After all, she had just given away her prized brooch, and she wasn't one inch nearer to saving her land.

But at least her integrity was back in place, and for that, she was grateful.

CHAPTER 13

THE OLD ROOSTER STRETCHED, FLAPPED HIS WINGS, and loudly crowed in another new day. Mellow rays of dappled sunlight spilled through the window of the soddy, spreading a warm golden path across the wooden floor.

With a groan Charity stirred on her pallet, reluctant to face the new morning. She knew it was late, but Mary Kathleen had cried most of the night. Finally the baby had quieted at dawn, giving Beau and Charity their first opportunity to sleep.

Charity willed her eyes open and glanced toward the bed. She was relieved Beau was still sleeping soundly. He was lying on his stomach, his golden hair tousled appealingly like a small boy's. His face was burrowed into the pillow, and his arms were wrapped snugly around it, revealing tight bunches of corded muscles in his forearms.

Her stomach danced about lightly. His sleeping position was a simple, masculine one, and yet somehow, though she had no idea why, it made a slow, languorous warmth spread sweetly through her body.

Memories of making love in the early morning flooded her mind until she struggled to block the stinging reminders. She warned herself it would be sheer tomfoolery to become physically attracted to Beau; still, she couldn't deny that she found him more fascinating every day. After making certain he was fed properly, she couldn't help but feel a twinge of pride as he began to shed his pitiful gauntness, and his body grew strong and sinewy again.

And every day he seemed more thoughtful. They'd taken turns walking the floor with the baby during the night and she'd been so grateful for his help. She thought again how thankful she was to have him around. Trading her emerald brooch had been such a small sacrifice for such a large reward.

A smile curved her mouth again. It had been a month since Laughing Waters and Little Fawn had attempted his abduction. Rolling over, she hugged her pillow to her tightly, her smile widening as she remembered how grateful Beau had been when he'd learned Charity had intervened and saved him from living like a Kaw brave.

He'd been too intoxicated to know he'd been captured or how Charity had accomplished his release. He couldn't remember anything beyond the first few swallows of potent *pi-ge-ne* he'd shared with the two squaws.

She thought of how sick he'd been afterward. He'd suffered a splitting headache for three days. Of course, she figured it only served him right. She couldn't imagine how he'd gotten drunk enough to let the squaws carry him off with his grinning approval!

She sighed. She couldn't blame Laughing Waters and Little Fawn for their infatuation with Beau Claxton. He was bathed, clean shaven, and breathtakingly handsome now.

He was truly an exceptional man.

And now that he was up and about, getting stronger all the time, Charity was achingly aware of how handsome and masculine he was. His tall, imposing frame loomed over her small one as they moved within the confines of the soddy. Although she warned herself not to, she found herself feeling content and secure again, the way she'd felt when Ferrand had been close by.

At times she caught Beau's blue eyes studying her as if he felt the same sort of contentment—or maybe that was only wishful thinking on her part. Regardless, he was polite and a joy to be with. They'd talk for hours on end, passing Mary Kathleen back and forth between their laps when she became fussy.

It was then that Beau would confide in her how he was looking forward to returning to his family in Missouri. He spoke fondly of his brothers, Cole and Cass, and told her of the stunts they'd pulled together on Willa, their family housekeeper.

He talked about his ma's biscuits and Willa's chicken and dumplings, and how much he loved them both. One evening he asked Charity to help him compose a letter to his family, informing them of his injury, yet assuring them he was healing properly. They moved to the table, and while Beau talked, Charity penned the letter in her neat, legible hand. The following day, Charity made the long ride into Cherry Grove and mailed the letter.

Charity sighed again, recalling how she had felt unusually lonely after that particular conversation.

When Beau had fallen asleep, she'd slipped outside the soddy and sat for a while, listening to the lonely wind on the prairie, broken occasionally by the howl of a coyote or the gentle whish of the tall prairie grass.

She found herself sinking even lower into self-pity as she reviewed her own gloomy circumstances. She missed her mother and father unbearably, and she thought it would be sheer heaven to curl up on her old feather bed beside her sisters, Hope and Faith, and pour her heart out to people who really cared. Then, after a visit with her family, and a good long cry, it would be nice to return to her homestead and find a man like Beau waiting for her.

Perhaps they could never love each other the way they'd loved Ferrand and Betsy, but it wouldn't be hard for her to adjust to living with a man like Beau, with his kind ways and gentle nature. In time, she felt sure their mutual respect could bring them a union that would be, if not passionate, at least comfortable.

Charity opened her eyes again, wondering why she was thinking such nonsense. The very best she could hope for from Beau Claxton would be an act of mercy in her behalf, not love and undying devotion, with a passel of golden-haired babies thrown in.

Still, she knew that once Beau was gone, there'd be a large void in her life again.

The sun went behind a cloud, and the room suddenly turned a dreary gray, as gray and sad as Charity felt this morning. She found herself deliberately dawdling as her mind turned to another weighty problem that only served to drag her sagging spirits even lower.

Something had to be done about Ansel. For the past week he'd visited the soddy daily. Though she hated to admit it, she'd concluded that Letty's death had left Ansel temporarily unstable.

At times he acted as though Charity were Letty. On other occasions he was totally at a loss as to where his wife had gone. He still paid little attention to Mary Kathleen, behaving at times as if he resented the child.

His continuing confusion worried Charity, but she didn't know what to do about it.

Once, she'd thought about asking Ansel to stay with her so she could take care of him until he could cope again, but she knew that would be improper; besides, the soddy couldn't shelter another person besides Beau and the baby.

On top of everything else, Beau's suggestion that she marry Ansel to get the help she needed with her land kept popping into her mind. Apparently, that was her only alternative. Once he returned to his old self, perhaps she could approach him with a reasonable offer of marriage. She realized she was trying desperately to persuade herself that it was the only solution left, since Beau wouldn't marry her.

Ansel was a reasonably young and vital man, and, once he got past the shock of losing Letty, he would be a good provider.

Ferrand surfaced in her mind, Ferrand making love to her during the long cold, winter nights. . . . She admitted she missed that part of her life. She and Ferrand had been shamelessly attracted to each other, making love at the most outrageous times. But performing such an act with another man? The thought was frightening.

Charity rolled to her right side, her eyes drifting over to the man on the bed.

She studied his sleeping form, trying to visualize what it would be like to be Beau Claxton's woman. She felt an ache growing deep within her, a painful reminder of how long it had been since she'd had the pleasure of knowing a man.

She knew she shouldn't be thinking of Beau this way—surely it was sinful, and disrespectful to Ferrand's memory, but her mind seemed bent on tantalizing her.

She imagined lying next to Beau, cradled within his arms. She could almost feel the thick mat of hair on his chest brush against her flushed skin. She thought of his mouth moving on hers, possessively molding and exploring. His hands would excite and demand, lifting her into a storm of passion that would—

A brisk rap on the door interrupted her fantasy. Charity bolted upright and guiltily pulled the blanket up to cover her budded breasts.

Beau stirred on the bed. "Someone's banging on the door," he mumbled after the knock sounded loudly again.

Charity glanced at him and blushed, hoping he couldn't read her mind. "I can't imagine who it would be."

"Better answer it before they wake the baby." He rolled to a sitting position and scratched his head.

He looked so masculine, so tempting, that for a moment Charity could only stare at his chest, the same chest she'd imagined herself being held against. She swallowed dryly.

The rap came again, and Beau glanced up to see what was keeping her. "You want me to get it?"

Charity sprang to her feet, forgetting for the moment that she wore only a thin muslin gown. "Oh . . . no. I'll get it."

Beau eyes reluctantly followed her as she scampered barefoot across the floor and reached for her wrapper hanging on a peg.

His breath caught in his throat as the morning light turned her gown transparent. He warned himself to look away, but found his gaze wanted to linger on the outline of her slender body blatantly displayed through the gossamer fabric. He felt an undeniable stirring of desire. It had been a long time since any woman had aroused him, and he found the feeling pleasant.

His eyes skimmed her high, firm breasts, her slender waist, her shapely thighs. There was a delicate, breathtaking beauty about her he'd never noticed before, and, for an instant, he wondered what it would be like to make love to her.

The idea astounded him. Since the day he'd married Betsy, he'd never speculated about another woman.

Charity was unaware of Beau's scrutiny as she pushed her heavy mass of dark hair over her shoulder and pulled the door open a crack.

Her mouth dropped open when she saw Reverend Olson and his wife standing on her doorstep, smiling at her warmly.

"Good morning, my dear. I hope we're not disturbing you." Reverend Olson's kind face reminded Charity of her father, and she was always glad when the reverend and his wife made their monthly visit.

But not this morning.

Charity was reluctant to reveal Beau's presence. Once the neighbors found that he was staying with her, gossip would be inevitable. As far as she was aware, only Ansel knew about Beau, and she preferred to keep it that way.

Cherry Grove was a small community, and its residents were unyieldingly straitlaced. For them, right was right, and wrong was wrong, and there was no middle ground.

While Charity thought her neighbors wouldn't judge her harshly for nursing an injured stranger, she knew there would still be some who'd argue that it wasn't proper for a man and woman to live under the same roof without the sanctity of marriage, especially when the woman happened to be a pretty young widow like Charity Burkhouser and the man was a handsome stranger like Beau Claxton.

"Reverend Olson . . . Mrs. Olson. How nice to see you." Charity felt trapped. Her fingers nervously plucked at the collar of her wrapper. "You must forgive me, I'm afraid I've overslept this morning."

"We heard you've been quite busy, dear." Mrs. Olson leaned forward, her blue eyes twinkling as she spoke in a soft, compassionate tone. "Has your unexpected visitor been keeping you awake nights?"

Charity smiled lamely. They already knew about Beau. "Yes . . . some . . . but I don't mind."

Reverend Olson looked hopeful. "Well, may we come in to see her?"

"Her?" Charity stared at him vacantly.

"The Latimer babe. We understand you're caring for Ansel's child." Reverend Olson inclined his head. "We were wondering if we might see the little girl."

When she realized they'd come to see Mary Kathleen, Charity felt limp with relief. "Oh . . . of course! But she's still asleep—perhaps you could stop by another time?"

For an instant she'd forgotten her main concern—Beau. If the Olsons came in, they'd find him. And what would they think, she fretted, when they discovered she and Beau were still wearing nightclothes in the middle of the morning?

Reverend Olson glanced from his wife to Charity with a benevolent expression. "I'm afraid that would be most inconvenient, dear. We plan to make several calls today. But I promise we won't take up much of your time, just a few minutes."

"But I'm not dressed."

"We'll wait in the buggy while you get yourself together," Mrs. Olson suggested brightly. It was plain to Charity, the elderly couple would not be easily deterred.

"Yes, well, I'll only be a moment." Charity gave them a hesitant smile, then, closing the door, she sank to the floor in despair.

Now what was she going to do? Reverend Olson and his wife would discover she was caring for a man in her house and then brows would lift with suspicion.

"Who is it?" Beau's voice drifted across the room, breaking into her frantic thoughts.

"It's Reverend Olson and his wife!" The fire in the grate had died, and Charity felt goose bumps rising on her arms. She hurriedly crossed the room to stoke the dying embers into a rosy glow.

"What do they want?" Beau discovered he was strangely disappointed that the wrapper she was wearing concealed her fully now.

"They want to come in and see Mary Kathleen. I don't know how they found out I have her, but they did."

Realizing the impropriety of his presence, Beau asked quietly, "Do you want me to hide?"

She added a couple of logs to the fire and turned back to face him. She knew she couldn't complain about the incriminating position she'd found herself in. It wasn't his fault, and nothing could be done to correct it now. She would just have to bluff her way through the visit and hope for the best. "No, that's impossible. Where could you go? We'd better get dressed. They're waiting."

Ten minutes later Charity opened the door and smiled cheerfully at the reverend and his wife, who were sitting patiently in their buggy. "You may come in."

For the occasion Charity had put on her best yellow calico and tied a matching ribbon in her hair.

Reverend Olson helped his wife from the buggy, and they hurried toward the soddy.

Rebecca Olson was making lively chatter as they stepped inside. "I just love the crisp snap in the air this morning and the glorious autumn leaves! I saw a field of ripe pumpkins on our ride from town. The reverend just loves pumpkin pie, don't you, dear?"

"My favorite."

Charity clasped her hands tightly and braced herself as Rebecca stopped short and gasped, catching sight of Beau.

Standing in front of the fireplace, he wore a pair of Ferrand's faded denim overalls and a dark cotton work shirt. To Charity he seemed unusually tall and handsome this morning. She suddenly wished he looked fifty years older, six inches shorter, with eyes that were pale and nondescript instead of vivid cornflower blue.

It would make her explanation much more credible.

"Why . . . hello." Rebecca smiled hesitantly and offered her small gloved hand to Beau. "You didn't mention you had company, Charity." The reprimand in her soft voice was unmistakable.

"How thoughtless of me," Charity apologized meekly.

"Good morning, ma'am." Beau stepped forward and took Rebecca's hand. "Pumpkin pie happens to be one of my favorites too." His voice dripped charm like molasses off hot biscuits.

Rebecca glanced at her husband again. "It is difficult not to like pumpkin pie."

Charity took a deep breath, unclasped her hands, and stepped forward.

"Reverend Olson, Rebecca, this is Beau Claxton. He's—he's been my guest for the past two weeks."

"Oh?" Rebecca's smile slowly faded. "Your guest, dear?"

"Yes, you see, Beau had the misfortune of meeting up with a wounded wolf in the stream, and, as a result, he was gravely injured. I've been looking after him until he regains his health." Charity tried to sound breezy and carefree, and as if it were the most natural thing in the world for Beau to remain with her.

Rebecca glanced at her husband. "Oh . . . do tell."

"Why, that must have been a terrible experience. It's a miracle you survived, young man." Reverend Olson reached out to clasp Beau's hand. "I guess that explains the bandages."

"I'm afraid without Mrs. Burkhouser's excellent care, I wouldn't be here right now," Beau admitted.

"Oh, dear." Rebecca's eyes anxiously surveyed the bandages still visible on Beau's face. "I do hope you're feeling better, Mr. Claxton."

"Yes." He flashed her a melting smile. "And please, call me Beau."

Rebecca blushed and her face turned three shades of rose. "Beau, what a lovely southern name. Are you from around here?"

"No, ma'am. I'm from Missouri."

"Missouri? How nice. I have a sister in Kansas City." Although the elderly couple was trying to be cordial, Charity saw the wary glances Rebecca was sending her husband. She knew they were unnerved by Beau's presence.

"Well, my, my, why don't we all sit down and have a cup of coffee?" Charity invited nervously, wishing she could smooth over the uncomfortable situation.

"A cup of coffee would be nice," Reverend Olson agreed. "But we mustn't stay too long, Rebecca. We do have other calls to make."

"Yes, dear. We'll only be a minute." Rebecca turned back to Beau. "Exactly where in Missouri do you come from, Mr. Claxton?"

"It's a small town, River Run—not far from Springfield." Beau held a kitchen chair for Rebecca, and she slipped into it graciously.

"Now, we'll only stay a minute," Rebecca reiterated as Charity began to pour coffee. "Claxton . . . Claxton—you wouldn't happened to be kin to the Claxtons of Savannah, would you?"

"As a matter of fact, I am." Beau smiled. "My father's family is from Savannah."

"They are?" Rebecca glanced at the reverend expectantly. "Did you hear that, Reverend? He's a Savannah Claxton."

To Charity's dismay Rebecca's minute proceeded to drag into an hour, then two, and before Charity realized it, suppertime was drawing near.

Rebecca had become enamored of Beau, as throughout the afternoon he entertained her with exciting war tales about his brother and himself and stories of the Savannah Claxtons.

Charity and the reverend shared Mary Kathleen, periodically changing diapers and warming bottles.

While Charity prepared the evening meal, Reverend Olson gave up on an early departure and dozed peacefully in the chair before the fire.

During supper the conversation was cordial, but Charity occasionally caught a renewed note of disapproval about Beau's remaining at the Burkhouser soddy while he recovered.

"The Reverend and I would be happy for you to stay with us until you're well. Isn't that right, Reverend?"

"Hummph . . . uh . . . well, of course, dear." Reverend Olson cleared his throat and reached for a third biscuit. "Mr. Claxton would be most welcome to share our home."

Beau glanced at Charity and saw her start to protest, and he intervened softly. "I surely do appreciate your offer, Rebecca, but I'd like to stay here awhile longer. I notice Mrs. Burkhouser has a few fences down, and I thought before I went home, I'd help out a bit to repay her for my keep."

Charity glanced up from her plate in surprise. Their eyes met and held for a moment as she tried to convey her gratitude. Why would he do this? Did it mean he actually planned to stay on and help her with the land, or was he only trying to pacify the reverend and Rebecca? Charity felt her pulse increase its tempo as she smiled at him, and he smiled back.

"But, Beau, dear. You're not going to be able to mend fences for weeks." Rebecca was clearly appalled that he'd consider remaining with Charity.

"I'm doin' better every day, ma'am, but I thank you for your concern." Beau's gaze slid easily away from Charity's and returned to the food on his plate. "Another week or two and I should be up to earning my keep."

Charity decided a change of subject was in order and promptly mentioned Ansel Latimer, inquiring whether the Olsons had noticed Ansel's strange behavior since Letty's death.

They said they had, and Charity discovered Ansel had told the Olsons of Mary Kathleen's whereabouts. She was relieved when they devoted the remainder of the supper conversation to that topic.

It was late when the reverend and his wife finally prepared to take their leave. Charity walked them to the buggy, while Beau put Mary Kathleen down for the night.

"He's a fine man," Rebecca remarked. "So tragic about his young wife."

"Yes, he loved Betsy very much."

Reverend Olson helped his wife into the buggy, then ambled around to check the rigging while the two women continued to chat.

Charity wrapped her shawl tighter in the crisp autumn air and smiled. "I'm so glad you stopped by, Rebecca."

"Why, thank you. We didn't intend to take up your whole day."

"We didn't mind at all." Charity was surprised how easily she'd begun to include Beau in her statements.

Rebecca glanced hurriedly toward the front of the buggy. Seeing her husband still busy adjusting the harness, she turned to Charity. "Dear, I don't know how to say this . . . but I feel as if I must."

"You know you can say what's in your heart, Rebecca."

At that moment Reverend Olson walked back to the buggy. "All ready, dear?"

"Well," Rebecca fretted, "I was about to remind Charity that while you and I find Mr. Claxton a perfectly delightful man, there will most assuredly be others in the congregation who'll question the propriety of this—this unusual arrangement. Don't you agree, papa?"

"Hummph . . . well, yes, dear, as a matter of fact, I've been thinking the same thing," he admitted. He turned to Charity, his faded eyes growing tender with concern. "Now, mind you, I'm not judging, but I'm sure you're aware it isn't proper for two . . . uh . . . unmarried adults to share the same roof, no matter how innocent it may be." He cleared his throat nervously. "Once the town hears a man is living with you, there will be talk, Charity, and I'm afraid it will be unkind, my dear. Mrs. Olson and I don't want to see that happen."

Charity lifted her chin, and a stubborn light came into her eyes as she met his gaze. "Talk doesn't bother me, Reverend."

"I'm aware of that, dear." He knew Charity Burkhouser was a courageous woman with a mind of her own, but that wouldn't prevent the storm of gossip that would surely follow the news that Beau Claxton was living at the Burkhouser soddy. "But we must protect your reputation," he reminded her.

"We're not alone," Charity argued. "I'm taking care of Letty's baby until Ansel returns, and Beau is a sick man. What could we be doing?"

Reverend Olson shook his head sadly. "I'm afraid that's beside the point, dear. There *will* be talk, so I'd like to suggest Mr. Claxton reconsider our offer to stay with us until his recuperation is complete."

Charity lifted her chin a notch higher, determined that gossips wouldn't control her life. "Are you saying you and Rebecca will inform the town about my houseguest?"

"Certainly not!" Rebecca objected, horrified that they'd be accused of such betrayal. "But you know a thing like this will eventually leak out. We're only thinking of you, Charity. We don't want to see you hurt."

Charity's face crumpled like a child's as her brave façade slipped away. "I know . . . but it's so unfair. We aren't doing anything immoral," she insisted in a small voice.

"We know that, but other people won't be as understanding," Reverend Olson predicted. "I want you to promise me you'll talk to Mr. Claxton about moving to our place, soon as possible. I'm sure your secret will be safe for a few more days, but after that . . ."

Charity looked deeply into his eyes and understood he wasn't being self-righteous. He was genuinely concerned for her welfare, and he was right. There would be talk, and it wouldn't be pretty.

"Promise us you'll at least think about it, dear," Rebecca coaxed. "I'll take excellent care of your young man."

Charity swiped embarrassedly at the tears starting to roll down her cheeks, wondering when she'd become such a crying ninny. "All right. I'll speak with Beau about your offer," she conceded.

Reverend Olson patted her on the shoulder and reached into his pocket for a handkerchief. "I think you'll see that it's for the best, dear."

But Charity didn't see it that way. When Beau left, she would be alone.

Again.

CHAPTER 14

AFTER CHARITY FINISHED THE DISHES, SHE SLIPPED outside to catch a breath of fresh air.

Reverend Olson's advice still drifted in and out of her mind. Moving Beau to the Olsons' residence would be the sensible thing to do, she realized. But could she let him go? She felt an inner peace when he was near, one that had been sadly lacking in her life since Ferrand's death. And if she wasn't mistaken, Beau felt that same harmony.

Should two lonely people be denied a friendship, a mutual understanding, merely to appease others who had nothing more to do than find guilt where there was none?

It seemed unjust to Charity that anyone should take this precious gift away from her. She and Beau weren't hurting anybody, so why, she wondered, should they be denied the pleasure of each other's company for the remaining few weeks before he returned home?

An hour later, Beau found her leaning against a bale of hay, staring up at the stars. "Mind if I join you?"

"No, I was just enjoying the night. It's lovely."

"Yes, it is." He sat, wincing as he slowly eased his injured leg into place.

"Is your leg bothering you today?"

"It stiffens up when I don't move around enough."

"But you're doing so much better." Charity wrapped her shawl snugly around her shoulders. "There's a chill in the air this evening."

"Won't be long till the first snow," he predicted.

An involuntary shiver traveled down her spine at the thought of another winter alone.

Winters in Kansas could be long and harsh, bringing numbing temperatures and unbelievable snowstorms. Charity knew a Kansas blizzard could be a terrifying spectacle. Without warning, dark billowing clouds would roar across the sky, unleashing blinding bursts of snow. The wind and snow could sweep across the plains with the force of a cyclone, taking a heavy toll on livestock and people. Communication with the outside world could be cut off for weeks at a time, and travel was impossible.

Nothing moved until hundreds of men could dig openings through the drifts.

She rubbed her hands down her arms to warm them, and turned her thoughts to a more immediate concern. "Is the baby all right?"

"Yes, I think the reverend and his wife wore her out." Beau chuckled and added solemnly, "Thank God."

Charity laughed at his open candor. "I thought you liked children."

"I do, but I was under the impression they slept once in a while."

"Well, I think most of them do, but Mary Kathleen seems to be a bit confused about when she should be doing her sleeping—day or night. But with all the excitement today, we should all be able to get a good night's sleep for a change."

They were silent for a moment, then Beau looked over at her. "What are we going to do about that situation?"

"The baby?"

"Yeah, I don't mean to criticize, but it appears to me that Ansel is a sick man. Doesn't look to me like he's going to be able to care for a baby for a long time."

Charity sighed. "He's troubled, all right."

"Well, what are you going to do? Keep the baby indefinitely?"

"Of course. I promised Letty I'd take care of her child," Charity told him. "Ansel's a good man. Given a little time, he'll get over Letty's death. It has just been so sudden for him."

"I'm not sure that's wise, Charity. You're gettin' mighty attached to the baby. It might be better if he hired someone to care for Mary Kathleen until he's better."

Charity confronted Beau with mock surprise. "*I'm* getting attached? I've noticed she has *you* wrapped snugly around her little finger."

Beau's smile was guilty as sin. "She's cute, all right."

"She's more than cute, and I wouldn't feel right about anyone else taking care of Letty's baby. I love caring for her."

"Seems like a lot of work on top of everything you have to do."

"I don't mind."

They sat in silence for a while, studying the star-studded sky, sharing a contentment that neither of them questioned.

"You're quiet this evening," Beau finally remarked.

"Am I? I guess I'm just thinking."

"Oh? Must be serious," he teased. "Usually you're a real chatterbox."

Charity shrugged good-naturedly. "Nothing profound."

"Your thoughts wouldn't have anything to do with the reverend and his wife, would they?"

Charity glanced up, surprised by his astute perception. "What makes you say that?"

"I noticed they weren't any too happy about me living here with you."

"I expected their disapproval."

"But it bothers you, doesn't it?"

Charity glanced at him shyly. "Well, surely Kansas isn't all that different from Missouri when it comes to morality."

"Morality? No, but we've done nothing to be ashamed of."

"Well, I see their point, Beau. I might think the worst if I were in their place and didn't know what the true situation was."

Beau stared into the darkness. As a rule he would ignore such misjudgment, but this was different. He couldn't stand by and let Charity be judged unfairly. "Now that they know I'm stayin' here, it'll make it hard on you, won't it?"

"Reverend Olson and his wife aren't gossips, but I'm sure the news will get around. But I'm not worried. I know I'm not doing anything wrong, and Ferrand always said that's all that counts."

They sat in silence until Beau finally stood up to straighten his leg. He winced, then said calmly, "I suppose I should give more thought about taking the Olsons up on their offer to move in with them."

Charity closed her eyes and bit her lower lip, forcing herself to reply. "I suppose that would be the proper thing to do, all right."

Beau jammed his hands in his back pockets and stared at the sky, resenting the fact that he'd have to leave her and Mary Kathleen all alone. It didn't seem right. On top of trying to run her homestead without the help of a man, she'd been good enough to take him in, nurse him back to health, and care for a newborn child that wasn't hers. And now the whole town would be down on her for what she'd done, when in fact she'd been the good Samaritan.

"You always for doin' the proper thing?"

"I—I don't know. Are you?"

"Well, don't tell my ma, but I've never worried much about it in the past," he admitted.

She glanced up at him and grinned. "I never was set on it myself—except in certain cases, of course."

"You consider this to be one of those cases?"

She sighed and turned her attention back to the twinkling sky. "Not really, though I suppose we could be faulted for it."

"Well, since neither of us is any too set on me movin', I suppose we could just sit tight for a while and weather out the storm."

Charity felt her heart leap with expectation. "You mean, you think you ought to stay . . . even if there will be talk?"

Beau gazed at her in the moonlight, watching her face grow unusually solemn. "If you have no objections, I'd like to hang around a while longer." He moved over to lean down beside her, his eyes growing solemn. "Mind you, I'd leave first light if I thought it was best for you. But, dammit, I'd worry about you and the baby if I up and done that. Now, I've been doin' some thinkin' since the reverend left." His voice softened in an attempt to spare her feelings. "I—I can't marry you . . . not that you wouldn't make a fine wife, but I guess Bets was sort of it for me . . . you know."

"I wasn't expecting you to—to offer me your love, Beau."

"I know . . . but I wouldn't marry any woman without givin' my all to her. It just wouldn't be proper. Marriage is . . . well, hell, it's special, and a man and woman should be in love before they enter into such an arrangement."

"I agree, but sometimes it doesn't work out that way."

"Well, just because I can't marry you doesn't mean I can't see that you're in a real bind, and I'd like to help you out. Since I'm goin' to be laid up awhile anyway, I could give you a hand. I know I've never said it in so many words, but I'm beholden to you for saving my life, Charity." The blue of his eyes deepened as he looked down on her, and she wondered if he could hear her heart trying to hammer its way out of her chest. "I'd like the opportunity to pay you back, if you'll let me."

"It wasn't all me," she reminded him.

"I know the squaws helped, but you're the one who took me in and sewed me up and sat up nights with me." He reached hesitantly and placed his hand over hers, sending a sporadic flurry of butterflies racing through her. "I won't be forgettin' what you've done for me, Charity. You're a good woman and I'd be proud if you'd let me repay your kindness before I leave. There's no reason I can't stay here till spring. By then I should have your land in good enough shape so's you can get your title. I'd be glad to do that for you, if you'd let me."

At another time in her life Charity might have refused his offer, pointing out that she neither wanted nor needed his sympathy.

But she'd discovered the hard way, no man—or woman, for that matter—could manage on the prairie alone.

She would've preferred he stay because he wanted her companionship. As it was, he would stay because he felt obligated to her. Nevertheless, she'd accept Beau Claxton on any terms he offered.

Her hand gently closed over his. "If you want to stay, I'll be grateful to have you."

Beau glanced down at her hand, and once more he felt a swift, tightening in his loins. Her touch was gentle, almost a butterfly caress. The feel of her warm flesh next to his rekindled desires of the flesh he didn't want to feel.

"You're sure? There's sure to be ugly talk when the town finds out I'm here," he promised. "Soon as I'm able, I'll be headed to town for wire to string fences. If they don't know about me by then, they'll be finding out."

"I don't care."

His hand gently squeezed hers, and he fought the overwhelming urge to take her in his arms. He was surprised to discover he wanted to, and he might have, if memories of Betsy hadn't kept appearing to remind him it wouldn't be fair to her memory. All he had left of Betsy was his memories, and Beau figured if he let those go, Betsy would be gone forever.

For one brief moment a flash of resentment shot through him. Hell, was he going to feel this way the rest of his life? Wouldn't the pain ever get any easier?

He took a deep breath, determined to clear his mind of the depressing thought. The least he could do was help Charity with her problems.

"I say we see this thing through together, if it's all right with you." He winked, and the butterflies in her stomach went crazy again.

She smiled and squeezed his hand tightly, unable to speak over the large lump in her throat. But it was more than all right with her. It was wonderful.

CHAPTER 15

THE FIRST SNOW OF THE SEASON FELL EXACTLY TWO weeks later. As the fine white flakes sifted down against the windowpane of the soddy, the predicted trouble arrived.

But it came in a form Charity would have least expected.

Beau was feeding Mary Kathleen her first bottle of the morning, while Charity bustled around the kitchen making breakfast.

The smell of fresh coffee in the pot, buttermilk biscuits baking in the oven, and bacon sizzling in the cast iron skillet filled the small, cozy room with mouth-watering aromas.

With a fire burning brightly in the grate, the relentless wind whistling across the barren land made little difference to the small, hapless family nestled inside the warm soddy. But outside, dwarfed by endless sky and sweeping plains, the Burkhouser homestead seemed hardly more than a clod of dust on the prairie.

Charity stole enough time away from the stove to stand on tiptoe and peer out the window at the swirling flakes of pristine white. "I love the first snow." To get a better look, she rubbed the steam from the window with her elbow.

"I thought you hated winter." Beau set the baby bottle aside. Tipping Mary Kathleen over his shoulder, he began patting her back gently.

Charity caught the endearing motion out of the corner of her eye and smiled. Beau performed the task so naturally now. Though he said Mary Kathleen was growing like ragweed, the infant looked tiny draped over his broad shoulder. And he had no room to talk. He was filling out rapidly these days, becoming an impressive man in his own right.

Charity couldn't help but feel a strong surge of pride as she watched the way her small family thrived under her care. It seemed she had to remind herself every day that they weren't really her family, only temporary gifts the good Lord had sent to see her through another long winter.

No one knew when Ansel would come to his senses and want to claim Mary Kathleen. And when spring arrived . . . well, she didn't want to think about spring and Beau's promised departure. She'd learned long ago to live for the day, and let tomorrow take care of itself.

"I don't like winter, but there's something about the first snow," she said dreamily. "It just makes me feel good all over."

"Well, if it makes you feel that good, maybe you ought to come out and help me today," Beau teased. "No sense sitting in the house and pining away."

Though Charity had argued that he wasn't strong enough yet to work, Beau had already begun some basic improvements. The day before, he'd patched the roof and set a row of fence posts. This morning, he planned to make some much-needed repairs to the lean-to.

Moving away from the window, Charity returned to the stove to turn the bacon. "I'd be happy to help you out," she said, "but I must insist that you let me do the hard part."

"Of course. I'll hold the posts while you drive them into the ground," he agreed wryly.

Charity knew he was teasing. Beau Claxton was not a man to stand by and let a woman do a man's work, even through his injuries still caused him considerable discomfort.

But she was certain she could do more than he permitted her to. While she couldn't wield a heavy sledgehammer to drive the posts into the hard-packed ground, she could lift the posts from the wagon and have them waiting in place.

But Beau wouldn't hear of it. He said she had enough to do taking care of the baby and running the household to keep her busy. While he was around, he'd do all the heavy work. Charity winced as she recalled one day the week before when they'd gotten downright snappish with each other concerning the subject.

Beau had been chopping wood, slowly and cautiously, until the pile beside the house had mounted steadily. Charity was sure that he was overdoing it and was bound to hurt himself, so she'd bolted outside four or five times to caution him to slow down.

"I used to help Ferrand all the time," she complained. Each time she'd appeared to give him advice, Beau had promptly, but politely, sent her back into the soddy. "Go bake bread or something," he'd said.

When she'd kept popping out the door to issue the same warning again and again, Beau had finally lost all patience with her.

He'd lowered the ax, leaned on the handle disgustedly, and fixed his blue eyes on her till the pupils had looked like pinpoints.

"Well, I'm not Ferrand," he'd stated calmly. "And I'd sure appreciate it if you'd march your fanny right back in the house and nail your feet to the floor so I can get my work done!"

Nail her feet to the floor! Why, that jackass! Willing her voice to remain calm, she'd replied in a strained but pleasant tone. "You don't have to remind *me* you're not Ferrand. Ferrand was always a perfect gentleman. Besides, I was only thinking of your comfort. You're a fool to be working this hard so soon after suffering such terrible injuries."

"I feel fine. I want you to quit actin' like a mother hen, cluckin' over me constantly," he ordered. "I'm gonna chop wood until I get enough to last us for a few days, and I don't want to hear that back door flappin' every five minutes like a broken shutter in a windstorm. Do I make myself clear?"

Charity took a deep breath and squared her shoulders defensively. Her eyes snapped back at him. "Well, I'll certainly see to it that you're not disturbed again, Mr. Claxton." She tossed her head, marched back into the soddy, and slammed the door loudly enough to send Mary Kathleen into a howl.

Beau calmly watched her fuming departure. When he heard the door slam and the baby screech, a slow grin tugged the corners of his mouth.

Serves her right, the feisty little heifer, he thought, but it had also occurred to him that she sure was cute when she got all flustered that way. It had been the first time he'd ever seen her lose her temper, and he'd discovered he rather liked her show of spunk.

They hadn't spoken to each other the rest of the day. By the following morning, they'd both concluded they were living too close in their tiny quarters to remain silent indefinitely, so they resumed talking.

Charity snapped herself out of her reverie to remind Beau that breakfast was on the table.

He was washing his hands as Charity took the pan of biscuits out of the oven and poured their coffee.

"Smells good," he complimented, and she realized he always had something nice to say about her cooking. He was a delight to cook for. He seemed to like anything she set before him. And since he was feeling better, he ate like a harvest hand at every meal.

"Thank you. I hope you're hungry."

"I'm always hungry for your cookin'."

As they sat down to eat, a knock sounded at the door.

"Now who could that be?" Charity glanced up from her plate with a curious frown.

"I don't know, but I'll get it." He winked at her solemnly as he pushed away from the table, sending her pulse thumping erratically. "If it's Santa Claus arriving early, I'd hide if I were you, Miss Charity."

"And just what have I done that I should have to hide?"

"The list is too long to go into right now."

When Beau opened the door, she saw his expression change from amused to puzzled.

Ansel was standing in the doorway, looking nearly frozen to death. Beau was surprised to see that he wasn't a wearing coat, only dirty overalls and a thin cotton work shirt. His shoulders were covered with a thick dusting of snow.

Ansel looked back at Beau, as his teeth began to chatter. "I—I—I want to se-e my ba-b-by."

"Good Lord, man. Where's your coat?" Beau reached out and pulled Ansel inside the shelter as Charity hurried to assist him.

"My goodness, Ansel! What's happened to you?" Charity had never seen him looking so disreputable—or so unkempt. He was filthy, and his clothes looked as if they hadn't been washed in weeks. They hung loosely over his skeletal frame, and the strong odor surrounding him was rank and offensive. His unusually long hair was dirty. Charity found it hard to believe that this was the same Ansel Latimer she'd known so well.

"I co-me to se-e my ba-b-by," Ansel repeated, his voice taking on an almost belligerent tone.

"Well, of course you can see Mary Kathleen—"

"Who?"

"Mary Kathleen," Charity repeated softly. "That's what we've been calling the baby, Ansel. It's what Letty wanted to name her. I hope you like it."

Ansel seemed to forget the topic momentarily as his gaze quickly shifted to appraise Beau. His eyes roamed over Beau's tall frame insolently. "Who's this man, Charity?"

"Why, it's Beau. The man who was injured. Don't you remember?"

"I don't know him." Ansel dismissed Beau abruptly as he glanced around the soddy.

Charity glanced at Beau uneasily.

"Where's my baby?" Ansel's demand grew louder. "I want to see my baby!"

"Ansel, let's all sit down and have a cup of hot coffee. You must be nearly frozen." Charity was beginning to realize how much worse Ansel had become. He was acting more strangely than ever before, and she was afraid he'd suffered a total breakdown.

She reached to take his arm, but Ansel jerked away as if her touch had burned him. He looked her up and down with the same contemptuous look he'd given Beau earlier. "You Jezebel," he accused hotly in a voice edged with hate.

Charity lifted her brows in stunned disbelief. "What?"

"You're a shameless woman, Charity Burkhouser . . . shameless!" he repeated, his eyes filled with rage.

"Now, wait a minute." Beau reached over and pulled Charity protectively to his side. "You have no right to speak to her that way."

"She ain't nothin' but trash!"

"Ansel"—Charity managed to find her voice— "what's wrong with you!" She was shocked by more than his language; she wondered what had prompted him to come with such outrageous accusations.

Ansel eyed her with disgust. "Don't try to lie to me, Charity. I've heard the talk. You're livin' in sin with this man, and you've got my baby daughter in your viper's nest," he sneered. "Well, I'm here to deliver her from the hands of Lucifer."

"Oh, Ansel." Charity sagged weakly against Beau. "I don't know what you've heard, but it isn't true—"

"Lies! Nothing but lies!" Ansel stepped back, his eyes flaring wildly. "They say this man's been livin' out here for weeks. Can you deny it?"

"He has been, Ansel, but we're not living together—not the way those people are implying."

"Lies! Nothin' but dirty, filthy lies, you sister of Satan!" He spat the words as if they'd made a bitter taste in his mouth.

"All right, I think that's about enough, Ansel. I want you out of here, or I'll throw you out." Beau stepped forward, his fingers curled into fists.

Charity reached to prevent him from carrying out his threat. "No, Beau. He's ill—"

"I'm know he is, but he's not going to talk to you that way," Beau warned.

"I come to get my baby," Ansel said calmly as all trace of emotion suddenly disappeared. "It's time I be takin' her home."

Charity glanced urgently to Beau. "No . . . he mustn't take her!"

Understanding the terror in Charity's eyes, Beau tried to stall for time. "You can't take your baby today." He hoped Ansel had not gone completely insane. "It would be better if you came back for her after the weather clears."

"I can take my baby any damn time I please!" Ansel's chin jutted out sharply.

"Look, you're a sick man—you need help. Let me take you into town and—"

Ansel started backing toward the doorway, his eyes growing wild again. Charity held her breath as he paused beside Mary Kathleen's bed. He glanced down and saw the sleeping baby, and his face suddenly took on the plaintive look of a small child's. "Ohhh . . . Letty . . . she looks like Letty."

"Ansel . . ." Charity eased forward, hoping to divert his attention so Beau could safely scoop the baby into his arms. "Why don't you let me fix you a cup of coffee and then you can hold her and see how pretty her eyes are. They're amber—just like Letty's."

Ansel looked up. "You'll let me hold her?"

"Of course you may hold her."

Suddenly, Ansel seemed as sane as could be. He straightened his stance and moved with somber grace to sit quietly in a kitchen chair. He drank the coffee Charity set before him and chatted amicably with Beau about the weather and spring crops.

When it was time for him to hold Mary Kathleen, tears came into his eyes as he gazed down at his baby daughter. "She does look exactly like my Letty." His voice held a reverent awe.

After he'd played with the baby awhile, Ansel asked if it would be possible to bundle her tightly enough to let her experience her first snow with her father.

"I know I've been actin' real strange, Charity, but I think seeing my baby has helped me understand that Letty's gone," he confessed. "Maybe as soon as I have a few weeks to get my life back in order, I'll be able to take my daughter home and be a proper pa to her." His eyes grew misty again. "Letty would've wanted that, wouldn't she?"

"Yes, she would."

"Losing Letty . . . well, I can't tell you what it's done to me."

"I know. You don't have to explain, Ansel." Charity patted his shoulder consolingly.

"Do you think I can take the baby outside?" he asked again. "The snow's so pretty. I feel like Letty would be there with us too."

Charity was touched by the earnest look in his eyes and hurriedly went about fetching the baby's blankets to comply with his request.

Beau followed Charity across the room. While Ansel cooed and talked to the baby, Beau whispered to her out of the side of his mouth. "I don't like the way he's acting, Charity."

Surprised, she paused to glance up. "Why not? He seems like his old self, Beau."

"That's my point. He was acting crazy as a loon ten minutes ago."

"I know, and I've been concerned about him, too, but I think perhaps seeing his baby has finally helped him to accept Letty's death."

"What about the way he was talkin' to you?"

"I'm sure he realizes he was mistaken. He'll apologize before he leaves; you wait and see. He's acting like the Ansel I've always known. I think with a little time, he'll be back to normal. You heard him. He's even planning on taking the baby home in a few weeks."

Beau was still skeptical, but Charity seemed to know Ansel better than he did. "I hope you're not being foolish. I don't want you or the baby getting hurt."

She reached out and touched his arm, deeply moved by his concern. "I can't deny Mary Kathleen's father the right to be with her, and it will probably do him a world of good."

"I'll abide by whatever you decide," Beau conceded. "I just hope you're not making a mistake."

She squeezed his hand. "Thank you."

She shook her head at the irony. If she was going to be hurt, it wouldn't necessarily be Mary Kathleen who'd break her heart. Come spring, Beau would be leaving. . . . She shook off the thought and hurried to bundle the baby properly for the brief outing.

"I'll only keep her outside for a moment," Ansel promised, worriedly tucking in Mary Kathleen's stray little hand that persistently poked its way out of the blanket after Charity finally handed him his daughter.

"A little fresh air won't hurt her, but she shouldn't be out but just a minute," Charity cautioned. "The wind's sharp today."

"Oh, I'll be careful with her."

Beau opened the door and Ansel stepped outside, still talking to his baby in low, soothing tones.

"I might as well fill the woodbox," Beau offered, reaching for his coat as Charity prepared to clear the table.

"Yes, it's getting low." She knew Beau wanted to keep a close eye on Ansel and the baby. If it made him feel easier, she wouldn't object. "Would you mind throwing these potato peels to the chickens?"

Beau crossed the room to take the small bucket out of her hand. Their fingers touched, and their gazes met unexpectedly. Charity felt her breathing quicken as she looked into his incredibly blue eyes. For an instant she found herself envying Betsy.

Strange, she thought, to envy a dead woman. But Charity realized that she'd gladly trade places with his deceased wife if, for only one second, for one brief second, Beau would look at her with the same love he had so fiercely reserved for Betsy. She knew it could never be, but it didn't keep her from wishing.

"This all you want me to take?" His voice was strained, and Charity thought his eyes looked vaguely troubled.

"Yes . . . that's all."

"I'd best see about Ansel." He started to walk away, but she saw him hesitate. He turned around and faced her, his face lined with worry. "I suppose the town is talkin' about us livin' together. That's what Ansel meant about hearing talk."

"It wouldn't surprise me."

"I don't like them thinking that."

"We agreed we didn't care," she reminded him.

"I know." He acted as if he wanted to say more, but changed his mind. "I'd better check on Ansel."

Charity watched as he walked to the door and opened it. He adjusted his hat low on his forehead, then smiled at her again. As the door closed behind him, she turned back to clearing the table.

Suddenly, the door flew open, and Beau stood looking at her, his face tight with fury. "The son of a bitch is gone."

"What?" Charity's hand flew to her throat.

Beau stepped into the room, removed his hat, and shook the snow off angrily. "He's gone, Charity. There's not a sign of him anywhere."

"Oh, dear God . . . the baby! He took the baby?"

Beau nodded curtly. "I'll saddle the horse and go after him, but I don't know . . . the snow's comin' down heavier now."

Charity moved across the room in a daze, trying to digest the meaning of his words. "Beau . . . Mary Kathleen . . ."

"You don't need to remind me, Charity. Damn it, I know he has her!"

At his sharp words Charity's composure crumbled, and as naturally as if it happened every day, she moved into the haven of his arms. He was taken by surprise and accepted her stiffly at first, until he heard her begin to cry. Then his arms folded around her, and he pulled her closely to him.

It felt unbelievably good to be in his arms. He smelled of soap and smoke and fresh outdoors. There were still traces of snow on his shoulder, and they were cold and wet against Charity's cheek as she buried her face in the warmth of his neck and cried harder. It was all her fault. She'd been foolish to let Ansel take the child, and now Mary Kathleen would pay the price of her misplaced trust.

"Now, now, there's no call to start cryin'," Beau whispered tenderly, smoothing her hair back with one large hand.

She had the same pleasant, lemony smell that always stirred him, and her hair felt like fine silk under his hand. With her small body pressed tightly against his, he could feel the gentle swell of her breasts through his coat.

"He couldn't have gotten far. I'll be able to find him and the baby before any harm's done."

"It's my fault," Charity sobbed.

"No, it's mine. I should never have taken my eyes off him."

"I want to go with you."

He grasped her shoulders and held her away from him gently, his blue eyes locking gravely with her green ones. "I think you should stay here in case he decides to come back."

"Oh . . . yes . . . I suppose he might come to his senses and bring her back."

Beau doubted it, but he didn't want her to know that. "I'll ride out and see what I can find." The blue of his eyes deepened to cobalt. "Will you be all right?"

"Yes, I'll be fine." She dabbed her eyes with the corner of her apron. "You'd better hurry. It's so cold out there."

Beau winked at her reassuringly. "The baby's bundled tight. She'll be fine."

Though Charity tried to muster a weak smile in return, two fresh tears rolled from the corners of her eyes. "I know."

Beau reached out and caught the two tears with his thumbs, tenderly brushing the dampness away. "I have to go."

Charity nodded, too overcome by emotion to speak.

He looked at her for a moment, then very slowly he pulled her face to his and touched her lips briefly with his own. Just as quickly, he stepped away, almost as if he had done something he shouldn't. "I'll be back soon as I can."

He turned, placed his hat back on his head, and opened the door. "Be careful if Ansel comes back. I don't think he'd hurt you, but you keep the gun close—and don't hesitate to use it if you need to."

Charity nodded, her knees still threatening to buckle from his unexpected kiss.

He went out the door, closing it firmly behind him.

Reverently, Charity's hand came up to touch her mouth while his taste still lingered. The kiss was only his way of reassuring her that everything would be all right.

She knew that.

But it was the most wonderful kiss she'd ever experienced, and she'd hold it forever within her heart.

CHAPTER 16

*I*T WAS NEARING DARK WHEN BEAU RETURNED.

Charity had spent the day alternately pacing the floor, praying, and wringing her hands in frustration. When she heard Beau's horse approaching, she rushed outside without bothering to put her coat on.

The snow was falling heavily, blanketing the ground with deep layers that made it difficult for her to walk. Beau was dismounting as Charity ran to him. Her eyes desperately searched his arms for a small bundle. When she saw there wasn't one, tears sprang to her eyes.

"You didn't find her?"

"No." Beau quickly led the horse into the lean-to, and Charity trailed behind.

"There wasn't a sign of Ansel or the baby?"

As he released the cinch and lifted the saddle, Beau glanced at her irritably. "You shouldn't be out here without a coat."

Charity wrapped her hands around her shoulders, trying to keep her teeth from chattering. The wind was whipping snow around the corners of the lean-to, making them raise their voices to be heard. "I'm all right!"

"Get back in the house!" Beau ordered.

"What are we going to do about the baby?"

Beau put the saddle away, slipped the bridle off, and pitched a forkful of hay to the horse. Without a word he drew Charity under the shelter of his arm and propelled her toward the soddy.

Once inside, he gripped her shoulders and turned her to face him. "I managed to pick up Ansel's tracks about a mile out, but then it started snowing heavier and I lost them."

"Oh, Beau!"

"He's taken shelter somewhere along the way. He knows the baby can't survive in this storm," Beau consoled.

"But he isn't thinking straight."

"I know, but he proved he can have his sane moments this morning. No, he's found shelter, and he and the baby are all right."

Beau wished he could be as confident as he sounded, but he could see Charity was near the breaking point. He had to act as if he believed what he said.

With a nod he released her, dusted off his hat, and stomped the snow from his boots. Quietly, Charity crossed the room to place another log on the fire.

When she turned around, she saw how deeply etched his face was with worry and fatigue, and she longed to go to him to offer comfort. She knew he'd grown as fond of the baby as she, yet she also realized it wasn't her place to take any liberties with him.

He moved closer to the fire to warm his hands, and she noticed his movements were stiff, as if the wounds were bothering him again.

"You must be exhausted." She stepped closer to help him remove his snow-crusted coat. "I'll dish up your supper," she said, hanging his coat on the peg.

After he'd eaten the stew and thick slices of white bread, still warm from the oven, she stood before him in the flickering firelight. Her expression silently begged him for some morsel of solace. "Well?"

"We wait, Charity."

"For what?"

"We wait until we hear something . . . one way or the other."

Mutely she stared back at him, aware he could no longer pretend that all would be well. He was being brutally frank now. He couldn't know any more than she what the next few hours would bring.

But Charity found comfort in the thought that she would not be alone during the wait. Beau would be with her.

She went silently into his arms, and they stood before the fire holding each other, trying to absorb each other's grief in the only way they knew how.

The night passed slowly. They tried to sleep, but found rest impossible.

Weeks before, when Beau had recovered enough to move about, he'd insisted Charity return to her own bed and he'd taken the pallet before the fire. Tonight, he tossed about on the makeshift bed, his mind restless and unsettled.

Charity stirred and called softly to him, asking him if he needed anything. His answer was no.

Thirty minutes later, he got up and came to sit on the side of her bed, and they began to talk. He reminisced about happier times, carefree boyhood days spent with his brothers. Charity spoke of her family, her sisters, and how she longed to see them all again.

The endless night dragged on, and they talked of many things. The wind howled and shook the soddy, and occasionally the sound of sleet hitting the windowpane caught their attention.

It occurred to Charity that neither she nor Beau had spoken of Ferrand or Betsy tonight, and the discovery encouraged her.

"How will he feed the baby?" Charity asked once, recalling the subject that was uppermost in their minds.

"He'll find a way. It's his child—a man takes care of those he loves."

By first light the knock they'd been praying for sounded at the door. Beau gently restrained Charity as she bolted forward. He went to answer it.

Reverend Olson stood on the doorstep, his kindly features lined with weariness. "I know you must be worried."

"The child?"

"She's with Mrs. Olson. Ansel brought her by late last night."

Charity joined Beau at the door, and he placed his arm around her supportively. "Is she . . . all right?"

"She was cold and hungry, but she'll be fine. Mrs. Olson is spoiling her outrageously right now."

Charity sagged against Beau's side with relief. "I'll get dressed and we'll go get her—"

"Charity"—Reverend Olson's expression changed—"may I step in, dear?"

"Oh, I'm so sorry. Of course. You must be chilled to the bone."

Reverend Olson stepped inside, and Beau hurriedly closed the door.

The snow was still coming down in large, puffy flakes, and the wind was bitter cold.

"Let me fix you something warm to drink," Charity offered, and the Reverend nodded gratefully.

While they sipped hot coffee, Reverend Olson told them how Ansel had suddenly appeared on his doorstep the night before, cradling the baby in his arms as he talked wildly.

"He was talking about Beau and me, wasn't he?" Charity's gaze was level and grave.

"Yes, dear. I'm afraid Ansel is very ill. Somehow he finally realized Beau is staying here, and he was convinced you two are living in sin."

When Charity started to protest, Reverend Olson stopped her with an uplifted hand. "Surely you must know what the town is saying, dear. We discussed this at great lengths during my last visit, and, if you recall, this is precisely what Mrs. Olson and I feared would happen. But apparently you preferred to take the risk of having Beau remain in your care rather than having him transferred to our home for safekeeping."

Charity's eyes dropped guiltily, but Beau met the Reverend's gaze straightforwardly. "We've committed no sin."

Reverend Olson's expression grew kinder as he shook his head sadly. "I know, my son, but surely you must see the impropriety of your situation. People are very narrow minded at times, and their tongues will continue to wag as long as you remain here with Charity."

"Then they'll just have to talk. We've done nothing wrong. Charity needs my help. Soon as I have her land in proper order, I'll be movin' on, Reverend—and not until then."

Charity watched Beau's eyes become as stubborn as his accuser's.

"You're making a grave mistake, young man." Reverend Olson shook his finger. "What you're doing will remain to haunt Charity long after you've taken your leave. You must consider that as well."

"Charity and I are in full agreement on what we're doing."

"Then I must warn you," said Reverend Olson, his tone turning grave, "the child cannot be returned to your care."

Though Charity had tried to remain silent, a low cry of protest escaped her now. "Oh . . . no. . . ."

"Ansel has left the child in my care, and I cannot, in good faith, let her be returned to such an atmosphere."

"Just exactly where is Ansel?" Beau demanded. "He has no right to take the child and give her to you! Charity has been the only mother Mary Kathleen has known. You have no authority to take her away from her."

"I'm not sure where Ansel is, but he has every right to place the child where he feels she will be properly cared for, Beau. He is Mary Kathleen's father."

"But he's insane," Beau argued heatedly.

"I certainly hope that isn't the case. I prefer to think he's a very troubled man, but, regardless, we have a search party looking for him at this moment. He was barely lucid when he brought the child to us last night. He wasn't even wearing a coat. The townsfolk are concerned he won't survive the storm unless we find him."

"I still don't see what that has to do with returning the baby to Charity. No one could give her any better care," Beau maintained.

"If she were married, there'd be no question," Reverend Olson reiterated. "Or if Ansel sees fit to return the child to her care, then I suppose there would be nothing I could say. We'll simply have to find Ansel and try to ascertain what is best for both him and the child at this point."

Charity glanced at Beau helplessly. He pushed himself back from the table and crossed the room to put on his coat. "I'll be riding back to town with you, Reverend."

"Oh, Beau." Charity stood, her features filled with concern. "You can't go out in this again. You were out all day yesterday—"

"I'll be fine, Charity." Beau cut her protest short, and she could do nothing but watch as the two men prepared to leave.

"I don't want you worryin'. I'll be fine." Beau faced her as they stood in front of the doorway a few minutes later. She handed him a sack of food she'd hurriedly assembled.

She knew her heart was in her eyes, but she couldn't disguise it. "You be careful." She handed him a warm red woolen scarf she'd knitted and given Ferrand on his last birthday. "Be sure to wear this. The wind is terrible."

Beau smiled and winked at her, his eyes silently conveying his appreciation for her concern. "Thanks. You take care too."

He tucked the sack under his arm, pulled his hat low on his forehead, and nodded to the reverend. "I'm ready if you are, sir."

The search parties had split off into small groups. Beau and Reverend Olson met up with two of the men as they rode into the outskirts of Cherry Grove.

All four men reined their horses to a halt. "Gentlemen, this is Beau Claxton," the Reverend introduced. Their horses pranced restlessly, their breath blowing frosty plumes in the cold winter air.

The two men assessed Beau silently, their expressions easily discernible. "You the one livin' with the Burkhouser woman?" Jim Blanchard finally ventured.

"Mrs. Burkhouser was kind enough to care for me while I was ill," Beau returned evenly. "And I sleep and take my meals there, but I don't 'live' with her." Though Beau spoke quietly, there was an unmistakable edge of steel in his voice.

Jim Blanchard looked at Troy Mulligan and gave him a knowing grin. Beau noted the snide exchange, and he eased forward in his saddle, casually resting his gloved hands on the horn. "And I'd appreciate it if you gentlemen would be so kind as to pass the word along. I'd not take kindly to anyone who'd say otherwise."

His smooth voice had such an ominous tone it promptly wiped the smiles from both men's faces.

"Gentlemen, we're wasting time," Reverend Olson reminded them patiently. "There's a sick man out here somewhere who needs our help."

The men agreed to search in opposite directions and meet back hourly to report any progress.

Beau rode north; the Reverend, south; Jim Blanchard, west; and Troy Mulligan headed east.

The wind continued to pick up, and icy pellets of sleet began to fall from the leaden skies. Beau rode for over thirty minutes without one encouraging sign to indicate Ansel had gone that direction. He realized even if there had been tracks, the snow would quickly have covered the trail.

The sleet stung his face, and he paused once to tie the woolen scarf Charity had given him. The faint smell of lemon lingered in the material, and Beau closed his eyes for a moment, inhaling her fragrance. The memory of her eyes, imploring him to find Mary Kathleen, lent him the strength to nudge his horse forward in the ever-deepening drifts.

It was nearing dusk, and there was still no sign of Ansel Latimer. When Beau had reported back to the other men, he found that they, too, had been unable to shed any light on Ansel's whereabouts, but they'd all agreed to keep looking.

Beau's face felt numb, and he could no longer feel his hands in the fleece-lined gloves he wore. The drifts were almost up to his horse's belly now, and Beau knew he was going to have to turn back soon.

The horse topped a small rise, and Beau reined him to a sudden halt. His eyes scanned the fields below him, and he felt his heart sink.

Silhouetted against the opaque sky stood one lone tree. In the stark branches of that tree was hanging the lifeless body of Ansel Latimer.

Beau felt a crushing sense of despair come over him as he sat atop his horse on that cold rise, watching the biting wind sway Ansel's limp body back and forth, back and forth, back and forth.

God, what an awful, lonely way to die. Why had he done it? he wondered. But he knew the answer better than anyone. Ansel didn't care about living, not without Letty.

Did any man have the right to judge another for taking his own life? Beau found himself wondering as he slumped wearily over the saddle horn, staring at what once had been a vital, loving man.

He searched his soul and found he couldn't condemn Ansel. It would take a higher source than he to pass judgment on such unbearable misery, and Beau could not help but feel Ansel had found a peace most folks would know nothing about.

Beau knew exactly how deeply Ansel had suffered. Hadn't he considered the same choice, not once, but many, many times after Betsy's death? But through the grace of God and, he was sure, his mother's prayers, some inner strength had kept him going for another hour, another day, another week, always with the muted hope that the pain would eventually ease.

The only thing Beau could fault Ansel with was that, like himself, he had loved too deeply.

It only took a few minutes to ride to the tree and cut the rope. Beau gently lifted Ansel's lifeless body into his arms, and carried him to his horse. He removed a blanket from his bedroll and wrapped it securely around the body, though he wasn't sure why. Perhaps, he thought, it was because Ansel just looked so cold.

Before he tied the body securely across the back of the horse, Beau stood gazing down into Ansel's face, which was surprisingly serene.

What had been his last thoughts? Beau wondered sadly. Didn't the man realize that by committing this final, irreversible act, he was leaving behind a young child to the mercy of a sometimes cruel and heartless world?

A new, even more disturbing thought came into Beau's mind. Had his own son or daughter been born, how would the child have suffered by his father's inconsolable grief? At that moment Beau's sobering revelations served to remind him that maybe it was time he put the past behind him and made an effort to live again.

Beau reached out and touched Ansel's cheek gently. "If it helps any, I understand why you did it. And I'll do my best to see your daughter's cared for."

Beau wanted to say more, but he didn't know what to add. Surely there had to be more profound words to say at a time like this, but he guessed he'd have to leave those words to the wisdom of Reverend Olson.

He rested the body across the saddle horn and made sure the rope was tied good and tight. Then he climbed onto his horse to take Ansel home.

CHAPTER 17

ONCE AGAIN THE FRIENDS AND NEIGHBORS OF ANSEL Latimer were called upon to assemble around a gravesite. In a matter of weeks fate had set aside these particular mourners to lay to rest another victim of what seemed like a never-ending tragedy for the Latimer family.

The snow lay deep on the ground as the small group huddled against the cold wind to listen to Reverend Olson intone about the "deeply troubled soul" of Ansel Latimer.

Beau and Charity stood side by side, solemnly listening to the minister's words. A weak sun slipped in and out of mushroom-shaped clouds which promised neither rain nor shine. The icy wind whipped the mourners' hats and coats about in a hapless manner, making the forced gathering more miserable than it already was.

Reverend Olson's words seemed far away to Beau as he painfully relived the moment he'd discovered Ansel's lifeless body.

He searched for a meaningful reason why so much heartbreak should come to one family, why so much misfortune should be thrust upon one innocent child. He could find none.

Mary Kathleen was alone now.

Who would see to her needs, rejoice over her first tooth, send her to school, or walk her down the aisle when she grew into a lovely woman? he wondered. With a pang he realized how proud he'd be to do all those things for her.

Although Reverend Olson hadn't spoken again of the baby's welfare, Beau knew Mary Kathleen wouldn't be returned to Charity's care. And judging from the sadness on her face, Charity knew it too.

Beau had watched her going about her work the past two days with a quiet despondency. When he'd attempted to cheer her, she'd politely dismissed his overtures with a wan smile and her soft reprimand, "Don't worry about me."

She missed the baby. At night Beau had heard her crying into her pillow, and he'd wanted to go to her. Instead, he'd lain staring at the ceiling, feeling her misery as deeply as his own, agonizing because he had no way of easing it.

Then the guilt had set in, keeping him awake long after Charity had dropped into an exhausted sleep. Deep within his soul he knew a way to spare her this agony.

It would only take a brief marriage ceremony.

A seemingly simple solution, yet by offering to marry her, wouldn't he inadvertently be allowing her to exchange one anguish for another? Granted, the Olsons would be happy to return Mary Kathleen to Charity's care if she were properly wed, but Beau knew it would be unfair of him to marry her. While he certainly liked and respected Charity, he wasn't sure if he could ever love any woman again. Since they both had experienced good, loving marriages, would it be right for them to settle for security and companionship and never again know the depth of love they'd each shared with their deceased partners? It seemed to Beau that neither he nor Charity would be happy under those circumstances.

He knew love came in many forms. He loved Wynne, Cole's wife, but not the way he loved Betsy. If anything ever happened to Cole, Beau knew he could marry Wynne and provide a good life for her and Cole's child.

Then why was he hesitant about showing the same compassion for Charity? She'd been good to him, as good as any woman he'd ever known. He owed her his life. And since he was relatively sure no other woman could fill Betsy's void, why was he being so damn stubborn about marrying her?

If he could save her land by sacrificing a few months out of his life, why shouldn't he? Once the land title was in her hand, and he was assured she could take care of herself, he could always go back to Missouri. She would never try to hold him against his will, Beau knew that.

Beau was pulled back to the present as he heard Reverend Olson inviting the gathering to pray. Heads bowed and Reverend Olson's voice boomed out encouragingly over the frozen countryside. "The Lord is my Shepherd, I shall not want . . ." The voices of the mourners blended somberly together as they recited the Twenty-third Psalm.

From the corner of his eye Beau saw tears begin to ooze from Charity's eyes. He reached to clasp her hand and squeeze it reassuringly as his deep voice joined with hers in the moving recitation.

"Yea, though I walk through the valley of the shadow of death, I will fear no evil: for Thou art with me . . ."

Beau could see heads begin to lift as Charity absently moved into the shelter of his side. He knew tongues would wag anew, but at the moment she needed someone to lean on, and he had about made up his mind— like it or not—that he was the only one she had left.

The top of her head barely reached his shoulder. The small feather on her black hat danced frantically as she huddled against his coat, seeking shelter from the blustery wind. She glanced up, and their eyes met. Her gaze searched his imploringly, crying out for his quiet strength, and Beau was more than willing to give it to her.

The dreary day was suddenly obliterated as he smiled, and as if they were speaking only to each other, they recited the comforting thought: "Surely goodness and mercy shall follow me all the days of my life: and I will dwell in the house of the Lord forever."

Beau believed those weren't just empty words written a long time ago, but a firm promise a man could depend upon, and his eyes lovingly brought the message home to her.

For Charity, that made Ansel Latimer's death a little easier.

Few chose to stop by the Burkhouser buggy to offer words of comfort after the service. Most of the mourners conveniently dispersed to the safety of their carriages for the return trip.

The Reverend and Mrs. Olson paused briefly, clasping Charity's hand. Their eyes spoke of deep sympathy because they knew she'd lost another close friend, and their words were kind and reassuring. Charity held tightly to Rebecca's hands. They couldn't have been more comforting had they been the hands of an angel.

When the last of the mourners had gone, Beau and Charity sat in the buggy staring at the mound of freshly turned dirt.

Ansel rested beneath a large oak, and the sound of the wind rustling through the brittle branches was a lonely one. Above, the sun had disappeared behind a cloud again, enveloping the earth in a shroud of gray.

"I hate death." Charity's voice sounded small and frightened in the frosty air.

"It's as much a part of life as being born."

She turned to Beau, her face childlike now. The wind had whipped her cheeks red, and her moist eyes reminded him of pools of sparkling emeralds. He had never seen her look so pretty—or so bewildered. Since coming to the Kansas frontier, she'd seen more than her share of death, and he knew she needed to know there was more to life than this terrible, crushing sense of loss. "But it hurts, Beau. It hurts." Her voice broke and tears began to slide down her cheeks again.

"I know it does." He reached over gently and cupped her face in his large hands. His gaze, as blue as periwinkles on a summer morn, held hers soberly. "I wish I could make it easier for you."

"You do, just by being here."

She smiled through her tears, and the sun suddenly broke through the clouds in a splendid array of light, bathing the grave and the small buggy in a pool of ethereal warmth.

Or did it only seem that way because that's how Charity made him feel? he wondered. When Beau glanced up, the clouds were as dark and dreary as they'd been before.

Charity noticed that he'd been staring at her a very long time. It seemed as if he were struggling to say something, but didn't know how.

Charity waited patiently but felt disappointment when, after gently brushing her tears from her cheeks with his thumbs, he reached to pick up the reins. The horse slowly began to move over the rutted hillside and out of the cemetery.

Charity turned, watching over her shoulder as Ansel's grave grew smaller and smaller in the distance.

"I hope he's with Letty," she whispered.

Beau hoped he was too.

A stray flake of snow fell occasionally as the buggy wound its way back to Cherry Grove. Charity had mentioned she needed a few supplies and would like to stop by Miller's Mercantile before they made the trip back to the soddy.

Beau readily agreed. He needed a new hammer, and he'd welcome the opportunity to purchase a quantity of raisins.

"Raisins?" Charity's brows lifted as he mentioned his strange request. "I love raisin pie. You know how to make one?"

"Why . . . I've never made one, but I'm sure I could."

"Good, then I'll get plenty."

But when the buggy rolled into Cherry Grove, Beau drove right past Miller's Mercantile, the Havershams' Restaurant, Dog Kelley's Saloon and Gambling House, the Parnell Clothing Store, the schoolhouse that served as the church on Sunday mornings, and the various other storefronts lining the almost deserted Main Street.

A plume of white smoke puffed out of the chimney of Miller's Mercantile, and Charity knew most of the townspeople who were brave enough to venture out on such a cold day would be huddled together around the old wood stove, exchanging tales of Ansel Latimer, and, no doubt, the scandalous Charity Burkhouser.

"You just passed the mercantile," Charity reminded him, thinking Beau had been lost in thought and missed his intended destination.

"I know."

The buggy rolled around the corner, and the horse trotted at a brisk pace down Larimore Street. Charity leaned over to assist Beau in correcting the oversight, her breath making white wisps in the cold afternoon air. "Just follow Larimore around, and it will bring you right back to Main."

"I know where I am."

"You do?" His air of confidence assured her that he did, but she didn't understand. As far as she knew, Beau had only been in Cherry Grove one previous time to purchase wire for the fences.

"How are you so well acquainted with the town?"

"I'm unusually bright for my age." He winked at her and began to whistle a jaunty little tune as he urged the horse to pick up its pace.

Charity sat back and enjoyed the ride, thinking how nice it was to get her mind off of the depressing events of the past few days. Beau seemed to be in an uncommonly good mood all of a sudden, and it made her own spirits lighter.

Still, when he pulled the horse to a stop in front of Reverend Olson's house a few minutes later, Charity glanced at him mystified.

"Are we going to visit Mary Kathleen?" She tried to conceal the sudden excitement in her voice. She knew he missed the baby as much as she did, and she didn't want to put a damper on his cheerful mood.

Beau set the brake and tied the reins to the handle. Then he got out of the buggy and turned to lift her down.

"Beau, I don't think we should drop in unannounced this way." Charity tried to slow her steps as he opened the gate on the white picket fence and ushered her hurriedly up the walk.

"A minister shouldn't be surprised by unexpected company," Beau soothed, and before Charity could protest further, he rapped briskly on the door to the parsonage.

The door was answered by Rebecca, whose face, upon encountering Beau and Charity on her doorstep, broke into a wreath of welcome smiles. "Land sake! Look who's here, Papa!"

"Who?" Reverend Olson poked his balding head around the door, and he smiled, too, when he saw the young couple looking back at him. "Well, do come in, do come in!" he invited, swinging the door open cordially.

Charity noticed he had a cloth draped over his shoulder, and signs of Mary Kathleen's recent dribblings were in evidence. "How very nice to see you!" Rebecca exclaimed as she bustled around collecting their coats and scarfs. "I never dreamed you'd stop by today!"

"Well, I had a few things to pick up at the mercantile," Charity offered lamely, never dreaming herself that she'd be standing in the reverend's parlor, inhaling the delicious smell of an apple pie simmering in the oven.

"Well, you must stay to dinner," Rebecca insisted.

"No, I'm afraid we have to be gettin' back soon," Beau refused politely. "It's startin' to snow again."

"It is? Oh, dear. I just hate winters, don't you?"

Charity nodded agreeably.

"Well, well. You must be here to visit with Mary Kathleen, but I'm afraid she just went down for her nap," Reverend Olson apologized. "She didn't sleep well at all last night. . . ."

Actually, she hadn't slept well since she'd arrived there, Reverend Olson wanted to amend, but didn't. He wasn't sure how many more nights he could walk the floor with a screaming baby and still retain a charitable attitude. The good Lord hadn't meant for old people to have babies—with the exception of the biblical Sarah, of course.

Charity was about to say they understood and would be happy to return as soon as they completed their shopping when Beau interrupted suddenly. "We'd sure appreciate seein' the baby, but that's not what we're here for, Reverend."

Charity's gaze flew up to meet Beau's expectantly. "It isn't?"

"It isn't?" Reverend Olson parroted.

"It isn't?" Rebecca echoed.

"No, sir . . . I . . . me and Mrs. Burkhouser want to—to get married."

"You do?"

"We do?"

"You do!" Rebecca clapped her hands together gleefully. "Wait just a minute! I have to take my pie out of the oven."

"Beau!" Charity looked at him dumbfoundedly. Her heart was beating like a trapped sparrow, and she suddenly felt lightheaded. He was going to marry her? The least he could have done was *tell* her.

"Yes. You don't have any objections, do you?" His eyes radiated that stubborn blue she'd come to recognize, and yet they looked a little sheepish too.

"No . . . I—I'm just surprised, that's all."

"Well, if you want to get Mary Kathleen back, it seems the only sensible thing to do." Beau took a deep breath and went on. "I figure since we're in town, we might as well get it taken care of."

"You—you don't mind?"

"Wouldn't be doin' it if I minded," he said abruptly.

"But, Beau, are you sure you want to do this?" Charity had no idea what had changed his mind, but she didn't want him to do something he would regret in the morning.

"I think it's the only thing left to do."

"But is it what you *want*, Beau?" She desperately wished he would say something more reassuring—anything—but could she really question his motives? If he was good enough to help her out, then shouldn't she just accept his kindness, and not worry why?

"It's all right with me, Charity, if it's what you want."

"Well, then, I suppose I don't have any objections . . . if you don't." She didn't dare press her luck by asking him if their marriage would be a permanent commitment or only a temporary arrangement. At this point it seemed immaterial.

Beau took a deep breath and straightened his stance bravely. "Then let's get on with it, Reverend."

Rebecca breathlessly returned after taking her pie out of the oven, and moments later the ceremony began.

Charity's hands trembled, and her voice could barely be heard as she nervously recited her vows. Beau's hands were steady as a rock, and he repeated his words woodenly, his voice never wavering.

How the vows were exchanged made little difference; for better, for worse, within a scant three minutes, Charity Burkhouser and Beau Claxton had become man and wife.

"Do you have a ring to give your bride as a symbol of your vows?" Reverend Olson asked.

"I'm sorry, sir. I don't."

"No matter. A ring is only a symbol; it doesn't insure love." Reverend Olson's gaze met Beau's kindly. "It will be up to you to cultivate love and make it grow, son."

"Thank you, sir."

"I wish you godspeed. You're both good people." Reverend Olson closed the Bible firmly. "You may kiss the bride."

CHAPTER 18

FIFTEEN MINUTES LATER, BEAU AND CHARITY WERE standing on the opposite side of Reverend Olson's front door with Mary Kathleen once again nestled snugly in Charity's arms.

"Did you get the impression Reverend Olson was anxious to return the baby to our care?" Charity asked with a cheeky grin.

"Sure looked that way." Beau and Charity had to laugh at the almost comical way Reverend Olson had hurriedly gathered Mary Kathleen's meager belongings, while insisting Beau and Charity get an early start for home.

"I'll bet he's already curled up in bed sound asleep," Charity predicted.

"I wouldn't doubt it."

They stepped happily off the porch together and walked to the buggy. Charity waited while Beau settled the baby comfortably on the seat, making sure the child was well protected from the inclement weather. Then he turned to assist her.

He lifted her slight weight easily, his strong arms suspending her momentarily in midair as the groom's eyes met his bride's shyly. Charity grew a little breathless as she stared back at her handsome husband. His eyes were a startling blue against the stark white of the frozen countryside, and she suddenly found herself wishing the unexpected alliance between them could somehow be a permanent one. She knew she would do everything within her power to make it so. Was it possible she was falling deeply in love with Beau Claxton?

"Charity . . . about the ring . . ."

"Yes?"

"I'm sorry I didn't have one to give you."

"It's all right. I don't have one to give you either."

"And . . . I'm sorry I didn't ask you proper . . . to marry me. I . . . well, this wasn't easy for me . . . or you. . . ."

"I understand." She smiled, trying to assure him that it didn't really matter. Her mind vividly replayed the kiss he'd given her at Reverend Olson's request. It was a brief, emotionless one, nothing more than a polite ritual, but it had sent every nerve in her body tingling.

"I've been givin' the problem serious thought." He hoped to alleviate any misconception that she might have that his was a spur-of-the-moment decision. The weighty conclusion had interrupted his sleep more than one night. "I think we made the only reasonable choice."

She nodded, wondering what it would feel like to touch his hair. Would it feel soft or coarse and springy? And his mouth. It was beautifully shaped, with full, clearly defined lips that looked unbelievably warm and sensual. What would it feel like to have his mouth fully explore hers?

Her eyes widened guiltily when she realized he was aware of the way she was shamelessly regarding him. A slow grin spread across his features, the devilish smile crinkling the corners of his eyes.

For a moment he looked as if he wanted to kiss her—really kiss her this time—but the moment passed, and before she knew it, he was quickly hefting her onto the buggy seat without further ado.

The stop by Miller's Mercantile was kept short because of the worsening weather. The store was busy, and Beau offered to hold Mary Kathleen while Charity made her selections.

He carried the infant around the store, acting very paternal, pointing out various articles to the child, which Mary Kathleen could not possibly understand or appreciate the meaning of. Charity watched as he paused and whispered conspiratorially to the child about a certain rag doll Santa Claus might be persuaded to bring her, if she promised to get her outrageous sleeping schedule back in order. His endearing petition warmed Charity's heart.

When Charity's purchases were completed, the baby exchanged hands so Beau could shop. Charity browsed through the bolts of brightly colored yard goods.

"This is the finest one we have in stock," the proprietor, Edgar Miller, proclaimed as he handed Beau a heavy hammer. "The head is forged iron, and the handle is solid oak."

Beau examined the tool carefully. Assured it would serve his needs well, he agreed to buy it and turned his attention to the vast array of hoes, rakes, spades, ropes, and kegs of nails. When he'd satisfied his curiosity about all the shiny new farm implements, he moved on to examine the food staples behind the counter on long rows of shelves.

There were large containers of soda crackers, coffee, tea—black and Japanese—starch in bulk, bottles of catsup, cayenne, soda, and cream of tartar, often used in place of baking powder.

The floor of the mercantile was lined with barrels. There were two grades of flour: white and middlings, coarse meal, and buckwheat flour. Large barrels of apples from Missouri, sacks of potatoes, turnips, cabbages, pumpkins, and long-neck squashes were in plentiful supply. There was more: salt pork, in a crock under a big stone to keep the pork down in the brine, vinegar, salt, molasses, and three grades of sugar: fine white— twenty pounds for a dollar—light brown, and very dark.

The counters were brimming with baskets of eggs—three dozen for a quarter—big jars of golden butter, selling for twelve and a half to fifteen cents a pound. There was cheese all the way from New York, maple syrup, and dried peaches and apples.

"Do you have any raisins?" Beau prompted.

"Raisins?" Edgar scratched his head thoughtfully. "Afraid not . . . but I could probably get some from over in Hayes."

"How long would it take to get them here?"

"Depends. If the weather cooperates, they should be here in a week or so. They'll be right costly, though."

"I'll take four pounds."

"Four?"

Beau nodded. "Four should do it."

While Edgar wrote the order, Beau looked at the row of watches and rings displayed in a glass case beneath the counter. His attention was immediately drawn to an exquisite emerald brooch that lay nestled on a bed of royal-blue velvet. Something about the brooch reminded Beau of Charity. The stones were elegant and the design most intriguing. Such a delicate piece of jewelry seemed out of place among the large watches and gaudy baubles surrounding it.

"May I see the brooch, please?"

Edgar glanced up and smiled. "Of course. Lovely piece, isn't it?" He moved over to unlock the case. Gently he lifted the box containing the brooch and placed it on the counter for Beau's inspection.

"Just got it in a couple of days ago," Edgar volunteered.

"It's beautiful." Beau lifted the brooch from the velvet box. The green stones caught the light and danced brightly. It suddenly occurred to him why the piece of jewelry reminded him of Charity. The stones were the exact shade of her eyes.

"Yeah, a couple of Indian squaws come waltzing in here day before yesterday and offered the brooch in trade for three bottles of whiskey and a handful of peppermint sticks."

"You don't say." Beau turned the piece over and examined the craftsmanship closely. Indeed, it was worth more than three bottles of whiskey and a handful of peppermint sticks.

"I'll make you a good deal on it," Edgar offered.

"How much?" Beau countered.

The price Edgar set was completely out of line, especially in view of the fact he'd just foolishly revealed to Beau what he'd given for the brooch. However, Beau knew the man would have no trouble finding someone who'd pay the exorbitant price.

"Well, thanks, but I'm afraid that's a little too steep." Regretfully Beau placed the brooch back in the box.

It would be Christmas in three weeks, and he didn't have anything to give his new bride. The brooch would have made a nice gift.

Beau started to walk off as Edgar slid the box back into the case. He suddenly turned and hurried back. "How much did you say those raisins would cost?"

Edgar repeated the price. The brooch would cost four times what the raisins would cost. But Beau had the money to buy the brooch; and he wanted Charity to have it.

"Then cancel the raisins, and I'll take the brooch," Beau said, grinning. He hadn't had a raisin pie in over a year; he guessed he could do without one a little longer.

Edgar smiled. "A gift for your lady?"

"Yeah. I married Charity Burkhouser about an hour ago, and I think she'll enjoy the brooch more than I'd enjoy the raisins."

Beau's grin widened as he watched Edgar's mouth drop open.

Beau noticed Charity was unusually quiet on the way home. It was growing dark, and they still had several miles to go before they reached the soddy.

The baby was sleeping and seemed unaffected by the cold as Beau urged the horse's steps to a faster cadence.

"You cold?"

"A little." The weather was uncomfortable, but Charity found she didn't mind. She was still enjoying such a warm glow from the unexpected turn of events, she barely noticed the discomfort. The baby had been returned to her care, and she and Beau were married. She didn't see how she could complain about a little thing like bad weather.

"I'd hoped to make it back before dark," Beau apologized.

"I don't mind. I'm fine."

"You think the baby's cold?"

"She doesn't appear to be." Charity reached down and adjusted the heavy blanket surrounding Mary Kathleen like a cocoon.

They'd ridden in silence for a few minutes when Charity remembered. "Were you able to get the raisins?"

"No . . . Mr. Miller would've had to order them."

"Oh. How long would it have been before they'd arrived?"

"He said about a week."

Snow began to fall again as the horse briskly trotted down the road, pulling the buggy containing the newly formed family.

Charity let her thoughts wander as the last vestige of twilight faded. The world around her became a fairyland of white as the snow began to sift down in earnest now.

She longed to snuggle closer to her husband's large body, but she didn't dare. He would surely think her forward, and just because they were married now, she couldn't start taking such wifely liberties. After all, it was still to be determined to what extent he intended to participate in their marriage.

Her gaze drifted shyly to him and she found him immersed in his own thoughts. His hands drove the buggy deftly, and she thought how nice it was to have a man perform that task for her.

Would he join her in her bed tonight? The thought jumped unexpectedly into her mind, startling her. It was shameful to be thinking such a thing, but the tantalizing prospect sent goose bumps skittering up and down her spine.

Would she object? The answer came more easily than the question: not at all. She was prepared to be his wife in every aspect he desired her to be. Even if he planned to leave her in the spring, it would not change her feelings. She would seek his comfort, tend his needs, and share his life for as long as he chose to remain with her.

And when the time came for him to leave, she would see him off with a smile and good wishes. She'd made herself that promise, and she intended to keep it.

Charity shifted around on the seat, adjusting the blanket more tightly around her. The darker it became, the colder it was.

"You might be warmer if we moved closer together." Beau's suggestion was spoken so casually that Charity wasn't sure if it was an invitation or not. "Just slide the baby onto your lap. She'll probably be warmer there anyway."

"Oh . . . well, yes. Thank you." Charity carefully repositioned the baby, then edged closer to him until she felt her hip make contact with his solid thigh.

She was so aware of him, not only aware of his masculine build, but close enough now to smell his distinct scent: a combination of soap, leather, wool, and the elements.

"Better?" Beau glanced at her and smiled.

"Yes, thank you."

They were closer than they'd ever been and Charity felt her limbs growing weak.

"Seems like we should be sayin' somethin' a little more meaningful, doesn't it?" Beau was the first to break the strained silence moments later.

"Meaningful?"

"Yeah, I mean, it is our wedding day. . . ."

"Yes, seems we should have something to say, all right." Charity fondly recalled the day she and Ferrand had married. Birds had been singing, and the grass had been a rich, lush green carpet for her to tread upon. The church had overflowed with well-wishers, and there had been baskets of flowers and a large wedding cake.

"Was the weather nice the day you married Betsy?"

Until now Charity had been able to view and talk about Betsy in a charitable light. But now, just the casual mention of her name sent streaks of jealousy shooting through her as she thought about the intimacy Beau and his first wife must have shared on their wedding night.

"Yes, it was. It was a warm fall day. The leaves on the trees were gold and yellow and brown. . . ." His eyes took on a faraway look, and Charity wished she hadn't brought up the subject.

"What was the date?" It shouldn't matter; yet, for some reason, she had to know.

"Second of October. What about you and Ferrand?"

"June second."

Silently each pondered the coincidence; it was the second of December—their wedding day.

"I—I was quite surprised when you asked Reverend Olson to marry us," Charity confessed. "But very grateful."

"The gossip was bothering you, wasn't it?"

"A little," she admitted. "But I would've seen it through." It hadn't been easy facing the accusing stares from the citizens of Cherry Grove. The few times she'd ridden into town for supplies had been disconcerting, but having Beau remain with her had been worth it.

"No need for either one of us to be the source of malicious gossip. Talk should quiet down now."

"I hope you don't mind, but I—I told several women at the mercantile we were married now."

"I don't mind. I told Mr. Miller myself."

Charity grinned. "You did? Well, thank you."

"It was my pleasure. You should've seen Edgar Miller's mouth drop open."

"Oh, he's the biggest gossip of all."

"That's why I made sure he was the first to know about us gettin' married. Maybe his tongue will have a chance to cool down now."

Charity sighed. "I surely hope so."

"By spring I should have the land in good shape," Beau predicted as he urged the horse across Fire Creek and headed north.

"With the two of us working it shouldn't take long," Charity agreed.

She wanted to ask if he still planned to leave then, but selfishness stopped her. She wanted nothing to interfere with the happiness she was feeling.

"Charity . . . about our marriage . . ." Beau paused, hesitant to approach the touchy subject.

Charity blushed, knowing the conversation was about to take a more personal turn. "Yes?"

"Well, I know you must be wonderin' if I expect to claim my . . ." Beau's voice trailed off uneasily, and she was sure that if she could see his features clearly, he would be blushing!

Her lofty spirits plummeted. She braced herself; next he would inform her that he had no intentions of claiming his husbandly rights because he didn't want to make love to anyone but his Betsy.

Beau started again. "I . . . well, I think we would . . . of course, we both need to . . . Well, hell, we should talk about . . . but then it's not gonna be exactly the same. . . ." He was having a horrible time making his point.

"Are you tryin' to say you don't plan to exercise your husbandly rights?" Charity offered gently, hoping to help ease his painful dilemma.

Beau's gaze flew to meet hers. "Well, no . . . I wasn't tryin' to say that."

"You weren't?" Charity's pulse jumped erratically with his rather adamant denial.

"No . . . I didn't mean that at all. I just meant it might be sort of . . . embarrassing at first. . . . Well, you know. . . . It might take us a while to get used to . . . get to know each other. . . ."

"You mean, you think we should sort of sneak up on it," Charity teased, delighting in the way he promptly scowled at her, clearly shocked by her brazenness.

"A Claxton never sneaks up on a woman," he stated. "Believe me . . . when it's gonna happen, you'll know it."

"I'm sure I will." And she could hardly wait.

She settled deeper into the blanket. A few moments later she scooted closer, pressing herself tightly against his side.

Beau was aware of her movements, and he shifted his leg so it was resting more fully against hers.

He felt desire begin to build, strong and powerful, making him feel almost giddy with the knowledge that once again he felt like a whole man.

"I was just thinking how nice it will be to get home," Beau remarked as the horse trotted along in the falling snow.

"Yes, it will be nice. The fire will feel exceptionally good this evening." Her hand reached over to shyly slip into his.

His hand tightened on hers perceptibly. He had no idea what was happening to him, but he was enjoying it. "The bed won't feel all that bad either."

"No, I find I'm rather looking forward to it."

"I was thinking the same thing."

Well, hell, why not, he argued irritably, trying to still the faint twinge of conscience tugging at him. Betsy was gone. And he was still a young man with some very fundamental, long-suppressed needs. It had been over a year since he'd been with a woman . . . and the woman he had in mind now was his wife.

But you haven't given one single thought to whether you'll be stayin' with this woman come spring, his conscience reminded. *You just went off half cocked and jumped into marriage without givin' the future much thought.*

And I don't plan to. At least not tonight, Beau thought stubbornly.

"I hope the baby decides to sleep tonight," Charity said softly.

"If we're . . . busy . . . it won't hurt her to cry a little. I think we're spoiling her," he blurted, his voice coming out louder than he intended.

"If we're . . . busy," she agreed, "it won't hurt to let her fret for a spell." His words, though innocent, excited her. He was sparring with her suggestively, and she loved it.

Charity's head had somehow drifted to his shoulder, and she turned and pressed her face into the warmth of his neck. She no longer cared if she was behaving improperly. "How much farther?" she whispered.

Beau felt his desire leap and tighten almost painfully. "About another mile."

He glanced down and caught his breath when he saw their mouths were only inches apart.

"Don't go to sleep on me," he urged in a voice that had gone husky with desire.

She looked up at him, her heart in her eyes. "I was just thinking how very nice that might be."

Beau's mouth lowered another fraction. "I was thinkin' neither one of us might get much sleep tonight."

"I'm not at all sleepy." Her tongue came out to boldly trace the outline of his mouth.

"Oh, hell, Charity." Beau's voice sounded shaken, raspy, as his lashes drifted closed and he allowed himself to become a willing captive of her sweet seduction.

"I . . . hope you don't mind," she whispered, her mouth moving over his experimentally. She was surprised to see how easily she could take such liberties with him. It felt natural . . . good.

"Mind? Do I look like a fool?" His hand reached to cup the curve of her face, making her mouth more accessible to his.

Their mouths touched, hesitantly at first, their tongues gently tasting and exploring.

"Charity . . ." He whispered her name again before his mouth covered hers hungrily.

Her hands came up to encircle his neck, and they became immersed in a firestorm of passion until the horse came to a sudden halt.

Beau opened one eye and groaned when he saw the buggy was stopped in front of the soddy. "We're home."

Charity smiled a little smile, pleased to discover the power she suddenly seemed to wield over him. "Uh-huh," she whispered, her mouth eagerly meeting his again.

"We'd better get in the house," Beau warned, when he was finally able to pull back from her embrace.

"Are you cold?" She gazed at him, her eyes hazy with unconcealed desire.

He placed her hand on the firm proof of his passion, and her breath caught. "No."

"Beau . . ." She wanted him.

"I'll get the baby." His voice held an urgency she'd never detected before.

"All right." She kissed him again, leaving her hand where he'd placed it, gently caressing his ardor. He was her husband. She longed to know every intimate part of him.

Beau's hands shook as he gathered the baby and stepped down from the buggy. "I'll take her inside and come back for you," he promised.

She watched as he started toward the soddy, her heart overflowing with love. She loved him. Maybe not in the exact way she'd loved Ferrand, but it was very, very close.

She began gathering the blanket, eager to become his wife in flesh, not just spirit, when she saw him come to a sudden, abrupt halt. He glanced back over his shoulder and called to her. "Did you leave a lamp burning?"

Charity glanced toward the window of the soddy and frowned when she saw the warm golden ray of light spilling out across the freshly fallen snow. "No."

He groaned. "I hope it isn't those two squaws again!" That was all he needed tonight. He returned to the buggy to grab his gun and hand the baby back to Charity before he turned toward the soddy again.

"You stay here until I see what's goin' on."

"Beau, wait. It may be dangerous!" Charity scrambled out of the buggy as Beau strode back to the soddy and kicked opened the door, gun drawn and positioned.

The young man sitting at the table looked momentarily startled at the hasty entrance. Quickly recovering, he invited in a dry voice. "Well, damn. Do come in."

Charity arrived breathlessly, quickly stepping behind her husband, her eyes widening as she viewed the splendid, dark-headed man in her home.

His boots were off, and his stocking feet were propped casually on the table. He had the tip of a cheroot stuck in his mouth, achingly familiar turquoise-blue eyes, and shamelessly long, thick black eyelashes. His hair was outrageously curly, and he looked as ornery as sin.

The man grinned, flashing a set of brilliant white teeth at her. "About time you and big brother was showing up."

CHAPTER 19

"CASS!" BEAU SHOT AN IRRITABLE SCOWL AT HIS younger brother. "You always did have a way of bein' in the wrong place at the wrong time."

Cass Claxton looked personally affronted by Beau's less than friendly greeting. "Now, what do you mean by that? Here I've ridden for two weeks, through rain and snow and dark of night, just to see how my big brother is gettin' along, and he acts like I was a some varmint come crawling out of the woods."

Cass was being melodramatic, and Beau knew it.

"How'd you find me?" Beau pulled Charity into the room and closed the door. "Don't mind him," he said, nodding toward his younger brother before he hurried across the room to lay Mary Kathleen down in her makeshift bed near the hearth. "He's harmless."

Charity smiled uncertainly as her frozen fingers worked to untie the strings of her bonnet.

Cass grinned and pushed back from the table to get to his feet. A cocky, devil-may-care attitude stood out all over him. "Well, hello, ma'am. You must be the lovely widow Burkhouser." He removed his hat and tipped it politely.

Charity smiled timidly, not at all sure how to take his cavalier attitude. She glanced to Beau for guidance.

"She used to be Mrs. Burkhouser," Beau said easily while busily removing the baby's warm bunting. He seemed to have fully recovered from the shock of finding his brother sitting at the table. "How'd you get here?" He hadn't seen an extra horse when they'd arrived.

"I brought a wagon. It's out back. I wasn't sure where to stable the horses." With undisguised curiosity Cass watched Beau settle the baby.

"And just how did you find me?" Beau turned his full attention to his brother.

"Your letter was pretty clear about where you were. When I reached Cherry Grove, I asked around. An old man gave me directions to the Burkhouser soddy. When it started gettin' dark, and you failed to show up, I began to wonder if I had the wrong place."

"We had business to tend to. Why'd you bring a buckboard?"

"Oh, you know Ma and Willa," Cass complained. "I had to bring half the root cellar, extra blankets, and medicine in case you weren't bein' properly cared for." Cass glanced at Charity and his grin widened. "All that worrying for nothin'. Looks to me like you're bein' taken care of real well."

Beau smiled, thinking how characteristic it was of his mother to think of everything. He left the baby's crib to walk over and clasp his brother's hand warmly. "Good to see you, Cass."

Charity looked from brother to brother and could see not only love but a deep mutual respect shining in their eyes. It was an intangible bond that would be hard for an outsider to penetrate. Loyalty was deep and strong.

Cass held Beau's hand tightly, his face turning somber. "Good to see you, big brother. You're lookin' a whole lot better than I'd expected."

Beau shrugged. "It was close, but, thank God, I'm on the mend."

"We've all been real worried about you," Cass confided.

"I'm sorry I haven't written sooner. I should have done better."

"Oh, we understood."

"The family all okay?"

Cass grinned. "Doin' fine."

"Ma?"

"Strong as an ox."

"Cole?"

"Healthy as a horse."

"And Wynne?"

"Pretty as a picture."

"Did your teachers ever mention anything about enlargin' your sentences?" Beau teased.

"Never said a word about it."

Beau slapped Cass on the back good-naturedly. "Come here. I have someone I want you to meet."

The two men turned their attention to Charity, who was standing by the fire with a smile on her face.

Beau walked over and placed his arm around her waist. "Cass, this is my wife, Charity."

For a moment Cass was clearly stunned by Beau's unexpected announcement, and his face showed it. But to his credit he managed to regain his composure quickly. "Your . . . wife! Well, I'll be damned." He quickly whipped his hat off again, brushed his hand down the side of his tight-fitting denims, and extended it graciously. "Welcome to the family, ma'am. You're sure goin' to be a lovely addition."

"Thank you, Cass. I'm so happy to meet you. Beau has spoken of you often."

"Oh, he exaggerates," Cass objected. "I'm sure once you get to know me, you'll find out I'm not at all like he's painted me to be."

Charity laughed. "I can assure you, it has all been very complimentary."

Charity thought Cass was as adorable and as strikingly handsome as Beau. If Cole, the older brother, was any more handsome, she didn't think her heart could stand the strain.

"Don't tell him that," Beau protested. "It'll only swell his puffed-up head."

"So, you've remarried." Cass's gaze drifted nonchalantly over to Mary Kathleen's crib. "Been . . . married long?"

Realizing what must be running through his mind, Charity spoke up quickly. "Oh, no! Uh . . . the baby . . . she's not Beau's."

Beau looked at her with a stunned expression. "She isn't?" Then he turned to Cass and, to Charity's horror, added, "Isn't that a hell of a thing for a wife to tell her husband?" he said in disgust.

"Beau!"

Beau grinned roguishly as he watched her face flush a bright scarlet. His arm tightened around her affectionately. "The baby's parents are dead, Cass, and Charity and I have been taking care of Mary Kathleen," he explained. "We're hoping Charity will be given permanent custody of the child, once things settle down."

Charity thought she detected Cass's quick sigh of relief. "You don't say? Been taking care of a new baby, huh?" He stepped over and peered down at the sleeping Mary Kathleen. "She's real cute."

"We think so," Beau said proudly.

While Cass filled Beau in on the activities currently taking place in River Run, Charity cut thick slices of pie and made a pot of fresh coffee.

"Wait till you taste her pie," Beau bragged. Charity bustled around the small kitchen, listening to the conversation with growing amusement.

"Good, huh?"

"Best I've ever eaten."

"Better than Ma's?"

"It's almost as good."

The lamp had burned low when it was finally decided that they had more than one night to visit.

"I hope I'm not puttin' you out by stayin' a few days," Cass apologized.

"Not at all!" Charity protested. "I'm thrilled to finally meet a part of Beau's family."

"Well"—Cass began to yank off the boots he had put on earlier—"just tell me where to roll up. I'm so tired I could sleep on a thorn and not know it."

Charity's eyes met Beau's expectantly. In all the excitement it hadn't occurred to either of them that their privacy was going to be drastically affected by Cass's unexpected visit.

With only one room, one bed, and one pallet, any hope of consummating their marriage vows seemed impossible.

"Oh . . . well, I suppose you'll be sleeping . . ." She grappled awkwardly with the problem of where to put him.

"Outside," Beau interjected hurriedly.

Cass's face fell. "In this kind of weather?"

"Beau, he can't sleep outside," Charity reminded.

Cass glanced down and saw the neatly made pallet by the fire, and a relieved smile replaced his worried frown. "Oh, you always did like to pull my leg. I see you've already made my bed. Well, think I'll turn in. I'm plain tuckered out."

Charity smiled lamely. "Yes . . . well . . . good night."

As she turned away, she thought her bed seemed to suddenly dominate the tiny room. She began to edge timidly toward the mattress while Beau banked the fire for the night.

Cass settled himself on the pallet as Charity proceeded to string a line across the room and hang a brightly patterned blanket over it.

Once she was assured of a modicum of privacy, she began to undress while listening to Beau bid his brother a good-night. A few moments later, he parted the curtain and stepped into the small cubicle.

Once again, the intimate area suddenly seemed stiflingly small.

"I'll get up with the baby for her night feeding," Beau offered. He sat down on the bed and began unbuttoning his shirt. "That way you won't have to . . . dress."

"Thank you." Her voice was so soft he could barely hear her.

"It's so late, I'm surprised she hasn't awakened before now."

"I'd have thought she would, too, but I guess she's real tired."

Charity stepped out of her dress and draped it neatly across a chair. She hurriedly fumbled for her gown hanging on a small hook and glanced at Beau self-consciously. "Would you mind . . . ?"

Beau looked up and saw her holding the gown to her chest protectively. "No . . . of course." He turned his head as she quickly slipped out of her chemise and pantalets, and pulled the gown over her head.

"All right . . . I'm through."

Beau stood up and peeled his shirt off and unbuttoned his pants. He glanced at her questioningly, wondering if she'd prefer to turn her head while he undressed, but she was busy turning back the blankets, keeping her gaze carefully averted.

A moment later, she scurried beneath the covers. The bed creaked as Beau sat down on his side to remove his socks.

Charity lay stiff with apprehension, awaiting the moment he, too, would be under the blankets. She had no idea where her earlier boldness had fled to, but it had completely deserted her now.

Beau leaned over and blew out the lamp, throwing the room into total darkness as he finished undressing.

Charity lay perfectly still, thinking how much she'd always hated darkness. Fears tended to be amplified, doubts reborn, and small problems inflated to overwhelming obstacles when there was no light.

Many nights she'd slept with a lamp burning, so she wouldn't have to face the emptiness. Now that she was married again, would that horrible loneliness finally be over? she wondered.

And then he was there beside her.

Just as she'd begun to worry about how she would act, he stretched out next to her, his body warm and reassuring—the way it used to be when Ferrand was beside her.

She could still hear the wind howling outside, the tick of the clock on the mantel, the baby making soft sucking sounds in her sleep, Cass's soft breathing as he dropped deeper and deeper into untroubled slumber. But with Beau beside her it was as if her life had been miraculously sorted out and put back into order.

For a moment Beau lay quietly, lost in his own thoughts.

She wondered if he was thinking of Betsy.

He wondered if she was thinking of Ferrand.

Finally, he rolled to his side and gently drew her to him. She could feel the outline of his body: the ridges, the sinewy muscles, the tuft of springy hair above the opening at the throat of his longjohns. She could feel the imprint of his maleness pressed against her side.

His familiar fragrance drifted pleasantly around her, and her hands trembled as her arms reached out to encircle his neck. Her breath caught as he pulled her flush against him and whispered into her ear. "I'm sorry about tonight. . . ."

His breath, rasping warmly and stirring her hair, caused a flood of sensations to seep through her like warm honey, all breathtaking, all mysterious, all inexplicably exciting.

"I understand. I guess the only thing that's really important is you're here . . . that we're together," she returned softly.

It occurred to her that neither she nor Beau had mentioned to Cass that this was their wedding night.

To her surprise, Charity felt her gown being moved aside, and she shivered as his hand found her breast. She hadn't expected him to touch her this way, but she found the gesture pleasing. Slowly, Beau began to explore her body, making slow, gentle forays up and down her silken flesh. Charity found she didn't object to his advances but welcomed the feel of his hands moving warmly against her flushed skin.

"You're at liberty to discover your husband," he reminded, his voice low and husky against her ear.

"But your brother . . ."

"Please, Charity . . . just touch me," Beau whispered. He had denied himself the pleasure of a woman for too long. Tonight, he desperately wanted and needed her touch.

Her hands shakily found the buttons on his shirt, and she slowly released them. His chest was broad and hairy just as she remembered. She pressed her lips into the mat of soft hair and breathed his name as his lips began to explore the soft skin down the column of her neck.

"You smell so good." He groaned and drew her up even tighter against him. She felt so good, so warm, so alive.

She whimpered and moved against him, their mouths meeting in hungry urgency. It had been so long since she'd been held like this, so long since she'd been made to feel like a whole woman.

His mouth suddenly turned hard and demanding as the dam of his own pent-up emotions finally gave way. A flood of desire came rushing in on them as he crushed her to him, his mouth devouring hers. She moaned as streaks of pleasure darted through her, so intense, so glorious, they left her lightheaded.

He could feel her trembling beneath his touch, and it aroused him more to know her passion was as great as his.

He took her hand and guided it to the undeniable evidence of his desire. "Touch me . . . here . . . and here . . . and . . . here," he urged huskily.

She did, and she heard his sharp intake of breath as his mouth melted back into hers.

Their kisses deepened as the old clock ticked, and the baby searched hungrily for her fist, as Cass began to breathe deeper, and as the wind shook the soddy with periodic gusts.

"He'll only stay a few days," Beau promised, when their mouths would part momentarily. There was an agonizing ache within both of them, one that begged to be fulfilled, yet Beau knew it would be impossible to make love with his brother lying on the other side of the thin, makeshift petition.

Charity sighed as he finally drew her into the shelter of his side, burying his face in her hair, breathing deeply of the fragrant, lemon scent that always surrounded her.

"Just a few days," he whispered again reassuringly.

It was, indeed, a strange wedding night; as the fire began to die down to bright, rosy embers, the bride and groom dispiritedly accepted the unkind twist of fate and began to drift to sleep.

Charity realized that it was almost a perfect night—at least, for her.

It was the first time, in a very long time, she'd fallen asleep with someone holding her in his arms.

Two weeks later, Cass was still there.

When Beau inadvertently told his brother of the large amount of work he had to accomplish by spring, Cass decided to stay for a while, and lend his brother a hand. It seemed to him the only proper thing to do.

Beau was grateful for the help, but his growing frustration at having no time alone with his bride considerably dimmed his enthusiasm.

Each night had become an exercise in self-discipline, one that Beau didn't relish having forced upon him.

And the enforced celibacy hadn't been easy on Charity either. Each accidental touch, each innocent smile, each unexpected brush of hands or coincidental meeting of gazes, only served to revive the deepening ache that screamed for fulfillment.

It was small consolation for her to know that Beau was struggling just as hard as she to remain pleasant until Cass decided to return to Missouri, but their combined attempt at tolerance was wearing noticeably thin.

"It can't be much longer!" Beau whispered fervently, his voice reflecting the anguish Charity felt.

They lay in the dark, closely entwined in their tiny prison behind the curtain. "He'll have to leave before winter sets in for good." The few insignificant storms they'd had would soon give away to howling blizzards, making travel impossible until spring.

The bed creaked, and Charity jumped uneasily. The noise ricocheted across the room like a loud rifle crack as Beau cast prudence aside and rolled her body on top of his. Before she could protest, and remind him that his brother lay only a few feet away, his hands came up to capture the sides of her face, his lips taking hers roughly in an urgent, seemingly insatiable kiss.

"Beau . . . please . . ." Charity tensed as she heard Cass stir on the pallet, and Beau's hands became more aggressive. She was certain Cass had heard the bed squeak. "He'll hear us. . . ." Her warning ran over Beau's lips like warm butter, and she found it hard to think, let alone protest.

"I can't stand this another minute. Let's go out to the lean-to," Beau urged, his hands beginning to take liberties that made her body grow warm and fluid. "I know it's cold, but we can stand it," he promised in a voice that was so suggestive Charity was sorely tempted to do as he asked.

"I'd want to, but Cass will hear us," she murmured as his mouth continued to tantalize and torment, "and the baby will wake up . . . and cry. . . ."

Chances were, they couldn't successfully slip out of the soddy without disturbing both Cass and Mary Kathleen, and both would be made to look foolish. Charity couldn't bear the thought. "Then Cass'll know. . . ." She moaned softly as his hands probed pleasure points that set her body aflame.

"No, he won't," he pleaded. "And even if he does, he's a grown man, he'll understand."

"Beau . . . please . . ."

"Charity . . . please . . ." His mouth slid down to nibble along the column of her neck.

"Beau . . ."

Then farther.

Her breath caught. "Beau . . ."

And farther.

"I'm your husband . . . I want you . . . all of you . . . right now!"

Cass stirred again, and Charity realized this sweet madness must stop before it robbed her of all control. Beau might be able to face his brother tomorrow morning without reservations, but she couldn't!

She cupped Beau's face in her hands and shook it gently. "Soon, my impatient husband, soon."

Beau groaned and flipped over on his back despondently. "I'm gonna die," he announced flatly, his voice holding not the slightest hope he would survive this harsh and unnecessary punishment.

Charity frantically clamped her hand over his mouth to prevent Cass from hearing, but Beau's overblown pessimism brought a reluctant grin to her face.

Beau was right. Cass *had* to leave soon.

The following morning Beau and Cass were sitting at the table finishing breakfast, and Charity was preparing to hang the wash.

While serving Beau's breakfast, she'd playfully heightened his over-stimulated senses. She'd pressed intimately against his leg and brushed her hand against his arm when offering him more biscuits. And when refilling his coffee, she'd made sure her breast rested on his shoulder.

The highly provocative gestures had been performed for purely selfish reasons. She loved the feel of him. She loved the deliciously giddy knowledge that at the end of the day, he would once again lie beside her, touch her, whisper tantalizing intimacies that only a man would whisper to the woman he desired. Making love would be wonderful, but she loved this hungry side of him as well.

Beau's eyes had instantly darkened with the knowledge of what she was doing, but she noticed he'd pretended to ignore her. She'd known it was wrong to arouse him when he could do nothing to alleviate his misery, yet the impish side of her had delighted in the way he'd shot her a stern warning before diverting his attention back to his plate.

Even Cass was beginning to notice his brother's unusually sour disposition. Beau had snapped at him twice over something so trivial it had made both his and Charity's brows lift in astonishment.

"Would you mind watching the baby while I hang the wash?" Charity inquired as soon as the last breakfast dish was washed and put away.

Beau was sitting in front of the fire, pulling his boots on.

"How long will that take?" he asked sharply.

Charity glanced up. "Not long. Why?"

"I can't get anything done if I have to stay in the house and baby-sit," he barked.

Charity sighed. Indeed he was in a very foul mood this morning.

"I'll watch Mary Kathleen," Cass offered.

"You can't watch Mary Kathleen and drive nails at the same time!" Beau snapped.

Cass looked at Charity and shrugged good-naturedly. "I can't watch Mary Kathleen and drive nails at the same time. Sorry." He held his forefinger up as an afterthought occurred to him. "But I would, if I could." Charity detected a mischievous twinkle in his eye now as he tried to smooth over Beau's uncharacteristic bad humor.

"I'm perfectly able to watch Mary Kathleen," Beau grumbled. "I merely asked how long it'd be before I'd be able to start on my work." The tone of his voice left no doubt that *his* work was far more important than hers, but she let the thinly veiled implication slide.

"Fifteen minutes at the most," Charity bargained.

"Try to make it ten."

"I'll pin as fast as I can." She shot him an impatient look, picked up the basket of wet clothes, and sailed out the door, letting it bang soundly shut behind her.

Still seething, she marched to the clothes line, flung the basket on the ground, and began haphazardly to pin diapers and washcloths in a long, disorderly row. She knew Beau's long-suppressed libido was the cause of his ill temper, and she could sympathize, but she was getting tired of his nasty disposition. The past two weeks hadn't exactly been a bed of roses for her either.

Submerged deep within her self-pity, she failed to detect the silent steps of a tall, muscular Indian as he moved away from a bush and began to approach her.

The brave's nut-brown hand suddenly snaked out and clasped her arm firmly, making her jump and squeal with fright. She nearly swallowed the clothespin she'd just wedged between her teeth.

"Mhhhhhhhhh?" Her wide eyes peered up at his imposing height helplessly. She prayed Beau was watching from the window, but she knew that was unlikely.

"You White Sister?" His voice was deep and gruff. Had he asked her if she was Mrs. Wah-kun-dah, she was so terrified she'd have agreed.

So she nodded wordlessly.

The brave's eyes narrowed. "Why White Sister have stick in mouth?"

"Mhhh . . ." Charity hurriedly reached up and removed the clothes pin. "I—I'm hanging wash."

"Hanging wash?" His black eyes grew confused. How White Sister hang "wash," he wondered. Red Eagle "wash" in water, and water cannot be hung up with funny-looking sticks.

Charity's heart was pounding, and her knees had turned to pulp as she looked at the exceptionally tall brave. He wasn't Kaw, she was sure of it.

Cheyenne, perhaps. He was breathtakingly handsome, with high cheekbones, a proud aristocratic nose, and long black hair that whipped freely about in the blustery wind.

He was wearing buckskins, moccasins, and a massive buffalo robe draped over his broad shoulders to ward off the chilly morning air.

"Did . . . can I do something for you?" she squeaked, wondering if he'd come here to harm her. Maybe he'd been hunting and when he happened to notice her hanging the wash, he'd become curious. She hoped that was the case.

"No can find Laughing Waters."

"Oh?"

"Laughing Waters say to Red Eagle, 'White Sister make good medicine.' "

"Oh . . . she said that, did she?"

The brave crossed his arms and stared back at her authoritatively. "Squaw heap big sick. White Sister make good medicine."

Charity decided he must be trying to tell her that his wife was sick and Laughing Waters was not available to tend her.

"Well, I'm not very good. . . . Laughing Waters and Little Fawn are much better at this sort of thing," Charity hedged.

"No can find cuckoo sisters," he announced flatly.

"Oh, dear. Well, I . . ." Charity searched for a reasonable excuse to deny his request but failed to think of one. "What's wrong with your . . . squaw?"

He rubbed his stomach. "Big hurt."

"Oh. Well, come with me, then." She had no idea what the problem could be, but she figured a good dose of castor oil couldn't harm and might cure his under-the-weather squaw.

As Charity traipsed into the soddy with the brave following close behind, Beau and Cass caught sight of the pair and their mouths dropped open.

Beau scrambled for his gun, while Cass sprang to his feet, every muscle tensed and ready for combat.

Without a word of explanation Charity hurried to the cabinet and extracted a large bottle, then poured a small portion of the contents into a fruit jar. Screwing the lid on tightly, she handed the jar to the Indian. "Make squaw drink."

The brave held the jar up to closely examine the thick, gummy substance. He scowled. "Make squaw drink?" He wasn't sure he'd heard her right. This did not look like something someone should drink.

"Yes, I know. It looks awful, but it might help."

The brave, taking her at her word, nodded. He looked sourly toward Beau and Cass, their bodies posed for immediate confrontation. Then he turned his gaze back to Charity. "Red Eagle no forget White Sister."

If the castor oil didn't do the trick, Charity sincerely hoped that, at least in this particular instance, his memory *would* fail him.

"Who in the hell was that?" Beau demanded after the brave made a quick exit out the door.

Charity shrugged. "I have no idea. I was busy hanging the wash, and he came up and said his squaw was sick and needed medicine."

Beau hadn't failed to notice how handsome the young brave was, and he found himself annoyed when he realized he was jealous of his wife's attentions toward another man. Just how well did she know that strapping, blatantly potent young buck?

"You mean, just out of the clear blue sky, he waltzed up and asked you for medicine?"

"He did, but that isn't unusual," she pointed out. "The Indians around here are rather straightforward when it comes to getting what they want."

"You've never met him before today?" Beau challenged again.

"If you mean, do I have any of his papooses running wild around here, the answer is no." Though she didn't understand or appreciate the insulting insinuation in his voice, she couldn't help but add, "But he was quite a striking man, don't you think?"

She was pushing her luck, and she knew it.

Beau looked back at her coolly. "I hope you mentioned you were under a man's protection now—just so he doesn't get the idea of comin' around when I'm not here," he countered tersely.

Cass watched the growing fracas with barely concealed amusement. Beau was jealous as hell, but didn't want to admit it, even to himself.

Charity's chin lifted with unmistakable defiance. "I don't believe we got around to that subject."

Their eyes locked stubbornly.

"Well, well." Cass awkwardly reached for his coat. "Guess we best be gettin' to those chores, Beau. We're burnin' daylight."

"I was thinkin' the same thing." Beau swiped his coat from the peg and opened the front door. "I suppose you're through hangin' wash?" He glared at Charity.

"It certainly looks that way, doesn't it!"

The door snapped shut briskly.

The next morning, bright and early, a brisk rap sounded at the door. Both Charity and Beau went to answer it.

"I'll get it."

"I'll get it," Beau corrected.

"I'm perfectly capable of answerin' my own door."

Their gazes locked obstinately.

Beau gave in first and Charity opened the door.

The handsome brave who'd caused all the trouble the day before stood before them, his face wreathed with an ecstatic grin.

"White Sister make good medicine." He held up three fingers. "Many papooses!"

CHAPTER 20

THE FOLLOWING MORNING, THE BELL HANGING OVER the door to Miller's Mercantile tinkled melodiously as Beau and Cass stepped inside. The store was empty, except for Edgar, who was busy putting turnips in a large barrel.

"Mornin', Mr. Claxton." Edgar wiped his hands on his apron and stepped behind the counter. "What can I get for you today?"

"I'm gonna need nails, wire, and a few more fence posts."

"Sure thing. Just got a new load of posts in yesterday. Who's that you got there with you?" Edgar eyed the tall, blue-eyed man with Beau, already deciding the two must be kin; there was a strong family resemblance.

Beau introduced Cass to the friendly little proprietor.

Edgar reached out and shook Cass's hand cordially. "Thought you two must be brothers. Where you from, Mr. Claxton?"

"Missouri."

"Missouri, huh? Never been there. Always wanted to, just never got the opportunity."

Beau told Edgar the amounts he needed, and Edgar wrote it all down on a large, thick pad.

"Got those raisins in," Edgar mentioned.

Beau gazed longingly at the large glass jar of raisins sitting on the shelf. He could buy the raisins, and Charity could make a pie . . . or he could save the money and apply it toward a new plow this spring. He quickly tossed the temptation aside. Charity needed a plow worse than he needed raisins. "Thanks, but I'll be passin' up the raisins today, Edgar."

"Just thought I'd mention it," Edgar replied easily.

"Appreciate it."

While Beau and Cass browsed, Edgar went about filling the order.

The door opened again, and a small, rather harried-looking man entered the store, accompanied by a girl who looked as if she must be his daughter.

She was a beauty with an exquisite figure and lovely, amethyst-colored eyes. Her golden blond hair, scooped up into a mass of ringlets, trickled down the back of her head beneath the brim of the latest fashion in Paris.

She had a wide, innocent-looking gaze, but her full lips formed a petulant look as if she'd just finished sucking a lemon.

Cass glanced up and took note of the new arrivals. Upon seeing the man and his daughter, he promptly returned his attention to the shirts he was examining.

The bell tinkled again, and Reverend Olson entered the mercantile. Catching a glimpse of Beau, he immediately came over and struck up a conversation.

"How's Mary Kathleen?"

"Growing like a weed."

"And your new bride?"

"She's just fine."

The reverend chuckled. "I hope the baby is allowing the newlyweds some privacy by sleeping longer periods at a time."

Beau flashed a tolerant grin. "She's not botherin' us."

And Mary Kathleen wasn't.

"Well, I haven't been able to locate any of Ansel or Letty's kin. I've sent letters, but as yet, I haven't received an answer," Reverend Olson admitted. "Now, the Farrises have offered to look after the baby, if you and Charity want, but with nine in the family and another on the way . . ."

"Mary Kathleen's doin' just fine with us," Beau dismissed abruptly. "Charity would be lost without her."

Reverend Olson gazed back at Beau kindly. "And what about you?"

Cass approached the two before Beau could answer. "I don't believe you've met my brother, Reverend. Cass, I'd like you to meet Reverend Olson."

Cass extended his hand, and Reverend Olson grasped it firmly.

The Reverend's smile was as pleasant as always. "Will you be staying in Kansas long, Cass?"

Funny. That was the question uppermost in Beau's mind too.

"I will *not* have that *filthy, disgusting,* piece of slime on my back!"

The men pivoted at the sound of a woman's shrill voice raised in self-righteous anger.

"Now, Patience, dear . . ." Leviticus McCord ducked hurriedly as a bolt of material came sailing over his head and landed with a thud at the feet of the three men, who stood watching the enveloping ruckus with growing curiosity.

"I am *sick* and *tired* of having to look like a—a common *peasant* all the time!" With one fell swoop Patience McCord angrily cleared the table of calico, cotton, and muslin. The floor of the mercantile suddenly looked as if it had been hit by a cyclone.

Cass watched as the girl turned tail and flounced over to rifle through the display of ribbons and fine laces.

Cass, Reverend Olson, and Beau haltingly resumed their conversation as Leviticus began to gather up the bolts of material, mumbling something softly under his breath about having only suggested the material might look nice on her—nothing to get all that upset about.

"I'm planning on headin' back to Missouri while the weather holds," Cass said, answering Reverend Olson's interrupted inquiry.

"Well, I'm sure Beau has appreciated having another set of hands to help with the work."

Reverend Olson cautiously eyed Patience, who, having moved to the rack of cooking utensils, was plainly trying to eavesdrop on the men's conversation.

"Patience McCord is a high-spirited girl," Reverend Olson whispered. "Extremely high spirited."

"Acts like a spoiled brat," Cass observed curtly. He was shocked by such an unladylike display of temper. "The woman has the manners of a goat."

Patience heard his remark, and her perfectly arched brows lifted with disdain. When Cass shot her an impervious look that not only matched hers but topped it, she quickly moved on.

"Oh, dear. Well, remember, *I* didn't say that," Reverend Olson insisted nervously. "The McCords are new in town. Leviticus is a retired circuit judge. He and his daughter came from back East, and it seems the girl hasn't quite made the adjustment her father had hoped she would."

The men began to drift apart, trying to remain nonchalant in the wake of a wildcat being turned loose in their midst.

A few minutes later, Cass was forced to duck again when he heard Patience scream and a bottle of perfume came sailing over his head to smash noisily against the west wall.

His head shot up, and his hands moved defiantly to his hips, but the girl had diverted her full attention to bullying poor Edgar Miller.

"*Why* don't you have something as simple as a spool of red thread? You have every other color," she accused. "*Why* don't you have red?"

"I did have red," Edgar said, eager to console her, "but Ethel Bluewaters came in yesterday and bought the last—"

"*Incompetent* fool! Sheer incompetence!" Her eyes narrowed threateningly. "It's a lucky thing you have the only mercantile in town, Mr. Miller, or I would certainly take my business elsewhere!"

Edgar prayed daily that such colossal good fortune would befall him. "Miss McCord, I have a new shipment of thread coming in next week, and I'm sure there will be plenty of red—"

Edgar's sincere apology was interrupted as she bombarded him with a barrage of spools. "I wouldn't buy your stupid thread even if you had it!"

He cringed and ducked, throwing his arms over his head protectively as the spools continued to bounce off the counter . . . and his balding head.

"Patience, dear! You must stop this!" Leviticus sucked in his breath and drew up his slight five-foot-two frame to boldly confront his daughter. Since the day his wife Althela had died, he'd had a terrible time controlling this unruly child. "Mr. Miller can't help it if Ethel Bluewaters bought his last spool of red thread!"

"The service here is *wretched*!"

Edgar was tempted to blurt that he was just thinking the same thing about her, but he valued his life.

"Now, dear"—Leviticus balled his fists up tight—"now, dear, we just can't have this! You'll just have to go back home until you can get yourself under control."

Cass leaned against the doorway, lit a cheroot, and watched the way the girl had managed to tree two grown men without firing a single shot.

It was amazing, he thought.

"That's perfectly all right with me." Turning her nose up haughtily, Patience lifted the hem of her skirt and swept past her father with the regal air of a queen holding court.

She paused momentarily when she came face to face with Cass, who by now had stepped over to deliberately challenge her path through the door.

"Get out of my way, cowboy." She spat the words out contemptuously, her violet eyes flashing with renewed anger.

Cass slowly placed the cheroot between his teeth, his dark eyes glittering combatively. Lazily, he reached up and pushed his hat back on his head. "And if I don't?" He grinned insolently. He'd put a stop to this real quick. No way would she push him around.

After a tense pause Patience hauled off and hit him squarely in the groin with her purse.

The blow was so unexpected, so explosive, that he saw stars. Staggering, he groped blindly for support as Beau stepped over and prevented him from falling down, face first.

Patience slammed out of the mercantile, rattling windowpanes and sending jars dancing merrily about on the shelves.

As Cass slid to the floor limply, Beau looked at his brother and shook his head sadly. "I don't suppose you've ever heard: 'Hell hath no fury like a woman scorned'?"

Cass shook his head lamely, not at all sure what had just hit him.

"Well," Beau sighed, offering him a hand, "you have now."

Charity opened the door to the soddy and scanned the flawless expanse of blue sky. It was an extraordinarily beautiful day.

She sighed. Christmas would be here next week, and she still didn't have a gift for Beau.

She'd finished knitting Cass a warm pair of socks, and Mary Kathleen a lovely new bonnet, but she wanted something special for Beau.

She wished now she'd ridden into town with the two brothers when they'd asked her to this morning. Instead she'd remained behind to do her weekly baking. By late morning she'd prepared six loaves of bread, and three sweet potato pies were cooling on the windowsill.

The pies reminded her of Beau's penchant for raisins, and the idea suddenly came to her that that's what she'd give him for Christmas: two large, plump raisin pies. By now Mr. Miller should have received the shipment of raisins.

Beau would be overjoyed when he woke up Christmas morning to the smell of his favorite pies bubbling in the oven.

First thing tomorrow morning she'd bundle up Mary Kathleen and make the hour's ride into Cherry Grove.

"You feelin' any better?" Beau noticed Cass wasn't quite as pale as he'd been earlier. He was still trying to ride easy in the saddle and having a hard time of it.

"That woman's meaner than a two-headed snake," Cass grumbled.

"You shouldn't have provoked her," Beau reminded him. "Women like Patience McCord you need to leave alone."

"You don't need to worry about that. I hope I never have the misfortune of meeting up with that hellcat again."

They rode on for a few moments in silence, enjoying the unseasonably warm afternoon. "You know, you've been as testy as an old cow standing on her bag," Cass accused, reminding Beau of his own display of bad temper of late.

"I know," Beau said simply.

"Well?"

"Well, what?"

"Well, what in the hell's gotten into you? You never used to be so short fused. I don't know how Charity puts up with you."

Beau shrugged.

"Just exactly how long have you two been married, anyway?"

"How long you been here?"

Cass glanced at him confused. "What's that got to do with anything?"

"Because we'd just gotten married the afternoon you arrived," Beau said curtly.

Cass was flabbergasted. "Are you . . . you've got to be pullin' my leg," he accused.

Beau shook his head.

"You mean to tell me . . . you and she . . ." Cass frowned. It was beginning to dawn on him what his brother's problem might be.

Beau nodded sagely as he watched Cass figure out the extent of his intrusion into their honeymoon.

"Well, I'll be damned." Cass absently withdrew a cheroot from his shirt pocket, mulling over this surprising bit of news. No wonder Beau had been on edge. He'd slept in the same bed with his bride for two weeks, and unless Cass missed his guess, Charity was too shy to let her new husband make love to her while his younger brother was sleeping not twenty feet away. "Why didn't you say something?"

"I don't know. Maybe I wasn't exactly sure if I would be doin' the right thing by her if we had consummated our vows," Beau confessed.

"Now what's that supposed to mean? She's your wife, isn't she?"

"Yes, but the marriage isn't what you think."

As the two men rode along through the bright sunshine, Beau began to fill Cass in on the past year of his life. At times his voice filled with emotion as he relayed how miserable he'd been until that fateful day the wolf attacked him in the stream.

He spoke of how Charity, along with two Indian squaws, had worked to save his life. Cass could hear gratitude and deep appreciation in his brother's voice.

Beau told him of how Charity's husband had been killed in the war, leaving his young widow to struggle through the hardships of pioneering a homestead.

He talked about Mary Kathleen and how Charity had been left to carry on when both baby's parents had died untimely deaths.

Beau said he felt sorry for Charity. He said he'd married her because there had been ugly talk about their living together and because he wanted to make repairs to her land that would enable her to have a clear title come spring.

Never once did he say he loved her.

Never once did he say he intended to make their marriage permanent.

The strange omission bothered Cass.

"Are you sayin' you plan to leave, once Charity has the title to her land?"

Beau fixed his gaze on the winding road. Cass could see a muscle twitch in his brother's jaw, and he knew he'd hit a sore spot.

"I'm sayin' I'm not sure what I'm gonna do."

"Well, hell, Beau. If you're not gonna stay with her, do you think it's fair to . . . to . . . bed her?"

"I don't know."

"Do you love her?"

Did he love her? It had been such a long time since Beau had felt love, he wasn't sure he would even recognize the feeling again.

"I don't know . . . I still think of Bets. . . ."

"She's gone, Beau," Cass reminded him gently. "We all loved Betsy, but you have to go on. She'd want it that way."

"I know. It's just been real hard for me, Cass."

"Well, I think Betsy would approve of Charity," Cass pointed out, trying to ease his brother's conscience. "She seems like a fine woman. And she's beautiful. You have noticed that, haven't you?"

"Of course I have. And I can't deny that I desire her," Beau admitted. "Living together all winter . . . well, it would be impossible not to want her."

Cass recalled how jealous Beau had become over the Indian brave the day before, and he wondered if Beau even realized he loved the woman. Apparently he didn't.

"So you're not sure you love her enough to make a lifetime commitment?" Cass prompted.

Beau laughed mirthlessly. "Hell, who knows how long a lifetime is gonna be?"

"Well"—Cass sighed—"you'll have to decide what to do about Charity, but I'll make it a little harder on you." He flashed his brother an enlightened grin. "The weather's real nice, and it looks like there's gonna be a full moon tonight. I'll just saddle up and ride out to do a little huntin'." He winked knowingly. "Been meaning to do that, anyway."

Beau shook his head, but he couldn't deny the thrill of expectation that shot through him at the thought of being alone with his wife. "Leaving me and Charity all alone," he concluded dryly.

"You'll still have the baby—unless Mary Kathleen wants to go huntin' with me."

"I doubt she will. She's out of bullets."

Cass grinned and spurred his horse into a faster gait. "Well, let's get going, big brother." His grin widened. "We're burnin' daylight."

CHAPTER 21

*W*HEN BEAU AND CASS ARRIVED AT THE SODDY, BEAU
asked Charity to prepare hot water for a bath.

Charity was surprised by his strange request, especially since it was the
middle of the week, but she quickly set about filling kettles and putting
them on the stove to heat.

After supper Beau dragged in the old washtub, laid out a bar of soap
and a fresh towel, and requested complete privacy.

He bathed, shaved, combed, and brushed. By six o'clock he was im-
maculate, though he wasn't sure what for.

Throughout his preparations he'd weighed the dangers of embarking
upon the course he had in mind.

Was it wise to consummate their marriage vows?

At first there had been no question in his mind. He would. He was a
man who'd been without the company of a woman for over a year. And
although his emotions had lain dormant during that time, his natural
desires had not.

Charity was a beautiful woman who, like himself, had missed the pleasures of the marriage bed. So would it be so wrong if they took refuge in
each other this long winter?

Neither he nor Charity had false expectations concerning their marriage. He'd been honest with her all along, and he understood she needed
a man to gain the title to her land.

Yes, they desired each other. The past two weeks had proven that, but
would desire be enough to see them through a lifetime, if he chose to
remain with her come spring?

And for that matter, although it'd sometimes seemed like ten years, it
had only been a little over a year since Bets had died. Fifteen months,
sixty weeks, four hundred and fifty days . . . it seemed like a lifetime,
yet it had been like only yesterday. Would it be a mockery of his vows to
Betsy to bring another woman to his bed this soon?

He wrestled back and forth with the weighty questions until he grew
short tempered again.

"I thought you were going hunting!" he snapped. Cass was contentedly sitting in the rocker, playing with Mary Kathleen, when Beau's accusation ricocheted across the room.

Charity glanced up from the sampler she was working on and frowned. "My goodness, Beau. Why would he be goin' huntin' tonight?"

"How should I know? But he said he was going." Beau focused a pointed look in Cass's direction.

"Oh, yeah. Well, listen, I am. I'm going," Cass promised. He sprang to his feet and carried Mary Kathleen back to her crib. After nuzzling her fat cheeks affectionately, he kissed the baby good-night, then reached for his coat.

"Don't look for me to be back till late," he warned. "I may even do a little fishin' while I'm out."

"Don't rush on our account," Beau told him in the most congenial voice he could summon.

Charity found Cass's odd behavior almost as puzzling as Beau's. "Fishing? Tonight?"

"Yeah, thought I'd take advantage of the mild weather. Won't be many more days like this one," Cass predicted as he pushed the brim of his hat high on his forehead. "Well, you two have a nice . . . evenin'."

"Cass!" Charity glanced at Beau worriedly.

Beau shrugged. "A man's got a right to go fishin' if he wants."

Cass jerked the door open before Charity could question him further. And came face to face with Patience McCord.

He drew back defensively, a sharp pain shooting through his still tender groin as he recalled his earlier encounter with her. "What are you doing here?" he demanded.

"Mr. Claxton?"

"Yes!"

"Mr. *Cass* Claxton?"

He frowned at her. "That's right."

Patience recognized him as the man she'd tangled with at Miller's Mercantile that morning. She'd thought all along that the blond-headed man accompanying him was Cass Claxton, not this arrogant mule. Apparently she'd been mistaken. "Oh . . . I didn't realize who you were," she murmured.

Cass's eyes met hers coolly.

Patience took a deep breath and drew her shoulders up primly. It didn't really matter which Claxton he was. She was here to speak to him on a purely business matter. "I wonder if I might have a word with you, Mr. Claxton?"

"Me?" Cass couldn't imagine what she would have to speak to him about.

"Yes, if I may."

Charity and Beau had come up behind Cass, catching part of the conversation.

"Won't you come in, Miss . . ." Charity smiled and looked to Cass to provide the girl's name.

His stubborn look indicated he wasn't going to.

"Why, yes, thank you. I will." Patience quickly stepped into the soddy before Cass could protest.

She nodded pleasantly at Beau as her skirts brushed past him, and he nodded back.

Quickly closing the door behind her, Beau wondered what Patience McCord wanted with his brother. He surmised that she must have come to apologize for her outrageous behavior that morning.

"May I get you something warm to drink, Miss . . . ?" Charity glanced helplessly to Cass again. Now that the sun had set, the air had turned frosty. She was sure the young lady would greatly appreciate a cup of tea or coffee to ward off the chill.

"Miss McCord won't be staying long enough to socialize," Cass stated firmly.

Charity was stunned by his lack of hospitality. She had no idea who this woman was, but it was clear that Cass did not like her.

Patience returned Cass's fixed gaze, her nose lifting a notch higher. "Why thank you, Miss . . . ?"

"Mrs.," Charity supplied warmly. "Mrs. Claxton."

"Oh . . ." Patience's eyes turned coolly back to Cass. She was surprised anyone would have the man. "I hadn't assumed you were married."

"Charity is my wife, Miss McCord." Beau stepped over to place his arm around Charity's waist.

"Oh . . . well, as I was about to say, I don't care for anything to drink, Mrs. Claxton. I'm just here to speak with Cass."

"Then Beau and I will take a short walk and let you speak with him in private," Charity offered.

"You don't have to do that," Cass objected. He had no idea what Patience McCord wanted, but he wasn't going to make her visit any easier.

"Thank you. I would like to speak to Mr. Claxton alone," Patience acknowledged stiffly.

Charity checked on the baby, then smiled encouragingly at Patience as she reached for her shawl. "Take all the time you need. We'll enjoy the outing."

"Thank you ever so much." Patience moved closer to the warmth of the fire as Beau and Charity closed the door behind them.

"Who is she?" Charity asked as they stepped off the porch and began walking.

"Patience McCord. She and her father were in Miller's Mercantile this morning where she made quite a scene." The recollection of Cass's unfortunate encounter with the highly temperamental Miss McCord brought a smile to Beau's face.

"Oh? She seems like a lovely young thing."

Beau wrapped his arm around his wife's waist and drew her ear up close to his mouth. "You think so? Well, let me tell you what that 'lovely young thing' did to *my* little brother."

Inside the soddy Cass squared off to meet his unwelcome adversary. "Now, what is it you wish to speak to me about, Miss McCord?" His gaze traveled impersonally over her petite figure, elegantly sheathed in an outfit he'd bet had set poor Leviticus McCord back a pretty penny.

Patience cleared her throat. "I understand you're from Missouri?"

"That's right."

"And you plan to return there soon?"

"I might."

He wasn't being the least bit cooperative, Patience realized, but then it really didn't matter. Her violet eyes were staunchly confident as she met his. "When you leave, I want you to take me with you."

Her pronouncement could have knocked Cass over with a feather. His forehead puckered, he shifted his weight to one foot, and stared at her as if he hadn't heard correctly. "You want *what*?"

"I want you to take me back to Missouri with you," she repeated.

"The hell I will." He turned and irritably jerked the buttons of his coat open and fumbled in his shirt pocket for a cheroot. The woman must be mad, he seethed.

"I'm prepared to offer you five hundred dollars if you'll escort me to my aunt's home in St. Louis."

Cass glanced up from lighting the cigar, and his eyes narrowed.

"Where would you get that kind of money?"

"That's none of your business," Patience informed him. "But I assure you I have it, Mr. Claxton. You see, it's imperative that I leave this little gopher hole they call a town and leave it immediately!"

"Imperative for what?"

"Imperative for my sanity," she snapped. "I simply cannot stand the thought of living in Cherry Grove, Kansas, another moment."

She eased forward, her eyes revealing her desperation as she reached out to clutch the sleeve of his coat imploringly. "You *must* help me. You are the only sane person in this hellhole who is wise enough to think of leaving. From what I can tell, the entire population of Cherry Grove is blissfully happy." She spat the words as if they left a bad taste in her mouth.

"When I overheard Reverend Olson telling Edgar Miller that you were planning to return to Missouri, I knew this was my chance to escape." Her eyes lit up like two Christmas trees at the exquisite thought of returning to civilization.

Coldly, Cass eyed the hand clutching his coat sleeve, and the hand dropped away. Patience began pacing the floor of the soddy. "You see, Mr. Claxton, if you'll get me safely back to St. Louis, I will pay you handsomely. Once I'm there, Daddy will understand how unhappy I've been in this—this rat's nest, and he'll let me stay. Oh! There will be parties and balls and lovely gowns once I'm under my Aunt Merriweather's excellent supervision." She gaily whirled around the floor, caught up in her fantasy.

Patience tactfully omitted that Aunt Merriweather tipped the bottle a wee bit more than she should, and that that was the reason Leviticus McCord had not left his daughter in St. Louis before. But it didn't really matter, Patience concluded. Mr. Claxton would never even have to meet Aunt Merriweather.

"Why, my daddy will surely be overjoyed to let me remain there once he comes to his senses and moves back there himself!" She paused, her face flushed prettily from the heat in the soddy. "Well?" She tipped her head flirtatiously. "Are you interested, Mr. Claxton?"

She didn't see how he could refuse. There was no way on earth for him to make such a vast amount of money by doing so little.

Cass stared at her while he slowly lifted his foot and struck a match across the bottom of his boot. "Not in the least."

Patience's brows shot up with surprise. "You're not?"

"Not on your life, sweetheart."

"What if I increase my offer to six hundred dollars?" It was a fortune, but she had part of her mother's inheritance left. She would gladly give every cent she owned to get out of Kansas.

Cass shook his head skeptically. "You don't have six hundred dollars."

Her eyes darted away momentarily, but seconds later they snapped back to meet his defiantly. "I do have that amount . . . and I'll give it all to you if you'll only take me with you."

Cass sighed. "Miss McCord. Not only will I not escort you to Missouri for six hundred dollars, but you could sweeten the deal with a herd of longhorns, a ranch in Texas, a chest of gold, and a lady of the night, and I *still* wouldn't take one step anywhere with you."

Her eyes turned icy. "You're despicable."

He shrugged and took a long draw on the cheroot. "So are you."

"Why won't you take me?" she demanded.

"Because"—he smiled, showing a row of even, perfectly white teeth—"I don't *like* you, Miss McCord." If she wanted him to be frank, he could.

She cocked her chin rebelliously. "I don't *like* you, either, Mr. Claxton, but I see no reason why that should interfere with your escorting me to

St. Louis. If it would help to persuade you to take me along, I'll promise not to even *speak* to you during the journey."

Cass drew on his cigar and walked over to stare thoughtfully out the window. "Does your daddy know you're running around asking men you don't even know to take you to Missouri?"

"No."

That didn't surprise Cass. "What would he do if he found out?"

"He'd be very upset, naturally. But he isn't going to find out, Mr. Claxton—unless you tell him." Patience doubted he would. He didn't seem the sort who'd want to involve himself in other people's lives.

"I'm not gonna tell him." Cass turned and walked back to the fire. "Your leaving would probably be the best thing that ever happened to him."

She shot him another scathing look. "Exactly why don't you like me? As you pointed out, we don't even know each other."

"I know you about as well as I plan to."

"Why?" she persisted.

"I don't like little girls with nasty tempers."

She sighed. "You're upset about what happened at the mercantile this morning. Well, it was your own fault. You should never have blocked my way."

"You're damn lucky you're still breathin'," he shot back irritably. "What kind of woman goes around hittin' a man in his—"

Patience blushed and tried to change the subject before he graphically described to her where she'd struck him. "Then you refuse to escort me at all?"

"That's about the size of it."

"You won't change your mind?"

He pitched the cheroot into the fire. "No, ma'am."

"Then I suppose I've said all I came to say."

Cass tipped his hat politely. "It's been a real pleasure, ma'am."

Patience brushed by him frigidly as she walked to the front door. She paused with her hand on the latch, refusing to look at him again. "If you should change your mind—"

"I won't."

Oh! The man was just damned hard nosed! She yanked the door open. "I'd appreciate it if you'd check my horse before I return to town."

"What's the matter with it?"

"He developed a slight limp just before we got here."

Cass grumbled something uncomplimentary under his breath, but she noticed he began to follow her out to the buggy.

After a hurried check he discovered the horse had thrown a shoe.

"What does that mean?" Patience inquired hesitantly.

"It means, you're gonna have to have it replaced before you go anywhere."

Her eyes met his expectantly. "Can you fix it?"

She saw him bristle again. "Lady—"

"I'll pay for your services, sir!" she snapped.

"Oh, brother." He took a deep breath. "All right. Wait a minute. I'll see what I can find to shoe your damn horse." Cass stalked away while Patience slumped wearily onto a bale of hay to wait. It was pitch dark, and she began to wonder if she could find her way back to town. Leviticus had moved her to this godawful Cherry Grove three months earlier, and she'd rarely ventured out on her own.

Beau and Charity returned from their walk and paused to chat with Patience for a few minutes. Informed of the problem, they moved on to the soddy to check on the baby.

Thirty minutes later Cass had the horse reshod and ready to travel.

"Which direction is Cherry Grove?"

Cass glanced up from a last check of the hoof. "What?"

"What direction is Cherry Grove?"

His expression turned incredulous. "You honestly don't know?"

She shook her head meekly.

"To the west," he said curtly, and returned his attention to the horse. "Okay," he said a minute later. "You shouldn't have any trouble."

He glanced up to confront two large, violet pools of tears.

"Now what's wrong?"

"I'm afraid. I don't think I can find my way back to town," she sniffed.

"Why not? Just follow the road."

"I—I have a terrible sense of direction," she confessed. "And this is the first time I've ever traveled . . . alone."

"You'll make it fine." Cass wasn't about to get stuck with her till morning. "Just give the horse his head. He'll find the way."

He noticed her hands were trembling as she reluctantly took the reins he was offering. He felt a tug of conscience and tried his best to dismiss it, but he found he couldn't.

"Well . . . look . . . what do you want me to do about it?"

"I—I don't know."

Cass glanced down the darkened road, then back to her. "You'll be all right. You have a gun, don't you?"

"A gun?" She shook her head. She'd never thought of bringing a gun. Besides, she wouldn't know how to use one.

Cass sighed and reached in his pocket for a cheroot, trying to buy some time to study the situation.

He could drive her back to Cherry Grove, but it was getting bone cold. Or he could let her stay here tonight, and she could drive herself back in the morning.

Neither solution suited him.

"You want to stay here tonight?" he finally asked when her sniffling grew more pronounced.

"I . . . whatever you think . . . but I have a horrible headache and I'm beginning to feel faint."

Cass groaned. Lord. He couldn't send her on her way in the dark if she was gonna faint.

"What about your pa?"

"Well . . ." She sniffed and blew her nose daintily into a lace handkerchief. "He'll be beside himself tonight, but I'm sure he'd be even more upset if I started out alone, got lost on the way, and was never found again."

Cass was annoyed by her simple-minded logic.

"Well, come on. It's cold out here." He helped her out of the buggy, and they walked toward the soddy.

"Will Mr. and Mrs. Claxton mind having an unexpected houseguest?"

Cass didn't even want to think about it. Beau was expecting a romantic evening alone with his bride, and now he was going to have not only his brother underfoot but Patience McCord as well.

"They won't mind," he lied.

As Cass and Patience burst into the room, Charity and Beau guiltily broke apart from their heated embrace.

On their walk Beau had explained to Charity why Cass was going hunting, and they were eagerly counting the minutes until they could finally be alone.

"Oh, you haven't left yet?" Charity blushed and made an attempt to straighten her mussed hair as Cass stalked over to the fire.

"Miss McCord's horse threw a shoe."

"We know."

"But you fixed it," Beau prompted.

"Yeah, but now it's dark, and . . . she's afraid she can't find her way back to Cherry Grove." Cass glanced at Beau apologetically. "She's gonna have to stay here tonight."

"You take her into town when you go huntin'!" Beau thundered, so loudly that the other three jumped with the impact of his sudden explosion.

Cass took a deep breath. "I can't. She has a headache and feels faint."

"You do?" Charity immediately forgot her own disappointment and moved to assist her guest. "May I do something for you?"

"If I could just rest for a moment," Patience said softly, her voice sounding very weak.

Beau looked at Cass helplessly as Charity moved Patience to the bed. "Now, now. You just lie down here, and I'll get you a bite to eat. Maybe you're just tired and hungry," she soothed.

"You're ever so kind." Patience shot Cass a smug look as Charity untied her leather kid shoes and removed them.

"Can't you do somethin'?" Beau demanded under his breath as the two women chatted.

"Well, what do you want me to do? Let her wander around on the prairie in the dark, threatening to faint?" Not that Cass would necessarily have objected, especially after the self-satisfied smirk she'd just sent him.

But he'd sure hate to face Leviticus McCord's ire if anything happened to his daughter because of Cass Claxton's negligence.

"I suppose this means the huntin' trip is off." Beau scowled at him sourly.

"I could go, but it wouldn't really do any good . . . would it?"

"Well, it's gonna be another damn miserable night," Beau predicted, in a voice that had turned as bleak as his face.

Cass felt bad about getting Beau's hopes up, then having to dash them this way, but what else could he do?

He wished he'd never heard of Patience McCord.

Beau watched as Charity turned the blankets back and tucked Patience in like a small child. "There, now. You just rest. You're not puttin' us out at all," she assured over Patience's constant fretting that she was. "You can sleep with me tonight. Beau and Cass can sleep on the pallet."

Beau glanced at Cass accusingly.

Cass shrugged and grinned back at him lamely. What could he say? He'd tried his best, and it just hadn't worked out.

CHAPTER 22

BREAKFAST THE NEXT MORNING WAS A SUBDUED affair. Charity and Patience were left to carry on the brunt of the conversation, while Beau and Cass silently ate their meal.

Beau had slept little the night before. He'd missed the warmth of Charity's body snuggled intimately against his. And more, he'd missed the smell of lemons, the clean fragrance of her hair, the feel of her hands caressing him gently during the night.

The moment breakfast was over, Patience announced she was leaving. Beau and Cass prepared to leave, too, saying they planned to spend the morning building fences on the north section.

When Beau found a rare moment alone with his wife, he drew her into his arms and kissed her soundly. "My, my." Charity was breathless when he finally relinquished his overly zealous embrace. "What was that all about?"

Beau sighed and blissfully nuzzled her hair, breathing its familiar fragrance. "I think I missed you last night."

She smiled, closing her eyes with ecstasy as his mouth played along the outline of her throat. "You think?"

He growled suggestively as he pulled her back for another long kiss that was disappointingly interrupted by Cass, who'd returned to the soddy to search for his forgotten gloves.

When Beau regretfully released her, affection was shining deeply in his eyes. "I wish Ferrand had built you a bigger soddy," he teased.

"I'm sure he would have if he'd known I'd need one so badly," she bantered back.

His good humor restored, Beau winked and swatted her fanny as he reached for his coat. "I'll see you at dinner. Looks like it's gonna be another fine day. Cass and I should be able to finish up the fence before dark."

"Mary Kathleen and I will be waiting for you."

Beau paused, realizing how good that sounded. He had someone waiting for him. It had been a long time since he'd had that warm, comfortable knowledge. "Good. I'll see you tonight."

When the house had settled down again, Charity quickly finished her chores and dressed Mary Kathleen. If she hurried, she could make the trip into Cherry Grove to purchase raisins and be back before Beau discovered she'd even gone.

The morning was unusually warm and balmy for December. The sun was shining brightly amid a scattering of fleecy clouds. It would be a perfect day to make the trip.

She selected a lightweight jacket—which she wouldn't need, but wanted to take along just in case. After harnessing the horse, she carried Mary Kathleen to the waiting wagon.

"Easy, now, Jack." She spoke to the horse reassuringly as she settled the baby, then climbed up on the seat beside her. Suddenly she thought to take a shovel along, in case she came across a few sassafras roots along the way. After she retrieved the shovel, the small party got under way.

Charity couldn't remember when she'd felt so good; it had been a long time. She hummed the hauntingly sweet melody "Aura Lee" to the baby as the horse trotted briskly down the road.

The wheels of the buckboard rolled effortlessly through Fire Creek and picked up speed as Charity urged the horse into a faster trot.

If she didn't dawdle at the mercantile, she'd have plenty of time. Beau wouldn't return to the soddy before noon. An hour into Cherry Grove, and an hour back, and she'd have the raisins safely tucked away and dinner on the table. Beau would never suspect she'd made a trip to town.

A small, puffy cloud passed over the sun, but Charity didn't notice. She was busy wondering if Beau would have a Christmas present for her. Quickly she reminded herself that all the work he was doing to the land was a gift in itself. It wouldn't hurt for her to surprise him Christmas morning with two delicious raisin pies even if he had nothing for her. Though she had to admit, a small, insignificant token would be nice. . . .

A second cloud skimmed over the sun and was quickly joined by two, then three. Charity glanced up as an unexpected chill crept into the air. Strange, the day had been perfectly clear a few minutes ago. Now it was becoming rather cloudy.

Deciding she'd better stop long enough to readjust Mary Kathleen's blankets and slip into her light jacket, she guided Jack to the side of the road. It took only a minute to perform the simple tasks, and she was ready to move on.

Glancing up again, she uneasily recalled how fast a Kansas blizzard could move in. But after careful study of the innocent-looking clouds, she concluded they were nothing to be concerned about. She clucked her tongue, and Jack's big hooves clopped noisily back onto the road.

Thirty minutes later, the first minuscule flakes of snow began to drift lazily down, melting as soon as they touched the ground.

Charity still wasn't worried about the abrupt change in weather. It would be about as far to turn back as it was to go on, and the snow appeared to be nothing more than a flurry. But she noticed it was getting noticeably colder, so she urged the horse to a brisker gait.

The snow continued to fall, but in the same gentle manner. The pristine beauty had always fascinated her, and Charity watched the pea-sized flakes float peacefully from the heavy, leaden sky, marveling at yet another one of God's wondrous creations. She hoped they weren't in for a big snow this time, but with Christmas only a few days away, it might be nice.

The wind suddenly shifted directions, and the snow began to fall more heavily. Periodic wind gusts whipped the wagon about on the road as Charity gripped the reins tighter and urged Jack to move faster.

The wind, steadily picking up in intensity, began to swirl snow back into her face, taking her breath away with its growing ferocity. It was becoming evident that once she reached Cherry Grove, she'd be forced to wait out the storm there.

She was a mile from the town when she began to panic. By now, Mary Kathleen was cold and crying, and Jack was becoming increasingly spooked by the freakish nature of the storm.

Drifts began to build beside the road so quickly that Charity found herself losing her perception. If it weren't for the aid of familiar posts and fences, she knew she'd soon be completely lost.

She reached over to try and soothe Mary Kathleen's frightened screams, finally admitting to herself that the trip had been a foolish mistake. At the first sign of snow she should have turned around and headed back to the soddy.

From all indications this was going to be a full-blown blizzard, and she and the baby would never survive the storm if she didn't find shelter—and soon.

Above all she must keep her head, she cautioned. She'd find proper shelter and wait for Beau to find her.

But Beau has no idea where you are, her mind shouted as stinging sleet turned her face a tomato red. She hadn't left a note or even the slightest hint of where she was going.

She pulled Jack to a halt in the middle of the road and gazed helplessly at the chilly alabaster prison she found herself locked into. She realized with sinking despair that Beau wouldn't have a clue where to begin to looking for her.

Not the vaguest idea.

The blizzard hit full force as Beau and Cass finished setting the fourth fence post.

"Looks like it's gonna be a real bitch!" Cass shouted over the rising wind.

"Yeah, we'd better be headin' in!"

The two men quickly gathered their supplies, loaded up, and kicked their horses into a full gallop.

The snow swirled around the riders, and by the time they reached the soddy, the horses were having difficulty plowing through the deepening drifts.

"I've never seen a storm move in so fast," Cass remarked as they rubbed down the horses.

Unexpectedly the image of Patience McCord's snippy little face crept into Cass's mind, and he wondered if the little twit had made it home before the storm hit.

"I've heard of such things happenin', but this is the first one I've ever been in." Beau glanced over and noticed Jack's stall was empty. "Where's Jack?"

"I don't know. Maybe Charity turned him out to pasture before the storm."

The men hurried toward the soddy, their heads bent low against the gale-force wind. Beau shoved the door open, puzzled that Charity hadn't opened it for him.

They stepped inside, and Beau paused when he saw the room was empty. The fire was flickering low, the soddy was chilly, and there was no sign of Charity or the baby.

Beau felt his insides knot with apprehension as he turned to Cass. "Where the hell is Charity?"

"I don't know. Maybe she's out trying to help the stock?"

"No, she wouldn't have taken the baby with her to do that." Beau jerked the door open and scanned the swirling mass of white. Encountering nothing but endless drifts of mounting snow, he felt the knot in his stomach grow tighter. Where was she?

Bounding out of the house, he made his way back to the barn, ignoring the howling storm. There wasn't a sign of the stock, except for the two oxen, Myrtle and Nell. They were in their stalls, contentedly munching on hay.

He stepped behind the lean-to, and his heart sank when he discovered the buckboard was missing too.

Cass followed Beau. As he watched his older brother resaddle his horse, Cass automatically reached for his saddle, too, trying all the while to calmly reason out the more positive possibilities.

"She's probably fine, Beau. She may be caught at one of the neighbors—"

"Charity wouldn't be socializin' on a day like this," Beau said shortly. "Besides, if she'd planned to go visitin' she would have said somethin' about it this morning."

The men remounted, and Cass handed Beau one of the two wool scarves he'd brought along. He tied one around his neck and pulled it up to cover his mouth. "Where do we start?"

Beau shook his head and remained silent as the full implication of Charity's unexplained absence closed in on him.

"Well, I say we try the neighbors first, then head toward Cherry Grove," Cass suggested.

"Cherry Grove? She wouldn't be going to town!"

"You don't know that."

"And you do?"

"No," Cass admitted, "but I figure that's where I'd be goin' if I had a husband and a small baby, and it was three days before Christmas."

"In a damn blizzard?" The horses shied nervously as a violent gust of wind threatened to collapse the drafty lean-to.

"Well, hell, Beau! It looked like a spring day just two hours ago!"

"Okay, okay, let's get movin'." Beau wasn't going to waste time arguing. Cass's reasoning might seem insane, but it was bound to be better than his own right now.

"We'd better stay together," Cass warned, the tone of his voice reminding Beau that they weren't embarking on a Sunday picnic. They were well aware how crazy it was to ride off in a storm this severe. Their lives would be at risk.

"Let's go." Beau viewed the worsening storm again, and a fresh feeling of despair threatened to engulf him. "Where are you, Charity?" he whispered brokenly. "Where are you . . . sweetheart?"

•   •   •

Charity was growing numb with cold. She'd searched for over thirty minutes, but had found nothing in the form of shelter. In the process she'd managed to get the buckboard off the road and into a steep ditch. One wheel had sunk into a deep drift, and the back end was gradually tilting grotesquely to one side. She crawled to the back of the wagon and placed Mary Kathleen on the floor, then lay down beside her. Huddled together in the warmth of the baby's blankets, she began to pray.

The day wore on, and the snow continued to come down in heavy wet sheets. Charity managed to stop the baby's periodic crying by letting her nurse from the bottle she'd brought along. The milk was icy cold, and Mary Kathleen spit the bottle out angrily several times, but Charity forced her to drink enough to pacify her hunger momentarily. She wondered what would happen when the bottle was empty. She'd only brought one.

An hour later Mary Kathleen had settled peacefully inside her blankets, her large eyes watching the snow with fascination. Charity knew the child was getting colder, and she had no idea how much longer an infant could survive in the falling temperatures.

By afternoon both Charity and the baby had begun to doze.

Charity lay next to Mary Kathleen, vacantly watching the snow slowly begin to bury the wagon. She tried to make herself stir, vividly recalling how Ferrand had once described a man who'd frozen to death. The man had succumbed to the temptation of sleep, an irreversible mistake, Ferrand had lamented.

Charity forced her eyes open, but her lashes were becoming frozen, and they soon drifted back to lie stiffly on her snow-covered cheek. Beau . . . don't let me die . . . don't let me die. . . .

Beau and Cass methodically made their way through the snow to the closest neighbors. Beau's despair increased with each worried shake of head, and the distressing news that virtually no one had seen Charity that day.

The two brothers had been persuaded to warm themselves and drink hot coffee at Jacob Petersen's dugout before starting out again. Ten minutes later, they were back in the saddle. "I think we'd better split up!" Beau had to shout to make himself heard above the shrieking wind. "Charity and the baby are out there somewhere . . . I know it, Cass. We'll have a better chance finding them if we ride in different directions."

Cass knew it was risky to separate, but he also knew they were running out of time. "I'll veer east; you take the road to town!"

Beau nodded as he reached across his saddle horn and clasped his brother's hand tightly. "Be careful, Cass."

"I will. You do the same." Their eyes locked silently.

"If we don't find them before nightfall, go back to the soddy. I'll meet you there." It made Beau sick to his stomach to consider the possibility, but he knew if they didn't find Charity and the baby by dark, it would be futile to continue the search.

Cass nodded. "Don't worry. We'll find them."

Beau acknowledged the statement with a brief nod, then reined his horse away and disappeared into the swirling mist of snow.

Cass proceeded in the opposite direction.

Charity woke with a start. She was in some sort of cave . . . a white one. And it was warmer.

Outside she could hear the wind screeching, but the sound seemed muted, softer somehow.

She carefully moved her hand to see if it was frozen, and, to her surprise, she discovered it wasn't. Though it was bright red and stiff, she could still wiggle her fingers, though it was painful to do so.

Her eyes moved slowly, and she found that she and the baby were completely buried under snow.

A scream escaped her, and she frantically began to dig her way out. But after a few futile attempts she sank back down beside the baby. It was hopeless. She didn't have the strength to break through the heavy drifts. Her gaze searched Mary Kathleen's face. The baby's eyes were closed, and she was very still.

Tears formed in Charity's eyes, and she felt a tremendous sadness overtake her as she laid her head beside the baby's, lovingly patting the small mound.

If Mary Kathleen died, she would be responsible. Once before she had risked the baby's life because of her foolishness, but mercifully, the child had survived. She supposed the good Lord could be getting tired of her blunders.

Charity knew she couldn't withstand the storm's fury for long, and she, too, might die. She lay limply across the foot of the blanket, peacefully awaiting the moment.

She thought of Beau, and how she'd come to love him. She wished now that she'd told him how much she cared. She'd started to, many times, but she'd always stopped herself because she was afraid he'd think she was pressuring him to make a similar declaration. She'd convinced herself he wouldn't want to hear her foolish prattle.

Betsy still lived so deeply within his heart, no other woman would ever be able to exorcise her ghost. Oh, Beau . . . oh, God . . . I love you. . . . Please find me so I can tell you. . . .

She thought of Ferrand. Would he be there, waiting to meet her when she passed from this life into the next? She heard herself chuckling, her voice sounding hollow against the walls of snow. Would she remember what her first husband looked like? she wondered.

Would Beau be saddened by her death? Had he made it back to the soddy before the storm hit? If she survived, would she ever be able to win his love? Her mind turned from tormenting her with questions to playing tricks on her. Strange tricks.

She saw Beau coming to her. A warm smile creased his face. She could see the way the corners of his eyes crinkled endearingly, and a small sigh escaped her as she eagerly reached out to touch him.

He caught her hand and brought it to his mouth. His eyes, his beautiful blue eyes, probed deeply into hers. They were in a room . . . alone . . . a lovely, quiet room with candles burning low in crystal holders . . . and flowers, lots of beautiful flowers filling the room with their perfumed fragrance. . . .

Her breathing became shallow as his mouth caressed the fullness of hers. He reached out to slip the straps of her chemise off her shoulders, his mouth eagerly acquainting itself with every inch of her silky skin.

She could see a bed, a large, comfortable bed draped in a rich, scarlet-red comforter . . . beckoning to them . . . beckoning. . . .

Charity could feel herself growing warm. Her strength slowly ebbed as the illusion wove its way in and out of her numbed mind.

She could feel Beau's mouth searching for hers as his hands slid down her back, cupping her buttocks tighter, pulling her against him, letting her feel his need. He was whispering his love for her. Her body ached, sensing that, through some merciful gift, she was to experience his love before she died, even if it was a hoax.

The wanting in his face made her tremble as he drew her across the bed, his gaze telling her more clearly than spoken words that he adored her. She came to him, raining kisses over his eyes, his cheekbones, the thick column of his neck.

And then the terrible waiting was over.

She felt his power encompassing her, drawing her into him, boldly claiming her as his wife . . . flesh of his flesh. . . .

She sighed, giving herself fully to him, joyously, wildly. . . .

Beau rode through the storm, stopping his mare frequently to cup his hands around his mouth to shout, "Chari–ty! Char–i–ty!" Time after time, the wind blocked his words and flung them mercilessly back in his face.

He nudged his horse forward, his shoulders hunched against the howling wind. "Please God, don't let me lose her."

Sometime during the fantasy it occurred to Charity that even if Beau was looking for her, he wouldn't be able to see the wagon. It was completely buried in the snow.

Feeling as if she were suspended from somewhere far above the wagon and looking down at it, she saw herself struggle out of her petticoat. She watched, spellbound, as she saw herself sit up and begin to feel around in the wagon for something to slide the petticoat onto.

Her hand found the shovel she'd brought along to dig sassafras roots, and with stiff fingers she tied the piece of fabric around the handle and hoisted the shovel into an upright position.

In the smooth, unbroken surface of snow, a lone makeshift flag began to flap at half mask.

She watched as she laid her head back down beside Mary Kathleen's, and closed her eyes once more.

Surely she'd still recognize Ferrand . . . he had blue eyes . . . no, green. . . .

Darkness was falling rapidly.

Beau's horse made her way laboriously through the tall drifts, moving noticeably slower. Beau knew the animal was close to dropping from exhaustion, and yet he couldn't make himself turn back and ride to the shelter of the soddy.

He knew he was running out of time, and he cursed himself for having listened to Cass. He should be searching south or west, not north. Charity had had no reason to go to town. Why had he let Cass talk him into riding to Cherry Grove when he knew better?

The horse squealed, her eyes widening in fright as she stumbled and suddenly went down, her heavy weight dropping wearily into the folds of the deep snow. Beau swore under his breath and waited until the horse struggled clumsily back to her feet.

This was insane. He was going to kill both the horse and himself if he didn't turn around soon, and yet how could he go back without Charity . . . and the baby?

God, he suddenly realized he loved that baby as if she were his own.

No, he wasn't going home till he found both of them. If the storm took his life, so be it. He'd already lost one wife and child; he wasn't strong enough to lose another.

He steeled himself against the bitter wind and rode on. His gloves had frozen to the reins, but he was past feeling the cold. He was aware of nothing except the pitch and sway of his horse as she labored through the drifts. He tried to ignore the deep ache growing in his heart.

Charity wondered if there would be a way she could leave Beau a letter. She knew it was impossible.

She wished she could, though. It would be a simple note. *I love you, Beau. Forgive me for never telling you so.*

She should have told him.

Beau had nearly given up hope when he saw the flag.

The horse slowed, and he squinted through the blowing snow at the piece of cloth flapping wildly in the wind. Leaning forward in the saddle, he tried to make out the strange signal but couldn't.

He clucked to his horse, and she eased forward. He held the lantern in front of him, watching its mellow beams spill out on the crusty snow. As he moved closer, he could see the flag was a woman's petticoat.

His pulse jumped erratically as he quickly slid off his horse and began to run toward the peculiar flagpole. When he reached the petticoat, he dropped down on his knees and began digging his way through the snowdrift with his hands.

"Charity! Charity! Are you in there?" He hastily pulled off his gloves so he could dig faster.

From somewhere far away Charity could hear Beau's voice calling to her, and she wondered why he was shouting so. Her head lifted weakly from the blanket. "Yes, darling?"

Beau's hands dug frantically through the drifts, tears blinding him as gut-wrenching fear turned to searing, white-hot anger and frustration. She had to be in there. She had to be!

"Charity, dammit! Answer me!" Snow flew in a furious white cloud as heartbroken sobs began to rack his large frame.

"I'm right here, Beau . . . there's no need to shout. . . ."

The wind continued to howl, and Beau continued to dig. She was there, beneath the snow. He felt it.

"Daddy's coming," Charity crooned, patting Mary Kathleen. "See, I told you he'd be here."

When his hand hit the side of the wagon, Beau was stunned for a moment. He glanced down and saw large red stains on the snow. His hands were raw and bleeding.

"Beau?" Charity called weakly.

Suddenly, he heard her.

His pulse jumped, and his sobs turned to hysterical laughter. He began digging again, ignoring the cuts on his hands, scooping the snow up in large armfuls and flinging it wildly into the wind as he shouted her name.

He saw her hand first, then part of her dress. He was alternately laughing and crying as he uncovered her and the baby and caught them both up tightly against his chest.

"Oh, God . . . oh, God . . . thank you . . . thank you. . . ." he cried.

He had the baby in one arm, and he was covering Charity's face with kisses, clasping her close against his chest, then releasing her long enough to claim her mouth again and again.

"I didn't think I was gonna find you . . . I was afraid. . . ." He cupped her face with one hand and continued to shower her with loving kisses everywhere. "Are you all right? Are you all right?"

"I'm . . . co-co-ld, B-B-B-ea-u."

"Oh, sweetheart, I'll get you warm," he promised.

"Th-th-the ba-b-by?"

Beau gently uncovered the thick layers of blankets to encounter a tiny pug nose which suddenly began to wrinkle in disgust at being awakened so abruptly. Mary Kathleen let out a wail that threatened to impair their hearing permanently.

The familiar bellow was music to Beau's ears.

His face broke into a radiant smile. "She's fine!"

He pulled Charity and Mary Kathleen back to his chest once more and squeezed his eyes shut in pure joy as he held them tightly in the shelter of his arms.

"Both my girls are just fine, Lord." His voice broke before he finished raggedly, "And I'm not gonna be forgettin' your mercy."

CHAPTER 23

REVEREND OLSON WAS SURPRISED TO FIND BEAU, Charity, and the baby waiting when he opened his door. He quickly called to Rebecca, and they warmly welcomed the small, half-frozen family in from the fury of the storm.

Hasty explanations were made, and Rebecca promptly put Charity and the baby to bed.

Dr. Paulson was rooted out early from his bed to make the cold trek to the parsonage to examine the weary travelers.

"I think they were both mighty lucky," he told a worried Beau as he entered the parlor an hour later and set his worn leather bag down. A fire blazed high in the hearth, and the smell of fresh coffee permeated the air.

Beau stood, his blue eyes penetrating the doctor's hopefully. "Will they be all right?"

The doctor could see Charity's husband was worse for wear than she was. His eyes grew kind. "They're doing fine, son. With a little bit of care, they'll both be able to go home for Christmas."

Beau visibly slumped with relief. "Thank you . . . thank you, doctor."

"I happen to have an extra piece of chocolate cake, Harlow." Rebecca had just returned from settling the baby. "I couldn't interest you in it, could I?"

"You know I'd come out in any weather for a piece of your chocolate cake, Rebecca. Thank you, I'd love some."

"How about you, Beau—won't you join us for cake?"

"No, thank you, Mrs. Olson. I'm waiting to see Charity."

Dr. Paulson followed Rebecca to the kitchen as Beau walked to the window and stared out thoughtfully. The storm still raged, but he felt an inner peace that he hadn't known in a very long time.

"You say your brother's still out there?" Reverend Olson inquired.

"No, I expect when it got dark, he went back to the soddy." Beau knew Cass was a reasonable man and that he'd have given up the search at dark as they'd agreed.

"By the way, Beau, I received news from Ansel and Letty's families." Beau turned slowly from the window. "And?"

"It turns out that Ansel's father passed away two months ago. Phedra Latimer is finding it hard to cope with her husband's death. Coupled with poor health, I'm afraid she'll be unable to take care of Mary Kathleen at this time."

"And Letty's family?"

Reverend Olson sighed. "Letty's parents are willing to take the child and place it with proper relatives because they, too, are in their mid-seventies, and physically . . ." Reverend Olson shrugged apologetically, "Children are for the young, Beau. When a person reaches his seventies, his body gives out, and he simply doesn't have the stamina to raise children."

Beau turned pensively back to the window, his eyes deeply troubled. "Place Mary Kathleen with strangers?"

"They wouldn't be strangers. They'd be Letty's kin. Of course, Mary Kathleen would have to grow to love them. And then there'd be the problem of sending the child back East. But these are decisions that don't have to be made tonight. You sure I can't have Rebecca fix you a bite to eat?"

"No, thank you. Maybe I'll get something later, but right now, I'd like to see my wife."

"Then you run along. Rebecca and I will see to the baby tonight. Mary Kathleen's sleeping soundly, and the doctor says she shouldn't have any lasting effects from her adventure." A tender light came into his faded gray eyes. "You know, son, it was the Lord's hand that allowed that wagon to be buried in the snow," he offered. "It surrounded your wife and the baby and conserved their body heat. It virtually saved their lives."

Beau's gaze met the reverend's solidly. "I know where the credit belongs, sir."

"Just wanted to make sure you did." Reverend Olson smiled. "See you in church Sunday morning?"

"Yes, sir, you will."

"Now, I believe you have a wife you want to see?"

Beau smiled. "Yes, sir."

"Then why are you hanging around here talking to an old codger like me? Go to her, son."

It was dark when Beau stepped into Charity's room to say good-night. She recognized his footsteps as he cautiously approached the bed.

"Hi."

"Hi. I thought you might be asleep."

"No, just resting."

The bed creaked as he sat down beside her.

"The baby all right?"

"She's sleeping. Reverend Olson said he and Rebecca would see to her tonight. You need your rest. Are you warm enough?"

She nodded.

"Good."

Charity reached out and took his hand. "Come to bed with me."

Beau's pulse jumped. "I—I thought I'd best sleep over by the fire and let you rest. . . ."

He couldn't see her face in the dark, but the plea in her voice drew him like a moth to a flame. "I want you beside me, Beau."

He stood and stripped out of his clothes, then crawled between the sheets beside her. He wrapped his arms around her small body and drew her close.

She sighed, burying her face in the warmth of his chest. "I love you, Beau."

"I love you, too, Charity."

She felt tears spring to her eyes. Her happiness was complete now.

His mouth searched and found hers, and he kissed her with a tenderness that overflowed with his love. They needed no words. They had nothing left to prove. Today had proven it all.

They fell asleep in each other's arms contentedly.

"We go home tomorrow." It was Christmas Eve, and as Beau sat on Charity's bed, an air of excitement dominated his voice.

"I know. I can hardly wait." She had weathered the close call amazingly well, and tonight the doctor had pronounced her well enough to travel.

Beau leaned over to steal a kiss, his eyes sparkling like a small boy's. "Cass was afraid you wouldn't make it home before Christmas, so he brought your and Mary Kathleen's presents by this afternoon."

"Wonderful! Where are they?"

"Not so fast." Beau drew back from her defensively. "I'd like to give you *my* present before you open his."

Her eyes widened at his sudden show of immaturity. "Why?"

"Because . . . mine's better than his."

"Beau!" She had to laugh. "How do you know?"

He shrugged. "I asked him what he got you; he told me, so I know mine's the best."

"You're terrible."

"Yeah, I know." He grinned and stretched out beside her, devilishly dangling a small, gaily wrapped box before her eyes.

She started to reach for the box, and he quickly withdrew it. "Not so fast."

"I thought you wanted me to open it."

"I do, but I want you to beg for it first," he teased.

"Beg for it?" Casually, she rolled over and slid on top of him, and his eyes widened as her mouth came down to meet his hungrily.

"What are you doing?" he sputtered.

She broke the kiss and traced a lazy finger across his cheek and over the outline of his lips. "What do you want me to do?"

"Well, that wouldn't take much thought," he admitted with a guilty grin. "I want to warn you, Mrs. Claxton—when we get home tomorrow, I have plans." His hands began to take liberties she adored.

"Tomorrow. Why wait so long to implement them?" Her tongue came out to tease his, and she felt him tense.

"Charity . . . remember, we're in Reverend Olson's house. . . ." His words trailed off weakly as she began to unbutton his shirt.

"You talk too much, Beau Claxton."

His hands came up to tangle in her hair, pulling her face closer to his. Their mouths were inches apart, his breath softly mingling with hers. "You think so?"

"I know so."

"What about the reverend?"

"I can't think of where you'd find a house more filled with love."

"You really think it'd be safe?" Beau groaned as she brought his mouth back to nibble at his lower lip.

"I think so, but we could always put a chair in front of the door . . . if you're worried."

"I'm not worried." Beau nuzzled her neck, drinking in her fragrance. "I was only thinking of your less-than-sterling reputation, Mrs. Claxton."

"Well, I would hate to have the reverend or Rebecca drop in unexpectedly," Charity retracted hesitantly. They slid off the bed together, and Beau walked her to the door, still kissing her.

He quietly moved the old chair against the door.

"Okay, now what?"

"Now"—she snuggled against him, her tongue teasing his ear suggestively—"I want you to make me your wife."

Beau caught his breath sharply. "My pleasure, Mrs. Claxton."

He felt her tremble as he slipped her gown over her shoulders and let the delicate material float to the floor. Their gazes met as he reached out and slid his hand down her hip, feeling the silken texture of her skin. Then his fingers skimmed up to her breasts and lingered.

He smiled, his eyes growing dark with passion. "You are so beautiful."

Her fingertips touched his lips. "You make me feel beautiful."

Her breasts filled his hands, and he dipped his head to kiss each one tenderly. It had been so long since her body had experienced such pleasure. She sighed as she buried her fingers in the thick texture of his hair. Slowly, she cupped his face in her hands and lifted his mouth back to hers.

His heart pounded as he began to kiss her, mindless kisses, filled with hungry urgency. He was aroused, magnificently so, and she could feel his need pressing against her bare skin, eager to claim her.

"Love me," she whispered.

"I do," he whispered back, "Oh, God, Charity, I do. When I thought I'd lost you and the baby . . . I didn't know what I would do. . . ." His voice broke with raw emotion as she drew his head against her breast to comfort him.

"Oh, my darling. I love you so very much. That's all I could think of as I waited for you to find me and the baby. I wished that I had told you of my love, long before now."

He guided her back to the bed, and they lay down.

With surprising efficiency he rid himself of his clothing. Then, with agonizing slowness, he began to take his pleasure discovering her body. His masterful touch made her grow weak with anticipation. The blue of his eyes darkened deeper with passion as his mouth caressed her silken flesh lovingly.

The feel of his lips moving against her bare skin made her catch her breath. She stared up at him helplessly, feeling as if she were drowning in his exquisite torture.

Silken arms twined around his neck; silken legs lay softly against his hair-roughened ones as their mouths met again and again.

A moment later she sighed, her breath softly stirring the hair on his chest. "Oh, Beau." She could not find the words to tell him of her joy.

"I know, I know. . . ." His mouth captured hers again, drinking in its sweetness as he levered his large frame above her small body. No longer could he think. He could only experience the essence of her, the sweetness flooding his body, crying for release.

"I love you . . . I love you. . . ." His whispers were muffled against her throat as he entered her. Fire flashed through them, searing, burning, driving all else from their minds.

The long wait had made their loving all the sweeter, Charity realized. And now the wait was over.

Beau was her love.

He was her gift.

• • • •

Though it seemed improbable that either of them could have forgotten how wonderful lovemaking could be, they lay in each other's arms afterward, marveling at what had happened between them. They had been good together. Unbelievably good. Sated and lazy, they continued to share long, languorous kisses.

"You know, I'm kind of glad it happened this way," Beau admitted. He toyed absently with a strand of her hair, intrigued by its softness.

"What way?"

"This . . . way."

She sensed he was trying to tell her something, so she waited.

"At first . . . well, I would have gladly taken my rights and not thought much about it," he began hesitantly.

"But?"

"But"—he sighed and rolled over to cup her face in his hands—"it wouldn't have been right. I still had Betsy in my heart."

She gazed at him lovingly. "And now?"

"Now"—he sighed—"I've let her go. Though I suppose she'll be with me from time to time." He paused, trying to sort out his feelings.

"Beau, I don't resent your feelings for Betsy. Betsy and Ferrand were our first loves, and they'll always hold a special place in our hearts."

Charity wasn't afraid to voice what he apparently couldn't. "But we're older now. We share a different kind of love. I'm content with that."

"I love you, Charity." Beau wanted that clear. "Maybe not in the same way I loved Bets, but what I feel for you is just as deep, just as right, as what I felt for her."

Charity's love shone brightly through her eyes. "I know. You don't have to explain."

"And Ferrand?"

"I will forever hold him in my heart." Her hand reached out to gently caress her husband's face. "Ferrand was my first love; you are my last."

Their mouths touched and lingered sweetly.

Beau reached for the small box he'd been about to give her before they'd made love. "I bought this for you several weeks ago."

She took the box and slowly slipped off the ribbon. "I'm afraid I have nothing to give you," she confessed. "I was going into town to buy raisins to make you a pie, when the storm came up."

"You were?" His eyes shone brightly with admiration. "You almost got yourself killed over raisins?" The realization only made him love her more.

"I wanted to do something special for your Christmas present." She thought about the raisins and wished she had the pies to offer him. She had nothing to show her gratitude, even now, after he'd risked his life to save her and Mary Kathleen during the storm.

"You saved my life . . . and I have nothing. . . ." She looked at him sadly.

He winked at her. "You've given me back my life. I think that's enough."

Smiling, she removed the paper and opened the box. Her breath caught. Nestled in the paper was her emerald brooch. Ferrand's grandmother's brooch.

"Oh, Beau." She was speechless.

"I hope you like it. I bought it one day at the mercantile. It seems two Indians had traded it." He reached out and gently caught the tears spilling from the corners of her eyes. "The color of the stones reminded me of your eyes."

Charity took the brooch in her hands and pressed it to her heart. She wouldn't dream of telling him that long ago another man had once given her the same gift with love. Beau's gift meant just as much, and she would cherish it as deeply as she'd treasured Ferrand's.

"My beloved husband, have I told you how very much I love you?"

He pulled her mouth back to his. "Yes, but I'd have no objections if you'd show me again."

"I still say you should wait till all the snow's melted." With a frown Charity passed the sack of ham sandwiches up to Cass. "It's almost January. There could be another storm any day!"

Cass glanced at Beau and shook his head. "Your wife frets too much."

Beau grinned. "I know, but I love her anyway."

"I need to be gettin' home before another blizzard hits," Cass explained patiently. "You two don't want me underfoot all winter, now do you?"

Beau and Charity looked at each other and grinned.

"That's what I thought." Cass climbed into the buckboard and tapped his hat back cockily on his head. "I'll probably be seein' you again one of these days. Ma'll have me draggin' another wagonload of them damn pickles and preserves out to you, thinking you all will be starvin' to death."

Charity pulled the blanket up closer around Mary Kathleen to shield her from the sharp wind. "You do that, Cass. We'll always be happy to see you."

Beau leaned over and kissed his wife. "I'm gonna ride out a ways with Cass. I'll be back."

Charity smiled. "Take your time. I'll be waiting."

He winked at her lovingly and swung into the saddle. "Let's go, little brother. We're burnin' daylight."

The wagon and rider moved out of the yard down the snowy pathway. For several miles the brothers traveled in compatible silence. Then as they crested a small rise, they reined their horses to a stop. Beau swung out of his saddle, and Cass got down off the wagon.

"Well, looks like I'll be goin' it alone from here on."

"Yeah, I best be gettin' back to Charity and the baby."

The two brothers shook hands. Beau remounted his horse, and Cass got back in the wagon.

"Oh, by the way, tell Ma I won't be comin' home this spring."

Cass grinned as he picked up the reins. "Didn't figure you would be."

"Yeah." Beau stared contentedly at the snow-covered countryside. "Sorta feels like I am home."

"Well, Charity's a fine woman," Cass acknowledged. "You going to adopt Mary Kathleen?"

"Figurin' on it."

"That's good. Ma likes bein' a grandmother."

"Yeah, can't wait till she sees my baby." Beau looked at his brother solemnly. "Mary Kathleen's about the cutest little baby you've ever seen . . . isn't she?"

"She's cute, all right."

"Yeah." Beau's grin widened, "I think so too. One of these days you'll settle down and have one almost as cute," he predicted.

Cass hooted merrily. "Don't count on it. No woman's gonna rope and hog-tie me till I'm good and ready."

Beau shook his head skeptically. "Don't be too sure. A thing like that can slip up on a man before he knows it."

"Not on me, it won't." Cass released the brake on the wagon. "Well, best be movin' on. I'm burnin' daylight."

"You take care. Tell Cole and Wynne we'll write. Maybe they can make the trip out to see us someday."

"Sure thing. You behave yourself, big brother."

"You do the same."

Cass grinned arrogantly. "Not a chance."

Beau threw his head back and laughed, his merriment rumbling deep in his chest as Cass's wagon rolled jauntily away.

Cocky kid, he thought affectionately. Some woman will come along someday and tie his tail in a bow knot.

He took a deep breath and held it, tipping his face up to drink in the bright sunshine. It felt good to be alive.

Damn good!

SWEET TALKIN' STRANGER

To the three Copeland sons:
Randall, Richard, and Russell,
Your papa and I are right proud of you.

PROLOGUE

Kansas Frontier: 1868

THE EARLY MORNING WIND HAD A SHARP BITE TO IT, but the sun shone brightly in the eastern sky. Guess a man couldn't ask for much more than that on the twenty-sixth day of December, Cass Claxton thought contentedly.

As the old wagon rattled along the road, a smile pulled at the corners of his mouth. He set the brim of his hat lower on his forehead as his cobalt-blue eyes surveyed the endless expanse of Kansas sky.

The visit with his brother Beau and Beau's new wife, Charity, had been good, but he was eager to get back home before a storm set in. Winters in Missouri were contrary, but he didn't think they could hold a candle to the full-blown blizzards of Kansas.

His face sobered as he recalled how Beau had nearly lost his wife and baby daughter the week before when they'd gotten stranded in a sudden blizzard.

The newly formed Claxton family had been lucky. Cass remembered the solemn way Reverend Olson had reminded them that it had been nothing short of a miracle that Charity and Mary Kathleen had survived after having been buried beneath the snow for half a day.

Cass's smile returned as he thought of how happy his brother was now. And it was about time. Beau had had a hard time getting over the death of his first wife, Betsy, but it looked like he'd make it just fine now.

The way Beau had loved his first wife and now Charity sometimes puzzled Cass. As far as women were concerned, Cass could take them or leave them. And he'd done just that, more times than he cared to admit.

There was no way a woman was going to hog-tie and brand him. He'd never met a woman he'd want to be around much longer than a week—with maybe the exception of Wynne Elliot.

Now there was a woman. The image of her crimson hair and dancing sea-green eyes came back to haunt him. He probably should have married her when he'd had the chance four years ago, but there was no use crying over spilled milk. Cole, his eldest brother, had married Wynne, and Cass had to admit he'd never seen a happier couple.

Of course, Beau's wife, Charity, wasn't all that bad either. She'd sure make Beau a fine woman—Cass couldn't argue with that. But taking a wife was the last thing on Cass's mind. He wasn't anywhere close to settling down and raising a family. He had a peck of wild oats to sow before any woman got him to the altar—if one ever did.

Cass gave a sharp whistle and set the horses into a fast trot. The old buckboard rumbled over potholes as he began humming a jaunty tune.

Directly ahead, he could see four riders approaching. Their horses were coming fast, and Cass wondered where they were headed in such a hurry.

As they drew nearer Cass frowned, noting that one of the riders was that infuriating Patience McCord.

The woman had been nothing but a thorn in his side since the day he'd run into her in Miller's Mercantile. He'd hoped to leave Kansas without encountering her again, but it looked like his luck had just gone sour.

Well, he'd tip his hat politely and ride on by, he thought, and was about to do just that, when the foursome reined up directly in his path. Caught by surprise, Cass hauled back on the reins, bringing his team to a sudden halt.

Leviticus McCord; his daughter, Patience; Reverend Olson; and a large man wearing a tin star sat stiffly in their saddles, staring back at Cass.

Cass tipped his hat. "Morning, Reverend."

"Good morning, Mr. Claxton."

The horses danced about, breathing frosty plumes into the brisk morning air.

"What brings you out this way so early in the day?" Cass carefully avoided looking at the young woman on the dappled-gray mare. He still seethed whenever he thought of how Patience McCord had hauled off and hit him below the belt with her purse during their unpleasant encounter a week ago. Then the silly twit had had the gall to look him up a few days later to offer him the exorbitant fee of five hundred dollars to escort her back to her aunt in St. Louis.

Cass had refused promptly and none too nicely. He wouldn't take Patience McCord to a dog fight, let alone ride all the way back to Missouri with her, and he'd wasted no time in telling her so.

But by then it had grown dark, and Patience had started to cry. She'd pleaded that she felt too faint and frightened to find her way back to town. Cass had had no recourse but to let her stay that night; he'd sent her packing first thing after breakfast the next morning.

But here she was again, looking down at him with that superior smirk of hers that made his blood boil.

"We're looking for you!" Leviticus roared.

"Me?" Cass's grin began to fade. Why would Leviticus McCord be looking for him, he wondered.

"Mr. Claxton, would you mind climbin' down off that buckboard?" The man with the double-barreled shotgun and tin star motioned for Cass to comply.

"Well, I don't know . . ." Cass glanced back to Reverend Olson expectantly. "What's going on?"

"I believe you've met . . . uh . . . hummruph . . . uh . . . Miss McCord?" Reverend Olson met Cass's gaze apologetically.

Cass glanced toward Patience dispassionately. "I've met her."

Patience nodded from beneath the veil of her ostrich-plumed hat, her violet eyes mocking him.

"Met her! Met *her!*" Turning scarlet, Leviticus shouted louder, "I should hope to heaven he's *met* her!"

Cass's eyes snapped to Leviticus. "Yes, I've met her!"

"Cass . . . uh . . . this is very difficult," Reverend Olson said in an uneasy tone. "Would you care to step down from your wagon for a moment?"

Cass obediently wrapped the reins around the brake, and in a lithe motion landed on the ground beside Patience, who was sniffling loudly into her lace handkerchief.

As she began to sob, her mass of blond ringlets trembled against her back like strands of spun gold in the morning light.

Something was wrong. Cass could feel it. "What's the problem, Reverend?" he inquired hesitantly.

The men dismounted and stared at Cass for a moment. Then Leviticus exploded: "*What's the problem?*"

Cass could sure see where Patience had inherited her volatile nature. The little retired circuit judge was now hopping around in the road with his fists balled into tight knots. "*What's the problem?*" Leviticus repeated in utter disbelief, pausing just long enough to draw an indignant breath before shaking his finger under Cass's nose. "I'll tell you what the problem is, you . . . you young whippersnapper! You sullied my daughter, and you're going to be held accountable!" He stomped angrily, nearly dislodging his felt bowler.

Cass shifted his stance and eyed the judge sourly. "I've what?"

"*Sullied my daughter!*" Leviticus shrieked. "Disgraced, soiled, *tarnished!*"

Cass's eyes narrowed. "I know what the word means, sir."

"*I should hope so!*" Leviticus shouted.

"Now, now, gentlemen, let's all calm down," Reverend Olson advised. "I'm sure we can settle this matter without hollering to raise the dead."

"What is he talking about?" Cass demanded calmly.

Reverend Olson glanced cautiously at Patience, then back at Cass. "Well, it seems that you and . . . you and Miss McCord spent a night together last week. Am I correct?" Reverend Olson sincerely hoped that he wasn't. He didn't know Cass all that well, but what he was here to carry out, he wouldn't wish on any man.

"Spent the night with her?" Cass shot a reproachful eye toward the lady. "No, I didn't spend the night with her."

"Oh, yes, you did!" Patience accused. Then she sniffed again.

Cass shifted his weight, and the blue of his eyes pinpointed her angrily. "I did not." Cass knew as well as anyone what her accusation could lead to.

Patience sighed tolerantly and dabbed at her welling eyes. "I told you he would take this attitude, gentlemen."

"Now just one minute." Cass turned to Reverend Olson. "I don't know what she's told you, but nothing happened that night—"

"So, you *did* spend the night with my daughter!" Leviticus accused indignantly.

"I didn't spend the night *with* her," Cass responded.

"She was gone all night!" Leviticus bellowed. "How do you explain that?"

"I was there . . . but so was my brother Beau and his wife. If you won't take my word for it, you can ask them . . ." Cass's voice trailed off as he began to realize that the more he tried to explain, the more he seemed to incriminate himself.

Leviticus glanced at the sheriff pointedly. The entire town of Cherry Grove knew that Cass's brother had lived with the widow Burkhouser for months before he'd married her. Did this young whippersnapper think he and the sheriff were foolish enough to take Beau Claxton's word about such an impropriety?

"Daddy"—Patience turned her watery eyes toward Leviticus—"don't you think it would be a waste of time to ride all the way to the Claxton soddy? You know good and well Beau Claxton would lie to protect his no-good brother." Her voice trailed off to a whine. "Can't we just settle this matter quickly?"

Cass shot her a scathing glare. "Patience, this is *not* funny," he warned. The seriousness of the situation was beginning to sink in, and Cass was feeling downright scared. "Nothing happened the night you stayed with me, and you know it. I should have sent you packing, and I would have if you hadn't lied to me when you said you were feeling faint."

Cass turned to Leviticus imploringly. "Sir, your daughter approached me that night and offered me five hundred dollars to take her to St. Louis." Cass straightened proudly. "Of course I said no." He didn't mind telling on the silly twit. Now Leviticus would see how rotten through and through his daughter really was.

Leviticus leveled his gaze sternly on his daughter. "Did you do that, Patience? Did you offer this man five hundred dollars to take you back to St. Louis?"

Patience gasped, batting her huge damp eyelashes. "Heavens, no, Daddy! Where would I get five hundred dollars?"

Leviticus turned to Cass. "Where would she get five hundred dollars?" Leviticus knew his daughter's penchant for lying, so he felt obliged to ask.

"I don't know!" Cass snapped. "She offered me money; she didn't say where she was going to get it!"

"Mr. Claxton." Leviticus stretched to his full five-feet two inches. Though his comical pose wasn't all that intimidating, it struck the proper respect in Cass. "I'm inclined to believe you, but I know for a fact that Patience doesn't have five hundred dollars. Good Lord, man! I barely have five hundred dollars! That's a fortune!"

"I know, sir . . ." And he did know! The little schemer had been lying about the money too! "But that's what she offered me—five hundred . . ." Cass felt a sinking sensation as he began to realize that he was in deep trouble this time.

"No, if my daughter says she didn't offer you the money, then I must assume she's telling the truth," Leviticus decided.

"But she's lying!"

Leviticus shot his daughter an exasperated look but continued, "Whether she offered the money or not, she says you took advantage of her that evening, and I can't risk the possibility of her coming up with a little blue-eyed bastard after you return to Missouri."

"Now, wait a minute—"

"No, you wait a minute," Leviticus said, his eyes narrowing. "You're about to take a wife, son."

"The hell I am!" This conversation had slipped beyond the point of reason. Cass whirled and was about to climb onto his wagon when he felt the cold barrel of a shotgun tapping him on the shoulder.

"You want to take a few minutes to reconsider your hasty decision, boy?"

Cass froze. The clear implication in the sheriff's voice made him pause.

"Son!"—Reverend Olson laid his hand on Cass's shoulder reassuringly —"I think you'd better think this thing through."

"But Reverend"—Cass looked at him helplessly—"I haven't touched Patience McCord."

Reverend Olson nodded sympathetically. "I'm sorry, but we have no way of proving your side of the story. In Cherry Grove, we tend to take the woman's word in matters of this delicate nature. I'd suggest you marry the girl, then try to resolve the matter in a more satisfactory manner later on."

Marry Patience McCord? Cass would prefer they throw a rope over the nearest tree and get it over with.

Leviticus helped his daughter dismount, and she rested her slender hand upon his arm. "You do believe me, don't you, Daddy? I wouldn't lie

about a terrible thing like this. I warned Mr. Claxton he'd surely be facin'
my papa's wrath. That's what I said . . . but I do declare, he just
wouldn't listen . . ." She broke off tearfully and covered her eyes with
her lace handkerchief.

Leviticus wrapped his arm protectively around her trembling shoulders. "I believe you, daughter," he soothed. Then he lifted his chin.
"Sheriff," he prompted in a righteous tone.

The sheriff stepped forward, and Cass looked at Reverend Olson
pleadingly. "Are you actually going to let them do this to me?"

Reverend Olson sighed and opened his Bible. "Do you, Cass Claxton,
take Patience McCord to be your lawfully wedded wife?"

"Hell, no, I don't!"

Reverend Olson turned patiently to the bride. "Do you, Patience Mc-
Cord, take Cass Claxton to be your lawfully wedded husband?"

"I suppose I'll just have to, under these dreadful circumstances. Don't
you agree, Daddy?" Her lovely amethyst eyes peered at Leviticus woefully.

He patted her hand. "You just relax, darlin'. Papa will see to it that
your virtue is protected."

"Virtue—that's rich! She doesn't know the meaning of the word!"
Cass accused.

"Oh, Daddy. He's just dreadful. Do I really have to marry him?"
Patience peeked out from behind her handkerchief at Cass.

"You don't have to marry me," Cass insisted through gritted teeth.
"All you have to do is tell the truth!" He'd never raised a hand against a
woman in his life, but given half a chance, he'd gladly have strangled
Patience McCord at that moment.

"Do you promise to love, cherish, and obey, till death do you part?"
Reverend Olson droned on, hoping to complete the unpleasant ceremony
as soon as possible.

"Wellll . . . I . . . I suppose I can . . . if I must . . ." Patience
glanced at Cass. "I *do*."

Reverend Olson turned back to Cass. "Do you promise to comfort,
honor, and keep her, in sickness and in health—"

"I wouldn't pull a mad dog off of her!"

"—forsaking all others, till death do you part?"

Cass glared at his bride heatedly.

The sheriff lifted the barrel of the gun a notch higher. "Say you're
gonna forsake all others till death do you part, boy, or I'll blow a big hole
through your chest."

"I will not!"

The sheriff pressed the shotgun between Cass's shoulderblades.

Cass darted a frantic look at Reverend Olson.

Reverend Olson sighed. "You must say you'll take her for your wife,
son. The marriage won't be legal otherwise."

The gun nudged him again. "Wanna live to see thirty, boy?"

"I do, but—"

Reverend Olson snapped the Bible shut. "I now pronounce you man and wife." He lifted his brows hopefully. "I don't suppose you'd want to kiss the bride?"

"*No*, I don't want to kiss the bride!"

Reverend Olson sighed. "I didn't think so."

Five minutes later Leviticus was placing the last of Patience's baggage in the back of Cass's wagon.

He knew he should be worried about his daughter's fate, but strangely enough he wasn't. Reverend Olson had assured him that the Claxtons were good people, and he could see for himself that Cass was a big strapping fellow who would hold his own with Patience McCord.

Lord knew she needed such a man.

"Take care of my daughter." Leviticus reached up to meekly shake his new son-in-law's hand. Cass sullenly ignored the gesture.

Leviticus laid a small pouch filled with several gold pieces on the wagon seat beside Cass. "She's a good girl," Leviticus told him in a hushed whisper. "Just a mite bull-headed at times."

Cass thought that had to be the understatement of the year.

Reverend Olson, the sheriff, and Leviticus remounted. With a nod, they prepared to leave the newlyweds alone.

"You be sure and write your daddy the moment you reach St. Louis," Leviticus reminded.

"I promise, Daddy. You take care now."

The small party turned their horses and trotted off toward town.

Cass whistled sharply, and the wagon lurched forward as the horses began moving. "You are not going to get away with this," he warned.

"I believe I just did, dear husband."

"Don't call me that."

"Why? I'll grant you permission to call me your wife . . . but only until we reach St. Louis." She laughed merrily.

"I'll be calling you a lot of things before we reach St. Louis," he promised.

"Tsk, tsk, such a sore loser! You should have accepted my gracious offer the other night," Patience pointed out, adjusting her skirts primly. "You'd have been much better off—five hundred dollars richer and still single."

"You don't have five hundred dollars!"

"But you don't know that for certain," she pointed out.

"Your own pa said you didn't."

"My own pa doesn't necessarily know everything," she reasoned sweetly. "You'll discover, Mr. Claxton, it's much easier to let me have my way."

"And you'll find your lying little fanny dumped on your aunt's porch so fast it'll make your head spin," Cass snapped. "I'll take you to St. Louis, but once we're there this absurdity is over. I want this so-called marriage annulled. Immediately."

Ignoring him, Patience turned and waved her handkerchief at Leviticus. "Bye-bye, Daddy. I'll write real soon!"

Leviticus waved back fondly.

"And you'll find"—Patience turned back to resume the conversation— "all I wanted in the first place was to go back to St. Louis." She sighed happily. "I'll be glad to have our marriage annulled, darling, just as soon as I reach my Aunt Merriweather's. However," she said, pausing to smile at him, "it was truly a touching ceremony—wouldn't you agree?"

Rotten. Cass had no doubt about it. The girl was just plain rotten.

CHAPTER 1

St. Louis, Missouri, 1874

A SHARP CRACK OF THUNDER RESOUNDED ALONG THE quiet residential street. A young woman hurried on her way, her hand placed strategically on top of her head to prevent the gusting wind from carrying off her plucky straw hat.

Patience McCord didn't mind the rain, but she did wish it could have held off for another thirty minutes. Fat drops began to pepper down on the cobblestone streets, filling the air with the tangy smell of summer rain.

Her shoes skipped gingerly over the gathering puddles as her eyes hurriedly scanned the numbers printed on the towering houses. The three-story frame dwellings nearly took her breath away with their lovely stained-glass windows and hand-carved doorways.

When lightning flashed as brightly as a noonday sun, she peered at the address scrawled on a scrap of paper that was fast becoming soggy in her hand.

Her feet flew purposefully up the walk as the heavens opened to deliver a torrential downpour. Pausing to catch her breath, Patience stood for a moment under the shelter of the porch eaves, watching the rain pelt down. She smiled as she saw an old lamplighter, already soaked to the skin, hastily making his way down the street.

She called out to the man, inviting him to take cover with her. He turned and scurried up the walk, his head bent low against the driving rain.

"Terrible, isn't it?" Patience commented as the white-haired gentleman removed his top hat and shook the rain off.

" 'Tis for certain, little lass." As he smiled his wizened face broke into a wreath of wrinkles. He set his lantern down and extended a friendly hand. "Thaddeus McDougal here."

Patience returned his smile as they shook hands. "Patience McCord. It looks like we're in for a good one." Patience had never acknowledged her married name, nor did she ever plan to. Since their journey from Kansas to St. Louis, she'd never seen Cass Claxton again. They had parted on bad terms, with Patience declaring she would see him again when hell froze over.

Thaddeus sighed. "Aye, it does at that, lass."

"Well, we can always use the rain."

" 'Tis true, 'tis true." Thaddeus glanced about the massive porch with mild curiosity. "Wasn't aware the old house had finally been sold."

"Oh, I don't think it has." Patience noticed that the house was not in the best of repair. The porch sagged; the paint was peeling; and several shutters flapped haphazardly in the blowing rain. It didn't matter though —it looked beautiful to her. "I'm here to see about acquiring the use of it."

"Eh? Well . . ." Thaddeus's pale gaze roamed over the peeling rafters. "Old Josiah would be real upset if he could see his house now. Used to brim with love and laughter, it did." His eyes grew misty with remembrance. "Josiah never had children of his own, you know, but he took in every stray he could find. Fine man, he was. The world lost a bit of sunshine when Josiah Thorton was laid to rest."

"I never knew him," Patience admitted.

"He was a good man." Thaddeus sighed again. "Well now, little lass, why be you tryin' to acquire such a big old barn of a house?"

"I'm looking for a place big enough to be a home for nine children."

"Nine children!" Thaddeus took a step back. The chit didn't look old enough to have nine children!

Patience smiled at his obvious bewilderment. "I'm overseer of a small orphanage. The bank has been forced to sell the home we're presently living in, and someone mentioned that this house was empty. Since I've looked unsuccessfully for weeks for somewhere to move the children, I hurried over to obtain the name of the owner." Her forehead wrinkled in a frown. "I'm sorry to hear he's passed away."

"Josiah died about a year ago."

"Then I suppose his family will be disposing of the property?"

Thaddeus frowned. "Josiah didn't have any family, leastways, not that I know about. Rumor has it he had a business associate though. Could be he can tell you what's to be done with the house."

"And how might I contact this business associate?" Patience hoped that wouldn't prove to be another time-consuming delay. The orphanage had to be out of its present location by the end of the month.

"Well . . ." Thaddeus stepped over to the legal notice nailed to the porch railing and peered through his wire-rimmed spectacles. "It says here that anyone wanting information about this property should contact a Mr. Daniel Odolp, Attorney-at-law."

Patience took a small pad from her purse and prepared to scribble down the attorney's address.

"Does Mr. Odolp reside here in St. Louis?"

"Yes, his office is close by." Thaddeus read the address aloud for her.

"Oh, that's not far."

"Just a wee jaunt."

"I wonder if Mr. Odolp would still be in his office?"

Thaddeus reached into his waistcoat and withdrew a large pocket watch. He flipped open the case and held the face of the watch toward the receding light. "Depends on how late he works. It's nigh on six o'clock."

Six o'clock. Patience doubted Mr. Odolp would be working this late, but since she'd be passing by his office anyway, it wouldn't hurt to check. "Thank you, Thaddeus." Patience replaced the pen and pad in her purse and reassessed the inclement weather. It wasn't raining too hard, just a nice, steady drizzle. "I'll just go by and see if Mr. Odolp is still in his office," she announced.

"But it's still raining."

Patience shrugged and gave Thaddeus a bright smile. "I won't dissolve."

She looked as if she might, to him. She was an unusually pretty piece of fluff with flaxen hair and the softest violet-colored eyes Thaddeus had ever seen. If she had wings, she'd look like an angel, he thought wistfully.

"It's been nice talking with you, Thaddeus." Patience reached down and quickly removed her shoes and stockings, then her hat. It was senseless to ruin them. Her toes peeked out from under the hem of her skirt, and Thaddeus had to grin. A barefoot angel.

"Nice talkin' to you, lass." Thaddeus reached down and picked up his lantern. "Guess I should get about my work. It'll be growing dark soon."

The old lamplighter and the young woman moved off the porch to go their separate ways.

One set out to light man's path, the other to find a home for nine children.

St. Louis, Missouri, was the gateway to the West for adventurers, explorers, traders, missionaries, soldiers, and settlers of the trans-Mississippi. It was founded in 1764 by Pierre Laclede Liguest, a French trader, as a settlement for the development of the fur trade. One hundred and ten years later the area had developed into a thriving waterfront town where cotton, lead, pelts, gold from California, and silver from New Mexico poured through shipping lanes along the busy Mississippi levee. It was said that St. Louis was admired for her hospitality, good manners, high society, virtue, and the sagacity of her women.

One such woman hurried through the night, intent upon her mission. Patience could hardly believe her good fortune as she rounded the corner leading toward the landing and saw the faint lantern glow spilling from a window on the second story.

Prominently displayed in bold black letters across the window was
DANIEL R. ODOLP, ATTORNEY-AT-LAW.

Quickly, Patience covered the short distance to the building and began
climbing the steep stairs leading to the second floor. A few minutes later
she tapped softly on Mr. Odolp's door.

"Yes?" boomed a deep voice that brought nervous flutters to Patience's
stomach. The man sounded like a giant.

"Mr. Odolp?"

"Yes!"

"I . . . I wonder if I might speak with you?"

Patience heard a shuffling, then the sound of chair legs being scraped
across a wooden floor. Heavy footsteps approached the doorway.

She swallowed and her throat went dry. The narrow hallway was dark
and foreboding, with only a small tallow candle splitting the shadows.

She suddenly wished she'd decided to wait until morning to make her
visit. Just as she was turning to leave, the door abruptly flung open.

"Yes?"

The man standing in the doorway was indeed a giant, at least six feet
five. Bushy dark eyebrows nested over his beady black eyes. His face was
pockmarked, and his jowls hung heavily on his neck. Sweat beaded pro-
fusely on his ruddy forehead. Patience thought he was the most unattractive and intimidating-looking man she'd ever encountered.

"Mr. Odolp?" she asked meekly.

"I am Mr. Odolp!" he barked. "Good Lord, woman, are you deaf?"

Patience drew herself up stiffly, perturbed by his appalling lack of
gentility. "No, sir, but I shall be if you continue to speak to me in that
tone."

"You called my name," he boomed, "and I answered. You implied you
wanted to speak to me, and when I opened the door, you asked *again* if I
was Mr. Odolp. Naturally, one would assume you have a hearing problem."

Patience jumped as he bellowed again, "*Yes*, I am Mr. Odolp!"

"Well, you needn't keep shouting." She lifted her skirts and brushed
past him irritably.

He closed the door and stalked back to his desk, his eyes grimly surveying her bare feet. "Where are your shoes and stockings, young
lady?"

Patience glanced down and blushed. Her shoes were still in her hand,
along with her hat and stockings. She must look as strange to him as he
did to her. "I'm sorry . . . it was raining."

"What brings you to my door at this hour?" he demanded, curtly
dismissing her stammering explanations. He sat down and reached for a
wooden box filled with cigars. He selected one, bit off the end, and spat
the fragment into the wastebasket as his chair creaked and moaned with
the burden of his weight.

Patience flinched at his lack of manners, but her demeanor remained calm. "I understand that you're handling Josiah Thorton's estate?"

"I am." The lawyer held a burning match to the cigar and puffed, blowing billowing wisps of smoke into the air.

The humidity in the room was stifling, and Patience fanned the smoke away from her face. "I was wondering if Josiah's house is going to be sold?"

"Which one?"

"Does he have more than one?"

Daniel turned his face upward and hooted uproariously.

" 'Does he have more than one?' You're not serious!"

"I'm afraid I didn't know Mr. Thorton personally."

"I'm afraid you didn't either." Daniel fanned out the match, propped his feet on top of his desk, and took a long draw on his cigar. "Exactly which house did you have in mind, honey?"

Patience felt her hackles rise with his growing insolence. "The one on Elm Street. And my name is Miss McCord, sir."

"Well, what do you want to know, Miss McCord?"

"Some details about the house. For instance, who will be disposing of the property?"

"The house was jointly owned."

"By whom?"

"Josiah and his business partner." Daniel brought his feet back to the floor and stood up. He lumbered to the files and rummaged for a few minutes before extracting a thick folder. "Since Josiah had no immediate family, we're waiting to see if anyone comes forth to put a claim on his estate." Daniel grinned as though he knew his next remark would certainly shock her. "Josiah's partner wants to be sure there aren't any little Thorton bastards waiting in the wings."

Patience wasn't shocked by his speculation, merely annoyed at his continuing audacity. "And if there aren't?"

"Then the Thorton estate goes to Josiah's partner." Daniel sighed, and Patience detected a note of envy. "A sizable fortune, I might add. The partner will then decide what he wants to do with the property."

"Exactly how long will it be before a decision is made?"

"Six months or longer."

Patience walked to the window and looked down on the rain-slicked streets. She pursed her lips thoughtfully. The house was exactly what she was looking for. Undoubtedly there were others available in town, but none so well-suited for her purpose.

She'd hoped to stay in the house longer, but six months would be sufficient. If she could persuade Josiah's partner to lease the house to her for six months, it would alleviate her immediate problem. At least she and the children would have a roof over their heads until she could make other arrangements.

"Would it be possible for me to speak with Mr. Thorton's business associate?" Patience requested.

"I see no need to bother him. What is it you want?"

Patience turned from the window, and her violet eyes met his beady ones. "I would prefer to speak to the partner in private, Mr. Odolp."

"And he would prefer you speak to me."

"Then let me phrase it differently." Patience's eyes grew noticeably cooler. "I *insist* on speaking to Josiah Thorton's business partner."

"You can't."

Patience arched one brow. "Does the name Silas Woodson ring a bell with you, Mr. Odolp?"

"The governor?"

"Yes, the governor of Missouri." Patience tapped her finger on her cheek thoughtfully. "You see, Uncle Silas would be quite distressed to learn of this conversation—"

Daniel Odolp's eyes began to widen. "Now, now, let's not jump to conclusions. I'll help you if I can." If the governor was the chit's uncle, then he'd better be a bit more cordial. "It's just that I don't like to have my clients bothered . . . but in this particular case I'm sure I can bend my rules a bit."

He reached hastily for a pen and paper. "Now, I'll just jot down the name and address of Josiah's partner. There's no need to tell him where you got this information, of course—"

"None at all."

Daniel slapped the piece of paper into her hand. "How is your uncle these days?"

"Oh, very busy."

"I can imagine."

Patience nodded. "He and my dear mama are brother and sister, you know."

"No, I didn't know."

"Well, I must be off, Mr. Odolp." She folded the paper carefully and slipped it into her bag. "Thank you for your cooperation."

Daniel rose and extended his hand pleasantly. "So happy to oblige you, Miss McCord. Must you be going so soon?"

Patience smiled. "I do wish I had time to stay and chat."

"Just stop by any time."

"I will."

Patience clutched her shoes, stockings, and hat as she walked to the door. She'd pulled it off! Aunt Merriweather would have disapproved of her tactics, but under the circumstances even she would tolerate this one tiny deception.

"Good evening, Mr. Odolp."

"Good evenin', ma'am. You say hello to the governor for me."

"I will. He'll be ever so pleased to hear from you."

Once safely outside, Patience hurried down the steep stairway and out onto the street, still grinning from her victory.

Pausing to catch her breath under the streetlight, she reached into her purse and carefully unfolded the paper the attorney had given her.

Her eyes widened, and she felt a hot flush creep up her neck as she read the name printed in bold black letters.

CASS CLAXTON.

Cass Claxton! She had to force back a rush of hysteria.

Great day in the morning! Her *husband* was Josiah Thorton's business partner.

CHAPTER 2

THE LATE AFTERNOON SUNLIGHT CLUNG IN DAPPLED ridges to the foot of the cherry fourposter bed. Golden rays bathed the man and woman who lay entwined in each other's arms in a warm, intimate glow. The storm of fiery passion was slow to subside as the couple stole a few more precious moments together.

"It is getting late," the woman drawled. The sound of her soft voice, heavy with a French accent and her still unsated passion, caused the man's arm to tighten around her possessively.

"So it is." His mouth took hers again, and she spoke his name softly as her fingers curled into his thick mass of coarse dark hair. Her small firm breasts, damp with perspiration, pressed tightly against the wiry mat of hair on his chest as they were caught up in a renewed fire storm of ecstasy.

The shadows had lengthened and turned to a rosy hue when Laure Revuneau finally summoned the strength to leave his arms. She slid quietly from bed, wrapped the sheet snugly around her slender frame, and walked to the small washbasin.

"*Mon chéri*, you will make me late for the party," she reproached.

Cass Claxton smiled up at her lazily, dimming her hopes of serious reprimand. "Laure, my love, I can think of a hundred things I'd rather do with you than attend another one of your Saturday soirees."

Stung by his honesty but accustomed to it by now, she began to gather her clothing, which had been earlier discarded in haste. "*Chéri*, I do not understand you at times. They are not merely *soirées*. As the daughter of the French consul, I have many responsibilities, not the least being to uphold Papa's image."

Cass reached out and caught the hem of the sheet as she brushed past the bed petulantly. Drawing her back into his arms, he kissed her until she became warm and willing again.

"*Mon pauvre chéri,*" she whispered when their lips finally parted. She sympathetically traced the tip of her finger around the outline of his sensual lips. "Do you truly hate my parties so?"

"Absolutely. So why do you insist I attend?"

"Because, it . . . it is something a man of your importance should do."

Cass threw back his head and laughed heartily at her simplistic reasoning.

"Do not laugh at me, *mon chéri*. Someday we will be called upon to host many parties in our own home," she said, pouting.

Cass tensed at her thinly veiled reference to marriage—her hints were coming up with unnerving regularity. "I'm sure having your social responsibilities must be burdensome, but may I say you handle it with an elegance and charm that other women can only envy," he soothed.

"Oh, *merci, chéri*. I have wondered if you'd noticed." Laure smiled seductively into his blue, fathomless eyes that were growing heavy with desire once more. Cass began to ease her back onto the bed when she thwarted his move effortlessly.

"*Non, non, non.* It is after six, *mon amour*. I must be going now. Papa will be worried."

She moved gracefully across the room to the small dressing area as Cass sighed and reached toward the bedside table for a cheroot. A match flared, and a moment later he lay back on the pillow to watch her dress.

"Would it honestly upset you if I failed to attend the party tonight?"

She was distressed but not surprised by his inquiry. Since she'd known him, he'd never enjoyed social functions. She lifted a delicately shaped leg to carefully pull a silk stocking over it. "You have other business?"

Laure knew better than to press the matter. She'd discovered months ago that he was not a man she could easily manipulate.

The sun's sinking rays formed a halo around her hair, making it appear as rich as black velvet. Watching her slip into her lingerie pleased Cass. He smiled as she diverted her attention to the satin corset. A tiny frown appeared on her flushed features as she studied it.

"Are you really going to put that thing back on?"

She turned and smiled. "It would be most improper of me if I did not."

"Since when have you ever been proper?" Cass said in a suggestive tone.

"Oh, yes, you are right!" She tossed the corset at him teasingly. "You may keep it to warm you on a cold winter's night!"

Cass chuckled as he caught the garment in one hand, then mockingly saluted her. Although there had been many women in his life, none could match Laure Revuneau's beauty, charm, and playfulness.

"I don't have other business," he said, returning to the subject. "I'm just not in the mood to socialize."

She tilted her head coquettishly. "But what are you in the mood for, *mon chéri?*"

Cass drew deeply on the cheroot as his eyes met hers hungrily.

She laughed softly, continually delighted—yet amazed—by his voracious appetite. Her eyes roamed over his broad shoulders, his wide chest with its dark springy hair, his lean waist, and she sighed wistfully. "You are a temptation, but I fear I would be delayed another hour if I were to stay."

"That's a strong probability." Cass sat up and stubbed out the cigar. "But the choice is entirely yours."

Laure finished dressing and walked over to the large looking glass. She peered at herself critically for a moment, then began to pull the pins from her tangled hair. "I wish you would change your mind about tonight. Many of your business associates will be there."

"I thought it was to be a charity function," Cass remarked absently as he lay back on the pillows and closed his eyes.

"*Vraiment,* truly, but the guest list is quite impressive," she encouraged. "I've invited everyone having the tiniest bit of social prominence—"

"And money," he speculated.

She laughed softly again. "*Oui,* most assuredly those who have *richesse.*" Not only was she in love with the handsome, charismatic Cass Claxton—considered to be the most eligible yet the most unobtainable bachelor in town—but it didn't hurt that he was a highly successful entrepreneur with valuable connections to the wealthiest people.

Cass had contacts that Laure drew upon regularly. Because of his various holdings in shipping, cotton, lead, and even silver from Mexico, Cass could be a real asset for a man in her father's position.

Laure's candid admission of where her values lay annoyed Cass. The last thing he wanted this evening was to mingle in a smoke-filled room with the idle rich. "Why don't I make a donation to whatever it is you're supporting and let it go at that?"

Laure turned, and Cass noticed that her lower lip was close to pouting again. "Please, *mon chéri* . . . say you'll come . . . for me?"

Cass hated it when she—or any woman, for that matter—tried to pressure him. "Laure, I don't want to argue about this," he warned.

"But papa will wonder where you are . . . and so will my friends." She crossed the room and knelt beside the bed, grasping his hand. "Please! It will be the last party I will ask you to attend this week." She stared up at him pleadingly.

"This week?" Cass shook his head with amusement. It was Friday.

"Say you will come, *chéri*," Laure caressed the palm of his hand imploringly.

"Laure . . ."

"*S'il te plaît?*"

Cass sighed, realizing she was going to be stubborn about it. "All right, but I won't promise to stay the evening."

"*Merci beaucoup, mon chéri!*" Laure wrapped her arms around his neck and kissed him breathlessly. "You will not regret it, *chéri* . . . I promise."

Cass wasn't optimistic, but it was difficult to refuse her when she looked at him with her wide turquoise eyes.

"I will instruct Mozes to prepare your bath." Laure rose and leaned over to kiss him fiercely. "Try to arrive before dinner. It will please Papa."

Blowing one final kiss, she hurried from the room, leaving a faint trace of her expensive French perfume in the air.

As the door closed behind her, Cass lit another cheroot and lay back against the pillow. He didn't plan to hurry.

He toyed with the idea of going back on his promise to attend the party, but after mulling over the ramifications such a reversal would bring, he concluded it wouldn't be worth all the tears and accusations.

He viewed the white satin corset lying next to his pillow, and a smile played at his lips. Her scent still lingered on the sheets, causing an ache deep within his loins at the memory of her satiny body next to his. He'd rather have Laure in a giving mood than a sullen one, so he would attend the party, but only briefly.

Afterward he would stop by the club for a game of cards and a bottle of his favorite brandy.

Having convinced himself that his concession was the only way to keep peace, he finally slid out of bed and went in search of the waiting bath.

It was growing dark as the carriage carrying Patience drew to a halt in front of an impressive rose-red brick home. The railing of its charming cupola matched the one along the length of its wide veranda. A beautiful rose garden on one side caught her eye. She had debated whether to postpone her business until morning, but had decided that since she was in the vicinity, she would approach Cass on her way to the charity function she was about to attend.

She sat for a moment staring at the lovely old two-story home, wondering when her estranged husband had become so prosperous.

She realized she knew nothing about Cass Claxton other than the bits of information she'd been able to extract when he'd escorted her to St. Louis six years ago.

Six years. It hardly seemed possible that the days and months had passed so swiftly. Patience felt a familiar prick of guilt as she thought about the way she'd tricked the man into marrying her. Now she was deeply ashamed of what she'd done when she remembered the selfish lengths she'd gone to get her way, but at the time she'd been desperate. She had been sure she couldn't have stood another moment in Cherry Grove, Kansas, and since Papa wouldn't hear of letting her return to St. Louis alone, she'd thought her only alternative was to use Mr. Claxton as a pawn.

She winced as she recalled the pall of black silence that had hung between them as he escorted her back to St. Louis. He had been justifiably furious and had spoken only when absolutely necessary, to bark a warning or issue her a brusque ultimatum. Then, on her Aunt Merriweather's front lawn, he had dumped her—and that was the most charitable way Patience could describe it—and tossed to her the small pouch of money Leviticus McCord had given him following their shotgun ceremony.

He had issued one final, tight-lipped decree: Have this outrage annulled!

A nagging twinge reminded Patience that she had never gotten around to it.

Not that she had taken her vows seriously, far from it, but she had just never filed for the annulment. She'd assumed there was no hurry. Cass had returned to his home in River Run, and she'd felt certain that she'd never see him again. A real marriage, a binding one, to Patience's way of thinking, began with a snow-white wedding gown, a church, flowers, and a host of well-wishers, not with an embarrassed minister, a sheriff carrying a loaded shotgun, and a bewildered groom—little more than a stranger—pleading for mercy in the middle of a dusty road. But she supposed she *should* have kept her promise before now. . . .

Stepping down from the carriage, Patience instructed the driver to wait, then turned and proceeded up the flagstone walk.

A lovely dark-haired beauty about her age was just coming out the front door. As Patience approached, the woman greeted her softly, "*Bon soir, madame.*"

Patience returned her smile. "Good evening. Is Mr. Claxton in?"

"*Oui.*" Curiously, Laure paused to study this stranger who was wearing an exact copy of a dress Laure had admired only that morning in the latest edition of *La Modiste Parisienne*. The pale rose dinner dress, with its off-the-shoulder neckline, cuirass bodice, lace trim, and long train of fine, pleated silk was breathtakingly beautiful. Rosebuds were entwined in the woman's shiny mass of blond hair, swept high at the crown to cascade down her back in golden ringlets. The stranger was simply exquisite.

"Thank you . . . *merci.*"

Patience continued up the walk as the young woman replied distractedly, "*Pas de quoi . . .*"

Moments later Patience stood before the brass door knocker fashioned in the shape of a lion's head, trying to bolster her courage. She knew that what she was about to do would not be pleasant. Cass would not be happy to see her again, and she couldn't blame him.

But the needs of nine homeless children were far more important to her than a bruised ego.

She turned slightly to watch the pretty young French woman enter the hansom cab waiting at the side entrance.

Who was she, Patience mused. A maid? She seriously doubted it. One of Cass's lady friends? Patience smiled. Apparently her dear "husband" was managing to amuse himself in his wife's absence.

She smothered a laugh, recalling her unusual marriage to Cass Claxton.

The philistine brute!

She drew a resigned breath and reached for the brass knocker. Cass Claxton be damned! Whether he was pleased to see her or not, they had business to discuss.

"Excuse me, sir, there's a young lady in the drawing room who wishes to see you." Mozes's giant frame dominated the doorway to Cass's bedroom.

The black man's height of six feet seven inches was a foreboding sight for all who were not acquainted with his genteel ways and impeccable manners. His hands were as big as ham hocks and his features were pinched and far from attractive, but anyone who knew Mozes could attest to his kindness and gentle heart.

For the past three years the tall black manservant had run Cass's household with a tenacious spirit and a firm hand. Cass commonly referred to Mozes as his right arm, and Mozes had more than earned Cass's trust and respect.

"What young lady?" Cass kept his attention centered on the stubborn cravat he was trying to tie.

"She says her name is McCord, sir."

"McCord?" Cass sighed and irritably jerked the cravat loose. The name failed to register with him. "Can you do something with this damned thing?"

Mozes stepped forward, and within a moment the task was effortlessly completed.

"I don't know how you do that," Cass reflected absently. "Would you hand me my jacket?"

"About the young lady, sir?" Mozes retrieved the double-breasted topcoat and held it as Cass slipped it on.

Reaching for a hairbrush, Cass tried again to control the springy mass of dark hair still damp from his bath. "Tell the lady I'm indisposed. She'll have to make an appointment to see me on Monday."

"Are you feeling ill, sir?"

"I feel fine, Mozes."

"The lady was quite insistent about speaking to you this evening," Mozes felt obliged to convey.

Cass laid the brush down on the dressing table. "That's too bad. It's growing late, and my business for the day has been concluded. If the lady wants to see me, she'll have to come back Monday."

"I'll tell her."

"Oh, and have the carriage brought around, Mozes." Cass reached for the black top hat lying at the foot of the bed. "I'm ready to leave."

"Yes, sir." Mozes bowed politely. "Will you and your lady want a bite to eat when you return, sir?"

"No. Miss Revuneau won't be returning with me. I think I'll stop by the club later." Cass glanced up and flashed Mozes a perceptive wink. "You and Sarah Rose can find something to keep you busy all evening, can't you?"

Mozes's grin spread guiltily across his face. "Yes, sir, I'm sure we can."

Closing the bedroom door, Mozes returned to Patience, who was waiting in the downstairs hallway.

"I'm sorry, madam. Mr. Claxton is not receiving guests at this time."

"Oh?" Patience lifted her brow with surprise. "Did you tell Mr. Claxton that *Patience McCord* wishes to speak to him?"

"Yes, madam, I informed Mr. Claxton of your wishes."

"And he refused to see me?"

"Mr. Claxton requests that you make an appointment to see him Monday morning."

"Oh, he does, does he!" Patience shot a reproachful glance up the stairway. Did she dare try to sidestep this giant and force her way into Cass's bedroom?

She measured the manservant with a critical eye. He was twice, three times, her size. No, there was no way she'd be able to make it up the stairs without his stopping her.

"Then I suppose I have no other choice but to bow to Mr. Claxton's request." She nodded coolly. "Good evening."

Mozes opened the door for her. "Good evening, Miss McCord."

About the time Patience was leaving by way of the front entrance, Cass was leaving from the side entrance of the house.

He paused momentarily to light a cheroot and enjoy the early evening air. The temperature was beginning to cool as a dark bank of clouds gathered in the west, hinting of rain before sunrise.

His attention was suddenly drawn to a young woman just entering a carriage at the front entrance.

A flash of rose silk, and the door to the carriage closed. Moments later the carriage disappeared in the growing dusk.

McCord. Cass frowned as the name Mozes had mentioned earlier popped unexpectedly into his mind.

McCord? Patience McCord?

Oh, damn! He shook away the alarming thought hurriedly. It couldn't be her again.

CHAPTER 3

THE FRENCH CONSUL'S ELEGANT MANSION WAS ablaze with light as Patience emerged from her carriage a short time later. She was in a decidedly foul mood.

Her husband's lack of cordiality hadn't surprised her, nor had his insolence. See him Monday, indeed! She didn't have the time or tolerance to play silly games with him.

Gathering her skirt in her hand, she started up a walk lined with towering hickory and walnut trees. The air was heavily perfumed with the scent of roses, and the occasional streaks of lightning in the west gave hope for relief from the insufferable heat the city had been enduring lately.

Patience dolefully recalled how Slader Morgan had asked to escort her to the party this evening. When she'd explained to him that she wanted to make a brief stop before the party, Slader had consented to meet her later. As it turned out, her stop had been so brief that he could have accompanied her easily, she thought irritably.

She nodded to a young couple who strolled past her arm in arm as she hurried up the walk.

Patience found herself wishing again that tonight's festivities were being held to benefit Maison des Petites Fleurs, or House of Little Flowers. But the small group of homeless waifs had been Aunt Estelle Merriweather's personal crusade, so the hodgepodge flock rarely received attention from outsiders. The nine children were viewed as less than ideal youngsters—street urchins who had stolen for survival, had eaten their meals from garbage cans, and had fought tooth and nail for the right to exist in a sometimes cold and callous world.

The memory of dear, colorful Aunt Estelle Merriweather brought the first smile of the evening to Patience's lips.

Estelle had had a heart as bottomless as her renowned brandy bottle. Patience fondly recalled how her aunt, without a word of recrimination, had welcomed the frightfully overindulged daughter of her baby brother into her home six years ago.

Over the years Aunt Merriweather had managed to channel Patience's zest and eagerness for life in more sweet-natured directions. She taught her niece the rewards of asking politely instead of demanding rudely. She had shown Patience the wisdom and power of a twinkling eye and a gracious smile. Gradually the young woman had given up the habit of stamping her foot and petulantly tossing her head of golden curls. No longer headstrong, she had become a lady. Estelle had watched proudly as a lovely, levelheaded woman had risen from the shell of the original Patience McCord, like a beautiful butterfly emerging from its unattractive cocoon.

Estelle had shown the same zeal and enthusiasm with the nine orphans. She saw them not as thieves and misfits but as needy children crying out for love. Society's lack of compassion toward those children had haunted her.

So one cold, snowy morning she had gone out into the streets, gathering the town's homeless lot to her ample bosom, telling them something miraculous, something they had never, ever heard before in their young lives: They were loved.

The dark eyes that had stared back at her with open skepticism had seemed forbidding; however, one by one, their small, dirty hands had clutched the material of her skirt, and like the Pied Piper, she'd led them down the street, past the shops and doorways of the town's most respectable and prominent citizens and into the first real home they had ever known.

She had secured an elderly couple to attend to the children while she personally handled the children's religious training and the financial burden. It had been a rigorous undertaking, born of love, but she declared it had been worth her every sacrifice to ensure the boys and girls a decent childhood.

When Estelle had passed away a year ago, the awesome responsibility of keeping the small group intact had fallen to Patience. At times, keeping the wolves from their door had seemed nearly impossible. Estelle had not been a rich woman, and she had left too little money to keep the orphanage operating.

Leviticus McCord had sent what money he could spare, but it was not enough. Estelle's house was heavily mortgaged in order to pay the orphanage bills. Finally the bank had been forced to sell it in order to settle her estate.

Patience had been able to keep food on the table by first depleting the small inheritance her mother had left her, then by working as a seam-stress. But now that they'd lost the very roof over their heads, she wasn't sure how much longer she could manage to hold on.

Harlon and Corliss McQuire, the elderly couple who had always helped look after the children, refused wages, saying that they were so old they needed very little. Patience knew the two of them had grown to love the children as their own, but she felt guilty about their working for nothing.

Just one fund-raiser like tonight's, and the children would be secure for a whole year, Patience thought wistfully as she stepped onto the large ve-randa. However, she would settle for the lease to Cass Claxton's rose-bricked house.

Slader Morgan was waiting in the shadows of the portico. As Patience approached he stepped forward and bowed graciously to kiss her hand. "How lovely you look this evening, my dear."

Patience's face broke into a radiant smile. The charming, debonair riverboat gambler managed to capture the attention, as well as the hearts, of most women. He had an easygoing manner and a silver tongue that rendered most women hopelessly smitten. His effect on Patience was no less stimulating. She had met Slader four months ago when he'd come to the shop to have a dress made for his mother. Since then, they had seen each other often.

She curtsied demurely. "Sir, you're ever so kind."

Slader gazed back at her fondly. "Kindness has nothing to do with it. You are, without exception, the most beautiful woman here tonight."

"May I take that to mean you have already examined the other ladies in attendance?" she bantered, knowing full well that he had.

"Only in passing." He grinned.

"Of course, only in passing." Patience was content with their informal relationship. She wasn't involved with Slader—or with any man for that matter. She wasn't sure she was happy with her present state, but between working and looking after the orphanage, there was little time to dwell on it.

Patience looped her arm through Slader's and smiled up at him as he guided her through open French doors into a large ballroom where ele-gantly dressed men and women were whirling around the floor to the strains of violins and harps.

The ballroom was splendidly opulent. The French-cut glass chande-liers flickered brightly overhead, their gaslight fixtures illuminating the rich red tapestries draped artfully at the great long windows. There were massive bouquets of summer flowers atop carved stone pedestals and priceless paintings on every wall. The marble floor was magnificent, hav-ing been polished until it reflected the pastel images of the ladies' gowns like a shimmering rainbow.

Patience found herself thinking that she could care for her nine homeless children for the rest of their lives with just a small portion of the money represented in this room.

"It's marvelous," she whispered under her breath.

"They're all stuffed shirts," Slader confided. "But I thought you might enjoy the change."

Didier Revuneau spotted Slader and Patience as they entered the ballroom. Taking his daughter's arm, he gently moved her through the crowd to greet the late arrivals.

"*Bienvenu*, my good friend, *bienvenu!*" The French consul reached out to grasp Slader's hand warmly.

"Good evening, Consul."

"You have met my lovely daughter, Laure?"

"We've met." Slader's eye ran over the dark-haired temptress with lazy proficiency. He bowed. "Good evening, Miss Revuneau."

Laure acknowledged the greeting graciously, her wide turquoise eyes openly admiring the handsome gambler. "*Monsieur* Morgan."

"Ah, such a lovely young flower you bring with you tonight." Didier's eyes were warm as he bowed and lifted Patience's hand to his mouth, lightly kissing the tips of her fingers.

Patience curtsied. "It is an honor to meet you, sir."

"Ah, but the honor is all mine, *ma chère*."

"Who is this lovely young flower, *Monsieur* Morgan?" Laure asked as she demurely slipped her arm through Slader's with such a familiar ease that it made Patience wonder exactly how well they knew each other.

It was rare for a man of Slader's reputation to be invited to such a prestigious gathering, but then Patience knew that he was widely accepted in the community, despite his questionable occupation.

Laure's smile was cordial, effectively covering the surprise she felt at seeing the same blond beauty she'd encountered earlier at Cass's.

Slader glanced down at Patience affectionately. "Miss Revuneau and Consul, may I present Miss Patience McCord."

Laure inclined her head demurely. "I believe Mademoiselle McCord and I share a mutual acquaintance."

"Yes, I believe we do." Patience had the distinct impression that the consul's daughter might be better acquainted with Cass than she.

"*Monsieur* Claxton," said Laure.

"Monsieur Claxton," Patience confirmed. So here was the reason— and a decidedly lovely one—her husband had been indisposed earlier.

"Did you see Cass?" Laure asked.

"No," Patience admitted, waiting to observe Laure's reaction.

"Oh," Laure's full lower lip formed into a pretty pout. "I am sorry."

"So was I."

"You are good friends with *Monsieur* Claxton?"

"I was there on a business matter."

Laure's expression was noticeably more guarded, but the tone of her voice remained pleasant. "Perhaps you will be granted another chance. Cass promised to come to the party. He should arrive very soon."

Patience felt her pulse take an expectant leap. "Oh?"

"Yes . . ." Laure's attention was momentarily diverted by the brocade gown Patience was wearing. "I was admiring your lovely dress earlier. Is it not the one shown in the recent issue of *La Modiste Parisienne?*"

"Oh, my, no. I could never afford to purchase such a gown. I'm afraid I only copied it," Patience admitted.

"You *made* this dress?" Laure's brows lifted.

"Yes. I'm delighted you like it."

"It is exquisite," Laure complimented, then returned her attention to Slader. "You must promise me a dance later."

Slader inclined his head politely. "Of course. I would be honored."

"Enjoy the evening," Didier said. Patience detected a merry twinkle in his dark eyes. "And your lovely lady."

"Thank you." Slader glanced at Patience again. "I'm sure I'll enjoy both."

Moments later the consul and his daughter merged into the crowd, leaving Patience and Slader free to mingle.

"She is lovely, isn't she?" Patience's gaze still lingered on the consul's daughter as Slader swept her onto the dance floor.

"Laure?" Slader chuckled. "Indeed, she is quite a woman." The tempo of the music shifted to a slow waltz, and Slader drew Patience more closely into his arms as they whirled beneath a canopy of shimmering lights.

"Slader . . ." Patience was annoyed to discover that she was actually curious about Cass's relationship with the French beauty, though she hadn't the vaguest idea why. She had never considered Cass appealing.

"Yes?"

"I was wondering about Miss Revuneau's friendship with Cass Claxton."

Slader's eyes met hers with a look of amusement. "Friendship?"

"I was on my way to speak to Mr. Claxton earlier, and as I was coming up his walk I saw Miss Revuneau leaving."

Ordinarily, Patience would have felt ill at ease prying like this, but she knew Slader wouldn't think her boorish—they always felt free to discuss their thoughts.

Slader lifted his left brow inquisitively. "Why would you be going to see Cass Claxton?"

"I told you, I had business I needed to discuss with him."

"And Laure was leaving?"

"Yes."

Slader's smile, overflowing with male perception, confirmed the obvious. "I would guess they'd spent the afternoon together." Slader felt a rush of envy as he recalled the many afternoons he had spent in bed with the hot-blooded young Laure.

"Oh . . . are they seeing each other?" Patience deliberately kept her inquiry casual. It was really none of her business . . .

"Yes, I believe you could say that." Slader smiled at her innocence.

It was Patience's brow that lifted this time. "Seriously?"

"If Laure has her way. Cass has been a difficult man to get to the altar, but Laure is a determined young lady." Slader leaned closer and whispered conspiratorially, "I've heard she's hoping for a Christmas wedding."

Patience glanced at the dark-haired belle whirling around the floor with one of her many admirers. "Oh, really? How interesting." How *very* interesting, she added silently.

Around ten, Slader suggested he go in search of something cool for them to drink. Patience agreed and drifted toward the veranda for a breath of fresh air while she waited.

She strolled along the railing, listening to the peaceful voices of nature blending in muted harmony. A full moon shone overhead, and she was disappointed to see that the earlier promise of rain had vanished.

She allowed her thoughts to drift. She was feeling relaxed and more optimistic about the children. Somehow things always had a way of working out, she assured herself. If worse came to worst, she could always take the children to her father in Cherry Grove. Leviticus had mentioned in his last letter that he would be willing to provide a home for the orphans, but Patience feared Harlon and Corliss were too old to make such a long trip, and she didn't have the heart to leave them behind. The children had become like family to her, and so had the elderly couple. It would be best for all if she were able to keep her flock in St. Louis where Harlon and Corliss could remain a part of their lives.

Directly ahead, Patience saw a man step onto the veranda and pause to light a cheroot. Her footsteps slowed as the light spilled out from the ballroom, and she recognized Cass Claxton's familiar figure.

For a moment she could do nothing but stare, taking in the head of curly dark hair and incredibly broad shoulders. The years had added an attractive, virile maturity to him. In fact, he now possessed devilishly good looks. He had been heavier when she'd last seen him, almost stocky from what she remembered, and now he looked leaner, older, wiser . . . more forbidding, for some reason. He was fashionably dressed, looking every bit the successful young entrepreneur he was reported to be.

Patience stood quietly in the shadows, not ten feet from him, afraid to breathe. What would he say when he saw her? She was afraid she knew. He would be none too happy.

He cupped his hand to the flame of the match and drew on the cheroot. The tip glowed a bright red in the darkness as he tossed the match away.

And their eyes met.

For a moment it seemed as if even the cicadas and tree frogs were holding their breath with strained anticipation as the couple stood staring at each other.

His eyes, even more of a vibrant cobalt blue than she remembered, narrowed as they coolly ran over her slim body.

Patience remained immobilized, holding her breath as she prepared herself for what was to come. Would he explode with pent-up anger? Or would he turn and walk away without a word? She hoped he wouldn't walk away. She didn't want to cause a scene, but she would if necessary.

Keeping his gaze centered on her, Cass calmly removed the cheroot from his mouth. In a voice as casual as if they had last seen each other only yesterday, he murmured, "As I live and breathe, if it isn't Miss McCord. I gather hell must have just frozen over?"

Patience swallowed hard and tried to summon her most charming smile as she responded, "Only temporarily, Mr. Claxton."

CHAPTER 4

*O*OH, THE INSUFFERABLE BRUTE HADN'T CHANGED one bit! Patience seethed, but wisely refrained from saying anything rude.

"I'm glad to see you're here," she greeted in an even tone. *Move carefully, Patience,* she warned herself. *You don't want to spook him.*

Cass drew on the cheroot as their gazes remained locked.

She was prettier than he'd remembered. Her once too slim body had rounded gently to form lush, ripe curves. Only her eyes were familiar, a defiant deep violet lined with long, sooty lashes. She was wearing her hair differently; it looked more refined and sophisticated than it had six years ago. But he'd be willing to wager she was still the devious little schemer she'd always been.

"Looks like the rain has passed us by," he remarked, hoping he could keep this unexpected encounter as impersonal and brief as possible. He hadn't seen Patience McCord or thought about her in years, but her appearance suddenly brought back the black day six years ago when, at the wrong end of a shotgun barrel, he'd been forced to marry the spoiled twit. It was a memory Cass did not hold dear. He had no idea what Patience McCord was doing here at Laure's party, but he didn't intend to stick around long enough to find out.

With a sinking heart, Patience realized that Cass intended to avoid her. His same casual, cocksure air of dismissal was there; it was just as infuriating as it had been years ago. She forced her voice to remain amiable, though she could see that he was already beginning to ease toward the doorway: "We certainly could have used a good rain."

Surreptitiously, she edged toward him.

She debated whether she should block his way to the ballroom. Such a move would undoubtedly upset him, and she didn't want to make him angry. He'd be impossible to deal with then, but she could see no other way; she had to talk to him sooner or later.

She would force herself to remain tolerant and cool, even though she was aching to inform him that she wasn't any more enamored of him than he was of her.

Taking another step closer, she decided to try cajoling him. "Cass, I'm glad you're here. I'd like to talk—"

"Sorry," he interrupted. "If you want to talk to me, Miss McCord, you'll have to make an appointment." He flicked his cheroot into the darkness, and with an insufferable smile and a mock salute, he turned and started back into the ballroom.

She gasped, hardly able to believe his impertinence. The deplorable swine!

After a second of indecision she bolted forward to thwart his escape, sensing that he would do everything within his power to avoid seeing her on Monday—or the day after or the day after that.

Cass caught her abrupt movement out of the corner of his eye and sidestepped defensively, his hands moving reflexively to shield his manhood from what he assumed would be another one of her brutal on-slaughts.

He hadn't forgotten the misery she had dealt him when he'd angered her by deliberately blocking her path in Miller's Mercantile six years ago. Out of the blue, she'd ruthlessly brought him to his knees with one swift, retaliatory blow of her purse. He wasn't about to let that happen again.

Facing her, he narrowed his eyes menacingly. "Just try it, lady!"

"Try what?" Patience's footsteps faltered as she watched him cover himself defensively.

"Try hitting me again in the . . ." His voice trailed off, then returned full force, "because this time I'll overlook the fact that you're a woman."

Though appalled that he assumed she would try such a thing again, Patience was determined not to let him rattle her. If there was even the smallest hope that he might lease Josiah Thorton's house to her, it was imperative that she remain calm. She fought to check her rising temper, even though her cheeks were flaming with embarrassment. "I wasn't going to strike you!"

The sharp exchange between the couple was beginning to attract attention.

Cass glanced uneasily at the growing cluster of curious onlookers. "What do you want?"

"I want to talk to you!"

"I'm busy!"

"You are not!"

Seizing her roughly by the wrist, he pulled her back out onto the veranda.

His resorting to barbaric tactics made Patience struggle all the harder to remain civil. She knew if she let her temper rule—as she was sorely tempted to do—all would be lost.

"Let go! You're hurting me!" She tried discreetly to free herself from his steely grip while sending a weak smile in the direction of the bewildered guests watching from inside the house.

Moments later Cass backed her against a baluster in a secluded corner of the porch, and their eyes locked in a glacial stare.

"What in the hell are you doing here, Patience?" His face was inches from hers now, his voice ominously low.

Her pulse sped as the manly fragrance of his soap and shaving cream surrounded her. With a jolt, she realized that, despite his despicable lack of manners, he had become a devastatingly handsome man.

"Let go of my arm," she demanded.

"The hell I will!"

"The hell you won't!" In self-defense, she dipped her head and sank her teeth into the back of his hand, then twisted her wrist from his grip so swiftly that he could do nothing but let go.

"Damn!" He sucked in his breath, viewing the row of small, even teeth marks on the back of his hand. "You little witch, watch your language!" he hissed.

Her eyes met his. "Why? Are you afraid someone will hear your *wife* cursing?"

Cass glanced over his shoulder, obviously alarmed that her remark might be overheard and misunderstood. "What do you want, Patience?"

Satisfied that she'd discouraged him from further attempts to intimidate her, she lifted her chin regally, snapped her fan open, and moved deeper into the shadows. "Why, dear, dear Cass, whatever makes you think I want something?" she inquired in her sweetest tone.

"Why, dear, dear Patience," he mocked in a tone far from sweet, "because you always do."

"Perhaps if you had consented to see me when I came by your house earlier, you'd know what I want," she reminded.

"I had no idea it was you."

"And if you had known?"

His eyes narrowed. "I would have set the dogs loose."

Somehow his answer didn't surprise her, and it confirmed that he certainly hadn't mellowed over the years. He was going to be about as easy to reason with as a grizzly bear with a thorn in his paw.

"You should have made an effort to see who it was before you sent me away," she reproached.

"I was busy."

"Yes, I met her on the way in."

Cass flashed a smile, a lazy, arrogant curve to his mouth that she could barely detect. "Then you understand why I didn't want to be disturbed by you."

"Tsk, tsk. I see you haven't changed." Her voice lowered, and she knew what she was about to add would most certainly cook her goose, but she was powerless to let her opportunity pass: "You're the same little weasel you always were."

She realized after she'd bitten him that she'd ruined any chance of convincing him to let her use Josiah Thorton's house, so there seemed little need for the pretense of civility now.

"Weasel?" Cass fumbled in his pocket for another smoke, fighting the urge to strangle her. He knew it was useless to try and outwit her in a war of insults—he'd tried that six years earlier and had lost every time. The best thing he could do was stand his ground.

Patience watched warily as he calmly lit another cigar. "What are you still doing in St. Louis, Patience?"

"I live here, remember?"

"I remember." He blew out the match and tossed it aside. "But I thought you'd be gone by now."

"Ah, then you've thought of me over the years," she said.

He removed the cigar from his mouth and smiled indulgently. "Not even once."

She sighed. "A pity. And here I thought you were pining away for me all this time."

Cass chuckled mirthlessly. "What a dreamer!"

"A better question is what are *you* doing here in St. Louis?" she challenged. "I thought you'd be in River Run."

Cass drew on the cheroot absently as he casually set a booted foot onto the rail next to her. He stared into the darkness for so long Patience thought he intended to ignore her again.

"It's none of your business," he finally said simply, "but if you must know, I went back to River Run for a few months before an old friend wrote and asked me to join him in a business partnership here in St. Louis. That's why I came back."

"Josiah Thorton," she murmured absently.

His eyes snapped back to meet hers. "How did you know Josiah Thorton?"

"I didn't. I just know that he was your business partner . . . and that he died, leaving you the executor of his estate."

"Just how did you find out about that?" Cass was clearly unnerved that she knew even that much about his business dealings.

"Never mind how, I just did. It was Josiah's house that I came to see you about earlier."

"Josiah's house?" Cass studied her guardedly. "What about it?"

"I want you to rent the house to me."

"Rent the house to you?" Cass found the request odd, even for Patience McCord. "I wouldn't rent my horse's leavings to *you.*"

"Nor would I accept them," she snapped.

"Then what makes you think I would rent Josiah Thorton's house to you?"

"I know you won't rent me the house for myself, but I'm hoping that when you hear that I have nine children who desperately need that house, you'll be willing to at least listen to what I have to say."

For a moment there was stunned silence as Cass slowly digested her words. She could see that her answer had taken him by surprise.

Suddenly he threw his head back and laughed uproariously, his white teeth flashing in the moonlight. His merriment continued to grow as Patience reviewed her remark to discover what was so amusing that it could send him into fits of mirth.

She could find nothing to warrant such an uncharacteristic show of hilarity.

"What's so funny?" she challenged.

Cass pointed at her, his eyes filling anew with unrestrained joviality. "You . . . and nine children!" He slapped his hand on his thigh and broke into another boisterous round of laughter as she watched with a jaundiced eye. She had a feeling that once she was able to discover the source of his amusement, she wasn't going to be half as lighthearted as he.

"What's so funny about the children and me?" she demanded.

As quickly as his gaiety had erupted, it came to a sudden halt. His eyes surveyed her dispassionately. "I can't imagine any man living with you long enough to father nine children. Is he addlebrained?"

Patience stared back at him the way she did whenever she was forced to deal with a simpleton, which at this point she was certain he was. "The nine children aren't mine."

"I didn't think so!" He roared again hilariously.

"If you can pull yourself together, I'll tell you why I have them," she said curtly. She was getting a little weary of his loutish behavior.

Cass gradually obliged, but with considerable difficulty. "Okay, humor me. Where did you get nine kids?"

"They're orphans. My Aunt Merriweather took them into her home to raise, and after she died I assumed the responsibility for their care."

"Of course you did! Grasping, conniving, spoiled Patience McCord giving unselfishly of herself to nine homeless children. Sounds exactly like you, my dear!"

He would believe that when it was announced that, through an unforeseen technicality, the South had won the war!

"You don't believe me?"

"I couldn't hope to *live* long enough to believe you, Patience!"

"Then I suppose it would do no good to plead with you to lease Josiah Thorton's house to me?"

"None whatsoever." Cass was not a heartless man, and he regretted that innocent children would suffer from his refusal, but he wouldn't help Patience McCord cross the street, let alone rent Josiah Thorton's house to her.

"Mr. Claxton"—Patience's eyes locked with his stubbornly—"I know you and I haven't exactly been friends." She stoically ignored the choking sound he made in his throat and continued, "But I fail to see how you could let our personal differences stand in the way of providing a home for nine helpless children. I beg you to reconsider. I understand you have accumulated wealth beyond what most people can imagine, and you surely have no need for that large house. Please reconsider. I'm desperate. In another week the children will have no place to live."

It went against everything in Patience to resort to begging, but if it was for the children, then she would.

"Come now, Miss McCord, if what you claim is true, and you've turned into an unselfish saint"—which Cass couldn't believe for one moment—"then why are you making it sound as if I'm the one responsible for the children's misfortune?"

"You have the house," she said simply.

He lifted his brows wryly. "There are no other houses in St. Louis with twenty-four rooms?"

"I'm sure there are, but none so ideal and none that I can afford. I'm afraid I can only offer a pittance to repay you for your kindness and generosity"—she nearly choked on the praise—"but the children and I will paint and clean and weed the gardens for a portion of our keep."

"What makes you think you could afford what I would ask?"

"I'm not sure that I can, for we have very little money. But when I saw the house, I knew it was exactly what I was looking for, even though it's old and run-down and needs lots of repair. Why, no one would think about purchasing it in the condition it's in now. Of course, I had no idea you owned it—"

"I don't. It belongs to Josiah Thorton."

"But he's dead, and you're the executor of his estate and the one most likely to inherit it, along with the rest of Mr. Thorton's vast holdings."

Cass's eyes narrowed again. "Who told you that?"

Daniel Odolp's face surfaced in Patience's memory as she quickly went on. "I can't say who told me, but wouldn't it be to your advantage to have people living in Josiah's house, people who would be able to care for it until the estate is settled?"

"And what happens once the estate is settled? Suppose I already have a potential buyer interested in purchasing Josiah's house. Would the kind-hearted, generous 'weasel' then dump you and your nine little orphans in the middle of the street?"

"Well . . . I'm not sure what would happen in that case." Patience had learned long ago to deal with life one day at a time. "It's possible that if I can't find another house at that time, I might be forced to take the children to my father in Cherry Grove, but I don't want to do that right now. With winter approaching, the long journey would be extremely difficult for the elderly couple who helps me run the home," she confessed.

"I hate to hear that, Miss McCord, because I'm not going to help you." Cass pitched his cheroot over the veranda and straightened to face her. "It looks like you're going to have to trick someone else into helping you out of your mess this time."

Her eyes narrowed. "You can't help me—or you won't help me?"

He grinned. "Both. I can't because Josiah's house is not mine to do with as I please—his estate won't be settled for months yet. And I won't because . . ." His eyes surveyed her insolently. "Well, I think we both know why I won't, don't we? Oh, by the way, I never received those annulment papers. Where are they?"

"You are heartless," she spat out. "So you'll just have to keep on wondering where those papers are."

He extended his index finger and tapped her under her chin warningly. "Watch it, sweetheart—your halo is wobbling." He grinned again. It felt good to turn the tables on her, for a change. After what she'd done to him, he was surprised she'd have the gall to come to him for a favor. But then he recalled that years ago she'd had the gall of ten women, and the way Cass figured it, refusing her tonight had just about evened the score.

Just about.

Patience felt her temper surfacing full force as he turned and started away from her.

Oh, she longed to shout at the top of her lungs where his precious annulment papers were, but she knew she didn't dare.

Squaring her shoulders, she called out to his retreating form pleadingly. "We don't have to have twenty-four rooms, you know. We can make do with far less!"

"Forget it."

"Don't you have *any* house you could rent to me for the children?"

"Nope, not even one. Good evening, Miss McCord. Real nice seeing you again." He threw his head back and laughed merrily.

Patience stamped her foot angrily. Good evening, indeed!

The man was an intolerable muttonhead who was going to pay for his highhandedness.

CHAPTER 5

TWICE IN THE FOLLOWING DAYS PATIENCE MCCORD went to Cass Claxton and begged him to reconsider. On both occasions he turned a deaf ear and told her in his most holier-than-thou tone that it would take an act of divine intervention for him to rent her a glass of water, to say nothing of Josiah Thorton's house.

She'd left enraged each time, to scour the town for another house, praying for that divine intervention he was so smugly sure she'd never find. And she didn't find it.

By Friday she realized she'd reached the end of the line. "I'm sorry," Patience told the children that night, "but we have no other choice. We must start for Kansas at first light Monday morning."

She sat with her hands folded at the dinner table, trying to gauge the reaction on the bright young faces before her. The children—Aaron, sixteen; Payne, fourteen; Jesse, nine, Doog, eight; Margaret Ann, six; Lucy and Bryon, five; Joseph, four; and Phebia, three—stared back at her with solemn gazes.

They were aware of her diligent search to find a home large and inexpensive enough to house them. The worry lines etched on Patience's forehead tonight told them that the miracle they had hoped for had failed to materialize. In three short days they must vacate Aunt Merriweather's house, so they realized that there was little Patience could do but transport them all to Cherry Grove.

The challenge was overwhelming, even for a woman of her fortitude, but they were confident she could get the job done.

"Are we gonna ride in a wagon?" Jesse picked up an ear of corn and began to gnaw the tender kernels thoughtfully.

"I'll be able to gather enough money to buy a wagon and a team.

Naturally we cannot hope for a wagon that will be large enough for all of us to sleep in, but the weather should remain mild enough so that we can sleep on pallets under the wagon at night. Corliss and Harlon will sleep inside."

Patience glanced over to assess Corliss's reaction to the news. She went about quietly dishing up potatoes onto the youngest child's plate.

Phebia was the baby of the household, a gurgling, brown-eyed, chubby-faced foundling who was left on the Merriweather doorstep three years ago by a mother who could no longer care for her. Estelle had been eager to welcome a ninth stray into the fold, and the other children had joined in to help with Phebia's upbringing.

"I know it's not the ideal time to embark on a journey," Patience admitted quietly, "but if all goes well we should reach Cherry Grove in six to seven weeks."

Patience knew they'd have to travel the length of Missouri, and then another hundred and twenty-five miles into Kansas; but it was only the end of August, and she figured they wouldn't have any trouble reaching their destination before the first snow.

She was relieved to see both Corliss and her husband nodding as she spoke, supportive as usual of any request she made of them.

"How are we going?" Harlon asked.

"I understand the most sensible way for us to go would be to take a boat to St. Joseph, then buy a wagon and supplies to transport us on to Cherry Grove, but because of our lack of funds, we won't be able to do it that way. We'll have to travel by wagon, keeping to the main route running across the state."

"All right. I'll see to getting the wagon and a team first thing in the morning," Harlon said.

"Thank you, Harlon. Wes Epperson over at the livery barn said he might have one he'd sell cheaply." Patience absently reached to cover Doog's fork in a mute reprimand as he prepared to launch a pea at an unsuspecting Bryon. "I think you'll like Cherry Grove," she told the children—although she herself had detested it.

Long ago, when she'd longed to return to the parties and gaiety of St. Louis, she'd begged Leviticus to let her go back to Aunt Merriweather's. Leviticus had ignored his daughter's pleading. He had moved his daughter to Cherry Grove to begin a new life, and he insisted she make new friends. The decision had forced Patience to take her own action. Cass Claxton was elected to take her back to St. Louis.

The marriage ploy had worked like a charm, though Patience realized now that using such underhanded tactics was unforgivable. She thought about her encounter with Cass two nights ago and felt sad. She was no longer the irresponsible, willful girl she had once been, and she had to admit her selfishness disturbed her deeply.

Now when she most desperately needed Cass's help—or more

accurately, when she needed the house he controlled—she knew she could never convince him that she had changed.

Patience sighed wearily. Her father's words came back to haunt her: "You've made your bed; now you must lie in it."

"Will them Indians git us?" blond, gray-eyed Jesse asked solemnly as he wrapped a string bean around his forefinger.

The same concern had kept Patience awake long into the night. "I'm not sure we'll encounter Indians, Jesse, but if we do, we'll just keep our heads, and I'm sure the good Lord will see us through."

Aaron, the oldest of the boys, said quietly, "Ma'am, I hear tell it's not our heads they'd be after. It's our scalps."

Patience felt a shudder ripple down her spine.

Lucy's brown eyes grew as round as saucers. "Really?" A piece of corn dangled from her one remaining front tooth.

"Well, of course there's always that danger, Lucy, but I'm sure Patience will make sure that we keep our hair," Margaret Ann soothed as she dabbed the younger girl's mouth with a cloth napkin.

Patience had always contended—out of Margaret's earshot—that Margaret was a thirty-year-old imprisoned in a six-year-old's body.

"What may I do to help, Miss McCord?" Margaret inquired sweetly.

"I plan to make a list tonight of the duties that will be assigned to each of us. I'll try to have it completed by breakfast tomorrow morning." Patience sipped her coffee, trying to read the children's faces again. She was relieved to see that they seemed to take the turn of events in stride. Over the years, under Aunt Merriweather's tutelage, they had become exemplary children.

Margaret and Payne stood up and began to clear away the dishes, while Corliss wiped Phebia's hands and face and lifted her out of the wooden high chair. She handed the child her favorite doll, Marybelle, and swatted her lovingly on the bottom.

"Jesse, it's gettin' late. Time for Phebia and Marybelle to be off to bed."

"Yes, ma'am." Jesse pushed back from the table and led Phebia, who immediately popped her thumb into her mouth, out of the room.

"The wood box be gettin' low." Aaron reached into his pocket and slipped his cap onto his head. "I'll be filling it up for you, Miss McCord, before I turn in."

"Thank you, Aaron. I'll see you in the morning," Patience replied absently as she reached for the small slate and piece of chalk.

The rest of the children dispersed from the table in an orderly manner as Harlon went into the kitchen to retrieve the coffee pot. He carried it back to the table and lifted his bushy white brows expectantly at Patience.

"No, thank you," she refused. "I've had plenty."

Corliss bustled off to the kitchen to supervise the cleaning as Harlon sat back down at the table. The clock on the mantle chimed seven times while he scraped out the bowl of his pipe. Patience was deeply absorbed in making the list of supplies she would need to purchase for the journey. Money was tight, but she had been known to stretch a dollar until it cried for mercy. Now she would just have to stretch it until it expired!

She knew very little about such things as wagons and teams and the proper food to carry on such a long trip, but she had spent hours that morning at the general store, talking to a family who had traveled to Oregon by wagon two years ago.

Clifford Magers had explained to her that when she went to select a wagon, she must make sure that it was strong, light, and constructed out of well-seasoned timber—especially the wheels, since they would be traveling through an elevated region that was exceedingly dry this time of year. He warned Patience that unless the woodwork was thoroughly seasoned, constant repairs would be inevitable.

She'd have to travel light, he insisted, no matter how strong the urge was to take along furniture, potted plants, iron stoves, and grandfather clocks. He emphasized that should she succumb to temptation, the heavy items would only have to be discarded by the wayside later in order to conserve the animals' strength for their long journey.

In selecting her team, Clifford advised mules rather than oxen because they traveled faster and seemed to endure the summer heat better. But when she'd gone to the livery later that day, she discovered that mules were priced higher than oxen.

Wes Epperson told her he thought she'd be smarter to buy oxen over mules, assuring her that oxen stayed in better condition and were able to make the journey in the same amount of time. He contended that oxen would be less likely to stampede if they were spooked by Indians.

Patience would have preferred mules, but with her limited funds, she supposed oxen would have to be her choice.

She glanced up, aware that Harlon had been watching her for the past few minutes. She smiled encouragingly. "Is there something you'd like to suggest, Harlon?"

"Yes, ma'am."

Patience lay the chalk aside and folded her hands over the slate. "I'm listening."

"Have you given any thought to the dangers a young woman and nine children will be facing once we're out on the trail?" he began quietly.

She sighed, sensing that all along Harlon had harbored misgivings about her decision. "I know there will be dangers, and I'm not happy about having to go, but taking the children to my father is our only hope of keeping them together."

"With all due respect, Miss McCord, I think we need a man—a good strong man who knows the wilderness to lead us on such a long journey."

Patience sighed. "I've thought about that, Harlon, but I have no such man, and it isn't as if we're traveling to some far away place like California or Oregon," she argued. "I'll have you to help me. You're a man."

"I'm an old man," Harlon reminded gently. "I can't do anything but hunt for fresh game and haul fresh water to the camp each night. You need a young man, a man strong enough to fight off Indians, wield a bullwhip, and drive a team of oxen."

Patience realized he was right, but what choice did she have? She didn't know such a man, and her scarcity of funds prevented her from hiring anyone.

"Maybe we can hire a bullwhacker to drive the team," Harlon mused.

"I don't know a bullwhacker, and even if I did, I wouldn't permit such a bully to travel with us."

Everyone knew a bullwhacker was the biggest show-off on a wagon train. His casual brutality to animals was deplorable, and he usually kept the women and children in constant fear. "Besides, I can use a bullwhip myself," she said. A former suitor had taught her how to handle a bullwhip almost as well as a man. She'd become accurate enough to swat a fly off the rump of an ox before the ox even knew a fly was there.

"Well, 'course, it's your decision," Harlon conceded. "I just wanted to make sure you'd thought about what we're gonna be up against."

"I have, Harlon, and I agree with everything you're saying, but I'm afraid we have no other choice. We will have to make the trip alone." She reached over and squeezed his hand encouragingly. "Aaron and Payne are developing into strong young men, and they will be able to drive the oxen. And though they haven't had much experience with a rifle, I'm sure they will learn quickly. The girls will pitch in to do all they can. You'll see, we'll be fine."

Harlon drew thoughtfully on his pipe as he listened to her rattle on about making a memorable adventure out of the journey.

It'd be memorable, all right! He'd traveled with a wagon train back in the fifties, and he could still remember the torrential rains, blazing sun, freezing winds, and the dust—miles and miles of swirling dust—that got into the eyes and clothes and food, tormenting the weary travelers until they thought they would lose their minds. He recalled the flies and the sickness . . .

"You'll see, we'll make it just fine," he heard her say again before she turned her attention back to her list.

"Well, I hope so," he muttered.

A few minutes later Harlon pushed away from the table and slowly got to his feet. "It sure would make it easier if you had a strong young husband to take us all to Cherry Grove," he said almost wistfully.

Patience glanced up from the slate. "Yes, it certainly would make it easier."

"Well, don't be frettin' none over what I've said." Harlon sighed as he stretched lazily. He stood and shuffled over to wind the clock. "Me and Corliss will do everything we can to help get those young 'uns to their new home. The good Lord will see us through. He always has."

"He always has." She nodded. "I've been praying about it, Harlon, and I don't think we have a thing to be concerned about."

Harlon nodded and announced he was going to turn in.

Patience bid him good night distractedly.

The lamp had burned low when she finally blew out the flame. She closed her eyes and clasped her hands around her waist, trying to ease the stiffness in the small of her back. Harlon's earlier comment drifted back to her: "It sure would make it easier if you had a husband."

Reaching for the candle, she rose to make her way to the darkened stairway, thinking about his observation.

Suddenly her hand paused on the railing.

It sure would make it easier if you had a strong young husband. Harlon's words echoed through her mind again, taunting, offering an almost prophetic challenge. *Someone who could take us to Cherry Grove . . .*

Her feet absently claimed a second stair, then hesitated again. It *would* make it considerably easier if she had a strong young husband to help out. He could escort them safely to Cherry Grove, and they could all stop worrying. She stood in the darkness, scowling thoughtfully.

Well, she *had* a husband. A good, strong, reasonably young husband who was more than capable of escorting them on such a journey. And why shouldn't he? Wasn't he partly to blame for her having to make the journey, since he'd refused to rent her Josiah's house?

Patience, there's no way on this earth that you could ever talk Cass Claxton into escorting you to your own lynching . . . well, maybe he would agree to take her to that, she amended grudgingly. But he would most assuredly refuse to lead her, two seventy-year-olds in failing health, plus nine homeless children safely across four hundred miles back to Cherry Grove, Kansas.

She took another step, then paused. No, he would *never* do it . . . unless . . .

Unless . . .

She smiled, and her feet began to move with purpose now as she hurried up the steep stairway, confident that if she put her mind to it, she might find a way he would.

Maybe it was time to show that smart-alecky Cass Claxton that Patience McCord *still* had the upper hand when she wanted it.

CHAPTER 6

MONDAY MORNING ARRIVED WITH A SLOW, STEADY rain falling from the eaves of the Claxton estate. In the distance occasional thunder rumbled unceremoniously, but all in all, the gray, cool morning was ideal for working. However, Cass found he had to struggle to keep his mind on the papers spread out before him.

He sat at his desk trying to concentrate while Laure draped herself over his shoulder, determined to offer him a tempting diversion.

"Oh, *mon chéri*, why must you always work?" she complained as she snuggled close against the broad expanse of his back. "Do you not think we could find more interesting ways to occupy ourselves?"

She nipped seductively at his left ear as her fingers began to nimbly work open the buttons on his shirt.

"Laure . . ." Cass warned, capturing both her hands in his. She giggled as he pulled her down onto his lap.

Her slender fingers threaded through the dark springy curls that grazed his collar as their lips met in a long, unhurried kiss.

Moments later he found himself gazing into her turquoise-blue eyes and admonishing her in what he hoped was his sternest voice. "What am I going to do with you?"

She pulled his ear toward her and whispered a suggestion that immediately brought an amused smile to his handsome features.

"Is not a morning more suited for making love than for working?" she whispered.

Cass's left brow lifted dubiously. "You left my bed not two hours ago, and now you're implying that I'm not paying enough attention to you?"

"Ah, but I am shameless when it comes to you, *mon chéri*." Her tongue seduced the outline of his lips while she twined her fingers into the thick mat of hair exposed by his open shirt.

Cass's ensuing laugh was that of a man who knew his power over a woman and delighted in it. His mouth took hers again in a hungry, masterful kiss that obliterated all thoughts of completing his work. Laure would easily have had her way and returned to his bed to spend the rest of the morning if it had not been for the sudden rap that sounded at the study door.

She groaned in disappointment as Cass cut short the heated embrace and glanced toward the sound of the intrusion.

"Tell Mozes we do not want to be bothered," Laure urged with a throaty command.

Cass grinned and eased her from his lap. "Don't be so eager, love. There is time for both business and pleasure." She affected a pretty pout as he rose and walked toward the door, as a more persistent knock sounded.

He found Mozes waiting with an envelope in his hand.

"Yes?"

"I'm sorry to bother you, sir, but a telegraph message just arrived. I thought you would want to see it immediately."

"Oh?" Cass took the envelope. "Thank you, Mozes." He closed the door and crossed the room again.

"What is it, *mon chéri?*"

"I have no idea." Cass ripped open the envelope. A frown began to form on his forehead as his eyes quickly scanned the puzzling message:

NEED HELP STOP COME AS QUICKLY AS POSSIBLE STOP BEAU.

"Is it bad news?" Laure came to stand by his side, hoping to catch a glimpse over his shoulder.

"I'm not sure. It's from Beau."

"Your brother?"

"Yes, my brother in Cherry Grove. He must be in some sort of trouble." Cass absently pitched the message onto the desk and strode briskly toward the doorway.

"Where are you going?" Laure demanded.

"To Kansas." He flung the door open and shouted for Mozes.

"*Kansas!*" Laure wailed. "But you cannot! You will be gone for weeks! And there is a party Friday night."

"You'll have to struggle through it without me," he said.

"But this is most terrible!" Laure ran out of the study, trying to keep up with his rapidly retreating form. "When will you be back?"

"I'm not sure," he murmured distractedly. "I'll let you know." Bounding up the stairs two at a time, he shouted, "Mozes! Pack my bag! I'm leaving in five minutes."

"But, *mon chéri!*" Laure paused and slapped her hand against the railing angrily as Cass continued his ascent. "*Cherry Grove, Kansas?*"

Grand Dieu! She'd never even heard of the place!

The rain was coming down in heavy sheets by midmorning as Patience and her small entourage left St. Louis. The eight younger children struggling to keep up behind the covered wagon were forced to step lively as the wheels of the large prairie schooner sluiced through the deepening mud holes.

"Keep moving, children. The rain will surely let up before long!" Patience glanced anxiously over her shoulder as she gripped the reins more tightly and urged the oxen up a steep incline. The creak of harness and leather filled the air as the massive animals labored to pull their heavy burden.

Harlon rode ahead, his hat pulled low on his forehead in an effort to shield his face from the rain. Corliss rode in the back of the wagon, popping her head out every now and then to keep an eye on the younger children. Patience could hear her calling repeated warnings: "Stay together, girls. Jesse, take Lucy's hand—she's fallin' behind again."

Because the weather was warm, the children had been instructed to tie their shoes around their waists to prevent them from wearing out the leather on the long journey. They knew Patience couldn't afford to buy new shoes this winter, so not one complaint was heard.

Phebia rode next to Patience on the wagon seat, hugging her doll, Marybelle, to her chest to protect it from the pelting rain. "Me want to go hooooome," she had been sobbing almost from the moment they'd left the city limits. "Me getting all wet!"

Patience had tried to explain that they couldn't go home—they *had* no home—but to Phebia's three-year-old mind, the journey was tiresome already. She couldn't understand why Patience wasn't doing something to ease her discomfort.

The oxen topped the rise, and Patience pulled them to a halt to wait for the children to catch up. She sat looking out at the rain-soddened horizon, trying to shake the depression that had been with her since waking that morning.

They'd been traveling for more than four hours, and she was certain they had barely covered two miles. How would she ever see them all safely across four hundred miles?

No matter how hard she tried to convince herself that she could do it, the ordeal loomed bleak ahead of her.

When the rain lets up, we'll be able to move faster, she reasoned. *If it ever lets up.* The clouds hung even lower, shrouding the earth with a dark gray mist as another heavy cloudburst assaulted them.

Harlon rode up beside the wagon and had to shout to make himself heard above the torrential downpour. "I be thinkin' it might be a good time to stop for dinner!"

"I think you're right!" Patience called back, thankful for any reprieve.

"There's a grove of sycamores 'bout a quarter mile on up the road. Looks like as good a place as any to stop."

"I'll follow you!" Patience fought to keep the animals moving as lightning streaked wildly across the sky, followed by deafening claps of thunder. Phebia started to scream as Marybelle's straw-colored hair wilted in the rain.

"Phebia, darling, Marybelle will be fine." Patience chanced a quick pat on Phebia's knee before she was forced to grab tighter hold of the reins.

Her sympathy only served to remind Phebia of how thoroughly miserable she was, and she bawled more loudly.

Patience herself was close to bawling a few minutes later when she felt the wheel of the wagon lurch, then slip deeper and deeper into a quagmire she'd been unable to avoid.

Corliss poked her head through the canvas opening. "What's going on?"

"The wheel—I thinks it's stuck!"

Climbing down from the wagon, Patience stood in the midst of the cloudburst, hands on her hips, surveying the wheel that was hopelessly mired to the hub.

Phebia was screaming even harder. There wasn't a thread of dry clothing left on Patience, and if she could have gotten her hands on Cass Claxton at that moment, she gladly would have strangled him.

Cass was traveling fast and light. His horse covered the ground in smooth, even strides despite the worsening weather. Within fifteen minutes from the time he'd received Beau's message, he'd started on his way. His mind raced with the possibilities that might await him when he reached Cherry Grove. Was Beau ill? Had something happened to his wife, Charity? Surely it wasn't their little girl, Mary Kathleen . . . She had been a healthy, rosy-cheeked infant when Cass had last seen her, but that had been more than six years ago. Had something happened to her— or maybe to the twins, Jase and Jenny?

He flanked the stallion harder, and the lines of worry on his face grew deeper. Maybe something had happened to Ma . . . or Willa, the family housekeeper . . . or Cole and Wynne.

God, he should have kept in touch with his family. How long had it been since he'd seen any of them? Four, maybe five years . . .

The horse topped a rise, and Cass abruptly pulled it to a halt. The animal was becoming winded, and Cass realized he was pushing too hard. Running the horse to death was not only cruel and senseless, but it would only cost him another delay.

He rested against the pommel of the saddle for a moment, letting the horse catch its breath and cool a little as his eyes surveyed the valley below him.

His gaze stopped suddenly as it fell upon a covered wagon in the near distance, leaning contortedly to one side. Several people milled around in confusion, while a couple of young boys tried to unhitch a cow and a goat that were tied behind the wagon. A large chicken crate remained lashed to the wagon's side, the occupants flapping their wings and cackling loudly in the confusion.

A pioneer family in trouble, Cass thought absently as he pulled aside his rain poncho and extracted a smoke from his shirt pocket.

When the cheroot was lit, he sat watching what appeared to be an elderly man and woman along with a younger woman struggling to free the wheel from its muddy confinement. He could see now that there were children, a whole slew of them, surrounding the mud hole that had firmly trapped the wagon wheel.

After studying the situation for a few minutes, Cass decided the wheel was going to be impossible to free, the way they were going about it. He shifted uneasily in the saddle, grappling with his conscience. His first instinct was to swing around the wagon and be on his way.

After all, it wasn't his problem. If he stopped to help, he could be delayed for an hour or longer, and he could hardly afford the wasted time. However, he could plainly see that at the rate they were going, the family would be stuck there until the sun came out and the road dried out.

And some of those kids sounded real unhappy. He could hear a little girl sobbing her heart out.

He pulled his hat lower on his forehead, hoping to overcome his conscience. He'd never claimed he was a good Samaritan . . . but he was a decent sort, and he knew he couldn't just ride by and ignore the situation, much as he wanted to.

Ma would wring his tail if she ever found out he'd ignored someone in trouble.

Sighing, he tossed the cheroot aside and picked up the reins. There were times he wished he'd been raised a heathen. It would have made his choice easier right about now. He clucked to his horse, figuring he might as well ride down there and get it over with so he could be on his way.

After all, how long could it take to get one wheel out of a simple mud hole?

CHAPTER 7

SIX AND A HALF WEEKS, CASS DISCOVERED. *THAT'S* HOW long he would be paying for his act of benevolence.

Riding up to the wagon, he'd quickly recognized Patience McCord and his expression had gone from guileless to horrified. "What in the hell are *you* doing here?"

Rain poured from the brim of his hat in rivulets as he sat on his horse and stared down at her. It was uncanny how this woman turned up to haunt him. He didn't know why fate had ruthlessly thrown her in his path again, but here she was, her wagon bogged down in a muddy slough, while nine children stood helplessly beside the road, looking to him as if he had just come off a mountain with stone tablets in his arms.

"Well, hello!" Patience greeted him brightly as she stood ankle-deep in mud. "How fortunate we are that you've come along!" She smiled up at him.

Eyes narrowing, Cass stared back at her coldly. "I fail to see anything fortunate about it."

She brushed the strands of damp hair out of her face, ignoring his brusque manner. She'd fully expected rudeness. "Well, as you can see, we are in a good deal of trouble. Your assistance would be greatly appreciated."

"Ha!"

Patience blushed, casting an apprehensive glance toward Harlon and Corliss, but they were so engrossed with the problem that they didn't appear to have heard the exchange. "There's no need for sarcasm," she reproved him quietly. "We are in need of a good strong back, and yours should do nicely."

Cass was about to tell her what she could do with that idea when his head turned sharply at the sound of Harlon, groaning with misery. The old man was straining against the large pole he was maneuvering in an effort to pry the wheel from the mud.

"Harlon, your heart!" Corliss said fretfully; fear for her husband's health deepened the furrows of her weathered face.

Cass glanced back at Patience, and she could see that he was struggling with his conscience.

Phebia began crying again, setting up a wail that could be heard for miles. "Me sooo wet and hungrrry!"

Her doll's flaxen hair trailed through the mud as the three-year-old dragged Marybelle by the feet in her hurry to seek comfort from Patience. Woefully the child buried her face in Patience's sodden skirt and howled.

"Please, Cass, we need your help. There are other people involved here, not just me," Patience pleaded as Margaret Ann, Lucy, and Bryon joined Phebia to comfort her.

Climbing down from his horse, Cass shot Patience a pointed look that clearly said, Just so you understand, I'm only doing this for them. Briskly he motioned for Payne and Aaron to step forward.

For the next few hours differences were set aside as they worked as a team to free the trapped wheel.

Harlon wanted to help but couldn't, so he and Corliss were put in charge of feeding the younger children their noonday meal.

More than once Patience found herself a hindrance rather than a help. Cass would gruffly order her to step aside as he and the boys heaved and tugged on the stubborn wheel. In an effort to appease him, she would obediently step away, but moments later she would be back in the thick of the action, working as hard as she could.

At one point she found her arms locked tightly around Cass's waist as the oxen, Aaron, Payne, Doog, Cass, and she formed a human chain of brute strength. She had never thought of Cass as a man—at least, not in the way most women would think of him—but the unfamiliar feel of his steely muscles pressed intimately to her bosom as they strained against each other caused a feathery flutter in the pit of her stomach, a feeling she found hard to explain.

Around three, exhausted and knowing that the animals had to have a rest, they stopped for a few minutes. Wearily they sank down onto the saturated ground to eat the fatback and cold biscuits that Corliss pressed into their hands. Since the downpour from the leaden sky had never slackened, a more substantial meal was impossible to prepare.

Patience found herself longing for a cup of scalding coffee to ward off the growing chill that enveloped her.

The children milled around, making the best of the situation, but Cass and Patience chose to eat their food in a withdrawn and uncommunicative silence.

Handing him another biscuit, Patience finally decided to make a small attempt at civility. "I'm sorry there's no coffee."

Cass accepted the offering distractedly, his mind intent on freeing the wheel and getting on his way. "I've lost a good four hours," he muttered.

"Oh?" Patience bit into her second biscuit. "Are you going somewhere?"

Cass turned to look at her balefully as rain spilled from the brim of his hat in torrents. "Now why would you think that? Isn't this the sort of day any man in his right mind would go out riding for the pleasure of it?"

She shrugged.

"Then obviously I'm going somewhere."

"Well, what a coincidence that we should happen to run into each other this way," she said.

"Yeah, what a coincidence," he returned dryly.

"It was a stroke of good luck for us. I'm sure we'll be able to free the wheel soon and then be on our separate ways." She lifted her brow inquiringly. "Where was it you said you were going?"

Cass swallowed the last of his biscuit and stood up. "I didn't say."

"Oh." It was apparent that he didn't care to elaborate, and Patience didn't want to push her luck.

"Let's get at that wheel again."

Struggling to her feet, Patience smiled back at him brightly. "I'm ready."

It was late afternoon before they managed to pry the wheel free. The old wagon lurched forward as Harlon, Corliss, and the children sent up shouts of elation.

Payne and Aaron stood back, laughingly surveying each other, and their faces broke into big grins. Only the whites of their eyes and teeth showed through the thick layers of muck encrusted on their faces.

Confident the crisis was over, Doog leaned down and scooped up a handful of mud and flung it at Jesse. The tensions of the day eased as quickly as they had come, and soon the ensuing mud war caught up everyone in its spontaneity.

Patience glanced warily at Cass, who looked no better than she, and suddenly they both joined in the fun.

Patience thought the mud balls Cass repeatedly sent in her direction had entirely too much velocity behind them, but she stood her ground and returned fire in a full-hearted attempt to go him one better.

When a truce was finally called, they were all a pitiful sight to behold. Even Corliss and Harlon were covered in mud, having been innocently caught in the cross fire.

"You look funnnny," Phebia drawled as Patience, trying not to gag, spat out a clump of mud.

"Land sakes, I never saw such goings-on!" Corliss complained. She began shooing the children to the back of the wagon where a bar of lye soap and the water barrel were waiting.

Cass followed the crowd, and belated introductions were made. Patience didn't go into detail about how she knew Cass, saying only that they'd met before.

As soon as he'd washed up, Cass walked away from the boisterous group and headed in the direction of his horse. The rain had turned to a slow drizzle as he heaved himself into the saddle and turned to leave without a word of farewell.

Patience was helping Lucy wash the mud out of her hair when she caught sight of Cass from the corner of her eye. "Margaret, come help Lucy," she said quickly under her breath. "I have something I must tend to."

Cass glanced up and saw her striding purposefully toward him. Hurriedly he reined his horse in the opposite direction, but her hand snaked out and grabbed the horse's bridle, preventing his departure.

"I want to talk to you," she stated flatly.

"Sorry, I've already wasted a whole day."

Her eyes sparked with determination, a sign that Cass had come to realize meant trouble. "I seriously doubt you'll consider what I have to say a waste of your time," she promised.

"*Anything* you have to say I'd consider a waste of my time, Miss Mc-Cord." He cut the reins to the left, and she was forced to step aside.

"Make that Mrs. Claxton," she corrected.

At first Cass thought he hadn't heard her right.

"Mrs. Cass Claxton," she repeated a little louder as he continued down his path of retreat.

The horse suddenly slowed again. Patience could see the muscles in Cass's back tightening, almost as if he knew what was coming. Without turning around, he spoke in a voice so ominous that it should have made her think twice about what she was about to do.

"*Mrs. Cass Claxton*—now what in the hell is *that* supposed to mean?" He didn't know what she was trying to pull this time, but she wasn't going to rile him.

"If you'll stop being in such an all-fired hurry to get away from me, I'll tell you what *that* means."

Cass turned his horse and walked it back to where she stood. He sat staring at her for a moment; then he slowly dismounted. His blue eyes fixed on hers with a silent warning; he prayed that her taunt didn't mean what he thought it did. "All right, what are you up to this time?"

"I need your help."

He made a disgusted sound in the back of his throat and turned to mount the horse again. "Don't you ever let up?"

She stepped forward, and her voice held an underlying urgency. "I will, I promise, if you'll help me just one more time."

He eased into the saddle and tipped his hat politely. "Can't do it, lady. Sorry. I've got troubles of my own."

Her eyes narrowed spitefully. "You have more than you think."

Cass knew he should ignore her and leave before it went any further.

She was spoiling for a confrontation, and he wasn't about to oblige her—but he couldn't ignore something she'd said.

"What did you mean by that 'Mrs. Cass Claxton' remark?" he asked, trying to remain unruffled.

She could see he was torn between tolerance and drawing his gun on her, so she decided to try a softer approach. She preferred not to antagonize him, but she wondered if that could be avoided. "You implied that you were traveling. Are you going to Cherry Grove?"

For one imperceptible instant she thought she saw his mouth slacken with disbelief. "No!"

"You're lying."

"I am not—but what if I were?" he snapped defensively. He swung out of the saddle again, deciding to stand his ground. If she wanted a fight, he'd give her one.

"You're lying. I know you are, and I want you to take the children and me to Cherry Grove with you," she demanded before she lost her nerve.

"Over my dead body," he vowed.

"Mr. Claxton, if I could have arranged that," she said calmly, "I would have long ago. I think for your benefit—and for that of your French lady friend—you'd better listen to what I have to say."

Cass shifted his weight impatiently. "Laure? What in the hell does Laure have to do with me taking you, two elderly people, and nine children to Cherry Grove, Kansas?"

"Listen and listen well, Cass Claxton. If you escort us there safely, then I in return will present you with papers confirming that our marriage has been annulled."

Cass stiffened resentfully. "You'll give them to me regardless," he demanded.

"Maybe I will and maybe I won't. It all depends on you."

Cass was still astounded that she knew where he was going. Switching subjects, he snapped, "Just what makes you so cocksure I'm even *going* to Kansas!"

"I'm not sure you are . . . I just assume you might be, since I know you have kin out that way," she said simply.

"Well, forget it! There's no way I'm taking you or anyone else to Cherry Grove. I plan to travel hard and fast. I can't be dragging along twelve other people."

"We'll keep up," she promised. "Just help us drive the team and make sure we're not killed by Indians or wolves or the like."

"Now, how in the hell am I supposed to do that?"

"You can," she said, firmly believing that even though he was a miserable excuse for a man, his knowledge of the land would be invaluable. "The boys and Harlon will keep us in fresh meat and water, and I promise we won't ask anything of you if it isn't necessary."

"Just that I get all of you to Cherry Grove with your scalps still intact!"

Patience didn't like to think of it that way, but that's what she was asking. "Yes."

"Well, lady, the day you hand over those annulment papers will be the day we'll discuss my escorting you to Cherry Grove."

"Darn it, I can't give you the papers!"

Cass turned back to mount the horse. "Then consider the subject closed."

"I don't have the papers, Cass." She lowered her eyes sheepishly. "I know you're not going to like this, but I . . . I never got around to filing for the annulment."

There! She'd admitted it, and now all she had to do was live through his fury. Once that was over, she didn't care—she was going to use the annulment as a pawn to get her brood to their destination.

She waited apprehensively for his reaction. When it finally came, it was nothing close to what she had expected.

He simply groaned, laid his forehead against the side of the horse, and beat his balled-up fist on the seat of the saddle.

"Cass?" She edged forward, extending her hand to him sympathetically, aware that her news had come as a shock. "I promise, I *will* give you the annulment . . . Please don't think I enjoy using underhanded tactics . . . but you must see that my situation is impossible without your help—"

"You never got the annulment?" His voice sounded hollow, stunned, disbelieving.

"No . . . Actually, I forgot all about you once you'd gone," she admitted. "Oh, I thought about the annulment occasionally, but to be honest, a marriage to me means a church and a gown and pretty flowers and . . . we didn't have those. Although"—her face puckered worriedly—"I suppose the vows were just as binding."

She supposed! He lifted his head to gaze tormentedly into her eyes. "We've been married for *six* years?"

She nodded hesitantly. "I suppose."

He moaned and dropped his head against the saddle again.

"But that needn't upset you," she soothed. "If you're on your way to Cherry Grove, then what can it hurt if we ride along with you? I think we could make it fine on our own, but Harlon is concerned that we need a younger man to see us through the wilds. But I promise you, the very day we reach Cherry Grove I will have my father immediately file for our annulment. There shouldn't be the slightest bit of trouble in obtaining one." She smiled. "After that, why, you'll never have to see me again!"

His head lifted, and his eyes gazed over at the covered wagon swarming with children, then on to Corliss and Harlon, who were sitting in the wagon, looking as though they were about to draw their last breath.

Escort Patience McCord and eleven others over four *hundred* miles of rugged territory? The old couple didn't look as if they could hold up for another four.

Could she force him to do this, he wondered frantically. Maybe she was lying again and in her twisted way had come up with this ridiculous scheme to blackmail him into taking her to Cherry Grove. He knew she was devious enough to try anything, and yet he wasn't sure that she would lie about anything as serious as their annulment.

Since the marriage had never been consummated, it couldn't be valid, he reasoned, trying to grasp at any glimmer of hope. The haphazard ceremony had taken place in the middle of the road at the end of a shotgun. How legal could that be? He wished now he had taken the time to find out, but the whole incident six years ago had seemed so ludicrous, and once he'd dropped her off at her Aunt Merriweather's, he'd barely thought about her again.

Maybe the ceremony hadn't been legal, and maybe he wouldn't have to yield to her high-handed tactics, but an inner voice told him that she would lie and say the vows had been consummated and then Judge Leviticus McCord would have made doubly sure that the marriage was duly recorded in the proper place in order to protect his daughter's sterling reputation.

No, as hard as it was for him to swallow, Cass was afraid she had trapped him again.

"Well? Will you help us?" Patience waited for his answer, not sure what she would do if he refused her again. She'd just played her last hand.

Cass shook his head wordlessly, too heartsick to reply. The way he saw it, he had no choice if he wanted his freedom. She had gotten the better of him.

Shooting her a look that could have sent a strong man to his knees, he began to climb wearily back onto the saddle.

"Aren't you going to say anything?" she asked nervously.

Glaring at her silently, he turned the horse toward the wagon and trotted off, his sagging shoulders clearly indicating how disillusioned he was with the world.

Patience sighed with relief. She assumed that meant he was going to help her.

CHAPTER 8

"YOU THINK THEM INJUNS WILL RIP OUR STOMACHS open with a knife, whack our scalps off till the blood runs down in our eyes, then string our guts out on the ground for the buzzards to peck on?"

Cass slowly opened one eye to stare back into a pair of solemn gray ones. "I thought you were supposed to be fetching wood."

"I was." Jesse gestured toward a small pile of limbs and twigs lying at Cass's feet. "Now what about the Injuns?"

"What about 'em?" A fly buzzed in a lazy circle above Cass's head as he lowered the brim of his hat to shade his eyes from the glare of the midday sun.

"They gonna kill us?"

"I don't think so."

"How do you know?"

Cass glanced at Patience, who was standing in the stream. " 'Cause they're never around when you need them."

Patience's lips curved into a smile as she busied herself helping Corliss and the girls with the wash. It was Sunday, a day of rest—if washing, cooking, and standing guard over the camp while the men went hunting could be considered rest.

The night before, they had been fortunate enough to have found a grove of tall pines next to a clear-running stream, and they'd made camp. After Bible study, the children wandered off to fish and swim, enjoying their reprieve from the rigors of the trail. Actually they'd made good time, considering the obstacles a group of their size was confronted with daily.

Patience's smile grew as she recalled the wide berth she and Cass had given each other. The others knew something was wrong, but no one had any idea what it could be.

Corliss and Harlon noticed the animosity between Cass and her, but they were polite enough to ignore it. Patience knew Harlon was too relieved to hear that Cass had agreed to travel with them to ever question why.

At least one thing was going right. Patience had been relieved to see the children take to Cass right away. Sometimes she worried that he might lose his temper with them, but she thought he'd shown a surprising amount of forbearance for their constant chatter and endless curiosity.

Aaron and Payne were clearly in awe of this man who seemed to know everything, and they were never far from Cass's side.

Phebia was the only one who still held herself at a distance. Although Cass had made several attempts to win her trust, she was still skeptical when it came to the tall, dark stranger who had come so suddenly into their lives.

But all in all, the days were beginning to settle into a routine, and Patience was thankful. She was beginning to think that her worries were groundless, that the trip might be made without incident.

She pretended to be unusually absorbed in her work as she listened to the conversation taking place a few feet from her.

"Bryon, leave my gun alone."

Bryon's inquisitive fingers had persistently crept over to explore the shiny Colt revolver Cass wore strapped to his right leg. The weapon was an enduring source of interest to the boys, who were familiar only with the old-fashioned muzzle-loading rifle Harlon kept in the wagon for protection.

Moments later Patience heard Cass warn Bryon again as the child's curious fingers began to creep in the direction of the pistol.

Even Doog and Jesse were eyeing the weapon with a determined look in their eyes.

"Can't you see Cass is trying to sleep?" Payne admonished the smaller boys. He was leaning against the trunk of a tree whittling a new whistle for Joseph. "Why don't you go find something to do?"

"Don't want to," Bryon said disagreeably.

"Then let's take a nap," Aaron threatened. He wanted to sleep too, but the younger children were making it impossible.

"Don't want to!"

Four-year-old Joseph walked up and straddled Cass's chest. "Don't want to either!" he joined in adamantly.

Satisfied that no one was going to get any sleep, Cass sighed as he sat up and lifted Joseph from his chest.

Corliss raised her head and admonished sharply, "You children, git! Let Mr. Claxton rest!"

"It's all right, Corliss. I promised Harlon I'd help him fix the broken harness," Cass said.

"Now that you're awake, will you show us your gun?" Bryon persisted.

Patience had to turn her head to keep from laughing aloud.

Even Margaret and Lucy glanced up when they saw that Cass was going to oblige. Dropping articles of clothing they'd been scrubbing, they scampered quickly from the stream as the shiny gun came out of its holster.

Cass squatted down on his haunches as the children gathered around him. Only Phebia, clutching her doll, chose to stand to one side and watch instead.

"A gun can either save your life or take it," Cass began. "You have to learn to respect whatever kind you decide to carry. This particular pistol is what they call a percussion revolver." He checked to make sure the cylinder was empty before he passed it to Aaron.

The young man's hands trembled with excitement as he examined the weapon closely.

"The fascinating thing about a percussion revolver is its fire power. Like a breech-loading weapon, a revolver can be loaded and fired rapidly. You can place six shots in the cylinder of a percussion firearm and fire it in a matter of seconds. That's quite an improvement over the time it takes to fill the chamber of a muzzle loader with powder and ball and cap it," Cass explained.

Doog, Jesse, and Bryon pushed closer, eager for their turn to hold the gun.

Aaron reluctantly passed the pistol to Payne for his inspection.

"But Mr. Claxton," Margaret Ann said primly, "isn't that dangerous?"

Cass flashed a crooked grin at her. "Yes, but like anything else, you have to take the bad with the good. There's a possibility of the revolver discharging several chambers at once. The flashback of hot powder and gases from the gap of the barrel and cylinder could seriously injure a man."

Lucy flinched and moved closer to Cass, draping her arm protectively around his neck. "Throw it away," she insisted. "Me don't want you hurt! I wove you!"

Patience wasn't surprised to hear Lucy's flourishing declaration of love. Clearly she'd been enamored of Cass from the moment he'd joined them.

"*I* don't want you to be hurt. I *love* you," Patience said absently, correcting the child's diction as she wrung out a muslin petticoat.

At the sound of her voice all heads shot up, and the chatter ceased.

Patience glanced up, startled to see that they were all staring at her. She flushed a deep scarlet when she noticed Cass's eyes fixed on the front of her dress. Her color deepened as she wondered exactly how much the wet material revealed of her breasts.

Cass met her disconcerted gaze, and his eyes danced devilishly as he recognized her discomfiture. Then she realized the cad was amused by her innocent blunder! They'd mistaken her statement for a declaration, not a simple correction.

Even Corliss had misunderstood. She stood gaping at Patience, long johns dripping a wet path down the front of her dress as she wondered if her hearing was failing her. It was the first time she'd heard Patience say one decent word to the man!

"Land sakes! You all know what I meant," Patience snapped before she dropped her head sheepishly and returned to scrubbing the collar of Harlon's flannel shirt.

The children's attention returned to the pistol, but Patience's unsettled feeling lingered. She noticed that though Cass continued to talk to the children, his eyes repeatedly strayed to the front of her dress.

Other than the fact that he was a man, she could find no other reason to explain his sudden preoccupation with her bosom. He had certainly given no prior indication that he'd noticed her except as a major annoyance to be painfully endured, yet the way he was looking at her now . . .

She ignored the tingling sensation at the bottom of her stomach but grimly conceded that, try as she may, she was finding it increasingly hard to ignore the fact that he was an exceptionally attractive man.

Patience wasn't aware of just how serious the attraction had grown until she stepped out of the wagon a couple of mornings later and saw him stripped to the waist, shaving.

She stood in the shadow of the canvas, staring at him as he lifted his chin, eyed himself in the small mirror tacked to the tree, and drew the straight-edged razor across his cheekbone.

The sight of his bare chest covered with a mat of curly, light brown hair caused her mouth to turn dry.

Other than her father's, Patience had never seen a man's chest—and most assuredly Leviticus McCord's chest had been nothing like the one she now found herself staring at.

She shook away the disturbing comparison, ashamed of herself. She should be about her work, not ogling the man, but her eyes refused to budge from the tight ridge of muscles that rippled along his arms when he leaned closer to the mirror to carefully shave his upper lip and then around the long, dark sideburns.

How many women had been held against that chest, and how many had explored those ridges of steel-banded muscles at leisure? Patience found herself wondering. The lovely French girl, Laure Revuneau, popped unexpectedly into her mind, and Patience felt a stirring that was very close to jealousy as she wondered how many times Laure had been held in Cass's arms and been adored and caressed by him . . .

Patience was startled to find that the question both intrigued and annoyed her, and she hurriedly forced her feet into motion.

It didn't matter how many women had been in her husband's life. He'd made it clear to Patience that *she* would never be one of them, no matter how badly she was beginning to wish that she'd started out on a better footing with him.

Patience walked around the wagon, pretending not to notice him as she filled the coffee pot and swung it over the fire.

Corliss appeared, and they exchanged greetings. Corliss started flapping the skirt of her apron and making clucking noises as she gathered the six white chickens, five hens, and one rooster that she released from the chicken coop each night. The chickens seemed to sense when it was time to move on, and they flew up into the portable coop at the sound of her voice.

Giving both women a perfunctory glance, Cass said good morning as Phebia came around the corner, dragging Marybelle by her heels.

"Poor Marybelle's going to have a knot on her head," Cass observed as Phebia came to a halt beside him. She stood staring up at his imposing height silently.

Cass finished shaving and reached for a towel to wipe the stray remnants of shaving cream from his face. Reaching for his comb, he noticed Phebia still staring at him.

"Something I can do for you this morning, Miss Phebia?" Patience was amazed at the way he handled the child's continuing reticence, allowing her ample time to warm to him. He would make a wonderful father, she realized, and was surprised by her observation. A few months ago she wouldn't have wished him on her worst enemy, let alone an innocent child.

Phebia remained silent, but a few moments later Patience saw her tug at Cass's trouser leg.

He glanced down, and Phebia cautiously extended the rag doll up to him. After a brief examination, Cass discovered that Marybelle was missing an eye.

He reached for his shirt, slipped it on, and acknowledged soberly, "Well, this looks serious."

Motioning for Patience, who had been listening to the exchange while she'd dropped slabs of bacon into a large iron skillet, he ordered briskly, "Nurse, prepare to operate."

Playing along with his theatrical manner, Patience dramatically passed the fork to Corliss and went to the wagon to fetch her sewing box.

Moments later Marybelle lay on a large, flat rock, her one remaining eye staring sightlessly up at the three onlookers.

A new button that almost matched the old one was hastily located, and Nurse McCord set about her work. Phebia watched with round eyes as Patience's nimble fingers worked the thread in and out of Marybelle's tender cotton face, proving without a doubt to be a true angel of mercy as her skilled hands efficiently provided a new eye for Marybelle.

After the operation was completed, the patient was resting comfortably —though with one green and one blue eye.

But to Phebia she was as beautiful as ever. Even before Patience could pronounce the patient fit, Phebia had already scooped the doll into her arms and begun squeezing her tightly.

Cass reached for his hat and adjusted it on his head as he smiled down at the elfin three-year-old. "You know, Phebia, if you carry Marybelle in your arms instead of letting her face drag on the ground, she'll be likely to keep her eyes longer."

Phebia started to skip happily away when she suddenly paused and turned around. Slowly she walked back to where Cass was standing. Crooking one finger, she motioned for him to lean down.

Thinking she was about to reward him for saving Marybelle's eyesight, he obligingly crouched to her level, where the child's brown eyes somberly met his blue ones.

Suddenly her forefinger and thumb darted out and clamped onto his nose like a vise and twisted. Cass teetered backward as he felt a rush of scalding tears flood his vision.

"Phebia!" Patience dropped her sewing basket and bolted forward to break the child's hold.

Her fingers wrestled with the child's to break her steely grip as Cass wobbled back and forth, trying to retain his balance.

Finally Phebia gave his nose one final jerk, then calmly released it, stuck her thumb in her mouth, and skipped away to join the other children.

Cass fell backward onto the ground and lay prostrate for a moment. He had fought with men the size of giants and had come out in better shape. He looked up to find Patience standing over him, grinning.

"What in the hell is so funny? That kid nearly took my nose off!"

"I think that's Phebia's way of saying she accepts you," she offered.

"Accepts me!" His fingers moved to check his smarting nose for broken cartilage. "I'll have to blow my nose out of my ear from now on. She's maimed me for life!"

Patience extended her hand to Cass. He grasped it and she pulled him to his feet, trying to ignore the way her heart jumped when their hands touched.

"You know something?" he asked, irritably slapping the dust from his pants with his hat.

Patience had to work hard to keep a sober face. His nose was fairly glowing. "What?" she replied, wondering if his eyes had always been that blue. They were beautifully expressive, even though what they were expressing at the moment was an anger that could make him spit nails.

"That kid reminds me of you!"

The comparison hit her the wrong way. Patience whirled and started back to the fire to help Corliss with breakfast. She wasn't about to pursue that remark because no matter *what* she did, he managed to find fault with her. Even though she'd gone out of her way to be nice to him lately, he hadn't bothered to say one kind word to her. His attitude was beginning to hurt her feelings.

"Don't walk away from me while I'm talking!"

"When you say something worth hearing, I'll listen," she tossed back over her shoulder.

"Women!" Cass muttered to himself as he watched her stalk angrily toward the wagon. He rubbed his throbbing nose dourly. At least he was thankful that Phebia had picked a less sensitive spot to pound than Patience had those many years ago.

His eyes inadvertently focused on the gentle sway of Patience's hips, and he was shocked to feel a faint stirring in his loins. The image of her at the stream, and her small, firm breasts revealed through the bodice of her wet dress came rushing back to agonize him further.

Damn! That was all he needed! It wasn't enough that she'd thrust the responsibility of nine children and two old people on him. Now all of a sudden *she* was beginning to look good to him!

Resettling his hat on his head, he walked to his horse and began saddling it.

His eyes strayed back to camp where Patience was bending over the fire, stirring eggs. Had she always been that good-looking, or was he just getting desperate for a woman's company?

Giving the cinch a hard jerk, Cass decided that it had to be the latter. Or at least he prayed that it was. Surely the Lord knew he'd had enough troubles.

CHAPTER 9

UNFORTUNATELY, TROUBLE CONTINUED TO PLAGUED Cass the next morning. He had reluctantly agreed to keep an eye on the child while Patience, Corliss, and the other children went to gather the last of the wild berries.

While he shaved, Phebia played with Marybelle around his feet. He had to sidestep twice before he could convince her that she should go feed Marybelle a late breakfast and get out of his way.

To his relief, the child bought the idea and raced to get a biscuit from the supply box. She sat on a nearby rock, taking intermittent bites, then squashing crumbs into Marybelle's unyielding mouth as Cass finished his shaving in peace.

As he was wiping soap from his face, he heard Phebia let out a scream that raised the hairs on the back of his neck.

He whirled. "What's wrong?"

"Caw-doo. Me want caw-doo."

Cass stared back at her blankly. "Caw-doo?"

She nodded succinctly.

"Caw-doo, caw-doo," Cass murmured as he glanced around the camp, wondering what in the hell *caw-doo* meant.

"Caw-doo!" Phebia demanded, her tone becoming more belligerent.

"Caw-doo . . ." Cass was getting frantic. A thought came to him, and his heart nearly stopped. Kneeling beside the rock where Phebia sat perched, he whispered hesitantly, "Did you do something in your britches?"

Lord, he hoped that wasn't it. He'd never had to deal with something like that before, and he wasn't sure he could.

Her eyes narrowed, and her face puffed with indignation as she shook her head and cried again. "Caw-doo!"

"Okay. Caw-doo." Relieved, Cass starting grabbing anything in sight, trying to figure out what she wanted.

He held up her bonnet.

She shook her head no.

He held up the remainder of the biscuit she'd been eating.

"No!"

A bar of soap.

"No!"

A towel.

"No! Caw-doo!"

"Why don't you sit there and suck your thumb until Patience gets back?" he said, knowing that he shouldn't be encouraging her to continue a habit that they'd all been trying to help her break, but he was stumped.

Phebia stood up and stamped her foot authoritatively, clearly outraged by his stupidity. "Caw-doo!"

Cass could feel the sweat beginning to trickle down his back.

After several more futile attempts, he finally sat down on the rock beside her, admitting defeat. "Phebia, I'm sorry, but I just don't know what you want."

He glanced up, relieved to see Aaron returning with a bucket mounded with berries.

"Hi."

"Aaron, what in the hell does *caw-doo* mean?" Cass asked wearily.

"Water."

Cass looked up, startled. "Water?"

"That's what she calls water." Aaron grinned at Phebia. "You want a drink of water, squirt?"

Phebia nodded eagerly. "Me want caw-doo!"

Cass watched as Aaron led her to the bucket and reached for the dipper.

Caw-doo, he thought irritably. Damn! He could have sworn that it would be something a child would step in, not drink.

A new, more disturbing kind of trouble arrived as four men came riding into camp around dusk the following evening.

It was a small party of buffalo hunters: one hunter, two skinners, and a cook. Their red wool shirts were dirty; their corduroy breeches stained; and the high Western boots they were wearing hadn't seen a coat of polish in years.

Corliss and Patience, happy to welcome company, cordially invited the men to stay for supper.

The hunters accepted their gracious offer and went about settling their stock for the night.

Had Cass been in camp, he would have sent the raw-boned buckskinners on their way. He felt nothing but contempt toward buffalo hunters.

The unscrupulous white hunters could present the first real threat to the group traveling by wagon. If there were Indians in the area, the sight of the hunters would be sure to provoke their fury, so when Cass, Aaron, and Payne rode in from hunting that night, Cass was none too happy to discover the four unwashed strangers in their midst.

"Patience, I want a word with you!" Cass ordered as he swung from his horse and handed the reins to Aaron.

He acknowledged the visitors' presence with a cool nod as he strode through the camp.

Patience rolled her eyes. Wiping her hands on her apron, she whispered to Corliss dryly, "The king has bellowed again."

Corliss chuckled. She was concerned and yet amused by the couple's open hostility toward each other. She and Harlon discussed the strange alliance nearly every night. Although they had no idea what was causing the couple to behave with such animosity toward each other, it was evident to them that Patience was attracted to Cass Claxton and that Cass was attracted to Patience. However, they had agreed that these young people were so mulish that they'd go to their graves before either of them would admit it.

Corliss knew that Harlon was beginning to fret about the growing stand-off between Patience and Cass. He'd taken an instant liking to the handsome young man who was deftly leading the group to its destination. More than once, he'd confessed that he hoped Cass might take a shine to Patience.

Corliss remembered Harlon's remark last night: "I just don't understand them, Corliss." He'd been brooding over the young couple while he was getting ready for bed. "Cass ought to be drawn to Patience like a magnet. She's pretty and smart, and I've never met a woman with a kinder heart. But instead of being attracted to each other, they both turn tail and run in opposite directions when one of them sees the other one coming."

"It's worrisome," Corliss had admitted. "They'd make a mighty fine couple. He's handsome, and she's as comely as a fairy-tale princess—and decent too. That little gal has worked hard to keep those children together. I tell you, Harlon, Cass Claxton could do worse than take Patience McCord as his wife."

A smile touched Corliss's lips as she remembered the way Harlon's faded eyes, for just the briefest of moments, had held a rejuvenated sparkle. "You know, Mama, her determination and zest for life puts me a whole lot in mind of you when you were her age."

Corliss found her face growing rosy at the way he'd looked at her. She hadn't seen that look in his eyes for a long time. "Oh, go on, now—I was never that pretty," she'd scoffed.

"You were," Harlon insisted. He gave her a jaunty wink that made her cheeks turn even brighter. "And you still are. Why, if it weren't for me being so bone-weary, I'd just prove it to you!"

Corliss knew that would be unlikely, but the thought was nice.

"My, my, aren't we feisty tonight?" Corliss said as she'd turned down the sheets and prepared to climb onto the feather mattress. His lighthearted banter had made her feel giddy—almost young again.

Harlon stood and stripped off his pants before climbing between the cool linens next to her.

"I hate to say it, but I've about come to the conclusion that it's Patience's age that's scaring Cass away." He'd removed his spectacles, folded them, and laid them on the floor of the wagon beside the bed. "She's in her twenties, you know, and the bloom has gone out of most women's cheeks by that age. Most are married by then and have children of their own. While Patience is still as pretty as a rose petal in the mornin' dew, I think her age is what's got Cass a little bit skittish."

"Could be," Corliss had acknowledged before yawning sleepily. "And her spunk might be worryin' him. I think it has him feelin' a mite cornered at times."

Harlon chuckled. "Yes, Patience's 'spunk' has had Cass more than cornered a couple of times."

They had lain quietly in the darkness, listening to nature's restful symphony outside the wagon. A smile tugged at the corners of Corliss's mouth as she recalled the days Harlon had courted her.

Those had been happy days, exciting days. 'Twas a real shame Patience couldn't experience that same joy, she mused. Lord knew, if anyone deserved happiness, Patience did. Corliss didn't know Cass well, but he seemed to her to be a decent sort of man. He was polite, always complimenting her after each meal, and doing more than his share of the work so that Harlon wouldn't have to overdo.

She concluded that it was just a shame that two such fine people were spitting at each other like two tomcats sitting on each other's tail.

Corliss's attention returned to the present as she heard Cass impatiently shout for Patience again.

"Better go see what he wants," Corliss encouraged. "Margaret Ann and I will see to the biscuits."

"It better be important," Patience muttered under her breath as she handed the spoon to Margaret.

She found Cass preparing to wash for supper. He'd stripped his shirt off, causing her another flash of momentary distress.

Why his bare chest should fascinate her she wasn't sure. She just knew that it did so increasingly.

"Don't you ever keep your clothes on?" she snapped.

He glanced up. "Who stepped on your tail?"

"No one stepped on my tail . . . I'm just concerned that the girls may see you this way."

He lifted a brow inquisitively. "Is that the reason for your concern, or does it fluster *you* to see me without a shirt, Miss McCord?"

"The name is *Mrs.* Claxton," she reminded in a carefully controlled tone, just in case he'd forgotten that she still had the upper hand, "and of course it doesn't 'fluster' me to see you without your shirt. I've seen jackasses without saddles before."

For a moment she thought she saw a hint of a smile involuntarily tug at the corners of his mouth, but then he turned away and began pouring water into the enamel washbasin. "I see you're in another one of your aggravating moods."

"Did you want me?" she said curtly. He had no right to ride into camp and bellow out for her as if she were his handmaiden.

"Afraid not, but it looks like I have you anyway." He glanced up as he reached for the bar of soap, unperturbed by her waspish disposition.

Patience could see the tight play of muscles in his forearms as he began to work up a thick lather. "I don't have time to play games. What do you want?"

"I see we have company."

"Then apparently there's nothing wrong with your eyesight."

He leaned over and scrubbed his face and neck with the white lather as he continued. "Do you know who those men are?"

Patience wasn't sure if it was disapproval or mere curiosity she was hearing. Her eyes traveled the width of his broad shoulders and lingered there.

"No . . . I mean, I assume they are four weary travelers who'll appreciate a hot meal and a bit of pleasant conversation."

Cass rinsed off his face and neck and reached for the towel. He rubbed the cloth over his face, eyeing her dispassionately. "Well, you assume wrong."

She found her gaze unwilling to leave his bare torso. There were tiny droplets of water interspersed throughout the cloud of light brown hair splayed across his chest. A thin line of the same hair ran down toward his trousers and disappeared into—

Patience caught her shameless reflections as her gaze dropped sheepishly to study her clasped hands. "Then who are they?"

Without taking his eyes from her, Cass reached for a clean shirt and slipped it on. "They're buffalo hunters."

Her gaze lifted back to meet his. The revelation meant nothing to her. "So?"

He finished buttoning the shirt, and with his eyes still firmly fixed to hers, casually unbuckled his belt. He made no attempt either to divert her attention or attract it as he loosened his pants and begin to tuck his shirttail into the heavy denim.

She was appalled to discover that his actions not only brought a disquieting lurch at the bottom of her stomach but caused her to grow uncomfortably warm.

"So," he mimicked softly, "by inviting those particular men to supper, we're now likely to attract the attention of every redskin within a fifty-mile radius."

Why was her heart suddenly hammering in her throat, she thought wildly, barely hearing his answer. He would surely see her reaction to his blatant maleness, and wouldn't that give him a good laugh, she agonized. Patience McCord practically swooning over him!

She could feel the color flooding her cheeks. "I'm . . . sorry . . . I didn't know . . ."

It occurred to her that he might be deliberately amusing himself. He knew what she was thinking, and he was taking delight in her wantonness! Yet nothing in his gaze indicated such deliberate cruelty. On the contrary, if Patience hadn't known better, she would have sworn that he was looking at her with the same undeniable interest that she felt toward him.

For an electrifying moment blue eyes seared deeply into violet ones, and Patience was aware of nothing more than his overpowering presence and the uneven cadence of her breathing.

Then, as if they simultaneously realized what was happening, their gazes split from each other. Cass reached for his hat as Patience eased to a safer distance on the far side of the makeshift washstand.

The incident left her puzzled and shaken. She found it hard to concentrate as Cass picked up the conversation in a tone that made her wonder if the events of the past few minutes had touched him at all.

"The harm is already done," he said. "We just have to hope there isn't a scouting party on these hunters' tails."

"Why would Indians follow them?" Patience was confused.

"Because they hate them. Unlike the Indian, who kills the buffalo for his own survival, the white man kills for business and pleasure." He picked up his gun belt and buckled it around his waist as he talked. "The Indians depend on the buffalo to supply medicine, cooking utensils, blankets, garments, boats, ropes, and even their tents. They use the sinews to make bowstrings and thread for sewing. Shoulder bones are used as hoes, and rib bones serve as sled runners. Even the animal's hooves are boiled down for glue. After the tribe has enjoyed the fresh meat of the kill, the women cut the meat into strips and hang them on racks to dry in the hot sun."

"To make jerky?"

"That's right, jerky. Later they pound it into powder and make pemmican, which will keep for years. Although there's still an abundance of buffalo roaming the plains, every buffalo killed is a direct threat to the Indians' existence. The white man's irresponsible slaughter continues to drive the herds farther afield, and I've heard some predict that the time isn't far off when the vast herds roaming the land will be only a memory."

"That seems impossible," Patience mused. "I've heard my father tell stories of seeing thousands of buffalo as they traveled across the plains."

Cass shrugged. "I'm sure that's true, but that will change. If the white man continues to kill buffalo for personal gain, how many will be left in ten, twenty years? Trust me, the Indian will do everything in his power to kill the men who threaten his survival."

"So if the Indians discover that we befriended the hunters, then our lives may be in danger?"

Absently he dusted his hat against the side of his legs. "No 'may be' about it. Our lives are in danger."

"Oh, Cass . . . I'm sorry. Corliss and I were just trying to be neighborly when we invited the hunters to stay for supper."

"Patience, I want you to listen to me." His tone was firmer than she'd ever heard it. "There's another danger I want you to be aware of. By their appearance, I figure these men have been on the trail for a while. My guess is they've been on a hunt somewhere in Kansas, Colorado, or Oklahoma, and they're on their way home. Now, I want you to heed what I'm about to say: A beautiful woman will be hard for them to ignore." His eyes locked with hers gravely. "I want you to go out of your way to avoid any personal contact with these men. Serve supper, then disappear and let Corliss and the girls clean up."

"All right." Her pulse fluttered at his admission that he found her attractive. Did he really think she was beautiful?

"With a little luck, those men will be on their way in the morning, and nothing will come of your misplaced hospitality. I've seen signs of a small wagon train ahead of us, four, maybe five, wagons traveling together. To be on the safe side, I think we'd be smart to catch up and travel with them for a few days."

"What about the Indians?"

"You let me worry about the Indians. You just do what I say and leave immediately after the meal. I don't want to have to save your hide if one of those men decides to haul your little fanny off for a romp in the woods."

Though he sensed that she was smart enough to see the wisdom of his advice, Cass waited for her chin to lift with her usual show of rebellion.

He didn't have to wait long.

"You sound as if you care what happens to my 'little fanny.' "

"*Your* little fanny?" He threw his head back and laughed. Patience gritted her teeth in an attempt to control her temper. She was trying hard to show him that she was not the same irresponsible, headstrong girl she'd been six years ago, but at times this man simply pushed her too far.

"Honey, if I were interested in lookin' for a fanny, I'd find me a sweet-talking woman," he assured her.

"Like Laure Revuneau?"

His sly grin spoke louder than words. "Like Laure. Now, there's a fine woman."

"Are you going to marry this fine woman?"

To her gratification, the question momentarily stilled him. "You didn't answer my question."

He tipped his head subserviently. "How could I marry anyone, my lovely, when it seems I am already encumbered by a previous commitment?"

"Well, you don't have to worry about me," she snapped. "I can take care of myself."

"I'm not worried. Even if a man in a moment of lunacy took a wild fancy to you and dragged you away, you wouldn't be gone long. After he spent a few hours in your company he'd be hauling you back so fast it'd make your head swim."

"Is that so?" She could feel herself slipping, but Cass was infuriating her. Squaring her shoulders, she made sure his eyes could easily detect the ripe fullness of her breasts. While she wasn't as well endowed as some, the good Lord had provided ample ammunition to back up her next volley.

"Well, how would you know what a *man* would do with me, Mr. Claxton?"

Unperturbed, Cass's eyes traveled lazily over the bait she was offering. Not that he hadn't noticed her charms before—he had. And he had to admit she wasn't all that bad. But he wasn't about to let her know it.

"Well?" she demanded. She had waited long enough. She knew he couldn't deny that she was a full-grown woman, and she wanted the satisfaction of hearing him say it.

"Well"—his gaze moved over her dispassionately— "is there something in particular that I'm supposed to find impressive?"

Her eyes narrowed warningly.

"Oh . . . I'm supposed to notice that you've . . . developed?"

"That's right. You might notice that I've grown up in the past six years."

"Is that a fact?" He took a step backward as she took a step forward. Indeed she had blossomed from what he'd remembered. He grew uneasy as he felt the first stirrings of longing.

"That's a fact," she confirmed.

Patience knew her Aunt Merriweather was probably rolling over in her grave by now, but she was determined to prove her point. Cass was the only man who had ever dared to ignore her. Men had been known to fawn over her and shower her with extravagant compliments to snare her attention. They had begged for her hand in marriage, but she had blithely broken their hearts. She had never met a man who matched her in spirit, with maybe the exception of this man, and *he* wouldn't even concede that she was a woman!

"Tell me, Mr. Claxton," she said, arching her back and tilting her breasts higher to attract his gaze. "Exactly in what way do you find them lacking?"

"Since I hadn't noticed 'them' before, and I'm certainly not interested in 'them' now, why are we going to all this bother?" he asked mildly.

Their gazes met in a defiant deadlock. "Are you saying you're *flustered* by them, Mr. Claxton?" she challenged.

"Only by the fact that 'they' are in my way and 'they' are delaying my supper."

Determined to beat him at his game, she edged closer. "Most men would be curious to know how well their wives are endowed," she dared. "But, then, maybe you're not a man."

He eased back a step, but their bodies were touching, and the objects of contention were pressed firmly against the front of his shirt.

"I don't have a wife," he stated calmly.

"Legally you do. But even if you didn't, you're surely man enough to at least be curious."

"But, Miss McCord," he reminded softly, "only moments ago there seemed to be doubt in your mind that I am a man."

"Mr. Claxton, you haven't shown any proof to the contrary." Her heart was fluttering and her legs were threatening to buckle, but she wasn't going to back down from him.

He smelled of soap and water and leather, and he was heart-stoppingly male. Why was she provoking him this way, she asked herself. Why wasn't she trying discreetly to catch his eye instead of trying blatantly to knock it out?

"Well, now, is that what all this is about?" Calmly he removed his hat and laid it on the washstand.

Her eyes widened as he turned and captured her breasts in his hands, exploring the soft mounds with breathtakingly slow strokes.

"You needin' a man, Miss McCord?" he murmured. His arrogance seared her, but she was mesmerized by the cobalt blue of his eyes.

He drew her closer but warned himself to go easy. This was only a game, one that he knew could quickly get out of hand. Though she rankled him, she was all woman—and he had been without the pleasures of one for weeks now.

"Let's just see how much woman you are, Patience McCord." His mouth lowered to graze hers softly. Her mouth tasted sweet and heady, and he had to remind himself that the purpose of this experiment was to teach her a lesson.

Patience's voice caught in her throat. The touch of his mouth sent fire racing through her veins. She could feel herself growing lightheaded and giddy. How long was she going to let this go on? And why had she taunted him, she thought frantically. He was not the sort of man who would permit such affronts to his manhood without turning the tables—she should have known that!

Cass felt her body go limp against his, and the sudden realization that she was not immune to his caress sent a feeling of masculine pride through him. He jerked her closer, surprised to discover how tiny she was. She felt exquisite and delicate pressed tightly against his large frame.

Willing to let her feel the unexpected effect she was having on him, he settled her closer between his legs, ignoring her murmur of protest. With a proficiency she found appalling, he slowly began to undo the buttons of her dress, one by one.

"If we're wantin' to consummate our vows, honey, don't you think we should find a little privacy?"

Gasping, she jerked away, her eyes flashing angrily. "You brute! *What* do you think you're doing!"

He stared back at her guilelessly. "Why . . . isn't this what you wanted? I'm only tryin' to keep my little wife happy."

"You're disgusting!" She spat out the words contemptuously. Her fingers were trembling so badly that she could hardly work the tiny buttons back into place. "We were talking about those *hunters* abducting me!"

"Oh, yes." His gaze lightly caressed her breasts. "Well, rest assured, Miss McCord, I have no interest in anything you might have. If one of those hunters should threaten you, I'll just be keeping my end of the bargain if I'm forced to rescue you. You do recall the bargain? I'm to escort you to Cherry Grove safely, and you'll hand me those annulment papers." He reached out and tweaked her cheek mockingly as she turned her face away.

"Miserable polecat!" she flung back angrily, forgetting all about the attraction she'd felt toward him just moments earlier.

He flashed her an exasperating grin. "What happened? I thought I was a weasel."

"Polecat is just one name for your miserable species!"

She whirled and nearly stumbled into Margaret Ann, who had silently approached the warring couple.

"What is it, Margaret Ann?" she demanded in a shaky voice.

"Corliss said to tell you supper's ready."

Shooting Cass a nasty glance, Patience picked up her skirt and marched away.

Cass was not as unscathed by the encounter as he would have hoped. His eyes followed her shapely form as she walked back to camp. He could still taste her on his lips, and he had a feeling that sleep wasn't going to come easily tonight.

"You comin', Mr. Claxton?"

"I'll be along in a minute, Margaret Ann," he said absently, reaching into his pocket for a smoke. A frown deepened across his forehead as he cupped his trembling hand against the breeze and lit the cheroot.

Leaning against a tree, he waited for the unexpected reaction Patience had caused in him to subside before he joined the others for supper.

He tried to sort out the confusion of feelings she stirred in him and decided the idea of a man carrying Patience off might not be so far-fetched.

She wasn't so bad. Actually, she'd developed into a good-looking woman.

He took another drag off the cigar. Too damned good-looking.

After supper the children gathered around the hunters' wagon, where gazing at .45 Sharps rifles, along with Winchesters, Remingtons, and Springfield trapdoor models held them spellbound.

Payne picked up one of the more than fifty Green River and Wilson skinning knives lying in the bed of the wagon and turned it over in his hands reverently. The wagon contained too many bull, calf, and cow hides to count.

"You say you've been in Colorado?" Harlon asked as he sat down next to the fire to light his pipe. He could hear the old cook begin to recite the tall, adventurous buffalo tales that were designed to make the children's eyes grow round with wonder.

"Yep, up near the border," Hoyt Willis replied as he stretched his long legs out before him and propped his head back on the seat of his saddle. His stomach was full, and he'd removed his boots for the first time in a week.

"I'd figure, with fall right around the corner, you'd be wanting to stay longer." Harlon assumed the hunters would follow the Indians' custom of hunting buffalo in September when the cows were fat and their wool the thickest.

"We'll be back once we've had time to visit our families and collect our money for the hides."

"You independent or working for someone?"

"Independent."

"Got a wife?" Harlon asked.

"A wife and ten young 'uns just waitin' for their papa to get home."

Harlon, who judged the hunter to be close to forty, thought the man stank something terrible. His shirt was saturated with animal blood and pieces of flesh where he'd wiped the skinning knife. His body was filthy, and his beard appeared to be matted to his face. Harlon hoped this man was thoughtful enough to take a bath and change his clothes before he saw his family again.

The night sounds closed in around them as the two men relaxed. The fire popped as a piece of wood burned through, sending a shower of sparks flying.

Hoyt's thoughts wandered to Patience McCord. He'd been disappointed that she'd upped and disappeared right after supper. His eyes hadn't left her all night as she'd moved around, ladling out stew and slicing corn bread.

Her waist was so tiny that Hoyt knew he could span it with both hands, and the thought of her in his bedroll brought a powerful surge to his groin.

The time he'd spent in a local thirst parlor in Hayes a few weeks ago suddenly seemed a long time ago. The measly couple of hours—and five dollars he'd paid for a crib woman in a curtained box in the back of the room—had barely slaked his hunger.

Images of the blond beauty with the violet eyes who'd darted curious looks at him during the evening meal rose to taunt him again. He could feel the tension in his body begin to build.

Damned if he wouldn't like to have her alone for a couple of hours.

"Where did the woman go?" he asked Harlon casually.

"Corliss? Why, I imagine she's getting ready for bed."

"Not your wife. The other one."

"Patience?"

"Yeah, Patience."

Harlon drew on his pipe and noticed it had gone out. "I'm not rightly sure . . . Why?"

"No reason." Hoyt tipped his hat over his eyes. "She and the Claxton man hitched?"

Harlon chuckled. "Nope."

"He seems right protective of her."

"Yes, that's his job."

A slow smile curved the corners of Hoyt's mouth. "She's not married, huh?" The thought sent a surge of anticipation through him. Was she still a virgin, he wondered. He reached to draw a horse blanket over the front of his breeches to cover the incriminating evidence of the path his thoughts had suddenly taken.

"Nope, she's not married."

Hoyt rolled to his side and settled his head more comfortably against the makeshift pillow. "Right nice-looking woman," he commented.

"That she is," Harlon conceded.

"Yessir." Hoyt's mouth curved into a satisfied smile as he settled deeper under the blanket. "Right nice."

CHAPTER 10

THE HUNTERS CLEARED OUT RIGHT AFTER BREAKFAST the next morning. Cass was relieved to see their dust. He neither cared for nor trusted the one called Hoyt, for he had a feeling the man could be as mean as sin if he took a notion to be.

Patience was still clearly peeved about the encounter she'd had with Cass the night before. Her anger was simmering barely beneath the surface as she went about breaking camp.

Cass ignored her. He hadn't slept but a couple of hours, and his disposition wasn't the best this morning.

Beau's telegram still worried him, coupled with the fact that he'd had to make two trips to the stream last night just to cool off.

That rotten Patience McCord. He could wring her neck for starting her silly "see how I've bloomed—too bad you can't do anything about it" nonsense.

He vowed he wouldn't allow himself to be caught up in another situation like that, no matter how much she egged him on.

He crouched beside the wagon to check the left front axle as Patience came sailing around the corner carrying a pan of dirty dishwater.

The sight of him with his usual cheroot wedged at a cocky angle in the corner of his mouth set her off again. Determined to avoid another scene with him, she whirled and started off in the opposite direction, but suddenly her footsteps slowed.

Cass was preoccupied with the wheel, unaware that she was even in his vicinity. Pursing her lips, she struggled against the overpowering urge to fling the greasy water at him.

It would serve him right for treating her the way he had last night, she fumed, though she knew if she did, it would be tantamount to waving a red flag at a salivating bull. But he *deserved* every nasty, revolting, repulsive, obnoxious ounce of water in this pan.

Before she fully realized it, she was tiptoeing closer to the wagon. When she was within firing range, she straightened and reared back to take aim. Cass stood up and turned to face her just as the water came soaring out of the pan, headed straight in his direction.

His features went blank momentarily before what she was doing finally registered. His eyes widened in disbelief as he dodged to one side in a vain attempt to avoid the onslaught, but his defensive action came too late.

The dishwater hit its target squarely on the bull's-eye, leaving a trail of soggy bacon rinds dangling limply from the front of his drenched shirt.

Jerking herself upright, Patience could see that he was livid. His cigar sputtered, then sent up a limp trail of smoke from the solid dousing.

"Dammit, Patience!"

She looked at him with round-eyed innocence. "Oh, my, I'm so sorry. I didn't see you."

He spat the soggy cigar onto the ground, then squared his shoulders wryly. "Like hell, you didn't see me! You always throw dishwater on the axle!"

Out of the corner of his eye, he caught sight of a revolting chunk of garbage dangling from his shoulder. He angrily flicked it off.

She smiled smugly. "Well, sometimes I do." She shrugged, ignoring the blistering looks he was sending her way. "Guess we'd better be getting a move on."

She turned as he began peevishly fanning the front of his shirt, mumbling things under his breath she was sure a lady wasn't supposed to hear.

"Sure has started off a fine day so far," she observed offhandedly.

He was still eyeing her with hostile intent as she sauntered away, swinging the empty dishpan in one hand.

Around midmorning the wind started to blow. Aaron was driving the team while Corliss rode on the seat next to him. Patience walked behind with the children.

Harlon wasn't feeling well this morning—summer complaint, he thought—so about an hour ago he'd climbed into the back of the wagon to catch a short nap.

Patience kept falling behind to oversee Lucy, Bryon, Joseph, Phebia, and Margaret Ann as they paused to gather armloads of wildflowers that grew wild along the pathway.

Cass rode his horse a good distance behind, keeping a close eye on the group. He'd seen nothing to indicate that Indians were in the area, but he knew that didn't mean they weren't there. Nor was he convinced he had seen the last of the hunters; he had a nagging suspicion that he hadn't. But for now, the small group was moving along smoothly. Any threat of trouble seemed remote for the time being.

As the wind picked up, he found his attention drawn more to Patience's skirt than to anything else. The heavy gusts would snatch up the flimsy cotton and toss it as high as her head, providing Cass with a glimpse of her shapely legs.

He tried, but found he couldn't ignore the recurring flash of bare skin that was as provocative—and as arousing—as any he'd ever seen. Although he hated to admit it, she was beginning to disturb him.

By the time her skirt soared a third time, his temper had risen along with other parts of his anatomy. It was plain he wasn't going to be able to cope with this misery all day.

He nudged his horse's flanks and quickly rode up beside her.

"Why aren't you wearing pantalets?" he asked.

Patience glanced up startled. "What?"

"Where are your pantalets?"

She drew back defensively. "I beg your pardon! What business is it of yours where my pantalets are?"

Truth was, she hadn't had the heart to put them on this morning. Her dress covered her decently, and it was just too hot for anything else. Besides, what she wore or didn't wear was certainly none of his business! The man had his nerve questioning her about her personal attire, she thought, but then, anything that scoundrel said shouldn't shock her anymore.

"Haven't you heard of sewing buckshot in your hem to keep your skirt from flying over your head?" he challenged in a tone that was almost belligerent.

She lifted her chin stubbornly. "No, I haven't heard of sewing buckshot in my skirt to keep it from flying over my head," she mimicked hotly.

"Woman, you're driving me over the edge."

"It wouldn't be a very long journey, now would it—"

Patience suddenly felt herself being scooped off her feet by a pair of incredibly strong arms and placed solidly in the saddle with him.

"*What* do you think you're doing? Put me down this instant!" she demanded as the children stopped walking and began watching the skirmish with wide-eyed fascination.

He had her wedged tightly between himself and the saddle horn. She was straddling the saddle, her skirt riding above her knees now. They were so close she could feel the solid imprint of his maleness pressing against her backbone.

She felt her stomach tighten as the reason for his outrageous actions suddenly dawned on her. The swine! He had been ogling her!

She twisted to confront him. Their faces were inches apart. The familiar smell of soap, leather, and maleness washed over her as she took a deep, self-righteous breath and said in a disgusted rebuke, "You should be *ashamed* of yourself!"

He grinned, aware that she'd guessed his motive, but not in the least disturbed by it. "That will be the day!"

"You . . . you heathen!" She struggled to free herself from the evidence of his blatant masculinity, angry to realize that she was actually thrilled by the effect she was having on him.

"You might as well pipe down," Cass warned. "If you don't have the good sense to keep yourself covered, then I suppose I'll be forced to see that you do."

"What do you mean *covered!* I was covered! I can't help it if your perverted mind—"

"Payne, you'd better see to Jesse and Doog. They're wandering too far ahead," Cass reminded, interrupting her heated tirade as he calmly reined the horse back in the direction he'd come. He gave the horse a little kick, and it trotted off, with Patience still protesting loudly.

"This is an outrage, and I demand you put me down this instant!" she railed.

To her dismay, Cass threw back his head and gave a wicked laugh, nudging the horse to an even faster gait. She gasped indignantly as she felt his hands slip beneath her breasts to steady her, then grow more daring as the soft mounds fell in and out of his palms with the horse's jarring gait.

"How *dare* you!" She struggled to salvage what little pride he'd left her as he laughed again and pulled her roughly against the front of his protruding breeches.

"Talk about an outrage—just look what you're doing to *me*, Miss McCord!"

"You . . . you barbarian!"

Undaunted, Cass pulled her closer to nuzzle her neck, calmly pointing out, in case she hadn't noticed, who had the upper hand this time.

Her hand shot out to slap his face, but he quickly thwarted the move.

"My, my!" he taunted with a crooked little grin. "I think the lady protests too much!" He drew her even more tightly against his maleness, his tongue beginning to explore the outline of her ear.

To Patience's horror, she felt herself growing limp in his arms. She *hated* what he was doing—or did she love it? The rogue was making her feel giddy and light-headed, and . . . and . . . unusually warm . . .

"You're disgusting!" she spat out, but Cass noticed she was struggling less now. His hands masterfully began roaming all over her body, delighted with her reaction.

"You're not going to pretend you don't enjoy my company," he murmured.

Patience kept her eyes fixed stoically ahead of her. "I don't enjoy it—I hate it!"

"Of course you do," he cooed sympathetically. His fingers lightly brushed the tightening tips of her breasts. "It's your little ol' body that's screaming for mercy," he whispered suggestively.

"Cad!"

"Liar!"

"You're perfectly disgusting, and while you may think you're bothering me, you couldn't be farther from the truth," she maintained loftily.

Lord, she wished he'd keep his hands to himself!

"Ah, my lovely, if you only knew how disgusting I can be!" he murmured, letting his tongue slide exquisitely over the delicate lobe of her ear. Chills ran up her spine, and she vowed she would get even with him for this outrage. His hand traveled lazily down the length of her rib cage as he whispered in low, soothing tones, "I can assure you, you would love every appalling moment in *my* bed!" He heard her soft intake of breath, and he chuckled.

"I want you to put me down!" she gritted through clenched teeth. She was appalled he could get to her this easily.

"Well, anything you say, darling."

Before she knew what was happening, she went sailing off the horse, hitting the ground with a solid thud.

"Cass Claxton!" she wailed.

Cass sat on the horse, grinning. At her!

All of the unexpected commotion caused Corliss to stick her head out of the back of the wagon. "Everything all right back here?"

"Everything's fine, Corliss. Miss McCord just insisted on walking again." Cass tipped his hat at Patience. "Don't tire yourself, darlin'."

Corliss looked blank for a moment, then shrugged and dropped the curtain back in place. She failed to understand what was going on.

Lucy grasped on to Margaret Ann's hand, looking as if she might burst into tears at any moment, as Patience picked herself up out of the dirt and stalked toward the wagon.

"Don't worry, Lucy," Margaret Ann said primly, but she looked a little concerned herself. She draped her arm around the smaller girl maternally. "I'm sure the weasel knows exactly what he's doing."

Late that afternoon the wagon topped a rise, and they spotted a small caravan traveling about a mile ahead. Cass was relieved to count five wagons and fifteen to twenty head of cattle in the train.

"I'm going to ride ahead and see if they'd mind if we joined them," Cass told Harlon.

"Seems like the smart thing to do," Harlon agreed. "We'll wait here until we get a proper invite."

Thirty minutes later Cass returned bearing the news that they'd been awaiting: They were welcome to join the wagon train.

That night, six wagons formed the customary pear-shaped corral, the pole of each wagon pointing outward, and the hub of the fore wheel of the next wagon set close to the hind wheel of the wagon just ahead of it. The exact placement of the wagons formed an enclosure large enough to pen the animals belonging to the train. It also provided defense: Indians rarely attacked a train when in corral.

The women of the train quickly formed a comfortable relationship. When the children had been safely tucked in that night, they sat around the fire, stitching handwork and exchanging small talk. The men enjoyed their pipes and cigars while they discussed the weather and how many hostile Indians they were likely to encounter.

It was decided that they probably wouldn't encounter any Indians until they reached Oklahoma. That bit of news relieved Patience because they would be leaving the wagon train when it reached St. Joseph, to veer north to Kansas.

She glanced up from the quilt she was piecing as she heard Cass excuse himself, saying that he was going to turn in early.

Ernest Parker's teenage daughter sprang to her feet to say good night. It was evident from the look in the young beauty's eyes that she'd developed an immediate case of puppy love for the dark, blue-eyed, curly-headed stranger, who promptly rewarded her with a smile guaranteed to melt any woman's heart.

Patience watched Cass's departure with mixed feelings. The events of that afternoon still lingered with her. It made her heartsick to admit that she'd actually enjoyed riding with the brute! The feel of his body pressed tightly against hers, the sensation of muscled thighs holding her firmly in place, masculine hands gripping hers solidly to prevent her from scratching his eyes out—all this had left her feeling unsettled. She had to admit no other man had ever touched her life in quite the same way, making her feel so aware, so vibrantly alive . . . so in need of . . . something.

She'd had to remind herself twice just this evening that she would be three times a fool if she were to let herself fall in love with Cass Claxton. He was a rogue and a rakehell who'd treated her as badly as she'd treated him.

When they reached Cherry Grove and she provided him with the annulment papers, she was certain that that would be the last thing he'd ever want from her, and she was confident she would never see him again.

She recognized he had every reason to want her out of his life, but the realization didn't make her growing feelings for him any easier to bear.

Why did I do the things I did, she silently agonized. *Why couldn't I have been the perfect lady, one who would have captured his heart instead of his ire?* Now it was too late to hope he would ever see her as anything but the rotten, despicable, strong-willed girl he thought her to be, and in her heart she couldn't blame him.

By an act of defiance and deceit, she still shared his name, but it was a woman like Laure Revuneau who would share his bed and eventually win his heart.

Ernestine Parker's lovesick gaze was not the only one that followed Cass's tall form as he strode toward the wagon tonight.

Patience was ready to admit, at least to herself, that she was falling in love with the very man she'd so foolishly forced to marry her.

And there was nothing she could do to hold it back.

The following morning Lucius Waterman's voice rang out a warning: "Steep hill comin' up!" And it ricocheted down the line of wagons.

Patience eased the team to a halt as Cass rode up beside their wagon.

"Better let Aaron take the reins. Looks like there could be trouble," he said.

Patience shaded her eyes from the hot sun with her hand and squinted back at him. "Do you think he can handle the team?"

Aaron was wiry and slight of build, although he insisted he was as strong as two grown men put together.

"He can handle it," Cass affirmed before he rode ahead to assess the hill. It was a bad one, steep, with little room for error. A frown creased his forehead as he tried to determine the safest angle of descent. There didn't seem to be one. Having the wagon fall and smash beyond repair while being windlassed down the steep grade wasn't something he cared to think about.

He returned as Patience climbed down from the wagon. Dismounting, he removed his hat and ran his sleeve over his forehead. "Get the children together and keep them at a safe distance," he said quietly. "Tell Harlon and Corliss they'll have to walk down the hill. I don't want anyone near this wagon except Aaron and me."

Patience's eyes lifted to meet his expectantly. "Is it that bad?"

"It isn't good," he admitted as he adjusted his hat back on his head. "Then I'll drive."

"I want you to do as I say. Aaron and I will take care of the wagon. You and the children stay back."

Realizing it wouldn't do any good to argue, Patience went in search of the children while Cass took Aaron aside.

She could see the two talking, and her heart filled with pride. It was almost as if he *were* her husband, instructing their son in a lesson of manhood. A terrible sense of dread began to fill her. If either one of them should be hurt, she didn't think she could bear it.

The train was alive with activity as the women called out to children and men started unloading some of the heavier pieces from the wagons and setting them beside the road.

When two of the women realized they were parting with their family heirlooms, they began crying and begging their husbands for compassion. The men managed to continue though they kept apologizing and assuring their wives that they were only doing what had to be done.

Since Patience and Corliss had brought nothing but the bare necessities, the McCord wagon was ordered to the head of the line.

"Payne, you and Jesse scout around for a full-sized pine tree," Cass instructed as he knelt to check the left front axle. There was even less lubricant in the hub than when he'd checked earlier that morning. "Doog, go tell Patience I need the bottom side of a bacon slab."

"Yessir!" Doog scampered off as Harlon hurried over to help. By the time Doog returned with the requested bacon rind, Harlon and Cass had removed the white oak wheel. Cass took the bacon fat and carefully wrapped it around the hub axle. Moments later the wheel was slipped back into place.

"Think that'll work?" Harlon asked.

"It should."

"Mr. Claxton?" Ernestine Parker stood at Cass's heels, her eyes wide with worry. "You do be careful, you hear?"

Cass winked, sending the poor girl's pulse thumping wildly. "I plan to do just that, Ernestine."

Payne and Jesse returned with the news that they'd found the full-sized pine.

Reaching for the ax, Cass told Payne to grab the long hemp rope lashed to the back of the wagon and follow him. The tree was quickly felled, then fastened to the back of the wagon to serve as a brake.

When he was confident that everything was in order, Cass swung up onto the seat of the wagon beside Aaron. He removed his hat and wiped his forehead on his shirt sleeve. "Well, I can think of things I'd rather be doing."

Aaron swallowed nervously. "Yeah, me too."

Cass turned to face him with a slow grin. He'd formed a real affection for the boy. "I suppose you know all about the birds and the bees?"

Aaron frowned and then grinned sheepishly. It seemed a strange question for a time like this, but he supposed Cass was just trying to make things seem normal. "Well . . . uh . . . there's a couple of things I've been meaning to have you clear up for me."

Cass chuckled ironically. "Son, there's a couple of things I still don't know."

Aaron's grin widened. "Yessir!"

"You've noticed that pretty little Ernestine Parker, haven't you?"

Aaron's Adam's apple bobbed as he flushed a deep red. "Yessir . . . a little."

"A little, huh?"

"Yessir . . . a little."

Cass grinned, deciding the boy was relaxed enough to start. "You about ready to get this wagon down the hill?"

"Yessir!" There was a slight tremble in the young man's voice, but Cass saw that his hands were steady as he picked up the reins.

His eyes locked on Cass with silent admiration. Aaron had never known his father, but if he had, he thought he'd have wanted him to have been exactly like Cass.

"Then let's get this over with so the women can stop their fidgeting."

"Yessir."

"I want you to take it real easy. Keep the reins good and tight, and ease the animals down real slow. The tree will act as a drag, but it's up to you to see that the animals don't get away."

"I can do that, sir."

Cass clasped one of Aaron's thin shoulders confidently. "I know you can."

Cass stepped off the wagon and turned to give a sharp whistle, indicating that they were ready to take the first wagon down. The other members of the train stopped what they were doing and came to watch.

"I'll need a couple of volunteers," Cass called out as he pulled on a pair of leather gloves.

Matt Johnson and Lewis Brown stepped forward. They were young men with strong, sturdy backs.

Glancing around to see where Patience and the children were, Cass found them standing off to the side, looking worried. Patience tried to smile as her eyes sought to convey confidence to Aaron. He was young to have so much responsibility thrust upon his shoulders, she thought sadly.

Aaron could feel sweat trickling down the back of his shirt as he gripped the reins so tightly that his knuckles began to turn white.

"Okay, son, let's—"

"Cass!" Patience suddenly shouted.

Cass glanced up. "What?"

"Please . . . be careful!"

He nodded curtly, surprised that, for a change, she wasn't cheering for him to fall down the hill and be trampled by a herd of longhorn.

"Let 'em roll!" he shouted.

The wheels on the wagon began to turn as Cass, Matt, and Lewis latched onto the rope tied to the tree, letting their weight act as an additional drag.

The crowd of onlookers held its breath as the wagon began to laboriously descend, rattling loudly down the incline. The hill wasn't long, just incredibly steep.

Aaron gripped the reins, keeping his eyes fixed straight ahead. Sweat poured down the sides of his dust-streaked face as he urged the animals in low, soothing tones to take it easy.

The harness creaked and the wagon tongue clanked as the team strained to control the heavy load. Overhead, clouds began to block the sun as a threat of rain sprang up.

Cass watched the clouds, praying that a thunderstorm wouldn't develop before they'd gotten all of the wagons safely down the hill.

Patience held her breath, trying to ignore the tight band of fear suddenly gripping her middle. Her heart was in her throat, and her eyes were riveted on Cass. She could see the muscles in his arms bunching tightly as he strained against the rope, while the weight of the wagon dragged him and the others helplessly down the hillside.

Patience wished she could take his place, that the dangers he was facing could be hers. It wasn't fair that he might be injured . . . or perhaps killed trying to help her.

Suddenly the wagon began to pick up speed, moving faster and faster. The anxious shouts of the men echoed through the countryside as Aaron threw all of his weight against the reins, trying to force the animals to slow down. A fierce gust of wind nearly pulled the canvas off the wagon as the first clap of thunder sounded.

Patience closed her eyes and began to pray aloud in a frenzied litany. "Don't let them be hurt, don't let them be hurt, don't let them be hurt . . ."

The minutes seemed like hours, and the heat closed in around her. She felt light-headed and faint, and the children's excited voices seemed to come to her from far away.

Suddenly a whoop went up, and Patience felt her knees buckle with fear.

"They made it!"

Her eyes flew open. Tears of relief began to stream down her cheeks when she saw that the wagon was safely at the bottom of the hill. She could see Cass, his clothes filthy now, but blessedly safe and sound, calmly untying the rope in preparation for the next wagon.

A flurry of clamoring feet swept her along in their wake as the children rushed down the hill to meet him.

Margaret Ann and Lucy descended like a whirlwind, throwing their arms around his waist, nearly dragging him to the ground in their exuberance.

Aaron hopped from the wagon, his flush of victory and his wide grin assuring the others that he was going to be hard to live with for a while.

Ernestine, who'd been headed for Cass, stopped and blushed prettily when Aaron turned his smile in her direction. He winked, a gesture he'd picked up from watching Cass, and her face turned a deep crimson.

"Was that fun?" Doog prodded Cass eagerly, his eyes conveying his deep longing to be old enough to do such an exciting thing.

"Never had so much fun," Cass teased as he tried to control the girls who jumped around his feet like grasshoppers.

Margaret Ann demanded a hug, then Lucy, then Phebia, and of course, Marybelle. Cass knelt down to good-naturedly oblige the ladies, though he was wary of Phebia's intentions. She still had an unnerving way of latching onto his nose when he least expected it.

Patience breathlessly arrived as Cass finished the hugs and stood up. With a cry of relief, she threw herself into his arms. "Oh, Cass . . . I thought you were going to be killed!"

His arm tightened around her as naturally as if he'd held her a hundred times before. "Why would you think that—"

She prevented him from finishing his sentence as she grasped the back of his head and hugged him with all her might. For a moment he froze. Then he pulled back as his startled eyes met hers.

Patience hadn't realized what she was going to do. She hadn't planned to reveal the depth of her feelings, but now she realized she was glad she'd done it. And she would die if he cast her aside in front of the children.

Cass's eyes filled with amusement, and a grin started at the corners of his mouth as he recognized the alarm growing in her eyes. "Why, Miss McCord," he challenged softly, "I didn't know you cared."

"I . . . I didn't know either," she confessed.

His amusement disappeared, and the blue of his eyes darkened as he contemplated the meaning of her admission. "Well, well, what do you know about that!"

She held her breath as he looked at her. It was as if he were seeing her for the first time.

Their gazes continued to do silent battle, and she prayed that he would be kind. Her eyes unashamedly issued a plea, one Cass found himself strangely powerless to refuse.

He glanced down at the children and winked; then, gathering her in his arms, he hugged her warmly. "Thank you, Miss McCord. Sure do appreciate your concern," he bantered.

For a moment she was caught by surprise, but then she enjoyed the unexpected. He felt exactly as she thought he would: splendidly male, superbly masculine, exciting, stimulating—wonderful.

She sighed as she stood on tiptoe, her arms encircling his neck more tightly.

"Thank *you*," she whispered into his ear.

If it hadn't been for the children, Patience would have stayed in his arms forever. But the sound of their embarrassed giggles broke the spell. Cass heard the children's snickers and suddenly broke the embrace as quickly as it had begun.

Clearing his throat, he tried to ignore the tittering still coming from the children. "Storm's about to break. I've got other wagons to see to," he said gruffly.

A new, headier thrill shot through Patience as she realized that he was as shaken by the encounter as she was. "Yes, of course," she murmured.

He turned to the children, who were still chortling. "If you children don't have anything better to do than stand around giggling at the old folks, I'll find something to occupy your time," he warned.

They squealed and scampered in all directions.

Patience watched him walk up the hill with her heart shining in her eyes. *The storm's already broken, Mr. Claxton*, she thought with a grin. *You just don't know it yet.*

CHAPTER 11

Sunday was a cool, overcast day with the wind blowing from the west.

Around noon Harlon was fording a creek when his horse lost its footing and fell. The sudden impact threw him, and in its struggle to regain its footing, the horse rolled on Harlon's leg and broke it. Cass had set the leg that evening.

It was just one of those accidents that can happen on the trail. Apart from Cass's concern for the old fellow's recovery, he realized that the accident meant there would be one hand fewer to help with the work.

At seventy-five, Harlon's bones were brittle and slow to heal. It could take months—or longer—before he'd be on his feet again. But everyone agreed that he was lucky to have come out of it with his life.

They had been on the trail for five weeks, and Cherry Grove was a little more than a hundred miles away. Cass was confident that he could get by without Harlon's help. Aaron and Payne were old enough to accept extra responsibilities.

The October mornings had a nip to them now. Cass knew it wouldn't be long before Indian summer would give way to the howling winter winds. But they should reach their destination long before that, so he wasn't concerned.

After supper that evening he walked to the back of the wagon to visit with Harlon, who lay on a mattress looking peaked, with his foot propped up on a pillow.

Patience had brought along a little bluemass for emergencies, but Cass could see that Harlon was still suffering.

"Can I do anything for you, Harlon?"

"Thanks, son, but I can't think of a thing I need."

Cass perched atop a bundle in the wagon and lit a smoke.

"I'm much obliged to you for settin' the leg," Harlon said. "I told Corliss I don't know what we'd have done if you hadn't been here to help us."

"You don't need to thank me. I was glad to help."

"You've been a real godsend to Patience—well, to all of us. I hope you know that."

Cass appreciated the praise but found he was uncomfortable with it. "Patience is a strong woman. She'd have made it with or without my help."

Harlon's old eyes twinkled. "She's not as strong as you might think, boy."

Cass was discreetly silent, and Harlon could sense he would prefer to drop the subject. Deciding to oblige, he glanced at the splinted leg resentfully. "I could just kick myself for breakin' this dad-burned thing! I won't be no use to anyone now," he complained.

Cass smiled. "Don't worry about it. It'll heal."

"Well, I shore hope so. I don't want to be no trouble to anyone."

"You're no trouble."

Harlon reached for his pipe and smoked in silence for a while, enjoying the distant sounds of someone strumming on a guitar.

"Gettin' colder," Harlon observed.

"Yeah."

"Seen any signs of Indians?"

"I saw a scouting party a few days ago."

"Think they'll be givin' us any trouble?"

"They watched us for a while, but they lost interest pretty quickly."

They listened to the voices of Patience and Margaret Ann as they approached the wagon.

"Margaret Ann," Patience was saying, "before you go to bed I want you to run over and ask how old Mrs. Medsker is this evening." The elderly woman had been ailing during the noon hour, and Patience was concerned that she might need something.

"Yes, ma'am," Margaret Ann replied and skipped off to do as she was told. She was back within minutes. "Mrs. Medsker said she didn't think it was any of your doin's how old she is," Margaret relayed.

Cass grinned as he heard Patience's sharp intake of breath before she hurriedly skirted Margaret off to Winoka Medsker's wagon to explain the misunderstanding.

"How come a nice-looking chap like you never took a wife?" Harlon asked. It seemed to him that a man Cass's age ought to have his own children's mistakes to chuckle about.

"Guess I just haven't found the right woman yet."

Harlon thought of Patience again and wondered if Cass wasn't missing a good opportunity to start a family.

"Harlon, I'd like to talk to you about something."

"Certainly."

"I guess I'm asking your advice."

"All right."

"Hoyt Willis has been following us for days."

Harlon glanced up, a frown furrowing his forehead.

"Is that right?"

"What do you think he wants?"

Harlon drew on his pipe thoughtfully. "Hard to say."

"I've been wondering whether I should let it pass or pay a visit to Mr. Willis one of these evenings."

"I don't know, son. The man 'pears as ornery as a freshly castrated bull to me."

"I don't want him disturbing the women," Cass warned.

"No, we couldn't put up with that."

"What do you think I should do?"

"Well, I think I'd wait him out. If he shows any sign of wanting to cause trouble, you can deal with him then. There's no use raisin' a stink if the man's merely travelin' the trail with us."

"Yeah, guess you're right."

"Just keep a close eye on him."

"I plan to."

Harlon drew on his pipe again, sending a plume of smoke rolling out of the wagon. "You don't suppose the women have noticed him?"

"I don't think so. Patience would have mentioned it if she had."

As much as Patience irritated him, Cass didn't want her subjected to a man like Hoyt Willis.

Harlon sighed. "Well, maybe we're just borrowin' trouble."

Cass's gaze followed Patience as she and Margaret Ann emerged from the Medskers' wagon. He didn't know why he found Hoyt Willis's presence so disturbing, but he did.

"Yeah, maybe we are."

But even Aaron mentioned Hoyt Willis's continuing presence a few days later as he watched Cass saddling his horse.

"Have you noticed that skinner's been following us for days now?"

"I've noticed him."

"What do you think he wants?"

Cass shrugged.

"You think he has his eye on Miss McCord?"

Jerking the cinch tighter, Cass frowned. "I think if he's fond of wild-cats, he's on the right trail." He swung in the saddle and adjusted his hat low on his forehead.

"You're not worried about him?"

"Not in the least."

Aaron grinned. He knew that it wasn't indifference toward Miss Mc-Cord that made Cass so sure of himself. It was plain old know-how that gave him the confidence to face up to any situation that came his way.

"Mind if I ride behind your saddle this morning?" Aaron asked.

"You're not driving the wagon?"

"No, sir. Miss McCord said she was going to."

"Then climb aboard."

As the horse trotted through camp, Cass spotted Patience rolling up the night's bedding and storing it in gutta-percha sacks.

Their gazes met, and he tipped his hat mockingly.

She stuck her tongue out at him.

"Miss McCord's a right fine-looking woman, isn't she?" Aaron remarked as Cass spurred the horse into a gallop.

"I suppose she'd do in a pinch," Cass allowed in a disgruntled tone.

Aaron's grin widened. He figured that Cass meant it'd depend on just who was doing the pinching.

Toward late afternoon the train of wagons stopped to water the stock in a wide brook they'd happened to find. The cool, clear water felt heavenly as the people splashed it onto their sunburned arms and faces. The children's delighted squeals were heard for more than an hour as they laughed and played in the bubbling water. Just as they were loading to leave, a new wagon came rolling in.

"Oh, brother!" muttered Patience irritably as she saw that the old buckboard was decked with an outrageously gaudy yellow-fringed awning.

It was a wagonload of fallen angels.

The women of the train hurriedly gathered the children and herded them into the wagons in an effort to shield their young eyes from the unsavory sight of *those women.*

A few of the husbands grudgingly followed suit, but not without one or two curious glances at the new arrivals.

However, the less-than-cordial welcome didn't dampen the spirits of these soiled doves. They piled out of their buckboard and headed straight for the water.

Within minutes they were cooling their ample assets in the stream, oblivious to the resentful looks fired in their direction. There wasn't actually a beauty in the lot, but that didn't seem to discourage the men's rapt attention.

Patience kept a close eye on Cass as he and Aaron sat on the horse with their eyes glued to the spectacle going on before them.

Even Payne's and Jesse's eyes were rounder than usual as they peeked around the corner of the wagon. Corliss hollered for them to *git*, and their heads quickly disappeared.

A buxom redhead seemed determined to capture Cass's attention. She gave the handsome stranger her come-hither smile, displaying her dazzling white teeth and full cherry-red lips as she dipped her lace handkerchief into the stream and let the cool water slowly trickle down into the deep, deep, deep—Patience wasn't sure it was ever going to reach bottom —crevice of her blouse.

Cass's mouth curved into a lazy smile as his eyes trailed the path of the water enviously. He leaned closer to the pommel, taking a slow drag on his cheroot.

It was clear to Patience that the redhead had snagged his undivided attention.

"Afternoon, ma'am. Mighty hot today."

"Yes, it is," she agreed in a sultry Texas drawl.

"You ladies traveling far?"

"Far 'nuff." She lowered her lids demurely. "Where you-all goin'?"

"Kansas."

"Sure 'nuff? Why I have a dear old grandma who lives in Wichita."

"That so?"

"Sure 'nuff. Are you by any chance going to Wichita?"

Cass shook his head, his eyes still traveling leisurely over her provocative display of swelling flesh. "No, ma'am, afraid not."

"Well, that's too bad . . . Listen, sugar, we'll be stopping not far down the road tonight. Maybe you'd like to drop by, so I could give you a letter to mail to my dear, sweet grandma once you reach Kansas." Her smile suggested that a letter was the last thing she planned to give him.

Patience had heard enough. Her hand reached for the bullwhip under the wagon seat. She stood up, whirled it around her head a couple of times, and let it fly.

Cass heard the deafening crack of the whip about the same time his cigar splintered into oblivion.

Stunned, he lifted his blank gaze to encounter Patience's snapping eyes as bits of tobacco fragments swirled to the ground.

"It's time to be on our way," she spat out.

The butt of his cigar dropped from his lips and rolled down the front of his shirt before it dawned on him what had happened. His face turned crimson, and for the first time in his life he was speechless.

Patience wielded the whip a second time, and the wagon lurched forward. The other drivers followed suit, and the train started moving again.

Once they were out on the trail Patience glanced back to see if Cass and Aaron were following. She was relieved to see that they were, but they were trailing at a distance.

"Guess I showed that cow-bagged Jezebel that she best not mess with my husband and expect to get away with it," she muttered tightly under her breath as she swung the whip again and sent it blazing over the oxen's heads.

She realized that her temper had gotten the better of her, that she'd gone too far this time. Cass would be mad as a hornet and probably yell at her for embarrassing him in front of the whole wagon train that way, but he'd deserved it.

A grin finally escaped its bounds as Patience recalled the horrified look on his face when he'd realized what she'd done.

But he *sure 'nuff* had it coming.

Camp was quieter than usual that night. Since Mort Harrison had the first watch, he was preparing to take up his post.

Meanwhile, Buck Brewster sat beneath a tree, playing his violin, a sweet, lilting refrain that floated pleasantly through the wagons.

Cass lay on his bedroll, looking up at the stars. It was a clear night, and the heavens were ablaze with God's handiwork.

Aaron and Payne had rolled up beside Cass tonight. He sensed that the two boys had something on their minds, but he could wait until they were ready to reveal whatever it was that was bothering them.

"You got a pa?" Aaron asked.

"My pa died just after I was born," Cass replied. "He was huntin' one day, and his gun went off accidentally. The bullet hit him in his left eye. The men he was with said they didn't think the wound killed him but that he died of a heart attack from the shock."

"I think mine's dead too," Payne admitted, though he couldn't be sure. He had been alone for as long as he could remember.

"Sure would be nice to have a pa to talk to or maybe a ma," Aaron mused.

"Mothers are special," Cass admitted, remembering his own mother and how long it had been since he'd last seen her.

A few minutes passed before Aaron finally broached the subject uppermost in his mind.

"Cass . . . those women we saw today . . ." As he sat up his voice trailed off hesitantly.

Cass felt himself start to grin and quickly squelched the urge. These boys were on the verge of manhood, eager to taste the fruits of life. They didn't have a pa to confide in, so Cass guessed he'd been chosen to answer their questions. "What about them?"

"Well . . ." Aaron cleared his throat, "they were prostitutes, weren't they?"

"Yes, they were."

Aaron was quiet for a moment, and Payne sat up. "A man's not supposed to be with that kind of woman . . . is he?"

"Well, I guess it depends on the man. Some men take their pleasure where they find it, while others prefer to find a good woman and settle down and raise a family."

"The Good Book says prostitutes are evil," Payne reminded them.

Cass nodded and added quietly, "The Good Book also says 'Judge not, lest ye be judged.'"

"Have you ever been with one of those women?" Aaron asked.

Cass sat up and reached into his pocket for a smoke, wishing the conversation were a little easier to handle. "Rule number one: A gentleman never says who he's been with."

"Even if he's been with one of them harlots?"

Cass eyed Payne dryly as he lit the cheroot. "You seem to be well versed on this subject."

Payne flushed. "Well . . . I saw this book one time . . ." He stopped and grinned sheepishly.

"Well"—Cass fanned the match out—"a man don't go spreadin' it around, especially not if he's been with one of those harlots. But the kind of woman you'll want to tie up with will smell like wildflowers after a rain; she'll have skin as soft as cotton; and her hair will feel like French silk when you run your fingers through it. She'll be gentle by nature, and she'll have a way of making a man feel eager to come home to her at night."

"What about the other ones?" Payne asked. He already knew what he was *supposed* to want.

"The other ones aren't that bad either," Cass admitted.

"Then you've been with the bad ones?" Aaron asked quietly.

"Boys, there are few 'bad' ones. Some are misguided, and some do what they have to to survive. Women have different natures. One will have needs as powerful as a man's, and the next one might shy away from the bed until she's properly wed."

"Which kind do you prefer?" Payne prompted.

Cass preferred not to answer that one. "I treat all women with respect, and I'd suggest you do the same. When you bed a woman, you treat her like a lady, no matter what other people think of her. And if you should accidentally father a child, then you must be man enough to accept your obligation. My brother Cole always taught me and my other brother that a man's a son of a bitch if he does any less."

The three lay back in unison to stare at the stars for a while, mulling over what had been said.

"What kind of woman do you think Miss McCord is?" Payne asked.

"Payne, she's a good woman!" Aaron gasped. "Isn't that so, Cass?"

"I would imagine."

"Don't you know?"

"Not really." Cass realized he didn't know anything about Patience, other than she was like a burr under his saddle most of the time. What sort of woman was she, he wondered. Beautiful, yes, he couldn't deny that. Over the last six years, she'd become a lovely, desirable woman, charming when she wanted to be, and a blessed saint when it came to dealing with children.

She showed no signs of being the spoiled-rotten, self-willed girl he'd been forced to marry, except when she had to deal with him.

However, the kiss they had unexpectedly shared had been warm and full of promise, revealing another side of Patience McCord that he'd never considered before. Would she please a man in bed? Cass feared she would—only too well. Had he enjoyed her kiss? He couldn't deny that it had stirred him. He couldn't deny that he'd liked it—was even beginning to like her. And that was worrying him.

"I think I'll just try out a few of those prostitutes before I look for a nice woman," Payne decided.

To him, it seemed like the only sensible way to handle the dilemma.

"Well, you better not let Miss McCord in on your plans," Cass warned.

He made a mental note to take Payne aside for a more detailed discussion of the subject. He had a feeling that the boy had missed a point somewhere.

"You think she'd be real upset, don't you?"

"Boys," Cass said, rolling to his feet and resigning himself to the fact that, between this conversation and his encounter with the redhead that afternoon, he might have to sleep in the creek tonight, "I try not to think of Patience McCord one way or the other."

Aaron looked up and winked. "But she's pretty hard to overlook, ain't she?"

That was another question Cass chose to ignore. "Go to sleep, boys. I think I'll take a ride."

Cass strolled off as Aaron, rolling up inside his blanket, closed his eyes and tried to conjure up an image of Ernestine Parker.

He wondered if she'd be a family-raisin' woman or one of them girls mentioned who had needs as powerful as a man's . . .

Well, it didn't really matter. Like Cass, there weren't *no* woman gonna hog-tie and brand him—not if he could help it!

CHAPTER 12

PATIENCE HAD JUST PULLED THE PINS FROM HER HAIR and was about to give it a thorough brushing when she saw Cass come walking back through camp. She was surprised to see that he was still awake.

The fires had burned low, and Buck Brewster was slipping his fiddle into its case, preparing to retire for the night.

Cass paused to speak to a young woman who sat in a large rocking chair just outside one of the wagons. She was trying to soothe her fretful infant who'd been ill for days.

"How's the baby tonight?" he asked.

"I think she feels a mite hotter than she did." Mardean Gibson's wan smile was mute testimony to the strain she was under.

Cass felt the baby's forehead, and his brow furrowed with concern. "Do you need another bucket of cool water?"

"No, thank you. Boyd said he'd fetch me one when he got up." Boyd and Mardean had been taking turns sitting up nights with the infant. Cass felt sorry for the young couple. At sixteen, they were barely more than children themselves.

"I'll hold your baby if you'd like to rest a spell with your husband," Cass offered.

Mardean gazed tenderly at the sleeping child on her lap. "I'm beholden to you, Mr. Claxton, but I want to stay with her," she said softly.

Giving Mardean's shoulder a friendly squeeze, Cass smiled. "If you need anything, you let me know."

Her face brightened momentarily. "Thank you. I surely do appreciate your kindness."

Patience watched the exchange out of the corner of her eye, and a feeling of envy engulfed her.

What she would give to have Cass speak to *her* with such compassion, such concern, such caring . . . Her thoughts wavered as she watched him walk to where his horse was grazing.

Now where did he think he was going at this hour, she fretted. She watched him pick up his saddle and sling it over his shoulder. Suddenly

Patience was sure she could guess. He had to be going to visit the wagon of prostitutes.

He was going to see that redhead, she thought frantically. And the two of them were not going to spend their time composing a letter to dear old grandma in Wichita!

Scalding tears sprang to her eyes, and she swiped them away angrily as she tried to tell herself that she didn't care. *Of course* he was going to visit that redhead. He was a man, wasn't he, and hadn't the woman issued him a blatant invitation that afternoon in front of the entire train?

Somewhere there existed a legal document verifying that Cass Claxton was her legal husband. However, Patience wouldn't even try to fool herself into believing that any document could prevent him from indulging in sins of the flesh. He was a young, virile man who'd been on the trail for weeks, and who by now—borrowing from one of her Aunt Merriweather's more colorful expressions—was probably hotter than a two-dollar pistol. The mere thought of this outrageous act of perfidy made her flush with renewed anger.

Well, she wasn't about to permit it. She would not allow him to disgrace her by running off in the middle of the night to cavort with one of those women of easy virtue.

As she began moving toward the wagon, she conceded to herself that her logic might be flawed. After all, no one on the train knew that she and Cass were married, so he could hardly disgrace her in their eyes.

But *she* knew they were married. And the thought of his being intimate with another woman, when he'd avoided her—his own wife—like the plague, set her blood boiling.

Sometime during the past weeks, she had unconsciously begun to think of Cass as her property—her man. Now she asked herself if a woman didn't have a right to protect what was hers, even though what was hers had never wanted to become hers in the first place!

She reached the wagon, and her hand fumbled under the seat for the bullwhip while she kept her eyes trained on Cass. He was acting just as if he were simply about the business of saddling his horse for an innocent moonlight ride!

He had one foot in the stirrup when he paused momentarily. Cocking his head to one side, he thought he could detect the sound of a whip oscillating in midair.

The meaning of the ominous whir suddenly sank in. He swore under his breath, and he braced himself mentally for what he knew was coming.

The soft *wisp, wisp, wisp* grew louder.

"Patience, you'd better think twice," he warned.

She wondered if he'd seen her coming or if he'd grown eyes in the back of his head. She stood behind him in her nightgown, whirling the whip above her head.

"Where are you going?"

"That's none of your business."

"Oh, yes, it is."

Wisp, wisp, wisp, wisp.

"Patience—"

"You bean-headed jackass! You're not going to that woman!" A menacing crack rent the air, and Cass clamped his eyes shut and gripped the pommel tightly as he felt the back of his shirt split in half. He sucked in his breath, waiting to feel his blood gushing in streams, but he gradually realized that she hadn't touched his flesh, a fact, he decided, which had most likely saved her blasted life!

"Don't push me, Cass. I can draw blood," she warned in a tight voice.

"What's this all about?" he demanded. She was glad to hear that, for once, his voice sounded thready instead of cocksure.

"You are not going to that woman."

"What woman?"

"*That* woman!"

"What woman? I wasn't going to meet a woman—I was going for a ride!"

He didn't know why he was bothering to inform her of where he was or was not going. She didn't own him. He started to turn around and tell her so when the whip cracked again.

This time it sliced through his sleeve and separated the fabric cleanly from his shoulder.

"Don't lie to me! You were going to see that woman!"

Cass had had enough. He whirled and lunged at her, and a struggle developed as Patience fought to retain control of her weapon. But his strength easily overpowered hers. They fell to the ground, and he landed on top of her.

"Get off me, you big oaf!"

Angry as she'd ever seen him, he sat up and snapped the whip in two.

"I have another one!" she said defiantly.

Casting the remains of the broken whip aside, he glared at her. "Miss McCord," he said in a voice so ominous that she felt the hair on her arms prickle, "you are sorely testing me."

"You were going to that . . . that woman," she accused. The little girl inside her wanted to cry, but the woman inside her refused to give him the satisfaction.

"I was not—and what if I was? You have no right to be telling me what I can do! I'm doing what I said I'd do. I said I would get you, the children, Harlon, and Corliss to Cherry Grove safely, and I'm trying my level best to do that. Now, woman, you've browbeaten me, badgered me, bullwhipped me, and badmouthed me about all I'm going to stand for. You're going to stop!" He was so angry that he began shaking her until she felt her teeth rattling. "Do you hear me?"

"If you want a . . . a . . . woman," she scoffed, "why don't you come to your wife?" Patience couldn't believe it was her voice offering him such liberties, but his resulting look of sheer horror confirmed that it was.

"My wife!"

"Your wife . . . I am, you know—no matter how hard you try to deny it!"

"I don't want you to be my wife! I've told you that a hundred times."

"But that doesn't change the fact that we are husband and wife," she argued.

"Let me get this straight. You're suggesting that just because of some idiotic, meaningless ceremony that took place in the middle of a road six years ago, I should want to bed you?" he echoed incredulously.

"Well . . . yes." Their eyes were still locked. "I . . . I wouldn't object to your demanding your husbandly rights," she said meekly. It would be a far better choice than letting him go to that woman.

"Bed you?" he repeated as if she had just volunteered him to be the prime target of a firing squad.

"Don't sound so shocked. Husbands and wives do it all the time."

She knew she was living dangerously. He would likely turn her over his knee and give her a sound paddling for even suggesting such a thing, but she didn't care. She would gladly follow through with her madness and pay the piper later.

"Oh, good Lord!" He slumped over, resting his face in the hollow of her neck, fighting to ignore her audacity. But he found he couldn't.

By some cruel act of fate Patience was offering herself to him; and when he weighed her proposal he was faced with the alarming fact that her timing couldn't have been better. Seeing those women today, talking with Aaron and Payne tonight—it wasn't fair. It just wasn't fair.

For a moment Patience thought he was going to break down and cry like a baby.

She lay immobile, reveling in his nearness as she felt his chest, then his shoulders, then his whole body begin to tremble.

His weight, though heavy, felt wonderously exciting pressed against her. She found she liked the feel of him, and she hoped he wouldn't be in any hurry to move away—at least, that's what she was hoping until she discovered that he was not overcome by sadness but by mirth. His body began to heave with barely suppressed hilarity.

"What is so funny?" she demanded when she realized that he was laughing at her.

"You!"

"I fail to see how my suggesting that you take me to bed should bring about such hysterics." She struggled to sit up, her pride mortally wounded by his rejection.

His hand snaked out. "Now wait a minute." Slowly he eased her back to the ground. "I didn't say I wouldn't accept your offer."

He managed to keep a straight face, knowing that to consider her offer seriously would be the act of a desperate man. Nevertheless he was not a fool: He had to admit that he was desperate for a woman's company.

This woman was a spitfire, a hellcat, and the biggest obstacle he'd ever tried to overcome, but she was also a beautiful, desirable woman—and she was his wife, albeit in name only.

He was fully aware that if he bedded her, he would surely consummate their union. However, once they reached Cherry Grove he could make it clear that he wanted a divorce instead of an annulment. So why shouldn't he bed her? Lord knew he'd earned the right.

"All right. I'll bed you."

She seemed pleased yet startled by his uncomplicated surrender. "Just like that?"

His eyes narrowed. "Yes. *Now* what do you want? Pretty words? Because if you do . . ."

Drawing a deep breath, she warned herself not to overreact—she was finally making some progress. "I don't expect pretty words."

The moment wasn't how she'd imagined it would be, but she conceded that it would have to do.

"All right." He released her from his hold and glanced around, seeking a private spot.

"We'll need privacy." He stifled the urge to throw her down on the ground and jump on her like a half-starved animal.

"I know the perfect place."

Cass followed her down a moon-drenched trail, still wondering if he had completely lost his mind.

There was a part of him that needed—*ached*—to be with a woman. Yet another part of him warned that he would be committing the worst mistake of his life. This could throw a kink in their agreement, but he hoped that it wouldn't. She seemed as eager to shed herself of him as he was her.

He was going to bed Patience McCord. *Bed Patience McCord!* The thought still astounded him. Yet concern over what he was about to do was overshadowed by just plain lust as his gaze focused on her feminine backside.

She hurriedly led him through the thickets and brambles until they reached a small clearing. As they turned, their eyes met, then glanced away discreetly. "Is this all right?"

Cass glanced around. "Yes."

They stood facing each other as moonbeams played on her hair. It turned the flaxen mass to spun gold. Cass found himself eager to touch it.

"Well?" she said.

"Well."

"I . . . I guess we'll have all the privacy we need right here."

"Yeah . . . I suppose we will." He didn't know why he suddenly felt as awkward as a schoolboy. He stepped closer to her. The fragrance of her lilac-scented skin gently teased his senses into painful awareness.

She looked at him, waiting.

Claxton, you can't take her without touching her, he thought. Reaching out hesitantly, he drew her into his arms.

Her small body fit against his surprisingly well, and the instantaneous tightening in his loins assured him that he had nothing to worry about. The act would be completed before he could think about the insanity of what he was doing.

Patience was seized by momentary panic as she felt a rush of heat. It was as if by this gentle but intimate gesture he had already begun to make love to her. *This is what you wanted,* she reminded herself. *He's a man, and you longed to be desired and enjoyed, to be fulfilled as a woman.*

Her arms slipped around his waist shyly as he hesitantly brought his mouth down to brush hers.

"Cass," she complained, "we are going to make love . . . Must you go about this so unemotionally?"

"All right." His mouth took hers roughly as he jerked her closer against him.

Her body suddenly went fluid as all her fantasies, all her needs, all her darker desires suddenly centered on him.

His first instinct was to take her quickly, reminding himself that there was no need for the usual niceties; he could just complete the act and be on his way.

She moaned softly as their kiss deepened, and her stomach knotted tightly as she began to experience the raw hunger of the man. It took her breath away, to feel his need—but she had hungers of her own that were begging to be explored. Her passion easily matched his, and she heard his sharp intake of breath as his hands began to skim across her breasts.

Cass could feel her heart racing against his hands. He was both pleased and alarmed by her swift response. He wasn't sure what he'd expected, but it wasn't this loving; this striving to please; this warm, giving woman he had in his arms.

She pressed closer, startled to feel the urgent pulsing of his need for her. Momentarily she was shocked—but the knowledge that she was the cause of this heated response excited her more than it frightened her. Closing her eyes, she allowed him—no, actively encouraged him—to begin taking liberties she had let no other man even dream of, savoring every delicious new feeling he was bringing alive.

Almost afraid of what was happening, Cass suddenly aborted the kiss, burying his face in her hair as he drew in a ragged breath.

This was not going as he'd planned. All of a sudden he had this crazy urge to take all the time in the world to make love to her, to savor the moment, to linger as he explored the lush curves and gentle swells of her young body. *Just get it over with, Claxton. Don't encourage her*, he berated himself.

"Do you want me to take off your gown?" he murmured raggedly.

"Yes."

Their gazes locked in the moonlight, and she felt complete abandonment as she saw his eyes grow dark with passion.

Not sure that it was the right thing to do, but wanting to do it anyway, she hesitantly reached out and guided his hands to the row of tiny buttons on her gown.

Touched by her honest simplicity, Cass gazed down at her, knowing he couldn't go through with it. He wasn't that much of a heel—yet. His hands dropped away guiltily. "Patience, this is no good . . ."

Recognizing the doubt in his eyes, Patience quickly grabbed his hands and brought them back to the row of buttons. "Please, Cass . . . If I were Laure Revuneau, you wouldn't hesitate," she baited.

Damn! Why did she have to mention Laure? He groaned silently. Just the thought of the hot-blooded French temptress automatically set his hands into motion again.

Slowly he worked the buttons loose, and Patience felt goosebumps rise on her skin. In a moment the gown fell away and dropped to the ground. For the briefest of moments she had to quell the urge to run, to hide her nakedness from him. She could feel the heat rising to her cheeks as she turned her head away, but quickly she straightened her stance, determined to prove to him that, with only a little coaxing, she could be every bit the woman he needed her to be.

Cass stood staring at her, the expression in his eyes telling her more eloquently than words that she didn't need to worry. He found her desirable.

Her young, ripe curves made him want to throw caution to the wind. His eyes lingered on the small, firm breasts, and his breathing grew more shallow as he slowly drew her back against the width of his broad chest. Gazing deep into her eyes, he asked again softly. "Are you sure this is what you want, Patience?"

His tone had changed. It was more gentle now, more forgiving.

She gazed up at him, finding it impossible to speak. She was overwhelmed with wanting him, needing him, but she didn't know how to tell him so.

But miraculously he knew.

His hands were unsteady as he began to unbuckle his belt.

"You're sure you're not having second thoughts?" He could see that she was trembling.

"No." She was trembling only because he couldn't seem to take his eyes off her, but she was happy she pleased him.

He smiled at her this time. Just at her. "Well, you can't ever accuse me of not trying to talk you out of it!"

She returned his smile faintly, feeling as if she were drowning in the blue of his eyes. "No, I certainly can't ever accuse you of that."

His belt fell away, and she saw him unbutton his pants, then step out of them.

Her heart lurched as she got her first real look at a half-naked man. Though he still wore underwear she could see he was all muscle and strength. The imprint of his maleness bulging against the front of his long johns suddenly seemed to jump out at her. She swallowed, unable to keep her eyes off the intimidating sight.

Her hands crept up to cover her mouth. "Cass?"

"Yes?"

She wet her lips nervously. "Exactly . . . exactly how does this work?" she whispered.

His hands paused. "Exactly how does *what* work?"

"Exactly how does . . . a man make love to a woman?"

His face went totally blank. "You don't know?"

"No . . . I don't." She thought she knew, but she couldn't be certain. Oh, she knew what parts of the body were involved—she just wasn't sure how they were all supposed to work together.

She felt foolish having to ask such a question, but after seeing his ample endowment . . . well, she simply had to know. Her parents had seen to it that she was well-educated in everything but life itself. Naturally, she'd heard whispers among her schoolmates. If what she had seen the animals doing in the barnyard was also the way *people* went about it— well, she just hoped it wasn't.

"You've never been with a man?"

"No."

"Your mother never spoke to you on the subject?"

"No." Shyness suddenly overcame her, and she snatched up her gown and held it against her breasts protectively. "I asked Mother about it many times, but instead of answers there was only this strained silence," she confessed.

If her scanty information about the act was accurate, she couldn't—not in her wildest dreams—picture her father and her mother participating in such a spectacle.

"What about your aunt? Surely she told you something."

"Aunt Merriweather?" Her eyes widened. "Dear me, no. She would never have spoken of such a thing."

Cass didn't want to believe what he was hearing. First Aaron and Payne; now her. Was there something in the air tonight that brought out the innocents of the world? And why should they all be thrown in his lap, he agonized.

He wasn't able, given his present condition, to give another lecture about intimacy between a man and a woman. For one thing, his own frustrations wouldn't permit it. Secondly, he wasn't her father. If she wanted to know about such matters, she'd have to ask someone else.

But she was looking at him with curious eyes as if she fully expected him to answer.

He sighed. "Look, Patience, you'd better let your husband explain this to you."

"But you *are* my husband."

"On paper only, dammit!"

For the moment she conceded the point. "All right, but you can't tell me you haven't been with many women, and you weren't *their* husband."

"Those women were different," Cass snapped. "I am not going to be the one to educate you."

Sensing his imminent retreat, she stepped forward. "Oh, please, Cass. I . . . I have to know. If you won't tell me, who else can I go to?"

"Talk to Corliss."

"Oh, I couldn't! I'd be embarrassed to tears."

"Then go to one of the other women on the wagon train."

"I can't do that. Please, Cass . . . you tell me."

"Surely you can find someone more qualified than I am to explain Mother Nature to you."

He swore tightly under his breath. If this wasn't just like her, he thought, getting him all stirred up, offering herself to him, then calmly dropping the news that she didn't know how. He should have expected as much, but he hadn't.

"There isn't anyone else I can go to." Patience knew he was angry with her again, and she didn't want him to be. Just once, she wished she could do something right where he was concerned.

"I'm sorry. I'm perfectly willing to go through with this," she pleaded, "but I have to know how!"

"Patience—"

She straightened, her eyes flashing with determination. "Tell me how, Cass—man-to-man, so to speak." She was not some empty-headed twit who ran from the truth. All he had to do was explain the procedure, and she was quite sure she could carry it out. She glanced at the front of his long johns again and frowned. Well, almost sure.

Cass sighed, realizing that she wasn't going to let up until he told her. "All right," he said calmly, pulling her down on a rock beside him. "You want it man-to-man, I'll give it to you—man-to-man. But remember, you asked for this!"

In the simplest, most basic terms—verging on the extremely blunt, at times—he proceeded to describe the act to her graphically and entirely from a man's point of view.

He didn't even try to soften the blow.

As he talked her eyes began to grow round. He could see her wide-eyed gaze darting wildly from the center of his underwear back to the front of her gown. She was clearly appalled by what he was telling her.

At first she was sure that he was making the whole thing up. She might be innocent, but she wasn't dumb. There was no way *that* could fit into *that*.

But he calmly insisted that there would be no difficulty.

When he was through, she looked at him for a long moment. "Well, I never!" she said.

He returned her look dryly. *"Now* you tell me."

"Why, it sounds perfectly revolting!"

"It isn't. It's enjoyable."

She knew he was lying this time.

Her ardor severely dampened, she hurriedly pulled her gown over her head. "It's late . . . I should be getting back to camp."

"Why, I thought you wanted to go through with this," he countered with mock surprise.

"Well, I'll have to give it some thought," she murmured distractedly.

Cass watched as she turned and beat a noisy retreat through the bushes.

Grinning, he reached into his pocket for a cheroot. *Claxton, you should be ashamed of yourself for scaring her that way,* he thought. But he wasn't. He was just miserable as hell now. He shifted about on the rock uncomfortably. He supposed he'd take that swim.

A devilish grin broke across his face as he thought about the look she'd had on her face when he'd explained how everything worked.

It *did* sound a mite hard to accept.

CHAPTER 13

*T*HE NEXT MORNING WHEN PATIENCE WALKED around the wagon, she found Mardean sitting in the rocker cradling her infant to her bosom.

Tears were rolling silently down the girl's cheeks as Patience knelt beside her. She reached out to smooth a stray lock that had fallen across

Mardean's forehead. The girl looked exhausted. "Mardean . . . is the baby worse this morning?"

Mardean lifted her red-rimmed eyes, and Patience saw in them the depth of human misery: Mardean's child was gone. She rocked back and forth, quietly holding her infant's lifeless body.

Sometime during the night, her baby had died.

Patience didn't know how things could get much worse. Last night with Cass and now this tragedy. Why did the world have to be so complicated?

There was a bright sun overhead, birds chirped, and the squirrels chattered noisily in the trees. It didn't seem a proper day for a burial.

The small group stood around the shallow grave as Lucius Waterman spoke the words of interment. His voice was solemn as he opened his worn Bible and read from Matthew 19:14: "But Jesus said, Suffer little children, and forbid them not to come unto me; for of such is the kingdom of heaven."

Patience stood between Cass and the children, wondering if she would be able to cope with such loss. The children that stood quietly beside her were not her own, yet she loved them all as dearly as if she'd carried them in her womb. Her heart went out to young Boyd. He stood tall with his arm around Mardean, who was sobbing openly. Patience could see that he was trying to be brave, even as his own grief streamed from the corners of his eyes.

Lucius spoke words of comfort and encouragement as Boyd and Mardean's family and friends listened in silent sympathy.

Patience could feel a kindness in all of them, a deep understanding. The grim reaper often lurked on the trail, and they were all aware of the dangers that could befall them.

Lucius closed his Bible and surveyed the small group. "Let us pray." Lifting his gaze upward, he began in a reassuring voice, "Father, we know not why You have called Susanann Gibson home today, nor do we question Thy will. Grant her parents the strength they will need to see them through their loss. Lend us the strength to give comfort and sustain Boyd and Mardean through the dark days ahead. God, we pray that You grant mercy upon us all. Amen."

Four men stepped forward, and as the mourners began to drift away from the gravesite, Patience could hear the scraping of the shovels. She knew each thrust of dirt would lay bare Mardean's heart.

After the service, the others broke camp, allowing the grieving parents the last remaining moments with their child.

Patience could see the young couple standing next to the mound of fresh dirt, holding onto each other tightly.

She wondered if she would ever receive the kind of love Boyd felt for Mardean. If a tragedy befell her, whom would she go to for comfort?

Her eyes searched for Cass. She found him busy hitching the team to the Gibsons' wagon. She suddenly needed the assurance that he was near.

Gathering the last of their supplies, she stowed them in their wagon, then ambled over to where he was working.

She perched on the tongue of the wagon and watched as he adjusted a piece of harness.

Phebia ran up, crying. She'd smashed her thumb—the sucking one. With solemn eyes, she silently extended her injury to Cass.

"I don't think it's serious, but I'll put a bandage on it," he reassured her.

Minutes later Phebia skipped happily away, dragging Marybelle by the hair. Her injured thumb was encased in a huge, snowy-white bandage.

"Maybe now she'll stop sucking the thing," Cass remarked as he turned his attention to the harness.

"She seems to rely on you more and more in all her crises," Patience teased.

Cass shrugged. "She's a good kid."

Patience sighed and clasped her hands together in her lap. "Real sad about the Gibson baby, isn't it?"

Cass glanced her way, but he kept working. "It is."

"I'll never get used to the thought of death." Her eyes grew misty as they wandered back to Boyd and Mardean. "I know we shouldn't question God's will, but you wonder why He would want to take a baby . . ."

"Losing someone is never easy, but when a child is involved, it makes it harder."

She looked at him. "You sound as if you've had firsthand experience."

"I guess I have. A few years back my brother lost both his wife and the child she was carrying." Cass jerked the leather straps together tightly. "The loss almost killed him."

"I'm sorry."

"Guess it was meant to be. After a year or so he remarried a little gal named Charity, and from what I hear, he couldn't be happier."

"Would that be Beau?" she asked softly. She'd met Beau Claxton years ago when she'd gone to Charity Burkhouser's soddy to ask Cass to escort her back to St. Louis.

"It was Beau."

"Do you have other family?"

"An older brother, Cole, and my mother. They live in Missouri."

"No sisters?"

"No sisters."

She was pleased to find that they could carry on a normal conversation without fussing. It felt good for a change. Maybe they were making progress, she thought wistfully, realizing that it would probably last only long enough for her to finish her next statement.

"Cass?"

He glanced up. "Yes."

"There's something I want to confess to you."

"All right." He wasn't overly curious. Nothing she could say would surprise him.

"I sent you the telegram from Beau."

Cass never even glanced up. The suspicion that she'd tricked him into taking her to Cherry Grove had entered his mind once or twice, but now the knowledge that she had actually done it was tempered more by a feeling of relief than of anger. "I see," he said quietly, relieved to learn that Beau wasn't in any trouble.

She blinked, stunned by his benign acceptance. "You're not angry?"

He looked at her this time, long and hard. "Would it do any good if I were?"

"No." She lowered her gaze to study her hands. "I realize that it wasn't a nice thing to do."

"You seldom do anything that's nice where I'm concerned."

She looked away again. "I know."

"Exactly why do you do these things, Patience?" he asked, wishing, for once, that she could explain what drove her.

"I don't know . . . I suppose because nobody ever cared enough to stop me."

"Your folks never taught you the wisdom of asking for favors instead of bullying your way through life?"

"I guess maybe they tried. But after Mama died, Daddy was so wrapped up in his grief that he just went off into his own little world. Seemed to me the only way I could get his attention was to throw fits, make demands, and act perfectly outrageous. When I found out that he wasn't going to come out of his shell long enough to do anything about it, then I suppose I just got worse."

She lifted her eyes, and Cass could see that they were bright with unshed tears. "What my father didn't realize was that I was hurting too. When I lost Mama, I didn't know where to turn or what to do. It isn't right to make a fourteen-year-old face death all alone. I needed him, Cass . . . but he wasn't there for me. Then he upped and moved us to Cherry Grove, Kansas, to begin a new life, and I didn't know anyone at all. I was sure that my world had come to an end."

"Did you ever let your father know you felt this way?"

"No." She sighed. "He wouldn't have understood. He's a good man, but he hasn't the faintest idea of how to deal with a child."

"So you were lonely and miserable, and you decided to trick me into marrying you and taking you back to St. Louis."

"I see how horrible that was now, but at the time I thought it was my only salvation. I knew if I could just return to Aunt Merriweather, then everything in my life would be all right again." She sighed, glad to have her weighty admission finally out in the open. "I always felt loved and wanted by Aunt Merriweather, but I guess she had a way of making everyone feel that way."

Cass stopped what he was doing and stepped over to tilt her chin up to meet his gaze. Her eyes were lovely, he realized with a start, violet-blue with long, soot-colored lashes. "Patience, I'm going to tell you something, so listen to me. You don't intimidate people into loving you. You earn people's love by being honest and decent, by being a woman of your word. That gets their attention every time."

"Maybe it isn't attention I want," she whispered. "Maybe I want to be loved the way Boyd loves Mardean."

"I know of nine children who think you've hung the moon," he reminded.

"I know . . . but sometimes I despair that no man will ever love me," she added softly.

"That's foolish."

She smiled, her eyes bright with tears as she gained courage. "Maybe I want to be loved by a man like you."

Their eyes met, and she wasn't sure of what she was reading in his gaze . . . pity . . . sympathy . . . maybe something entirely new. Could it be a grudging realization that she wasn't as bad as he'd thought she was, she wondered.

"Then I suggest you give a man like me a reason to love you," he said simply.

They studied each other, unprepared for the swift response they were triggering in each other. He recalled the way she'd looked the night before, standing before him in the moonlight, naked, innocent, vulnerable. He wished now that he'd been gentler with her.

"Cass! Cass!"

Cass and Patience glanced up to see Jesse dashing headlong in their direction.

Cass frowned. "What is it, Jesse?"

"Doog . . ." Jesse was panting so hard he could barely get his breath. "Doog . . . fell . . . down a big hole."

"A hole?" Startled, Patience sprang up from the tongue of the wagon. "Where? When?"

"Just . . . now . . . Come on . . ."

Cass paused long enough to grab a rope; then the three raced through camp, shouting for extra hands to help with the rescue.

Corliss poked her head out of the canvas flap. "What's going on now?"

"Doog . . . he's fallen into a hole!" Patience shouted.

"Land o' mighty!" The flap fell back into place as Corliss began to search frantically for her shoes.

The growing assembly fought their way through dense briars and thickets, tearing off the prickly vines that angrily snatched at their clothing. A stitch formed in Patience's side, but she ran on, her shorter legs barely able to keep up with Cass's long-legged strides.

They ran for more than a half mile before Jesse skidded to a halt. With wide eyes, he pointed to the ground expectantly. Noting the thin beam of light shining down through the opening, Cass determined that Doog had fallen into the shaft of a deserted well.

Dropping to his stomach, Cass narrowed his eyes and peered down the hole. "Doog?"

"Yessir?"

"What are you doing down there?"

"Just sittin' here."

"Is he all right?" Patience crowded closer, trying to hear the exchange. "Are you all right?"

"I'm not sure . . . I—I want out of here!"

Patience glanced up to see Ernest Parker and Boyd Gibson already tying a loop on the end of a rope. She was stunned to see Boyd, but here he was, temporarily casting aside his grief to help another.

She felt a gentle hand on her shoulder, and she turned to find that even Mardean was there, lending her silent support.

"Doog, I'm going to lower a rope. I want you to grab it and loop it around your waist," Cass ordered.

"I can't . . . My arm is all funny-looking, and it hurts real bad!"

"Is it broken?"

"I don't know . . . Maybe."

Cass hoisted himself to his feet, his eyes gauging the size of the shaft's opening. It would be tight, but he could fit through it. He turned back to Patience. "I'm going to have to go down there."

"Oh, Cass . . ." Patience edged forward, concern for his safety etched on her face. "Be careful . . ."

A loop was quickly tied in a second rope and dropped around Cass's waist. Ernest, Lucius, Boyd, and Laurence Medley, Mardean's father, took hold of the other end.

"We're ready anytime you are." Ernest handed Cass a rifle. "You better take this."

Cass accepted the rifle, then removed his hat and handed it to Patience. "Here, make yourself useful and hold this for me."

"Please"—Patience's eyes locked helplessly with his—"please . . . I'm so worried . . ."

He grinned. "You worry too much."

Seeing her lower lip begin to tremble, his smile faded. "I'll be all right . . . okay?"

She nodded wordlessly.

In a completely uncharacteristic gesture—at least toward her—he reached out and tugged her nose playfully, then turned to face the four waiting men. "Gentlemen, I hope you have strong grips."

Moments later the men began to carefully lower Cass down into the dark shaft.

Patience couldn't bear to watch. She turned and buried her face against Martha Waterman's shoulder.

The hole was close to fifty feet straight down. Loose rocks bounced and skidded off the walls as Cass began to maneuver his way slowly down the sides of the shaft.

"You still down there, Doog?"

"Yessir."

"Any particular reason you picked this day to fall into a hole?" Cass asked, trying to keep the boy's mind off the problem.

He was about a fourth of the way down when he felt the rope give. A fine sweat broke out across his forehead as he braced his feet against the wall, tightened his grip, and waited. Seconds later, the rope went taut again.

"No, sir . . . I was just a chasin' a rabbit, and I was runnin' real hard . . ."

As Cass eased down another few feet, a barrage of loose rocks clattered noisily down the sides of the walls. When the dust finally settled, Doog called out expectantly, "Cass? You still there?"

"I was the last time I looked. How about you?"

"I'm still here."

"Good."

"You scarit?"

"A little . . . What about you?"

"A little."

"Your arm hurting you?"

"Yessir."

Cass was halfway down the shaft.

"Is Miss McCord up there?"

"Yes, she is."

"I'll bet she's scarit, huh?"

"She looked a mite peaked . . . Doog, can you see me yet?" It was the longest damned shaft he'd ever seen, Cass thought.

"Yessir."

"Well, hold on. I'll be there in a minute."

"Okay."

"How much water's down there?"

"Not much . . . just a little."

Cass could hear the faint trickle of running water. The well being almost dry would make the rescue easier.

"Cass?"

"Yeah?"

"Better hurry. Them snakes are making me kinda nervous," Doog admitted.

"Snakes?" Cass paused, his heart sinking.

"There's three great big ol' ones just kinda layin' here lookin' at me."

Cass muttered an obscenity under his breath. He wasn't afraid of snakes, but he didn't necessarily cherish the thought of having a tea party with three of them at the bottom of a well.

"What'd ya say, Cass?"

"Nothin'."

After a few minutes Cass could see the bottom. Doog was sitting with his feet drawn up on a ledge, staring up at him. "Where are the snakes?" Cass asked, trying to adjust his eyes to the dim light.

Doog pointed in front of him. "Right there."

They were there, all right. Cottonmouths. Coiled up and waiting for company.

"Listen, Doog, I'm going to brace myself, and I want you to swing yourself out to me."

Cass deliberately kept his tone neutral, hoping to keep the boy from knowing what they were up against. Apparently the child couldn't determine from the snakes' thicker, shorter bodies, from their darker coloration, from the cotton lining in their mouths that they were any different from other water snakes. But they were very different.

"My arm hurts."

For a moment Cass had forgotten about the child's injured arm.

"All right . . . Let me think for a minute." He could feel the sweat trickling down his back as his eyes went back to the snakes. This was not going to be his day—he could feel it.

"Cass, are you all right?" Patience's anxious voice came to him from far up the shaft.

"We're doing fine!" he called back.

One of the snakes opened its mouth, displaying the white markings on its upper lip as if to warn the intruders that they were asking for trouble. Cass felt his skin crawl.

"Just fine," Cass repeated softly, hoping to make himself believe it.

"Them snakes dangerous?" Doog asked when he noticed Cass's preoccupation with them.

"They're cottonmouths, son."

Doog's eyes widened, and he jerked his feet back closer to his body. "They're poisonous?"

"Now, listen. It looks like I'm not going to be able to come all the way down to get you. I know your arm hurts, but I'd like for you to try and jump to me," Cass said calmly.

Doog stood up slowly, his gaze still fixed solidly on the snakes. "Well . . . all right . . . I'll try . . ."

The boy was light, maybe sixty pounds, Cass estimated. His weight would be easy to handle if the men above could control the unexpected jerk on the rope.

"Patience!"

"Yes!"

"Tell Lucius I'm going to have Doog jump to me. I figure he weighs around sixty pounds, so tell the men to brace themselves!"

Seconds later she returned. "They say they're ready!"

Cass looked at the snakes, then back to Doog. "It's important for you to be real accurate. I'll try to get as close as I can. All you have to do is latch onto my hand."

"Yessir."

Cass got a good grip on the rope with one hand, and stretched the other one down to the boy.

Doog glanced back at the snakes.

"Don't look down," Cass cautioned softly.

Doog obediently lifted his eyes. "I'm scarit," he whispered, "real scarit, Cass."

"I know." He motioned with his hand. "All you have to do is grab onto my hand."

Doog swallowed.

Cass waited. The sound of a snake's hissing echoed through the dark chamber.

"Okay, I'm gonna jump," Doog decided. He edged closer to the ledge as one of the snakes began to uncoil.

It slithered across the body of the smaller one and paused.

Taking a deep breath, Doog shut his eyes.

"Doog, take your time." Cass could see the boy was nervous, and they couldn't afford a mistake.

Doog suddenly leapt, his hand grappling wildly for Cass's. Their fingers brushed in midair moments before Doog plummeted to the floor of the shaft.

Screaming, the child flailed wildly in the stagnant water before springing to his feet and backing fearfully away from the snakes that were beginning to move in for the strike.

"*Cassss!*" Doog's voice was bordering on hysteria.

Cass swore under his breath as he slid the rest of the way down the wall, dropping the rifle in his hasty descent. His boots hit bottom, and in a running dash he caught Doog up by the seat of his pants as two of the snakes struck out.

Jerking the boy aside, he swore as the snakes struck again.

Cass jerked frantically on the rope. "Pull!" he shouted.

Sweat ran down the sides of his face as Doog screamed again. Cass glanced down and saw one of the snakes slithering across the toe of his boot.

The rope jerked once and went slack.

"Doog, can you reach the rifle?" Cass shouted as he kicked out at one of the snakes, catching it with the toe of his boot and sending it through the air.

Doog was terrified. He clamped his eyes shut and shook his head. "Noooo . . . I'm scarit!"

The second snake lunged again as Cass jerked backward, unable to hold on to the rope this time.

He could hear voices coming from above as his feet slipped out from under him. He fell into the water, still trying to hold onto Doog.

Cass thrashed about in the water, his hand groping for the rough hemp as the snakes came swimming toward them. His hand froze as it closed over something alive. Swearing, he flung the snake against the wall and searched for the rope again.

Doog screamed as all three snakes struck again, one catching the edge of Cass's boot this time.

"Tell us when you're ready to come up!" Patience shouted down the shaft, unaware of the drama taking place below.

Cass swore as one hand finally located the rope and his other hand grabbed the rifle that was tilting precariously on the ledge. "We're ready!" he shouted.

"You ready?"

"Pull, dammit!"

Suddenly the rope went taut, and Cass with his arm around Doog went sailing up the side of the wall. Doog clutched on to Cass and the rifle with his good arm, his injured one dangling at his side. His eyes were riveted to the snakes that were still determined to punish the trespassers.

About halfway up, the rope slipped down again, leaving them dangling helplessly in midair.

Cass held tightly to Doog as the boy buried his face against his neck and shook like a leaf in a high wind.

"Don't let us fall," the child moaned.

Cass hazarded a cautious glance down the long, narrow shaft where the snakes lay waiting. "Lucius will see to it that we don't."

Moments later the rope began to move again.

"Listen, Doog, I don't see any need to let Miss McCord know about our little friends down there," Cass said as they neared the top of the opening. "It would only upset her—women are real funny about snakes, you know—so why don't we just keep this between us men?"

Doog nodded without raising his head, confiding in a muffled voice, "I think from now on I'm gonna be real funny about snakes too."

Seconds later Lucius lifted Doog out of the shaft and pried the rifle from his fingers.

A cheer went up as Cass emerged into the bright sunlight. He gave a sigh of relief. He couldn't remember when daylight had ever looked so good to him before.

It was all Patience could do to keep from rushing over and throwing herself into his arms. Instead she hurriedly embraced a sopping-wet, much-relieved Doog.

Corliss ran her hands over the boy's upper body and diagnosed his injuries as a sprained shoulder and a bruised arm. As she prescribed a sling and a period of rest, Doog, who was openly distressed by all the fuss that the womenfolk were making, tried to wriggle from her grasp and edge toward the other boys.

Assured that the child was none the worse for wear, Patience released Doog to Corliss's care and hurried to Cass's side. At least she would be able to see for herself that he wasn't injured.

Ernestine Parker was fawning over Cass again. Had the child been one year older, Patience swore that she'd have told the girl to find her own man.

"Are you all right?" Patience asked, placing her hand on Cass's wet sleeve possessively.

"I'm fine." Cass and Doog exchanged a conspiratorial glance, and they both grinned.

"Well, I appreciate your going down there in that awful, dark hole to get Doog." Patience surveyed Cass's wet clothing expectantly. "I'll bet it was just terrible down there."

Cass shrugged.

Phebia marched over and immediately demanded that Cass remove the bandage from her thumb. Since it had only been for show anyway, he complied.

"Good! Now I can suck it again." She popped the thumb back into her mouth contentedly.

"Folks, we best be gettin' on the trail," Lucius warned. "We've lost nigh on to four hours today."

The group began to trail off toward their camp, talking among themselves about all the strange happenings the morning had brought.

The children clustered around Cass and Patience as they started walking. Cass casually placed his arm around Patience's waist as Corliss fell into step, carrying Phebia and Marybelle.

Doog was busy extolling his adventure to the other boys, obediently omitting the part about the snakes, though Cass could tell it pained him to have to leave it out. Without that exciting part, it sounded as if he'd simply fallen into a hole and Cass had come down to fetch him.

Patience smiled contentedly as they walked along enjoying the lovely fall day. She thought they looked like a real family as the twelve of them sauntered down the road together.

A real family.

CHAPTER 14

THE NEXT DAY, HOYT WILLIS MADE HIS MOVE. HE crouched behind a tree, watching Patience as she went about her work. One hour—twenty minutes at the least—and he'd show Patience Mc-Cord what a real man could do for her. He wiped the back of his hand across his stubbled chin, trying to control his eagerness.

It was Sunday, and the men were off hunting. The women had gone to the river shortly after their church services to do the week's wash. It was about the only time they had to catch up on the week's gossip without the men being around to scowl at them. They were chattering like magpies as they went about their work.

It wouldn't take Hoyt long to do what he was here for. All he had to do was get the little missy alone.

Patience helped Corliss most of the morning, but shortly before noon she announced that she and Phebia were returning to camp to begin the baking.

Corliss absently waved her off, never missing a lick in telling her story about how Jesse had put a frog in Bryon's bedroll two nights ago. She was describing the howl the five-year-old had sent up.

After feeding Phebia a biscuit and a cup of milk, Patience put her down for a nap. Almost everyone had drifted out of camp by the time she turned her attention to making bread. She had just dumped several cups of flour into a large wooden bowl when she heard footsteps approaching. She glanced up and was startled to see the buffalo skinner she'd be-friended several weeks earlier.

Hoyt Willis stood looking at her, a grin spreading across his dirty features. He tipped his hat politely. "Afternoon, ma'am."

Patience stepped back as his foul smell washed over her.

"Mr. Willis . . . what are you doing here?"

Hoyt's eyes traveled hungrily over the bodice of her dress. "I thought you might be sparin' me a cup of coffee, ma'am."

"Well . . . I suppose I can." Patience didn't like the idea of the man being around while Cass was gone, but she didn't want to be rude.

She walked to the large pot hanging above the fire and poured coffee into a tin cup. Hesitantly she handed it to him.

His fingers brushed hers intimately as he took the cup. "Thank you, ma'am. I'm right beholden to you."

Patience nodded and moved away quickly. She was dismayed to see him amble over and settle himself comfortably upon a rock a few feet away from where she'd planned to work.

Deciding she could do little about it, she returned her attention to mixing the bread.

"Right purty weather we're havin'," Hoyt remarked as he took a sip from the cup.

She nodded, not looking up.

"Sure was sorry 'bout the old man a breakin' his leg. At his age it'll take a spell to heal."

Reaching for the salt, Patience felt a tightening in the pit of her stomach. How would he know Harlon had broken his leg—unless, of course, he'd been following them?

"Where is the rest of your party, Mr. Willis?"

"Jest call me Hoyt, honey."

A warning light entered her eyes as she turned and met his gaze evenly. "My name is Miss McCord."

"Yes," Hoyt's eyes focused on the gentle rise and fall of her breasts. "I know what your name is." His gaze never wavered.

"Then use it when you speak to me."

Hoyt grinned. He liked a woman with spunk—made his effort more worthwhile. "The other fellers are camped down the road a ways."

"I'm surprised. It was my understanding that you were eager to get back to your families. I would think you could travel much faster than we can."

"Oh, we ain't in no hurry," Hoyt said. "I just kinda like to take my time and enjoy the scenery—you know what I mean?"

Patience knew.

"Where's your man today, Miss McCord?" His tone remained friendly, but Cass's earlier warning about the man was making Patience feel uneasy. She wondered how far away Cass was.

"Are you referring to Mr. Claxton?" she returned coolly.

"Yeah, Mr. Claxton. Where he be off to on such a fine day?"

"He's hunting nearby."

"That so?" Hoyt peered at her over the rim of his cup as he took another swallow of coffee. "You know, if I had me a fine-lookin' woman sech as you, I'd be sending them young bucks off to do my huntin'."

The implication in his voice hung heavily between them.

Patience continued her work, ignoring the innuendo about how he'd spend that time.

"I suppose the old man is around?"

"Harlon's . . . resting in the wagon." Patience didn't want this man to think she was alone without protection, so she quickly added, "He's here in case there's any trouble."

Hoyt glanced toward the wagon about thirty feet away. "Is that a fact! 'Course there ain't much an old feller with a broken leg can do, now is there?"

"Not much," Harlon's voice suddenly agreed as the barrel of his gun slid out of the back of the wagon and leveled at the center of Hoyt's chest. "But ol' Myrt here can sure get her point across!"

The tin cup clattered to the ground as Hoyt sprang to his feet. He jumped back as the hot coffee seared through the material of his shirt. "Here now, I was just makin' conversation. T'ain't no call to be gettin' all riled up!"

"You git on out of here, Mr. Willis. We don't take to the likes of you comin' around botherin' our womenfolks," Harlon said calmly, keeping the gun firmly on its target.

By now Jesse, Doog, and Joseph had returned to camp for dinner. They stood watching the tense exchange with wide-eyed curiosity.

Hoyt cast an uncertain look in Patience's direction.

"He means what he says, Mr. Willis. You'd best be moving on."

A look of sheer hatred flared unchecked in the skinner's eyes. "All right, but you'll be regrettin' this, missy!" He yielded in a voice so tight that Patience barely caught the message. Then he whirled and walked away.

The boys came running to Patience, their eyes aglow with excitement. "What'd he want, Miss McCord?" Doog asked.

Patience drew the boy close, distractedly giving him an assuring squeeze. "Nothing, Doog . . . Just a cup of hot coffee."

But Patience knew what he had wanted, and the realization sent a cold chill down her spine.

The men had a good day of hunting. Laurence Medley had even killed a small doe.

That night there was fresh venison steak for all.

After supper Cass took Aaron and Payne down to the river to wash. The three whooped and yelled as they plunged headlong into the icy water, the shock nearly stealing their breath away. Hurriedly they waded to the bank to lather themselves with the bar of soap Patience had supplied.

Jesse and Doog sat nearby, skipping rocks on the water. They didn't see any sense in washing again. They'd just bathed last night, so they had a whole week to go before they had to subject themselves to such misery again.

The sun was sitting behind a row of towering trees, casting its mellow glow on the red and gold leaves shimmering with vivid splashes of color. The air already had a sharp bite to it, and being wet didn't help matters, Cass thought as he washed faster.

"How many rabbits did ya kill today, Payne?" Doog wanted to know.

" 'Bout six, I guess."

"How 'bout you, Cass?"

"Twelve rabbits and four squirrels."

"Gosh!" Doog would be glad when he was old enough to go hunting with the men. Fact was, he'd be glad when he was old enough to do anything.

"What did you boys find to do to keep out of trouble?" Cass asked.

"Nothin'. We just sat down here and threw rocks in the river, whilst we listened to them women cacklin' like a bunch of ole settin' hens." Doug and Jesse giggled.

"Hear anything interesting?"

The two boys looked at each other sourly. "Not a thing."

Satisfied that they were socially acceptable again, Cass, Aaron, and Payne waded out of the water. They shivered as they dried off and put on clean clothes.

"That skinner came to camp today," Doog announced.

Cass's hands suddenly paused in buttoning his shirt. "Hoyt Willis?"

"Boy, is he nasty dirty!" Jesse observed as he made a disgusted face.

"What'd he want?"

"Miss McCord said he just wanted a cup of coffee," Jesse relayed.

"But Harlon had to turn the gun on him," Doog said.

Cass finished dressing and sat down to pull on his boots, trying to digest the news. He hadn't talked to Harlon tonight. The older man was asleep during supper. Since his leg was keeping him up nights, Corliss hadn't wanted to disturb him.

"Why did Harlon turn the gun on him?" Cass finally asked.

Doog was about to skip another rock when he let his arm slip back to his side. "Don't know . . . 'cept I think the skinner wasn't bein' real mannerly to Miss McCord."

Cass stood up, his eyes suddenly flashing with anger.

Aaron, sensing trouble, reached out to put his hand on Cass's arm warningly. "Best check with Harlon afore you get all riled. Doog's stories aren't too reliable at times."

"They are so!" Doog turned to Jesse. "Didn't that ole skinner come to camp today?" Jesse lifted his eyes to Cass. "He did, Cass. Honest!"

"Aaron, look after things here," Cass said. "I have business to tend to."

"I'm coming with you." Aaron stepped forward, meeting Cass's eyes solemnly.

"I appreciate your offer, but I can take care of this matter myself," Cass refused quietly.

"I know you can, but there be four of them. I figure that's two apiece."

Cass grinned. "You think you can handle two?"

Aaron drew his unimpressive stature to its full height. "Yessir."

"Then I guess you and I better go teach a certain skinner a few manners."

"Can I go too?" Payne was on his feet, eager to do his part.

"I'd rather you stayed here," Cass said as the five began to walk back to camp. "With Harlon down, we need to leave a man here to help the women."

"Oh . . . all right." Payne didn't think the job he'd been delegated sounded half as exciting as going out to knock that skinner's brains out, but he supposed it was just as important. Someone should be here to look after the women, and, like Cass had said, it needed to be a man. Payne's chest puffed with pride.

"Gentlemen, I think we'd better keep this under our hats," Cass advised as they drew closer to the camp. "The women will get all fussy if they know where we're going."

The four boys nodded, giving their unspoken promise to keep the mission quiet.

"Gosh, I don't like girls!" Doog complained. "They're always taking the fun out of everything."

Cass clamped his hand on the boy's shoulder sympathetically. "Try to hold that thought, son."

Patience glanced up as her men came walking back into camp. She felt such a warmth when she thought how the boys idolized Cass. It was apparent that Aaron respected and loved Cass deeply, and she wondered what the boy would do once they reached Cherry Grove and Cass left.

She watched as Cass and Aaron broke away and paused to converse with Harlon for a moment. Seconds later, the two emerged from the wagon and matched strides as they went to saddle the horses.

Realizing they were about to leave again, Patience abandoned her dishwashing to run to catch up with them.

"Cass!"

He turned and saw her hurrying toward him. Pausing, he waited until she had caught up.

"Where are you going?" she asked, fighting to catch her breath.

"Aaron and I have a little business that needs tending," he said easily, his tone never giving away their true intent.

She frowned. "Business—tonight?"

"We shouldn't be gone long."

"Well . . ." She looked from Cass to Aaron doubtfully. "You be careful . . ."

Cass nodded. "We plan to."

She turned and started away, then paused. She reached out and put her hand on his arm.

Cass looked at Aaron and grinned as he pulled her close for a reassuring hug. "You're worrying again."

"I just can't help it. It seems to me you're storying about where you're going." Patience had an uneasy feeling that Cass was keeping something from her.

Cass drew back and grinned at her innocently. "Me? Story to you?"

"Don't you look so innocent, Cass Claxton!" She placed her hands on her hips. "You'd story to me in a minute." She turned to Aaron. "Is he storying to me?"

Aaron shrugged and grinned sheepishly.

Cass chuckled and reached out to draw her back into his arms. He gave her another hug, then turned her in the direction of camp and smacked her fanny. "Go wash your dishes, woman."

Patience still had a niggling feeling in the pit of her stomach that something wasn't right as she watched him walk away.

Exactly *what* it was she wasn't sure, but she had a feeling it wouldn't take her long to find out.

CHAPTER 15

IT WAS GETTING CLOSE TO MIDNIGHT BEFORE CASS and Aaron returned to camp. Patience thought she'd never seen two more disreputable-looking characters in all her life.

Their clothes were filthy; their shirts were torn at the shoulders; and both were sporting what would turn out to be the biggest, blackest shiners Patience had ever seen.

They got off their horses and turned to face her guiltily. She saw that each had a pumpkin tucked under his arm.

"You've been fighting!" she accused, drawing her wrapper closer against the night chill. She'd lain awake for hours, listening for their return.

"Fighting?" Cass shot a knowing glance at Aaron, and they both grinned. "We have not. We've been picking pumpkins." He gallantly extended his bounty to her.

Corliss emerged from the back of the wagon. Seeing Aaron's sorry condition, she squired him off to patch him up. That left Cass in Patience's care.

"I have never seen such going-ons!" Patience usually borrowed one of Corliss's standard sayings when she didn't know what else to say. Quietly she set the pumpkin aside and stepped over to help him to the washstand.

He good-naturedly shrugged her away, insisting that he didn't need any help.

Patience decided that whatever he'd been doing, it had left him in a good mood. He was buoyant and elated, completely unconcerned that she'd been up most of the night, worrying herself half to death.

Pouring water into the enamel basin, she reached for a bar of soap.

"If you've been out all this time consorting with that woman . . ." she began, remembering the redhead who'd just been itching to get her hands on Cass. If that woman continued to fool with her man, she'd break her in two! "Why . . . why I can't believe you'd subject Aaron to such—"

"Redhead, redhead! Is that all you can think about?" Cass complained. "Do you honestly think I'd let a woman do *this* to me?" It was a low blow to Cass's pride.

Patience wrung out the cloth and began scrubbing his face just as she would have scrubbed Phebia's. "I don't know what to think of you! And I didn't say anything about a redhead—you did!"

"Ouch! That hurts!" His voice was muffled by the flying cloth.

"You'd better not have taken Aaron out to teach him things he shouldn't know yet!"

"Aaron is sixteen years old. What he doesn't know, he should be learning." Cass sucked in his breath painfully as the soap seeped into one of his open wounds. "Will you stop it! I can wash my own face, woman!"

"What *have* you been doing, Cass?"

"I told you. I had business to take care of." He wasn't about to tell her where he'd been, because if she found out that he'd gone out to take care of Hoyt Willis, then she'd assume he'd done it as a favor to her—which he hadn't. Anyway, he didn't think he had. He was pretty sure that he'd just wanted the skinner out of his own hair.

"And you involved Aaron in your rowdy mission?"

"You bet! He's a great kid." Cass had a new respect for the boy. He'd witnessed grown men tumbling tonight under the hands of a youth filled with sheer grit and determination.

Patience didn't know what the two had been up to, and it didn't seem likely she was going to find out. But there was no way on earth she believed they'd been out picking pumpkins.

"You should be ashamed of yourself!"

Cass sighed, realizing that she wasn't going to let up until he appeased her. "All right, I'm ashamed of myself."

"You are not!"

"I know it, but I figure you're not going to pipe down until I say that I am."

Patience irritably dabbed white salve on his cuts, silently admitting that she'd been more scared than angry. From every appearance they had been fighting. She found a smile threatening as she wondered what their opponents must look like now.

"It's a wonder you weren't shot."

"Not a chance. I'm smarter than that."

She helped Cass out of his soiled shirt, handed him the washcloth, and went to get a clean shirt from his pack. By the time she returned he was looking more presentable. Handing him the clean shirt, she walked to the dying fire to pour a cup of coffee.

Frost was settling on the ground, and a bright harvest moon was hanging overhead. The midnight hour gleamed as brightly as day.

She turned and finally smiled. He accepted the unspoken truce with a feeling of relief. She handed the tin cup to him. "Drink this. It'll help to warm you."

He slipped into his coat, his gaze locking with hers gratefully. "Thanks. Why not stay and share a cup with me?"

She was surprised by his invitation. It was the first time he'd ever asked her to join him, and she fought the urge to read more into his unexpected request than he might mean.

"Thank you. That would be nice." She busied herself pouring a second cup of coffee as he walked over to pick up his bedroll. Moments later they left camp so that they wouldn't disturb the children who were sleeping beneath the wagon.

They walked side by side until they came to a grassy knoll where Cass paused. Patience helped him unfold the bedroll.

"It's getting chilly," she remarked as they sat down and settled their coffee cups on the ground beside them.

"Another month and the snow will be flying." He glanced at her, suddenly aware that she was wearing only her nightgown and a flannel wrapper. "Would you like my coat?"

"I'm warm enough, thank you."

They sat for a moment in an easy, compatible silence as they sipped the coffee.

"Hoyt Willis paid a visit to camp this afternoon."

"That right? What'd he want?"

Patience frowned as she thought about the vile buffalo skinner and his crude intentions. "He asked for a cup of coffee, but I think he was up to no good. Harlon had to ask him to leave."

"Oh?"

"Aren't you a little surprised he's still around?"

"No."

"You don't think he might be intending to cause some kind of trouble?"

She thought about mentioning the insinuations Hoyt had leveled at her, but she knew if she did it would only add to his troubles, so she left out some details about the incident. She was confident that Harlon had properly discouraged the vulgar man from coming around again.

Cass tipped his hat forward and lay back on the bedroll. "I'm not worried about Hoyt Willis, and there's no need for you to be either."

"Well"—Patience was confident that Cass could handle whatever trouble Hoyt Willis could cause—"I'd sure be happier to know that he was a hundred miles on down the road."

They shared the silence again.

When Patience finally turned to say something, she had to cover her mouth to stifle her giggles.

Cass raised himself halfway up, his brows drawing into an affronted frown. "What's so funny?"

"You . . . you look like you tangled with a wildcat!" *And lost*, she added mentally.

A muscle quivered in his jaw, and she could tell that he was trying to restrain his amusement. "You think it's funny, huh?"

Her eyes gleamed with merriment. "Yes . . . I never knew a jack-o'-lantern could be so ferocious!"

He shrugged and lay down again. "Go ahead and laugh."

"Thank you, I believe I will!" She broke into another round of mirth, and by the time she was near tears he'd decided to join her. He knew that he looked a sight, but it had been worth it. He and Aaron had taught Hoyt Willis a lesson tonight that the man would never forget.

"You remind me of the time Jimmy Lonigan pushed me into a mud hole," she teased. "I declare, I was a mess. My face was caked with mud; my dress was ruined; and the lovely yellow ribbon Mother had tied in my hair that morning looked like a soggy noodle. I was never so humiliated! I pitched a temper tantrum of such magnitude that my teacher was forced to send one of the younger boys rushing out the door to get my mother to come take me home." She laughed merrily. "I didn't return to class for a week, and I'm sure the teacher thought that was too soon."

Cass grinned as he pictured her fit. "What made Jimmy Lonigan want to push you into a mud hole?"

Patience looked down at him, managing to keep her features deceptively composed. "Why, I just can't imagine! I was such an angel!"

They laughed together, and Patience thought it had the nicest sound.

"I remember being embarrassed in front of the whole schoolroom once." Cass gazed across the moonlit meadow as the corners of his mouth lifted with amusement. "My brother Beau had brought a frog to school one day and stuck it in Elsbeth Wilson's lunch pail. Elsbeth was a real pain. Her folks were rich, so she always had more than the rest of us, but she was miserable. She always looked like she'd been eating persimmons. When she opened up her pail, that bullfrog jumped out onto her desk and swelled up with a loud *barrroopt!* You could have heard Elsbeth screaming for miles."

"What did the teacher do?"

"Because I'd laughed the hardest, the teacher thought I'd put the frog in her lunch pail, so she made me sit in the front of the room all afternoon, holding that frog on my lap, apologizing to Elsbeth every few minutes for being 'unsociable and crude.' "

Patience giggled. "And your brother didn't say a word in your defense?"

"Are you serious? Beau sprang out of his seat, pointed a self-righteous finger in my direction, and hollered that I shouldn't have been so mean, and that he was gonna tell Ma on me when we got home!"

They had another good laugh together. Patience couldn't remember when she'd had so much fun. When their merriment had died away, Cass swiveled to look at her.

"I'll bet you were one of those prissy little girls, in your frilly dress, with your hair in big blond curls that hung down to your fanny."

She nodded. "Mother insisted on my wearing my hair that way. Butch Michaels was forever dipping one of my ringlets into his inkwell," she admitted.

"He was probably sweet on you and just wanted to get your attention."

"Oh, he got my attention, all right! I gave him a black eye every Monday morning. It got to where he'd run when he saw me coming out the door."

Cass grinned. "I bet!"

She cast her eyes down shyly, knowing that he was teasing her this time. "I was pretty terrible most of the time."

"You haven't improved a whole lot since."

Patience glanced up, and he winked at her.

"Oh, you . . . how would you know what I'm like?" she accused. "You've never taken the time to get to know the real me. You're always blustering around, shouting at me, acting as if I'm about to give *you* a black eye every Monday morning."

"Butch Michaels has my complete sympathy," he said dourly. "I've experienced a couple of your black eyes."

Patience knew that he was speaking figuratively, of course.

"I'll admit that in the past I gave you reason to feel that way about me, but I wish I could convince you that I've changed, Cass . . . Even if I do backslide a teeny bit occasionally."

"A teeny bit? I'd say your lapses are more like rock slides!"

"Nevertheless, I am better."

Than what, he wondered to himself. "Well, if that's what you think . . ." he said indulgently.

"It's what I know. I'm really not a bad person."

He shrugged. "Who am I to argue? You were the perfect lady the day we met," he conceded dryly. "You remember? I just happened to step into your path while we were in Miller's Mercantile—"

"You didn't just happen to step into my way," she corrected. "You deliberately blocked my way."

"But you do recall the incident? You had just bounced fifteen or twenty spools of thread off Edgar Miller's bald head because he didn't have a certain color you wanted."

Patience blushed. "That was a long time ago."

He eyed her evenly. "I sang tenor for months after that!"

"I said I was sorry."

"Since then you've tricked me into marrying you at the point of a shotgun, maneuvered me into taking you to Cherry Grove, deliberately thrown that nasty dishwater all over me, and with the aid of a bullwhip, thoroughly humiliated me in front of the whole wagon train and seven prostitutes. Then that same night, you turned the whip on me again, nearly peeling the hide off my back because you'd gotten it into your head that I was riding off to meet a redhead—"

"That whip never touched your back!"

His eyes narrowed. "A fact, I might add, that saved your life!"

Her eyes dropped sheepishly as he continued, "In the time I've known you, you've browbeaten me, cussed me, spat on me, threatened and co-erced me more times than I can count on both hands—now tell me again how you've turned into such a nice person! I'm having a hell of a time believing that!"

She knew he was right. She had treated him terribly. "I wish we could just start over," she confessed as a heartfelt sigh escaped her.

He was silent for a moment, and she wondered if he was angry with her again. Then he said quite calmly, "Well, I guess there's no law that says we can't."

Her eyes flew to his face, and his steady gaze assured her that she hadn't heard wrong. "Do you mean it?"

"I mean it. I don't enjoy this bickering any more than you do, and for the sake of everyone else, I think we should try to get along with each other. I can't say I'm ever going to forget what you've done, Patience, because I'm not sure I ever could. I'm the kind of man who likes to control my own destiny—and I damn sure plan on having the *only* say about whom I marry. No woman's ever gonna hog-tie and brand *me*. But I'll concede that people can change, if they want to."

Patience's heart tripped and thudded at his words. "Thank you," she said softly. "Does that mean you do believe I've changed?"

"That means I'm going to work on it a little harder."

"Thank you . . . because I'm beginning to care for you quite deeply."

"Well, just don't let it get out of hand," he warned.

"What would you say if I told you I needed you?" She knew the question was wanton, shameful, but it popped out anyway.

He slowly lifted the brim of his hat to look at her.

"I do, you know," she said.

"You mean emotionally?"

"I mean physically too."

He lowered his hat again. "I thought we'd been all through this. We're not going to bed with each other. A man doesn't take a woman—at least not a woman like you—unless he plans to make her his wife. I don't plan to make you my wife, Patience."

She reached out, tipped his hat up. "Right now, for this moment, I'm going to forget you said that, Cass Claxton! Once we reach Cherry Grove, you'll be a free man—no matter what you choose to let happen here . . . tonight."

Love shone brightly in her eyes, and she prayed that, for once, he would recognize it. They gazed at each other as they had done many times before. His eyes were shadowed by the moonlight, making them seem darker. Still, she could see in their depths that he wanted her, perhaps more desperately than he would allow himself to admit.

"Patience . . . nothing is going to happen here tonight. It would be senseless . . . I'll admit I'm beginning to like you, but it isn't love." The very word scared the devil out of him.

"Cass, right now I don't care how you feel about me. I'm lonely . . . very, very lonely, and I'm beginning to wonder if I'll ever be able to make a man happy. I need you to hold me, to love me. I need someone to care just for me, even if it is only for tonight."

In a vague way Cass understood how she was feeling. The children and the trail made demands on their energy every day, and there were times when he, too, wished he could go to someone to ease his troubles.

"Surely I'm not so unlovable that you couldn't want to be with me," she argued. "You're a man, I'm a woman."

"Patience . . ." He *did* want to hold her, make love to her. He knew it wasn't right. In fact, it was wrong—but she was making it impossible for him to say no.

Sensing his growing weakness, she leaned over and her mouth brushed his persuasively. "Cass, please . . . just for one night . . . teach me how to be a woman."

Her lips continued to brush back and forth with lazy seduction.

"I thought after our talk the other night—" Cass objected weakly.

"I thought it over," she murmured. And she *had*, many, many times. "What a man and woman do when they make love doesn't sound all that bad. Besides, if Corliss lets Harlon and my mother let my father . . . it can't be that bad!"

They exchanged a slow, tantalizing kiss, and desire began to override common sense. "It isn't bad," he relented as their lips parted briefly. "It's pleasurable, and I'm sorry I misled you about it—"

Her hand came up to cover his mouth. "Then love me, Cass, now . . . tonight . . ."

He groaned, and she suddenly found herself lying on the ground beneath him. She caught her breath, whispering his name.

She was innocent and he was worldly. He knew it wasn't a fair match, but he was blinded by the feel of her warm and willing body as she lay beneath him. Her urgent, whispered pleas were more than any man could ignore.

Her lips parted, and her eyes glowed with desire as her breasts rose and fell with each breath.

His eyes flashed a gentle but firm warning as he gazed into her eyes. "All right, but *I* make love to *you.*"

"Meaning?"

"Meaning I consent because I want you, Patience . . . maybe I have for a long time—I don't know. But we're going to make love for no other reason than that I care for you, desire you, want you—but *not* because you've asked me to." His brow furrowed sternly. "That's a habit you're going to have to break. Other men are not going to have to be asked twice."

A satisfied light entered her eyes. "Maybe I won't be asking other men."

A muscle quivered in his jaw. "I'll whip your fanny if you do." His lips recaptured hers, more demanding this time.

When they parted many long moments later she whispered, "I promise you, Cass. I will never, ever deceive you again." And she meant it. Never again would she manipulate him. Never again would she impose her selfishness on him. From this moment on she would love him as deeply and wholly as she knew how.

He said nothing because he knew nothing to say, but she saw that the look in his eyes was one of understanding. "I hope you know what you're doing."

"I don't," she admitted with a cheeky grin. "But I figure you know enough for both of us."

A slow grin replaced his frown of worry. "Oh, you think so!"

She sighed. "I'm afraid I know so."

He pulled the pins from her hair, allowing the fragrant mass to tumble around her shoulders in a glorious cloud. His fingers slipped through the silken mass, and he drew her face slowly back to meet his.

The kiss ignited an ember that had been smoldering for weeks, and Patience knew that what she was about to do was right.

Their lips parted, and he brushed a kiss across her forehead as he began slipping her gown slowly—ever so slowly—over her head.

"You want to learn to please a man, huh?"

She nodded.

He drew her to her feet. Their eyes met and held as his large hands began a leisurely exploration of her body. He brushed his fingertips across the tips of her breasts, causing her to catch her breath with expectation. The crisp night air made her even more sensitive to his gentle ministrations.

"Are you afraid?"

"No . . . well, maybe a little."

His eyes darkened even more as his hand ran over her flat stomach, her tiny waist, along her arms.

"You can't hazard a guess what a man might like?"

"Well, if I were a man I would probably like to be touched here . . . and here . . . and maybe here . . ."

Cass's soft intake of breath told her she was probably right. His hands drifted over her bare bottom, squeezing her, then moved up her spine to send tingles racing through her.

"Yeah," his voice dropped to a husky timbre as his eyes lowered to caress her nakedness. "You're getting close."

"And maybe here . . . and here . . ." He caught her hand and steadied it momentarily. "Most men are kinda partial to right here."

Her body seemed weightless, light, wanting him to seize control as their mouths came together again.

He was like a rich, heady wine drugging her with pleasure. His hands, gentle before, now began to tease, to excite, to take. Though Patience didn't have the slightest knowledge of this form of love, she trusted that he would be gentle with her.

"I don't want you to think about what I told you the other night . . . Making love can be beautiful."

"Oh, Cass, I knew you would make it so," she whispered as her own hands became bolder. He was all sinewy muscle and warm, pulsating flesh.

Cass wasn't sure he deserved the trust he saw in her eyes, but he was moved by it. "I won't hurt you. I want you to remember this night and know what it means to be a woman."

She smiled up at him, her heart overflowing with love. He knew her better than anyone. He knew all her weaknesses, and yet he still wanted her. The realization made her want to cry.

Their lips met again, all restraints abandoned this time. Though he knew he had to move slowly, his body was hungry to take, to possess, to control. Taking her hand, he brought it back to him, murmuring softly, "You realize this may hurt."

Nodding, she closed her eyes. The feel of him pressing against her bare stomach suggested that pain might be inescapable.

Their mouths suddenly became inseparable, hungry, searching. There was so much for her to absorb: his scent, his taste, the unfamiliar feel of his manhood throbbing to claim her.

His hands explored, probed, paid homage to what had before been only a mystery. Her breathing was faster, more pronounced. Cass realized it was the first time in a long time that he was doing the leading with a woman. The teaching and the knowledge of her innocence made him heady with desire.

"Patience . . . I'm sorry . . . There are times when a man can't take it as slow as he would like to . . ."

Whimpering, she anchored her fingers in his hair and cradled herself more deeply into his arms. Desire, hot and urgent, raced unchecked through her. "I never thought . . . I never imagined it would be like this . . ."

Their kisses deepened, their tongues tempting, tantalizing, teasing, making them grow bolder, more daring with each passing moment.

They joined slowly, he keeping the rhythm easy and gentle. He had never had a woman be so giving, respond so completely and with so much love—but then nothing about her surprised him any longer.

She squeezed her eyes shut. The pain was there, as he'd said it would be, and suddenly his gentle motion took on an urgency that could no longer be contained. Her eyes suddenly opened, and above her she saw the velvety black sky and a million twinkling stars. And Cass was looking down at her with a look she couldn't quite make out—of tenderness, of hunger, of pride. Then he cried out her name, his arms imprisoning her trembling body as the pain dissolved and turned to ecstasy.

Her eyes closed again as she felt herself tumbling over and over into the inky blackness, willing the delicious sensations bursting throughout her body to go on forever.

The tenderness lingered long afterward. Patience lay beneath Cass, trying to make sense out of what had just happened. She didn't regret one moment, but she wondered what must he think of her now.

She took small consolation in the fact that he seemed in no hurry for her to move, and she herself was in no hurry to break away.

"Well, what do you think now?"

She sighed. "I think you were trying to scare me the other night."

He chuckled as his hand caressed her bare bottom. "I'm sorry."

"You should be. I think I'm going to take to this quite well."

They rolled onto their backs on the blanket and gazed at the stars. As they exchanged kisses, he drew her closer to whisper into her ear. He told her things any woman would long to hear.

The magic of the night slowly slipped away; and long before she welcomed it, dawn signaled the coming of a new day.

"I have to be getting back. I don't want Corliss to know I've been gone." She slipped into her gown, aching to hear him say that the night had meant as much to him as it had to her, but he didn't.

They stood and he gathered her into his arms for one final long kiss.

"I'll be along shortly," he said when the kiss ended.

"Yes, breakfast will be ready soon," she said, disappointed. As she turned she was suddenly overcome by emotion. For one brief moment she thought she might fling herself back into his arms and beg him to tell her that she meant something—anything—to him. For him she felt a most incredible love, and she knew that what they had shared was the most wonderful thing that had ever happened to her. But she also knew that, as kind and gentle as he had been, what they had shared had not touched him.

"Patience?"

She turned. "Yes?"

"You can stop worrying," he said softly. "You're going to make some man very happy one of these days."

A smile, tiny though it was, came forth. "Thank you."

Squaring her shoulders, she lifted her head and walked back to camp, determined, painful as it would be, to try and put the events of this night behind her.

CHAPTER 16

*B*Y THE END OF THE WEEK, THE WAGON TRAIN reached St. Joseph, Missouri, where Patience, Harlon, Corliss, the children, and Cass were preparing to say good-bye to their new friends before veering east toward Kansas.

Patience was going to miss Mardean, Winoka Medsker, Lucius Waterman, and Buck Brewster's sweet fiddle music. The group had formed close bonds, and Patience knew she would miss the ones who had become like family to her.

But they were all determined to substitute happy faces for tearful good-byes. After they cleared supper away that Friday night, the women brought out the pies and cakes that they'd managed to bake during the week. Meanwhile, Buck tuned up his fiddle for dancing.

The camp took on a festive air as the weary travelers set their troubles aside and, as Corliss put it, 'just let their hair down for a spell.'

Patience became breathless and rosy-cheeked by midevening. Though they'd traveled more than fifteen miles that day, the men had kept the women dancing nearly every jig. Patience thought Cass had forgotten her by the time he got around to claiming her for a dance.

"Miss McCord, may I say you look right fetchin' tonight," he complimented as he whirled her beneath an ebony sky full of twinkling stars.

"Oh, I do thank you, kind sir," she returned, matching his airy tone. "Your silver tongue just makes me feel ever so giddy, but I *was* beginning to fear that you were never going to come over and 'fetch' me."

"Been waiting for me, huh?" He threw his head back and laughed, whirling her around merrily, and she thought she would burst with happiness.

She gazed into his eyes and grinned. A change had taken place in their relationship since the night they'd made love. He was more at ease with her, less prone to being provoked, more willing to cooperate. "I thought I was going to have to whip Ernestine Parker and take you away from her," she said.

He winced. "I thought I was going to have to ask you to."

The music suddenly slowed to a waltz, and Matt Johnson stepped over to claim Patience. Cass motioned the other man away as he drew her possessively back into his arms, settling her closer this time.

Smiling, Patience laid her head against his shoulder and closed her eyes contentedly as he moved her away from the fire, into the deepening shadows.

"Sorry I didn't have time to eat dinner with you and the children," he apologized as the darkness wrapped its silky arms around them.

"We missed you, but I'm sure Laurence appreciated your helping him repair his axle."

"Lucy still cranky?"

Patience nodded, mechanically carrying on the conversation, but her thoughts were wandering. She loved his scent, his smell, the feel of his broad chest pressed tightly against her breasts.

"Maybe she's just tired of traveling," Cass said.

"Maybe, but it won't be long now before we're home."

They became lost in the sweet strains of the violin as he drew her even closer, drinking deeply of the intoxicating fragrance of her hair. Through her skirt she could feel the imprint of his maleness, barely restrained, exciting.

"Cass?"

"Hmmm?"

"Do you ever think about the other night?"

He appeared to be weighing his answer, and she wondered if she had overstepped her bounds. Finally he said, "If I were to be completely honest, Miss McCord, it would only make your head swell."

She savored a flood of satisfaction as she drew back to gaze into his eyes. "Then you do."

"I never said that."

"But you do." She felt her stomach tie in knots as he gazed back at her.

"All right," he confessed. "I do."

Her breath quickened as she reached out to trail her fingers tenderly down the side of his face. He moved back as if her touch had unnerved him.

"Then meet me again tonight."

"No."

She wasn't discouraged, wouldn't allow herself to be. "Please."

"Patience, no." She recognized the familiar stubbornness in his voice and steeled herself for a fight.

"Why not?" She knew it was madness, but she wondered how she'd lived so long without love.

"I don't want you to be hurt," he told her, his tone becoming more gentle.

"You would never hurt me." Her fingers lightly stroked his shoulder blades. "Don't you know how I ache to be with you, to lie in your arms once more?"

"I want you to stop talking like that." He bent close, his lips perilously near hers. "We'll reach Cherry Grove in a few days. No matter what has passed between us"—his voice lowered—"I'll expect you to hold to your promise concerning the divorce."

"I intend to."

"The minute I get you and the children settled, I'll be on my way."

"I understand that."

Their mouths moved nearer.

"I don't want you going all hurt and weepy when I leave," he warned. He paused and gazed deeply into her troubled eyes. "It's going to be hard enough to leave the children. I've lain awake the past few nights, trying to sort through my feelings, and I realize I've grown more attached to all of you than I should have. Aaron and Payne look up to me as the father they've never had. And I'm sorry, really sorry, that I can't be here for all of them . . . Jesse, Doog, Joseph, Bryon, Lucy, Margaret Ann—God, Margaret Ann!" A look of respect came into his eyes. "What a match she'll make for a man someday—Lucy, Phebia . . . you."

In many ways Cass knew that Patience had come to depend upon him as much as or more than the others. "But I *will* be leaving, and should I take you to my bed again, though I can't deny that it would be my pleasure, it would only make our parting harder when the time comes for me to go."

"Then don't go!" she urged in a broken whisper, suddenly wishing she had more control over her emotions. She had been struggling so long to find herself, to know the real Patience McCord, but it had taken this man to show her that she could be the woman she'd always longed to be. She didn't know how she could bear losing him now, so soon after he'd taught her the real meaning of love.

"I have to leave, Patience. I'm not ready to settle down to one woman . . . I may never be."

"Not even Laure Revuneau?" Patience knew she was out of line, but she had to know what he felt for Laure.

"Laure?" Cass realized that he hadn't thought of the French beauty in weeks.

"I believe she was hoping for a Christmas wedding, with you."

She felt him grow tense. "I guess she's free to hope all she wants. No woman's gonna hog-tie and brand me."

Her pulse leapt expectantly. "Then you aren't planning to marry Laure?"

He sighed. "My only plans are to return to St. Louis and attend to my business, which has been sorely neglected of late."

Her eyes met his unashamedly. "I'm going to say something you're not going to like."

"Then don't say it."

"I'm in love with you, Cass, deeply in love."

His face changed and became hard. "Patience . . . don't do this—"

"I am, Cass. I'm sorry, but I am." She stopped dancing and caught his face in both her hands, not caring that others were watching them now. "I love you and I will never, ever give up hope that someday, no matter what I've done in the past, you will return my love."

"Patience," he warned, pulling her hands away and drawing her face to his chest. "You're making me nervous as hell!"

"I know you always have been a mite skittish," she acknowledged with a broken sob, "but you can't stop me from loving you. You're the best thing that has ever happened to me."

"No, Patience. It'll do no good for either one of us to think that way. I can't return your love. We're no good for each other," he said sternly, and she wondered if he wasn't trying to convince himself more than her.

She thought of all the times she had rejected other men—easily, cruelly, and without much thought for their feelings. She guessed the good Lord had had His fill of her nonsense and had sent Cass Claxton for her penance.

But if He had, she would gladly accept her punishment and pray that the Lord would see fit to extend it.

"We could meet tonight."

"No."

"We have only three days left. We could slip away for just a little while and . . . and I would have something to remember you by." Patience knew she was sounding like a shameless hussy lately, but she didn't care. She loved Cass so fiercely, so completely, that she was willing to endure any name anyone wanted to call her if he would spend one night with her again. "Please, Cass, what could it hurt? If you're worrying about my virtue, the damage has already been done."

"Patience, how many times do I have to tell you no—I won't be asking you to my bed!"

"I'm asking you to *mine!*"

Cass was not sure how long he could keep refusing. He wanted her. He ached for her, but he knew that if they made love again, it wouldn't satisfy the hunger in him but only nourish it.

His need for her was becoming a raw craving, one he had to fight daily. He cared for her—maybe he did even love her at times—but there was still a part of him that wouldn't accept the verdict. She had tricked him more times than he could count, and he wasn't sure he could ever really trust her. And when it came down to it, what good was love without trust?

She sighed. "You might as well give in to me. I'll ask again."

"And I'll just keep refusing."

And she did. And he did. And she did. And he did. Every night, until Cass thought he would lose his mind. But he took hope in the knowledge that if he could make it through one more night, then the battle would be over.

It was the last day out, and Cass deliberately rode well ahead of the wagon. At noon, he took his meal and ate with Aaron and Payne under a distant tree.

Surprisingly Patience left him alone.

Later that night, when everyone was safely tucked in bed, Cass took his bedroll and went in search of a place to sleep. All during supper he had watched Patience move about camp. His passion demanded that he ask her for a moonlight walk, then passionately fulfill her every need, yet his common sense told him that he only had to make it through one more long torturous night, and he would once again have his freedom.

Spreading the blanket on the ground, he went to the creek to wash up. When he returned five minutes later, Patience was already lying on the blanket.

"Oh, hell!" He stared down at her, shifting on one foot impatiently. He just didn't have the strength to go through this again!

"Hello." Her smile was beguiling and meant nothing but trouble. "Isn't it a lovely night?"

"What are you doing here?"

Her lower lip formed a teasing pout. "Why are you always so cranky?"

He looked down on her dourly. "I guess a man wouldn't need one of those crystal balls to see what you're up to."

Her smile turned wicked as she rose and presented her back to him. She began to remove her shirt, then her blouse.

"Patience," he warned.

A camisole sailed against his chest, and he groaned.

Deciding he was simply going to ignore her, he dropped to the bedroll and jerked his hat determinedly down over his face. If she wanted to catch her death, he wasn't going to waste his breath trying to stop her.

He suddenly tensed as he felt her hand on his belt.

"Patience, don't make me get mean with you," he growled.

"Now, now, darling," she purred throatily. The belt suddenly loosened, and he felt the top button of his breeches give way. "I know you must be exhausted from trying so hard to ignore me. I'm just going to help you relax a little."

He was aroused instantly, and the sight was encouraging to Patience.

"I don't need any help, and it wasn't a bit tiring to ignore you."

Her hands began to ease his breeches down. "Well, you just did a wonderful job," she praised, sliding her body up his long length, her mouth coming to rest against his with a long, unhurried kiss.

Cass's lips parted for one blissful moment as he moaned, his hand slipping up to capture a bare, satiny globe.

"You're naked," he accused resentfully against her lips.

"My, my, so I am! How do you suppose that happened?" Her fingers loosened the buttons on his shirt. "You know, you almost had me believing your little act until I saw the way you were looking at me during supper tonight."

"I wasn't looking at *you*. I was watching the dog."

"No, you weren't watching the dog. You were looking at *me*. You couldn't take your eyes off me, not once." She placed her hands on his hard flat belly, caressing, taunting.

"You're really asking for trouble, lady."

She smiled and leaned down to kiss him. "So humor me."

Moments later his flannel shirt came off, and her hands made quick work of peeling back his undershirt. Spreading her hands across his bare chest, she nipped his rib cage painfully with her small, even teeth.

"*Ouch!*"

"That's for ignoring me all day." She kissed the place she nipped, then nipped again.

"You are shameless!" He chuckled, feeling his body tremble as she began kissing her way across the dark hair on his chest.

"Tell me you're sorry."

"For what?"

She nipped again, only lower this time.

"Lord!" He caught his breath as her hands and her mouth grew bolder. "You realize you're acting like that redhead you found so offensive?"

"No, I'm nothing like the redhead," she said, moving back up to cover his mouth with hers. "I can't come close to her experience," she whispered. "But I don't think you'll ever notice the difference."

He sighed and completely gave up as his hand moved downward along her body in a soft caress. "Where is everyone?"

"Asleep in the wagon."

"Harlon and Corliss?"

Their mouths touched, teased, became more intense.

"Sound asleep."

Cass could not suppress the glow in his eyes as he finally rolled her over on the blanket, gazing deeply into her slumberous violet eyes with a lusty perusal. "Then I suppose I'll have to let you have your way with me, Mrs. Claxton."

He'd finally gotten her name right.

"Yes, darling." She yielded with mock subservience. "I guess you will."

CHAPTER 17

*T*HE MAISON DES PETITES FLEURS ORPHANAGE ARRIVED in Cherry Grove a little before noon on Wednesday. It was a dreary, overcast morning, and a bone-chilling wind blew from the north. October had finally gotten down to business, and the earlier reassuring rays of sunshine had been violated by clouds.

As the wagon rolled down Main Street, Patience took in the familiar sight of Miller's Mercantile, and she breathed her first sigh of relief since she'd left St. Louis forty-one days ago. The journey was finally over, and the Lord had seen them safely through.

Patience pulled the team to a halt. Corliss lifted the flap, a big smile settling over her tuckered features as her eyes took in the row of storefronts. "Lordy, Lordy, am I ever glad to see this!"

Patience sighed, her own smile projecting relief. "We're home, Corliss. We're finally home."

"Praise the Lord!"

Edgar Miller was sweeping his porch, his gaze darting to the wagon every once in a while as he tried to see who the new arrivals were.

Patience saw his balding head bobbing up and down with curiosity, and she lifted her hand to give him a friendly wave. "Hello, Mr. Miller!"

Eyes widening, Edgar nearly dropped his broom when he recognized Leviticus McCord's daughter. He suddenly turned tail and shot back inside the mercantile, slamming the door firmly shut behind him.

Cass rode up beside the wagon and stopped. Resting his hand on the saddle horn, he grinned down at Patience lazily.

"You'd better raise a white flag, Miss McCord. I believe the troops are getting nervous."

Meeting his laughing eyes with an impervious look of her own, Patience firmly gathered the reins in her hands. "Very funny, Mr. Claxton."

Cass was still chuckling as she clucked her tongue and urged the team to begin moving again.

Nothing had changed in Cherry Grove. The sleepy little town wasn't much, but she knew there were a lot of good, God-fearing people residing here, people who would see to the children's physical and spiritual welfare. She saw that the Havershams still had their restaurant and that Doug Kelly still ran his saloon and gambling house. She wondered if the saloon still served as a church on Sunday mornings. The town wasn't nearly as bad as she'd thought it was six years ago. It was a nice place, actually, one she was sure that she and the children would grow to love.

Once they were settled, the children would come to know and respect Leviticus, and she and Cass could—

Her newfound enthusiasm was suddenly overshadowed by an unsettling thought. In a few days Cass would no longer be with them. He had become so much a part of all their lives that it was hard to imagine how she and the children were going to manage without him. Patience didn't want to imagine a day without him, let alone the rest of her life, but she admitted that she had no magical power to prevent him from leaving.

The wagon turned the corner, and Reverend Olson's house came into view. Patience could see Rebecca standing on a chair, cleaning windows. The parson's wife glanced up, startled when she recognized Patience driving the wagon. She quickly recovered and began tapping on the panes of shiny glass, making staccato sounds as Patience smiled and waved at her.

Moments later the door to the parsonage flew open, and Reverend Olson came hurrying out, still struggling into his coat.

Patience was eager to see Leviticus again. Though they'd corresponded regularly, she hadn't seen him in six long years. She wondered how much he'd changed. He'd always had a penchant for gooseberry pie and lemon cake, and she giggled as she pictured her wiry little father having developed a round belly and rosy cheeks.

She couldn't wait until the children met him. Patience knew they would adore him, and Harlon and Corliss would welcome the hours of companionship Leviticus would provide.

At Christmastime, he would see to it that the orphanage had the biggest, brightest, most beautiful tree in all the town. There would be apples, nuts, and oranges to fill each stocking, and the house would be bursting with the mouth-watering smells of succulent roast duckling, tasty mince pies, delectable spice cakes and—

Her thoughts wavered as Leviticus's house suddenly came into view. Unconsciously she pulled back on the reins, bringing the team to a halt. For a moment she sat dumbfounded staring at the scene before her. There was nothing there except a smoke-blackened chimney standing alone in the pile of burnt rubble.

Patience heard Corliss's sharp intake of breath, then her awestruck "Dear God in heaven!"

The chimney, silhouetted against the gray sky, was the only thing left of Leviticus McCord's house. The rest had burned to the ground.

Whirling, Patience saw Cass riding up beside her. Speechlessly she looked at him.

Climbing off the horse onto the wagon seat, he drew her into his arms as Reverend Olson came hurrying up to the wagon.

The reverend appeared momentarily taken aback as he saw Cass Claxton holding Patience McCord in his arms. But he quickly pushed aside his astonishment and said, "Oh, Miss McCord . . . I'm so sorry I wasn't able to stop you."

Lifting her face from the haven of Cass's chest, Patience stared back at the reverend, still unable to comprehend what was happening. "Stop me?"

"Yes . . . your father . . . he's . . ."

The meaning of what he was trying to say slowly began to penetrate her numbed senses, and her face suddenly crumpled. "Daddy?"

Reverend Olson glanced at Cass guardedly. "You'd better bring her to my house. We can talk there . . ."

Patience peered expectantly up at Cass. "Cass . . . where's Daddy?"

"Come on, sweetheart." Cass lifted her gently off the wagon seat and drew her protectively against his side. "Corliss, you'll see to the children."

"Of course."

"Aaron, you drive the team and follow us back to the reverend's house."

"Yessir."

Cass mounted his horse, then reached down and lifted Patience as he would a small child, placing her in the saddle in front of him. Stunned, she wrapped her arms around him, holding on tightly. "Cass . . . Daddy . . . what's happened to him?"

Nodding solemnly at the children who were staring up at him with open curiosity, Cass reined the horse around and walked it back in the direction they'd just come from.

When they arrived, Rebecca was waiting with a pot of hot tea and a heart filled with compassion. The reverend suggested that he and Patience step into his study. Alarmed, she glanced to Cass for assurance and he nodded. "You want me to come with you?" he asked.

She shook her head dazedly. "No . . ."

For a moment he wasn't sure she could make it on her own, but he should have known better. He had come to realize that there was more to Patience McCord than met the eye.

The door to the study closed as Rebecca reached out and pressed a reassuring hand on Cass's shoulder. "Come sit beside the fire. You must be weary."

Cass belatedly removed his hat. "Thank you, ma'am. I'd be obliged."

When they were seated, Rebecca reached to pour the tea, but Cass suddenly jumped to his feet, his tormented gaze focused on the study door as the sound of Patience's anguished cry tore through his heart.

"Please, Mr. Claxton," Rebecca urged softly. "This is very difficult . . . Later she will need you more."

Cass sank down slowly, stunned by what had happened. His blue eyes pleaded with Rebecca, trying to make sense of it all. "How . . . when . . . ?"

"Two weeks ago, in the middle of the night. No one is sure how the fire started. By the time it was discovered, it was well out of hand."

"And Patience's father? He wasn't able to escape?"

Rebecca shook her head sorrowfully. "They found Leviticus still in his bed."

Cass woodenly accepted the cup of tea she offered, wondering how he was going to get it down.

"We were aware that Patience was on her way here. That's all Leviticus talked about after he'd gotten the news she was coming. We've felt so helpless knowing we could do nothing to prepare her for the tragedy that awaited her."

Rebecca blotted her eyes. "My, how Leviticus looked forward to seeing his only child again and the children she was bringing to fill the emptiness in his life." Overcome by emotion, Rebecca tried to stem the flow of tears rolling from the corners of her eyes. "He had such fine plans, such high hopes. He would sit for hours and tell anyone who would listen how they were all going to be so happy . . . And now . . . now what will happen to all of them? Leviticus and the home they were coming to are gone. Everything is gone."

Cass's gaze traveled back to the study door as Rebecca's words drove deeply into his heart.

The children were homeless. Again.

Later that afternoon Patience asked Cass if he would take her to visit her father's grave. He said he would, and they left just after supper.

Rebecca had insisted that they stay the night at the parsonage, saying that they'd all put their heads together the next morning and come up with some solution.

At the sight of the fresh mound of dirt, Patience caught her breath and turned away, realizing that she'd been praying all afternoon that it wasn't true. But it was. Her father was dead.

Cass silently drew her back into his embrace and held her tightly as her anguish overflowed, and her tears came again.

"He never really knew me," she whispered brokenly. "And I never really knew him."

She was heartbroken that Leviticus would never know how much she'd loved him, how much she'd appreciated all the love and devoted care he'd given to her. And she had never once thought to say thank you.

Was it possible for a child to fully realize how deeply and unselfishly a mother and father had given their love, never asking, but freely sacrificing whatever was required to see the child happily and safely to adulthood? What other relationship on this earth could boast of such love, such unending commitment that asked nothing in return? How strange, she thought, that children failed to understand such love until they had children of their own.

She recalled how one day she had selfishly demanded that her papa walk through snow up to his hips to buy a silly little bauble she'd decided she had to have. He'd worked all day and walked home, but at her insistence he'd trudged back out into a blizzard to do her bidding.

Hours later he'd returned, cold and exhausted, bearing a red peppermint stick and the shiny spinning top she'd wanted. She'd jumped up and down with joy in their warm, cozy parlor while Leviticus had shed his sodden clothing and Mama had wrapped a warm blanket around his shoulders. Patience could still hear the way Leviticus's teeth chattered as he stuck his feet into a basin of hot water to thaw out.

Mama had raced around the kitchen, fixing tea and liberally lacing it with brandy to keep him from catching his death, while Patience had watched the colorful top twirl round and round in the middle of the floor, unconcerned about her father's near-frozen state.

She could recall thinking she was the luckiest little girl in the world to have such a fine papa who would buy her such extravagant things. Now she knew how fine Leviticus really was, not because he could afford to buy his daughter a spinning top but because he'd loved her enough to walk three miles in the snow to purchase a silly toy that meant nothing to him but everything to his five-year-old child.

Leviticus McCord, Patience could still hear her mother scolding, *you're spoilin' that child somethin' terrible!* But Leviticus had only laughed and candidly admitted that it was true, but that he didn't care. Then he had taken Patience onto his lap, opened the family Bible, and as her chubby fingers had worried the top round and round in her hands, he'd begun to read her favorite story to her, the one about Mary and Joseph and the little Babe born in a manger.

The tears came harder now, and Patience desperately wished she were that child again.

Drawing her gently away from the graveside, Cass supported her slight weight back to the buggy that the reverend had lent them for the journey. He lifted her up onto the seat, and their eyes met and held.

"Tell your papa good-bye, Patience."

Drawing her shoulders up determinedly, Patience turned, and with tears streaming down her cheeks, she said loud and clear, "Good-bye . . . and thank you, Papa!"

She glanced back to Cass, and a radiant smile suddenly broke through her tears. "Do you think he might have heard me?"

Cass smiled back at her lovingly. "I think he heard you."

As darkness closed around them, Cass picked up the reins, and the horse began moving away, leaving only Leviticus—and the good Lord— to know for sure.

"Good Lord! Look what the dogs have dragged up!" Beau Claxton stood gazing at his brother, shocked to find him standing in the doorway of his soddy.

The two brothers began slapping each other on the back, laughing and whooping like two young boys as Charity moved away from the stove to see what all the commotion was about. About the time she discovered that it was Cass, she was already being swept off the floor and tossed into the air by a pair of powerful arms.

"Cass Claxton, put me down!"

"Lordy, you're fat as one of ma's old sows!"

"Beau!" Charity wailed. "Tell your brother that I'm not fat; I happen to be carryin' another child of yours!"

Retrieving his wife's squirming body in midair, Beau lowered Charity to her feet, kissing her soundly on the way down.

"*Another* young'un?" Cass teased, his eyes surveying the three children looking up at him with wide-eyed innocence. "Haven't you people ever heard of moderation?"

Beau looked at Charity and winked. "Not with this woman I haven't."

"Well, control yourself," Cass admonished with a grin. "I can only stay for a little while."

"You'll stay the night, won't you?" Charity protested. "We haven't seen you for years!"

"Sure." He reached out and ruffled the youngest child's head of blond hair. "I have to get acquainted with my nieces and nephews, don't I?"

"You'd sure better!" Wrapping his arm around Cass's shoulder, Beau walked with him over to the fire. "What are you doing here? Children! Come over here and meet Uncle Cass." Beau motioned for the children to come to him. "You remember Mary Kathleen? She was just a baby last time you saw her, and these are the twins, Jason and Jenny."

Cass grinned and shook each child's hand solemnly. "Nice-looking family, Beau."

"Thank you." Beau beamed with fatherly pride. "It is, isn't it?"

While the men caught up on the news, Charity fixed supper. After they'd eaten the thick slices of cured ham, hot cornbread, and steaming bowls of brown beans, she sensed that Cass wanted to talk to Beau alone.

Around eight, she hugged each man, then discreetly excused herself, saying she wanted to put the children to bed early.

When she'd disappeared to the far corner of the room, Cass sat staring pensively into the fire as Beau got up to wind the clock.

"So, what brings you back in our direction?" Beau asked as he finished with the clock and reached for another stick of wood to throw on the fire.

"It's a long story, but at the moment I'm trying to find a home for nine children."

Beau's hand paused in midair, and he grinned. "Nine, huh? Your women all catch up with you at one time?"

"No, my women didn't all catch up with me at one time," Cass mimicked.

"Whew!"—Beau's brow lifted curiously—"we're a little touchy, aren't we?"

Cass supposed that he was, but he was tired and he had to get the children settled somewhere. Phebia had cried for two days, wanting the home she'd been promised.

"I'm in one hell of a mess, Beau."

Beau's eyes met his brother's solemnly. "You're serious, aren't you?"

"I'm serious."

Beau sat down to give his full attention to whatever was bothering his brother. "All right, I'm listening."

Cass took a deep breath, then began to talk of his recent journey from St. Louis, of the orphanage, the children, and the fire. He was candid about everything except Patience McCord and her forcing him to marry her six years ago. That was too humiliating to admit, even to Beau.

"Why would *you* agree to escort a pack of orphans to Cherry Grove?" Beau wondered aloud.

"I did it as a favor."

"For those old people you mentioned—Harlon and Corliss?"

"No, it wasn't for them. I agreed because the woman who runs the orphanage was in a bind," he mumbled.

"Really!" Beau stared into the fire thoughtfully. "What's her name, and how good-looking is she?"

"That didn't have anything to do with it," Cass shot back defensively.

"I'll bet!"

"Seriously, Beau, it didn't. I ran into their wagon outside of town on my way to—on a trip I was taking. They hadn't gotten two miles out of town, and already they were stuck in a mud hole. When I stopped to help, the woman made me see how desperate they were for a man to help them make the trip to Cherry Grove. Well, I couldn't just ride off and leave them stranded, now could I?"

"Since when?"

"Come on, Beau, you know me better than that."

Beau chuckled. A year ago it wouldn't have surprised him one bit to hear that Cass had left twelve people stranded along the road. "So you agreed to bring nine children, two seventy-year-olds, and the woman back to Cherry Grove." Beau had to wonder about that.

Cass nodded. Suddenly, he sat up straighter, his face animated. "You wait until you meet these kids—you're going to love them! There's Aaron —he's sixteen—and Payne—he's fourteen. I've been teaching them all about hunting and women! Then there's Jesse, Doog, Bryon, Joseph, Margaret Ann . . . Wait till you meet Margaret Ann—you won't believe this child. She thinks she's thirty years old—and you will too once you talk to her—but she's only six. Then there's Lucy and Phebia. Phebia is three and still sucks her thumb, although we've all been trying like hell to break her of it. And then there's Joseph who's as cute—"

"Whoa! Wait a minute!" Beau glanced up expectantly. "Are you *sure* these aren't your kids?"

"Of course they're not my kids, but lately I've been thinking it wouldn't be so bad having a couple of my own," Cass admitted.

Beau thought he detected a defensive note in his brother's voice. "Ma would insist you marry first."

Cass sighed. "I'm aware of that."

"So, you were bringing the kids and the old people and the woman from St. Louis, and when you got here, you found that the house that was meant to be the new orphanage had burned down?"

"That's right. And I've looked everywhere for the past two days to find a house large enough to serve as an orphanage, but there just isn't any-thing." He had debated about taking them all back to St. Louis to give them Josiah's house, but with winter coming on, he realized that Harlon and Corliss would be in no shape to make the return trip.

Beau seemed pensive as he thought about the problem. "I can think of only one fire that's happened around here lately, and that was Judge McCord's house over in Cherry Grove—you remember him? He had a daughter named . . . what was it? . . . Patience, that you had that run-in with at Miller's Mercantile one day."

Cass blinked. "Seems like I do recall meeting her."

"You *recall* meeting her!" Beau hooted. "Why she about knocked your—"

"I *said* I remember Patience McCord," Cass interrupted tersely. How could he forget her? It wasn't enough that she'd been on his mind; now she and her nine kids were in his heart.

"I just asked." Beau had never seen Cass so edgy.

"Look, I might as well tell you because there's no way I'm going to be able to keep it from you: Patience McCord runs the orphanage. I said I would help her get the children to Cherry Grove safely."

Beau cocked his head wryly.

"It's the truth."

"How many guns did she have pointed at you?"

"None!"

"All right, all right, you don't have to take my head off!"

"I need your help, Beau. Now let's stop messing around and get down to business. I'm running out of time."

"How can I help? I don't have a house big enough for three kids, let alone nine!"

"Then you're going to help me build one."

"You and me? Build a house that big?"

Cass nodded. "And however many men I can hire to help us. Patience needs a home for those kids, Beau, and I'm not going back to St. Louis until I know they have one."

"Well, I'll be damned!" Beau said softly. He was beginning to wonder just what Cass's main concern was—the kids or Patience.

"You can be anything you want!" Cass grunted irritably as he reached inside his shirt pocket for a cheroot. "Just have your tail end in Cherry Grove first light tomorrow morning."

CHAPTER 18

WITH THE HELP OF BEAU, AARON, PAYNE, AND THE twenty additional men that Cass was able to hire, the house was completed in two weeks. It took five men alone to build the fireplaces.

And what a glorious house it was. Fifteen rooms, seven fireplaces, five spacious bathrooms complete with claw-footed tubs for bathing, and the most modern, up-to-date kitchen conveniences Edgar Miller could have shipped from Hayes on such short notice.

The house even had running water piped straight to the bathrooms and kitchen, provoking the envy of every housewife in Cherry Grove.

Cass wouldn't let Patience see the house until it was almost completed. But her excitement and enthusiasm surpassed even the children's, so late Saturday afternoon he borrowed the reverend's buggy and drove her out to the building site.

The orphanage was situated just outside of town on thirty-five acres of prime land. The house was built in a grove of towering oak trees, providing cool breezes in the summer and a sturdy windbreak in the winter.

The horse's hooves clopped up the winding drive as Patience's hands came up to cover her mouth. She tried to keep from squealing when she saw the magnificent sight spread out before her. The house was as large as a palace!

Cass grinned as he watched her grow speechless in wide-eyed wonder. "I wanted it to be larger, but the men told me that would require several additional weeks to complete, and I figured that Rebecca and the reverend couldn't stand the strain."

Having thirteen unexpected guests for two weeks couldn't be pleasant, Cass had reasoned, especially since four of the children were either ill with chicken pox or coming down with it.

"Oh, Cass, I've never seen anything like it!" Patience exclaimed, her eyes alight with joy. "It must have cost a fortune!"

Cass reined the horse to a stop in front of the house, and they sat for a few moments, admiring the carpenters' craftsmanship. The dwelling was superb, both in quality and construction. It had two stories of wood and stone, with tall columns supporting the sweeping verandas.

"The men will finish up the stonework by late tomorrow. The remainder of the furniture will be here Monday, and we should be able to get you moved in on Tuesday morning," Cass said simply as he set the brake and stepped out of the buggy.

"Oh, it's lovely . . . simple lovely . . ."

He turned to lift her down but instead held her suspended in the air for a moment, his dancing eyes meeting hers teasingly. "Is that all you can say—that it's lovely?"

She smiled down at him affectionately. "How about, thank you, Sir Galahad." For indeed she thought he was the noblest knight in all the land.

Cass shook his head, indicating that she needed to do better.

She shook her head inquiringly. "No?"

"No."

"Then perhaps a kiss from the fair maiden?"

"Perhaps you know one?"

"Sir"—she dropped her gaze demurely—"I *was* one, until Sir Galahad rode into my life." Her mouth dipped to brush his lightly, and Cass could feel the thunder of his heartbeat.

"I guess I should apologize, fair maiden. I don't know what came over me," Cass said, his voice becoming husky with desire. The last two weeks had allowed them no time alone, and he'd discovered that he had missed his sweet temptress. "Can you forgive me?"

"The fair maiden not only forgives you, but longs for more," Patience whispered.

"Come here, my little seductress." His mouth took hers and she responded. With a sigh she melted against him, refusing to admit to herself that they were spending their last few days, maybe hours, together.

The house was so close to completion. Once he had her and the children comfortably settled, she knew he would be gone, leaving her with only a memory to ease her aching heart.

Their lips parted, and he let her slide the rest of the length of his body. The intimate motion left them both breathless with wanting.

"I believe you were interested in seeing the house?"

"Oh, yes . . . I can hardly wait."

Tucking her against his side, he led her up the steps leading to the circular veranda.

"Cass, has Reverend Olson ever said anything to you about why we're together?"

"No, but I've noticed that he and Rebecca have exchanged a few inquisitive looks."

Patience and Cass shared a good chuckle as they imagined the kindly minister's confusion. Though the reverend had presided over their hasty vows six years ago, neither Cass nor Patience had expected him to think their marriage would last.

"I suppose I should sit him down and explain what's happened," Cass conceded.

"I think you should." Patience looked up at him and grinned. "Then come and tell *me*, because I still can't understand it."

"Someone will have to explain it to me first." Cass had lain awake nights, wondering how he'd suddenly found himself so entangled with Patience. They shared an easy camaraderie now, one that he knew he was going to miss.

They opened one of the two large doors and stepped into the front parlor. Long, elegant windows lined the room, bringing in the light from the east. A huge fireplace to lend warmth in the winter centered on the west wall.

Patience's hands flew up to cover her mouth again as she viewed the mammoth room. "Oh, my . . ."

"Come Christmas Eve, I want Aaron and Payne to cut the biggest, nicest tree they can find," Cass told her. "When they bring it home, I want you to make it a night the children will always remember. They can string popcorn and berries and make chains from colored paper. I'll send some of those tiny candles they can put on the branches, but you'll have to watch and be sure that they don't burn themselves. And be sure to make Phebia take a nap that day, so she won't be so cranky that she can't enjoy it. And have Jesse and Doog hold Joseph up to the tree, so he can get his share of the fun and—"

Patience laughed delightedly. "Cass Claxton, I never dreamed you were so sentimental!"

Cass grinned sheepishly. "Christmas is a special time for family. I want this year to be the best the children have ever had."

They walked toward the kitchen holding hands. Patience was taken aback when she saw the long work counters, the two ovens in the walls, two cookstoves, three sinks, and a colossal-sized icebox to keep the milk, butter, meat, and vegetables cool.

"I've never seen such luxury," she murmured, her eyes taking in the rows and rows of copper-plated pots and pans hanging over the cook-stoves.

Taking her arm, Cass led her to the window and pointed to a large structure still under construction behind the house. "That's going to be the washhouse. I wanted it to be away from the main quarters so that you and Corliss won't be bothered."

"Bothered?"

"I've arranged for three women to come in four times a week to do the wash."

Patience turned, flabbergasted. "For how long?"

"From now on."

"But Cass, I can't afford to pay three women to do our wash!"

"I know you can't, but *I* can. There'll also be a couple of men who'll do the yard work, two who'll keep you in wood, a man who'll supply fresh meat year-round. Three local farmers will keep you in fresh vegetables, milk, eggs, and the fruit in season. Sadie Withers and Wanda Mitchell will be coming in daily to do the cooking so that you and Corliss won't have to work so hard. I've arranged for you to have unlimited credit at Miller's Mercantile, so you can buy staples and the children's clothing and shoes. Use it. I've also spoken with the doctor in town, and he's been instructed to forward any bills pertaining to the orphanage to my offices in St. Louis, including those incurred by Harlon and Corliss and yourself. You'll also be receiving a sizable check each month for any incidentals you might need." He paused and lifted his brow inquiringly. "What have I overlooked?"

She gazed back at him in awe. "Your sanity! I can't accept such gener-osity."

He drew back, affecting a mock bow. "I'm not bestowing all this on you, fair maiden. I'm giving it to the children."

"Cass . . . I don't know what to say. Your kindness is overwhelming, but—"

Cass took her arm again and guided her to the next room. Their footsteps echoed hollowly across the gleaming pine floor as they walked. "No *buts*. You should know by now you're not going to win an argument with me."

"Ha, ha! Aren't you the dreamer!"

The dining room came next, large and airy with space enough to seat fifty guests. "The children will be needing the extra room for all the friends they'll be bringing home over the years," Cass explained.

An adjoining room with back-to-back fireplaces looked out over a meadow, providing the children with restful surroundings to do their schoolwork. Next to it was a medium-sized study where Patience would transact business pertaining to the orphanage. The room had a smaller, more intimate feeling, with a cozy fireplace tucked into one corner and four large windows across the south wall.

To the left, a separate wing housed Patience's and Corliss and Harlon's bedrooms.

Cass suggested that they view Patience's quarters after they'd taken a tour of the upstairs.

Escorting her up the long, winding staircase, Cass then led Patience down the hallway, where they peeked into each of the bedrooms the children would occupy. Every room was large, bright, and cheerful. Patience could just visualize the looks of astonishment on the children's faces when they saw their new home.

Patience thought her heart would burst from happiness. There was only one thing to mar her joy: the knowledge that Cass would not be there to share it with them.

"Now I'll take you to see the best part," he said.

"There couldn't be more."

"Ah, but there is."

They went back down the stairway, arm in arm. At the bottom Cass turned her in the direction of the wing he had left for last.

"I thought you might enjoy having the bedroom on the left, though you're free to choose any one you want."

He paused before a closed door and gave her a wink that threatened to make her heart stop beating. "For some reason, I'm partial to this one." He reached out, turned the handle, and the door swung open.

Patience was unprepared for the sight she found. The four-poster bed, the armoire, the chiffonier, and the dressing table were made of the finest, richest walnut. The draperies, the bedspread, the pillows, the fabric on the settee in the adjoining sitting room, the chaise longues, and the numerous chairs scattered about were all done in delicate shades of lavender and blue. Lush baskets of ferns hung in the corner windows where the last rays of daylight shone through the windowpanes. Outside the window was a large pond where three graceful swans glided on the peaceful water. Patience's eyes took in the small dressing room, a closet the size of a room, and the private bath with handles and faucets shaped in the form of swans.

The room was so beautiful that she felt tears welling in her eyes.

Cass leaned against the doorway, viewing her emotion with tenderness. "The lavender reminds me of your eyes; the blue warns me how much I'm going to miss you and the children," he said softly.

Not daring to look at him, she kept her eyes fixed on the swans and said in a broken voice, "You're leaving, aren't you?"

"First light, Wednesday morning," he verified softly.

"Must you go?"

"Patience . . . I warned you this would happen."

"I'm not trying to stop you . . . I just wish you didn't have to go."

"There are times I wish I didn't have to either, but I do." He wasn't sure if he *could* love one woman after so many years of running from them. But he knew that what he was feeling for her must come powerfully close.

Swallowing the lump crowding her throat, Patience turned, smiling. "Then we don't have much time, do we?"

"No." He drew her into his arms, his eyes growing dark with his need for her.

Placing her hands on either side of his face, she closed her eyes as he pulled her to him, his lips skimming over hers in something more provocative than a kiss. Suddenly he drew back as he felt the salty wetness begin to slide down her cheeks. "What's wrong?" he probed gently.

"I'm sorry. I'm doing exactly what I promised I wouldn't do."

"Going weepy on me?"

"Yes."

Stemming the flow of tears with his thumbs, he asked softly, "But why are you crying now? I haven't left yet."

Her heart was in her eyes. "You've brought me here tonight to say good-bye, haven't you?"

He sighed, tenderly drawing her head back down to his chest. "Yes. It's not easy for me, Patience, but I'm just not ready to settle down. Can you understand that?"

"Yes." Patience understood, but it didn't make it any easier for her.

For a long moment they said nothing; then he gently tipped her face up to his and kissed her. Her breath fluttered unevenly through her lips to his, "I never knew it could hurt so bad."

"What?"

"Loving you."

"Please, don't make this any harder," he whispered raggedly.

Tears ran unabashedly down her cheeks. "I'm afraid I'll never see you again."

His breath was warm and sweet against her mouth. "I won't ever be very far away from you."

"Oh, Cass, how will I ever let you go?"

They sank to the floor, holding each other tightly. Soothing her hair from her forehead, he touched his lips to her nose, her cheeks, then her mouth. It was the first time he had taken such infinite care in loving her. It was as if he wanted to memorize every inch of her, the texture of her silky skin, the scent that she'd bathed in, the knowledge that she willingly waited for him.

"I can't seem to stop wanting you," she confessed. "Is it always like this?"

"Yes."

He drew back as if there was something more that he needed to tell her. But words failed him, and he shook his head wordlessly, burying his face in the haven between her breasts.

Trying to control the tears that rolled silently from the corners of her eyes, she tenderly soothed the top of his head, sharing his agony yet lost in her own.

They clung to each other, needing to assure each other that everything would be all right, that first light on Wednesday morning would never come. But Patience knew it would and he would then be gone, never to hold her in his arms again.

Cass lifted his eyes to gaze at her, realizing that torture could be exquisite.

She smiled through her tears, cupping his face between her hands gently as she sought to ease the hurt and confusion she saw in his eyes. "We have so little time. I don't want you to ever forget me, Cass Claxton."

"Forget you?" His gaze grew even more tender. "Can a man forget a sunrise or a baby's smile?"

She felt his fingers skim down the front of her dress, releasing buttons so that he could find her. His mouth returned to take hers with heat-soaked passion as they rolled over on the floor. Her body began to respond wherever he touched her, the response becoming more eager, more anxious as his hands took on a renewed urgency. There was nothing soft, nothing gentle in what they brought to each other now. His caresses drew her upward, filling her with a deep, searing need. She could hear his sounds of pleasure as his mouth took hers with a building passion.

Her breath caught as he tore at her dress with a primitiveness he had never shown before. He was ravaging her, and even as he realized it he could do nothing to prevent it. He wanted her, had to have her.

They began to kiss with reckless abandon. His mouth worshiped, devoured hers as he tried to say her name but couldn't. His clothes fell away; then the remainder of hers followed; and they became mindless with desire.

He rolled on top of her, and they were no longer aware that they were breathing.

"Don't leave me," she whispered fervently.

"No, let me go, Patience. You have to let me go . . ."

Soft sobs engulfed her as he passionately sought to ease her sorrow.

But Patience knew it would take more than kisses to erase his memory. She would never lie in his arms again, never feel the touch of his hand, never know the joy of his crooked smile.

She couldn't lose him, an inner voice screamed helplessly, and yet she knew she had, as he masterfully drew her into a sheath of satin-coated oblivion, muffling her sobs with his kisses. Come Wednesday morning, he would ride out of her life, forever.

CHAPTER 19

I**N THE END SHE HAD NO CHOICE BUT TO WATCH HIM** leave. Wednesday's dawn was as bleak and cold as the cloak of loneliness settling around Patience's heart. The first snow of the season was beginning to sift down in fine, powdery flakes as Bryon, Joseph, Lucy, and Phebia huddled around her skirt, their eyes openly indicting Cass for desertion as he went about saddling his horse. Even Margaret Ann had shed some of her sophistication as the knowledge that he was actually going to leave them began to sink in.

A cold wind whipped the tails of the heavy sheepskin jackets that Cass had recently purchased for the boys as Jesse, Doog, Payne, and Aaron stood by, anticipating his departure with stony silence.

After delaying as long as he could, Cass finally found enough nerve to turn and face his accusers. The forlorn faces he found waiting weren't encouraging.

He cleared the sudden lump in his throat and adjusted his hat, settling it lower on his forehead, carefully avoiding meeting any one particular gaze. "Well, guess that about does it."

Corliss offered him the sack of food she and Patience had prepared earlier. "Just some chicken and biscuits—won't last long, but it'll be more appetizing than jerky."

"Much obliged, Corliss. I appreciate it." Cass tucked the food away in one of the saddle bags. "I talked to Harlon earlier, but tell him I said good-bye again."

"Shore will . . . You take care now, you hear?"

His eyes softened. "I will, Corliss."

"How long will it take you to return to St. Louis?" Patience asked, finally stepping forward.

Cass was forced to meet her gaze, though he didn't want to. They had said their final good-byes toward dawn, and it hadn't been easy. "Ten, twelve days . . . Depends on how good time I make."

"You could sell your horse in St. Joseph and take a boat the rest of the way," she said. "It'd be faster."

"No, I don't mind. I need the time."

A faint smile touched her lips in an effort to make it easier for him, because she realized that he was hurting as much as she. "You take care of yourself. The weather looks like it doesn't plan to cooperate."

"I will." He gazed down at her, wondering for the thousandth time if what he was doing was right, and he came up with the same unyielding answer: He just didn't know.

"You'll write?" she whispered as her bravado began to slip.

"Yes . . . You do the same."

"Of course."

Turning to face the children, he looked at the faces he had grown to love, fighting the building emotion that was pressing heavily against his chest. "You kids mind your elders."

There was a combined mumbling of "yessirs" before Phebia buried her face in Patience's skirt and began to cry.

Reaching out, Cass lifted her into his arms and forced her to look at him. "You're a big girl now, Phebia, and big girls don't cry."

Tears of misery rolled silently out of the corners of the child's eyes. There were many things the three-year-old couldn't comprehend, but Phebia sensed that Cass would no longer be there to patch her small hurts and make them better.

"You want to pinch my nose?" he bantered lightly.

Phebia shook her head no.

"Will you give me a kiss before I go?"

She nodded. Cass removed the thumb from her mouth, and she leaned over and pecked him on the mouth.

He winked at her. "Not bad. With a little practice, you'll be breaking some man's heart before we know it."

Margaret stepped forward shyly to offer him a kiss. She was joined a few moments later by Lucy. God, he loved these kids, he thought as he held on to the three small bodies tightly.

Phebia suddenly backed away and extended Marybelle to him. Cass grinned and obediently gave the chosen one a kiss. But Phebia emphatically shook her head. "Marmarbelle go with Papa," she said firmly, extending the doll to him again.

Cass lifted his brows, stunned. "You want me to take Marybelle?"

Phebia's face broke into a radiant smile. "You Marmarbelle's papa!"

Gazing at her lovingly, Cass nearly broke down. "You sure you don't want Marybelle to stay here and live with you?"

Phebia shook her head again.

"All right. I'll be a good papa to Marybelle." Cass stood and carefully tied the doll onto his saddle horn.

Openly shaken now, he turned and knelt down to hug Joseph, then Bryon. Rising to his feet again, he shook hands with Doog and Jesse. "You boys behave yourselves."

"Yessir."

"Yessir."

He could feel his eyes beginning to water as he reached out and clasped Payne's hand in his tightly. "I'm depending on you to keep the smaller ones under control."

"I will, sir."

"You see that you do."

And then it was time for Aaron.

Aaron's eyes remained stoically fixed straight ahead as Cass, too overcome by his deep feelings for this young man, simply reached out to squeeze his thin shoulder. Then he turned and walked blindly to his horse.

"Cass."

His foot paused in the stirrup as he heard Patience's voice.

"Yes?" he answered without turning around.

She was suddenly by his side, her hand gently on his arm, silently willing him to turn and look at her.

But he steadfastly refused. Keeping his head down, he said in a voice growing gruff with emotion. "Patience . . . let's just get this over with."

Wordlessly she pressed an envelope into his hand.

Recognizing the significance of the long, legal envelope, a blanket of pain suddenly covered his features. The divorce papers.

"These are the papers I promised you. All they need is your signature," she said softly. "I signed them a few days ago."

For one fleeting moment Patience thought he might relent and stay with her, but the moment was brief. He swung up onto the saddle, tucking the envelope inside his jacket dispassionately. "See that you write."

Her eyes reaffirmed her love for him, told him that she would always love him. "You do the same."

He kicked his horse in the flanks, and the children stood huddled against the driving wind, watching him ride out of their lives as simply and as uncomplicatedly as he had ridden in.

"*Mon chéri*, I do not know what has gotten into you!" Laure Revuneau paced the floor of Cass's study, wringing her hands with frustration. "I did not hear from you the entire time you were gone. And now that you're back, you've been ignoring me for weeks."

Cass sat at his desk, staring out the window at the snow coming down in a heavy blanket. A sense of depression, one that had plagued him since he'd left Cherry Grove ten weeks before, was with him again.

Crossing the room to drape her arms around his neck affectionately, Laure sighed. "You have not made love to me since you returned. Have I done something to offend you, *mon chéri?*" She nuzzled his neck invitingly.

Cass pushed back from his desk, hoping to remove himself discreetly from her embrace. He didn't know why, but Laure no longer held her former appeal. In fact, no woman did. He had begun to compare each one he encountered with Patience, and it annoyed him. "You haven't done anything wrong, Laure. I've just been busy lately." He stood and walked to the fire and picked up the poker.

She followed him, her mouth curving in a provocative smile. "You are not so terribly busy now, *n'est-ce pas?*"

He studied the fire, realizing that the time had long passed to be honest with her. He had told her nothing of Cherry Grove or Patience McCord, and he didn't plan to. But he also realized that he had no plans to continue their relationship. "I'm sorry, Laure." He knelt to poke the fire. "I'm leaving for Atlanta within the hour."

She was stung by his rejection. Her startled face was suffused with disappointment. "You're leaving again?"

"I'm sorry. I'm afraid my business has suffered since I've been away, and I will be traveling often in the next few months."

"But . . . *mon chéri* . . . what about us?"

He straightened, turned, and his eyes met hers steadfastly. "I think you would be happier if you sought more reliable companionship."

Lifting her head proudly, Laure realized that she was being dismissed. It was a compassionate dismissal, but nevertheless it had become apparent over the past few weeks that he no longer cared for her. She knew she could plead with him to change his mind or she could accept his decision with the grace befitting a lady of her stature. She chose the latter because she sensed, though she hadn't the vaguest idea why, that this decision had not come easily to him.

"If that's what you want," she said.

"Laure . . ." He sounded tired, discouraged, and she heard a familiar note of despondency creeping back into his voice as he sighed. "I wish to hell I knew what I wanted."

A tap sounded at the door as Laure gathered her ermine cloak and prepared to leave. "Perhaps you will reconsider when you return from Atlanta."

"I won't reconsider."

Laure opened the door to find Mozes waiting. She turned back to Cass and smiled bravely. "I do not give up easily."

Cass lifted the corners of his mouth in a wan smile. Then he winked. "Take care, Laure."

"I shall, *mon chéri.*" Her eyes softened perceptively. "Whoever she is, I hope she deserves you."

Mozes stepped back to allow Laure room to exit. When she was gone, he walked into the room as Cass turned back to the fire.

"Another letter has been delivered, sir."

Cass glanced up expectantly.

"Again it's postmarked Cherry Gro—"

Mozes didn't get to finish before the letter was snatched from his hand as Cass tore into it eagerly.

"Will there be anything else, sir?"

Cass wasn't listening as he strode toward his desk, his eyes hungrily roving over the piece of paper.

"Very good, sir." Mozes closed the door, grinning. He had no idea what was in Cherry Grove, Kansas, but it had to be something special.

Seating himself at the desk, Cass began hungrily reading Patience's neat handwriting:

Dearest Cass,

I hope this letter finds you happy and well. The Christmas tree fit in the window just as beautifully as you predicted it would. Aaron and Payne took the smaller boys, and they scouted the woods on Christmas Eve looking for the perfect pine to cut.

That evening we placed the lovely candles on the tree, and the children strung popcorn and made chains from the colored paper you'd sent them. When they were finished, the tree was truly a magnificent sight.

Aaron and I took turns holding Phebia and Joseph to the top of the tree so they could place Baby Jesus in the manger. Joseph was so proud after we gathered around the tree later that night, when I opened the Bible to read to them about the angel appearing to the Virgin Mary, telling her she had been chosen to be the mother of the Christ Child and how Joseph and Mary had made the long trip to Bethlehem only to find no room at the inn.

For days afterward, our Joseph was quite adamant that he had a wife named Mary and that they had journeyed to Bethlehem on a donkey, where they'd developed bad head colds because they'd had to sleep in a stable.

Corliss and I finally got the children to bed and asleep by midnight, only to be up again before five. The older boys were ecstatic over their new rifles, and the girls simply adore their dollhouses. Of course, Bryon and Joseph thought their bicycles topped everything. Where in the world did you find such silly contraptions?

Well, I must close and get to bed. Tomorrow Doog and Jesse are in a spelling bee at school. Can you imagine that?

We think of you every day, and your name is mentioned quite frequently in Margaret Ann's prayers.

> Respectfully Yours,
> Patience McCord

The first buds of spring were just bursting open on the oaks when Doog came running up the drive, waving a letter in his hand.

"It's here!"

Patience dropped her sewing, and children started flying out of every door. Making her way carefully down the steps, she prayed that it was news from Cass.

"Is it from him?"

"Yes!" Doog answered.

When Cass's letter was in her hand, Patience closed her eyes and held it close to her heart for a moment, imagining that she could smell his familiar scent. Of course she couldn't, and at the children's indignant insistence, she ripped into the letter and began to read aloud:

> Dearest Patience, Harlon, Corliss, Aaron, Payne, Doog, Jesse, Bryon, Joseph, Margaret Ann, Lucy, and Phebia,
>
> Please do not take in any more children until I can acquire a longer pencil.

Patience paused to glance up sheepishly. "He's silly, isn't he?"

"Read us more," Joseph demanded.

"All right." She went on:

> I have been traveling for many weeks now, and I am very weary. At times I think I will sell everything I have and retire, but after a good night's rest, I change my mind again. Hope you children are minding well and keeping up with your homework.
>
> Take care of yourselves.

> Love,
> Cass

Margaret Ann frowned. "Is that all?"

Patience sighed. Cass couldn't be accused of being long-winded. "That's all."

Dearest Cass,

Is it ever hot! If we owed someone a hot day, we could have paid him back a hundred times lately. The temperature has soared above one hundred for days, and the children are getting cranky. Aaron and Payne have taken the smaller ones to the pond to swim every afternoon, though I had to scold Joseph again today. He chases my pretty swans until their tongues are dragging the ground.

Harlon is up and about. Feeling right perky, he says to tell you. Corliss says to tell you that she's feeling tuckered out because of all the heat. Phebia has just about stopped sucking her thumb, though she does have an occasional relapse.

I received the signed divorce papers. Thank you.

Hope you are well. I had a spell last week of not feeling so well, but I'm much better now.

We thought of you the other night at supper; we were enjoying that stew you like so much.

Take care.

Respectfully,
Patience McCord

P.S. I almost forgot! Bryon and Lucy wanted me to tell you that they've each lost another front tooth. You should see them when they grin! They insisted that I enclose their teeth—hope you don't mind.

The oaks were bursting with color as Doog came running breathlessly up the drive again.

Patience ran out of the washhouse. "Is it here?"

"It's here!"

She flew across the yard, her heart thumping erratically.

"Give it to me."

Not waiting for the other children this time, she tore into the letter, her eyes eagerly reading the words:

Dear Ones,

Since I'm in California, I decided to visit the ocean today. I sat for a long time looking out across the water, thinking of you. I was reminded of what a great distance separates us. Sometimes I worry that you don't have everything you need, and that makes me worry even more. If you should ever want for anything, you have only to ask. And don't be concerned about money. I have all we could ever need and more. I used to think money could make a man happy, but I'm beginning to realize that there are more important things in a man's life.

Take good care of yourselves—I miss all of you in a way I find hard to put on paper.

Love,
Cass

P.S. Patience, be sure that the kids have *big* pumpkins for Halloween. I mean it. I'm getting tired of you being so frugal.

Dear Cass,

The children had the biggest pumpkins in town. I hope you're happy. Do you realize you are spoiling these children shamelessly? Take care.

Respectfully,
Patience McCord

Dear Patience,

I'll spoil the children if I want to. God, I miss you.

Cass

"The old-timers are predicting at least nine inches by morning," Mozes remarked as he set a tray filled with sandwiches and a pot of tea on the study table.

Cass answered absently as he sat before the fire, his fingers folded above the bridge of his nose, staring unseeingly at the glowing embers. Patience was on his mind constantly lately. Her memory tortured him at night, and today he'd passed a woman on the street who'd reminded him of her. The response he'd had to seeing the look-alike had been mighty painful.

What was he going to do about Patience McCord? About the children?

He got up and walked to the window, where he began to pace restlessly. It had been close to a year since he'd seen them. A year. How much the children must have grown! Why didn't he go to them? How much longer was he going to feed his senseless pride that no longer required feeding, he wondered.

Regardless of what she'd done to him in the past, he could no longer deny that he was in love with her. She had changed. He had seen her change from a spoiled brat to a compassionate, loving woman. So what in the hell was he waiting for? Why did he keep torturing himself like this?

Suddenly he stopped pacing. By God, he wasn't going to wait any longer. He was going to go after her.

His eyes caught sight of a buggy pulling up in front of the house, and he groaned.

Company, the last thing he needed or wanted. He was about to tell Mozes that he wouldn't see anyone, when he noticed a boy stepping down from the carriage.

Whirling back, Cass leaned closer to the window, his face breaking into a big smile when he recognized the visitor.

"Aaron!" Cass bolted from the window as Mozes glanced up from pouring the tea.

"I beg your pardon, sir?"

"Mozes, it's Aaron!" he exclaimed as he ran across the room and out the door.

"Aaron?" Mozes lifted his brow curiously.

Aaron was just coming up the walk when Cass flung the door open. The boy broke into a grin as Cass rushed out to engulf him in a warm embrace.

Clapping him heartily on the back, Cass exclaimed, "Aaron, what are you doing here, son?"

"Come to pay you a visit!"

Cass held the boy away to get a good look at him. He'd grown at least two inches! "Lord, it's good to see you—"

His smile suddenly froze as one possible reason for Aaron's visit crowded in on him. "Is everything all right at the orphanage? Has anything happened to Patience or one of the children?"

"No, sir, they're all doin' fine," Aaron insisted with a good-natured grin.

"Are you sure?"

"I'm positive."

Cass began moving the boy toward the house, keeping his arm firmly around him as if he might somehow slip away. "How did you get here?"

"By boat."

"Boat? From St. Joseph?"

"Yessir, I have a part-time job working at Miller's Mercantile, and I used some of the money I've been earnin' to buy my ticket."

"You didn't need to do that. I would have sent you the money to come for a visit."

"I couldn't do that, sir. Miss McCord says I need to be man enough to stand on my own two feet."

"Well, she's right, of course—are you hungry?"

"Yessir."

They walked inside the house, and Cass shouted for Mozes to bring more food. Mozes stuck his head out of the study, wondering who this young lad was who made his employer so happy.

"It's cold out there—and snowing." Cass hurriedly drew Aaron closer to the warmth of the fire.

"Yeah, but Missouri's not as cold as Kansas."

"Take off your coat and warm yourself. How in the world did you find me?"

"I asked around. You weren't hard to find."

Mozes returned with a large tray laden with food, as Cass began to fire a million questions at Aaron about the other children.

When he'd answered all of them to Cass's satisfaction, Aaron tore into the slice of steaming hot apple pie that Mozes had just placed before him.

Cass lit a cheroot and settled himself behind the desk. "Well, how have you been?"

"Real good. You remember Ernestine Parker?"

"Sure, I remember Ernestine."

Aaron grinned. "Well, me and her just might be marryin' up next spring."

"Is that so!"

"Yessir. We've been writin' back and forth, and I'm thinkin' real strong 'bout askin' for her hand."

Cass shook his head, grinning. It was hard to realize that the boy was old enough to think about such things.

"How old are you now?"

"Seventeen. Ernestine is younger, but I plan on takin' real good care of her."

Cass smiled. "Ernestine's a fine choice, Aaron. I'm sure she'll make you an excellent wife."

"Thank you, sir. I hope she feels the same."

"Where do you plan to live?"

"In Cherry Grove. I think Miss McCord can use my help raising those kids. Corliss and Harlon are getting so old, and the kids are a real handful at times."

Cass nodded, glancing out the window, fondly recalling how there was rarely a moment's peace when the children were around. "How are Corliss and Harlon?"

"Just fine."

"And Patience?" Cass's tone softened as he turned and leaned forward in his chair. "How is she?"

"She's fine, sir. Had you a fine son a few months back."

"Oh, yeah? Well that's goo—" Cass started to lean back when he suddenly froze, his face draining of all color. He sat up straight. "Had me a *what?*"

Aaron looked at Cass directly, and his tone changed from friendly to cool in the blink of an eye. "I said, she had you a fine son, sir." After all the times Cass had told him he was to do right by a woman, Aaron found it ironic that *Cass* had walked out on Patience, leaving her to raise his child.

Cass could not find his voice.

Moving the slice of half-eaten pie aside, Aaron stood up and drew a deep breath. He didn't cherish what he had to do, but someone had to do it. "Sir, I want you to know I've thought a lot about what I'm about to say —and I know you might not be real happy to hear it, but I've come a long way to say it, so don't try to stop me."

Cass glanced up, still in shock by the news that he had fathered a son. "I don't mean no disrespect, sir, but you've got this comin'."

"All right." Cass stood up to meet Aaron's stringent gaze expectantly. "Say what you've got to say."

"You're a no-good son of a bitch . . . sir." Aaron struck out at Cass blindly.

"Aaron!" Cass dodged the flying fist, astounded by the boy's actions. "I've whipped men for less than this."

Aaron braced himself, fully prepared to fight. "Then you'd better get to whippin', sir, because it's the truth." The boy's face was flushed with anger.

"The truth!"

"Yessir, it is."

"You want to tell me why you think it's the truth?"

" 'Cause of what you did to Miss McCord."

"What do you think I've done to her!"

"Sir, I may not know a whole lot, but I think it's plain to everyone what you did to her."

Cass had the grace to blush. "That's not what I meant. What's all this nonsense about me being a son of a bitch?"

"You are one, sir, sure as I live and breathe."

"Why?"

Aaron kept his eyes solidly fixed to the snow falling outside the window. "You told me you'd been taught that if a man accidentally fathered a child, then he should be man enough to accept his obligation. Otherwise he was a son of a bitch."

"And you think I haven't?"

Aaron's gaze focused on Cass accusingly. "I *know* you haven't."

Cass leaned back in his chair, trying to grasp what had happened. He was quiet for a long moment, trying to muddle through what Aaron was saying. "Does Patience know you're here?"

"No, sir! And she'd skin me alive if she knew. She thinks I've gone to visit Ernestine, but I had to do this for Sammy."

Cass glanced up again. "Sammy?"

"Yessir, Samuel Casteel Claxton. I believe Miss McCord figured you might want your son named after you and your pa, seein' as how he's dead and all."

Samuel Casteel Claxton. God, Cass thought, *I have a son*. Patience had had the perfect way to trap him again, but she hadn't. She *must* have known or at least suspected that she was carrying his child when he'd left her. She'd let him ride away that day, divorce papers in hand, and never said a word.

"Aaron"—Cass's voice broke with emotion—"believe me, I didn't know . . . She never told me . . . I never dreamed . . ."

Aaron studied Cass's reaction quietly, realizing with a jolt that the news had come as a complete shock. Had he really not known about the child?

"You mean, she really never told you?" Aaron asked.

"No . . . She never said a word. I wouldn't have left if I had known . . ." Cass's eyes turned pleading. "You have to believe me, Aaron. I didn't know."

Stepping forward, Aaron laid his hand on Cass's shoulder, squeezing it reassuringly. "Well then, I think it's time you met your son." Aaron smiled into Cass's eyes, and Cass saw that the smile was no longer that of a child but of a man.

"I think so, too, son."

The expression Aaron saw in Cass's eyes reminded him of five-year-old Joseph, when he had done something wrong. "You think Patience will forgive me?"

Aaron grinned. "Shoot, yes. She's always been down right silly about you."

A proud grin spread across the new papa's face. "When's the next boat leave from St. Joseph?"

Reaching into his back pocket, Aaron drew out two tickets. "Tomorrow morning—and I'd be much obliged if you would pay me back for your fare, because I'll be needin' money when I have my own son"—Aaron flashed him an embarrassed grin—"sir."

CHAPTER 20

THE SOUNDS OF A MOTHER CROONING A SOFT LULLABY to her child filtered softly through the room. The fire popped in the grate, and the house had settled down for the night.

Patience cuddled the child in her arms lovingly, her hand supporting the head of dark curly hair as she gazed into an achingly familiar pair of blue eyes and sang softly, "Hush, little baby, don't you cry; I'm gonna sing you a—" Patience glanced up as she heard the sound of a match being struck.

Her heart leapt to her throat when she saw who was standing in the doorway.

Cass leaned against the frame insolently, his gaze focused on the child she was holding. "Forgot to mention something, didn't you, Miss Mc-Cord?"

She managed to calm her pounding heart long enough to return his gaze innocently. "No, Mr. Claxton, not that I can think of."

He motioned with his eyes to the child. "No?"

"No."

He drew off the cigar thoughtfully. "Where did you get the baby?"

Patience smiled. "Oh . . . he just sort of came . . . one day."

Cass's gaze traveled lazily over her fuller bustline. "I'll bet."

Patience realized that, somehow, Sammy's father had found out about him. "Who told you?" she asked softly.

"Does it matter?" Tossing the cheroot in the fire, Cass walked into the room and came over to kneel by her chair. His presence suddenly filled the terrible emptiness in her heart, and she murmured a silent prayer, thanking God for sending him back, even if he didn't plan to stay.

Cass gazed down on his son, his eyes growing tender. "God, Patience, he's beautiful!" The child had big blue eyes and a head of dark, curly hair.

Sighing, she drew the blankets aside for him to examine their perfect creation. "We did do good work, didn't we, Mr. Claxton?"

"We sure did!" Cass reached out and touched his son under the chin reverently. "Hi, son."

The child puckered up and started to cry, distressed that his dinner was being delayed.

Mother and father laughed, momentarily easing the tension.

"How old is he?"

"Three and a half months."

"No kidding! Why, he's big for his age, isn't he?"

"Of course." She was deliberately avoiding his eyes. She wasn't sure she could keep her emotions under control. "Samuel Casteel Claxton is going to be just like his father. A fine, strong man."

Cass leaned closer, and she felt faint as she drew in his familiar smell. She longed to throw herself into his arms and let him kiss away the loneliness of the past year, but she knew she wouldn't. Not this time.

His gaze had returned to the infant to study the shock of dark hair and arresting blue eyes. "He looks like me. Ma will be pleased."

Patience sighed. He didn't have to remind her of how much the baby looked like him. Sammy was a daily reminder of what they had once shared. "Yes, he does, and he has your streak of orneriness too."

"Mine!" he grinned, that ornery crooked grin that tore at her heart-strings. "I'd say he takes after his mother in that department."

"Oh, now, now," she cooed as the child began to sob harder. "Is this any way to act in front of your papa?"

Cass suddenly caught her hand, demanding that she look at him. "Why, Patience? Why didn't you tell me about our son? Did you think you could keep this from me forever?"

Swallowing the lump crowding her throat, she brought the baby up to her breast to nurse. "No . . . I just wasn't sure how you would feel about it, Cass. I know you aren't ready to settle down, and a baby certainly does call for a certain amount of permanence in one's life."

Cass tried to ignore the sight of her bare breast. He struggled with the urge to touch her . . . to hold her in his arms again. "Feel about him? He's my *son*."

Patience drew a long breath, and finally turned to face him. "Yes, but he's my son too, Cass. Now, how does *that* make you feel?"

They looked at each other, their gazes locked in anguish.

"Maybe that just makes him that much more special," he admitted in a shaky voice.

"*Maybe?*" She wasn't sure what he was trying to say. Was he here to claim his son? If he was, he'd have to claim her too. She wanted Cass Claxton, and this time she was willing to fight for him. "I didn't tell you about our child because I didn't want you to think I was trying to trick you again."

"I wouldn't have thought that—"

"Yes, you would have. You know you would have."

"Well, I don't think that now," he said gently.

"Cass, I love you so deeply it's a physical ache at times," she blurted out. "I pray every night that someday you'll return my love, but I'm tired of using tricks and deceit to hold you. I'm afraid if you want your son, you have to take me too."

"I'd be grateful to have both of you."

"And you'll have to want *me* because we agree our lives will be empty and meaningless without each other," she warned, his ready acceptance failing to register with her. "I'll settle for nothing less."

His gaze traveled adoringly over her, then on to his son nursing at his mother's breast. "You'll have nothing less. I'm sorry it's taken me so long to realize how I feel, but I had to be sure—for both our sakes. I love you, Patience Claxton—so damn much it hurts."

"Well, as I say, if you ever want—" She suddenly paused, his words finally sinking in. Her eyes widened. "You love me?" she whispered.

He nodded, slowly drawing her mouth down to meet his. They kissed for a long moment, deeply and with a hungry urgency.

"Oh, Cass, why did you leave?"

"I had to. It's taken me a year to realize what's important in my life, but not a day has gone by that I didn't know, deep down in my heart, I loved you."

"But you signed the divorce papers."

"Yes, because I wanted *that* marriage over and done with. I want us to start again. I want our love to be the ruling force this time, not manipulation. I'm deeply in love with you, Patience." His hand reached out to touch her face reverently. "I hope you can forgive me."

"Oh, Cass, if you only knew how long I have waited to hear you say you love me."

His smile was as intimate as the kiss he was about to give her. "Get used to it—you're going to be hearing it a lot for the next fifty years."

When their lips parted many long minutes later, she prompted softly, "Does this mean you're home to stay?"

"It does."

"What about your business—?"

He placed his finger across her lips in an effort to allay her concerns. "I've already consolidated a lot of my holdings, and the rest of my business can be handled from here in Cherry Grove. I'm closing the house in St. Louis, and I've arranged to have Mozes brought here to help with the children—if you have no objections."

She gazed back at him, her heart overflowing with joy. "No, of course I have no objections, but Cass . . . are you sure it's me you want, or is it because of your son that you've changed your mind?" She had to know for sure.

"I want you, my love, and my son . . . and my nine other children."

"Oh, Cass . . . are you sure? The children will be overjoyed. They love you as much as I do . . . ." She paused and smiled, drowning in the familiar blue of his eyes. "Well, almost as much."

"Woman, I've never been more sure of anything in my whole life—and don't start arguing with me." His lips pressed, then gently covered her mouth.

"Then each and every one of us is yours," she said a moment later. "You don't mind being hog-tied and branded?"

"Not by you."

He reached out to pull her and the baby onto his lap as Sammy grunted and began struggling to keep his supper from disappearing again.

"Hey, kid, me and your ma are getting married—not in the middle of a road at the point of a shotgun, but she and I and our ten children are going to plan the biggest, rowdiest wedding this old town has ever seen!" Cass told his son. "I want the whole world to know she's mine, and she's going to stay mine for the rest of her life!" He paused and grinned engagingly at his son. "What do you think about *that*, Samuel Claxton?"

Sammy Claxton burped.

Cass and Patience laughed delightedly as they began kissing again. "That means your son thinks *that* sounds just grand," Patience clarified.

Cass winked lovingly at Sammy's mother. "So does his papa."

•   •   •

Cass stood at the bedroom window, looking down on the activity, shaking his head with amazement. The orphanage was decked out in its very finest. Greenery and colored ribbons adorned each room, and the smell of fresh-cut flowers filled every nook and cranny.

The parlor was filled with tables stacked high with gaily wrapped presents awaiting the bride and groom's attention.

A magnificent eight-tiered wedding cake kept Corliss and the women who scurried about the kitchen busy trying to keep the children's fingers out of the icing.

There had been a solid stream of buggies arriving for the past hour, with people alighting from the carriages in their Sunday best to witness the exchange of vows between Miss Patience McCord and Mr. Cass Claxton.

A knock sounded at the door, and Patience swept into the room like a bright ray of sunshine.

"Hello."

Cass turned, a smile surfacing on his face when he saw her. "It's about time you got here. Come here, woman."

She went willingly to him, and his arms encircled her, one hand at the small of her back as they exchanged a long, thorough kiss.

"Patience, please! I can't make it through another four hours," he whispered, completely miserable now.

"Oh, it will be more like six hours," Patience told him solemnly.

"Six hours?"

She nodded.

He began drawing her toward the bed purposefully. "There is no way on earth I'm waiting *six* more hours to make love to you. I've already waited over a year. Enough is enough!"

She laughed, gently thwarting his efforts to wear her down. "You promised."

"Promised what?"

"You promised we could have a real wedding night."

"I'm a man in love—I can't be held responsible for what I say," he excused himself. His mouth captured hers again relentlessly.

Patience wasn't buying his sad story. She laughed, pushing him away firmly. "But you're a man of your word."

"Our wedding night is going to be real," he coaxed as he drew her back into his arms persuasively. "Real long, real passionate, real unforget-table, real—"

"*Real* real, with the bride coming to the groom unsullied."

"Patience." He shifted to one foot tolerantly. "I seem to recall a time when you were not half as worried about your virtue."

"But I didn't have to be." She pecked him on the mouth affectionately. "That was when I was married to you," she reminded him.

"Well, hell! You're going to be married to me again in another hour."

"I know." She rubbed against him, pressing her lips to his throat. "Think about that while you're waiting for the ceremony to take place."

He groaned, pulling her to him tightly, hungrily crushing his mouth against hers. Scooping her up in his arms, he started for the bed.

"Cass."

"No."

"Cass!"

"Don't argue with me."

"Your mother, brother, sister-in-law, and family housekeeper have just arrived," she gasped laughingly. "They're waiting to see you."

She felt the enthusiasm suddenly draining out of him. "Damn!"

Rubbing her cheek against his, she hugged him tightly around the neck. "You need to have a little patience, my love."

He groaned painfully. "That's what I've been telling you."

There was a lot of back-slapping and hugging as the Claxton family was reunited.

Cass drew his mother, Lilly, into his arms and held her tightly. He hadn't seen her for more than five years.

"Now where are all my grandbabies?" Lilly turned to Cole's children, engulfing them in big grandmotherly hugs.

"Ma, you better ease up," Cass warned. "You still have my ten to go."

Lilly threw her hands up in despair. "Lordy, lordy, I always said you'd be the one to turn my hair gray!"

Willa, the family housekeeper who'd been like a mother to the Claxton boys, was there, beaming with pride as she swept Cass into her arms and gave him a big kiss.

Wynne was standing by, eager to talk to the lothario who had jilted her at the altar nine years before.

"I can't wait to meet the woman who's finally snagged you," she teased, going into his open arms.

Cass grinned as he good-naturedly drew Cole's wife into a tight embrace. "Wynne, sweetheart, look at it this way: If I hadn't have left you standing at that altar, and you hadn't traipsed all over the country looking for me, why, where would my brother be today? In the arms of one of those wild, wicked women—"

Wynne poked him soundly in the ribs. "All right, all right. How many times do I need to say thank you?"

Cass laughed and knelt down to greet his nieces and nephews. "Jeremy, look how you've grown—and your sisters, Tessie and Sarah!" He stood up again, shaking his head with disbelief. "Boy, they make you realize you're getting old, don't they?"

Cole was suddenly forced to sidestep as Doog, Jesse, Bryon, Joseph, and Lucy came hurtling down the stairway. "Damn, did school just let out?"

Cass threw his head back and hooted. "No, those are just more of mine!"

Cole looked at Wynne and grinned. It was hard to imagine Cass with a wife and ten children!

Beau and Charity arrived with the children, and the hugs and kisses started all over again.

"You're expecting again!" Wynne exclaimed.

Charity nodded, her eyes sparkling with happiness. "Beau says it's a boy this time, for sure!"

"It'd better be, I've sure worked hard enough on it," Beau teased, giving his wife an adoring squeeze.

Events began to go by in a blur. Greetings were exchanged, and Cass grew more nervous. He kept anxiously dragging his watch out of his vest pocket to check the time.

When he was sure he couldn't wait another moment, the music suddenly sounded the wedding march, and Cass straightened his tie, took a deep breath, and stepped into place next to Aaron and Payne under the wide arch of greenery in the parlor.

Phebia had reclaimed Marybelle, and she carried her as she came walking down the stairway first, dressed in a little replica of the bride's outfit. She entered the parlor hesitantly, scattering rose petals along the pathway while sneaking an occasional suck on her thumb.

Margaret Ann and Lucy followed, wearing circlets of fresh flowers around their heads, and dressed in long lavender-blue gowns.

Jesse, Doog, Bryon, and Joseph came along next, spit-shined and polished in their new blue suits. Corliss followed carrying Sammy, who didn't care one bit for all the commotion. The latter group didn't have any official role in the wedding, but it had been agreed by all that the ceremony should be a family affair.

And then the moment Cass had been waiting for finally arrived.

Patience came down the stairway, a vision of loveliness in her ivory bridal gown.

Cass's eyes locked with hers as she walked slowly toward him, supported by Harlon's steady arm. They smiled at each other, savoring the heady moment, anticipating the hour they would be back in each other's arms forever.

Reverend Olson performed the ceremony, and this time he didn't have to prompt the groom to accept his vows, or kiss his bride.

In fact, the guests were beginning to wonder if Cass was ever going to stop kissing her.

Patience finally broke the heated embrace and covered her face with embarrassment amid the sound of loud applause.

Wine began to flow, and the wedding cake was cut, though the groom seemed a bit too eager to dispense with the ceremonies and be on his way with his bride.

The guests crowded around as Cass lifted his glass, his eyes overflowing with love as he made the first toast to his bride. "Here's to our first happy year of marriage." He winked, then leaned over and whispered in Patience's ear. "One out of seven's not bad, is it?"

She laughed and kissed him this time.

"Well, little brother," Cole said to Cass as they caught a rare moment alone a few minutes later, "I guess I worried about you all these years for nothing!"

Cass gazed lovingly at his new bride, who was busy trying to excuse herself in order to slip away. "Yes, she's something, isn't she!"

It had taken a considerable swallowing of pride, but Cass had finally told his family about his earlier marriage to Patience and how he'd come to love the children of the orphanage as much as he loved his own son. He'd had to. Lilly had nearly fainted when she'd found out he had ten children.

Beau drifted over to join his brothers. "I guess Patience will do in a pinch, but have you two *really* looked at my Charity? Now, gentlemen, there's a woman!"

"Hell, men, Wynne's got your women beat, hands down!" Cole stated flatly.

Beau and Cass both turned to give him a dour look.

The three brothers suddenly exchanged identical devilish winks. As far as they were concerned, they *all* had done all right.

Samuel Claxton Senior would have been right proud of his sons.

ABOUT THE AUTHOR

Winner of a Career Achievement Award for Love and Laughter from *Romantic Times*, LORI COPELAND is the acclaimed, bestselling author of nearly fifty contemporary and historical romances, including such immensely popular works as *Sweet Hannah Rose*, *Fool Me Once*, *Promise Me Today*, *Promise Me Tomorrow*, *Promise Me Forever*, and *Forever, Ashley*.